REG RAWLINS, PSYCHIC INVESTIGATOR

REG RAWLINS, PSYCHIC INVESTIGATOR

13 - 15

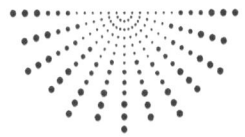

P.D. WORKMAN

ISBN: 9781774683187 (KDP Paperback)

ISBN: 9781774683194 (Kindle)

ISBN: 9781774683200 (ePub)

ALSO BY P.D. WORKMAN

FIND MORE BOOKS AT PDWORKMAN.COM

MYSTERY/SUSPENSE:

Reg Rawlins, Psychic Detective

What the Cat Knew

A Psychic with Catitude

A Catastrophic Theft

Night of Nine Tails

Telepathy of Gardens

Delusions of the Past

Fairy Blade Unmade

Web of Nightmares

A Whisker's Breadth

Skunk Man Swamp

Magic Ain't A Game

Without Foresight

Careful of Thy Wishes

Time to Your Elf

Undiscovered Tomb

Missing Powers (Coming Soon)

Thrice Spared (Coming Soon)

Auntie Clem's Bakery

Gluten-Free Murder

Dairy-Free Death

Allergen-Free Assignation

Witch-Free Halloween (Halloween Short)

Dog-Free Dinner (Christmas Short)

Stirring Up Murder

Brewing Death

Coup de Glace

Sour Cherry Turnover

Apple-achian Treasure

Vegan Baked Alaska

Muffins Masks Murder

Tai Chi and Chai Tea

Santa Shortbread

Cold as Ice Cream

Changing Fortune Cookies

Hot on the Trail Mix

Fateful Plateful (Coming Soon)

Cut Out Cookie (Coming Soon)

On the Slab Pie (Coming Soon)

Recipes from Auntie Clem's Bakery

Kenzie Kirsch Medical Thrillers

Unlawful Harvest

Doctored Death

Dosed to Death

Gentle Angel

AND MORE AT PDWORKMAN.COM

CAREFUL OF THY WISHES

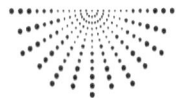

REG RAWLINS, PSYCHIC INVESTIGATOR
#13

For those who have wished to help

CHAPTER ONE

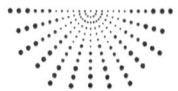

*R*eg had been putting it off for too long. She had been spending more, knowing that she had the gems to fall back on, so, although she had been doing okay with her psychic services business, she had been spending more than she was making, which wasn't a great way to keep her bank balance in the black.

She kept putting off cashing in a couple of the gems because of the work involved. She hadn't ever done it before, for one thing. She had used pawnshops in the past to get a bit of cash for jewelry she had acquired through one means or another, but she knew that she didn't get anywhere near what they were worth. And she couldn't take cut, unset gemstones to a pawnshop. They weren't jewelers. They wouldn't know how much they were worth or give her a fair price.

That meant that she had to figure out where to go to sell the gems. She found several gemstone buyers in nearby cities; that was an easy enough internet search. The problem was finding one that would not only give her a fair price, but would look the other way on gems that might not have come through *regular channels*.

The stores in Black Sands would be more understanding about how she had acquired the gems, but she didn't think it was a good idea for anyone in Black Sands to know about the fact that she had a small chest of cut gems in her possession. She hadn't yet rented a safe deposit box like Sarah, her landlord, had suggested, which meant that the box of gems was in Reg's closet. Or under the bed. Or whatever other place she had chosen to hide it in temporarily. She moved it around regularly because she knew it wasn't safe. There wasn't anywhere secure to hide it within the guest cottage she rented from the older woman. If word got out that she had the gems, she could have a problem.

Of course, the cottage was protected with magical wards and charms, but Reg knew that there were still ways for less-honorable thieves to find their way around the wards, or for powerful beings to break them. She knew because it had happened before. Sarah had helped her to set new wards several times. She always rolled her eyes and gave Reg a stern lecture on not allowing herself to be talked into releasing the wards, allowing a pixie into the house, or surrendering by any other means to which the wards were vulnerable.

So Reg knew that she couldn't liquidate any of the jewels in Black Sands. It was too risky. She would have to go into one of the bigger cities where she was unknown and where she would not be required to explain how the stones had come into her possession. And those kinds of places didn't advertise the fact on public websites.

But she couldn't afford to wait any longer.

There were a few interesting listings on Craigslist and eBay. Reg made screenshots of them and looked up the addresses on the maps app on her phone.

"What do you think?" she mused aloud.

Starlight looked at her, blinking first his blue eye and then his green. She didn't know how much of commerce or the internet he understood. His psychic powers might not extend that far.

"I need money if I'm going to get you food and kitty litter. So you want to help me with that, right?"

He blinked again, both eyes together this time. Reg focused on the white mark in the third eye position on his forehead. The star that gave him his name. She squinted her eyes slightly and let them go out of focus, thinking about the listings that she had just found on her phone, trying to sort out which of them was the best bet. She brought up the first one in her mind, a David Price of Rite Price Gem Exchange and immediately felt a sense of foreboding. Her stomach tied itself in a tight, heavy knot that nearly made her physically sick.

She didn't know what the danger was in going to Price, but she knew it was not a good idea. She mentally struck that one off her list.

"Okay…"

She opened her eyes for a couple of seconds to check out the next listing. *Dreame Jewelry. Achieve your highest dreams.* That one sounded even sleazier than the first. But she focused her eyes on Starlight's white star again and thought about it.

She had never dreamed that she would come into possession of such a fortune. There had been plenty of times in the past when she had dreamed of somewhere safe and sheltered to live and a bowl of warm soup in her hands. Reg had found that and more in Black Sands, a little Florida community that had seemed ripe for all kinds of paranormal cons. But, as she had soon discovered, there was more to Black Sands than just a high percentage of practicing psychics and retirees with thick wallets that needed unburdening. Instead, she had found a community that had not only accepted her as a bona fide psychic, but had opened up to her a whole new world of paranormal practitioners and experiences that were often difficult for her to believe existed.

She still woke up some mornings wondering if the past year had all been a dream and she didn't really possess any unusual psychic or paranormal abilities. Maybe there were no witches, fairies, sirens, or immortals. Maybe it was all just a very detailed and involved hallucination.

And then she talked to her cat and pulled out the little chest of gems and looked out the window at Sarah's backyard garden, flourishing under the care of Forst, the garden gnome. And she knew that it was all real.

"Do you think they would give me what the gems are worth?"

Not what they were worth, of course, but at least enough that she wouldn't have to worry about her bank account again for a few months.

She had a good feeling about Dreame Jewelry. Maybe it was the right place to go.

There were still more places on her list, but she didn't want to go over all of them with Starlight. Using her psychic powers, even with Starlight, was tiring, and she couldn't maintain her focus for that long.

Besides, it was nearly noon, and she was ready for some breakfast.

CHAPTER TWO

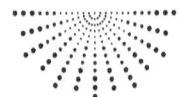

$\mathcal{I}$t had taken Reg a couple of hours to get to the city and locate the little store front that Dreame Jewelry worked out of. When she saw the dingy front window with dusty displays of what clearly was not real jewelry, she nearly changed her mind. There were several other jewelers on her list. Dreame really did not live up to its name.

But she was there. She might as well at least check it out. She'd had a good feeling about the place initially. Maybe it was a diamond in the rough. So to speak.

Reg pushed open the door. A bell tinkled, announcing her arrival. The interior was dim after the bright Florida sunlight outside. She couldn't see much at first. She closed her eyes, then opened them again and squinted around.

There were a few display cases with much the same kind of product as she had seen in the window. Maybe a few real pieces, but even the ones that appeared to be real weren't spectacular. They needed a good cleaning, to begin with. The store smelled dusty and old and sort of oily. A jewelry store shouldn't smell oily, should it?

Reg browsed through the displays. When she looked up, she saw a man standing behind the one that had been on her right when she had pushed her way through the door. She was sure that he hadn't been there, standing in the dim recesses of the room, when she had arrived. But he had either appeared out of nowhere or had crept in from the back of the store so quietly that she had not heard him or been aware of his presence.

"Oh. Hi there. I didn't see you."

The man was dark-skinned and had a short black beard that was not properly trimmed. Or maybe it was just a few days' growth of whiskers that didn't count as a beard. His face was round and his body wide.

"Good afternoon," he greeted in a resonant, surprisingly reassuring voice. "Jean Beaugrand at your service. How can I help you today?"

"Well, I was just looking…" Reg indicated the display cases, not yet showing her hand. Maybe she was just a tourist who had wandered in off the street.

The man's eyes traveled over Reg, from the multicolored headscarf around her head, to her red box braids, to her flowing peasant shirt and skirt. Maybe she didn't look like a tourist. But Beaugrand would have no way of knowing who she was. She didn't know anyone in the area and she wouldn't tell him that she had come from Black Sands.

"Are you here to buy or to sell?" he asked, getting immediately to the crux of the matter.

Reg pursed her lips, thinking about what to say. Admit that she was there looking for a buyer? Or continue to look at his wares and feel him out before revealing the fact?

She didn't say anything at first. She ignored his question as if she hadn't heard or understood it and browsed through the display case that he was standing behind, getting closer to him, reaching out with all of her senses to examine him, to read and classify him. She was good at cold-reading people. Or what she had always thought of as cold reading but might actually have been using her psychic powers before she knew she had them.

"Like what you see?" the man inquired mildly.

There was more to Beaugrand than met the eye. Few people showed their true selves to the world, but she sensed that he was hiding more than most. While his face and voice suggested that he was open and honest, there was a cloak of mystery and secrecy around him. Something stopped her from being able to probe him further.

"Well, there are a couple of pieces," Reg said, turning her attention back to the jewelry and pretending that was what he had been asking. She indicated a necklace that was almost directly in front of him. The ruby in the pendant was real. She could feel that. After having handled her own gems regularly, she could sense the power of a real stone. "This one…"

The man smiled, showing two rows of white, even teeth. "That is a very nice piece," he agreed. "Are you interested in buying?"

There was no price tag on it. Reg studied his face. He did not appear to be sarcastic or judging her as being too poor to afford it. It was a simple question about her interest in it.

"No," Reg admitted. She pulled a small velvet pouch out of her pocket. "I saw on Craigslist that you purchase gemstones. I don't see any out, so I was just wondering…"

"I do not display them," Beaugrand agreed. "I sell them privately to silver- and goldsmiths. People don't generally walk in off the street looking for unset stones."

Reg hesitated for another instant, reaching out to assess his feelings and intentions again. Either he was very good at blocking her, or he was an honest man. She loosened the strings on the pouch and spilled the gems she had brought with her onto her palm. She didn't know if he would be interested in everything, or whether he only bought certain gems. Or perhaps only what he knew his smiths were currently looking for.

The man leaned forward to look at them. He opened a drawer and put a shallow tray on top of the display case. "You can put them in there, and I will have a look."

He pulled a loupe from a pocket and picked up a ruby. He looked at it for a few moments, then put it back and picked up a blue gem, a sapphire, Reg assumed. He studied it for only an instant before putting it back.

He shook his head slowly. The opening move of his negotiation. Reg was familiar with negotiation, and he wasn't going to scare her away by declaring that her gems were worth very little or nothing. She could be hard-nosed and get a fair price. She'd had a lot of practice when she had been a lot more desperate than she was now.

"They are real," Reg asserted, looking him in the eye.

Beaugrand nodded. "Oh, yes. They are real. And good quality."

She was surprised to hear him concede that. But maybe it was part of his strategy. A little carrot to tempt her.

"Then what is the problem? They're good stones, you purchase stones for your smithies. Why wouldn't you be interested?"

"Do you know anything about the provenance of these stones?"

She had sold enough family heirlooms to know that provenance referred to being able to prove where the goods had come from and what hands they had passed through. She hadn't bothered to doctor any papers to give the gems fake histories.

"I understood from what I read that you... will purchase gems without provenance," Reg said delicately. She didn't want to imply that he was doing something against the law, or even unethical. But she'd done her research. She knew that Dreame dealt in... shadier areas.

"This is true," he tilted his head in a slight nod. "However, I wondered if you know *anything* about these gems. How did they come into your hands?"

"They are not stolen."

"That is good, but does not answer the question." The man pulled a stool over and sat down, resting his meaty forearms on the top of the case.

"They were given to me as a gift."

She doubted he would believe that, but he didn't give any sign of disbelief. "And did you accept them? Or did you say that you would check them out first?" He looked down at the gems in the tray.

"They are mine. I can sell them or do whatever I like with them."

"So, you accepted the gift."

Reg nodded impatiently. "Yes. Of course. Who wouldn't?"

Beaugrand smiled, showing his teeth again. "Perhaps someone who is not as rash as you."

Reg's stomach knotted. This did not sound good. Why should it be a problem that she had accepted the stones that were given to her as a gift? Unless they were stolen property, she couldn't see what was wrong with her owning them. The police couldn't do anything about that.

"Why? What do you mean?"

"I cannot buy these stones from you. You will need to find another avenue to rid yourself of them."

Reg stared at him, frowning.

CHAPTER THREE

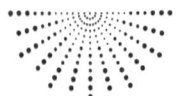

*R*eg left the man in Dreame and returned to her car with the gems back safely in the pouch in her pocket. She sat in the driver's seat and considered the situation.

The man had not given her any further information on why he would not or could not take the gems, or why Reg should not have accepted the gift from the fairies. She thought about all the rest of the gemstones in the small chest under her bed at the cottage. If she would be in trouble for accepting the small sampling of gems that she had shown to the man in the store, then how serious of a position was she in for having accepted hundreds more?

She rubbed her temples, trying to think. She'd been having a lot of issues since her encounter in the graveyard. Apparently, being possessed for more than a few minutes could do that to a person. She had holes in her memory, problems with concentration, and a certain level of decision paralysis in going ahead with anything. She didn't know whether the paralysis was the result of the other issues or a separate issue all on its own. It was hard to make a decision or be motivated to proceed with a plan of action when she wasn't sure that she had considered all the important points.

She thought back to the arrival of the gems, trying to remember every detail. She'd thought at first that it was a package from Amazon, but hadn't been able to remember anything she'd had on order. Sarah had brought it in to her, so Sarah was the one person who knew that she had them. Reg was sure that she would have been very careful not to mention them to anyone else. She didn't want the cottage to be broken into.

The gems had come in a small wooden chest, which they were currently stored in. There had been no explanatory note, just a small announcement card that said they were from the Papillon family. It had made perfect sense at the time. Reg had helped save their daughter Calliopia, who had been suffering from a nearly-fatal knife wound. No one else had given adolescent Callie any hope of survival, and Ruan, her mate, had even been willing to dispatch her himself rather than to let her continue to suffer.

But Reg had done it. She had been able to save Calliopia when no one else could, and Callie's parents had rewarded Reg with the gift of the gemstones. While it was a very lavish gift for a human, Reg had assumed that the fairies had far more access to jewels and that it was probably just a trifle to them. A small thank you for what Reg had done for their daughter.

She couldn't think of any reason she should not have accepted the jewels. Sarah had not said that she shouldn't, and Sarah was the one Reg relied on to tell her about things in the magical world. Reg had not been raised in a magical household, so she had no idea about many of the things that other practitioners thought normal or that anyone would know.

If there were something wrong with accepting the gift, then Sarah should have told her.

But there was something niggling at the back of Reg's mind, and she couldn't put her finger on what it was.

Maybe if she just relaxed and didn't try to think about it, it would come to her later.

* * *

But Dreame Jewelry was not the only purchaser on her list. Just because he had refused to buy the gems, that didn't mean that she couldn't sell them. There were plenty of others who were, she was sure, less scrupulous than Mr. Beaugrand.

She hadn't told him her name, so he wouldn't be able to report her to the authorities if there were something wrong with the gems. He had asked her about their provenance, so she had to assume there was something wrong with the chain of ownership of the gems. Had the Papillons reported them stolen after giving them to Reg? Though she knew that the fairies did not have the same ethics as humans, she couldn't see Mr. and Mrs. Papillon doing something to harm her after what she had done for them.

Reg clicked on her phone and looked at the various listings she had captured earlier. The next closest one was The Sapphire Exchange. The listing said that they dealt in all kinds of precious and semi-precious stones, and they were only a few minutes away, so they seemed like a good bet.

The contrast between the two stores was startling. The Sapphire Exchange was brightly lit, with lots of lights and white counters and reflective surfaces. Reg couldn't imagine working there and having to deal with the bright lights all day long. It was enough to give her a headache just walking into the store.

It had a spacious, open plan that made Reg think of a spa or an exclusive perfume store. Very high-end furnishings. There was a uniformed guard at the door who looked at Reg with suspicion but did not challenge her. A willowy young woman stepped forward to meet her, taking Reg's hand in her slim one.

"Welcome to The Sapphire Exchange," she said in a musical voice. "We're so delighted to have you here. Would you like to speak with one of our consultants?" She motioned to a counter where a man sat waiting, a tray like the one Beaugrand had used in front of him awaiting the next customer.

He gave her a pinched smile and tilted his head back so that he was looking down his nose at her even though she was standing and he was sitting on a stool.

"Come," the woman encouraged, touching Reg on the arm to encourage her forward.

Reg resisted, not liking the looks of the man.

"Ignore the sourpuss," the woman whispered in Reg's ear. "Mr. Cuttleby will be happy to serve you."

Reg let herself be urged forward to the counter. Unlike at Dreame Jewelry, there were trays full of row upon row of cut gemstones for buyers to see. But Reg didn't get much of a feeling from them. There was a certain feeling that they were genuine stones, but no power, as she got from Sarah's emerald, or her own gems, or the ruby necklace at Dreame Jewelry. They felt... common and... Reg couldn't think of the right word for them. *Farmed? Cultivated? Domesticated?*

Mr. Cuttleby continued to smile in his narrow, pinched way at Reg. His eyes went briefly to the young woman who had escorted her over.

"And what do we have here?"

Reg hadn't told her escort anything about who she was or what she wanted, so she didn't expect her to be able to tell the man anything. The young lady grabbed one of the tall stools ranged throughout the store and placed it in front of Reg.

"A seller," she told Cuttleby. "I'm sorry, I didn't catch your name, Miss...?"

Reg was so startled by the woman knowing that she had something to sell that she didn't have the sense to make up a name.

"Rawlins."

"Miss Rawlins is here looking for a buyer," she told Cuttleby with a nod. She put a hand on Reg's shoulder as she slid onto the stool. "Mr. Cuttleby here will be happy to help."

She nodded and drifted away from the two of them. Reg swiveled to watch her go. She turned back to Cuttleby. "How did...?"

"She is very... intuitive," Cuttleby explained carefully. "So, what are you trying to sell today?"

The woman was clearly a psychic, and yet Reg hadn't felt anything from her. No probe into her mind and consciousness. If the woman had read her, she had a very light touch.

Reg tried to force her attention from the woman to Mr. Cuttleby, but found it difficult. While she was talking to him, her mind was still whirring away in the background, trying to analyze the woman and to keep track of her behind Reg, supervising, welcoming other customers, and keeping everything running smoothly.

Mr. Cuttleby waited. Reg pulled out the little pouch of gems.

Did she still want to sell them to The Sapphire Exchange? It felt dangerous that the woman had read her so easily. But there were only two reasons for someone to go into the store. She was either buying or selling, so the woman automatically had a fifty percent chance of getting it right. She only had to read a few indicators to guess which Reg was doing. She wasn't wealthy; the clinking bracelets and other bits of jewelry she was wearing were all just costume stuff. Nothing of any value. Perhaps she looked more desperate than she had realized.

She loosened the strings of the pouch and emptied it into the waiting tray. She was reassured that they were all there. Nothing had disappeared into Mr. Beaugrand's palm or been lifted by the woman as she helped Reg across the store.

"Ahh." Cuttleby leaned forward and looked at the stones. "Some very handsome specimens."

Reg couldn't help leaning forward to look at them as well, feeling warm and validated by Cuttleby's manner.

Cuttleby examined each stone one at a time with a loupe and the aid of glasses with a complex eyepiece. Reg had performed her own examination of the stones and had not been able to identify any flaws or identifying marks. They were, as far as she could tell, perfectly cut to show off their color and clarity and should be the envy of any collector or jeweler.

Eventually, Cuttleby laid his loupe aside and folded his hands. He looked at Reg.

"We cannot buy these."

CHAPTER FOUR

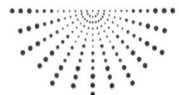

*R*eg stared at him. "What are you talking about? What do you mean, you can't buy them?"

He raised one eyebrow, looking at her. As if she were trying to scam him and already knew the answer to that question herself. "I'm sure you must understand that we cannot buy every stone that comes into the store…"

"No, I guess not, but these are really good quality. They are genuine. There must be a good market for them."

"You have proof of the provenance of the gems?"

"No… but I understood that…" Reg shifted uncomfortably on the stool. "I thought that there were ways *around* that."

"We understand, of course, that sometimes stones have been in the family for a long time. They are not new imports and are therefore not etched with an identification number."

Reg nodded her agreement. He was feeding her everything she needed to say. Providing a pathway through all the red tape for her. "Yes. They've been in the family for decades. Centuries. Before they started tracking gems like that."

She wondered if she had gone too far. Centuries? Would he believe that?

"And documents are sometimes lost during wartime or other unrest," Cuttleby provided.

"Yes. Exactly. When you are fleeing for your life, you're lucky to be able to hold on to the gems themselves."

"But these gems," Cuttleby indicated the stones in the tray. "These were clearly not in your family originally."

"Originally?" Reg echoed.

Of course they had not been in her family originally. Gems passed through many different hands. Her family had clearly not mined them personally. They had to have come from somewhere.

"These stones will need to be... *cleansed* before you can get anything for them."

Cleansed?

Reg slowly started to pick up the gems and return them to her bag. Was that some sort of certification process they needed to go through? Was it like laundering money? Using them for some kind of legitimate purpose before they could be sold? But that didn't make any sense.

"Do you know of *anyone* who would be willing to buy these?" she asked Cuttleby, desperate for more information. If she couldn't liquidate some of the gems, she would be in a very tight position. She wouldn't be out on the street, because Sarah would be willing to let her rent slide if she weren't able to raise it. But Reg had been feeling very proud of herself for being able to have a house of her own and be able to afford not only enough food, but the clothing and other little luxuries that she'd never been able to afford before, taking care of a cat and running her own business. She was acting like an adult, a respectable adult, for once.

If she couldn't sell the gems, all of that could come to an end.

What was the good of a chest of jewels if she couldn't do anything with them?

CHAPTER FIVE

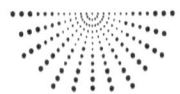

*A*t Cuttleby's grave head shake, Reg slid the bag of gems back into her pocket and stood up from the stool. She was shaken by the experience. Both of the places she had picked out so far had been a complete bust. Neither one even considered buying the gems. Neither was even willing to negotiate. Reg had expected some haggling, but she hadn't even considered that they wouldn't want to buy the gems at all.

She headed for the door. The young greeter turned and met her eyes, smiling. As Reg got closer to her, the smile faded.

"No luck?" she asked, brows drawn down in puzzlement.

"No," Reg agreed. She didn't want to talk about it. She didn't know how to deal with it. She had to rethink her entire life in Black Sands. She'd been letting her psychic business slide a little since people had found out that her mother was a siren. With the amount of hate and prejudice aimed at her, she hadn't been advertising, worried that it would draw more people out against her who would damage her property or cast spells or even to take it a step further and commit direct physical violence against her.

It was beginning to look as though she might have to leave town. Try again another place. She had thought that she had found her niche in Black Sands, but with each revelation about her past and her own nature, it was getting harder and harder to stay there and pretend that she was just a regular psychic like all the others who were already practicing there. It was bizarre that having additional powers would make her as much of a pariah as being poor and homeless had been before arriving in Florida.

The woman took Reg's hands in her own as if they were old friends greeting one another at a funeral. Her eyes were clear and focused on Reg, as if she were looking into her soul.

"You have friends. Ask your friends."

"Um…" Reg wasn't sure how to respond to this. "Okay. Thanks."

She pulled her hands out of the woman's grip and walked away.

* * *

She could have tried a couple more places, but Reg could already see the pattern. And if she continued to go to other jewelers and exchanges, she would become known, and people would refuse to deal with her. She had to go home, reevaluate, and figure out what she needed to do to cleanse the gems so that they could be sold. Once they were clean, then she would be able to go to other dealers and see about selling them. Quietly and without attracting attention to herself. If she went to every shady dealer in the city with what she had now, it would be just like shining a spotlight on her gems. Which clearly was not a good idea.

So she turned her car around and started driving toward home.

The weather was idyllic. She had the windows down and she could smell the salty tang of the sea on the breeze. It made her want to drop all responsibilities and just go to the ocean. She could walk along the beach with her feet in the water.

She could go for a swim. For a boat ride. She could go *hunting*.

Reg immediately pushed these thoughts away and walled them off. She was not a predator. She was not going hunting. She was going home to figure out how to deal with the gemstones so that she would be able to sell them. Either that, or to figure out how to get her business off the ground again and start making some money the old-fashioned way.

The trip home seemed to take much longer than the journey out had. When she had left, she had been anticipating a big payday. She didn't know how much the gems were worth, and she knew that it would be work to get them liquidated, but she had figured that she would be going home with a stack of cash.

Not with the gems still in her pocket.

She swore to herself several times.

How could she have screwed it up? She had looked at the gems with an eyepiece that would magnify them enough to see any identification numbers etched into them. She knew that there were no markings on them. So what had Beaugrand and Cuttleby seen when they had looked at them? What had told them that there was something wrong with the provenance of the gems and that they couldn't purchase them?

It didn't make any sense.

* * *

Reg stalked from her car toward the back yard where her cottage was located behind Sarah's big house. Her thoughts were confused and angry and she wasn't paying much attention to anything around her.

She didn't see or sense Corvin until he stepped out from behind a bush right in front of her. She was moving so quickly, her anger burning so hot, that he was lucky she didn't mow him right down. As it was, Reg gasped and brought her hands up to protect herself against him.

When she saw Corvin's incredibly handsome face, the clear bright eyes and neatly-trimmed beard that she had come to know so well, her anger flared even more. Corvin raised his hands defensively.

"Reg—it's me."

"I know it's you," Reg snapped. "I don't know what you're doing here, but I cannot deal with this right now. Get out of my way."

He raised one eyebrow, surprised. He poured on the charm, so that Reg could feel the heat emanating from him and smell the scent of roses. Her anger dampened, her body betraying her, heart beating faster in anticipation and endorphins flooding her brain. Reg tried to steel herself. She could resist him. She'd done so countless times since she'd come to Black Sands. But her unchecked anger had apparently opened the emotional connection between them, and she felt the attraction even more strongly than usual.

"Stop that," she told him. They were standing too close together.

She wanted to step right into his arms. She had been through a big disappointment. Anyone would want the comfort of a friend. To be swallowed up in his arms and to give herself to him. "Stop," she repeated in a quieter, more subdued voice.

"I'm not doing anything." His voice was rich and soothing. It always sent a wave of warmth over her, as if she were being wrapped in a warm blanket on a chilly day. Or slipping into a warm bath.

The thought of sliding into warm water helped clarify her thoughts. She needed to fight back against him. He was dangerous, but so was she, if she called on her powers to fight back against him. Or to entrap him, as he was trying to entrap her.

"You are too. Turn it off."

"I can't help my natural reactions," he reminded her. An excuse he had given repeatedly in the past for stepping over the line. "When you come storming over here, act like you're going to attack, my natural defenses…" He held his hands palms-up in mute appeal. "Would you blame your cat for raising its hackles at a threat?"

"I didn't threaten you. I just told you to get out of my way. So that I can get home and relax. You know that I wasn't attacking you."

"What the brain knows and what the body perceives are very different. I'm not trying to do anything to harm you." He leaned forward despite his words, the heady scent of roses swirling around her. Reg could almost see the pheromones, like in a cartoon where a stream of perfume snakes through the air and beckons to the target, physically lifting him off of his feet and transporting him. She drew the warm air into her lungs and savored it like a smoker.

"Stop." Her protest was faint.

"Why don't we go to your house, and you can tell me what's got you so riled up today."

He backed up so that she could continue down the pathway toward the cottage. Reg didn't hesitate to close the distance between her and her house, though her strides did seem more difficult than usual. Swimming through setting concrete might have been faster. She knew that if she got through the gate, she would enter the space that was protected by Sarah's charms and wards, and Corvin would not be able to follow her. No one who intended her harm would be able to get into the yard. A necessary protection after everything that had happened recently.

But as she reached the gate, Corvin was right behind her, and he put his hand on her arm as if to escort her to her cottage in safety. Reg passed through the portal and, with his hand on her, Corvin was able to enter with her. Reg turned her head toward him.

"You can't do that! You're not welcome here!"

"And yet, here I am." He smiled, his eyes dancing. His amused, little-boy smirk just pulled her in harder. Was there no end to the wiles he could use on her?

"And you can go right back out." Reg gave him a shove with one hand. Even with a layer of cloth between them, she could still feel the buzz of electricity that always sparked between them. He resisted, his muscles contracting under his cloak and shirt. Reg wanted to explore all his muscles. Very slowly. She pushed harder. She marshaled all of her willpower to push back against him mentally. She could protect herself. She could make an envelope of power around herself that would prevent her from falling victim to his entrancing scent and magical charms.

It was difficult. After her fruitless errand to the city, Reg was tired and frustrated and didn't have the patience to deal with the unbelievably gorgeous warlock. She knew that she was only seeing and feeling what he wanted her to. It wasn't real. Her perceptions were magically enhanced. She was already partially under his spell.

But she worked hard to reflect back the heat he was generating and the rest of the charms, to force them back upon him like a weapon. Corvin stepped back slightly. It was barely perceptible, but she felt his muscles slacken under her hand as he tried to defend himself against her considerable skills.

"There's no need…" he purred in protest.

"Get back from me. Get out of my yard. And don't try to use your charms on me!"

"Regina." He said it in that alluring way he had, reaching into her soul, looking for another way in. "I'm just here to talk. I'm your friend."

"You're not being my friend. You're trying to ensorcel me. Again."

"As I said, it's just my body's natural defense. We both know what I am…"

"You have plenty of other defenses. Aren't you claiming to be one of the most powerful beings in the world, with all the power you absorbed from the Witch Doctor, and his horde, and everything else you have consumed? From me when you took my power in the mountain?"

"That was at your request. I took nothing more than I was allowed."

"Huh. We both know that's not true. And even if it was, that's not what I asked. If you're so all powerful, then why do you have to use your charms against me? If you really needed to defend yourself, you have plenty of ways to do that."

He shrugged and smirked.

"I don't need your help," Reg asserted.

"Another thing we both know—that it isn't true. You do need my help. You are still weak from being possessed by another. Your mind is damaged. There are holes in your memories and knowledge…"

The wizard had taken more from Reg than she was willing to admit. But Corvin wasn't there to help her. He was there to take advantage of her in her weakened state.

"You can't help me. And I don't want your help even if you could. I want you to stay away from me and my house. What are you even doing here?"

Reg would admit that she had called Corvin in the past when she needed company, usually late at night when she didn't know who else would be up, or to ask him a question that he, as a professor and a scholar of magical history, might have the answer for. She could see him in her mind when she wanted to, to know whether he was up and what he was doing. But she called him on the phone, so it was safe. She didn't ask him to come over in person.

Usually.

Almost never.

"Like I said," he leaned against a tree, "I came to see whether I could help you. I know how much trouble you have been having lately. I can feel…" He trailed off, and she could feel him poking at her consciousness, prodding and trying to find his way in that way since his pheromones had failed. "I can feel how much difficulty you are having, how many roadblocks you are running into. I can help."

It was tempting, but she knew that his "help" would only lead to further harm. Yes, he had helped her in the past, but she had needed others there to help her, or else she had unleashed the siren powers inherited from her mother, which she did not want to do. If she used them, there was no guarantee that she would be able to stop herself, either. She might go too far, and although she feared what Corvin could do to her, she worried more about what she could do to him.

She would never forgive herself if she let those instincts take over and irreparable harm were done.

Reg forced these thoughts from her mind and pushed Corvin's consciousness as far from her as she could too. "Stay out of my brain. Go home. Or to look for other prey. You can't have my powers. That will never happen again."

He slunk back from her, still eyeing her as if wondering what other strategy he could use to get what he wanted. He wouldn't give up. However close they became as friends or however distant due to both of their natures, they would always be inseparably connected by the powers they had shared in the past.

No one could undo that.

CHAPTER SIX

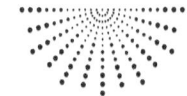

*E*ventually, Corvin left the yard and Reg was able to relax. She was pretty sure that she understood the wards that Sarah had set well enough to know that even though Corvin had entered the yard once on her arm, they would not allow him in again alone. She was pretty sure of that.

Mostly.

She monitored Corvin's position as he headed back to his car, making sure that he actually left and didn't stick around, waiting for round two. Once she was sure he was gone, she headed to the cottage. But upon reaching her doorstep, Reg changed her mind. She needed to learn more about the gems and what she would have to do to be able to sell them, and she would not get that from an internet search.

Sarah had a very powerful emerald that helped to keep her young and vibrant. Sarah knew about stones of power, and she would be able to help Reg. She would know what to do about it.

Reg went to the back door of the big house, knocked, and entered. "Sarah? Are you home?"

Reg could feel her presence in the house, so she didn't really need to ask. She was just being polite and announcing herself.

"Reg? I'm just getting dressed, come on up."

Having seen Sarah's rooms full of clothes, Reg knew that getting dressed was something that might take Sarah a few seconds or a few hours, depending on where she were going. If it were out on a date with one of her younger men or to a community dance or event, she might go through a dozen different outfits before settling on one.

Reg climbed the stairs and followed the sound of hangers sliding and clicking along rods, to find Sarah going through a rack of formal wear.

"Hi. Going out?"

"Well, I'm not decluttering, I'll tell you that!" Sarah laughed merrily.

Reg laughed. Sarah's house was packed to the gills with her possessions. She wasn't a hoarder exactly, everything was neat and clean and properly stored, but if a hoarder could be neat, then maybe she was.

"You could probably get rid of a *few* things," she ventured.

"Reg, dear, once you have lived out of a tent, you learn the value of having everything you need right at hand. If I got rid of all the 'extras' around here, you can bet I would end up needing it again the next week."

Reg nodded. She hadn't lived out of a tent, but she had lived rough on the street. And it hadn't been easy. She could relate to Sarah's desire to hold on to as many possessions as she could. Reg too had a difficult time letting things go, even when they were old and worn and no longer useful. She would have a very difficult time packing up and leaving Black Sands if she had to. She had gotten used to having *things.*

"So, what's up with you?" Sarah asked.

"Just ran into Corvin in the yard," Reg said with a grimace.

"What's he doing down there? Get me my broom and I'll send him packing!"

Reg laughed. She remembered the way Sarah had wielded her broom when chasing a stray cat out of her garden. The devastation had been significant. But she also remembered how Corvin had helped Sarah out when she had been sick, and that despite her warnings for Reg to stay away from him, Sarah still seemed to have quite an affection for him.

"He's gone now. He said he wanted to 'help' me."

"Help himself *to* you, more like." Sarah pulled a dress off the rack and held it up to her shoulders. It was black with sequins and Reg thought maybe a bit young for a woman of Sarah's age. Or a woman who looked Sarah's age. Reg had no idea how old she really was. From the picture of Sarah that she had seen in a history book about the settlement of Black Sands, she was very old. But she only looked about sixty. She was a little overweight, with gray hair, and looked very grandmotherly. She treated Reg like a daughter, but at other times her behavior was not quite so age-appropriate.

Sarah put the dress back.

"Good for you. We don't want his kind hanging around here. We have quite enough troubles without him adding to it."

Reg bit her lip and was quiet. She was the one who was causing Sarah most of those problems. It was because of Reg that Sarah had to deal with vandals and witches trying to vanquish Reg from the community.

Sarah looked at her. "Nothing to do with you, Reg. Now, what can I help you with? Are you looking for a dress?"

"No. Thank you. You sure have some nice ones, though."

"You should feel free to borrow them anytime. I may be quite a bit thicker than you, but it is easy to alter the size of a dress, if you know how." Reg suspected she was talking about witchcraft rather than sewing alterations. "You know I have more here than I can ever use and I won't miss anything you borrow."

"Yes. I will, sometime." If she stayed in Black Sands. "Actually... I wondered how much you know about gems."

"Not my area of expertise. The emerald is one of the only stones of power that I have. Lesser stones look nice in jewelry. Some can be used in meditations or magnifying spells. Why?"

"I was trying to liquidate a few of the gems that I got from the Papillons. The fairies."

"Oh."

Sarah turned away from Reg to look at the dresses she was going through. She didn't offer any immediate advice. So maybe she didn't know that Reg would have problems selling them. Maybe Sarah had never had a stone she wanted to sell, only ones she intended to keep.

"I went into the city today, hoping to find a buyer."

Sarah said nothing.

"I went to a couple of places, but they both said that they wouldn't buy them," Reg went on. "I guess they saw something that they didn't like. I knew there might be problems with not being able to prove their provenance, but that's why I picked the buyers I did. They were places that were supposed to be more accepting of… unpapered stones."

"Yes. Very interesting."

Reg was getting frustrated. Sarah was usually very helpful, offering more suggestions than Reg needed. Her stubborn silence grated on Reg's nerves.

"Do you know of anyone who would buy them? Or can you explain to me what the problem might be?"

"I don't have any suggestions for buyers, I'm sorry. That's not something I do."

"Okay… I was hoping you would at least have some suggestions. I thought you must have heard about someone, after all the years you've lived in this community…"

"No."

Reg blew out her breath and shook her head. "Well, maybe you could help me to understand why they would not want to buy them. I mean, I've done my homework. I know that they take older gemstones that don't have any provenance. It's only the new gems that need ID numbers etched onto them."

"Not really my area…"

"You don't know anything about it?" Reg challenged, getting the feeling that Sarah was intentionally blocking her. It wasn't that she didn't know what Reg was talking about. It was that she didn't want to talk about it. Maybe didn't even want Reg to talk about it.

"No."

"You don't know why no one would buy my gems."

Sarah finally turned her face toward Reg. She blinked several times, focusing on her accuser. Her face was devoid of expression, as if she were wearing a mask.

"Because they are cursed."

CHAPTER SEVEN

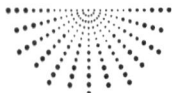

*I*f Reg had been chewing gum, she would have spat it out. Or swallowed it. She stared at Sarah, who did not change her expression, but went back to examining the clothing on the rack.

"They are *cursed?*" Reg repeated.

Sarah nodded. "Yes."

"How do you know that?"

"They have a certain… feeling. Once you have held a cursed gem in your hands, you will know it again."

Reg thought about the way she felt when she handled the gems. She had been able to feel their power, just like with Sarah's emerald, but she hadn't felt anything bad.

"Are you sure? Maybe they're just… they have power."

"I can tell the difference between a powerful gem and a cursed one. Not that the two are exclusive. They are not."

"Can you look at me, Sarah? Can you explain it to me?"

There was silence as Sarah continued to look through the clothing, ignoring Reg's question. Reg said nothing, standing there waiting. Finally, Sarah turned her face toward Reg, though she didn't move her body, so she was just looking back over her shoulder at Reg.

"We don't talk about such things."

Her words lay heavily in the air for a long time as Reg tried to decide what to do about them.

"We don't talk about them. Why not?"

"There are some things that are just not... discussed in polite company."

Reg remembered another such comment. "Some things," she repeated, "like about people like Corvin? The way you don't discuss what his abilities are, what his 'curse' is, not warning the innocent people who could become his prey?"

Sarah nodded. "Certainly not. It would be extremely gauche to bring up such a thing. It's like..." Sarah shook her head as she tried to think of a comparison that Reg would understand. "It would be like discussing sex at the dinner table. It simply is not done. There are some things that are... simply too delicate."

"So it's more important to avoid making people uncomfortable than it is to prevent them from being hurt."

"I did warn you," Sarah reminded Reg. "I told you more than once that he was dangerous and that you should not go out with him or be left alone with him. You cannot deny that."

"No. But you didn't tell me why. I thought you were just saying that... he might take advantage of me. But I'm a big girl and I can take care of myself. I didn't understand his... gift, or curse, or whatever you call it. Because people thought it would be impolite to tell me."

Sarah shrugged. "We can only do what we can. If you do not want to listen or do not understand, then that isn't on us. That's on you."

"How could I understand if no one would tell me?" Reg demanded, the frustration that she had previously put aside on the topic coming to the surface again. "Explain that to me."

"By listening to what you are told. I told you enough for you to understand that he was a danger to you. You are the one who chose not to listen, to go out with him and then to bring him back here, by yourself, and to break the wards that I had set to protect you."

"I didn't bring him back here, I..." Reg faltered under Sarah's glare. "Well, I did, but that wasn't because I wanted to, he had control over me."

Sarah's eyebrows lifted in disbelief.

"You know what effect he has on people. How was I supposed to resist that?"

Sarah said nothing, but Reg heard again her accusation, that Reg should have listened to what she was told. That if she didn't, then she was the one who was at fault. Not the people who didn't explain it to her in detail. The people who should have known that she didn't understand and that she was treading on thin ice.

"You're blaming the victim," Reg pointed out.

"Yes." Sarah agreed.

"I didn't ask for him to take my powers."

"Well, that is debatable."

They were at a stalemate. Reg knew that she wouldn't convince Sarah of anything. She had already made up her mind.

"Fine, then. But I need you to explain to me about the gems being cursed."

Sarah took a couple of dresses off the rack without even looking at them, much less holding them up to herself. She sighed and walked out of the room. Reg assumed she was to follow, and did so.

"As I said, it really is not seemly for me to be discussing it with you."

"Then how am I supposed to know that the gems are cursed or what I can do about it?"

"You should be able to sense it yourself. You have psychic powers. Are you telling me that you feel nothing when you hold the gems?"

"Well... no. I can feel that they are powerful, like you said. But that doesn't mean that they feel... dangerous. Or cursed or whatever."

"What did these buyers tell you?"

"Nothing. One said..." Reg tried to remember the words that had been used. "That I should not have accepted a gift. And that I would have to show their history. The other one said that they had to be cleansed."

Sarah nodded and shrugged as if that explained everything.

"That doesn't help me!" Reg snapped. "I have no idea where they came from, other than from Calliopia's family, and I don't have the first clue how to cleanse gems. They're *cursed*? How do gems get cursed?"

"You would have to look at their history to find that out."

Reg shook her head. "How do I do that?"

"I have never accepted a gift of cursed gems," Sarah said, raising her brows. "So I'm afraid I cannot help you with that."

Reg folded her arms across her chest. "So once again, it is my fault. Because no one will talk to me. You are the one person who knew about me getting the gems. You couldn't have given me a heads-up? You couldn't tell me that you thought they were cursed and maybe I shouldn't accept them, or I would have to *cleanse* them before I could use them for anything?"

"I fail to see, Reg, how it is my fault that you did something rash."

Reg tried to figure out a way to explain to Sarah that it was clearly her fault, and not Reg's own, if no one had taught her about cursed gems and what to do about them. But she couldn't find any argument that Sarah wouldn't just throw back in her face. Why hadn't Reg educated herself? Why had she just assumed that it was okay to accept such an elaborate gift? Hadn't she seen that there was something wrong with it? Didn't she sense that the gems were cursed, with all that psychic power she was supposed to possess?

One of her foster mothers had once told her "If it sounds too good to be true, then it probably is."

It was advice that Reg had used, not necessarily in her own purchases and ventures, but as a guide to conning other people out of their money. Make something sound *too* good, and people wouldn't do it. They would pull back, suspecting that something was wrong. Make it just a little better than they could get anywhere else, with a good sob story as to why you were willing to give them what they wanted at such a low price, and they were far more likely to buy into it. Give them just the barest hint that the reason the goods or services were lower was that they *might* have fallen off the back of a truck or because Reg was in desperate need to pay her rent the next day, and they would willingly accept it. Make it too low and they would know they were being conned.

And the fairies giving Reg a chest full of jewels? Reg hadn't thought that was too good to be true?

In fact, the thought had crossed her mind. But she knew that the fairies were fabulously wealthy compared to her and that she had nearly killed herself trying to bring the Papillon's daughter back from the brink of death, and it didn't seem to be that much out of proportion. She definitely deserved more than a simple thank you. She had put herself in considerable danger more than once to save Calliopia.

She deserved a reward. And maybe the Papillons had meant her to split the treasure between all the people in her company, everyone who had helped to save Calliopia. There hadn't been any instructions, and Reg hadn't distributed the gems, even though she had thought more than once that she probably should. It was hard for her, after being so poor her whole life. She was used to taking care of herself, to considering her own need for safety and stability, not anyone else's.

"You're not going to help me?" she asked Sarah.

"I'm afraid I can't, Reg."

Reg was pretty sure that she could. If she wanted to.

CHAPTER EIGHT

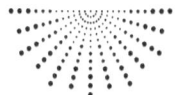

*I*f Sarah wouldn't talk to her about the gems, then there was another party that already knew about the jewels that Reg could talk to. She didn't look forward to going back to the Papillon mansion to try to get some information on the history of the gems, but she didn't want to reveal the fact that she possessed the gems to anyone else. If she went to Davyn or Corvin or someone else who might be able to help her to cleanse them, then more people would know about her treasure. With every person who knew about the gemstones, the odds of their getting stolen skyrocketed. She might trust Davyn, but she didn't trust that he wouldn't just happen to say something to his new friend Julian or to someone else who would spread the word around.

So, it was time to see the fairies and ask them about it.

Mrs. Papillon had told her that she was welcome at the mansion anytime. Reg had, of course, never taken her up on it, and Mrs. Papillon had undoubtedly expected that she never would. Reg really didn't have any reason to go to the mansion. Except now she did. She would have to put that invitation to the test.

Reg first returned to her cottage to pet Starlight and make sure that his dishes were freshly filled with adequate nourishment. She had only been gone for a few hours, but these things were important to a cat. Reg didn't tell him what she had discovered so far. It was one thing when

Sarah looked at her with that expression of disdain when she had done something stupid or not known the most basic of magical traditions and practice. It was quite another when her cat did it.

"I'll be back later," she told Starlight breezily. "Maybe we'll put on a movie tonight. Pop some popcorn."

Not that that was any different from any other night they spent together. Sometimes Reg invited a few of her friends over to watch the movie with her. And on occasion, she had gone to a community event. She was supposed to be meeting new people, expanding her business base, but Reg was currently trying to stay low until people forgot about her mother being a siren and started treating her like a normal person again. The same person she had been when she had first arrived in Black Sands.

The trees and vegetation growing beside the road were green. Everything in Florida was green. It was one of the few places Reg had ever been where they didn't have to worry about what to do if there were a drought.

Her surroundings grew wilder, but she could also tell that she was getting close to the mansion. They were wild in a perfect way, as if they had been grown and trimmed to the exact shape they were in order to look wild. Window dressing or camouflage? Did the fairies want to be seen or to be hidden? Reg couldn't figure out which it was.

She watched carefully for the turnoff, and then took the pathway that went deeper and deeper into the forest. It wound around, and the foliage around her grew even more gorgeous. It was really stunning, comparable to the garden Forst had created at Sarah's house. Though Reg would never tell him that. Or the fairies. They would probably both take it as an insult.

She didn't know how fairies and gnomes got along together, but she knew that fairies and pixies didn't get along. Or fairies and cats. Fairies and humans weren't the best of friends, for that matter. So it was entirely feasible that fairies didn't get along with gnomes or any of the other races in the area either.

Reg pulled into a clearing in the forest to see the Papillon mansion towering above her, looking just like the castle out of a fairy tale. The lawn and trees and gardens around the mansion were all groomed and manicured and trimmed to look absolutely perfect. She was almost afraid to get out of the car, for fear that the illusion would break and she would find herself looking at a normal yard and house.

She sat there for a moment and then forced herself to get out.

She rang the doorbell and knocked for good measure. Sometimes the butler was inclined to be condescending and pretended he didn't hear her or said that she would have to come back another time, when she had actually been invited. But she hadn't been back since Mrs. Papillon had told her that she was welcome there anytime, so maybe things had changed.

The tall, pale-faced butler swung open the door and looked down his nose at Reg.

"Is Mrs. Papillon in?" Reg inquired. "I'd like to speak with her for a few minutes."

He appeared to be considering the question, and Reg didn't want him to come to the wrong answer. "She said I could visit anytime."

His lips puckered sourly and his nostrils flared. He still said nothing, but eventually opened the door the rest of the way and stepped back to allow her to enter.

Reg stepped into the mansion and looked around. It was a big house and she wasn't sure where the proprietors would be. The greenhouse where she had watched them pot plants? One of the arboretums she had previously visited Calliopia or her parents in? She would not be going to Calliopia's bedroom this time. Callie was no longer there. She had broken away from the community, committing an unpardonable offense.

"This way," the butler told Reg haughtily, as if he'd been trying to get her attention earlier and she hadn't been paying attention. In all honestly, she hadn't been, but neither had he said anything to her aloud. If he expected her to read his mind or some nonverbal signal he had given her, he would have to be more clear. She had been taught that it was rude to read people's minds without their express permission. And usually she didn't. If she could help it.

Reg swiveled and followed the tall fairy, feeling like a child being left behind by his long strides.

He waited at the entrance of one of the rooms. Reg caught up with him and tried to slow her breathing. She didn't want to run into the room out of breath, scaring people into thinking there was something wrong or that she was being disrespectful by running in their house.

She walked into the room at what she hoped was a stately speed, and found Mr. and Mrs. Papillon sitting among the indoor trees, deep in discussion.

They stopped speaking when they saw Reg. Mrs. Papillon rose swiftly to her feet and extended a hand to Reg.

"Welcome, Reg Rawlins. You honor us with your presence."

Reg wasn't sure whether Mrs. Papillon was expecting her to shake hands, or to kiss her fingers, or if it were just a grand gesture. She bent her knees in a small curtsy and hoped that would be enough to show her hosts respect.

"I'm sorry to come here without an invitation. I hope I didn't interrupt anything."

"Of course not. You are always welcome here."

Mrs. Papillon motioned to another seat, a white wicker chair that was nestled under a tree with long, broad leaves. Reg sat perched on the edge of it. She didn't intend to get comfortable. It wasn't exactly a comfortable topic that she had come to speak to them about. They might just throw her out the moment she opened her mouth about the gemstones.

Reg looked around, wondering if she needed to start with some small talk. She didn't know if that were customary with fairies, or just a human thing. When she had talked with fairies before, it seemed that there had always been some special reason to meet and they had gotten directly to the topic. When Calliopia had been on her deathbed—well, they didn't begin with discussing the weather.

"How is Calliopia?" Reg tried. "Have you talked to her at all?"

"She is not in contact with the kin," Mr. Papillon said archly. "She has chosen to live outside our community."

Because she had chosen a pixie for a partner. Something that was taboo in both communities. By choosing each other as mates, Calliopia and Ruan had been expelled from both of their families. Reg wondered how many other fairy and pixie couples there were out there, on the outskirts of society, choosing to live in exile rather than complying with the expectations of their magical races. She was sure that Calliopia and Ruan could not be the only ones. But such things were not discussed.

Yet another topic that was forbidden in polite company. Like the one that Reg was planning to bring up.

"Yes, I just wondered whether… word had gotten to you. Sometimes children still write letters home… or get a message to you through another source. Or maybe you just hear rumors through a messenger. Someone who has happened to see her."

Mr. Papillon looked at his wife and did not say anything. She gave Reg a bland, beatific smile, and did not fill her in on any knowledge of Calliopia's life.

"Is that all that Reg Rawlins came to inquire about today?"

"No," Reg admitted. "That's not why I am here."

They looked at her, faces blank, waiting for her to tell them her reason for the visit.

"I neglected to thank you for the gift that you sent me after Calliopia's recovery," Reg said slowly. Since there had been no accompanying note with the gems, she was feeling her way through the subject, and thought it best not to say that it was compensation for her healing Calliopia or anything that they might take umbrage with. "That was a very generous gift."

Mrs. Papillon inclined her head in a brief nod of acknowledgment but didn't say anything else about their gratitude for what Reg had done or that she deserved the rich reward they had given her. Reg rubbed her sweating palms along her thighs, drying them on her skirt. Her palms were wet and her mouth dry, and she desperately wished that she had brought a water bottle or that they had offered her some refreshment.

"It was really too generous," Reg suggested. "I should probably have returned them to you right away. I should not have accepted them."

Mrs. Papillon glanced at her husband.

"Why should you return what was freely given?" Mr. Papillon asked. "The stones now belong to you."

Reg felt as if a weight had been added to her shoulders. If the gems were cursed, it was clear that the Papillons wanted nothing to do with them any longer. They were happy to have transferred ownership to another being. She had been a dupe. They had known or hoped that she wouldn't recognize that they were transferring a curse to her, so that they could be rid of it.

Reg hadn't asked Sarah what kind of a curse it was. Something that would make her sick or cause her early death? A bad luck curse? She hadn't exactly had an easy life since she had acquired the gems but, on the other hand, she hadn't contracted some rare disease that was rapidly subtracting years from her life.

At least, not as far as she knew.

Maybe the recipient of the curse had to know about it for it to be effective. Maybe there was a psychological aspect to it. A person was only cursed if they believed in the curse. Maybe by being unaware, she had avoided any negative effects up until then.

"I was hoping to be able to sell some of the stones. I'm short on cash, and humans need a certain amount to be able to pay the bills. House rental, utilities, internet..." Reg trailed off, knowing that the fairies would know next to nothing about these human concepts. "So anyway. I took them to a couple of places in the city to see if I could get some money to pay the bills."

They both just looked at her, not filling in the empty space, not acknowledging that they knew where she was going with this. Maybe they thought that humans could sell anything, that the curse wouldn't have any effect on commerce.

"But I was told by the jewelers I talked to today that they could not buy the stones, because of the curse on them."

Mr. Papillon nodded slowly. Not a surprise, then.

"I need to be able to sell them," Reg pointed out. "They are useless to me otherwise. Just having them doesn't do me any good."

"They do have power," Mr. Papillon pointed out. He shook his head slightly. "Humans are so avaricious... they see only the opportunity for profit. But the stones have value in themselves. Power and beauty. You do not need to sell them to profit from them."

"But I do. And I need to understand what this curse is. I don't get it. I didn't even know that they were cursed until today. Can you tell me what it is? Where it came from? What does it mean to me?"

He was silent, gazing at her.

"Please," Reg tacked on. "This is very important to me."

"We... cannot help you," Mrs. Papillon said.

"You must know something about this curse."

A shrug.

"Did you know that they were cursed?" Reg tried. "Or is that just a human thing?"

"The stones belong to you now."

"Yes, okay. But I need to know something about their history. The jewelers said that I needed to understand the history of the gems and where they came from. But the only thing I know about is that they came from you. I don't know where they came from before that."

She was met with blank faces and stares. No sign that they understood her need to know this information or that they intended to help her.

"Have they been in your family for long? They are quite old, right?"

"All gems spring from ancient lineage," Mr. Papillon said logically. Of course they hadn't just been created recently. They had been formed in the earth thousands of years before and had waited there for someone to dig them up. They were all old.

Reg thought that he knew what she meant, though. Fairies and some of the other races were very pedantic and expected everyone to follow their rules and conventions, and anything that fell outside those parameters was wrong and needed to be corrected, until the person could say or do things the way that the kin did. They weren't willing to bend to human conventions, but expected other races to conform to theirs.

"Right. And they've been in your family for...?" Not a flicker on Mr. Papillon's face to indicate that he intended to fill in the blank. "For how long?" Reg prompted, hoping that he was just waiting for her to finish the question properly.

"They are yours now," he repeated firmly. "They are your responsibility and we have nothing more to do with them."

"I could really use your help, though."

No answer.

"Your advice." Reg hoped that if she didn't imply that he still had some responsibility for the gems that he would soften. "Your race is so wise in these matters. If you could help someone who has not grown up in the magical community..."

"We keep to ourselves. We do not wish to be involved in this matter."

"You didn't keep to yourselves when you needed help finding

Calliopia. And you were happy for my help when I came to see her, when she was hurt. I've given you a lot of help and advice. I would think that you could reciprocate."

"We have paid you handsomely for your services," Mr. Papillon disagreed. "A king's ransom. We do not owe you anything further."

A king's ransom? Was it just a figure of speech, or was it literal? Was it a clue?

"If there is anything you could tell me about the gems or about their origin or this curse, I would be really grateful," Reg said earnestly, putting as much emotion and sincerity into her words as she could. "It would be really helpful for me."

"I am sorry," Mr. Papillon said again. "I cannot help you."

He stood up. An unmistakable signal that it was time for Reg to leave. Reg stayed where she was, resisting.

"Maybe Callie would be able to help me," she suggested. "I could find her and see if she knows anything about the provenance of the jewels."

Mr. Papillon's expression was thunderous. "Our daughter knows nothing about these stones. You will leave her out of it."

Reg didn't really intend to track Calliopia down and find out if she knew anything about the gems, but it was interesting to observe Mr. Papillon's reaction to the suggestion. Was he angry just because she had mentioned Calliopia? Because she was no longer part of their household? Because he saw it as a threat? Or was there any possibility that Calliopia really did know the secret the gems held and might be able to tell Reg what she needed to know?

"She is no longer part of your household. I didn't think you considered her part of your family anymore."

Mrs. Papillon looked at her husband, weighing her words against his reaction. "Calliopia will always be a part of this family. No matter how far away she is."

"No matter what she does? No matter what your community thinks of her?" Reg knew that the Papillons were concerned with how they looked in their community. It had been obvious to her in her previous interactions with them that they had been unwilling to go against any of the conventions of their race.

"She is our daughter. No matter what the kin say," Calliopia's mother said firmly.

Mr. Papillon's eyes flashed to his wife, but he did not dispute what she said. There might be a discussion about this matter after Reg had left, but he would not call her out in front of Reg.

"There are only so many places I can go to find out what the problem is with these gems, what the curse on them is all about. So if you don't want me to make any inquiries, then you should tell me yourself. That would be the logical thing to do."

"We cannot help you with this."

Reg finally rose to her feet as well. She didn't even come close to matching Mr. Papillon's height. He towered above her. She felt like a child standing next to him. And he had always treated her like a child; all the fairies did. Reg's limited human years meant that she would always be a naive young child compared to the longer-lived races. Sarah, with her centuries, might be someone worth speaking to. But not Reg.

The butler appeared in the doorway, stiffening and waiting for Reg to follow him. Reg looked at the Papillons, hoping against hope that they would throw her a bone. Just one little tidbit that would get her started in the right direction.

But there was nothing. They both watched her impassively, waiting for her to leave. Mrs. Papillon did not bother to tell Reg this time that she would always be welcome.

Reg followed the butler to the front door.

CHAPTER NINE

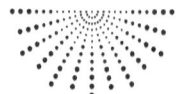

*R*eg bought a big, greasy burger on the way home, and when she arrived at the cottage, plopped herself down in front of the TV and didn't move for a couple of hours. She was discouraged about the whole gem thing and determined to put it out of her mind and not think about it anymore.

But her brain was not cooperating. Reg sat with Starlight in her lap, petting him and trying to remain focused on the miniseries she had turned on. But she still had the little bag of gems in her pocket, and it was like they were burning a hole there. She couldn't think of anything else.

Eventually, she got up to have a drink, then sat again, flipping through channels to try to come up with something better. Anything that would keep her attention. But all the shows she turned on just seemed to remind her of her own troubles and she couldn't get into anything else. She could have a warm bath and head to bed, seeing if sleep would erase the subject from her mind, but of course she knew that would not work. She would just toss and turn, thinking about the gems and how she would rid herself of them. It would keep her from being able to get to sleep, until she was too exhausted to stay awake anymore.

She turned the TV off, grumpy and dissatisfied. Starlight put his ears back, listening to her. He didn't turn to look at her, but his ears gave him away. He wasn't used to her turning off the TV in the evening unless she were getting ready for bed or a visitor.

"What do you think I should do?" Reg asked him, although she hadn't explained the problem to him at all. Exactly how did she expect him to give her advice on a human problem when she hadn't told him anything about it?

Starlight purred and curled himself into a ball, showing her his white tuxedo chin and throat.

"Yes, you're cute." She rubbed his jaw and chin. "But that doesn't really help me."

He purred more loudly.

"Cute kitty isn't solving any of my problems."

Although stroking his silky soft fur didn't make things any worse, either. What was it like to be a cat? Nice not to have all of the human worries? Or harder because they were not in control of anything and had to get humans to do everything for them?

Starlight twisted to look at her with one slitted eye. She bent down and kissed him on the nose, which caused him to snort and shake his head, flapping his ears.

Reg got out her phone and thumbed through her mail and her social networks. Nothing important going on there. Nothing that interested her, even when she went to YouTube to check on her favorite channels.

The phone rang.

Reg didn't need to look at the picture on the screen to know who it would be. Only one person could read her mind well enough to know that she was restless and out of sorts. Only one person would intentionally call her when she was in that kind of a mood and risk how she might react.

"Corvin."

"Regina," he purred. "How are you this beautiful evening?"

"Ugh. Angry. Irritated. Depressed. What makes you think it is such a beautiful evening?"

"The sky is clear; the moon is out. Jupiter is rising. Why would I not be in a good mood?"

His cheer just put her into a worse mood. And he probably knew that. He liked to poke at her, irritate her.

"Why don't you go jump in a lake?" Reg suggested.

"Is that an invitation? Do you have any particular lake in mind?"

Reg wondered fleetingly if a freshwater lake would set off her siren instincts like the saltwater of the ocean. Probably. Did Florida even have freshwater lakes?

"Did you call me because you wanted something?"

"No. Just thought you might enjoy a chat."

"Well, I'm in a pretty bad mood right now, so it probably isn't a good idea."

"You were upset earlier today too. What's going on?"

"You ambushed me earlier."

"Well, it wasn't meant that way. I was just staying out of Sarah's way until you got home. I didn't mean to be… lurking."

"You're lucky she didn't see you. She was talking about going after you with the broom when I mentioned you were around."

"I've seen that witch wield a broom. I wouldn't want to be on the other end of it."

"Me neither," Reg agreed, allowing a small laugh.

"She should be out enjoying the night life by now. I could come over and try to cheer you up."

"No, you couldn't. I wouldn't let you in."

"We could sit outside in the garden and enjoy the night air."

"Not even that." She knew only too well that he could charm her almost as easily outside as in.

"What is on my sweet Regina's mind?"

"Your sweet Regina?" Reg snorted. Had he been drinking? "I don't think you've ever tried that one before. I'm anything but sweet. Especially today."

"Then tell me about it, sourpuss."

Reg thought about it. Corvin had been more forthcoming in the past than some of the other witches and warlocks she was acquainted with. Being somewhat a pariah anyway, he was more likely to flaunt the rules of the society and step out of bounds. Maybe that meant that he would be more willing to discuss gems and curses with her too. Reg got comfortable and started scratching Starlight's ears again.

"Well… let's say I have a friend who has a problem."

"A friend. All right. You have a friend with a problem. What sort of problem is this?"

"He has come into possession of some… *artifacts*."

"Yes? What sort of artifacts?"

"Well, these artifacts are valuable. But where they came from and how they ended up in his possession is not very clear."

Corvin chuckled.

"And your friend is looking for a way to *rehome* these artifacts? Or does he want to keep them?"

"Well, he needs to liquidate some of them, at least."

"There are places one can go. Certain dealers who are willing to overlook a less well-known history."

"But let's say that one or two of those places say that… there are issues that they can't overlook."

"Hmm. That could be troublesome."

Reg waited for further information, but it did not appear to be forthcoming.

"So… what could he do?"

"What kind of problem is he having?"

"Well…" Reg hesitated. Corvin knew, of course, that she was talking about herself. Even if her explanation hadn't been transparent, he could access her thoughts and feelings only too easily.

"What kind of artifacts are we talking about?" Corvin tried.

"Some… gemstones."

"Oh." Corvin sounded surprised and interested. "And where did your friend get these gemstones?"

"They were… a gift."

"From a friend or an enemy?"

"Hmm." Reg stroked Starlight's first slowly. "Someone… he thought was friendly."

"That's not quite the same thing as a friend."

"No. I wouldn't say… a friend."

"Your friend should beware of taking gifts from people who are not exactly friends."

"So I gather. My friend didn't know she—he—had to be careful."

"Regina. Have you learned so little in the time you have been here?"

"Don't blame me," Reg snapped. "It's not my fault. It isn't as if anyone told me!"

"Some things you would be expected to understand."

"But if you haven't grown up in a community like this, in a household where that kind of thing was taught, then how are you supposed to know? Is that something that's just built into your DNA?"

"Most practitioners have grown up in practicing households," Corvin admitted. "It can be hard to understand what someone who was raised in a conventional home would know or not know."

"How about you assume that I don't know anything? Because I don't. I wasn't taught any of this stuff. And if my friends aren't up to telling me, then how am I supposed to figure it out on my own?"

"You *are* a psychic." He sounded amused. Just the attitude Reg didn't need from him.

"But apparently, reading people's minds without their permission, delving down into their psyches and all their life experiences, is frowned upon."

"Yes," he agreed, more soberly. "I can see how that would not be an option. It was just a joke."

Reg sighed. "So you can't help me."

"I didn't say that. We haven't really even gotten to the problem yet. Where did the jewels come from?"

"I'm not going to tell you that."

"Then how do you expect me to offer you any advice?"

"I already went to the person who gave them to me, and they were not helpful. They wouldn't tell me anything about their history or what to do about them being... a problem."

Corvin sighed. "I don't suppose you've ever heard of blood diamonds."

"Of course I've heard of blood diamonds. Everybody has."

"Oh. Well, as you know, I'm not a good judge of what you might know or not know about the magical world."

"The magical world?" Reg repeated. "Blood diamonds don't have anything to do with the magical world."

There was only silence in response.

Reg pounded her fist against her forehead. Was she ever going to understand the ins and outs of the community she was a part of?

48

"Okay, explain to me how blood diamonds are a part of the magical world."

CHAPTER TEN

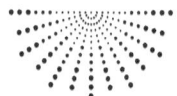

*W*hat do you know about blood diamonds?" Corvin asked. "Maybe we should start there."

"I know that... you're not allowed to buy diamonds from certain countries, because of the way they are used to fund wars. Because of the way the people who mine them are taken advantage of. So there's a certification system to make sure that all newly imported diamonds are etched with a serial number. Then they can be traced so you can be sure you are getting stones that haven't been used to fund war. Where people haven't been treated badly to get them."

"That's a reasonable description," Corvin agreed. "As far as the non-magical world understands it."

"But there's something missing from it."

"Yes." Reg pictured Corvin in her mind's eye. Stroking his neatly-trimmed beard while he thought about what she knew and what he needed to explain to her. "What is missing is that many of these wars are funded by practicing warlords. That stones are mined not just for their monetary value as trinkets for men and women in the western world, but also for their magical properties. Their innate power. Those who are obsessed with gaining power—" It was almost funny that he would refer to other people as being obsessed, when Reg didn't know anyone who was more focused on the acquisition of power than

Corvin himself. "—they will go to great lengths to mine and buy these gems."

"So… what kind of power? You mean like Sarah's emerald? The one that keeps her from getting older?"

"There are as many different powers as there are gems. But as the gems are added to existing hoards, there are fewer and fewer in circulation that have any significant power. This forces warlords and other practitioners to dig deeper and deeper to find new ones."

"And since they are scarce, the price goes up," Reg suggested.

"Basic economics. And the more valuable they are, the more warlords are willing to risk to find them. The dirtier the game gets. The more desperate the miners' circumstances become."

Reg didn't like to think of the trouble that the gems she had in her pocket might have caused. She had been thinking of them only as a means to plump up her bank balance. Not as artifacts with a history. Not of the blood that might have been shed to obtain them.

"But not all gems are blood diamonds, right? There are plenty that have been in families for generations. Just because a gem isn't etched, that doesn't mean that it came from one of these countries. That there was any blood shed over them."

"No," Corvin agreed. "There are certainly gems that were obtained without being part of one of these conflicts. But many of them, even ones that have been passed down through the generations, have long histories of bloodshed. Look up any of the larger gems currently on display in museums, and you will see long lists of battles fought over them and kings and queens and royal progeny who were killed for them."

"But these gems that I have—that my friend has—"

"Really, Reg, you can drop the subterfuge. You aren't actually very subtle."

"Well, okay. These gems that I have, there is no way to know what their history is. Whether they were part of any conflict. Right?"

"There are several ways that their pasts, or parts of their pasts, can be revealed."

"How?"

"The battles that have been fought, the owners that the gems have been torn away from, they leave a…" Corvin hunted for the words.

"They leave a sort of a psychic imprint on the gems. They are not unaffected."

"And how would anyone know that they had a psychic imprint?"

"Well, someone like you, who has psychic powers, and has been trained in reading gems. They would be employed by any of the practicing jewelers so that they could analyze the gems brought in for trade."

"So when they were looking at the gems, they weren't just checking color and clarity."

"No. The people that you consulted with were psychic themselves, and recognizing the history of these gems, they would have... *scruples* about buying them."

"But there have to be people who were still willing to buy them. Right?"

"I wish that I could just say yes. There may be. But it will depend on the level of damage to the stones."

"They are damaged?"

"This psychic imprint is not just a mark on the surface of the gem. It affects the power of the gem. And the effect of that power on the possessor. A gem that has a long history of violence becomes—"

"Cursed?"

There was a long pause.

"Cursed," Corvin said finally. "If that's what you want to call it."

"Would you call it something different?"

"No. I don't suppose so. Mostly... we avoid saying anything at all. It isn't something that is discussed."

"So I've found out." Reg sighed. "You know, all these things that are not discussed in polite company in the magical community...? It would be nice to have a list of them. And maybe some kind of primer about not getting involved with warlocks of a particular ilk. Or giving anyone your keys. Or accepting gifts from fairies."

"You got these gems from fairies?"

CHAPTER ELEVEN

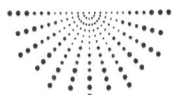

"Well…" Reg didn't want to give him any details.

"I'm sure we've talked before about gifts from fairies," Corvin said. "Haven't you ever read a fairy tale?"

"I know fairy tales," Reg retorted. She might not have read any herself, but she'd heard fairy tales. She'd watched the Disney movies. She knew as much as the next person did about them.

But maybe not as much as a magical practitioner.

"I'm not talking about the pap on TV and at the movie theater," Corvin said, sensing the direction of her thoughts. "I mean real fairy tales, in their original form, or at least before they were watered down for modern children."

Reg shook her head and didn't say anything. She had not grown up in a magical home. She had not gone to university or studied literature. Corvin knew all those things. If he expected her to know what he was talking about, he would have to explain it clearly.

"The older versions of the fairy tales are closer to the truth," Corvin said. "Fairies don't grant wishes. And when they give gifts or perform magic, there is always a catch. Always. They are not humans. They don't give gifts out of tender feelings. They do it because there is something in it for them. They give with one hand and take away with the other. Bartering with a fairy is never a good idea. They will always end up with the better end of the bargain, even if you think you have thought everything through and that you are getting the better deal. It isn't going to happen. You will always lose."

"But it wasn't just a gift. And it wasn't something that I asked for or bartered for."

"You think it was just something they gave you because they thought you deserved it? Showing gratitude or helping you out?"

"Well, yes. And what about Lord Bernier? He helped me and testified against you at the tribunal. Why did he do that? What did he get out of that?"

"I don't know, Reg. But you can bet that he got something out of it. Maybe just the opportunity to stick it to someone like me. Whether you can see his reason or not, you can bet that he had one. He had an ulterior motive. Fairies don't do anything for anyone other than the kin out of the goodness of their hearts. You can bank on that. They come from a different culture."

Reg wiped her hand across her face, mentally pushing the topic away and trying to reset. They weren't talking about fairies and the consequences of taking gifts from them. Reg had already made that mistake, so there was nothing she could do to change the past. And she already knew that even if she tried to gift the gems back to the Papillons, they would not take them. They had passed the responsibility for the gems on to Reg, and they didn't want them back.

"But that doesn't answer my question. What can I do about the gems? How can I cleanse them so that I can cash them in? I don't want to hang on to them. They don't do me any good just sitting there. I need to be able to liquidate them. And if they are cursed—what does that mean? Am I going to die? Have a run of bad luck? What?"

"Much like people who have been traumatized, gems that have violent histories can be very unpredictable. You don't know what consequences might result from owning cursed gems until you do…"

"Are you telling me that these gems have PTSD?" Reg barked out a laugh.

Corvin chuckled. "More or less, yes."

"The jeweler I talked to said that they can be cleansed."

Corvin pondered this. "I am not an expert in gems and curses," he said finally. "I might be able to offer some suggestions if I saw them, but you understand that it is not my area of expertise. I can go back over some of the stories and legends about fairy gifts and cursed gems and see whether I can find anything in the historical records I have gathered, but..."

"That sounds like something that will take a lot of time."

"It sounds as if you've got nothing but time."

"I need to sell them to pay my way," Reg said. "I can't live on nothing."

"Sarah would let you ride for a while. I don't think she needs the money at all, she just wants to have someone close, and not leave the cottage standing empty. What I'm saying is, if you can't sell them, then what's the difference between sitting on them and not doing anything, and sitting on them while you wait for me to do some research?"

"I guess if you're doing the research, at least I have a better chance," Reg admitted. "But I was hoping that you—or someone else—might have the answer more quickly."

"I wish I could offer a name. This is an area that most practitioners that I know of stay well away from."

Reg sighed heavily. "Why do things have to be so complicated? I thought that fairy tales were simple. They're for children. They can't be that complex."

"But the reality behind the fairy tales can be very complex. Fairy tales are just a window for us into the magical or paranormal worlds. You wouldn't expect a painting of a house to show you everything in the world. Just the house."

"You need to see the gems to figure it out?"

"I can't really read them from here, can I? I won't be able to read them as clearly as your jewelers, but I should be able to sense something. Maybe what effect they are having on you. Maybe what happened to them or how to cleanse them."

"Can't you just take the power out of them?" Reg asked, and then regretted it. She didn't want to give Corvin any more power than he already had. He was too strong as it was.

"I expect I could," Corvin said slowly, "although the power of a cursed gem might be locked up tight inside, like a turtle in a shell. A self-defense mechanism."

"You make them sound as if they are alive. Being traumatized. Hiding inside themselves. They're rocks, not people."

"I'm sure they're just as alive to a practitioner who understands them as Forst's plants are to him. You told me that Forst said that his plants have feelings and preferences."

Reg nodded in response, thinking about it. Just because she couldn't hear or feel the feelings of an inanimate object like a gem, that didn't mean that it didn't have any. Sarah could not hear the thoughts of her garden gnome, and so she thought that he chose not to speak to humans any more than necessary. She hadn't known that the gnomes spoke to each other with telepathy, or their "inside words," and just were not very adept at speaking in their "outside words." The fact that Corvin didn't know anything about what Starlight was thinking or feeling didn't mean that her cat didn't have any thoughts or feelings, just that Corvin didn't have the skill or power to feel them.

"You still there, Reg?"

"Yeah. Maybe… I could bring them to you tomorrow. Would that be good? We could meet at The Crystal Bowl."

Then Reg remembered.

"Oh, maybe somewhere else, since The Crystal Bowl has decided that they don't serve my kind."

"Dinner tomorrow somewhere more accommodating?" Corvin asked.

"Do we have to wait until evening? We lose another whole day. I know Sarah won't push it, but I'd like to move these gems as quickly as I can. I don't like not having anything to fall back on. I thought that I had enough that I didn't have to worry. No one said that I would have any trouble liquidating these stones."

"How many people know that you have them?"

Reg bit her lip. "No one."

"No one? I know now. And the fairies. And someone else must know, or you wouldn't have said that someone should have told you about them."

"Sarah," Reg admitted finally.

"Sarah and who else?"

"No one else. I haven't told anyone. I didn't want to have them stolen."

"No. That's a good point. Although, at least that's one way to rid yourself of a cursed treasure."

"I don't want to just get rid of it. I want to be able to use it. I haven't been making very much as a psychic lately. Not with people deciding that I'm too dangerous. Word spreads, so that even the non-practitioners think that I can't be trusted, even if they don't exactly know why."

"Maybe phone or computer consultations would be a good idea. If you don't have to meet with them face-to-face, then they don't have to worry about... other things."

Reg wrinkled her nose, considering it. She'd always hated phone line psychics. She liked the personal touch, being able to see people face-to-face. The psychic hotlines had always seemed like too obvious a scam. It was a lot harder to read someone over the phone. But it might be the only option she had. At least a video chat would give her a little bit more information and a better chance of reading the person. With Starlight's power and her crystal ball, maybe it would be enough to remotely read someone.

"I guess. I'll have to look into it."

"Make it about them," Corvin suggested. "Market it as a new service that serves their needs. Readings from the comfort of their own homes. No need to drive anywhere. No matter how remote or hermit-like they are, they can still access your services."

"Thanks. Yeah."

"So if you don't want to wait until tomorrow night, then why don't we meet tonight? It isn't that late. I know you stay up until the small hours of the morning anyway, whether you have clients or not. I won't be disrupting any planned seances. So how about it?"

"Where? Your club?"

Corvin considered this. Reg pushed harder to sense his feelings. Did he want to take her home? To somewhere more private than his club, where Reg always insisted on using the main dining room where there were other people around to act as witnesses or to help her if Corvin decided to take advantage of her proximity?

"The club would work," Corvin decided. Maybe best not to try to introduce her to somewhere new or to invite her to his house. She wouldn't accept. And she wouldn't invite him to the cottage, which was where he would really have liked to be. "Shall we say an hour? I need time to get ready. I'm not exactly prepared to entertain at the moment."

Reg sensed the humor in his voice and wondered briefly why he wasn't prepared to entertain. He was deep in some experiment or spell, with ingredients spread out around him? He was in his jammies, a housecoat, or sky clad, reading a book in his library? She withdrew her psychic connection with him as much as possible rather than using her vision to see him. She really didn't want to know.

Corvin chuckled. "No need to get shy now, Regina."

"An hour is fine," Reg agreed. "I need to get ready too."

"I'll pick you up."

"No. I'll meet you there. I don't want you driving me home."

That always seemed to end up being a problem. The enclosed space of his car, the proximity of her cottage while she grew intoxicated with his charms—not a good idea.

CHAPTER TWELVE

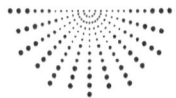

*A*fter Reg hung up the phone, she tried to shift Starlight from her lap. The cat clearly did not want to move, comfortable where he was.

"Come on," Reg groaned, sliding her hands underneath him and trying to avoid his kicking feet with their razor-sharp claws. "I need to get up. You can curl up and go to sleep here. Or on the bed. But I need to go out tonight."

She put him down on the couch beside her. Starlight sneezed, snorted, and jumped to the floor, stalking off grumpily into the kitchen.

"I'm sorry. But you know I have to figure out what to do with these gems."

Or maybe he didn't. That was a pretty complex thing for a cat brain to understand, even if Starlight had been a more complex being in previous lives. Commerce didn't mean much to cats. They understood whether there was any fish in their food bowls, but not the fact that she needed money to buy the fish, that she hadn't gone to the ocean to catch it herself.

Reg's mouth watered at the thought, and she tried to put all thoughts of the ocean and hunting and fishing out of her brain. She wasn't going to the ocean any time soon. Not until she could be sure that she wouldn't do something she would later regret.

She ignored Starlight's snit and went to her closet to find something suitable.

Maybe it was having seen Sarah's rooms full of clothing earlier in the day, but the little collection of dresses and skirts in her closet looked very small and pitiful. It was probably more than she had ever owned before, but compared to even some of the single moms who had fostered her, it was not a very grand offering. And Corvin had probably seen each piece she owned.

Not that it should matter. She wasn't going on a date with him. She was consulting with him on a financial matter, that was all. Men wore the same suit to all kinds of meetings, Corvin usually wore the same cloak with the same or similar clothing beneath it. If men could wear the same outfit on multiple dates—*business meetings*—then why couldn't women?

Still, she tried to pair a dress with a headscarf and wrap that she hadn't worn on any previous occasion with him, doing her best to make it look fresh and new. He probably wouldn't even notice. All he would care about was her warm body close to his and her powers just tantalizingly out of his reach.

* * *

One of the gorgeous, sexily-clad hostesses at the club met Reg at the door and knew immediately to escort her to the dining room. Either Corvin had called ahead to let them know that they would be there, or Reg had been there enough times with him that they knew Reg's preference for a public meeting. She didn't like the possibility that she was meeting with Corvin often enough for people to remember her from one time to the next. She told herself that she only saw him once in a blue moon, when it was really necessary for the two of them to meet. And it was only because it wasn't safe for her to meet him at her home or his that they always ended up going out for dinner together at his club.

She missed The Crystal Bowl. At least that had been a casual, pub-like atmosphere where she felt comfortable. She hated the feeling that she was on display and being evaluated when she was at Corvin's private club.

Corvin was there ahead of Reg, even though it had not yet been the hour that he had suggested. He stood immediately when Reg entered the dining room and pulled a chair out for her. Reg let him push it in as she sat down, ignoring his body heat next to her and the scent of roses that already infused the air.

"Thank you." Reg looked at the waitress who approached the table. "Can I get a glass of wine? Actually…" Reg checked herself. She should know by now that alcohol went to her head much too quickly when she was around Corvin. "Just, uh, water. With a twist of lemon."

The waitress nodded, smiling.

"No wine?" Corvin demanded, looking at Reg with his brows drawn down. "How about a little scotch in that water?"

"No. Not today."

She didn't tell him that she wanted to keep a clear head. He would just argue with her. Corvin stood there next to her, waiting for an explanation. Reg smiled and nodded at the waitress, waiting for her to take Corvin's order. The woman looked at Corvin expectantly.

"Well, I'm not teetotaling," Corvin said. "Single malt on the rocks."

She nodded and fluttered her lashes at him. "Right away, Mr. Hunter."

Corvin sat down next to Reg, already looking disgruntled. Reg reminded herself that he was there to help her. She should at least try to make it a pleasant evening. She blew her breath out and tried not to breathe in any more of his enchanting pheromones than she absolutely had to.

"Do you think you could turn down the charm?" she suggested. "You've already got the waitress swooning."

"She wasn't…" Corvin looked in the direction the waitress had gone. "Well, she might have been a little smitten. But that could just be my ruggedly handsome good looks."

Reg had to admit that he was among the most attractive men she had ever known. Maybe the most handsome she had ever known in person, rather than just worshiping from afar.

"I'm sure that doesn't help," she agreed as coolly as possible. "But seriously. We're not going to be able to get anything productive done here if I'm all fuzzy-headed."

He smiled, eyeing her. Enjoying the fact that she was as much as admitting her attraction toward him. It made sense to build up his ego. He was far more likely to help her if he felt flattered and appreciated.

Reg could feel him dialing back the charm a little, though she still felt an intense attraction toward him, which she strove to ignore.

The waitress returned promptly with their drinks. She stood a little too close to Corvin, bent down just a little too far, and held on to his glass for just an instant too long. She met his eyes and smiled, then reluctantly straightened.

"Did you want dinner?" she breathed.

"No. Just the drinks."

The waitress gave a small pout and withdrew.

Reg watched the waitress go. She reached into her purse and took out the little bag containing the gemstones.

"Really," Corvin said, putting his hand over hers before she could open the bag to show him the gems. "You don't want to be flashing those around here. Not if you're hoping to keep them a secret."

"Well, we can't exactly do this in private." It was too dangerous for her to be alone with him. She was strong enough to fight back against his charms. Most of the time. If she were focused. But she wasn't confident that she would always win. The more he grew into his powers, the more reason she had to be concerned.

Corvin's hand slid under hers, so that the bag was under his hand, Reg's hand resting over his. As usual, the touch of his skin to hers was like an intense electrical shock. It was difficult not to react to it by jerking her hand back away. Corvin smiled, enjoying her discomfort.

He closed his eyes like a purring cat, focusing on the gems in the bag.

"Nice," he breathed, "very nice."

She wasn't one hundred percent sure that he was talking about the gems. She tried to withdraw her hand, but he put his other hand over it, sandwiching her hand between both of his.

"Stay. I want to feel the effect of the stones on you."

That made some sense, so Reg left her hand where it was, although she was very self-conscious with both of his hands touching hers. She felt the eyes of the others in the dining room upon her. As if she had been caught in a compromising position.

Did everybody else there know what kind of a warlock he was? Did he bring other women there other days and then take them home with him and steal their powers? Were they used to seeing him there with vulnerable women, knowing what would happen next?

She hated the idea of their watching and being complicit in his predatory behavior.

There should be rules against it. But as she had discovered in the past, the rules that governed Corvin were too lax to provide anyone any real protection.

CHAPTER THIRTEEN

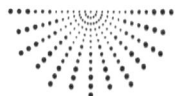

*R*eg waited, watching Corvin's face, trying to shut out everything else in the dining room to feel what he was feeling and learn more about the gems. That was what she was there for.

"They do have... a history," Corvin confirmed.

"Well, we knew that. How could they not have a history?"

He removed the hand that was on top of hers, but left the other in place. "A violent history, I mean."

Reg nodded. They had already guessed as much. Maybe the confirmation was important. He had said that the gems were affected by the violence. She tried to think of it in a scientific way. They absorbed the negative energy or were imprinted with the violence that went on around them. But the picture that came into her mind was not of rocks absorbing the heat of a fire or mirrors reflecting their surroundings, but that of a child, knees drawn to chest, hiding her eyes, as the world exploded around her.

Corvin looked at her curiously. "You can feel it too."

"I can? I can feel that they have power, but that they are cursed?" Reg shook her head. "I don't think so. They don't feel... evil."

"No," he agreed.

Reg looked down at her hand, warm beneath his. "Can you do something about it? Can you cleanse them?"

Corvin's eyes were focused somewhere else. No longer on Reg's face. He turned his hand over, palm up, with the bag in it. He squeezed Reg's hand with the bag of gems sandwiched between them. Reg tried to focus her attention on the stones. She could help with whatever it was Corvin was doing.

Eventually, Corvin shook his head. "It will take someone with more skill than I." Removing his hand from hers, he picked up his glass and took a drink. "But then, you knew it was a long shot. I told you that I am not experienced in this sort of work."

"So I have to find someone who can do... a special kind of magic on gemstones?"

"It isn't the magic that is special... just the expertise. I wouldn't want to experiment, get it wrong, maybe devalue the gems." He had another drink of his scotch. Reg picked up her own glass and had a sip of the cold water. It tasted horrible; she regretted not ordering a real drink.

"If you had more, I might suggest some experiments," Corvin said. "But as you have only a few gems to start with, I wouldn't recommend it. If you take a misstep, you could lose a large portion of your fortune." He said fortune with an ironic twist of his mouth that told her that the money she got from the gems would not be very much. But it didn't really matter how much one gem was worth. Not when she had as many as she did.

"What would you suggest?"

"There are more, then?" His tone of voice told her that he had already guessed that. Maybe from the gems themselves. Maybe Reg had given it away herself, not guarding her thoughts and feelings carefully enough. But it was impossible to shut Corvin out completely and she had stopped trying.

She shrugged. Let him think what he liked. She wasn't going to quantify it for him. He didn't need any more explanation.

"If it was me... I would try a few different... exercises. Try giving one away as a gift. Try giving one as payment for services, without cashing it in first. Maybe Sarah would take one by way of payment for your rent."

Reg shook her head. "How would that help anything?"

If it worked, it might relieve some of the financial pressure that she was under, but she couldn't pay for everything using gemstones. She would still have to be able to get cash for some of them. She couldn't use a diamond to pay for her groceries.

"I told you that the magic, the *curse* on these stones could be unpredictable. I can't tell, just holding them, what effect they might have on the owner," he gave a nod to Reg herself. "Or to your ability to traffic them. You may be able to give them away, so that the curse does not fall on the person you give it to. And if that works, then maybe they could gift a portion back to you, now cleansed, and keep a portion as payment for laundering the gems for you. If you are able to use them as payment, even better. You don't need to worry about getting money back for them, or getting the gems themselves back, because you are able to get something else of value."

Reg nodded. "I guess."

"It's an experiment. I don't know how these gems are going to behave."

Reg laughed. "You make them sound human."

"I have possessed many different gems and have found that their properties are extremely varied. They each seem to have their own... personality. A temperament that I can't really explain any other way. The races that traffic in gemstones regularly treat them as their children. As if they are sentient."

"Okay. So you don't know how they will behave." Reg shook her head in amusement. "Should I... give one to you? As the first experiment?"

His eyes glittered. "Are you giving it freely as a gift? Or are you expecting something in return?"

"Maybe as payment for you examining them for me," Reg suggested. "Services performed."

Corvin shook his head. "That was done as a friend. If you muddy the waters, that will mess with the experiment. If you pay for something that I was not expecting payment for, then what is it?"

"Okay." Reg shrugged. She didn't care or see what difference it could make. "Then how about... as a gift. Can I give you one of them?"

He considered for a moment. Reg had expected him to jump at the chance to get one of them for himself. Corvin was nothing if not greedy. But maybe receiving the gift of a cursed gem was different. If Reg should not have accepted them from the fairies, then maybe Corvin should not accept them from her either. Even if she was giving them freely, not expecting anything from the transaction.

"All right," Corvin said eventually. "How about the sapphire?"

Reg tried not to show her surprise. "How did you know there was a sapphire?" He had never opened the bag and set eyes on them.

Corvin smiled. "I could tell."

Reg shook her head. She glanced around to see whether anyone was watching them or if the waitress was headed back over to refill their drinks. Reg had barely touched hers. She wished she had gone with her first impulse and ordered a glass of wine. She could have kept it to one glass. That wouldn't have been a problem, even dealing with Corvin's proximity.

No one appeared to be watching them. Reg loosened the strings of the bag and tipped it so that the gems fell close enough to the mouth to see which was which. She pressed her finger into the blue sapphire, and the moisture of her skin provided enough adhesion for her to lift her finger and turn it over, the sapphire sticking to it. She offered it to Corvin.

He put out his hand, palm up, to receive it. Reg transferred the gem to him, dropping the stone into his outstretched hand. He jumped and quickly tipped his hand to roll the sapphire off of it and onto the table. Reg looked at his face.

"What is it?"

"It's hot."

Reg did what any self-respecting child would do when told something was hot and reached out her finger to touch it herself. It was still cool to her touch.

She looked at Corvin, raising an eyebrow. "Seems fine to me."

Corvin put his hand over it for a moment, then touched it again, with just the tip of his finger. As before, he jerked back.

"Nope."

Reg studied it. So her first little gem had a hot temper. "We should try another one," she suggested.

Corvin shrugged and didn't agree or disagree. Reg picked the sapphire up and put it back into her bag. She gave the bag a little shake and the ruby came up close to the mouth. She picked it out, pinched between two fingers, and offered it to Corvin. He touched it, but this one did not seem to be too hot for him to handle. He put out his palm, and she again deposited a gem into it. Corvin held on to the ruby for a moment, as if waiting for it to do something. They both watched it carefully.

Reg felt a little silly. What were they waiting for? Did she think it was going to jump from his hand back into the bag? She'd accepted Corvin's description of their having feelings and desires a little too quickly. As a scholar and a professor, he should have been more objective about it. And she shouldn't have been so quick to buy into his description.

"There. That's better. So… how do we tell whether it is still C-U-R-E-D?"

"Cured?" Corvin said with a smile.

"No." Reg scowled, trying to picture the word in her mind to figure out how she'd screwed it up. Spelling—anything to do with reading and writing—was not her strong point. And spelling out loud required her full concentration as she tried to picture the word and sound it out at the same time as keeping track of which letter she had said and which came next. "*Cursed*. You know what I meant."

"Do yourself a favor and don't bother trying to spell in front of the stones. It isn't as if they understand what you are saying."

"How do you know? If they understand that they were stolen, or whatever it was that happened in the past, then how do we know they don't understand what we are saying? They could!"

Corvin shrugged. He studied the ruby, tilting his hand back and forth, catching it in the light. "It is a very pretty little jewel."

"Do you want a loupe?" Reg patted her pockets, then went to her purse. "I think I put it…" It took her a minute rummaging through the clutch purse she had brought with her, small though it was, to find the jeweler's loupe. She didn't like to think of how long it would have taken if she had her main shoulder bag with her. It was so full of stuff that she was afraid to dump it out and start inventorying it. Who knew what had been left there over the past months? It would be like an archaeological dig.

68

Corvin took the loupe from her, looking amused. Reg realized he wasn't trained in what to look for in a gem. Was there actually something she knew more about than he did?

"You're looking at the color, cut, and clarity," she told him. "Looking for any visible flaws, how rich and even the color is, how it catches the light."

Corvin adjusted the focal distance, squinting slightly, eventually settling on the best distance for him to examine the stone. He shrugged and handed back the loupe.

"That's a really good ruby," Reg told him. "It should bring in a lot of money. If I can find someone to buy it. If we can cleanse it."

"I understand what you're trying to do."

"Okay, well… so what can you tell? Do we have to wait for something? Can you tell whether it is still cursed or not?"

He closed his eyes for a moment, then opened them and nodded. "Yes. Still is."

Reg swore. "I guess it couldn't be that easy, could it? What if you keep it for a while? Maybe you haven't really accepted it yet, because you are thinking of giving it back. How does the ruby know if you've accepted my gift or not?"

"I don't know if there are any particular rules or guidelines, why it works one time but not another. It isn't like a computer program or code. You can't be sure what will happen."

"Maybe you could talk to it."

"Talk to it?"

Reg nodded. "Tell it… that you like it. Take it home with you and find a special place for it and tell it that you're keeping it." Reg tried to think of what else might make the gem feel like it had been accepted by a new owner. What things had made her feel better about a family when she was in foster care? What things had made her feel more at home? "Tell it that you'll take care of it and protect it so that nothing bad happens to it again."

Corvin's eyes rested on Reg's face. She looked away, embarrassed, her face warming. Probably blushing brilliantly.

"I'm just trying to think of what might work," she said, trying to brush it off. "I've never had any gems before. I don't know how it all works."

69

"I think we're going to need to find an expert. I'll do like you said, and you can try some more experiments, but I think that you need someone who really knows what they are talking about."

CHAPTER FOURTEEN

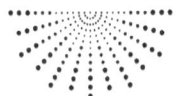

*R*eg was glad that she had brought her own car and that she
hadn't had any wine, even though the water had been awful.
She was still clear-headed at the end of her consultation with Corvin. It
was not a date. She wasn't going anywhere with him afterward, regard-
less of the sad eyes he made at her when she refused. She was just going
home. She could smell the roses as he attempted to talk her into it, and
stood up.

"I've got to go home. Let me know if you make any progress with
that ruby or find someone I can talk to about the gems."

"What's the hurry, Regina? You don't have anywhere to be tonight."

"It's been a long day,"

"Don't try that 'I'm tired and I'm going to bed as soon as I get
home' crap with me."

Reg shrugged. "Would you rather hear the truth?"

He glared at her. Of course he knew why she wouldn't get into the
car with him, wouldn't let him into the cottage, or go anywhere they
were alone and he could try to overcome her resistance and steal her
powers. Was it better to say that than that she wanted to go home
because it had been a long day and they hadn't succeeded in figuring
out how to cleanse the gems?

"You are strong enough to resist me," he pointed out. "You've done it enough times. So why do we have to keep up this charade of the help-less female? If you want your sex to be equal and respected, then why don't you drop the victim role?"

Reg's anger flared. Despite his challenge, Corvin leaned away from her, his eyes sharp and calculating. Things happened around Reg when she got really angry.

"Staying out of the tiger cage isn't playing a role," Reg snapped. "It's being smart."

He chuckled, a low, warm sound. "Comparing me with a cat? Not the most appropriate metaphor. Besides, don't you like to play with furry kitties? Come play in the tiger cage, Reg…" he wheedled.

Reg laughed and shook her head. "Not a chance."

She turned and walked away from him.

The air outside the dining room was more breathable. When Reg got into her car, she cranked the windows down and let the breeze blow in her face, even though it was a little chilly. When she got home, she was feeling awake and alert, and knew it would be a long time before she could get to sleep.

* * *

When she eventually went to bed, the sun was up over the horizon. She still didn't feel particularly tired, and tossed and turned trying to find a comfortable position and to get settled in for sleep. Starlight sat on the windowsill and watched her, meowing a couple of times that it was time for her to get out of bed and to feed him, even though it was much earlier than she ever got up. Cats really did seem to think that humans only existed to feed them and change their kitty litter. And maybe to play with them and groom them when they were in the mood.

Starlight watched her, ears pricked forward, knowing that she was thinking about cats. But when it didn't lead to her getting up to feed him, he eventually jumped down from the window and walked his rounds of the rest of the house.

She wished that Starlight could talk, and then immediately rescinded the wish. It would be much worse if he could order her around and tell her all his opinions of her. A person had to be careful what she wished for.

That was when she remembered.

It hadn't been that along ago, just at winter solstice. But so much had happened since then and Reg's brain *had* been inhabited by an evil entity during part of that time, which had made it almost impossible to access the memories she wanted when she wanted them. It was as if he had taken all the filing boxes that held her memories in neat, orderly sections and had dumped them all out on the floor and stirred them around. She didn't know how many memories might be gone forever, and how many of them she would be able to recover and eventually put back in order again. But until she could, she would have to put up with not being able to access them when she wanted to and having them surface at unexpected times.

But she had just remembered that Harrison had put in an appearance during their Yuletide celebration. Even though she had invited him, she hadn't expected her immortal godfather to show up, not being limited to a linear timeline like Reg.

And he had asked her what her wish was.

"My wish?"

"Is there not…" he made a twirling motion with his finger to indicate the Yule decorations and guests, "…a wish made for this observance?"

"Well… I don't know if there usually is or not." No one had mentioned making a wish, but Reg wasn't about to turn it down. "I wish… for safety for Starlight. And wealth. I could use a little extra money, just to make sure I have something to fall back on."

Fir had been kneeling down to talk to Starlight. He rose to his feet. "Be careful of thy wishes. You never know which ones will be granted."

Reg sat up in bed and stared at the closet. Not a very inspiring sight. But that wasn't really what she was looking at. She replayed the memory several times. She had wished for wealth. And it was after that she had received the gift of gems from the fairies. She hadn't connected the two incidents. There was nothing about the fairy gift that had made her think back to the spur-of-the-moment wish she had made at Yule.

"Harrison!"

She said his name out loud. Not really calling him or reprimanding him for what he had done, if he had been complicit somehow in the gems coming to her. But at the same time, she did want him to come to her and to reassure her that he'd had nothing to do with the gift.

If fairy gifts were dangerous, immortal wishes could be even more devastating. She had learned that from the experience of Vivian, a client she had tried to help.

Reg swung her feet over the side of the bed and got up. When Harrison came, he didn't always show up in the room that she expected him to. In fact, she should probably not even bother to call him from any room other than the kitchen, with his being so enamored with mortal food.

She didn't find him in the kitchen eating a chocolate cake or pizza that he had produced out of thin air. Reg breathed out slowly, not sure whether to be irritated or relieved. She wanted to talk to him, but she didn't want to at the same time. She didn't want to have to deal with the problem or to find out that again, it had been her own doing. Or that it had been partially her own fault for making a wish that had kicked off a series of events that ended up with her being burdened by a chest of cursed gems that she couldn't do anything with.

"If you do not want them, then do not wish them," Harrison said logically.

Reg turned toward the living room, where Harrison was sitting on the couch with his long legs stretched out on top of the coffee table. Starlight was in his lap. Of course.

Harrison's long, spindly legs were encased in black and white horizontally striped tights. On top, we wore a long-sleeved yellow shirt and a black vest bedazzled with jewels. He twirled the ends of his long thin mustache, smiling at her.

"Uncle Harrison!"

"You called?"

"No. Yes. I guess maybe I did."

"You did," he confirmed.

"Okay, well, I just didn't know whether I really wanted you to come or not."

He shook his head. "You should only ask for that which you really want."

"Probably. I'm worried that's what got me into the middle of this mess in the first place."

"Mess?" Harrison looked around the tidy room.

"Not that kind of mess. The kind of mess where I have a hoard of cursed gems."

"Ahh." Harrison nodded sagely. "That mess."

"Is this because… did I get those gems because I wished for wealth? Is that the way that you granted my wish?"

He considered this thoughtfully. And Reg really knew better than to ask him questions, because he never gave her a straight answer when she did, and she always ended up more confused than she was when she started.

"Perhaps," Harrison said eventually. Which was more definitive than many of his answers.

"But I wanted wealth that I could use. So that I could pay my expenses. There is no point in having a bunch of jewels that I can't do anything with."

He nodded. "That is a problem."

"Then why did you do that? Why not give me money that I can use? Just drop it into my bank account or give me gold. Or jewels that I can actually use."

He waved his hand as if it were of no consequence. "That is not what happened."

"No, it isn't," Reg agreed dryly. "But that's what I want."

"Perhaps when you make your next wish. Is it your birthday?"

"No, it's not my birthday or any other wishing day. And I don't think I'll be making any other wishes, because who knows how they might be fulfilled."

"Yes."

"If you knew what I wanted, then why couldn't you give it to me? Is there some rule in the universe that you can never give me what I really want?"

Harrison petted Starlight with long, slow strokes. "Why do you not wish for what you really need?"

"I did! But you didn't give me what I needed. You gave me cursed gemstones."

"No, I did not. The fairy folk did."

"I know that's who they came from, but it was because of you. Because of the wish that I made. Isn't it?"

He twirled his mustache. "The universe," he said thoughtfully.

"What about the universe?"

"Are there rules? In your universe?"

"Well… yes. *You* have rules you have to follow, don't you?"

She knew that there were rules governing some of the immortals' behavior. A rule that they weren't supposed to do anything to harm another of their kind, which seemed to Reg to be ignored more often than it was followed. And a rule that they were not supposed to procreate with mortals. Ditto. They clearly didn't obey that one either. Were there rules about what wishes they could grant? Or how they were allowed to grant them?

"There are rules among my kind," Harrison confirmed.

"Rules about granting wishes?"

"Oh, yes."

"Like that I can't ever get what I wished for?"

He blinked at her. For a moment, he looked away from her, lavishing attention on Starlight, scratching his ears and jaw.

"You did get what you wished for."

"No, I didn't."

He shook his head.

"Maybe you should try again," Reg suggested. "You can take the gems back and give me cash instead. Cash that isn't cursed. I don't care if it's in my bank account or in hard currency. Just as long as I can spend it."

"Humans are very shortsighted."

Reg closed her mouth and considered that for a moment. Harrison was not constrained by the same natural laws as she was. He could travel back to the past, and she assumed to the future too. He could go anywhere and make things happen as he pleased. Was he saying that humans were shortsighted in general, or was he referring specifically to her insistence that she needed cold, hard cash? Was something going to happen in the future that would render the money useless, and there would be something else she wished she had asked for instead?

"What do you mean by that?"

Harrison raised one eyebrow. "They cannot see very far. Only what is in front of their own faces."

"I know what shortsighted means."

He shrugged. If she knew, then why had she asked?

"I mean… why did you say it now? Is there something that I'm being shortsighted about?"

"Yes."

"About the money?"

His head tilted to the side. *Maybe yes, maybe no.*

"Why am I being shortsighted?" Reg tried.

"It is only human. You can't help it."

"Can you tell me what's going to happen? What it is you think I am being shortsighted about right now?"

But she should have known that there was no way to pin an immortal down and get a straight answer. Even when it was a clear answer, it wasn't the one she wanted.

"Yes."

Reg waited. Harrison shifted Starlight from his lap to the couch beside him. And then he vanished.

CHAPTER FIFTEEN

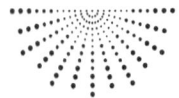

*a*rgh!"

Reg looked around for something to throw. She was still standing near the kitchen island, and she grabbed a spoon and fired it across the room in the direction of the couch. Starlight jumped down from the couch and crouched down, looking at her with his ears back.

"I unwish it!" Reg shouted. "Do you hear me, Harrison? I take it back; I don't want the gems anymore. You can take them away and give them to someone else!"

But she knew what he had said in the past. There was no unwishing. She couldn't change what she had wished for, get him to change things back to the way they had been. Even though he had returned to the past before and changed things around. If he could do that for his own reasons, why couldn't he do it for her? Just run back in time, and when she was about to voice her wish about wealth, warn her that she didn't want to make a wish like that and get her to wish for something less controversial. A wish that an immortal couldn't screw up.

If there was such a thing.

"Stupid immortals!" Reg growled. She knew she wouldn't be able to get to sleep, so she started tidying up the kitchen to burn off her angry energy. Maybe it was time for her to start behaving like an adult with adult responsibilities instead of sitting around feeling sorry for herself because a box full of gems weren't going to change her life. Why would they? How often had she heard that money wasn't the solution to life's problems?

She had never believed it, but she'd heard it enough times.

When a person was barely scraping by, having trouble just getting enough food to subsist on, there was no point in saying that money wouldn't solve her problems. When eating was the problem, money was definitely a solution.

But she wasn't in that situation. Not again. Not yet. She had a place to live that was warm and safe and there was a friend nearby to keep an eye on things and to give her advice or other help when she needed it. She had all the food she really needed, between the little that she had stocked herself and the various leftovers and other bits that Sarah brought over from time to time. Really, despite her low bank account, it was the wealthiest she had ever been, even without the jewels.

By the time she burned out her anger, the kitchen was spick-and-span. Sarah would be impressed.

* * *

It was a while before Starlight was on speaking terms with Reg again. He didn't like her shouting and throwing things around. And she could understand that. She had never liked it when she had lived in homes where people shouted and threw things either. She knew better and shouldn't have let her anger and frustration get the better of her.

But eventually, with Reg sitting sideways on the couch with her feet up, browsing through funny YouTube clips on her phone, Starlight decided to forgive her. He jumped up onto the couch and curled up in her lap, purring away as if he were perfectly contented. Reg vowed to herself that she would never throw something in his direction again. He hadn't done anything wrong. And even if he had, that wouldn't excuse throwing cutlery at him.

There was a knock on the door.

Reg sat up, surprised. Starlight looked toward the door, his ears pointing directly at it, listening intently. Was it a client? Reg looked down at herself. She was still dressed in her pajamas. It wasn't as if they were indecent or even revealing, but it was obvious from the style and fabric and the muted colors that it was her pajamas. She had been up for several hours; why hadn't she bothered to change?

She hadn't been expecting company.

There was another knock followed by the chime of the doorbell. Reg put Starlight gently to the side and got up. She left the chain on and opened the door a crack to see who it was. Best not to open it all the way in case it was a witch who intended her harm, or Corvin, or someone else she didn't want to let into the house. They shouldn't be able to get into the yard if they had evil intentions toward her, but Reg had seen too many magical loopholes to trust that the wards set to protect her would do it flawlessly and continue to work forever. Mortals made mistakes. All mortals, including Sarah.

She peeked through the narrow opening at a woman with long, spiraling blond hair and an all-black cat in her arms.

"Oh! Francesca!" Reg shut the door to slide the chain and opened it up to allow Francesca and Nicole in. Nicole pronounced in Francesca's beautiful Haitian accent, of course, as NEE-cole. "Was that today? I totally lost track of time!"

"Yes, today," Francesca agreed in a clipped voice. "You put it in your phone. You said you would put it on your client calendar so that you would not forget." She nodded to the date book that lived on Reg's kitchen island, where she and Sarah both wrote down any client appointments they made for psychic services. Of course, it had been completely blank lately and Reg hadn't opened it, even if she had written it down.

Francesca bent over as she let go of Nicole, so that Nicole and Starlight could play together. The two cats touched noses and rubbed against each other, purring and chirping greetings. Reg couldn't help laughing at their joy over seeing each other. It had been a long time since their last play date.

"Come on in, have a seat," Reg invited, motioning to the couch. "I'll put on the kettle."

Francesca obeyed, alighting gracefully on the couch and watching the two cats until they retreated to the back rooms of the house for some privacy.

"Nicole is very happy to see Starlight," she observed.

"Yes. I forgot how much fun it is to get the two of them together.

After all the hassle with the kittens, it's nice to have just the two of them again."

Francesca nodded.

"How is Nicole doing? Does she miss them?"

"She does sometimes, I think… but she is also happy to be on her own again. It is not easy suddenly being the mama of nine kattakyns!"

The kittens were not actually Nicole's. Rather than being normal kittens, they were draugar—a sort of a zombie creature—that had transformed into cats and had been charmed and locked into that form by Francesca as part of their efforts to defeat Samyr Destine, one of the immortals, also known as The Witch Doctor. After binding his essence to the kattakyns, Francesca had found new homes for the kittens around the world, distributing them as far apart as possible, to prevent the immortal from re-forming. As long as Destine was bound, the world was safe from his evil.

"I'm sure she's probably happy to be able to get a good sleep," Reg agreed. "It must be murder trying to get enough rest with nine kittens to look after. Especially when one of them is Nico."

Reg had a special place in her heart for Nico, who had been very difficult to manage. Reg could relate to the poor guy and had fostered him for a short time when he became too much for Francesca. Reg was happy that she had found a place for him in the dwarf mountain, where he was revered as a warrior cat instead of constantly being yelled at for climbing the curtains and knocking over vases.

"That little fellow was a challenge," Francesca agreed, rolling her eyes.

Reg busied herself with getting the tea tray together while she waited for the kettle to whistle. "Any preferences for your tea today?"

"Maybe something citrus?" Francesca suggested.

Reg nodded and got out a couple of lemon or orange teas to add to the tray. Though Francesca was a charmer rather than a psychic and could not read tea leaves, she still preferred the loose-leaf tea. Reg made sure that there was plenty of honey for her own tea. While she regularly drank tea with Francesca or her clients, Reg had a sweet tooth and found the teas more palatable with a significant amount of sugar.

The kettle whistled. Reg poured the hot water into the teapot and took the tray over to the coffee table, where she set it down. She sat on one of the wicker chairs and, after preparing her cup of tea, tucked her feet up on the seat beside her to get comfortable.

"You know, I really appreciate that you still bring Nicole here to visit with Starlight. After... everything that has happened... there are a lot of practitioners who won't have anything to do with me anymore."

If she were perfectly honest, Reg would have to admit that she was fishing for reassurance. She wanted to hear Francesca say that Reg was the same person she had always been, and Francesca trusted her completely. That her possible parentage did not make a bit of difference.

Francesca stirred her tea thoughtfully for a few moments, appearing to give it all of her attention. But Reg could tell that she wasn't thinking about tea. Or about the cats.

"Life... is very complicated," Francesca said finally. "As much as you would like everything to be black and white, it is not." Her lilting accent took a bit of the sting out of the fact that she had not said that she liked or trusted Reg and would never let anyone sway her opinion of her friend. "You are a friend. You have done nothing to harm me. I have not seen any of this... worrisome behavior. If ever I do... I will judge by what I see."

"You know what kind of a person I am," Reg asserted, hoping for a stronger message of support.

"I think I know."

Francesca wasn't going to go any further than that. And if Reg kept pressing her, she would probably be disappointed when Francesca was forced to admit that no, she didn't trust Reg and could no longer be so sure that she was a friend or would remain one. And Reg didn't want to hear that.

"So... have you heard from any of the kattakyns' owners? How they are settling in?"

Francesca nodded and took a sip of her tea. "Yes, I occasionally hear from them. The ones who don't call me, I like to reach out to now and then just to make sure that everything is going well and that... they haven't decided to give the kittens away to someone else. That could be disastrous."

Reg nodded. While the kattakyns could not exercise all the magic that the Witch Doctor had once held, much of which had now been transferred to Corvin, they each did have a part of him. And if that power ended up in the wrong hands…

Reg didn't like to think about what could happen. That was why they had been so careful to hand pick the kattakyns' human companions.

"But they haven't, right? The kittens are still in the homes we placed them in?"

It had really been Francesca's project, but Reg had helped out a bit. As much as she was able. And she was the one who had found Nico a home. Nico had been the most difficult.

"So far, they are all where they should be." Francesca took another drink and licked her lips. "I am concerned, though…"

"Not about Nico…?"

"Not Nico in particular." Francesca pressed her lips together, trying to decide what to tell Reg and what to hold back. "It is… the immortal that is of concern."

CHAPTER SIXTEEN

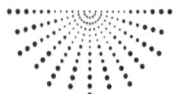

he immortal?" Reg asked, a sinking feeling in her stomach. "Which one?"

She hoped that it was someone other than Harrison or Weston. An immortal she had never heard of before. Someone less closely connected with her. She didn't like the idea of there being even more immortals around poking their noses into human business, she really didn't want to deal with the news that Harrison or Weston were, once again, causing chaos.

"You know which one," Francesca said darkly. "Your Harrison."

"Harrison?" Reg grimaced. She held herself back from protesting that he wasn't *her* Harrison. She didn't have any control over him. She didn't own him. She barely had any influence over him. But he was her Uncle Harrison. Her immortal godfather. She couldn't completely disclaim any relationship with him. "What has he done now?"

Francesca shook her head grimly. "He has been to visit several of the kittens."

"Several of them?" Reg echoed in dismay. She searched for a reasonable explanation. "But just visiting… that's not dangerous, is it? He couldn't do anything…"

"You do not know the power these immortals have. *I* do not know the power the immortals have, and I have been close to them. Too close to them. It is not good. I fear for what he could do."

"He doesn't want The Witch Doctor to re-form," Reg pointed out. "He knows that evil, the problems that were caused by Destine trying to gather so much power to him."

"They do not believe in evil, these immortals. They do not understand it the same way as you or I. To them... these are just games they are playing. Poking a stick into an anthill and watching all the little creatures scurrying around in panic. Is someone who pokes an anthill evil?"

"Well... to the ants, I guess."

Francesca nodded. "To the ants. But not to themselves. They see no harm in it. Humans to them are just pests. Little, scurrying pests that have overpopulated the world that the immortals once claimed as their own. They do not care whether the Witch Doctor remains bound. Harrison is probably bored. Looking for a new playmate."

Reg shook her head slowly. "I'll talk to him. I'll tell him that he can't do anything to free Destine. He'll listen to me."

"Will he?" Francesca raised one brow skeptically. "This... I do not know."

"But he can't. I'll talk to him. I'll explain it. He'll listen."

Francesca shrugged. She sipped her tea. "If you would do that, perhaps there is a chance. Otherwise... there is nothing we can do. We cannot hide the kattakyns from him. We cannot stop him from gathering them and allowing the Witch Doctor his freedom. It is very bad."

Reg did not like hearing "very bad" from Francesca. The battle against the Witch Doctor had been hard won. Francesca had assured them that there would be no way for Destine to form again for another thousand years. But if another immortal aided him, bringing the kattakyns back together and releasing him from his prison...

They had enough to worry about with Weston being free. And Harrison, for that matter. Even when he was trying to help Reg, he was just as likely to screw it up and make things worse for her or her friends. Even when he granted Reg's wish, it ended up coming back to bite her in the butt. Suddenly, instead of being wealthy, she had a bunch of cursed gems she couldn't get rid of or cash in on. A responsibility that she had never wanted.

"Hey, I have something for you," she told Francesca, thinking about the gems.

"Something for me?" Francesca gave a little smile, surprised by the segue, curious as to what it was. Reg had never given her a gift before. They didn't normally have that kind of a friendship. They talked on the phone. Rehomed kittens. Brought the adult cats on play dates.

"Yes. Just wait here for a minute."

Reg went to her bedroom, where she found the two cats together on the bed, cuddled up and grooming each other.

"Don't do anything I wouldn't do!" Reg told them with a laugh.

She found the skirt she had worn the previous day on the floor and searched through the folds for a few minutes before finding the little bag of gems in one of the pockets. Had she become so careless about the gems that she would just leave them in a pile of clothes on the floor?

She remembered that she had, in fact, nearly forgotten them under the bed when she had left Black Sands in a hurry to avoid trouble. How could someone forget something so priceless? She hadn't even known back then about their being cursed. She had thought they would be easy to sell, that she would be able to live off of them for the rest of her life.

Reg opened the bag and shook it until one of the gems tumbled into her waiting palm. An emerald. A beautifully cut teardrop shape. It would look lovely in a pendant on a necklace. It was nothing like Sarah's emerald, of course, but it was still beautiful and would bring in a good amount of money if it weren't cursed.

She took it back out to the living room, and handed it to Francesca, keeping her movements as casual as possible. As if she gave her friends expensive gemstones all the time.

Francesca looked down at the stone in her hand. "Why, this is lovely, Regina. Where did you get it?"

Reg didn't tell her where. "I wanted you to have it," she said. "You've been such a good friend to me. I came into... I inherited... received several stones, and I thought you would like that one."

"Oh, I could not accept it," Francesca said, trying to hand it back. "This is yours. If it is real, it must be very valuable. I couldn't take something like that from you."

"I want you to have it."

"Really… I have nothing to give you in return."

"I don't expect anything in return. I just want to share with my friends."

"I don't know…"

"I was thinking it would look nice on a necklace. Don't you think so?"

Francesca played with it in her hand. "Well, yes. It is very pretty."

"I think it would look really good on you," Reg said. "It complements your eyes." She was using all the con skills that she had learned over the years. Putting it into Francesca's hand. Making her imagine how she would use it, how it would make her look and feel beautiful. Few people could turn you down once they had held the product in their hands and imagined how they would use it.

But she saw Francesca's shoulders square and heard her take a deep, bracing breath. She held it out to give it back to Reg. "No. I cannot accept this."

Reg didn't put her hand out to take it back. They looked at each other. Eventually, Francesca placed the emerald on the tea tray in front of her. She would not accept it. Somehow, she had known or felt what Reg had not, that accepting the gem as a gift would not be a good idea. It would not end well.

Reg shook her head. She was the psychic. Shouldn't she have had a feeling about the gems? If it was unwise to accept gifts from fairies or to make wishes, then why hadn't she sensed that? When she held the gems in her hand, why didn't she feel a sense of foreboding, a knowledge that they were cursed and that they would not bring her the wealth and security that she desired?

It had been the same with the key that had released Weston from his self-imposed prison. Even though Forst had warned her that it was a dark key, she had felt attracted to it. She had known that she wanted to possess it, even when it had been dirty and corroded. She should have felt something from it other than attraction. The knowledge that it didn't open the door to a great treasure, but to an immortal who could affect the course of her life if she released him.

But when she'd held the key, she had known that she was destined to use it, to match the key to the lock that it would eventually open.

And when she held the gems in her hand, she felt their power and potential, not an evil force or the dark cloud of a curse over her life.

What did that say about her nature?

"What is it?" Francesca asked, drawing Reg away from her contemplation. "I am sorry if I have insulted you. But it is not wise to accept such things."

"To accept what things?" Reg probed. Gems? Cursed objects? What did Francesca sense when she held the emerald in her hand?

"To accept gifts of such value without having earned them." Francesca shook her head. "It is not wise," she repeated.

If it sounds too good to be true, it probably is. Reg heard her foster mother's words in her head once more. Words that she should have heard when the gift from the fairies had first arrived. She had known that it was too much, even for having saved Calliopia's life. It was a king's ransom, and Calliopia was only an adolescent fairy from a household that, as far as Reg knew, was not of royal lineage. Reg had explained it away to herself. She'd told herself that it had not been worth that much to the Papillons. Fairies owned a lot of jewels, and as a product that was not scarce to them, it was of less value. It was valuable to her as a human because humans did not have such hoards.

Reg sighed again.

It wouldn't be as easy to give the jewels to others as gifts as she had hoped. Not if everyone were as savvy as Francesca.

CHAPTER SEVENTEEN

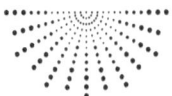

*A*fter Francesca and Nicole had gone home, Reg went for a walk in the garden. It was an enchanted place, the plants practically vibrating with magic and vitality. Sarah had been right when she had said that a garden gnome would be able to do a much better job with the garden than any human could. Forst had turned a broken, desolate wreck into a paradise.

She stooped to smell a flower, then continued to walk, keeping an eye out for the little red-capped old man who seemed to be able to blend in with the plants and the dirt in a way that should have been impossible. She wondered sometimes if he could actually enter into the plants or the soil he tended and become part of their structure. There was definitely magic at work there that she couldn't fathom.

Reg sat down on the stone bench that was surrounded by heady blooms in a riot of colors, buzzing bees, and fluttering butterflies. She closed her eyes and breathed in the sweetly scented breeze. She could smell not just the flowers, but the green of the leaves and the moist soil they sprang from. She felt as if she could almost drink the smells, they were so rich.

Reg Rawlins is welcome here.

Reg opened her eyes and smiled at the little gnome in front of her.

While his words might have startled her if they were said out loud, she was not surprised at hearing them inside her head.

Good morning, Forst.

It is early for Reg Rawlins to be enjoying the garden.

It is, Reg acknowledged. Forst, like many others, probably thought her a slob for sleeping so late most days. But that was just the schedule that her body preferred, and a schedule that allowed her to do late-night seances. When she actually had clients calling her. *Would you believe I've already had company today? I don't think I actually got to sleep last night.*

Take care of thyself, he warned solemnly, pulling out his curved pipe and filling it with tobacco. *You have but one lifetime in this body.*

I know. It wasn't on purpose, believe me.

Something is on your mind?

Reg nodded. *Lots of somethings. I wish that I understood the magical world better. It seems like I am always getting myself into trouble one way or another.*

You cannot fight your nature. He lit the pipe and took a few puffs. The comforting smell of the tobacco merged with the other smells in the air. *The many great things you have done would not be without the choices you have made.*

Reg laughed. *The many great things?*

He looked at her, gaze unwavering. Reg was the first to look away. She knew that Forst and others believed she had greater powers than she did. She had skated through some of her more difficult adventures, surviving just by the skin of her teeth and a few happy coincidences or a bit of quick-thinking and deception on her part. She was not nearly as powerful or smart as he thought. But as she had once helped Forst's twin, Fir, when he had been in police custody, he revered her. It was something that any other human could have done just as easily, not actually requiring any magic, only a familiarity with the legal system and human nature, but she was the one who had stepped forward to help, so she had earned Forst's loyalty.

Reg put her hands down beside her on the bench as she leaned back, turning her face up toward the sun. As a redhead, she couldn't spend much time worshiping the sun, but the warmth on her skin did lift her mood.

There was a sharp bit of gravel on the bench under one hand, and Reg drew up her hand to brush it away. She frowned, looking down at the red stone that had embedded itself into her palm. A ruby.

Where did this come from? Reg demanded.

Forst chuckled as he drew on his pipe. *I found it as I was working this morning, dropped on the pathway. I knew it must be thine, so I left it here for you to find it. Or for it to find you.* His eyes twinkled.

How did you know it was mine? Reg asked, staring at the ruby. It was, she was sure, the same one she had given Corvin the night before. How had it found its way back into her yard?

Forst shrugged. *Sarah would not have dropped it back here. She uses the front sidewalk to get to her car and would not bring an unset gem into the back yard.*

Well, she could, Reg countered.

Is it not thy stone?

Yes. I mean. It was. I gave it away, which is why I don't understand how it could be here. What's going on?

I know not, it has not told me its story. He smiled and blew a couple of smoke rings. Reg watched them drift up into the sky, expanding and breaking apart.

I gave it to Corvin. Reg looked around, as if he might be hiding in some shadow of the garden. But she knew he couldn't get into the yard and, if he were there, she would be able to feel his presence. He couldn't get close to her without her knowing it. *It doesn't make any sense.*

You give gifts to the power drinker? Forst's bushy brows drew down and he shook his head. *You should not have anything to do with that one.*

I am careful. We were not alone. Reg paused, thinking about it. *Is there a reason I should not give him something? I don't understand all the magical rules. It doesn't… I haven't entered into some kind of contract by giving him a gift?*

Accepting the gift of the fairies had been a mistake; was the same true of giving a gift? Especially to someone like Corvin? He had argued in the past that she had given her permission for the liberties he had taken, and she didn't want to think that her gift to him might mean that they were now engaged or had made some other kind of agreement.

They are cunning, his kind. You don't want to get too comfortable around him, thinking that he is just another human, another warlock. Forst shook his head. *Encouraging his interest in you is very unwise. You have shown him too much courtesy in the past.*

But you don't think that I did something wrong. That I contracted with him for my firstborn child or anything.

Forst stroked his beard and shook his head. *No, no. He is not a fairy.*

Having had some dealing with the fairies about changelings before, Reg had an idea of what Forst was talking about. The fairies did not reproduce quickly enough to support their population, and so they found ways to get the babies of other species and turn them into fairies through their magic. Calliopia had been one such child.

How did the ruby get back here? Corvin couldn't get into the yard. The wards keep him out. Reg looked around her, reaching out all of her senses to make sure the barriers were still there and had not been broken. Everything seemed warm and safe and protected.

Perhaps he sent another. Or perhaps it was taken from him without his knowledge. Or he lost it somewhere else, and it made its way back here.

Reg laughed. *It doesn't have legs,* she pointed out. *Or movement or will of its own. So how would it get back here by itself?*

Not by itself. But make no mistake, such a stone can have a will. Forst gazed at the stone, nodding sagely. *Many humans believe only what their eyes can see and ears can hear, but you are not one of those people, Reg Rawlins. Use your other senses and do not be deceived.*

Reg wasn't sure she would ever get used to the magical world. Gems that could make up their minds and transport themselves from one place to another? It didn't make any sense. Not logically.

But the magical world frequently defied her logic.

CHAPTER EIGHTEEN

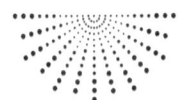

*R*eg had another cup of coffee before calling Corvin. She wasn't sure how to begin a conversation with him about the delinquent ruby. It seemed silly to be calling him to ask whether he had the ruby. If it was the same ruby, how it had ended up in her possession again?

By the time she reached the bottom of her coffee mug, her phone was ringing, and Corvin's face was on the screen. Reg put her empty cup on the coffee table, pulled her feet up on the couch, and answered the call.

"Corvin."

"Regina. I trust you slept well."

"No. I don't think I got a wink of sleep. What about you? Were you up wandering all night?"

Corvin cleared his throat and Reg waited for his explanation. "No… I was not wandering. I returned home."

"Really? You went directly home? And didn't go anywhere else?"

Corvin was slow to answer. They shared enough that he probably knew that lying to her wasn't going to work. "No. Not directly home. Why?"

"Because strange things are happening, and I don't know how you are involved."

"Strange things? Do tell. What sort of strange things?"

"Have you had any luck with that ruby? Figuring out how to remove the curse?"

"No. I haven't spent any time on it yet. These things take time, and I will need to do a considerable amount of research to come up with some ideas."

"And you will need the ruby."

He was silent for a few beats, then cleared his throat. "Yes, of course."

"And you don't, do you?"

"I don't what?"

"You're as good as Harrison at not answering questions properly. You don't have the ruby anymore."

"What makes you think that?"

"Because I do."

"How did you get the ruby back?" His tone was sharp, as if she had done something wrong. All Reg had done was go out to her garden for a stroll and found the ruby there.

"It was in my yard. Were you here? Before you went home last night? Did you come by to make sure that I was safe and settled for the night?" She offered a reason for him to have been by, the type of excuse that he often gave her.

"No. I wasn't in your yard."

"Not in the back yard, no. But I wonder if you were in the front. Or maybe stopped to visit Sarah. Or just pulled over for a few minutes to... check your email."

"I wasn't there," Corvin growled. "Not at all!"

"Where did you go, then? Because despite appearances, I'm sure this ruby couldn't get all the way back to me all on its own."

"Cursed gems," Corvin muttered. "You never know what they will do. I warned you about that. Don't know what I was doing, taking it from you in the first place."

"How did you lose it, then?"

"I don't know. A pickpocket?" He considered. Reg could feel his seething beneath the surface. "I stopped for a drink. Talked to... a couple of people. Maybe somebody managed to take it off me. Or it fell out of my pocket." As if anticipating her skepticism, he repeated, "You don't know what a cursed gem will do. You may think you've got deep pockets, or it is locked away safely, but if it has other ideas…"

"I don't quite buy the idea that a stone could have a mind of its own."

"When you've lived a few centuries, maybe you won't be so naive. I would think that from what you have seen of the paranormal world so far that you wouldn't be quite so quick to declare what is possible and what is not."

"So someone just happened to guess that you had a ruby in your pocket and lifted it. Or you dropped it. And then what? It sprouted legs and walked to my house? Jumped out of the next person's pocket all on its own? What?"

"I don't know how, and I wouldn't want to say. Somehow… maybe it fell on the ground and a bird picked it up. Or another creature that likes sparkly things or was attracted to its power. I told you that cursed gems are unpredictable. And they are not quite as easy to rid yourself of as you would like to think."

Reg thought about it. It wasn't exactly as though she was worried about having the gems in her possession. It was irritating and inconvenient if she couldn't liquidate them somehow, but she didn't see the harm in simply possessing them. Despite everything that Harrison and Sarah had said so far, nothing really bad had happened to her. She hadn't had the best of luck recently, but when had she? After the life she had led so far, Reg didn't expect things to be easy.

"Okay," she sighed. "I guess that experiment is finished, then. I can't give the jewels away. But that was never really what I wanted to do anyway. I was hoping that after I gave them away, they would be clean, and I could work out some kind of deal to still make money off of them. But if that doesn't work… then it doesn't work."

"I think… you're taking the matter all too lightly," Corvin warned. "You seem to think that you can keep holding on to the gems forever. That you won't suffer any harm or setbacks because of them."

"Well, I've been okay so far. Nothing *terrible* has happened."

Just minor things. Like being poisoned by a serial killer. Being kidnapped by a swamp goblin. Being investigated by the magical equivalent of the FBI. Fighting sirens. Being made an outcast. And being possessed by an evil wizard. Minor stuff.

Reg sat there thinking about it. Of course, she couldn't attribute any of those things to owning the gems. It had all seemed like a natural progression from the things that had happened to her before she had been given the gems. It wasn't as if she'd been living a charmed life before that.

"Reg, just because nothing terrible has happened, that doesn't mean that it won't. Have you read any of the accounts of what has happened to people who have possessed cursed stones in the past?"

"Well, no." Reading wasn't Reg's thing, and even if it had been, what reason would she have to study up on cursed gems?

"We're not talking about minor inconveniences," Corvin explained. "The owner or their families getting killed, the gems stolen in bloody wars, plagues and sicknesses. Financial ruin."

"I don't have any family, money, or a kingdom," Reg pointed out. "I could get sick or die, but… what are the chances of that?"

"Pretty good, I'm thinking. These gems you are in possession of are a pretty powerful source. You may only have a small number, but it isn't really the quantity that makes the difference." It was probably a good thing he didn't know that she had a whole chest of them. "But think about the fairies you got them from. I assume it was Calliopia's family?"

Reg made a noncommittal noise.

"What happened to them? Their daughter was kidnapped. When she was returned, she ran away. And then she was mortally wounded. If it weren't for you, she would have died. It was a near thing."

"Then why did they give them to me? I was the one who saved their daughter. Why would they reward me by dumping a cursed treasure on me?"

"You're thinking in human terms. I told you before, the fairies don't think that way. They think about themselves. How they can get the best deal out of every transaction. If they could get rid of cursed gems by giving them to you, why wouldn't they? Humans like gems, you clearly don't know a lot about their world, hopefully you would take them."

Reg rested her forehead on her knees. "So I can't use the gems. I can't give them away. And I can't keep them. Does that about sum it up?"

CHAPTER NINETEEN

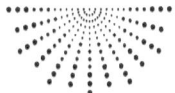

*R*eg worked out a new plan.

She went to a thrift store she had previously been to in Black Sands. There were not many places that sold clothing and accessories at reasonable prices, and she didn't have much capital. She would use the last of her cash, and then she would have to rely on her credit cards. She knew from experience they wouldn't last long and the fees would add up quickly.

But if she couldn't use the gems, and the curse on them had resulted in the loss of her clientele, then she wouldn't be able to raise any new capital without first ridding herself of them. So she had to spend money to make money, eventually.

The woman at the register looked at the pile of wallets and purses that Reg had placed there, bemused.

"Are you… having some kind of theme party?" she guessed.

Reg nodded, smiling pleasantly. "Yes, exactly, how did you guess?"

The cashier wanted to ask her more questions about it, but since she was the one who had suggested it was a theme party, she couldn't then claim that she didn't know what someone would do at such a party.

"Oh, that sounds like a lot of fun!"

"If it all works out, it will put a smile on my face," Reg confirmed.

The woman began to scan the items through. Reg watched the

numbers carefully, pointing out if one of them was supposed to be reduced or had a broken clasp or some other reason she could ask for it at a lower price. Eventually, they were all tallied up, and Reg counted out every penny like a grandma on a fixed income. The cashier put all the purses into a big shopping bag and Reg took them home.

There, Reg went to work filling the purses with bits of paper and items from the junk drawer, as well as a small handful of gems in each. With a determined smile on her face, she drove around town, stopping every few minutes to leave a purse or wallet in a strategic area, somewhere it would look natural, as if someone had dropped it or left it behind by accident. Places that were sheltered enough that whoever found it could be assured they could walk away without anyone observing them.

The whole process from start to finish took most of the day. Or at least, until she was ready for supper. The whole venture had given her an appetite, and she was smiling as she sat down for a fish fillet Sarah had left her.

Starlight meowed around her feet, begging for his portion, and Reg put a piece of the fish patty in his bowl for him. With a sigh of satisfaction at having rid herself of the jewels, Reg checking her social networks on her phone.

She had barely started to scroll down when she saw a couple of FOUND notices, with pictures of the purses she had left behind. She shook her head in disbelief and kept scrolling. The good Samaritans could look for her all they liked, and then they could keep the cursed gems. What else could they do?

Hopefully, most of them did not have the special powers they needed to recognize the gems as cursed and would just be thanking their lucky stars that they had made such a find. Or maybe they would think that the gems were fake, because no one would leave such a precious possession on the ground like that. They would end up in the garbage, glued to a child's paper craft, sewn into a glamorous outfit, or glued into a cheap jewelry setting for dress-up. Reg took great satisfaction in the thought.

She was most of the way through the fish when she started getting instant messages and emails. Surveillance camera pictures of her dropping the wallets, or photos of the receipts and bits of paper that she had left in the wallets, with questions like "Is this you?" and "Is this your wallet?"

Reg didn't answer them, but the pictures and inquiries tumbled through her head. How had people identified her so fast? Had all the wallets been found by private investigators? People who somehow managed to trace them back to her name or social media? It was unbelievable that they could identify her so quickly from a grainy photo or faded receipt from three months before. It shouldn't be possible. She had assumed when she had been dropping them that it would not be possible.

She shook her head. Let people pursue her. They couldn't force her to take the wallets back. And if she didn't take them back, they would bear the responsibility of ownership of the gems or would have to find another way to get rid of them. It was out of her hands.

* * *

A couple of hours passed before her phone started ringing. Reg looked at the phone number. A number that she didn't know. And then another. Then a blocked number. Reg rolled her eyes. Too bad. She wouldn't answer the calls. There was no way she was taking those gems back.

Half an hour passed without the phone ringing, and Reg just started to settle into a show on the TV. Her phone buzzed again, and she looked at it reluctantly. Marta Jessup.

That would be Detective Marta Jessup.

Reg wasn't sure whether to answer it at all. Jessup might just be calling to see whether they could get together sometime. They had enjoyed a few girls' nights out, but Reg was rather irritated with having been hauled in for questioning on a murder recently. Jessup hadn't exactly extended her any courtesies for being her friend.

But if she ignored Jessup's call, then likely the next step would be finding the woman on her doorstep, inquiring to see whether she was okay.

And she did not want that. The only way to get rid of her was probably to talk to her, tell her that she was too busy to get together, and set up something indefinite in the future. If Jessup insisted on a date, then Reg would call back and break it in a day or two.

Reg swiped the screen. "Hello?"

"Reg! Good to hear your voice!"

"Yeah. You too. Are you off tonight?"

"Actually…. no. I'm on duty."

"Oh, we'd better make it quick, then." Reg couldn't exactly say "I've kept you long enough" and hang up when it was Jessup who had called her, and she hadn't said what she wanted yet. But Reg wanted to signal her that she wanted to get off the phone quickly.

"What's going on tonight, Reg?"

"Uh… I don't know. Just watching a new series."

"I'm not talking about what you're doing right now, I'm talking about this growing pile of wallets at the precinct."

Reg gulped. "What?"

"Have you been dropping purses all over Black Sands?"

"I don't know what you're talking about. Why would I do something like that?"

Jessup snorted. "That's a really good question. I have a couple of theories, but it is pretty bizarre behavior, even for you."

"Even for me?"

"Well, you have to admit, some pretty strange things have happened to you since you moved here."

Reg couldn't exactly argue with that. "Well, I'm not sure what's going on with these purses. Sorry."

"Reg, we've got surveillance pictures of you."

"It's not me. Must be someone who looks like me."

"There really aren't that many people around who could pass for a redhead in box braids wearing a flowing yellow and orange skirt."

Reg looked down at her knees, tucked up under the skirt. At least Jessup wasn't at the cottage. Reg could still deny it.

Jessup wouldn't believe her of course, but she could try to bluff her way through.

"Maybe someone is impersonating me. Trying to set me up. Or it is a doppelgänger. Do doppelgängers really exist? Maybe we should call Corvin in for a consult. He could tell us the entire history of doppelgängers since the beginning of time."

"I'm sure he could," Jessup agreed. "But on the other hand, it's not a doppelgänger. It's you. And I want to know the meaning of this."

"I don't know. The meaning of what?"

"Of the purses that you bought from Sandy Claws Thrift Shop today. It didn't exactly go unnoticed."

"Uh…"

Caught. But Reg hadn't done anything wrong. If anything, she had done something nice, spreading her wealth around the community, sharing it with people who might have less than she. Surely people weren't complaining about it.

"So, what's the deal?" Jessup demanded. "Is this some kind of joke? A social media game? Some weird new form of geocaching? What?"

"No. I just… felt like doing something nice."

"By leaving wallets all over town."

"Yeah. I figured people would be excited to find them. That maybe they would get into the hands of the people who needed them the most. Like social programs never do."

Jessup sighed heavily. "Yeah. Sure. Well, you're going to have to come to the police station to claim them."

"I'm not claiming anything."

"You need to. We can't just keep them here. Come and pick them up and we'll forget about this."

"Forget about what?" Reg asked sweetly.

"Forget about any charges of… I don't know. Littering. Wasting police time and resources. Interfering with a police investigation."

"Interfering with what police investigation?"

"I don't know, maybe the sudden appearance of dozens of abandoned wallets?"

"No way that ever gets to the court system."

"Maybe not. But I know where you live."

Reg choked. "What?"

"If you won't come here to get them, I'll bring them to you. They can't just stay here. And you've been identified as the rightful owner, so you need to be responsible for them."

"But I don't want them."

"Then throw them in the garbage."

"Like that's gonna work," Reg muttered.

"What?"

"You go ahead and throw them in the garbage there. I don't want or need them. If you don't want them around there, then throw it in the police department bin. Why bother loading them into the car and driving them here?"

"Reg!" Jessup said firmly.

"What? I don't want them. Just throw them out. I guess my little game didn't pan out. You go ahead and just dump them."

"I'm not authorized to do something like that. It's destruction of evidence. Or of personal property. You need to take possession of this pile and throw them out yourself."

"I'm not going to."

"You have until the end of the day. If they're still here at the end of my shift…"

"Then you have my authorization to throw them out. And to go home and get a good sleep."

Reg could see that the conversation wasn't going anywhere. She hung up the phone. Jessup tried to call her back twice, but Reg didn't answer it.

She wasn't an idiot.

CHAPTER TWENTY

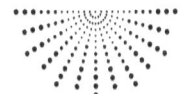

*R*eg kept an eye on her phone around the time she knew Jessup would be getting off of her shift, but there was no further call from her. Maybe she had accepted Reg's instructions and would just discard the wallets at the end of her shift. Then Reg would be done with them forever. She could start taking clients again and everything would go back to normal.

Or paranormal.

The way they had been before Reg accepted the gems from the fairies.

She started getting ready for bed. She had not slept well that last couple of nights and was looking forward to climbing into bed and falling asleep. Her body and her brain needed a good rest.

Starlight joined her on the bed and cuddled up with her, purring with contentment as she scratched his ears and chin. Just a regular night, like any other. Everything back to the way it should be.

* * *

When she got up in the morning, Reg felt as if she had been sleeping for days. She stretched, petted Starlight when he jumped down from the window to see her, and lazed in bed for a while longer before her body forced her to get up to use the john and scavenge in the kitchen for something suitable for breakfast. Since she didn't usually wake up hungry, she thought this was a good sign that she had caught up on the sleep she needed, and her body was ready to put energy into other things.

She found some leftover fish sticks, which she fed to Starlight, and started the coffee brewing. There wasn't anything that looked even remotely like breakfast in the fridge, so she settled for a bowl of cold spaghetti takeout from a few days earlier.

There was a knock at the door and the sound of Sarah's key in the lock.

"Just a minute!" Reg called, and hurried over to unlock the bolt, which could only be locked and unlocked from the inside.

She opened the door to Sarah, but her landlord didn't immediately step in as she usually did. Instead she looked down, frowning.

Reg followed her gaze and saw the pile of purses and wallets on the doorstep.

"Oh."

"What is all this?" Sarah asked. "What's going on?"

"Well... just a sort of a... social experiment," Reg explained. She supposed she couldn't just leave them all on the doorstep. Sarah would have something to say about that. She bent down and gathered them up in her arms, bringing them back into the cottage.

"What kind of a social experiment?" Sarah persisted.

"Seeing whether people would return lost wallets."

"I would say it was successful."

"Yeah." Reg dumped them all in the middle of the kitchen table. She would sort through them later, after Sarah was gone, and figure out what to do with them. After she emptied them, maybe she could return them to the thrift store. She didn't have any further use for them. And then she would have to figure out what to do with whatever gems had been returned.

"Any appointments today?" Sarah asked, moving over to the date book on the island to flip to the current day. Reg wasn't sure when she had last looked at it. She had broken the habit when her business had dropped off. If she wanted to get it back again, she would have to get out there and hustle. She couldn't just rely on past clients or word of mouth to do her marketing. She'd always had to hustle business before; there was no reason it should be any different now. That was why her business had dropped off. Nothing to do with cursed gems.

"I don't think so," Reg told Sarah, as they both looked at the blank page. "Why, did you have someone to schedule in?"

"No… but I think it is time to get the word out that you are accepting new clients. No need to say that the old ones have all disappeared. But I do think that we've both fallen behind on drumming up appointments."

"It isn't your responsibility," Reg protested, embarrassed that Sarah had to point this out. "You're my landlady, not my employee. I should be doing that myself."

"You know I don't mind. I like being involved in something. A person can get bored just sitting around the house all day. I'd like to know that you're going to stay around. If there's no business, I suppose you'll want to move on to somewhere there is."

"I'm not going to abandon you…" But Reg knew that Sarah was right. If they couldn't drum up any new business, she would have to consider other possibilities. One of which was leaving the cottage and Black Sands behind and finding a new center of operations where people didn't know so much about her and her family background.

"You don't owe anything to me, either," Sarah said with a sad smile. "If things aren't working out here, you aren't obligated to stay for an old woman like me. You'll need to move on."

"Well, let's not talk about that right now. I'm going to start putting up new posters and talking to people. Maybe some internet advertising too. I'll get more clients. And like Corvin said, I can do work as a phone hotline psychic. No one will care about my parentage if they're just calling in on a hotline."

"That doesn't sound very fulfilling. I suppose young people don't mind being on the phone all day, but I would want face-to-face meetings at least some of the time. It would be very isolating to only talk to people on the phone."

Reg shrugged. She would have to do what she had to do. She'd been on the streets before. She didn't want to return to that kind of life. She would definitely choose being a hotline psychic over that kind of life.

Starlight was meowing at Sarah, rubbing against her ankles and winding around her legs as he told her all his woes.

"He's been fed," Reg said, giving Starlight a glare. "Don't let him tell you that he's hungry and I never feed him properly."

"He's just saying hello," Sarah said, and bent over to give Starlight a scratch behind the ears. She didn't like cats as a rule, but she had always behaved kindly toward Starlight, spoiling him by giving him treats that he didn't need.

Starlight glared at them both and stalked off, in a huff that he wasn't getting extra food.

Reg laughed and poured herself a cup of the freshly-brewed coffee. "Would you like a cup?"

"No, no. I just came over to see how you were and to check the calendar." Sarah looked over at the pile of wallets on the table. And to find out why there was a bunch of wallets and purses on Reg's doorstep, of course. Who wouldn't be curious about that?

Sarah checked the fridge. "I left some cabbage salad in here the other day. It really needs to be eaten in the next day or two or it will be too late."

"Okay. I'll have some," Reg agreed. "Thank you."

"Of course, dear. Always happy to help out." Sarah nodded and took her leave. She was always happy to help with everything, except for helping Reg to cleanse the gems or even to find an expert who could. Reg appreciated everything that Sarah did for her, but was frustrated with the way Sarah refused her in other areas. It wasn't the first time that Reg thought Sarah was able to help, yet wasn't willing.

People had to have boundaries, though. Sarah couldn't let Reg walk all over her. She had her health and her own responsibilities to consider. It just seemed like she was willing to offer help in everything except for when Reg really needed it.

Sipping her coffee and taking a bite of spaghetti every few minutes, Reg went through the wallets and purses, making piles for the jewels and for the junk that she had stuffed into the wallets. Who would have thought that the random bits of paper and objects would be enough for people to trace the gems back to her?

When she was finished, she put all the wallets back into the shopping bag for later and retrieved the wooden box that the jewels had been previously housed in and filled it with the jewels. Starlight jumped up on the table to look at them. He didn't normally jump onto the table; but then, Reg didn't normally use it and he was probably curious.

"Nothing to eat here," she told him.

Starlight poked his nose into the box, then looked at her. Reg looked at the little wooden chest.

"I think there are more gems in there now than when I started."

Was it possible that she had actually gotten more jewels back than she'd had to start with? Had people added their own cursed gems to the wallets? She had assumed, even when Jessup had said that she'd received all of those wallets, that she wouldn't get them all back. People would keep at least some of the wallets and gems. But her hoard of cursed gems didn't appear to have diminished.

Reg rubbed her forehead, trying to figure out what to do.

Where was a pixie when you needed one? The pixies thought they had the right to claim anything that was buried in the earth, which was their domain. And that included gemstones that had originally come out of the ground. Maybe instead of leaving wallets around town, she should have left the chest of gems in the pixie territory. It had been a while since she had been to their burrows, but she still remembered the general area, and she knew that there were plenty of pixies around guarding them and keeping a lookout on everything that was going on in the neighborhood. She didn't imagine it would take very long for them to snatch up a box of gems.

Although maybe they wouldn't if the gems were cursed. They would surely be able to sense the curse on the stones, perhaps even faster than the experts who had looked at them so far.

But maybe they would have the means to remove the curse as well, so they wouldn't care.

An idea started to form in Reg's brain. Pixies. Maybe she already knew someone who was an expert on gems and could tell her what to do about her little problem.

Ruan, Calliopia's mate, had come to Reg when she had been injured, looking for her help. And she had saved Calliopia and gotten her back on the road to recovery when everyone else had said that it was impossible. Ruan himself had been ready to end her suffering. So he owed Reg. And Ruan was a pixie.

CHAPTER TWENTY-ONE

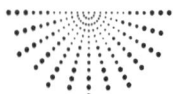

*R*eg had no idea where Ruan might be. They had left town once Calliopia was well enough to travel, and they had not, as far as Reg knew, told anyone where they were going. They were outcasts in both the fairy and the pixie communities, so there was no point in telling anyone where they planned to go, if they planned for their nomadic lifestyle to carry them anywhere in particular. Reg suspected that they simply went whatever direction the wind blew them.

Which meant they could be practically anywhere. Or at least, anywhere Ruan's rickety old car would take them.

Reg went to her living room and took the crystal ball off its shelf. She had been able to see Calliopia and Ruan in the crystal more than once before. She had a connection with Calliopia that they couldn't seem to break, and that would be enough for Reg to trace her, no matter how far away she was. And Ruan should be with his mate. Divorce was not a thing in the pixie and fairy worlds. Once the two were mated, that was that.

Reg got comfortable and focused her eyes in the depths of the crystal.

Where is Calliopia?

The scar on Reg's hand where she had been cut with Calliopia's fairy blade had faded until it was barely visible after the blade had been destroyed, but as she focused on the crystal and Calliopia's name, her hand began to throb. She tried to use the pain to sharpen her focus. Calliopia was out there somewhere, and the pain and the connection they had previously shared on more than one occasion should lead Reg directly to her.

She started to see images in the crystal. The pain in her hand grew hot, getting sharper and sharper until it felt as it had when she first was cut. She didn't look at her hand, afraid that if she did, she would find it once more open and bleeding.

Starlight walked over and, after standing up on his hind legs to look into the crystal, he jumped up beside her and snuggled close while she tried to focus the images. Finally, Calliopia came into focus. The pretty girl with light brown hair smiled and said something to the figure beside her. Ruan, of course, with messy brown curls and a cherubic, apple-cheeked face that made him look like a little boy, though he was undoubtedly older than Reg, probably by decades, and had a mouthful of sharp predatory teeth.

I need to speak with Ruan. Reg focused on him, trying to project her thoughts to him. She knew that he had some capacity for telepathy, but didn't know how clear it would be over the miles.

She could see Calliopia and Ruan exchanging a few words, but then the vision started to fade. Reg tried to hold on to it.

Ruan!

But it had faded into mist, and then she was just looking at the reflection on the shiny surface of the crystal ball. Reg swore. She shook her hand, trying to relieve the pain. It would fade, since she was no longer trying to reach Calliopia. She rubbed her palm with the thumb of the other hand.

Her phone started to buzz. Reg sighed and flopped her head back, tired and frustrated. She didn't want to talk to anyone on the phone. She didn't want to deal with an inquiry from Jessup or someone else who had found one of the wallets and wanted to return it to. Or talk to Corvin or anyone else. Not even a client.

But thinking about a client made her galvanize herself, and Reg reached for her phone to see who was calling.

It was a Skype call, with Ruan's dirty, laughing face on the screen.

Reg stared at it for a moment, then finally moved in order to catch the call before it failed. She swiped the call and held the phone up in front of her. Ruan's picture was blurred to start with, then came into focus. He leaned toward the camera on his own phone.

"The great sorceress Reg Rawlins calls," he observed.

"I was trying to reach you!" Reg agreed. She felt a little silly for not trying to reach out to him using technology. But she didn't have his phone number and hadn't realized that he would have a phone. The pixies she had met in the underground burrows where Calliopia had been held lived without any kind of technology. She hadn't seen as much as a hand-cranked wheat grinder. The pixies were omnivorous, eating things like bugs and grubs, and she didn't know whether they ate grains, or just tuberous things that grew under the ground. Ruan had been familiar with fruit juice, but that was probably from his time living aboveground with Calliopia.

"Phones are easier," Ruan said. "And with Skype, no roaming fees, even if we are outside of human-erica."

"You're out of the country?"

"We come; we go." He made a careless gesture with his hand. "It makes no difference to our sources."

"No… I guess not. It's nice to see your face. How are you? And how is Calliopia doing? Has she completely recovered?" Fairies were quick healers, but the wound she had sustained had been very serious.

"She fares well." Ruan considered, obviously holding back. "The wound heals. It no longer pains her, except at night."

That might psychological rather than physical pain, if it was only at night. Or maybe she only noticed it when she was not distracted by her daily activities.

"Is she sleeping better?"

Ruan shook his head. "Demons yet plague her sleep. But I do not let her sleep alone and she does not sleep with a weapon."

Callie had by now, presumably, replaced the dagger that Reg had destroyed. But they had learned the hard way that she could not be trusted with the weapon while she slept. Reg wondered how they had sorted out the sleeping arrangements, with Calliopia unable to abide the night shadows and Ruan, a creature who would normally have spent most of his time in underground burrows, needing somewhere dark and close to rest and regenerate. Maybe he built himself a little blanket fort in Calliopia's bedroom. Or slept with an eye mask on to block out the never-ending light.

"I wish there was something I could do to help," Reg said. "She really should be seeing a therapist. Someone to help her with all of this stuff."

Reg's amateur armchair diagnosis was that Calliopia suffered from some fairy form of PTSD since her kidnapping. She had found that fairies responded well to human medicine, and wondered whether anti-depressants and a sleep aid might help her. Or seeing a therapist.

"Fairies do not do such things," Ruan disagreed, shaking his head.

"I know. But I think it might help."

He shrugged his thin, waifish shoulders. "But that is not why you reached out to Ruan…?"

"No." Reg squared her own shoulders, remembering the task at hand. "I don't know whether you will be able to help, but…"

"Of course I will help all I can," Ruan said, giving a small, formal bow.

Reg was glad that he was on her side. When she had been looking for Calliopia and the pixies had been holding her, he had been on the opposite side, and she had found the pixies to be an angry, bloodthirsty group. But since she had healed Calliopia, Ruan no longer considered Reg an enemy. At least, she hoped that if she were ever to meet him face-to-face again, he would still be friendly and on her side. But she would always have to be careful, because as Corvin had pointed out repeatedly, non-human creatures did not have the same morals and rules as humans did. Perhaps someone who was a friend one day would be dinner the next.

"Okay. You are a pixie, and pixies are experts of things under the earth."

He nodded his agreement. No false modesty. The underground was his domain.

"And… gems. You're familiar with precious stones and their powers and… natures."

Ruan raised an eyebrow, looking comical to Reg rather than wise. "Piskies know gems."

"I have… come into possession of some gems and I don't know if you can help and give me some advice, but…"

"What is the problem?"

"They are apparently cursed."

His previously pleasant and interested expression grew dark. He turned away from the phone camera and said something in a low voice to Calliopia, who was off-camera somewhere. Reg couldn't tell what he had said. Perhaps something in a pixie or fairy language. She realized suddenly that maybe Ruan and Calliopia were not the best ones to be talking to about the issue, when the gems had been given to her by Calliopia's family. Who knew what kind of complications might arise if Calliopia knew what her parents had done, or if they knew that Reg was consulting with a pixie about how best to remove the curse.

"Cursed gems," Ruan said darkly, shaking his head. "You should not accept them. Give them back."

"I've tried. I didn't know they were cursed until now, I accepted them as a gift a while back." She shrugged and shook her head, trying to look casual about it. "I just didn't know. I don't have a magical background. I didn't know about cursed gems."

"Didn't know about them?" Ruan's tone was scathing. "Even humans know of cursed stones."

"Well, some humans do. I didn't really know they were a thing. I mean, I knew about blood diamonds, and I knew there are stories about treasures being cursed when someone steals them from a tomb. But I didn't know… I thought that was rare, and that it didn't happen anymore, I guess."

"Reg Rawlins should not accept such gifts."

Reg nodded. "You mean something that seems so extravagant? I guess I should have realized. But I didn't stop to think about it. I was just glad… I thought it was a nice gift, that's all. I knew it was expensive, but I thought that they just weren't that valuable to… the person who gave them to me."

He shook his head. "You are like a child. Even a pixie child of a few years would know better than that."

"Okay." Reg was getting impatient with his criticism. "I realize now that I did something stupid. But we can't change that. I want to know what I can do now. To cleanse the stones."

"This is not done. Humans cannot do such a thing."

"You said I couldn't cure Calliopia, either. That I couldn't unmake the blade. But I did."

Ruan pondered this. Calliopia said something to him, but he looked lost in thought. He answered her faintly. It was some time before he focused on Reg's face on his phone screen again.

"Reg Rawlins *is* a great sorceress," he admitted. "Perhaps it is something that a great sorceress can do, even if a normal human could not."

"Right! How are we going to know if I don't try?" But she was a little worried about what he would tell her to do. Was it complex magic? Something dangerous? She didn't want to risk her life on cleansing the gems, however much she would like to be comfortably well-off and not to have to worry about raising money again.

CHAPTER TWENTY-TWO

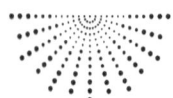

"*R*eg Rawlings should give the stones to the piskies," Ruan suggested. "They will take care of them."

"By take care of them, you mean that they'll take them and not give them back, right? I won't ever see them again? That's not cleansing them, that's just taking them."

If there were any chance that Reg could still get something for the stones, she didn't want to overlook it. If Ruan could tell her how to cleanse them properly…

"By giving away, they can be cleansed," Ruan asserted.

"Yeah, Corvin thought that might work too, but it doesn't. Every time I give them away, they come back."

Ruan snickered. "Cursed stones can be very stubborn."

"Well, I guess I got some really stubborn ones, because I've tried all different ways of giving them away or having someone take them, and it doesn't work. In fact, I think I ended up with more than I started with."

"Reg Rawlins must have a very inviting home."

"Well, great. I have a good home for cursed stones. I'm not sure I'd tell that to the real estate agent."

Ruan considered, rubbing his hairless chin. "Reg Rawlins has great powers. Perhaps you can use the elements."

"What elements? How would I do that?"

"You can perhaps fire them, as you did Calliopia's blade. Burn away the impurities. This is often done with precious stones and metals."

"I'm not planning on a trip back to the dwarf mountain to use their forge. How hot do I have to burn them?"

"Very hot. Reg Rawlins can do this."

"Yes," Reg had power as a firecaster, so this was right up her alley. "I can try that for sure. And that's all there is to it? I don't have to say a spell or make a potion?"

"No." Ruan rolled his eyes at her naiveté. "Just fire. If that works not… best to throw them into the sea."

"I don't want to do that. I still want to be able to use them."

"Use them?"

"For money. To pay for things."

"Ah." Ruan nodded his understanding. "Not if you throw them into the sea."

"Yeah. So is that it? If firing them doesn't remove the curse, then my only option is to throw them into the sea, to get rid of the curse? So that I don't have a bunch of bad luck?"

Ruan hesitated, looking off-camera, then nodded.

"That's it?" Reg demanded. "There's nothing else I can do to remove this curse?"

Ruan shook his head slightly, but Reg thought he was shaking his head in answer to a question Calliopia had asked, not her. She waited for him to turn his attention back to the small screen.

"Ruan."

He looked at her. "Humans do not cleanse gems," Ruan asserted again. "It is not done."

"But I can try if I want to. And I'm not exactly human. Or all human. So maybe I can."

"From whence came the stones?"

"I don't know, exactly. I mean, I know who had them last, before they were given to me, but I don't know their history."

"They have been stolen? How were they mined? From where?"

"I don't know, Ruan. That must have been a long time ago. I have no idea where they came from. Or if they were stolen at some point. I would guess so." She shrugged. "Gems that have been around for a long time, you would think that they might have been stolen at some point, wouldn't you? Spoils of war, maybe?"

"Sometimes from temples," Ruan said. "Offerings to gods or statues in temples."

Reg had seen Indiana Jones. She shrugged. "Yeah, I guess. But there's no way for me to know. And it's... not just a couple of gems. It wouldn't be possible to trace the histories of all of them. I don't know how I would even trace the history of one. They wouldn't be cataloged somewhere, would they? You can't just search on the internet for an emerald pendant of this size and cut and find out where it came from, can you?"

"Internet is an amazing thing," Ruan said with some reverence. "But no, I do not think so."

"What difference would knowing their history make? Would that give me another way to remove the curse?"

Ruan nodded reluctantly.

"It would? How? What would I do?"

"Returning the stones to their rightful owner, or to their birthplace, that could remove the curse."

Reg couldn't even fathom how she would do that. "The last owners don't want them back. I already asked."

"But they did not have them from the source," Ruan speculated. "They are not the rightful owners."

Reg blew out her breath. "No. Probably not." The fairies might have had them for generations. And the Papillons did not even want to talk to her about them. So how would she get the information about where they had come from so long ago? And who would be the rightful owner after so long? If hundreds of years had passed since they were stolen from their rightful owner, then how would she be able to find the heir they were to go to? It was an impossible task.

"Well... you're right. That is probably not possible. Even for the great Reg Rawlins."

Ruan nodded solemnly. "Return them to the piskies," he suggested again. "They will take care of them."

"You make it sound like putting babies to bed at night."

Ruan laughed and nodded. "Yes, like that," he agreed. "The gems need a... different kind of home. Someone who understands where they came from and what they went through. A piskie could take good care of them."

"Well, not if I have any say in it. I'm not going back there anytime soon. I want to be able to get some money for them. What is the point in a treasure if you can't pay for anything?"

"Treasures are… to be treasured."

"Hmmph." Reg didn't know that she agreed. Merely owning a treasure wasn't enough for her. But maybe with the information Ruan had given to her, she would be able to do something.

CHAPTER TWENTY-THREE

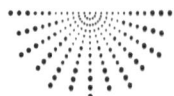

*R*eg had one small problem with firing the gems. Besides the fact that she wasn't sure if she needed any special equipment or how hot she needed to get them in order to purify them as Ruan had suggested.

And that was, being a newbie firecaster, she was not allowed to "play with fire" by herself.

Because, of course, there was always the danger that she would burn down the house and everything in it. Or, as she had when she was trying to unmake the fairy blade, that she would pull energy from everyone around her and risk burning up half the planet in a massive fireball.

These things were tricky.

Not being allowed to use her power on her own, she had to bring another firecaster into the growing circle of people who knew about the gems. Sarah, Corvin, the Papillons, Jessup—though she might not know that they were real, and Reg was sure she didn't know that they were cursed—Ruan and Calliopia, and now Davyn.

She didn't have to show him the entire hoard. Not initially. They could try firing just a few of the gems, and then if it worked, she could get Davyn to help her with the rest.

"I have a special job today," she told the warlock, who was the head of Corvin's coven. "But I'm going to need help."

"What kind of job?" Davyn asked.

Dark-haired like Corvin, Davyn wasn't nearly as handsome and had a bit of a geeky look when he was dressed for his day job. Which he wasn't, but having seen him at work, Reg couldn't help seeing that sort of "accountant" appearance even when he was in his robes.

"I have these gemstones... but they are, well, cursed, I guess. I've been talking to Ruan, and he said that I could try cleansing them with fire."

Davyn's brows drew down. "You have cursed gems. Where did you get those?"

"It's a long story," Reg said. Although it wasn't. He'd gone with her to the dwarf mountain. He knew all about her helping to cure Calliopia. He'd assisted her in the unmaking of the blade. How hard was it to say that she had received a gift of gems from Calliopia's family after that?

But she didn't want to tell him. That might open her up for questions as to why she hadn't shared the gems with the others who had gone on the quest with her, which she was sure was probably the standard practice. But they all had money. Or most of them. And Reg didn't. It had been her idea, her quest, and she was the one who had provided the firepower to melt down the dagger. The gift was hers.

Besides, if she had shared it with them, then they would all be cursed now too. They wouldn't have wanted that.

Davyn gave Reg a doubtful look. "Well... I know how it works in theory, but I've never tried it myself. And I don't know how reliable a method it is. It isn't as though it's endorsed by the Magical Jewels Association or something."

Reg gaped. "There's a Magical Jewels Association?"

"No." Davyn chuckled. "It was a joke. I was being facetious."

"Oh." Reg shook her head. "I thought you meant there really was. After meeting Julian, I thought there might be all kinds of regulatory agencies out there that I know absolutely nothing about."

"No, there's not really much regulation of practitioners. Usually, it is left to the leader of a coven to address any problems. Or to take it to a tribunal, like we did with Corvin. Magical Investigations is the exception rather than the rule."

Reg nodded slowly. She still really didn't have much understanding of how the paranormal world worked and how they kept it from collapsing into chaos. With all the non-human races, powers, and methods of communication, it was a wonder that things were as orderly as they were.

"Why don't you show me your gems?" Davyn said, bringing her back into focus. "I'll take a look at them, and we can see whether we can purify them."

"Does it really work like that? Burning up the bad stuff?"

"No… cursing doesn't really leave any physical impurities in or on the stones. Which is one reason that I'm a little reluctant to believe that fire will accomplish anything. But fire has other purposes too. It can help with focus and concentration, can magnify other powers, can help to soothe negative emotions. So maybe there is something to it. We won't know whether there is any efficacy until we try it."

"Okay. I'll be right back." Reg withdrew to her bedroom and picked up the little bag with the stones in it that she had already dealt with. It made sense to her to use the same stones for each experiment. It might be that different things would work on different stones, so she didn't want to take the chance of missing the one thing that would work on the stones she had taken to the jewelers on the first day.

She returned to Davyn and put the small bag on the kitchen table, from which she had previously cleared all the wallets and piles of gems and debris. Davyn looked at it.

"Get them out so we can see what we are dealing with."

Reg loosened the strings on the bag and spilled the gems out into her hand. She showed them to Davyn. He leaned closer for a look, but didn't use or ask for a jeweler's loupe. She wondered if he had any more experience with gems than Corvin did. Maybe all that either had ever done was to polish up their family heirlooms.

"Very nice," Davyn proclaimed.

"Can you tell that they're cursed?"

He passed his hand a couple of inches above Reg's, as if feeling for heat. He nodded. "I'm no expert, but I can feel something."

"Okay. So how do I do this? Do I need to heat them to a certain temperature? For a certain length of time? Am I supposed to hold them or put them into an oven safe dish?"

"Let's go with you just holding them. You can withstand more heat than any cookware you have, I would think."

Davyn rubbed his hands together, then started to move them around as if manipulating an invisible ball. The fire started to grow between his hands, a friendly flicker of flames that immediately called to Reg's own fire.

Without Reg even making an effort, a flame sprang up in her hand. She looked down at the fire dancing in the palm of her hand, the gems scattered on her palm beneath it.

"Let's grow the fire a little, but mostly, I want you to make it hotter."

Reg focused her attention on the fire. She grew it into a fireball like Davyn's and watched it rotating just above her hand. She poured more heat into it.

The fireball grew significantly bigger, and Davyn was immediately assisting her, trying to bring it down in size again, to keep it small and compact, while simultaneously allowing her to bring up the temperature.

"That's right," he murmured. "Let's go white hot, but then I want you to hold steady."

It was a struggle. Not to get it hot enough, but to keep the fire small and then to hold at the level Davyn wanted her to. The fire within her, always eager to be called upon, did not want to be regulated. It wanted to burn wild and rampant, consuming everything in its path. What did that say about Reg's nature?

She tried to keep the fire calm and maintain the temperature. She had thought that the way Corvin had referred to the stones as having thoughts and feelings had been funny, but at the same time, she saw her fire as having its own personality, its own thoughts and preferences. And wasn't it just an extension of herself?

"Hold there," Davyn encouraged.

Reg tried to hold on, not letting it get hotter or letting it drop off. She needed to keep a tight focus.

"Now," Davyn's voice was slow and soothing, like he was talking to a wild animal or trying to hypnotize Reg. "Think about the gems in your hand. They are getting warmer. You were able to put power into Calliopia's medallion. Remember how that felt. Start to transfer the heat from the fire to the jewels."

Reg nodded. She looked through the fireball at the gems. The sapphire that had burned Corvin. The ruby that had come back to her. The emerald she had tried to give to Francesca and been refused. A few other gems that she had placed in the bag, thinking that she would be able to cash them all in to get the money she needed to pay her expenses. Had she been naive to think that a person could just own gems and cash them in whenever they wanted to? Maybe owning a gem was more like owning a cat, with extra responsibilities and effort required to maintain them.

She pushed fire into the stones.

Or maybe like welcoming a new child into your home. Reg herself had been introduced to one foster home after another, traumatized by her violent past, unsure what to think of the new parents and family she would have to get along with and be expected to obey.

What kind of harm had the gems experienced in the past? Did they remember all their owners? Everything that had been done to acquire them?

The stones grew exponentially hotter in her hand. She remembered Corvin not even being able to touch the sapphire without burning himself. Maybe the stone had been trying to tell her something. That she could cleanse it not by giving it away, but with her fire.

But even though she could feel the heat, it didn't bother her, didn't hurt her. She was in control of it.

"Now hold again," Davyn suggested.

Reg felt a twinge of doubt. While he had been calm and focused guiding her through the exercise, she couldn't help but notice the uncertainty in his voice. He had been honest with her. He knew how the cleansing should work in theory, but he'd never done it himself. He was winging it.

"They need more," she countered.

"*You* want more," Davyn countered with an amused chuckle. "Stay focused."

Reg obeyed. Despite not being bothered by the heat, she was starting to sweat. Producing a hot fire and holding it steady for so long required exertion. It wasn't like running or jumping rope but, in its own way, it was a physical exercise.

She focused on each of the gems in turn, checking on how they held the heat and if they were changing. Perhaps it wouldn't be possible to tell if there were any change until they were finished with the experiment. She couldn't detect any difference yet.

"Okay." Davyn was looking at his watch. "That should be long enough. Dial it back slowly, and then extinguish your fire."

Reg's instinct was to do the opposite. To let it burn with a stronger furor and intensity. To let it get just a little bit out of control. Davyn was there to pull her back, after all, so she could be a *little* reckless.

"No," Davyn told her.

Reg breathed out in a carefully controlled breath. She lowered the temperature of the fire, then started to reduce it in size until it was just a glimmer above her palm. She extinguished it, feeling a sharp pang of loss as she did so.

CHAPTER TWENTY-FOUR

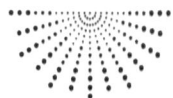

ood," Davyn proclaimed. "How is the temperature of the gems? Are they still hot?"

Reg rolled them in her palm. "No. They're cooling."

They didn't look any different. But they wouldn't, would they? Reg tried to reach out with her other senses, but found them too difficult to reach.

Davyn went to the sink and started running cold water. He opened and closed a few cupboards until he found a mug. He filled it and brought it to her.

"Rehydrate."

Reg nodded and obeyed, taking the mug with her other hand. Davyn watched her carefully.

"Your control is getting better."

"About time." Reg was impatient with herself. She thought it should be easier to control her powers. If she had special gifts, then she should be adept at controlling them. If she weren't, then it was her own fault.

Davyn shook his head, smiling. "How can you be good at something that you have not practiced? You wouldn't expect to be good at basketball or cooking without some practice. Or playing the piano."

"You're lucky you haven't tasted my cooking."

"It's just an example. Even if you have a talent for something, you cannot expect to be good at it, or even proficient, if you've never had the opportunity to exercise and grow your skills."

"I guess. It just feels like it takes me way too long to learn."

"Keep in mind that children in our community are carefully watched for their talents and once those gifts are identified, are trained up from the time they are very young. Your background is completely different. Your gifts were not identified and encouraged. From what you have said before, they were actively discouraged and beaten down. It takes time to overcome that kind of conditioning. To go from not being allowed to access your powers at all to trying to take control of them and nurture them. It takes a lot of time and effort."

"And in the meantime, I'm like a toddler trying to get his legs. It's so frustrating."

"Like a toddler who is already man-sized," Davyn said, "One of the reasons they are so hard to control is because they are so strong."

Reg looked down at the gems on her hand after chugging a couple more swallows of water. "They don't look any different."

"The difference would not be in their appearance." Davyn leaned closer to peer at them himself. After a moment, he hovered his hand over Reg's, frowning.

"Is it gone?" Reg asked. "Did it work?"

Davyn shook his head slowly. Reg's heart sank. She had guessed as much, but had hoped that he would tell her that it had worked. She was so tired of trying to overcome the curse on the gems. Wouldn't anything work?

"If anything," Davyn said, "I would say they are stronger. They have absorbed some of your energy. But the darkness is still in them. And that's not good."

"Because that means the curse is stronger," Reg deduced.

"Yes. Do you mind? May I take them for a moment?"

Reg held them out to him. "Have at it."

She didn't warn him about the sapphire. Even if it got hot, it couldn't do much harm trying to burn a firecaster. Davyn took the gems from her and handled them carefully. It wasn't long before he was putting them back in her hand.

"You'd better hang on to them."

Reg looked at him, trying to read his expression or his aura. "Why? What's wrong?"

"I don't think... they like me."

Reg raised her brows. "They don't like you?" She gave a short laugh. "Everyone keeps making out like they have thoughts and feelings. But they're stones. They're just... inanimate objects. They don't have feelings."

But she couldn't deny that they were warm in her hand and that she felt a great sense of relief when Davyn handed them back to her. Despite her inability to get rid of them, she found that she had some anxiety over their finding their way into someone else's possession.

But of course she felt that way. They were her treasure. Her way of staying independent and living the kind of life she wanted to, sheltered and protected, off the streets. With friends who cared about her. People she didn't have to leave as soon as she had pulled off a money-making scam.

"It's a bad habit," Davyn admitted. "Ascribing emotions to the gems instead of admitting that they are our own feelings. When I hold these gems, I feel... anger and injustice. They provoke a feeling of dissatisfaction and the desire to... get rid of them and go somewhere safe."

Reg closed her cupped hand around the gems and thought about it. They did not make her feel that way. She couldn't feel any evil or darkness or even anger when she held them. She felt... a sense of longing. An even stronger desire to be kept sheltered and safe.

"Well... thank you, I guess. I mean, yes—thank you! Now we know that fire won't work. I'm disappointed, but I wouldn't have known what to do without you. Now I guess... I try something else."

"Good luck. I hope you can figure it out. I imagine you would like to be able to use them. Or to build a nest-egg for the future. I'm sorry it didn't work out."

"Yeah, it would be nice," Reg agreed with a sigh.

But maybe it wasn't to be. Maybe the only thing she would be able to do was to get rid of them, so that she wouldn't be plagued by any further bad luck. She would be sorry to see all that wealth go out of her life, but it wasn't as though she was losing anything. They had not been of any value to her before, and they would not be after she got rid of them. Her possession of them was fleeting and temporary.

* * *

After Davyn had left, Reg sat down with Starlight to chill out and regain her strength. A bit of ice cream with chocolate syrup would help her to recover more quickly, she was sure. And Starlight liked to lick out the bowl afterward when she had ice cream. Though she'd have to make sure there wasn't any chocolate sauce remaining.

She had the TV on, thinking that she would be able to forget the pressure to supplement her bank account soon. At least the cable was paid for by Sarah, so Reg didn't have to feel like she was paying for unnecessary luxuries. But she found the TV annoying, and shut her eyes to concentrate, thinking over the session with Davyn and her conversation with Ruan. Ruan was the only one of her contacts who seemed to actually know anything about cursed gems and was willing to talk about them. Maybe in pixie society, it wasn't considered inappropriate to talk about cursed gemstones.

Ruan's next suggestion had been to throw the gems into the sea. While Reg had dismissed this on principle, it was beginning to look like her only remaining option. And it wasn't something that she would be able to do by herself.

Getting close to the ocean was one of the triggers that activated her siren instincts. The last thing that she needed while she was trying to get people to forget about her siren parentage was to go on some kind of murderous rampage at the harbor.

CHAPTER TWENTY-FIVE

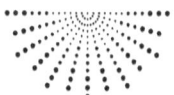

*R*eg knew she was compounding one bad idea with another. She couldn't go to the ocean alone and hope to be able to avoid triggering any siren-like thoughts or actions. There were few people who would be able to help her if that happened. And she didn't want to involve anyone who didn't already know about the gems or to have a whole group of people with her to watch the fun. So she asked Corvin if he would go with her.

"Of course," Corvin purred into the phone, always happy for any excuse for the two of them to be together. "A little jaunt out on the water is just what you need."

Reg tried to figure out whether he was being sarcastic or genuinely thought it was a good idea. "I'm worried about what might happen," she told him. "And you're going to be on the boat alone with me, which isn't a really safe place for you to be. If the water makes me... do things..." She trailed off and grimaced. "We already know that you are... susceptible to sirens."

"But I will be prepared. And you're not a *mature* siren and your blood is more diluted than your mother's. I was able to resist you before."

"Yes," Reg nodded to herself. "That's why I thought... maybe you would be okay. But I don't want to just invite you and have you come out there, thinking that it's going to be a piece of cake. We don't know what could happen. You're putting yourself at risk."

"I realize that. Just like you realize that *you* will also be at risk."

"Yeah. But the same thing applies. I can resist you, if I'm prepared."

"What an interesting dance this will be," Corvin chuckled.

"Are we both crazy? This is the stupidest thing we could be doing."

"You only live once."

Reg wasn't sure that was strictly true after the things she had seen in the paranormal world. But she wasn't going to argue it.

"We should probably sleep on it," Reg suggested. "You're not supposed to make big decisions like this on an impulse."

"It's not such a big decision to go for a sail. And I can tell you that my answer wouldn't be any different tomorrow, or the next day, or the day after that." She felt like his lips were right against her ear as he whispered into the phone. "The answer will always be yes, Regina."

Reg couldn't suppress the shiver that ran down her spine or the goosebumps that popped up all along her arms. And she was going to trust him?

No, she wasn't. Neither one of them would trust the other, no matter how attracted they were.

* * *

It was getting dark when Reg arrived at the harbor. Maybe not the best time to be going out on a boat, but they didn't want other people to observe what they were doing. Especially not if things got out of hand.

It was a clear night, not a cloud in the sky overhead, although there were some gathered at the horizon, catching the last few pink rays of the setting sun. Reg just stood and drank in the scene before her for a few minutes. She had been keeping away from the water, worried about how she would react to it, but being close enough to see the water stretching out in front of her and to breathe in the salty tang of the water made her wonder what she had been so afraid of. It was beautiful. She felt as though she were coming home.

She should spend every day at the waterfront. Even just a few minutes to walk by the water and breathe in the air, listening to the mewling of the waterbirds flying overhead and the waves lapping against the land. She almost wanted to sleep in the water, it was all so peaceful and idyllic.

Maybe there was no reason for her to worry about the gems after all. What did she need money for? She could sleep on the beach all year long. She would have everything she needed there. Her food within hunting distance. Who needed gemstones?

"Regina."

Corvin had nearly snuck up on her. Reg startled and turned to look at him. He was, as usual, perfectly attired. Not for a dinner out this time, no tux and tails, but casual clothes that would allow him to pilot the boat and have freedom of movement. The black t-shirt he wore clung to his chest in a way that made her want to peel it right off and lay her cheek against him.

Reg resisted the image, trying to wall it off in her mind. She was there for a job. They both had to be on top of their game, aware of every movement and shift in mood of the other. It was not a pleasure-cruise, and letting it become one would lead to her downfall. She would lose her psychic powers to him just as she had once before, and she would be left a hollow shell, the silence echoing in her head, lonelier than she had ever been in her life. Without the voices of the spirits who all vied for her attention, the world was a vast, empty place.

"Did you rent a boat?" Reg asked crisply, taking one step away from Corvin. If she didn't step farther away, she was going to step closer, and she couldn't let that happen. She would stay in complete control of herself, just like she had when she had been firing the gems.

"Of course. I told you that would not be a problem."

"Good. Lead the way."

His gaze wandered over her face, in no hurry to get to the boat. "Maybe a drink first?"

"No. No drinks. I need to stay alert, and so do you."

"Milkshakes?"

"No," Reg said firmly. "This is not a date. This is a job. Trying to get rid of the gems."

He started strolling toward the boats. "I don't see why you're in such a hurry to get rid of them all of a sudden. I haven't had a chance to finish my search of the literature. And you said that the curse hasn't affected you, so it isn't as if you are trying to rid yourself of bad luck."

"Well... maybe I spoke too soon. Without thinking. Because... there has been some stuff lately. I don't know whether it is all because of the gems, or if it's just... the way things would have gone anyway. And if I can't rid the stones of the curse, then I need to rid myself of the cursed stones."

Corvin shrugged with one shoulder as he watched to make sure she was following him. He would obviously rather have her walking with him arm-in-arm, but Reg wasn't about to risk it just for appearances. People who saw them walking together, a few feet apart, without any touching, could think that they were fighting with each other. Or that they were family rather than dates. Or that they were just not *that kind* of friends.

A few of the boats were strung with lights that the owners were turning on as the sun dipped below the horizon. They looked magical, twinkling in the night, the gentle sounds of waves lapping and boats bumping against the dock playing what sounded like a lullaby to Reg.

Corvin pointed to one. "Right there. The White Lady."

"Great."

Reg walked out onto the deck. She felt grounded by the boat lifting and falling with her breathing. Why didn't she live on a boat? Plenty of other people in Florida did. What had made her rent Sarah's cottage instead of a boat?

She watched Corvin untie the boat. His movements were quick and sure. Familiar with ropes and all things nautical. He jumped aboard and held up the boat keys for her to see. "Let's get this lady on her way."

Reg moved to the front of the boat and stood watching while Corvin pulled it away from the dock and out into the open water. The harbor was protected by a strip of land that ran most of the way around it and, once they got past that, Corvin opened up the throttle and took them away from the lights and out into the deep, dark water.

It was so beautiful. The stars were coming out overhead. The waves were low, slapping against the boat. The wind was a little chilly and made Reg pull her wrap around her a little more tightly. A fine mist of saltwater blew in her face. Reg licked her lips, tasting the salt and the sea.

CHAPTER TWENTY-SIX

*A*ll of Reg's senses sharpened. She could see and hear things she hadn't been able to moments before. Things behind them on the shore. Things under the water. Corvin at the wheel humming to himself, his cologne or deodorant almost intoxicating. Even though Reg had been sure to eat before they headed out, she was suddenly starving.

Corvin shifted his gaze from his navigation to her face and smiled. "How far do you want to go?" he shouted over the noise of the engine.

He didn't need to shout; she could have heard him even if he had whispered. Reg surveyed the water ahead of them. She stretched out her senses and felt under the water. She could visualize the bottom of the ocean in her mind, like a radar map. She pointed to a spot ahead of them and to the right.

Corvin raised his brows, but he didn't argue with her or demand to know why she wanted that spot in particular. He adjusted his course appropriately and slowed so that Reg could tell him where to stop.

Reg watched the water, breathing in the damp spray and growing increasingly restless.

Corvin throttled down still more, and Reg kept her eyes on the spot she wanted. When they reached it, she raised her hand and Corvin stopped. He looked out over the water.

"Do you want to drop anchor?"

"No, just let it drift."

He nodded and walked out to her. "Enjoying our little trip?"

Reg nodded. "It's beautiful. I could stay out here forever."

"We could come more often."

It was a tempting offer. But Reg needed to remember her purpose. They were not there just to take in the night air and the smell of the sea.

"Ruan didn't say there was any kind of ceremony or ritual," she said, taking out the little bag of gems.

Corvin looked down at it. "It's really too bad... I think we could spend longer looking for an answer."

Reg shook her head. "I want to get it sorted out. I can't wait forever."

"I didn't say forever. But a little longer."

She shrugged and didn't argue the point. Corvin held out his hand, not to take the bag from her, just getting close to it. Feeling the power emanating from the stones. It was strange that Reg had not noticed before how easy it was to feel the power of magical artifacts. When she had met Corvin, she had thought it such a strange talent. She hadn't been able to feel then what was so obvious to her now.

"They're stronger," Corvin said with surprise. "Or are there more of them here than you originally showed me?"

If he examined them for long, he would know the answer to that question. "They are stronger," Reg admitted. "Apparently the fire... increased their power."

Corvin nodded. "That makes some sense. But not the results you were expecting."

"No. So now..." She looked down at the little jewelry bag and addressed them directly. "It's time to say goodbye."

Corvin's mouth quirked up at the corner, amused. "Aren't you the one who said that gems are inanimate objects without thoughts or feelings?"

"Well... maybe someone who looks and sounds like me said that."

He chuckled. "Something like that."

Reg sighed. She loosened the strings of the little bag one more time and spilled the stones out into her palm. "If they're in the ocean, no one will bother them again. They'll be safe from plunder. They can rest."

Corvin nodded. Reg held her hand out over the rail and sprinkled the gems into the water. They fell with little plops into the ocean and sank rapidly to the bottom.

Reg felt the pull of the long, deep trench beneath them. She could dive to the bottom. It would be quiet and dark. She would float there like a baby in its mother's womb. And if she had a mate, she would have everything she needed.

She grasped the front of Corvin's shirt. He jerked back abruptly, eyes widening.

"Come on, Corvin," Reg said in a low, coaxing voice. "Come with me."

"We're not staying out here."

"You will if I ask you." She reached for him again and he retreated several steps. Reg looked him in the eye, pinning him down. She knew he was vulnerable. Even though he was on guard now, she was sure she could overcome any resistance. "Don't you want to go for a swim?"

"And stay under water for the rest of my life?" Corvin asked. "No, I don't think so."

"Don't be so stubborn." She stepped toward him, drawing his scent down into her lungs in a long, slow breath. "You have spent so long pursuing; wouldn't you like to change the game for once?"

Another step. The smell of his body was almost overpowering. The blood pumping through his veins in an endless hot, salty tide. His breath. His sweat. And the smell of flowers. Roses.

Reg's brain clouded. She shook her head, trying to clear the fog. "Stop that."

"You don't want to take me," Corvin warned. "That's not what we came for. You came to get rid of the gems. Remember?"

"I could have thrown them into the harbor. We didn't need to come all the way out here for that."

"Then why did we come all the way out here?"

She took another heavy step toward him and he didn't retreat. Reg drew up to him, nearly touching. Their faces were inches apart.

"Regina." His voice was hoarse. Not pushing her away. She could have what she wanted. Reg took another deep breath and wobbled, losing her balance. She felt as if she'd had too much to drink, when she knew she hadn't touched a drop.

Corvin took her hand. Electricity buzzed between them, jolting Reg back to some sense of reality. Corvin pulled her against him, bending his neck to kiss her. Reg struggled, trying to pull away from him and to push away her desire for his blood at the same time. What had made her think that her siren desires and his hunger for her powers would cancel each other out?

"No." She pushed against his chest; against those perfect pecs she had been admiring under his t-shirt. She could feel the blood flowing through his veins, right under her fingertips. "You'd better stop," she warned.

A war raged within Reg. The desire to take him under the water and satisfy her hunger, the intoxicating smell of the pheromones he exuded, the charms he worked on her, and the little voice in the back of her brain that reminded her she was in danger, both of losing her humanity and of losing her powers. She reached for her powers, reflecting the waves of heat coming from Corvin back at him to fend him off. Corvin stepped back, withdrawing until Reg's hands fell free from his chest and she stood there, almost immobilized, taking in deep breaths and trying to bring her body back under her control.

Galvanized by the space between them, Corvin withdrew, returning to the ship's wheel. The engine roared to life. Reg's nostrils flared at the choking smell of the exhaust from the engine. Why did humans pollute the environment with their stinking, belching machines? They fouled the water and the air. What other creatures were so enamored with their own technology, their own ability to destroy everything around them?

She grasped the rail, feeling suddenly nauseated. The loss of the gems, the warring attractions, and Corvin speeding away from the place she had selected for his watery grave all converged at once, over-whelming her.

They weren't far from the shore. They would return the boat to its place in the harbor within an hour of having taken it out. So little time had passed, and yet it had been a lifetime. Reg clung to the railing, looking at the water and at the stars in the sky, fixing her eyes on the horizon in an effort to overcome the vertigo. What kind of siren was she, getting seasick?

She saw the lights of the harbor, and then they were there. Corvin carefully returned the boat to its place along the dock. He shut off the engine, threw a rope onto the dock, and jumped out to secure it. He returned to the boat a couple of minutes later and approached Reg warily.

"Are you okay?"

Reg cleared her throat. "Sure. Of course." She still held tightly to the railing, the rise and fall of the boat no longer exhilarating, but barely tolerable.

"You ready to go ashore?"

"I might need a hand."

He looked as though he doubted this was a good idea, and of course he was right. At the best of times, allowing him to touch her was a bad idea. And when she was surrounded by sea water and the smell of the ocean so pungent in the air, it was not a good idea for him to allow her to touch him.

What a crazy, tangled-up world they lived in.

"Just help me off the boat," Reg instructed. Her legs wobbly, she grasped his arm, first with one hand and then both together. Reg was acutely aware of the buzz of electricity, the heat of his body, and the thrum of the blood in his veins. She closed her eyes most of the way as he walked her slowly toward the dock. He stepped onto solid ground first, then before she knew what he was going to do, picked her up and set her onto the dock next to him. Reg swayed.

"Take a minute to get your land legs," Corvin advised.

"Whew... I don't know what happened... everything just suddenly went wonky," Reg explained.

"Yeah. It's okay. There were a lot of things going on at once there."

Reg leaned against him, appreciating his size and strength and the fact that his body seemed to know which way was up.

"You're getting better," she told him with a weak smile. "You didn't let me seduce you."

Corvin's brows went up. "You don't know how much I wanted to."

Reg smiled in appreciation. But she knew which of them had been stronger. He was the one who had been able to walk away and start the engine of the boat. If it had been left to Reg, they would probably both be at the bottom of the underwater trench she had chosen. And that would not be good.

"How about something to eat?" Corvin suggested.

CHAPTER TWENTY-SEVEN

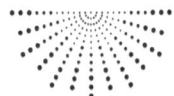

*R*eg was famished. Which was funny, because she had intentionally eaten before going on the cruise so that she wouldn't be starving when her siren instincts kicked in. And then the nausea had hit. She wouldn't have predicted that having dinner with Corvin would be such an attractive prospect. She hadn't thrown up during her bout of seasickness, so she should still have been full.

"Yeah," she told him immediately. "Let's find somewhere to eat. Is there somewhere close?"

Corvin looked surprised, but he grinned down at her, pleased.

"There is a place just down the road," he offered. "Florida is full of seafood joints, but nothing compares to Seaman Jacks. No seafood more than two hours old. He's got fishermen in the water the whole time the kitchen is open, bringing in fresh catches throughout each shift. It's basically direct from the ocean to your table."

At other times, Reg might have been disturbed by this image, thinking of the live fish in the ocean, minding their own business until they were suddenly caught on a line or in a net. She didn't like to think of the live animals that ended up on her plate and had contemplated the idea of becoming vegetarian like the fairies or gnomes.

But she was starving. And the thirst for blood still lingered. She didn't want salad. She didn't want limp, stringy leaves on her plate. She needed flesh. And next to the smell of Corvin's blood, fish fresh from the ocean seemed the best thing.

"Yes," she nodded vigorously. "Let's go there."

Corvin chuckled. "No need to twist your arm today, huh? Well, let's get something into that bottomless pit."

It wasn't ladylike to have such a big appetite, but Reg didn't care at that point. She just needed to fill the void. Corvin's description was apt.

They walked together to the parking lot.

"Let's take my car," Corvin suggested. "When we're done, I can bring you back here for your car, assuming you're feeling up to driving."

"No." Reg's protest wasn't very forceful. "I should take mine now."

"You're not feeling well. Once you've had something to eat and been able to sit for a while, you'll feel much better. Then you can drive. Right now... I don't think I would trust you not to drive right off the road, maybe straight into the ocean. And neither of us wants that."

"Well..." Reg let Corvin steer her to the sleek black car that he reserved for dates and special occasions. He walked her to the passenger side and opened the door for her.

"Your carriage."

Reg smiled. She slid into her seat and Corvin carefully closed the door.

* * *

"What should I order?" Reg asked as she looked over the menu. "Everything sounds great, and if it's all as fresh and good as you say..."

"Do you trust me to order for you?"

Reg had previously been furious when Corvin had done so without asking. What he might consider old world manners were, to her, just misogynistic male presumption, and she wasn't having any of it.

"Just this once."

Corvin smiled and closed his menu, setting it aside. Reg closed hers and set it on top of his. The waitress saw that they were ready to order and approached, order pad in hand.

"What can I get you?"

"The next thing that comes out of the water."

The waitress smiled. "Catch of the day," she agreed. This was apparently not an uncommon request at Seaman Jacks. "For two?"

Corvin nodded.

"We should have someone in shortly, so I don't think you'll have long to wait."

She took the order to the kitchen. Corvin picked up his tumbler and had a drink. "You're in for a real treat."

* * *

Reg tried not to give away how hungry she was waiting for their meals. She should have insisted on an appetizer, at least. Something to hold her over until their catch of the day got there. She could still smell Corvin, across the table from her, even though they were away from the water now. Her stomach felt like it was going to consume itself.

What if the fisherman didn't get in when he was expected? What if he hadn't caught anything or his boat had broken down? She couldn't bear to be waiting there for hours.

"Reg?"

Reg tried to turn her attention back to Corvin, who was looking at her with his head tilted slightly to the side.

"Sorry. What?"

"How do you feel? Now that you got rid of the cursed gems. Do you feel any better? Luckier?"

Reg gave a little laugh. "I doubt it works that quickly." She shrugged as he kept looking at her, waiting for a straight answer. "No. I don't feel any different now."

He nodded.

"Do you think I should?" Reg asked. "I never felt like they were bad for me. I didn't feel... cursed or unlucky."

"Well, that's fortunate. Some of the stories that I have heard about people who have received cursed gems... illness and death of family members, terrible accidents, financial ruin. You've had some weird things happen, but it's hard to say whether any of it has been something to do with the stones."

"I don't think so. Don't you think that most of that stuff is just coincidence? People thinking they are cursed, so they start adding up all the stuff that's been going wrong? I mean… I've had lots of bad stuff happen. It didn't just start when I got the gems. Probably the worst things were way before that, when I was in foster care. Or before that, when I was with Norma Jean."

"So you expect bad things to happen."

"Sure, I guess. I don't expect my life to go smoothly, that's for sure. Those stories… they're probably just the worst ones. Things that were really nasty. There are probably lots of other people who held cursed stones who never had any bad luck." Reg thought about it. "Maybe I was too quick to get rid of them. Maybe they wouldn't ever have caused me any trouble. It was people like you who kept saying that I'd better look out. I'd better be careful, get rid of them as quickly as I could before they caused any real damage."

Corvin looked slightly guilty at this. "They can be very dangerous," he said. "Even if yours weren't."

"Hmmph. Maybe I should have waited."

He shrugged and played with the dessert menu on the table. Reg looked away from him, letting her eyes wander over the interior decorating of Seaman Jack's. As with many of the seafood restaurants on the waterfront, it had been decorated with a nautical theme. Lots of nets and ropes and mounted fish. Bit of weathered boards and starfish and shells.

Reg stared at a large net draped over one wall, imagining what it would be like to be in the water when one of those came down. Did mermaids or other sentient creatures ever get caught in the nets? What would the fisherman do if he hauled one of those up?

"What are you thinking?" Corvin asked.

"Just…" Reg broke off when she saw the waitress coming toward her. Making eye contact this time, two plates and a large platter stacked on her hands. She gave them each a plate and put the fish platter down in the middle of the table with a flourish.

It wasn't a sort of fish that Reg recognized, but she wasn't a great connoisseur where fish were concerned. The waitress gave a little introduction about the fish and how it had been prepared. Reg was just eager to get something into her stomach.

The fish had been cleaned and cooked, but the head was still on it, and it was otherwise intact. Reg would have preferred that it not be recognizable. But who was she to complain? She was going to eat it either way.

"Enjoy," the waitress finished, giving Reg a little bow and beaming like a proud parent.

When she was gone, Corvin gave Reg a nod. "Help yourself. First choice is yours."

Reg wasn't sure if there was a particular protocol that he expected her to follow, demurring or asking him to carve it for her or taking a less choice bit so that he could still have the best of it. And she didn't care what he thought. She needed to fill the hole in her gullet. She carved out a portion from the middle of the fish's body and transferred it to her plate.

"Smells great," she commented. She didn't wait for him to dish up before digging into her meal. She forced herself to slow down after the first couple of bites. To enjoy the flavor and texture of the food, the freshness that Corvin had bragged about, rather than just inhaling the whole thing.

"Good?" Corvin asked around a mouthful of food.

Reg nodded, not bothering to swallow before answering. "Great!"

He nodded. They ate in silence for a few minutes. Reg was eyeing the rest of the fish that remained on the platter. There was still plenty more, at least a full helping for each of them. After finishing what was on her plate, she helped herself to more. There was a clink on the plate like a bead falling, and Reg looked to see what had hit the ceramic. It didn't sound like a fish bone or the clink of her fork. As she touched the serving fork to the fish's head to look under and around it for the foreign object, she heard the noise again. Reg turned the platter to get a better view of it. At the very end of the platter, near the fish's mouth, were a couple of bits of rock or glass.

Reg frowned and pushed them around for a better look. Corvin stopped eating and squinted, studying them.

"What did they put in this?" Reg asked. "Is this normal? Some regional dish?"

"No." Corvin poked at them with his fork, and then at the fish's mouth, causing more to fall onto the dish. He and Reg both realized at the same time what they were.

The gems she had thrown into the ocean just an hour before.

CHAPTER TWENTY-EIGHT

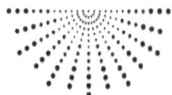

*T*hat's not possible," Reg blurted.

"No?" Corvin questioned. "I think it's just been proven possible."

"But no, it can't be. There's no way. How?"

"Apparently the fish caught your gems before it was caught by the fisherman."

"That couldn't happen. Is this all some kind of joke? Did you set this up?"

"It's got nothing to do with me, Reg. You dropped those gems into the ocean yourself. You know that was no sleight of hand. And if you want to gather those up and clean them up, I think you will find that they are the same gems that you threw away, not replacements."

"How would I be able to tell that?"

"You are the one who knows how they feel."

Even with her hand just close to the gems, Reg could already feel their auras. She knew without cleaning them off and concentrating her attention on them that they were the very same gems. Which, of course, was impossible.

There was no way to even calculate the odds that the gems she had thrown into a deep trench in the ocean would be scooped up by a fish, who was then caught by a fisherman and fed to Reg for supper. And that in all of his careful preparations, the cook would not have found the stones himself. They should have been in the fish's stomach or intestines, thrown directly into the garbage, because who would examine fish intestines for gemstones? A fish wouldn't just hold them in his mouth.

"This is crazy," Reg said, shaking her head.

"It is," Corvin admitted. "I knew that the stones were powerful, and that you are powerful, but I didn't foresee that they would be able to make their way back to you after being thrown out into the middle of the ocean."

"They couldn't," Reg agreed, even though they had. She couldn't think of any other explanation.

She gathered the gems and put them onto a napkin, then rubbed them to get the fishy residues off. After making sure that they were as clean and dry as she could get them, she dumped them into the little bag she had tucked back into her pocket. Corvin's eyes followed them.

"So, it would appear that you have been given yet another chance to handle this differently. Throwing them into the ocean is not the answer."

"Yeah."

Corvin shook his head. "You don't need to sound so gloomy about the prospect. If they haven't been causing you any bad luck, as you say, then you don't need to be in such a hurry to get rid of them. There has to be another way to cleanse them."

"No."

"What did Ruan tell you?"

"That they would have to be returned to their rightful owners."

Corvin was silent.

"How could I possibly do that?" Reg demanded. "I have no idea where they came from originally, who they should have rightfully belonged to but were stolen away from. How could I possibly figure out who they should go to now?"

"We could probably figure out some general information to start with," Corvin said. "We may not know exactly which mines they came from, but an expert might be able to look at the composition of the gems, any impurities or other clues, and tell what country or what part of the country they came from."

"How would that help me? Then I could go to that country and advertise, asking them if they were the rightful owner of a bunch of precious gems." Reg's mouth twisted itself into a pretzel, the sarcasm was so bitter.

"I'm not saying that. Identifying the country they came from would be the first step."

"But they're not all from the same place. They've been collected over the years. They all started out in different places."

Corvin sighed. "You don't know that. And there are few enough gems that even if they are from different parts of the world, we wouldn't be totally overwhelmed with the job of identifying what those places were."

Reg slumped back in her seat. Did he really think that she had only the gems she had shown him? He knew better than to trust her and take her word at face value.

Corvin studied Reg's face and body language. The hopelessness of the situation.

"Reg… that *is* all of the gems, isn't it?"

Reg shook her head. "Not even close."

CHAPTER TWENTY-NINE

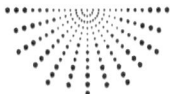

*R*eg didn't tell Corvin everything he wanted to know about her gems. He already knew too much, more than anyone else. He didn't need to know how many stones she had or exactly where they had come from. Of course, Sarah knew that, so it wasn't like Reg was the only one who knew. She didn't like other people knowing so much about her business but, as the girl at the gem exchange had told Reg, she needed to reach out to her friends for help.

And now, she needed more. She wasn't sure how she would be able to find anything out about where the gems had originated from. And as far as she knew, they could all have come from different places over hundreds of years. How was she going to trace the origin of every gem?

She started thinking about the individual gems on the way home. She had, up until then, been thinking about them only as a collection. Her hoard. Her treasure. But it was made up of individual gems, which had all come from different backgrounds. Like the children she had known in foster care, some of them might be sibling groups who had come from the same time and place, but each individual or group could have a different history. Different damage. Different curses.

Maybe she had made a mistake in considering the whole of the collection and assuming all of them were cursed and that they would all need to be treated the same way. But what if that weren't true? What if the gems and their issues were just as individual as children?

Upon arriving home, she retrieved the small wooden chest and started going through the gems. Not just running her fingers through them and laughing at the amount of wealth that they represented, but actually looking at each gem individually and classifying them.

Chances were that they were all cursed. Why would the Papillons have given them to her otherwise? They had wanted to rid themselves of the curse. Maybe it was what kept pushing Calliopia away from the family. Maybe it had caused them other grief. They didn't want the gems in their home, in their possession any longer. They saw an opportunity to dump them on Reg, and they would not take them back. They were hers for good, until she could figure out the best way to handle them.

But maybe a few had slipped through that were not cursed. Or maybe the Papillons had justified themselves in giving Reg the treasure by including non-cursed stones as well as the cursed ones. Maybe they weren't all bad. As traumatized and damaged as many of the kids Reg had known in foster care were, there were still those who had somehow overcome all their challenges, who had studied and worked hard and pulled themselves up by the bootstraps to qualify for scholarships that would open a pathway out of poverty and homelessness that was closed to so many others. Sometimes those with the worst stories still made it out and got ahead in life. Maybe some of Reg's gems were overachievers and could provide her with a little liquidity while she worked on the others.

She hadn't invited Corvin into the cottage or offered to show him what she had.

Starlight crouched on the kitchen table, watching what Reg was doing with great attention. She had been afraid at first that he would think that the gems were something to play with and would bat them off the table, but he was still and watching her curiously as she scooped and sorted the stones.

Some of them were very powerful, like the ones that she had initially picked out for her trip to the jewelers. It made sense that she had been attracted to the more powerful gems when she had selected which ones to liquidate.

But others were smaller or had less power when she reached out her psychic senses to examine them. Some of them barely stirred any response. So she kept the powerful ones separate from the weaker ones. Maybe the weaker ones would be easier to purify. Maybe if she tried firing those ones, she would have more success.

An idea tickled at the back of her mind that if Davyn had just let her do what she wanted with the gems, that she might have been able to cleanse even the most powerful ones. He had forced her to hold back, and to give up when she felt that she might have been able to achieve her goal if she'd just been given a free hand.

But she couldn't practice firecasting by herself, and she didn't know of another firecaster who could help her. It was not a common gift.

She sorted the larger piles of gems into smaller piles. She couldn't always define what it was she was dividing them by. It wasn't their appearance or the type of stone. Sapphires were mixed with quartz and garnet. Diamonds with zircon and topaz. She couldn't put into words exactly what it was she was looking for or feeling when she considered each of the gems. She didn't stop to think about it too much, not wanting to get derailed trying to figure it out. She just kept going.

Reg was getting tired. Her eyes were itchy, and she could barely see straight, let alone study the gems through a jeweler's loupe. But if she stopped in the middle, she wasn't sure if she would be able to pick up on it again. She didn't trust herself to get back on task once she lost momentum.

Starlight jumped down from the table and prowled around the house, only to return a while later and sit on the table again, looking at all the piles of glittering stones. But not once did he lay a paw on any of the piles to mix them up or to play with the precious gems.

At some point, he disappeared, and Reg supposed he had gone off to sleep for a few hours. It was light out when Reg started going through the cupboards and drawers in her kitchen looking for bags to sort the gems into. She found half a box of zip-top sandwich bags, and used them to segregate the gems, one pile per bag. She was exhausted, but had a great sense of accomplishment as she looked over all of the bags piled up on the table.

She wasn't really sure what she had accomplished. She had sorted the gems based on how they felt to her. Maybe she was drunk. Maybe she was still under the influence of the sea air and Corvin's charms. She was tired, that was for certain. Any or all of those things might have impaired her gifts or influenced her in some way. The gems might just be separated into random groups, and when she'd had some rest and a chance to think, it might all just be nonsense. Like looking back on a bad trip. Knowing that she had believed everything she saw was real at the time, and yet simultaneously had known that it was not.

The sun was already coming up when Reg collapsed onto her bed to try to get a bit of sleep while she still could. Pretty soon, Sarah would probably be coming around expecting to have a chance to visit with her. Jessup might decide she wanted to continue the conversation about the wallets and just what exactly Reg had been doing with them. Corvin might call to discuss the evening and go back over the pertinent details.

She could shut off her phone so that none of them would disturb her, but Reg did not like to be cut off from the rest of the world. She didn't like to think that she was isolated. She would rather be woken up if something happened.

CHAPTER THIRTY

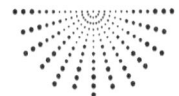

$\mathcal{S}$tarlight was curled up on the bed snoring and, pretty soon, Reg was right there with him in dreamland. So thoroughly zonked out that if Sarah had come to the cottage that morning to check Reg's calendar, deliver the mail, and have a visit, Reg had slept right through it. And she imagined that Sarah would probably have woken her up, once she saw the gems, to ask her what was going on.

She had only gotten a few hours of sleep when her body woke her up and she could not find a comfortable position to go back to sleep. Reg dragged herself to the kitchen, promising herself coffee if she could stay awake long enough to brew it. Starlight had been looking out the living room window, and plopped down to sit in front of his food dish and yowl at Reg if she didn't fill his dish in 3.5 seconds.

"Yeah, yeah. I know. It's coming."

She found some tuna, which made her feel queasy all over again, remembering how she had felt on the boat after they had turned around to go back to shore, with no idea that she would see the gems again in just a short time.

That fish had to have grabbed the gems the moment she had tossed them in, and then gone on to find the fisherman who had hooked or netted him. And how could that be, when she and Corvin hadn't seen anyone else close by? It was impossible, just like she'd told Corvin. She knew that magic didn't have to be logical, but it was still an impossibility that it had happened.

Reg just dumped the tuna into Starlight's bowl, not trying to calculate how much he needed. Let him get fat. She couldn't be bothered with fussing.

Starlight happily gobbled the fish, making loud chewing noises that did not improve her nausea.

The coffee had not yet finished brewing when Reg's phone started to vibrate. She looked at it, deciding even before she saw who was calling that she wouldn't answer it. Whoever it was would have to wait until she'd had her morning—afternoon—coffee and had a chance to wake up properly.

But she saw Ruan's picture on the screen and scrambled to pick it up.

"Ruan!"

"Reg Rawlins." The pixie licked his lips. "Reg Rawlins is a deep sleeper."

"Did you call earlier? Yeah, sorry about that. I was up all night..."

"Night is easier on piskie skin," he commented. "The moon's face is better than the sun's burning gaze."

"Yeah, well, that isn't why I stayed up, but you're right. It wasn't nearly so bright and..." she squinted at the bright sunlight in the garden outside, "...so *glaring* last night."

"Better for dealing with gems."

Reg looked around, afraid that she would find Ruan in the house with her. How had he known anything about what she'd been doing?

"What makes you think I was dealing with gems?"

"Reg Rawlins is already finished cleansing her gems?" Ruan asked. "I do not think so."

"Well, no, I guess when you put it that way. No, I haven't finished cleansing the gems yet. Although... I've been working on it."

"They are difficult?" Ruan asked.

"Yes. I've tried a bunch of different things, based on what you said, but I guess now I'm down to... trying to figure out where they came from. How am I supposed to find their rightful owners when they are hundreds of years old? I don't know how long they were in possession of the—their previous owners. They might have been stolen ages ago. And they might have gone through several different hands after that. I was looking on my phone at some of the gems that people said were cursed, and it seems like they just get stolen one time after another."

She remembered what Corvin had said about warlords stealing them not only for their monetary value, but also for their magical properties. One gem might have changed hands a dozen times in the midst of wars and raids.

"The gems do not belong to you. Or to the one who owned them before you."

"No."

"But you can find a rightful owner."

"I don't know." Reg shook her head to herself. Such a venture felt as though it might take a lifetime. Especially if she had to trace each stone's individual history. Why wasn't there just a depository that cursed gems could be taken to, and someone there could be tasked with the job of finding out where they belonged? "These aren't big gems like you would find in a crown. I mean, some of them are a good size, but not *that* big. How can I find the rightful owner for something like that?"

There was silence from Ruan for a few moments while he considered her question. His answer surprised her.

"I think Reg Rawlins has already started to trace the gems to their sources."

She looked around again, sure that he must be watching her. How else could he know that she had even been working on the problem? She looked at the baggies of gems spread out over the kitchen table. She had done her best to sort them into groups, but she couldn't be sure that the gems she had grouped all came from the same owner or even the same country. It had all been done by feel, and it was completely possible that she had been sorting them based entirely on her own preferences and impulses.

"I've been trying," she said carefully. "But how could anyone do that? Especially someone like me, without any training."

"Perhaps Reg Rawlins would like some help."

"I'd love some help. But I don't know any experts, and I'm not sure who I could trust even if I did."

"You could call Ruan."

Reg laughed. "I'm already on the phone with Ruan."

"Reg Rawlins the sorceress could *call* Ruan."

Reg realized he was talking about transporting him to her magically. She had done it once before, though she had been told afterward that it was extremely powerful magic, and she wasn't sure whether she would be able to do it again. And the first time, she had been calling Calliopia, not Ruan. She had a better psychic connection to Calliopia because of blood magic.

"I don't know. I don't remember exactly how I did it the first time."

She tried to remember the details, but they were foggy. It was incredibly frustrating to deal with the holes in her memory. She had looked in her crystal ball for Calliopia and Ruan. And then she had called Calliopia's name.

Reg walked across the room and set her crystal ball on the coffee table. She sat down on the couch and stared into it. She still held the phone to her ear, which would probably distract her and keep her from seeing anything clearly.

"If I call you... that won't screw up your plans?" Reg asked. "And what about Calliopia? You don't want to be separated from her, do you?" She had been told there was no equivalent of divorce among the fairy and pixie folk. But they also strictly forbade pairings between fairies and pixies. Reg hoped that Ruan had not abandoned the young fairy.

"We will not be separated," Ruan assured her. "You will call us both."

Which was what she had done the first time, when she had called Calliopia and Calliopia had grabbed hold of Ruan to bring him with her.

"Reg Rawlins needs help. We owe for the healing of Calliopia."

"You don't owe me anything." Reg was about to say that she had been paid for the service but, looking at the gems, thought it was probably best not to mention the fact.

But Ruan would probably figure out on his own where the gems had come from, if he hadn't already.

And she hadn't considered the danger that Ruan might try to steal the gems. As far as he was concerned, it would not be stealing, because pixies believed that anything that came from under the earth belonged to them. He would believe that he was simply taking back what was already his. And she didn't think that his gratitude for what she had done for Calliopia would necessarily have anything to do with the decision.

"Ruan, if I call you, you cannot take the gems," she warned. "If you want a few of them, I will give them to you, but you can't take all of them."

If she were going to have to give most of them back to the rightful owners, she couldn't afford to give away all the rest.

"The gems are not thine to give," Ruan countered.

"Maybe not. But they're not yours to take, either."

There was a low chuckle from Ruan. Something that didn't sound as though it should come from the round, childish face. Something deeper and much more grown up than his appearance.

"Humans think they own what they take from the earth, but they do not."

"Pixies can't have everything that comes from the earth just because that's where their burrows are. That doesn't give them ownership over everything."

"Humans do not even know how to access the power of precious stones."

"Some humans know how to access some of the powers," Reg countered. Sarah knew how to access some of the youth-giving powers of her emerald, though Ruan's sister had been able to access much more of it. And Corvin had said that the warlord wanted the powers of the stones. Reg assumed that the warlords he was talking about were human. She was pretty sure they couldn't all be pixies. And there was Corvin himself, who could absorb the powers of other humans and of magical artifacts. She assumed that he could take something from stones of power as well. "If you are going to come and take the stones from me, I'm not going to call you here."

Ruan said something in an undertone that was probably a swear word in pixie. Or maybe a disparaging comment that he made to Calliopia who was undoubtedly there with him, holding his hand, waiting for Reg's call.

CHAPTER THIRTY-ONE

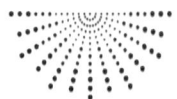

*E*ventually, Ruan's grudging voice came over the line. "If Reg Rawlins calls, Ruan will not take the stones. But *they are not thine.*"

"Okay." Reg accepted his viewpoint. She knew that they had been given to her and she had accepted them, but it was also true that the stones had probably been stolen and were therefore not the fairies' to give to her in the first place. "Finders keepers" wasn't exactly a legal precept she could rely on. "Maybe some of them have a different rightful owner. That's what you're going to help me to figure out, isn't it?"

"We will find their source," Ruan agreed. Which Reg wasn't sure was quite the same thing.

"So you promise me that you will not take the stones. You *promise.*"

She felt a certain amount of uncertainty that a pixie would keep a promise, even if she wrung one out of him. Pixies and other races had different moral strictures than humans. A pixie would probably consider a promise made to a human to be worthless and unenforceable.

"Ruan promises on his honor."

"And there aren't any loopholes? You don't have your fingers crossed?"

"Why would Ruan cross his fingers?"

"To get out of keeping the promise. You aren't going to turn around and tell me that you're not going to keep your promise because I am a human or because I let you into my house or anything stupid like that."

"No," Ruan huffed. "I said *on my honor.*"

What was this, Simon Says?

"Okay... I'm going to hang up now, so I can focus. Are you ready? I don't know if I can do this again, but I'll try."

"We await."

Reg terminated the call. She slid the phone into one of the pockets of her skirt and breathed out slowly, trying to calm any anxieties or doubts about what she was doing.

She stared into the crystal ball and saw nothing. She kept breathing slowly, forcing the air to move in and out in a focused rhythm, fixing her gaze on the ball.

There was nothing to worry about. Once she was relaxed and focused, she would be able to call Ruan. Ruan would be able to help her with the gems, and everything would work out as she had hoped.

The phone rang again, the buzzing distracting her. Reg hesitated, thinking that she should just ignore it. But what if it were Ruan again, with further instructions? She worked the phone out of her pocket and looked at it. Not Ruan again. Corvin this time. Hadn't she spent enough time with him the evening before? She could use a little breathing room.

But he knew more about her problems than anyone else, including Ruan. Reg groaned and swiped the screen to answer.

"Corvin? I'm kind of in the middle of something here. Is it important?"

"What are you doing that's so important?" he challenged, which Reg thought was more than a little insulting. She didn't have important things to do? Did he think that she just sat around all day and waited for him to call?

"None of your business." Then she bit her tongue and waited for him to state his business. She would not babble excuses and sound like she was his inferior. He didn't have any authority over her, and she didn't owe him any explanation.

"I have been doing some more research on your gems," Corvin said finally, sounding irritated.

"Oh, great. Did you find something in your historical records?"

"Well… no, not exactly. I was looking at some more modern literature."

"What does that mean?" Myths and fairy tales were his usual purview. She had no idea what "more modern" meant. 1800s?

"Scientific literature." Corvin sounded a little embarrassed that he'd had to stoop to reading such things in order to find his answers. "There are some methods for tracking down where gems came from, sometimes right down to the exact mine, if they have enough information in their databases."

"Really?" Reg was skeptical. Science promised a lot of things that it didn't quite follow through on. Whatever futuristic methods Corvin was looking at were probably years away from actually being commercialized and available to someone like Reg. "How do they do that?"

"It's called spectroscopy. They use a laser to vaporize a few atoms of the gemstone, and they can tell by the composition of the vapor—"

"You want to use a laser on my gems?"

"It wouldn't damage them or reduce their value in any way. It would just be a few atoms from the surface of the gem, and they would be able to tell by the elements present—"

"No. No way. I don't want them harmed any further."

"I told you it doesn't do any damage."

"I don't believe it. And I don't want anyone messing with them. And… I don't know how anyone would test all of them, anyway. The cost of something like that is probably astronomical."

"Well, it might be pricey if you tested every one, but maybe if you tested just a few, you would be able to tell where *all* of them came from," Corvin pointed out, in his ultra-smooth voice, acting as if she were being unreasonable. Just a hysterical woman. She hated it when he got all professorial and acted as if he knew so much more than she did. Reg knew stuff too. It just wasn't the kind of stuff he learned from books.

Reg looked at the bags of gems on the table. All from one place?

"They aren't all from one mine. Or even all from the same country. It's not like someone just mined all these stones and kept them together in one collection."

"Well, it's not likely, no. But if you can test a few, and then you could move those stones, then you would have more capital to test the next ones."

"Do you know someone who does this spectral-whatever?"

"Spectroscopy," Corvin repeated, enunciating it carefully. "Not spectral, that would be ghosts."

"Uh-huh." Reg waited. Corvin had a bad habit of not answering her questions.

"And no… I'm just in the research stage. I don't know anyone who does this, and we'd have to be careful of who we approached about your… gems of unknown origin."

The fewer people who knew that she had them, the better. Reg wasn't particularly interested in having some unknown scientist laser off chunks of her gemstones to identify their origin. She had Ruan. With Ruan's skills coupled with her own, Reg didn't think she needed anyone else's scientific crap.

"I don't think I need that."

"I thought you were convinced that tracking the origins of your gems was the way to go."

"Yeah, but I'm on that. I went a different way than spectral analysis."

Actually, what she had done probably *was* closer to spectral analysis. She just wanted to get under his skin.

"Spectroscopy," Corvin corrected, an edge to his voice.

"Whatever it is. I don't need it. And I'm in the middle of something, so if that's everything…"

"I'm trying to help you."

"Yeah. I appreciate it. But I need to go now. Maybe if this doesn't work, we'll try your thing."

Corvin saved her the trouble of having to hang up. She put the phone down on the coffee table and waited for a moment to see whether it would ring again. She didn't expect it to, since he was the one who had broken the connection. After a half a minute of silence,

Reg turned her attention back to the crystal ball and refocused her attention on it.

As she tried to breathe calm into her body and consider what she might see in the crystal, she heard Starlight's paws on the floor as he padded over to her. He jumped up beside her, and Reg put her hand on him, petting him as he snuggled close, purring.

He always knew when she could use the boost to her psychic senses.

Reg immersed herself in the warm, sharpened sensations, gazing into the crystal. Gradually, the shapes deep inside began to shift until she could see Ruan and Calliopia. They sat somewhere outside, Calliopia in the sun and Ruan in the shade, with his hoodie pulled up over his head and dark sunglasses on. Fairies needed sunlight and pixies shunned it, but Ruan was willing to do anything for his mate.

It might just have been the effect of the crystal ball, but Calliopia seemed taller than Reg remembered her. She was only an adolescent, so Reg supposed she might still be growing. They held hands, sitting as close to each other as the arrangement would allow. They were talking, but Reg couldn't hear what they were saying as she focused in on them, becoming part of the world they were in, wherever they were. She concentrated on Calliopia, rubbing the faint scar in her hand with her thumb. The bond between the two of them was still there, despite Calliopia's efforts to break it.

Reg saw Calliopia's lips form the word *now* and didn't know whether it was an instruction to her or a warning to Ruan that they were going to be called. Reg took a deep breath, fortifying herself the best she could.

Calliopia, come.

CHAPTER THIRTY-TWO

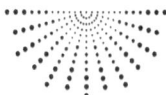

There was a jumble of images, the whole world going sideways. Reg was overwhelmed with a rushing, whirlwind feeling, tripping and somersaulting along through space until, eventually, something large fell onto the floor beside the coffee table. Good thing they hadn't actually landed on the coffee table; that would have been painful. Reg opened her eyes and looked at the pixie and fairy, upended on her floor, looking thoroughly undignified. They righted themselves as quickly as they could, Calliopia releasing Ruan's hand. She brushed at her clothes, straightening her dress and wiping away any dust from Reg's floor. Ruan jumped to his feet, laughing.

"What a ride is that!"

"I imagine so!" Reg agreed. She felt bad about pulling them to her, dumping them in the middle of her cottage like that. But it had been Ruan's idea. His request.

The couple looked around. They had been in Reg's cottage a couple of times before, so it was not unfamiliar to them. Calliopia saw Starlight sitting on the couch and hissed at him. Starlight hissed back.

"Mind your manners," Reg warned the two of them.

Cats and fairies did not get along. Nor did pixies and cats, for that matter, but Ruan had spent some time with Starlight and had grown to accept him, if not to like him. He delved into one of the pockets of his pants and pulled out a small jar. Reg did not look to see what he shook out onto his hand and offered to Starlight as a treat. Probably a spider and, if so, Reg didn't want to know about it. She was better off not seeing that. Starlight eagerly snarfed down whatever delicacy it was, and the pixie downed one himself.

"My gems," Calliopia said, looking at the stones arranged on the table, sorted into bags.

Reg's stomach clenched. While she knew that they had come from the Papillons, she had hoped that Calliopia wouldn't recognize them. She had certainly not expected the fairy to claim them.

"Not your gems," she countered, keeping her voice even. "They were given to me. By your parents. They are no longer the property of your family. If you don't like it, take it up with them."

Calliopia walked over to the table and looked through the bags, her eyes bright and interested. Reg watched her carefully. As much as she had tried to get rid of the gems, she wasn't prepared to let Calliopia just walk away with a bag or two of them. She was getting closer to finding the way to cleanse them.

Ruan joined Calliopia at the table as her hand lingered over one of the bags, fingering a couple of the gems under the plastic.

"Reg Rawlins has been hard at work," Ruan said with an approving nod.

"I have," Reg admitted. She yawned. "Stayed up late last night trying to get them sorted."

Ruan looked carefully over each bag. He pulled one of them toward him. "These ones are not cursed," he observed. "Reg Rawlins cleansed them?"

"No. Those ones were not cursed to begin with. Or if they were… it wore off. I will use those ones to get myself some money." She motioned to the cottage. "So I can pay for the rent and my food."

Ruan nodded. Reg didn't know how much he understood commerce. She didn't know if he still had a car, but he had once, so he must have had to pay for gas and repairs, if nothing else. She assumed that when he and Calliopia traveled, they must have to pay for at least some of the places they stayed, even if they found free shelter at others. So Ruan understood money and the need for it more than other pixies, living in burrows and eating grubs.

Reg put out her hand and took the baggie of clean gems from Ruan. Even if those were the only ones she managed to hold on to, she had to make sure that he couldn't take them. Calliopia's eyes lingered on them. She gave Reg what looked to her like a pout.

"Those too were cursed."

Reg looked at them through the bag before putting them into a pocket. "These ones? Are you sure? Maybe… the curse wore off over time?"

"No. Curses do not wear off," Calliopia insisted.

Maybe something that Reg had already tried, maybe dropping them all over town in wallets, had done the trick. Only Reg hadn't realized it at the time.

"Well, it doesn't matter either way. I'm just glad that these ones are curse-free so that I can use them. It is all the others that are a problem." Reg eyed the mess. "I sorted them, but I don't know whether it is right. Do you?"

Ruan nodded, while still looking the bags over carefully. Reg suspected that he was itching to take at least a bag or two.

"They hail from many places," Ruan observed.

"Yeah. I don't know how I'm supposed to find the rightful owners for all of them. It's impossible."

He shrugged. "Perhaps not all. Perhaps only some."

"Even that seems… impossible. How am I supposed to figure out who is supposed to own something that was stolen generations ago? I would have to find the original owner, and then find his heirs… over generations… it isn't possible."

"If you do not start…" Ruan gave an expressive shrug.

If Reg didn't at least give it a try, there was no way she would succeed. Not even with one stone.

"So what do I do?"

"Go there."

"Go where?"

"To their source," Ruan said, rolling his eyes as if the answer should have been obvious.

"The countries they came from? The mines?"

He nodded.

Reg sighed, shaking her head. "How can I do that? I don't even know which countries they each came from. And to travel there... I have to cash in the other gems to get enough money, find out what the travel requirements are, visas and identification and all that. I don't even know whether they'll even let me on a plane." What if they identified her as someone with outstanding warrants? What if they fingerprinted her or used facial recognition and decided to hold her for things she had done in the past? "Can you even get on a plane with gems like this? They'll want to know where I got them. And I can't explain it."

Ruan shook one of the bags of gems. He picked at the plastic. "How does it work?"

"Traveling with gems? I have no idea!"

"No," he scowled. "Opening the bag."

Reg laughed. She took it from him and showed him how to separate the two sides of the zipper to open the bag he had picked up. Ruan held the bag up to his face, sticking his nose into the mouth of the bag and inhaling deeply. Reg scratched the back of her neck. Exactly what did gems smell like? She couldn't believe that they had a smell at all. There hadn't been any particular odor when all the gems had been stored together in one chest. There was no mustiness or other smell that Reg associated with old things. Gems didn't rot or disintegrate. That was one of the things that made them retain their value. As stones, they would stay in the same form for centuries without any degradation.

"You," Ruan told Reg, holding the bag up to her.

Reg took it uncertainly. "What? Am I supposed to smell them too?"

He nodded.

Reg inhaled, pulling the smell in and holding her breath, trying to identify a particular nuance.

"And now," Ruan explained, "Reg Rawlins takes us there."

CHAPTER THIRTY-THREE

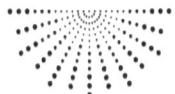

*R*eg snorted. "I what? I take you where?"

Ruan pressed the bag upward again, toward her nose. "Smell, smell! Take us there! To their source!"

"I can't take anyone anywhere!" Reg protested.

Ruan pushed the bag back up toward her nose again, insistent.

"Reg Rawlins can call Ruan and Calliopia here," he pointed out. "She can take us elsewhere!"

"No…"

Ruan went to Calliopia and took her hand. "We all together. Join together."

Ruan resealed the bag of gems, put it into Reg's pocket and took her hand in his. Reg took Calliopia's in the other. Ruan's hand was moist and bony. Too hard for the hand of a little boy, which was what he looked like but was not. Calliopia's hand was smooth and soft, and her strength was different. Not gristly like Ruan's, but Reg could still tell that she was much stronger than a human.

Reg looked at Ruan, not sure what to do. She had never transported herself along with someone else.

"How do I do this?"

"Close thine eyes," Ruan instructed. His tone was not sharp, but patient, like a parent walking his child through tying her shoes or riding a bike for the first time.

Reg closed her eyes, and breathed in and out, trying to settle herself and feel comfortable holding on to Calliopia's and Ruan's hands.

"See the gems in thy mind."

Reg pictured them, trying to make the image as clear as possible in her mind.

"Smell them."

Reg did her best to bring the smell into her mind. Green and fresh and warm, like spring air.

"See the source from whence they came."

That was more challenging. Reg focused on the smell, felt the weight of the gems in her pocket, and pictured them in her mind. But she had to picture where the gems came from, not the gems themselves. She didn't even know what a diamond mine looked like, other than a vague Disney-esque picture of dwarfs plucking gems from the inside of a dark tunnel. She inhaled again, trying to cement the smell of the place in her mind. Green. Wild. The air thick and hot around her.

"Yes, you see?" Ruan chuckled. "Much smoother when Reg Rawlins is with us."

Reg was reluctant to open her eyes. Ruan let go of her hand, and then Calliopia did the same. There was something buzzing in the air. A bug. Reg swiped at it.

"We are here, Reg Rawlins," Ruan called softly. "Open thine eyes."

Reg didn't want to, but eventually, she did. The cottage was gone. Everything familiar was gone. She was in the middle of a hot green jungle. And it was not somewhere she wanted to be.

"What are we doing here? This doesn't make sense. We don't want to come here. I want to go back home."

"First-time traveler," Ruan said with a laugh. "It will get easier."

"I don't want to travel. I don't want to be here. I'm doing just fine without any more gems. We can just leave these ones here and go home." Reg took the baggie of gems out of her pocket and looked around. If she left them there and transported herself back home, the gems would be sure not to follow her again. It was much too far for them to go. She would just dump them and run. Someone else would find them, and his life would be blessed because of them.

"Hold, Reg Rawlins," Ruan said, putting his hand on her arm, his words pitched low and soothing. But Reg was not a horse or whatever other kind of animal might be spooked by sudden movements. She was a human, and she didn't want to be stuck in the middle of a jungle she had never seen before.

She started to flash back to the Everglades. Lost in the midst of the swamp with no idea which way to go to get home. Predators around her, both of the magical sort and the conventional kind that would just tear her to shreds and eat her. She panicked, remembering being tied up and drugged or enchanted. Seeing the rows of human skulls in Tybalt's vault.

"No," she insisted. "I have to go home."

Ruan patted her arm. "Shh. No danger here. Let us look around and find the source."

Having a job to do made Reg feel a little bit more stable, but she still wanted to go home where she knew she was safe. She looked around for a mountain with a hole in the side of it. A mine, like she had seen on TV. If she had transported them there based on what she had learned from the gems, then they must be close to the entrance of the mine.

"This way," Ruan suggested. "We will follow the water."

CHAPTER THIRTY-FOUR

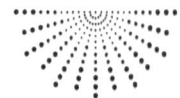

*R*eg stuck close to Ruan as he led the way. No way was she going to be left behind, fending for herself alone.

The canopy of trees shaded them from the hot sun. Ruan adjusted his sunglasses on his nose and tugged his hood down farther.

Calliopia looked back at Reg, her irritation clear. "Try not to crash through the jungle like a buffalo."

Reg's face heated. She tried to step quietly. The pixie and the fairy seemed to have no trouble slipping silently through the vegetation, but every step Reg made seemed to broadcast her presence to anyone who was nearby. Calliopia didn't criticize her further, so Reg hoped that she at least only sounded like a *small* buffalo.

They were on a slight downhill slope. It was a while before Reg's dull human senses could discern what the pixie's already had. The sound of water splashing somewhere close by. As they got closer, she could smell the water. She hesitated, worried about triggering her siren instincts. Ruan and Calliopia didn't know about her parentage and how she might react. Would a siren attack a pixie or a fairy? Or only a human? She didn't imagine her instincts were that discriminating. Blood was blood.

As they drew closer to the water, she could hear voices. More potential victims. Reg resolved to stay well back from the water, which would hopefully keep her from being triggered. The others were going more slowly as they reached an embankment that was just above the river. There was a sharp drop-off of eroded earth and rock. They followed the embankment downriver, toward the voices, staying just under the edge of the trees, hopefully out of sight of the people down below them.

Fairies and pixies were good at blending with their surroundings. Even walking so close to them, Reg lost sight of Calliopia or Ruan as Callie's green dress and Ruan's dirty brown clothes blended with the jungle. Reg was sure that she, on the other hand, stuck out like a sore thumb.

She wanted to ask Ruan where this mine was that they were supposed to be visiting. Had she taken them to the wrong place or was it close by and she just couldn't see it because of the denseness of the jungle vegetation? Did Ruan have any idea where he was going?

They reached a place where they could see men down in the river. They stood in water up to their mid-thighs and called back and forth to one another as they worked. They had shallow boxes and they stooped into the water to fill and then held up high, shaking them slowly back and forth.

"What are they doing?" Reg whispered. "Panning for gold?"

Ruan raised an eyebrow at her. Calliopia scowled and held a finger to her lips.

Reg shook her head and turned her attention back to the men in the river. They were tall and very dark-skinned, their bodies impossibly thin, dressed in clothing that was almost as ragged as a pixie's. They continued to fill their boxes and to shake them. It didn't take long for Reg to realize that the bottom of the box was a screen, so that the boxes acted as sieves, allowing the men to strain the mud from the river bottom, looking at the larger bits of stone and debris. Reg still had in mind that they were looking for gold. She'd seen old Western movies where prospectors had panned for gold.

One of the men moved differently from the others and, at the distance Reg was from them, it took her a few moments to realize why. He handled his sieve differently because he had only one hand. The other arm ended in a stump. Reg was about to point this out to Ruan, then decided that he had probably noticed the fact before she had and kept her mouth shut. The man used his stump to hold the sieve against his body and plucked something out of it. He put it into his mouth to clean it off and held it up to the sun with a shout to the others.

They moved closer to see what he had found, and high-fived each other, their voices rising excitedly. Reg leaned closer, trying to get a better view of what was happening. Ruan glanced at her.

"A diamond," he told her.

"Really? People get diamonds out of rivers? I thought they had to go down mining tunnels, really deep."

Ruan shrugged. "Sometimes. And sometimes, like here, they have a river mine." He looked over at Calliopia and said something to her.

Calliopia considered for a moment, then offered, "Alluvial."

Ruan nodded. "Alluvial mine."

"So all they have to do is come over here and strain the muck to find the diamonds? That sounds a lot better than going down some hole in the ground."

Ruan did not say anything. Reg turned her attention back to the men congratulating the one-handed man who had found the diamond. She didn't think that they would have been so excited if it had been a common occurrence. Maybe they pulled only a few diamonds out of the river each day, so each one was reason for celebration. Maybe it only came out to one diamond each at the end of the day. But Reg knew what diamonds sold for. That would still make each man a very good living.

There was a shout from the shore. Reg had to lean out over the embankment to see the man standing beside the river. Unlike the men in the river, he was dressed in army fatigues, and in his hand he held a large gun. Reg couldn't see it very well and she didn't have much knowledge about guns, but she knew enough to identify it as a machine gun. Something big and very deadly. He held it pointed at the group of men in the river. They turned and looked at him, each of them falling back a step or two and raising his hands in the air, separating from the man who had found the diamond. The man with the gun barked orders, gesturing at the one-handed man.

He was, Reg supposed, asking for identity papers or a permit to mine in that river. Some law enforcement officer who patrolled the river to make sure that everyone was properly authorized and behaved fairly.

The tall man who had found the diamond walked slowly through the water toward the army man, protesting or explaining, his words quick, asserting his rights. The man with the gun was insistent, repeating his demand. Eventually, the man with the diamond reached out and handed it to the soldier on the shore. The soldier folded it into a piece of paper and put it into a pocket, grinning. He motioned with his gun to the man who had found the diamond, threatening.

Reg realized with a sick heart that the soldier wasn't there to enforce some regulation, but to steal the man's treasure. His means to make a living.

CHAPTER THIRTY-FIVE

*R*eg turned to Ruan, her mouth dropping open. She tried to put together the words to express how she felt about this injustice. Nothing came to her. Ruan shrugged.

They continued to watch. The mercenary walked away from the river. It was some time before the men resumed their search for diamonds. Reg hoped that they would find enough by the end of the day to make up for the loss. Ruan and Calliopia stood there watching with Reg, their faces somber.

"Can we go talk to them?" Reg asked. "Do you think it would be safe?"

Ruan rubbed his chin. "As long as Reg Rawlins can touch us, we can return home."

They were relying upon her for their transportation back to Black Sands. If they got separated, Reg would not be able to take them back. She wasn't completely confident in her ability to return to her cottage at will, but Ruan seemed to take it for granted that she would be able to.

Reg nodded her understanding. "We'll stay close together."

They started to pick their way downriver again, getting closer to the men and the place where the soldier had stood and made his threats and demand. She wasn't sure how she would introduce herself to them, but they spotted her little company and started to talk excitedly again, pointing her out to each other and chattering in their native tongue. Reg had second thoughts. She hadn't even thought about the language barrier. She could sense the men's emotions and read what she could from their actions and body language, but it would take more than that if she wanted a conversation with them.

The man who had lost his diamond walked up the shore out of the water and approached Reg. Speaking, he touched her red hair, done up in tiny box braids, and motioned to his own face, almost black in comparison with her pale white skin. He had probably never seen a white person before, let alone a white woman with red hair. It would be something to tell his children and grandchildren about.

"You don't... do you speak any English?" Reg asked.

He said a few more words that she didn't understand, then addressed her. "My grandmother teach me. She work in big house for white man." He smiled proudly, a broad, toothy grin.

Reg breathed a sigh of relief. "We saw what happened. That man who just stole your diamond."

He nodded, face falling. "First stone we find in... five weeks." He held up the five fingers of his remaining hand to make sure she understood.

Reg quickly revised her ideas about how much money the men would be able to make searching the river for gems. One diamond in five weeks, split among—she did a quick head count—six men. Far less than she had speculated. It would be much harder to support themselves and their families on that. But depending on the size of the diamond, they could still make a living.

"I am Joseph," the man said. He looked at his friends. "We will go back to the village. Show you to our families. It is a great honor to be visited by a witch."

"I'm not..." Reg decided that it would be too difficult to explain to them that she wasn't really a witch, just a psychic, who happened to have parents who were... she didn't want to get into all that. She would let them call her a witch, just as she had stopped protesting Ruan calling her a sorceress. She had red hair, she had appeared there magically, she wasn't sure what the right word was to describe herself simply in his language. Or in English, for that matter. Sometimes it was just easier to take the path of least resistance. They were offering to show her hospitality, and she wanted to talk to them further, to get to know them. "My name is Reg. And this is Ruan and Calliopia." She motioned to the pixie and fairy.

Joseph's eyes got wider as he studied her two companions. He bowed low to them, muttering something to his friends. They all followed him out of the water and bowed to both Reg and the others. Ruan gave a low bow back, his eyes glittering. Calliopia gave a scarce nod, her head held high. Reg nodded and shrugged, unsure how to respond to their actions.

The men led them back to the village. It felt as though they went a mile or two through the jungle, following no pathway that Reg could see. But it might have been much shorter than that and she was just out of shape and not used to walking through such heavy vegetation. At least she didn't have to try to walk quietly anymore, which helped. Though she couldn't help noticing how quiet and catlike the men were.

Eventually, they reached a small clearing with several shacks or huts clustered together. Young children, tiny, with arms as thin as sticks ran to greet the men, who smiled and lifted them up and spoke with them. Women in colorful dresses, many with head scarfs, stood back, watching Reg and the other visitors with wary, distrustful eyes. Reg knew fairies and pixies stole young children, so maybe they had reason to be wary.

The men sat down on the ground, motioning for Reg and her companions to join them. Reg felt a little awkward at first. She clearly stood out, and the women and children watched from a distance, fascinated with the white woman with the red hair. But Reg soon became engrossed in the conversation with Joseph and forgot about everything else.

She couldn't help but notice that Joseph was not the only one who was missing a limb or part of one. She wasn't sure whether it was a birth defect, common to this village because of their isolation from others, or perhaps a disease or bacteria that had resulted in their having to be amputated. There were some in the village missing both hands, and even one man missing both arms with only stumps extending from his shoulders.

Joseph caught her looking at the man. He tapped his own stump with the other hand. "Mbombo's army," he explained. "Cut off, prevent men from joining the rebels against him."

Reg's eyes widened. She couldn't imagine someone having men's hands amputated just to prevent them from rising up against him. And clearly, it was not only men who had been maimed. A number of women and even little children had been victims as well.

"How could he do that?" Reg shook her head in disbelief.

"Machetes," Joseph explained, making a chopping motion. He had mistaken her horror for a query as to how it had been done. "Many people, very fast. Must bind them up quickly, see doctor, or…" He rolled his eyes and made a slumping motion, indicating death.

"That's horrible!"

He nodded his agreement and conveyed her comment to the other men, who talked among themselves and nodded. Reg looked at Ruan and Calliopia, gauging their reactions to this news. They nodded as if it didn't come as a great surprise to them. Reg supposed that if they had lived for hundreds of years, they had probably witnessed all kinds of barbarity. Despite media coverage of mass killings at schools or nightclubs, the world did seem like it had become more civilized in the last few centuries. In Reg's world, she did not expect to encounter villages filled with people who had been mutilated by a warlord.

CHAPTER THIRTY-SIX

*a*nd I am sorry that man took your diamond," Reg said. "Does that happen a lot?"

Joseph nodded. "Very difficult to hold on to a stone until you can sell it," he admitted. "Hide it under your tongue so no one sees it... we should have been quiet and not given ourselves away. But it is very hard when you have been looking for so long without finding a stone."

Reg remembered their cheers and high-fives. Relief and joy that they had finally found what they had been seeking for weeks.

"How much would you get for a diamond like that?"

Joseph looked around at the others in the circle. "The last one we got eight hundred dollars." He indicated himself and the other men. "For six men."

Reg was not great at math, but calculated that to be just over one hundred dollars per man. For five weeks of work. She was quickly realizing that her initial thought that it would be an easy life, just pulling diamonds out of the river, was totally off the mark. A hundred dollars to support a family for a month. All around her were indicators of the poverty they lived in, from the shacks to the children with arms like sticks and swollen, malnourished bellies.

"How much would someone pay for it?" Reg asked.

"Pay for it?" Joseph looked confused, having just told her what they had gotten for it.

"I mean… the man or the woman who buys it to put in a ring on a necklace, what would they pay?"

"Oh." He shook his head. "I do not know that." He relayed the question to his friends, who mostly shook their heads in response.

One leaned forward though, and spoke to Joseph with his eyes fixed on Reg. He was older than most of the others. His chest looked as if it were collapsing inward. He had a lot of scars on his face.

Joseph looked back at Reg. "He says his nephew lives in the city, and that he talks to the diamond brokers and the men who sell the stones when they are cut. He says ten thousand." Joseph shrugged and shook his head. "I do not think that can be."

"If it go to a jeweler," Ruan told Reg. "But maybe to a wizard, if a stone of power."

"For more money?" Reg demanded.

"For more…" Ruan's mouth twisted as he searched for the right English words and construction. "…other trade. Slaves, crops, weapons, sorceries."

Reg didn't like the sound of that. She put her hand to her head, which was aching with the heat and with the weight of the village's sorrows.

"You are tired," Joseph observed. "You have come a long way. You will come into my home and rest."

"Oh, no…" Reg protested weakly.

"You should come," Joseph told her. He stood up and extended a hand to her. Reg rose to her feet. She looked at Ruan and Calliopia.

"What about you? You'll want to go back."

"We wait," Ruan told her. "Reg Rawlins cannot travel unless rested."

"Well… you're probably right." Even just a psychic reading for a client could tire her out. Traveling across the ocean must take more energy than that.

She conceded and let Joseph lead her to his shack, where she met his shy wife and was shown to a mat on the floor where she could sleep.

Reg had slept on the streets before. She knew that if she were tired enough, she could sleep practically anywhere. It didn't need to be a comfortable soft bed in a darkened room. So she lay down on the mat, turned on her side with her back to Joseph and his wife, and listened to them conversing in a language she could not understand as she drifted off to sleep.

* * *

She awoke disoriented, unsure of where she was or what had happened. She listened to the noise of a fly buzzing and children's voices in the distance and tried to reconstruct her day and how she had ended up there. She couldn't help worrying about losing significant chunks of her memory, but it all came back to her quickly. Ruan's arrival, traveling around the world to the river mine, Joseph's village.

Reg got up from the mat slowly and looked around. Joseph and his wife were gone, and she was alone in the little shack. She took a quick look around, not wanting to be caught snooping. There was a fire pit in the middle of the floor. A small supply of grains and roots on a counter. There was a plastic basin, but no sign of plumbing. Water was probably carried in from the river, or a smaller stream closer to the village.

She walked out of the shack and looked around for the others. Ruan and Calliopia sat under a tree as they often did at home, with Ruan shaded and Calliopia in the sun, which was starting to descend. A lot of children were gathered around them, looking at them curiously, talking to each other and occasionally approaching the couple, then withdrawing in alarm if either of them moved or looked at them.

Reg approached them, smiling at the children who swarmed around her, touching her white skin or reaching up to examine her red hair. They were older than the children they had seen earlier.

"You must have all been at school," Reg observed. She didn't know whether they knew any English. But maybe they taught a bit at school, or the children had learned some from American music or TV.

One of them, a boy who Reg thought might be about ten, laughed. "No school. We do not go to school."

"Oh. You were out...?" Maybe they worked in fields or gathered fruit or did some other chore for their families.

"In the mine. All must help in the mine."

"In the river?" Reg asked in confusion. She had only seen the grown men working in the river. There hadn't been any children around. But maybe they worked another part of the river, where the water was shallower or the adults could watch over them and keep them safe from soldiers.

"No," a little girl with big black eyes shook her head at Reg and wound one of Reg's red braids around her finger, looking at it raptly. "Under de ground."

Reg looked around at the children to see whether she was being teased, or whether they supported what the little girl said. Several of them nodded. A few commented, but none of the others in English so she could understand.

"You work in an underground mine? All of you?"

They nodded. "We are small," the boy said, "we can go in holes too small for grown-ups."

"You are too big," the girl told him, poking him in the shoulder. "You getting too old."

The boy nodded, lowering his eyes. "Yes. I go soon to the river with the men. Or join the army."

"The army? You're too young for that," Reg laughed.

He shook his head vigorously. "The other boys, they already go. I stayed here because my leg hurt." He pointed to ugly, puckered scars on his leg. "But I am strong now. Big enough and strong enough to go."

Reg looked around for the adults, hardly able to believe what the children were saying. Was it all a big joke? Were they seeing how long they could string along the strange white lady? She had heard of child soldiers, but she thought that UNICEF and all the other organizations had lobbied to have such practices banned. They were well into the twenty-first century. How could such barbarity still be going on in the world?

She looked back at the scars on the boy's leg. She had a sneaking suspicion that they were from bullets, but she was afraid to ask. She knew about blood diamonds. Conflict gems. But she had never really pictured what that meant in terms of human life.

Reg walked over to Ruan and Calliopia and sat down with them. For a while, none of them said anything.

CHAPTER THIRTY-SEVEN

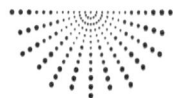

*T*he stones came from here?" Reg asked eventually.

Ruan nodded.

"From the river or from the underground mine?"

"They are the same source," Ruan explained. "The water pounds the rock and gathers the stones that wash out of the ground. Two mines with one source."

"And just the diamonds, or the other stones too?"

He shrugged. "They come from these people. Whether out of the same mine or nearby."

Reg looked around at the children still gathered close to them, so curious about the strange visitors. Who knew how much English they understood? "Can we talk without little ears listening?"

Ruan looked at the children. He suddenly bared his sharp teeth and let out a snarl that sent all of them running away, shrieking. Reg giggled and hoped that they hadn't been too traumatized by the sudden show of aggression.

"Children everywhere are the same," Ruan advised with a shrug.

"You're pretty scary. I nearly ran away myself."

"The first day Reg Rawlins met Ruan Rosdew, she was afraid."

Reg thought back to that first day. Not as afraid as she should have been. She had almost let him mesmerize her. She was lucky that he hadn't harmed her. Strong as pixies were, he could have done her damage. If Calliopia's blood had not burned him.

"You are very strong and dangerous," she told him.

Ruan looked pleased.

"So..." Reg touched the bag of gems in her pocket, which drew both Ruan's and Calliopia's immediate attention. "If these gems came from here, then can I give them back? I don't know who they were stolen from originally, or how long ago. But these people... they are the rightful owners. Just like Joseph and his friends are the rightful owners of the diamond the soldier stole today."

Neither of them agreed. Reg supposed that was a bit too much to expect from them. Ruan believed that the pixies should own anything that came out of the earth, and Calliopia had been part of the family that owned them before they had been given to Reg.

"They are the rightful owners," Reg asserted, looking at both of them for some sign of disagreement. It was too much to expect them to agree, but maybe if they didn't disagree, that was confirmation enough. "How do I give them back? Is there a ceremony? A spell? And..." Reg searched for the words to express what she wanted to say. "If I give them back, how do I make sure that they make things better for these people? That they won't just get stolen by the guys with guns and then the people are beaten down and worse off than they were to start with?"

* * *

Reg approached Joseph after the evening meal had been served. She and her company had refrained from eating anything, knowing they could eat however much they wanted when they got home. The villagers needed every bite of food they could get. Reg despaired over the little children, some of whom seemed to have no energy and who were, she feared, already at death's door. Mothers looked away from the children they held, maybe off into a future they hoped might exist, and not down into their dying children's eyes.

"Do you have... a medicine man or a holy man?" Reg asked Joseph. "Or woman?"

Joseph nodded slowly. "Yes. We have Benji Kongolo. But… his power…" Joseph was apparently looking for a polite way to say that the elder wasn't able to perform the protective or healing rites that they hoped for. "It is *limited*. He is not powerful like you." Joseph indicated Reg, sweeping his hand down and up to indicate Reg's entire body.

Reg wanted to protest the declaration, but she kept her mouth shut. If she said she had no power, then why would Joseph let her see him? Why would Benji want to see her?

"I would like to talk to him."

"He does not speak your language."

"Then I would like to sit with him. Privately."

"I could translate for you."

Reg shook her head. "No. I need to see him alone."

Joseph nodded, accepting that Reg might have good reason to talk to the holy man on her own. "I will take you."

He got to his feet. Reg followed suit. Joseph led her beyond the small circle of huts, into the jungle. Reg kept her mouth shut and followed. She was sure it was not safe to be outside the village as night fell. Besides the night predators who might be stirring, there were also humans out there. They type of humans who shot at or recruited young boys to fight their wars, and girls to be their wives and slaves. Who stole gems at gunpoint and would be delighted with the haul they would find in Reg's pocket. Both Corvin and Ruan had warned about supernatural warlords wielding gems of power. Where were they? In the cities where they had all the modern conveniences? Or in the jungle, close to nature, able to hide in the shadows and watch unobserved?

Reg had thoroughly freaked herself out by the time they reached a camper shell in the middle of the jungle. A camper shell there in the middle of nowhere? Joseph walked Reg to the door of the cabin and stood to the side of it, knocking and raising his voice to say something to the occupant.

Reg waited anxiously for the answer. Eventually, a gruff man's voice responded. She looked at Joseph, who nodded. Reg stood there for a moment, unsure how to proceed. Gathering her courage, she stepped forward and tried the door handle. It moved when she turned it. The door clicked open.

"Mr. Kongolo?" Reg looked into the camper, then poked her head in to look down the length of it. "I'm sorry to bother you, but..."

He said something to her from within the darkness at the back of the camper. Feeling only slightly encouraged, Reg forced her feet to move, stepping farther into the home. It was getting dark outside, and it was pitch black away from the small windows at the front of the camper. Reg walked toward the sound of the voice. In a few steps, she reached the sleeping area, an upper and lower bunk. The upper bunk was filled with boxes and books.

On the lower, she had to squint to make out the shape of a man. She couldn't see any of his features, only the dark shape against the lighter sheets.

A voice encouraged her again. Old and gravelly, but friendly. A pat at the edge of the bed, close to where Reg stood.

Sit down.

Reg sat awkwardly, feeling like it was too close, too intimate to be sitting on the man's bed, only inches from him.

"I'm... I'm Reg," she told him, pointing to herself. "Reg."

"Benji."

"Joseph said that you are a holy man."

"Joseph."

"Yeah. So. Here's the thing..." Reg touched the bag of gems in her pocket. "These belong to you." She hesitated for a moment, then drew the bag out. He wouldn't be able to see it, so she didn't know why she bothered. Were there no lights? Lanterns? Candles?

She put them down on the bed, next to his hand. They glowed slightly, seeming to produce their own light.

"These stones are not mine," Reg said. "They are from your people. They belong to you."

Knowing that he could not understand her words, she concentrated on projecting her feelings to him, and trying to read his in return. She pushed the gems toward him in her mind, showing them to him, offering them.

He reached over and grasped the bag. He pulled it in to his body and hugged it against himself. The whole camper shell began to shake. Reg wondered briefly whether Joseph, still outside the camper, was shaking it for effect. Maybe some of the children from the village had followed them and thought it would be funny to scare the stranger.

But she knew that wasn't what was going on. The shaking originated inside the camper, not outside of it.

The holy man began to hum. Reg looked around her, wishing that she could see something in the dark interior of the camper. The stones glowed more. Reg focused her attention on them, on magnifying the light, and it increased again. She could see the bottom portion of Benji's face, lit up in grotesque detail by the underlighting. He was older than Joseph, but not a grizzled old man with gray hair and no teeth. And not, she didn't think, someone who had seen the centuries pass, like Sarah or others that Reg knew. Magic seemed to slow the progress of time in those people, but Reg felt like Benji's aging process had been sped up rather than slowed down.

Will you accept these stones? Reg tried to convey the thought to him.

He began to chant. Reg closed her eyes, listening to the syllables and rhythm of the chant. She couldn't understand it, but she wasn't sure she was meant to. Maybe it was words, and maybe it was just meaningless syllables, and the magic was contained in the cadence and tones. She could see colors in the darkness behind her eyelids, flashing and changing and growing with the chant, becoming more and more clear.

She saw brown hands of varying different sizes and tones pulling gems out of the river, and gems catching the light in the rock walls of underground tunnels.

And she saw the people in the village, but they were different from what she had actually seen with her own eyes. Whole families were together, the babies, children, and teens with their parents. Their bodies whole, not scarred from bullets or missing limbs. Their faces were happy, their eyes not hollow and sad. The mothers smiled and gathered their children in rather than staring off into the distance, looking for something to hope for, anticipating the next death.

Reg's cheeks were wet. She didn't rub the tears away, but let them fall, listening to the man's chant.

Can you use them? Reg wanted to know. *I don't want them to bring more suffering, more death.*

She opened her eyes. Benji pulled open the zipper on the bag and put his hand into it, running his fingers through the gems. He pulled out one stone and held it toward Reg. Reg hesitated, then took it from him, wondering why he had given it to her.

She let it warm in her hand. She closed her eyes once more, feeling the stone. It was a diamond. One of the largest stones. Why had he given it back to her? What did it signify?

Reg saw a man. He was unlike any of the men she had seen so far in the jungle. His skin was dark like those of Joseph and the other villagers. He wore army fatigues like the soldier who had stolen the diamond from Joseph. And he was fat. Everyone she had seen there had been thin, accustomed to eating meals that were scant with long periods of hunger between them. Someone who was that fat clearly had no trouble getting enough to eat.

Who is this?

You will find him. They were the first words that Reg had felt from Benji. They were strong and resonant, and she had no doubt that he spoke the truth.

He pulled another gem from the bag and put it in her hand. Reg concentrated on it. Not another diamond, but an emerald. Rich and green and warm. Like the lush growth of the jungle. A picture of Joseph came into her mind. Reg didn't have to ask questions this time. She would give the emerald to Joseph. That would be easy, and she felt confident that he would know what to do with it, how to use it to the best benefit of the village. He wouldn't let anyone take that stone away from him.

Benji ran his fingers through the gems that remained in the bag. There were still plenty of them. Enough to sustain and bless the village for a long time, if they were carefully guarded and used the right way. Benji drew a third gem out and put it into Reg's hand with the others.

A ruby this time. Red like Reg's braids.

For you.

"No." Reg tried to give it back to Benji. "No, these are for you. They belong to your people."

For you, he insisted firmly.

Reg didn't argue. She felt the three gems in her hand. Each different. Each very valuable. Each with a different purpose, though she wasn't one hundred percent sure what each purpose was.

Benji did not remove any more of the gems from the bag. His fingers worked to close the zipper at the top to seal them up again. He would, she hoped, find a suitable hiding place to store them in to ensure their safety. She wouldn't want them to be stolen from the villagers again.

Benji nodded reassuringly. He hummed some more, and then the sound gradually died away.

CHAPTER THIRTY-EIGHT

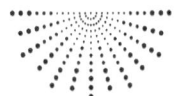

*R*eg turned the handle and pulled the camper door open, letting in the cooler night air. It was quiet, the sounds of bugs and birds and activity that she had become accustomed to quieted. There were a few unfamiliar night sounds, which made her anxious to return to the village, where she would at least have some protection from predators that slunk through the jungle looking for the weak and vulnerable.

There was a movement to her right and she turned quickly, panicking. But the tall, slim shape spoke in a reassuring voice.

"It is Joseph."

"Oh." Reg blew out her breath. "Thanks for waiting for me. I'm glad you didn't go back to the village."

"Of course not. You are ready?"

"Before we go…" Reg pinched the emerald between her fingers. "Put out your hand."

It sounded like a game. Or like one of those tortures that fellow foster children dreamed up. "Put your finger here," one would say, displaying an empty palm. Curious, Reg would do so, only to have the child close his fingers around it and give it a sharp jerk or twist, forcing her to her knees in pain.

But Joseph did not suspect any deception on her part. He put out his hand obediently. Reg placed the emerald in it.

"You must keep that safe. Find a way to sell it in the city, where you'll get a good price for it. Buy food, build a water pump, get the other things the village needs."

Joseph looked down at the gem, his night vision clearly better than hers, used to navigating at night without a light. "Where did you get this?" He rolled it around in his palm. "I have not seen a cut stone before, except in a rich man's jewelry."

"It is yours. It belongs to your people. If you have questions, you can talk to Benji, he can tell you what you need to know."

Joseph slipped it into his mouth, placing it under his tongue, where he had told her that he should have hidden the diamond instead of advertising its existence to the soldier.

"I will keep it safe."

Reg nodded. "Let's go back to the village."

They went slowly, Joseph quickly figuring out that Reg couldn't see where she was going. She remembered Ruan addressing her as "oh blind one" on their previous quest to the dwarf mountain and she smiled to herself.

"Is there a man around here, not in your village, a man who wears army fatigues and is very fat?"

Joseph turned to look back at her curiously. "How do you know of General Mbombo?"

"Benji—" Reg started to motion back to the camper and to explain, then remembered that Benji could not speak English and it might be difficult to explain the matter to Joseph. "Well... I heard of him. The General. Is he..." Reg cast about, finding it awkward to ask the question. She didn't really understand the politics and factions in the area. "Is your village for or against him?"

Joseph didn't answer immediately. They continued to walk through the jungle, Reg regularly stubbing her toes, tripping over something, or having a branch slap her in the face.

"The people in my village are not... aligned with the army or the rebel groups," Joseph said finally. "But the rebels often recruit them to fight, and some choose to join one side or the other. And sometimes they switch sides, if they are left behind or captured. It is not easy to answer."

Reg nodded thoughtfully. "But he is not good for your village. He does not protect you."

"No." Joseph gave a sharp laugh. "The General does not help anyone but the General."

Then why had Benji asked her to give one of the gems to the General? And how was she going to find him and get him to meet with her in order for her to give him the gem? Reg tried to think of a story that would make sense. How she had heard of him and wanted to help his cause. But she was sure that wouldn't make any more sense to the General than it did to Reg herself. A white woman showing up out of the jungle and offering him a large diamond? There was no reason for her to even be in the country.

She frowned, pondering on this while she trudged after Joseph. She swore as she barked her shin on a log that jumped in front of her. Joseph looked back at her. She could see little but the whites of his eyes.

"Are you okay?"

"Yes. Just a klutz."

"Klutz," Joseph repeated.

"It's… someone who is clumsy."

"Ah." He didn't argue that she wasn't clumsy, just blind as a bat. Reg wondered how much farther the village was.

* * *

She didn't know how much of the story she should tell to Ruan and Calliopia. Neither one was particularly happy with her returning *their* stones to the country they had come from. If they knew that she had been given a ruby in return, they would probably try to steal it from her. Since she'd been given it by the rightful owner, Reg assumed that she would now be able to use it as she pleased. She didn't want to lose it to a quick-fingered pixie or fairy.

So she gave them a brief description of the camper and the man she had found there. As much as she could tell them about the little she'd been able to see. She told them that she had given him the gems, but not that she had been given any of them back again.

"We go home now?" Ruan asked.

"Uh... I still have something else to do here. I guess that means sleeping here tonight, and then hopefully... tomorrow..."

"Something else?" Ruan lowered his brows, looking suspicious. "What else?"

"I can't discuss it. Something that the holy man wanted me to do."

"We should go home."

"You and Calliopia are nomadic. Why does it matter to you where we spend the night?"

"Reg Rawlins gave him the gems, we go home."

"He asked me to do something for him."

"Dangerous." Ruan shook his head. "This be a dangerous place. Not a good place to sleep, and Reg Rawlins should not make promises to medicine man."

"Why not?" That feeling in the pit of her stomach again. The beginnings of dread. How was it she kept making these mistakes over and over again? Don't take gifts from fairies. Don't go out with men of Corvin's ilk. Don't go to the Everglades looking for a lost wizard. There should be a rule book somewhere.

"Why does medicine man need Reg Rawlins to do something?" Ruan asked. "Medicine man has his own magic. And all of the stones. Why does medicine man not do his own magic?"

Ruan had a point. Reg shrugged and shook her head. "I don't know. I didn't ask. We didn't exactly have a detailed conversation. I gave him the gems, he asked me to do something for him. I didn't think... that it might be a problem."

Calliopia looked around them. The jungle was dark. The shacks were darker blots in the night. There were a few flickering lights; candles or lanterns inside the huts. They cast long, flickering shadows across the central clearing where Reg talked with them. Reg could feel Calliopia's anxiety at the shadows. She remembered Calliopia's fear of being attacked by shadows in the night. And she had been attacked in the night. She clearly hadn't gotten over it.

"I'll ask Joseph where we can stay for the night," Reg said. She was surprised that they hadn't been asked. Weren't poor villagers always supposed to be hospitable? Inviting strangers to share their food and homes? It wasn't very hospitable to leave Reg and her company with nowhere to sleep.

And Reg was hungry. She had thought they would be going home right away and hadn't wanted to take food out of the mouths of the children. But now her stomach was growling, and it hurt, and there was nothing to eat. She hadn't even managed to bring her purse with her, where she always stowed a couple of granola bars or some food she could eat in an emergency. She'd had too many hungry nights herself as a child to take it for granted that she would always have something to eat.

She found her way, mostly by feel, to the shack that she thought was Joseph's, the one that she had napped in earlier in the day. She knocked quietly on the door, hoping that she wasn't disturbing anyone's sleep. Like the other men who had been digging in the river, Joseph had at least a couple of young children.

The door opened a crack. Joseph put his face to the door. "What is it?" he whispered.

"My friends and I... we need somewhere to sleep."

"Yes?"

Reg stared at him. He didn't invite her in.

"We are strangers here. We don't know the area. Where can we sleep?"

He gestured to Ruan and Calliopia and nodded. "There is fine."

"There is not fine!" Reg disagreed. "It's dark and we can't just sleep in the dirt."

"You can light a fire."

There was a pit in the middle of the ground, where some families had cooked and shared their dinners. Reg supposed there was enough fuel stacked nearby that she could light a pretty decent fire. It would provide some light for Calliopia. It might not be enough to banish her nightmares, but it was the best they could do.

"Do you have some blankets or sleeping mats we could use?"

"One moment."

He shut the door. Reg waited outside impatiently. Hospitality. They should be taught a lesson on hospitality. In all the TV movies she had ever seen, poor villagers had been welcoming and helpful, giving up their own food and beds for strangers.

But that was TV, and she was now confronted with real life. And real life had plenty of bumps and unexpected turns along the way.

After a few minutes, Joseph opened the door again, and he pushed a few blankets into her hands. Reg had expected them to be hand-woven, like the Mexican blankets she had seen in craft sale stalls and roadside tables in the south. But they were more like the rough blankets that she had slept in when sent to summer camp in the hopes that she would behave herself and stay out of everyone's hair.

"Thank you. And—"

Joseph shut the door and Reg heard him latch or bolt it on the other side.

She could probably still get the door open. Failing that, she could probably just kick a hole in the side of the shack. But she was supposed to be a good guest, and good guests didn't do that, even if their hosts didn't think to provide them with pillows and more comfortable bedding. Reg took the blankets back to Ruan and Calliopia. She put them down on the ground in a pile without any comment. She went to the fire pit and started to stack bark and wood in it.

CHAPTER THIRTY-NINE

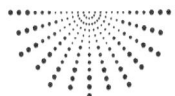

e are staying here?" Calliopia asked.

Reg nodded. "It will be fine. I'll get a fire going, and we'll be nice and toasty."

Ruan took Calliopia's hand and murmured to her.

Reg knew it wasn't the first time that they'd had to sleep under the stars. It had taken a long time before Calliopia had been able to sleep under a roof, worried about being ambushed in the night as she had been when she was kidnapped. She had needed to be outside, under the sun and the stars. So there shouldn't be any reason for her to be averse to sleeping outside in the village. She wouldn't have to worry about anyone coming in through the windows, since there were no windows.

"Do either of you have any food or any way to get food?" Reg asked.

In *The Hobbit* the elves had Lembas, a kind of cracker that never got stale. Shouldn't Ruan and Calliopia be carrying something like that with them? They were the ones who had chosen a nomadic lifestyle. So they should be prepared for unexpected travel or to occasionally run into a few bumps.

She looked over her pile of wood. It was a nice big pile. It would burn all night and keep away the jackals and lions and whatever else roamed the dark jungle at night.

"We have no food," Calliopia said, her tone accusing.

"Well, I'm providing the fire. You see if you can think of a way to get some."

"There is not much to steal," Ruan said logically.

"I don't want you to steal it. Aren't there all kinds of foods that grow in the jungle around here? Fruit and nuts and leafy things?"

Not that Reg liked to eat leafy things. But her stomach was really hurting. If it were all she had, she might break down and eat even leafy things.

"We cannot find them at night," Ruan said scathingly.

"You're the one who can see in the dark. What does it matter to you whether it is day or night?"

Ruan looked around. "Not safe to wander in the jungle at night."

"What could happen? You can make yourself disappear. And Calliopia..." Reg couldn't think of what Calliopia could do. "She has magic."

"We will not hunt at night," Ruan said firmly. He looked at Calliopia, who looked as though she might argue and order him to go find her something to eat anyway. He shook his head and said something to her. Calliopia looked away, arms folded, and scowled.

It amazed Reg that Calliopia could scowl and still look so beautiful. In the dark, with shadows flickering across her face. What would it be like to be that beautiful? Reg had always thought herself quite plain, even though Corvin and others had told her she was pretty. Corvin was just attracted by her powers, not her looks. Or if he was attracted to her looks, it was just the influence of her siren parentage. Sirens always looked beautiful to their prey. That was how they attracted them. As a child, Reg had been skinny and gawky and awkward. Not very impressive.

"Well, if you won't gather any fruit at night, then you might have to go hungry."

Reg rubbed her hands together and then began to form a ball of fire between her palms, gradually making it bigger and pulling her hands farther apart. It was so warm and friendly; it instantly made her feel better. She could banish the darkness and gloom. They would have a pleasant night, sitting by the fire. There was nothing as relaxing as staring into the flames.

"Big enough to light the wood, Reg Rawlins," Ruan warned.

Reg pulled back, becoming aware of the size of the fireball she had created. She squeezed it back down to baseball size, then reached into the wood and let it go, lighting the prepared fuel quickly.

The wood was dry and burned bright and hot. Reg basked in the glow. She went over to the blankets she had put on the ground and picked one out.

It was one night. It wouldn't hurt her to sit or lie on the ground for one night in the open air. It was still warm. But she was hungry. Where was Harrison and his chocolate cake when she needed him?

"Harrison," Reg whispered, and looked around, wondering whether he would come to her. Even though she knew that he was an immortal and his powers were beyond her comprehension, she was still surprised to have him appear somewhere other than Black Sands.

Harrison sat next to her, his long skinny legs encased in chaps and a large cowboy hat on his head. His shirt, rather than one of the prints or styles that Reg associated with western wear, was a bright blue and orange Hawaiian print. Harrison's long fingers strummed a banjo. She wasn't sure if it was a child-sized banjo, or if it just looked small because of how long his arms and legs were.

"A camp out," Harrison said enthusiastically. "You have not done a camp out for many years."

Reg opened her mouth to answer him, but he cut her off.

"You have slept outside, though. Is it a camp out when you don't have a campfire?" He looked thoughtful, considering this. "Or if you don't sleep in tents?" He looked around at the shacks, shaking his head. "These are not tents. But sleeping in a blanket on the ground... that *and* the campfire make it a camp out, right?"

"Uh, right," Reg agreed. "We are having a camp out."

"Oh, good. I love a camp out."

"You know what we need, though? Wieners to roast. And marshmallows. *Not* together."

"Wieners and marshmallows," Harrison agreed. "Yes."

Reg found a package of wieners and one of jumbo marshmallows at her feet. She looked around for a stick to roast them. Ruan picked up the package of wieners and smelled it.

"Meat? What kind?"

"We never ask."

"Oh." He nodded. "And what for Calliopia?"

Reg had forgotten that fairies didn't eat flesh. She thought about other traditional campfire foods. Most of them seemed to involve roasting meat.

"These fruits?" Ruan asked, tearing open the bag of marshmallows and pulling out one of the marshmallows. He squished it between his fingers several times, apparently fascinated by the texture. He took a small bite and looked surprised.

"Uh, no, they're not fruit. But they're good. I don't know whether they're vegetarian, though. How about... bananas or potatoes? Those are good roasted in the fire. Or... pineapple. Or some kind of stew. Those brown beans—cowboys ate those, didn't they?" She looked at Harrison in his *unique* cowboy getup.

"Beans," Harrison agreed with a nod. He moved a pot of bubbling baked beans closer to the fire. Reg wasn't sure why they needed to be move closer to the fire if they were already boiling. Calliopia leaned forward and sniffed at the pot delicately. She looked back at Reg as if suspicious that Reg was trying to fool her.

"This is good human food?"

"Yes. Beans. You've eaten beans before, haven't you?"

"Not this kind."

"They're really good. Grab yourself a plate and a spoon and have some," Reg suggested.

Still looking dubious, Calliopia picked up one of the provided tin plates and ladled some of the beans into it.

Ruan looked at Harrison. "Energy drinks," he said distinctly, as if speaking to a computer that wasn't very good at voice recognition.

"No!" Reg objected. She remembered what Ruan was like after a couple of cans of energy drinks. "Fruit juice. Or milk. Or pop."

"Milk," Calliopia echoed. She dipped her spoon into the beans and delicately ate a few. She didn't look pleased, but she didn't spit them out either, so Reg figured that counted as a success.

"No energy drinks?" Ruan asked, looking disappointed.

"We won't get a wink of sleep. No."

Harrison passed out glasses of milk. Reg passed a couple down to Calliopia and Ruan, and then ended up with one in her own hand. She didn't like milk. She hadn't thought when she blocked Ruan's request that Harrison would give them all the same thing.

"Can I at least have chocolate?" she asked Harrison.

She was left holding a chocolate bar, which was ten times better than chocolate milk, so Reg was okay with that.

"I want candy too," Ruan insisted.

Before long, every demand had been satisfied, other than the one for energy drinks, and everyone was quiet as they ate.

"Do you remember camping out?" Harrison asked Reg. "Your brain is not holding as much lately."

Reg choked on her wiener covered with ketchup. That was one way of putting it. She knew that Harrison didn't mean it in an insulting way, he was just having a normal immortal-type conversation.

She cleared her throat. "Yeah. I remember a few camp outs. Mostly being sent away to camp."

He nodded agreement.

"Some of those were okay. I liked it when we did crafts or hiking or swimming. But *not* getting up early or having to go on runs or do calisthenics." Too many of those camps had been intended to reform the troubled and the troublemakers. Inevitably, that involved trying to work them so hard that they didn't have the energy to get into any trouble.

Which inevitably failed. At least with Reg.

"And the food," Harrison suggested. "Always lots of food. Tables piled high with it."

Reg nodded, remembering. For someone who had been through several periods when food had been scarce or nonexistent, that had been very important for her, and she had not overlooked it. "Pancakes and bacon and eggs," she remembered, salivating even though they already had too much food for all of them to eat before morning. "Sausages, macaroni and cheese, sub sandwiches filled with whatever you liked. The food was great."

* * *

They all ate until they were stuffed. Reg lay down, her hand over her bulging stomach, and felt guilty for eating so much when the children in the village had probably never had the opportunity to fill their bellies until they were full. If they tried to eat all the food that Harrison had provided, they would probably go into shock. She'd heard about that happening after WWII. It could kill someone who was starving to suddenly eat normally.

Ruan and Calliopia were talking together, speaking pixie or fairy so that Reg could not understand them. She kept her voice low and spoke to Harrison.

"Do you know the General?"

"The General?"

"There is a man who lives somewhere close by. He is not skinny like the people who live in this village. He's fat, and wears army fatigues, and he is called the General. He probably lives in a palace. Or at least a bigger house than any of these." Reg gestured to the shacks around them.

Harrison nodded.

"Does that mean yes, you know him?" Reg demanded.

"I could," Harrison said obliquely.

Reg shook her head. "Do you or not? Can you tell me where he lives?"

Harrison waved in the direction Reg thought the river was. "It is not far."

"I need to see him tomorrow. I have something to give to him. Do you think I could walk there? Or he might come here to me?"

"Human time is very linear."

"Yes. It is. Do you think I might see him?"

"You might."

Reg wasn't satisfied with the answer. But she didn't want Harrison to magically transport her to the General or to transport the General to her. Using magic on him would probably just cause trouble. Reg was hoping to avoid as much trouble as she could. Get to the General's house, give him the diamond, and then return home with her companions. Quick and simple.

"I don't know whether I'm going to get to sleep tonight," Reg said with a yawn. "With everything that has happened today, and what else I have to do. My stomach hurts and I don't even know what time it is supposed to be."

"Humans don't know anything," Harrison said agreeably.

CHAPTER FORTY

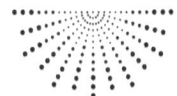

*D*espite her worries and her grossly overstretched stomach, Reg was able to sleep. Maybe Harrison had put a spell on her to stop her from talking to him and asking more questions. More likely, he just got bored and disappeared. He was nowhere in evidence in the morning.

Sometimes when he disappeared, all the food disappeared with him, and sometimes it did not. This time, perhaps he had seen the need of the villagers, and he had left the food behind. The children gathered up all the scraps and leftovers and divided them up. There was no fighting and competition, they just split it up and took it to their various homes, to eat or to share with their families.

Joseph and his men were up before the sun had risen much over the horizon and were preparing to leave. Back to the river to look for more gems, Reg assumed. Had Joseph hidden the emerald somewhere safe, or was he still holding it under his tongue?

"You are still here," he said to Reg, seeming a little surprised by this. Maybe his inhospitality of the night before had been designed to make her go home. Reg folded her blanket carefully and offered it to him.

"I am still here. I need to see the General today."

"The General. You do not want to see him."

"I need to."

Joseph shook his head. "That is not a good idea."

"Even if it is what your holy man wanted me to do?"

Joseph's eyes went to her face, surprised, then he looked down at the ground. "I am not a holy man. Or even a good man. But… I would not see the General without protection. Will your companions keep you safe? The General is a powerful man. Not just in politics."

"Well, I guess I'll have to do my best." Reg wasn't nearly as confident as she tried to sound. She did not want to face a powerful warlord. She wanted to go back home and forget that she had ever been there. Benji could have the ruby back. Or she could give it to Joseph or to one of the women in the village. That would be more equitable. Why did it have to be the men who held the gems?

"I cannot help you with this thing," Joseph said. "We go to the river to dig."

He nodded to his companions, and with their screens in their hands, they started on their trek back to the river to search for precious stones.

Reg looked around at the villagers who were watching her, though they dropped their eyes or looked away and pretended they were not.

"Can somebody tell me the way to the General's house?"

None of them offered anything in response. Of course, they probably didn't speak English. It seemed that only a few had any fluency. Though maybe they understood more than they pretended to, and it was just a good blind. It was always a good idea not to give too much away. Let your opponent underestimate you.

Joseph didn't want her to go to the General. Ruan and Calliopia didn't want her to go to the General. The villagers didn't want her to go to the General.

And Reg didn't want to go to the General.

She closed her eyes and pictured the man that Benji had showed her in her mind the night before. She focused on making the picture very clear, seeing every detail of his face and body, the way his clothes stretched around his fat middle. Then she expanded her view out, looking at the room around him. Then waiting, feeling for a tug in a certain direction. He was there. She could feel him. Reg started to walk.

She'd been pushing her way through the jungle for a while before she realized that she was being followed. Reg looked behind her and saw that Ruan and Calliopia were a few paces back, walking silently in her footsteps. She was crashing through the bush like a buffalo and hadn't even heard them.

There wasn't anything to say that hadn't already been said, so Reg just kept walking. Eventually, she stumbled into a clearing.

It wasn't just a natural break in the trees, a natural little grove. It had been clear cut, maybe even burned, so that all the space around the compound was flat and empty. To prevent anyone from being able to sneak up on them. Anyone approaching the buildings would have to make themselves visible.

Unless it was someone like Davyn, who could cloak himself. Or a pixie. Reg turned to the others. "Ruan… can you go to the world of shades?"

Maybe it was surprising that he hadn't already.

"And can you take Calliopia with you?"

Ruan studied Reg. "Calliopia can no longer enter that world. She is full fairy now."

"I thought maybe if you were holding on to her, it would work like it did when I called her and got both of you."

"No."

"I can hide," Calliopia offered. She made a motion that was half-shrug, half-indicating the greenery around her. "A fairy can easily hide from human eyes."

Being as blind as they were.

"Yes. The two of you. I want both of you to hide yourselves. I don't know what will happen, but we have an advantage if they don't know that you are here."

Calliopia nodded. She withdrew from them and, in a moment, Reg could no longer follow her movements. Her dress and hair and even her pale face blended in with the dappled light and she was gone. Reg nodded. She looked at Ruan. Ruan spun in a circle, gaining speed and, in a moment, he too was gone. In the right conditions, Reg would still be able to see his shadowy shape, but with the contrast of the dark jungle and bright sunlight in the clearing, her eyes couldn't adjust well enough to make him out.

"You two wait here," Reg told them, talking to the air. "I will… hopefully not be too long."

She began her walk across the empty space, knowing that she would be spotted by the soldiers immediately.

The insects continued to buzz, and the birds continued to chirp and sing. Nothing had changed. But Reg felt as if she were walking into a void. Everything was different.

She was not approached, but could feel eyes on her. She strained to see anyone in the compound up ahead, but if they were watching her, it was through viewing slots or peepholes or hidden cameras. Or maybe some of them were in the jungle behind her, watching from high perches or dark shadows.

The compound was enclosed by a wall and the outer walls of the buildings. Reg aimed for a large gate, where she assumed there was a checkpoint where they would want to see proper ID or credentials. How was she going to get past there? She was a con. She would try to con her way in.

It seemed as if she would never get there. She covered the first half of the distance, and then half again, and again, each fraction seeming to take longer and to be more difficult. Even though she was walking on flat ground and then pavement, she felt more tired than she had been walking in the jungle, climbing over obstacles and pushing her way through dense brush.

CHAPTER FORTY-ONE

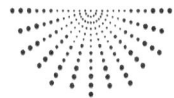

*F*inally, she was at the gate. A soldier was there waiting for her, his weapon cradled in his arm. Was it the same man as had taken Joseph's diamond the day before? Reg wasn't sure whether it was him or just another with the same uniform.

He looked her over with hard eyes. Eyes that looked on all the suffering in all of the villages and were not moved. He had grown up in a war-torn country, and he'd had to be strong and hard to earn his place in the General's forces. Like the children from the village, he had probably been recruited when he was a young teen and had worked his way up the ranks to gain a position where he always had enough to eat and could, as a bigger predator, live off of the people beneath him.

But he couldn't hide his surprise at seeing Reg. Her white skin and red hair were enough to make her stand out anywhere. They certainly did not belong in the jungle or in the General's citadel.

"Who are you?" he demanded.

Reg tried not to betray any surprise over his use of English in addressing her. His accent was heavy, but his words and meaning were clear. "Reg Rawlins. I am here to see the General."

"What about?"

"That's between me and him."

"You have no business here."

"That isn't for you to say. Take me to see him. I am sure you will be rewarded if you do."

"Rewarded." His eyes glittered. "By you?"

Reg's skin crawled. She couldn't wait to get out of there. To get back home where she was safe and didn't have to deal with predators. At least, not ones like him. "By the General. He will reward you for bringing me to see him. Richly rewarded."

"Why? What makes you think this?"

"Because I have brought him something of great value."

The guard looked skeptical. "What?"

"If I showed you, he would probably kill you. He will not want anyone else to see what I have."

Not a bad bluff. She could see his concern over this dilemma. How could he know if Reg had something that the General would want to see if he couldn't see it? But insisting that he see it could lead to losing his life, which wasn't high on his to-do list. Could he take her word that she had something of value? Or should he insist on seeing it? Even take it from her and deliver it to the General himself? That would earn him points.

Then again, if she had something of great value, maybe he could take it for himself and, with enough money and power, he could overthrow the General and take his place. It was always a possibility.

"Not a good idea," Reg told him. She pushed emotions toward him. Fear and anxiety, worry about his precarious position in the organization. He was the first line of defense, but the first line of defense would always be the first to fall. The higher-ranking men were not placed at the outer doors, but inside where they were better protected. With the General at the center of the citadel like a spider in the middle of his web.

The anxiety took hold quickly. It was a familiar feeling for the man. Something he fought off every day, worrying that he was not good enough, that he had risen as far as he could go. That he had left behind his mother and his brothers, betraying them to work for the man who would happily kill every villager in the country if it brought him more money and power. And so far, he was succeeding.

"You don't want to make him angry," Reg warned. "If he finds even that you have delayed, he'll have your head."

"You do not know anything. You are not from here."

"I know things that you do not. And I know what I have."

"You will wait here," he said abruptly, turning away from her.

Reg watched in surprise as he retreated to a guardroom. Maybe to consult with a superior? To make a phone or radio call outside her hearing? There were other guards in the hall beyond the guardroom, watching Reg carefully with their guns on their hands. Thin rangy men like coyotes.

In a few minutes, the guard was back. He had a wholly different aura. Instead of the fear and anxiety, he was angry, heedless, confrontational. Reg wasn't sure what had changed, but he was not the same man as he had been when he had disappeared into the guardroom.

"You don't frighten me," he blustered. "You don't know anything about the General. You aren't from here."

"That doesn't mean I don't know anything about him."

The guard leaned closer to her, getting into her face, intentionally invading her personal space in order to intimidate her. She stared into his eyes. A sea of dark brown that she couldn't even see the pupil in. Reg tried to keep her own anxiety at bay. This was more what she had been expecting to run into. Angry, violent men who didn't have the same rules and morals as the law enforcement back home. Men who wouldn't hesitate to go way over the line.

He sniffled and wiped at his nose, and Reg suddenly understood the pinpoint pupils. He hadn't gone into the guardroom to talk to a superior, but to work up a little courage through other means. And whatever he had snorted had done the trick. He would not be intimidated by a strong woman who pretended she knew more than she did now.

"Well, if you won't take me to him…" Reg shrugged, pretending to withdraw. When advancing didn't work, retreat was always an option.

He glowered at her suspiciously. He'd expected her to fight more. To insist that he would regret it if she didn't let him see his boss.

"Tell me why you want to see him."

"I told you. I have something of great value. I thought… never mind. There are others I can offer it to. Your General is not the only powerful man in the country."

He grabbed her arm, holding it tightly. "You're not going anywhere."

She didn't pull away, just looked at him. "It doesn't make much sense for me to just stand in the door, does it? Either in or out. Which is it going to be?"

He looked undecided for a few seconds, then his lips pressed together into a straight line, and he jerked her toward him. Over the threshold. Reg could feel herself slipping through an invisible barrier as she allowed him to pull her in. It was a good thing she hadn't tried to just walk in while he was in the guardroom and had not tried to sneak through a back gate. She would not have been able to get through the magical protection and they would have had her for trying to break in rather than just asking at the door.

Reg let him pull her along, and eventually he decided that dragging her wasn't giving him the upper hand and he let her go, allowing her to walk beside him. Reg looked around at the building as she walked through the various passages. The walls were bare, not adorned with all manner of rich art and tapestries. Despite his apparent power and wealth, the General wasn't living in a kingly mansion. It was utilitarian. A stronghold.

They went through many twists and turns, moving from one building to another until they reached a waiting room or antechamber where the soldier stopped and spoke with another guard. He was deferential, but his face and his movements still gave away the fact that he was high on some kind of opiate. Reg was sure the inner guard could see that as well as she could. They spoke together in low voices, and eventually the inner guard approached Reg.

"Who are you?"

"My name is Reg Rawlins."

"But who are you?"

"Someone with something of value for the General."

"Show me."

"He will not want anyone else to see or know about it."

The new guard thought about this. He knew, of course, that his boss had secrets. Anyone who had attained that kind of standing had to have secrets. Dirt on other people, leverage, booby traps, secret plans, powers, and weapons. Secrets were the currency of power.

"He was not expecting you."

"Of course not."

"I could beat it out of you." The guard's eyes traveled up and down Reg's body, assessing her, imagining what he would do to her.

Reg suppressed her reaction to him and stuck to the same line. "He wouldn't want you to know about it. What good would that do?" She laughed. "Is it worth it to beat a defenseless woman so that you can see something secret before you die?"

She wasn't defenseless, of course. He might be stronger than she was physically, but Reg could overcome him with magic any day. She didn't sense that he had any powers himself. He was a physical being. Someone used to using his physical strength and intimidation to get what he wanted. Maybe he was wily and smart too, to have achieved a high standing among his peers, the last guardian of the General, but he didn't have any magic that she could sense.

He stared at her boldly before finally making his decision. "You will wait here." He pointed to the guard who had brought Reg from the front gate. "And you will watch her. Make sure that she does not try anything."

At the nod of agreement from the front gate guard, he turned and withdrew into the chamber behind him. The General's office? Or was there yet another layer of protection before reaching him? He was very well-protected.

Reg didn't say anything. The high guard didn't say anything, but jittered and vibrated as he walked around the antechamber, looking for something of interest within its bare walls. Reg could hear him grinding his teeth, and it set her own teeth on edge like fingernails on a blackboard. She tried to wall off his emotions to keep them from affecting her. She needed to stay sharp during her conversation with the General, if she got in to see him.

CHAPTER FORTY-TWO

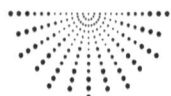

*T*he door opened, and the inner guard stepped out. He nodded to Reg.

"Enter."

She walked by him, into the final room.

The General sat behind a desk. Exactly as she had seen him. A pristine camouflage uniform that did not appear to have ever seen the battlefield or a hike through the jungle growth. Plenty of meat on his bones. It wasn't all fat; she could see that. He undoubtedly worked out as well, lifting weights or wrestling or doing something else to help him to increase his muscle size. A powerful man, both politically and physically.

"Has she been searched?" the General barked.

The guard, who had entered behind Reg, shook his head. "She said… she has something for you that you would not want us to see."

"And you just took her at her word? Assumed that she does not have a knife or a gun? Or enough explosives to blow this building sky high?"

The soldier nodded stoically. "Yes, sir."

"Is that really wise?"

"If she has something you would not wish us to see, then it would be unwise for us to search her."

The General laughed. "And you feared me more than the possibility she might set off a bomb?"

"Yes, sir."

He chuckled again. "Very wise," he agreed. "You are dismissed."

The guard withdrew and shut the door, leaving Reg alone with the General. He looked her over thoughtfully. Reg wondered if he had ever seen anyone like her before. A white woman, certainly. But a redhead? A powerful psychic, firecaster, and part-siren? There was a lot more to her than met the eye.

"What is your name?"

"Reg Rawlins."

He considered this. Reg waited for him to think through whether he had ever heard of her or should have.

"And have you brought a bomb to blow us all up?"

"No. I have brought you a powerful stone."

The General's brows went up, and he leaned forward on his desk, studying her intently. "A powerful stone?"

Reg stayed where she was for a few minutes, then decided to approach him. He didn't draw back or tell her to stop. If she had a weapon, then now was the time to pull it and see whether she could get the drop on him.

But Reg didn't.

She stopped right in front of his large, heavy desk and delved into her pocket. She withdrew the large diamond and displayed it to him, pinched between thumb and forefinger. The General's eyes were greedy.

"Give it to me."

"I have to warn you, before I give it to you…"

"Warn me what? You think you can intimidate me? I am not afraid of a little girl like you." He shook his head. "You may think you have power, but you have nothing. I have had more power than you from the day I was born. A girl like you? You can't even comprehend the kind of power I have."

Reg tried to keep a straight face. Despite his bluster, she didn't sense much magic from him. Maybe he could keep his gifts hidden to an extent, but she didn't think he would be able to keep very much hidden. Maybe he was strong in the family he came from, in his own village, and he had amassed enough soldiers to be able to command what he wanted. But that didn't make him a powerful warlock or wizard.

"This stone is cursed. If you accept it, you will take that curse upon you."

"Cursed?" He laughed. "I am not afraid of your little trinkets. Let me see it."

Reg handed it to him. It at least didn't burn his palm when she placed it in his hand. Better if it behaved itself until he acknowledged that he accepted Reg's gift.

The General turned the stone in the light, examining it. He didn't pull out a jeweler's loupe to examine it. Reg didn't know whether he just saw a large, precious stone, or whether he could feel the magical potential it had. Either one was fine, as long as he accepted it. He would run into problems if he tried to sell it, just as she had. And Reg had no doubt that he would feel the full force of the curse. The man was oppressing the land that had produced the stone. He was terrorizing the people who were the rightful owners of the gem. There was no distance between the gem's past and the General's actions, as there had been with Reg. He was, by his position in the power structure, the one who had stolen the gem from its rightful owners, and it was the holy man's intention that he should suffer the consequences of those actions.

"It is beautiful. Is it real?"

Reg stared at him. He couldn't even tell whether it was real? How would he know whether it had any powers if he couldn't feel it?

"Yes. It's real. Do you need an expert to certify it?"

"I normally only see uncut gems in these parts. Sometimes they fall into my hands, and I sell them in the rough. I don't usually get to see them after they have been cut like this." He turned it in the light to catch the light, sending a shower of reflected light on his desk.

Reg looked away from him. There was a window behind him, and she tried to figure out what direction she was facing. The sun was shining directly in, so it must have been mostly east facing. She tried to remember which side of the citadel Ruan and Calliopia were on. How long would it take her to get back to them once she was done? She wanted to get home. She'd had enough of the poverty and fear. She needed to get out of there before something really bad happened to one of them. It was tempting fate to think that they could stay there and be fine.

"Why did you bring this to me?" the General asked sharply.

Reg looked back at him, startled out of her own thoughts. She considered her answer. "I was asked to."

"Why? A bribe? Who is it from? I've never even heard of you before."

"No, it's not a bribe. I don't think so. One of the villages… they wanted to make a gift to you. But I wasn't given any explanation. I guess they just… felt you deserved it. Maybe it is a thank you."

He shook his head. "Somebody wants something of me. And you have to know. You're the one who brought it."

"You can take it or refuse it," Reg said with a shrug. "It's up to you. Do whichever you want. If you don't want it, I'll take it back away with me. If you want it… it's your choice how you use it. Maybe you want to sell it. It would fetch a king's ransom. Or maybe you want… to put it in a ring and wear it. Or use it in some other way."

"Yes? Like what?"

"I don't know."

The General's expression was hard. He looked at Reg fiercely and, though she tried to avoid his accusing eyes, there was nowhere to go. The room was without adornment; there wasn't even anything interesting to look at, other than the window. Reg stared down at the diamond in his hand instead.

She could feel the General's mind in hers, looking for a way in, probing and pressing and looking for the answers he needed. She could resist him. She had defended herself against much stronger attacks in the past. She didn't know whether he was aware of what he was doing, or if he were just trying to read her face and, in doing so, probed her mind. Or maybe he was aware, but was trying to do it covertly and not to tip her off. She hoped that it was the third option—that he didn't have any powers to speak of. He was just powerful because he had money and a lot of firepower behind him.

"How could I use it?" the General pressed.

Even though he was on the other side of the desk and wasn't touching her, she felt as though he held her pinned. He was stronger than she had given him credit for.

"I was told it was a powerful stone," Reg said. "I don't know what that means. I don't know what you can use it for."

"I think you do."

Reg was itching to get out the door and away from him. What was he going to do? Have her arrested for bringing him a gem more expensive and powerful than anything he had ever seen before? He didn't have any reason to detain her.

"Do you accept the stone? Or should I take it back?" Reg didn't put out her hand to take it from him, but her intention was clear.

The General's lips pursed. "I accept," he agreed finally.

Good. Reg relaxed. She breathed out a long stream of air, relieved. She had been afraid that he wouldn't. That he would send her away with it.

"Then I am done here," Reg said. She nodded to him and took a step back, toward the door. She felt her back hit something and stopped, startled. She hadn't realized she was that close to the wall. She glanced over her shoulder to confirm her position in the room but, in doing so, saw that the wall was still several feet behind her. She had run into nothing.

CHAPTER FORTY-THREE

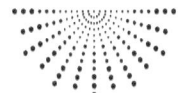

*R*eg reached out all of her senses, trying to verify what was going on. She had run into something, and yet there was nothing to run into. She was standing in the middle of a nearly-empty room. She wasn't against the wall. The General or someone else in his staff had put a force field there to prevent her escape.

"You have the jewel," she told him. "I am leaving now."

"I have the jewel," he agreed. "I would have gotten it out of you one way or another, so you haven't done me any favors. This *gift*, this bribe, is something that I would have gotten anyway. And now I want to know what else you have. What weapons. What valuables. What *power*."

Reg again tried to step back, but her feet felt as if they were glued to the floor, and she still couldn't move past the barrier behind her.

The General heaved his bulk up, pressing his hands against his desk for assistance. Reg struggled against the force that held her in place. Was the General doing it himself or was there someone else she didn't see who was holding her in place? She was strong. She could break free. But it would help her to know who it was that held her.

He walked around his desk to her. He touched her face. "You are very white. I don't think I have ever seen someone with such white skin."

Reg pulled away from him. She could still do that, at least.

"And you braid your hair. Your *red* hair." He ran one thin braid through his fingers. "Is it naturally that color? Or do you color it?"

Reg didn't bother to answer. She didn't see or sense any other opposing force in the room or close by. So he must be acting alone, using his own powers. She tested her powers against his consciousness. He had already opened the door between them, which made it that much easier for her to work her way inside unimpeded. He looked momentarily uncomfortable as she slipped past his defenses. Like he didn't know whether to burp or sneeze. When she was in his mind, he made a snuffling snort and shook his head, then continued as if nothing had happened.

"You come in here, a little girl like you," he sneered, still trying to physically intimidate her. "Against someone like *me*! Didn't they tell you anything about me, these friends of yours? Did they send you in here like a lamb before a lion, as a sacrifice? So defenseless."

Reg ignored his words, exploring his mind instead. She wasn't particularly careful. She knew that it was against the magical community's rules to invade someone's mind without their permission. At least, it was in Black Sands.

But she wasn't in Black Sands anymore.

His mind was full of dark places, fractured and broken. Not the mind of someone who was strong and powerful, but a bully who had been able to make everyone think he was something he was not. He was happy to take the diamond, to magnify his power. Reg wasn't sure, as Benji had been, that it was a good idea. Giving a man like the General more power did not seem like the way to bring him down. He wouldn't stop recruiting the villagers' children and using them to fight the rebel forces. He would keep putting weapons into their hands and seeing how much destruction he could cause. Because he wanted more power and more of everything.

Reg did not like violence. And violence against the General's mind seemed even worse than violence against his body or the security of his fortress. She should not have let anyone put her in this position. She should have told the holy man no. She should never have gone to the General. Someone else could have taken the jewel to him. She should just have gone home.

She steeled herself and pushed hard against his consciousness, letting him know that she was there. If she were going to break free from his grip, she needed to distract him and force him to turn his attention elsewhere.

The General jolted and looked at her in shock. "What...?"

"Knock knock."

His mouth formed a *what* shape and opened and closed like a fish's. Reg did her best to disrupt him, striking out against random memories and processes. The General's hands opened and closed, grasping at something in front of him, maybe trying to stabilize himself somehow.

"Stop!"

Reg didn't. But she shuffled her feet and stepped backward, finding herself free from his hold. She struck out again, stirring up dark memories, triggering a fear response. She could feel it not just in his mind, but pouring off of him in waves, his aura darkening. She backed away from him more quickly, scrabbling behind her for the doorknob. Finding it, she twisted it and pulled the door open.

The General started to bellow. Reg didn't know whether it was gibberish or his native tongue. To her, it just sounded like incoherent shouts. The soldier who had let her in looked up from his post, his eyes wide.

"You'd better get in there," Reg prompted.

He hesitated for a moment, trying to decide whether to detain and question her or to go to his boss, then made the decision to go to the General. Of course he knew that there was no way Reg could find her way out of the compound without help; she would have to get past numerous guards to do so.

Reg hurried to the next door, which opened into a corridor. She lifted her skirt and sprinted down the hall to the next, then hesitated which way to go. She had tried to keep track of the twists and turns, but hadn't been able to hold them all in her head.

A hand grabbed hers. Not the big, iron hand of a guard detaining her, but a small one like a child's. Reg looked down, but didn't see anything but a faint shadow.

"This way!"

She followed the tug on her hand, and they worked their way through the corridors of the place. Reg was sure they weren't going out the same way she had come in, and there were not nearly as many guards to avoid as she had expected. Whenever she slowed, the hand pulled on her hand harder, making her work hard to keep up. She was puffing like a train engine, but at least there was no one around to hear her.

They went through a long underground tunnel—Reg had definitely not gone through any underground tunnels when she had arrived—and when they reached the end of it, climbed the rungs of a ladder into a cave, then followed the dim light and smell of fresh air until they reached the outside, somewhere in the jungle, the compound nowhere in sight.

CHAPTER FORTY-FOUR

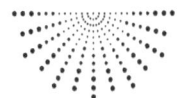

*R*eg collapsed, sitting down on a log and trying to catch her breath. She wiped tears of exertion from her cheeks. "Well. That was fun."

Ruan appeared beside her. "We should not stop here."

"I'll go on in a moment. Please."

He nodded and waited for her to catch her breath. Reg definitely needed to get into better shape. Especially if she were going to be running away from bad guys very often.

"How did you know the way out?" Reg asked. She didn't need to ask how he had gotten in. Clearly, he had followed her while invisible. She wasn't sure how he had gotten through the magical barrier at the gate. Maybe he had been touching her when the guard escorted her through, the three of them entering in a chain. The same way Corvin had been able to get past Reg's gate.

Ruan considered his answer. "By smell. And by memory."

Smell, Reg could understand. His senses were much more sensitive than hers. He could probably smell the guards a mile away. And even Reg had been able to smell the fresh air that led out of the cave.

"By memory? You've been here before?"

"No. But the underground tunnels are more ancient than the buildings. They are in piskies' memories."

Reg frowned. She rubbed more tears away from the corners of her eyes. At least they were slowing now so she didn't look like she was a damsel in distress. "You remember them? How old are you?"

"Not *my* memories." Ruan looked at her intently to see whether she discerned his meaning. He shook his head. "It is a wonder humans live as long as they do. Reg Rawlins has *no* ancestral memories?"

"Uh... no. I mean, I've heard of things... instinct, and genetic memory, and stuff like that. But science can't really tell us anything about how they work. And they aren't memories like the memories that I have from my life."

"Such big brains for so few memories," he said in a tone of awe.

Reg put her fingers to her temples. Her brain was, at the moment, feeling way overtaxed. The struggle with the General, though only brief, had been difficult. And running with Ruan had tired her body. It was still early in the morning, and she wasn't used to getting out of bed early, let alone trekking to a military compound, doing mental battle with a warlock of some sort, and then making her escape.

The ruby had better be worth it.

"We go on now," Ruan suggested. "You are breathing again."

"Yes, okay." Reg pushed herself up from the log. "Lead the way."

He did so and, in a few minutes, they were joined by Calliopia, who rolled her eyes like a bored teenager.

"You take a long time."

"Sorry. I had a job to do. And then there was the escape..."

She shook her head, expressing her irritation. "Now we go home?"

"I was planning to go back to the village first..."

"Why?"

They both looked at her expectantly. Reg thought about it. "Well... I was going to pass the message along that I have given the diamond to the General, like Benji asked. And... to say goodbye. They didn't have much, but they did show us hospitality. I should tell Joseph—"

"The diggers will not be back until the evening. And the village will know that the fat man has the diamond." Ruan shrugged. "Everyone will know that he has the diamond."

"How? Because he'll be looking for a buyer?"

"I do not think he will sell."

"You think he'll use it then, its powers?"

Ruan nodded. Reg felt anxiety land in her stomach again. "Why would Benji ask me to give it to him if he is going to use its powers for his own purposes? Won't that make things worse for him and his people?"

Neither of the others answered immediately, and Reg was afraid she was right. Now, not only did the warlord have a choke hold on the villages in the area, stealing their children for slave labor, soldiers, and wives, but now he had a stone of power that would extend his reach and his abilities. How could that be a good thing?

"The stone is cursed," Calliopia pointed out eventually. "The more he uses it, the more it will enslave him."

"How will it affect him? The cursed stones didn't really affect me."

Calliopia looked at Reg speculatively. She licked her lips. "You did not *use* the stones. You only held them. They like you."

"They like me?" It was the most blatant personification of the gems yet. Reg shook her head and laughed. It was true that she had not used the stones for their power. And she had not tried to acquire more. She had only hidden them away, and then when she had the need, tried to trade them in for money. Apparently, that had kept the gemstones happy.

But she was sure from other stories she'd heard about cursed treasure that the treasure was still cursed and made the owner unlucky even if she didn't know anything about the curse and had come by the stones honestly. Unwitting owners and their family members died because of the curses on them.

"They like you," Calliopia repeated. She looked at Ruan, who nodded his agreement.

"They are... at rest," Ruan said, trying to explain it further. "Not active."

"So I'm safe? I don't have to worry about finding the rightful owners of all the rest?" Reg dreaded having to travel to dispose of each little bag of gems. That was a lot of work. And a lot of danger, if this first trip were any indication.

Maybe just the one quest would be enough. The gemstones would see that she was willing to return them to their original countries, to the people who should have held them, and...

"They will not stay at rest," Ruan explained. "Maybe for a short time. But not forever. They will one day activate."

It sounded like Reg was still in the honeymoon period with her stones. Sooner or later, they would begin to test her. It would be better if she could return them to their people before that happened. She didn't really want to find out just how dangerous the curse of the stones could be.

"Okay. Well, great. Maybe you can help me with the rest?"

Ruan didn't jump at the chance. And why would he? It didn't benefit him if she returned all the gems to their rightful places. He had his own life with Calliopia. They didn't have to answer to anyone and could come and go as they pleased.

"Do we go home now?" Calliopia asked plaintively.

"Yes. Yes, let's go home," Reg agreed.

She reached for both of their hands and thought about home.

CHAPTER FORTY-FIVE

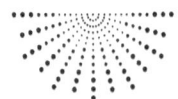

*T*he landings were getting a little smoother. Reg found herself sitting on her couch, with Calliopia and Ruan standing holding her hands. They let go immediately and looked around. Reg gave a long sigh of relief. She was so glad to be back home, like Dorothy at the end of *The Wizard of Oz*.

Starlight jumped up on the kitchen island, where he really wasn't supposed to go, and gave a long, low yowl of disapproval. Calliopia made claw hands and hissed at him. Ruan just looked and said nothing.

"Yes, I'm sorry," Reg apologized. "I know I left you all alone here without any planning. But I'm sure you had enough food in your dish, and Sarah probably gave you more anyway." Reg stood up and went over to him, but he rebuffed her, turning his back to her to jump down from the island and then marching over to his empty bowl.

"I said I'm sorry. But it was only one night. You didn't starve."

Reg turned on the kitchen light. It was dark outside, and the interior was lit by a single lamp in the living room. She opened the fridge and found something that looked like stew. It smelled meaty, so she put a few spoonfuls into Starlight's bowl and set it down on the floor. "There. Okay?"

"We have not eaten," Calliopia pointed out.

Much like a cat.

Reg opened the fridge again and looked for anything that might be suitable for a fairy. She didn't buy milk, but she did get cream for the coffee and tea. And there were a few raw fruits and vegetables, though they were a little more wilted than "crisper drawer" would have one believe. Reg put some cream into a cup and arranged the produce on a plate and took them over to Calliopia. She wrinkled her nose when she looked at them, but she sat down and put them on the coffee table and started to eat.

"What about you?" Reg asked Ruan.

"I am prepared. I saved food from last night." Ruan pulled a few wieners out of his pocket. Reg tried not to roll her eyes or gag. That was just one less body she didn't have to feed. And she herself wasn't ready to eat yet, so she could sit down and relax for a few minutes while Calliopia ate, and then see the couple off. She wasn't sure what she would do then. Maybe watch some TV or lie down for a nap. She was tired and sore after her encounter with the General.

There was the sound of a key in the lock, and Sarah entered. She looked in consternation at the pixie and fairy for a moment, then saw Reg.

"I saw the light. So, you're back."

"Yes. Sorry to disappear without any warning. We had... something that had to be taken care of."

"I tried to call you. But I couldn't get your cell. It said you were out of range."

"Yeah. I guess I was. Sorry about that. But we weren't gone for very long, and I'm back now. Thank you for seeing to Starlight while I was gone."

"A cat doesn't require much care. Though I think he missed you. He was not very happy."

Sarah didn't look very happy herself as she looked at the kitchen table, still occupied with the bags of gems that Reg had sorted earlier.

"You really shouldn't leave these out. I told you before to get a safety deposit box. Leaving them here like this, out in the open. Someone could see or sense them."

"But there are already wards protecting the house and the garden. Who would be able to get in?"

"Someone with more powerful magic. Just because I have woven a spell, that doesn't mean it cannot be defeated or broken. You should know by now that you can't rely upon such things. You still need to beware that someone else's spell could be stronger or there could be a way around it. A spell is only as strong as the person who wove it and the time they put into it."

"Well… okay. I'm sorry about that. I'll take care of them. It won't be a problem."

Sarah glanced at Ruan and Calliopia and didn't say anything, but her mouth was a stern, straight line, a change from her usual demeanor.

"Are you finished with your meal, Calliopia?" Reg prompted. "The two of you will be wanting to get on your way."

Calliopia took a deep drink of the cream. When she put the cup down, she was sporting a white mustache. Reg wondered if it were deliberate defiance or if she were just unconcerned with appearances. "I will take the fruit with me?"

"Yes, go ahead," Reg agreed impatiently. Why not? Reg wasn't going to eat it herself.

Calliopia picked up what remained of her meal. She nodded to Ruan, and the two of them left the cottage, Ruan giving Reg a brief nod as he left.

Sarah waited until the door was shut, but the pixie and fairy were probably not out of earshot, considering how sensitive their ears were. "You really should not have folk like that in the house."

"I needed Ruan's help."

Sarah looked at the gems on the table. "With your stones? You couldn't find a human who could help you?"

"Well, no. Since it's apparently bad manners for humans to discuss cursed stones. You didn't have any suggestions. Corvin was going to look some stuff up, but it sounded like that might take forever and a day. So I talked to Ruan, and he helped me."

"Helped himself to the stones, more likely. How many did he take with him?"

"None."

"You'd better make a thorough search of the house to make sure that he hasn't left something behind. If he did, he can come back later when there is no one here, and he will make off with all of them."

"I'll look. But I kept a pretty close eye on them. Besides, he knows they are cursed, so why would he bother to steal them?"

"Pixies are not like us. Don't judge what one of them would do based on what a human would do. They believe that all gems belong to them."

"I know. But I really don't think he's going to try to steal my gems."

Sarah just raised an eyebrow.

"I'll look," Reg promised again. "I will."

Sarah looked around one last time, but apparently couldn't think of anything else to warn or criticize Reg about, and left it at that.

"Well, you can feed the cat now, so I'll leave you to it. I'm glad you're back safe and sound from… wherever you were."

* * *

Reg gathered together the bags of gems, putting them one at a time into the small wooden chest. She had the ruby she had gotten back from the holy man, together with the gems that she and Ruan had both sensed were not cursed. When she was up to it, she could go back to Dreame or The Sapphire Exchange and sell one or two of them to get her bank account balance up to a level that made her comfortable so that she could buy groceries and kitty litter.

She wouldn't sell the ruby, which she sensed she was supposed to hang on to. Maybe she could learn about its powers or the powers of hers that it could magnify. But there were also multiple bags of gems from other locations around the globe. They weren't active yet, so she could afford to take a little while, maybe just take one trip every few weeks to repatriate a bag of gems to its rightful owners. And sooner or later, she would be done and wouldn't have the threat of gems possibly becoming angry and making her or someone in her circle of friends sick.

As Reg packed the last couple of bags into the chest, she realized she was not alone. She whirled around, immediately thinking of Sarah's warning that someone who was more powerful than she was might be able to break through the protective wards to steal the gems. It wasn't so much that she was afraid they would be stolen, as what else a powerful witch or warlock might do to her. If someone stole cursed gems... he would get what he had coming to him.

But there was no burglar behind her. Instead, Harrison sat watching her, his long legs stretched out with his feet resting on the coffee table. He was wearing a pink silk shirt with something printed on it and flowing black pantaloons. Reg took a step or two closer, squinting at the shirt. It looked suspiciously like the patterned print was of black cats. Maybe tuxedo cats like Starlight. Or were they pure black cats like the kattakyns?

"Get your feet off the table," she told Harrison firmly.

He looked at her for a moment, then pulled them off and bent his knees to put his feet on the floor where they belonged.

"Why are feet not allowed on the table?" he asked seriously, as if it were an important question he had about the universe.

"Because feet are dirty. It is rude to put them on the table, where people eat."

"But my feet are not dirty. And this is not an eating table."

"It's still rude."

He raised his brows, but didn't argue about it.

"I didn't call you," Reg said. "Are you here for a reason?"

"There is always a reason."

Reg waited for more, but Harrison did not explain. "I suppose there is," Reg conceded. "Are you here to talk?"

"I am talking."

"Why did you come?" Reg demanded, frustrated.

"I came to see my goddaughter. And her cat." Harrison looked around, but Starlight had not come out at Harrison's appearance, as he normally did.

"He's pouting. He's upset with me for leaving."

"Perhaps you should not have left."

Was that a warning? That she had done something she shouldn't or that she would run into problems if she continued to try to repatriate all the cursed gems? Or was it just an inane comment by an immortal who didn't understand the ways of humans?

"Starlight?" Reg called. "Aren't you going to come out to see Harrison? Harrison didn't do anything to bother you."

He didn't come out. Reg frowned, starting to feel anxious about

Starlight's reluctance to come out. He always loved it when Harrison visited.

"Perhaps he has gone somewhere else," Harrison suggested. "Maybe to go see one of the kittens."

Reg shot him a look. "How could he go see one of the kittens? He doesn't have any way to get out of this house without me seeing him. And how would he travel all around the world on his own?"

"The same way you did."

"But I... he's a cat. He doesn't have the same powers."

Reg hurried to the bedroom to reassure herself that Starlight was there and hadn't magically disappeared to visit one of the kattakyns or someone else. She knew he was upset with her for leaving, but it wouldn't have prompted him to leave, would it?

Reg pushed the bedroom door open the rest of the way, holding her breath, worried she would find the room empty.

Starlight was sitting on the windowsill where he often did, watching out the window.

"What are you looking at?" Reg asked, relieved. "Didn't you hear me? Harrison is here. Don't you want to see him?"

Starlight licked his white tuxedo bib, then jumped down from the windowsill, taking his own sweet time about it. He followed her out to the living room and approached Harrison, not even looking at Reg.

"So, you can come here when you want to visit a cat," Reg suggested. "You don't need to go where the kattakyns are."

"The kattakyns?" Harrison asked innocently.

"Destine's kattakyns. You know you need to stay away from them, right?"

"Do I?"

"Yes. You do. We can't risk doing anything that might allow him to re-form as the Witch Doctor. It's too dangerous."

Harrison shrugged. "Perhaps he could take another form," he suggested. He picked Starlight up and held him in front of his face in an undignified pose. "As a cat!" he suggested.

"No. We don't want that. We don't want him to re-form at all. He needs to stay bound."

"An immortal cannot be bound forever."

Francesca had said that the binding might give way in a thousand years. By that time, Reg expected to be dead and gone and forgotten. She wouldn't have to worry about the Witch Doctor and his powers then. She wasn't keen on anything that might reduce the Witch Doctor's term of imprisonment to a year or two.

"Maybe not, but he can be bound for a thousand years. And that's the way we want him to stay. Got it?"

Harrison lowered Starlight to his lap. "Got it?" he echoed.

"No. You say 'got it,'" Reg told him.

"I did."

"No, you didn't. You said it as a question. I want you to say it as a statement. As an agreement that you won't do anything to allow the spell to unravel before that. You won't go visit the kattakyns, and you won't move them to other places, and you won't unbind them so that they can find each other and re-form the Witch Doctor. Or any other form."

Harrison gazed at her, looking perplexed. He petted Starlight in long, even strokes.

"Tell me you got it," Reg encouraged. "You won't do anything to change that."

He didn't answer. Reg closed her eyes, shaking her head. She opened them again, drawing in her breath to give him clear instructions, but he was gone.

Starlight lay on the couch by himself, his tail whipping back and forth.

TIME TO YOUR ELF

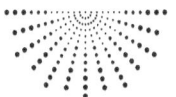

REG RAWLINS, PSYCHIC INVESTIGATOR
#14

To those who want to move forward instead of back

CHAPTER ONE

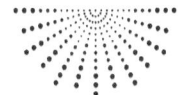

The sun was down and Reg was feeling energized as she looked through the appointment book on her kitchen island. It felt good to have some business coming in again. Her bank account had almost dwindled away to nothing and she had been feeling the pinch.

But she had come back from her most recent adventure determined to get things running again, and her efforts were definitely paying off. There was at least one appointment scheduled every night for the next couple of weeks, and in some cases a couple of readings and a seance.

She had been worried that she wouldn't be able to get any work. There had been quite a reaction in the paranormal community when they discovered that her mother was a siren, and the backlash had not been pleasant. But her landlord, Sarah, had been correct when she had said that it would settle down and people would forget all about it in a few weeks when it was no longer big news. The work was coming back in, and Sarah's wards and charms kept the more militant witches away from the yard and cottage so that they didn't have to keep cleaning raw egg off Reg's front door and the remnants of spells and curses that had been left behind in the yard. All in all, things had been pretty peaceful the last couple of weeks, letting Reg get back into the swing of things.

There was a tap on the door and Sarah let herself in. The older woman was dressed for a night out. A green sequined dress clung to her curves and, despite her more mature figure and a bit of extra padding around the middle, she looked very fetching. Reg was sure that she would have a fun night with whatever group of friends she was hanging out with.

"Just thought I would check in before we go," Sarah announced, smiling. Starlight came running in from the bedroom and jumped up on the island counter, yowling at Sarah in a pleading, plaintive voice that clearly announced that Reg had been neglecting him and no one ever fed him when Sarah was not around.

"Don't believe him!" Reg warned.

"Oh, I know he exaggerates," Sarah agreed. She petted Starlight. "But I don't think it would hurt for me to give him a little treat, do you?"

"For a beast who is starving, he's getting pretty fat," Reg observed. "You'd better not give him too much. I'm going to have to start giving him that special food for overweight cats." She looked Starlight in the eyes, one of them blue and one of them green. "That low calorie, high fiber kibble."

Starlight made a cross meow and turned to look at Sarah and to rub lovingly against her hand.

"You're all ready for your readings tonight." Sarah looked Reg over and gave an approving nod.

Reg didn't know how Sarah could get up so early in the morning when she stayed out half the night with her friends. Weren't old people supposed to need more sleep than younger folks? Even if Sarah only looked to be in her sixties, Reg knew—or at least had been told—that she was actually centuries old. So she should need a lot of sleep, shouldn't she?

But Sarah was always up before Reg was and *tsked* and shook her head over the fact that Reg didn't usually manage to get dressed for the day before noon. Young people these days.

"Good to go," Reg agreed. "I'm just going to grab a bite to eat before my first appointment arrives." She looked down at the book. "Eugene Franklin."

"Eugenia," Sarah corrected. "You'd best get that right!"

"Oh." Reg looked at it again. The letters were carefully printed, but Reg had only glanced at the first few letters and assumed the rest. She was not the best reader and used a lot of shortcuts. Sometimes that worked and sometimes it didn't. "So… Eugenia. That must be a woman."

"Yes."

"Got it."

There was another tap on the door, and Reg looked over to see Letticia, the older witch who led Sarah's coven. While Letticia's lined face always looked serious and foreboding, Reg had learned not to make assumptions from her looks. Letticia had helped Reg out in the past and was not quick to prejudge her as others had. She was a lot more compassionate than she looked.

"Are we ready?"

"Just one moment. I need to get the cat something to eat."

Reg rolled her eyes.

Letticia tilted her head and looked amused. "I don't think that cat is going to starve. For someone who claims not to like the creatures, you do tend to put a lot of time into this one."

"Well, somebody should keep an eye on things."

Letticia shook her head slightly, but didn't point out that Reg was standing right there and the cat was clearly not starving to death as he claimed. She waited patiently while Sarah found some tuna and put a spoonful in Starlight's dish. Starlight jumped down from the counter and started to wolf it down.

"What are you guys doing tonight?" Reg asked.

It was probably not a coven night, since Sarah usually dressed in formal black for those. But Reg supposed some of the witches from the coven might go out together for a social activity. It wasn't all chants and spells.

"There is a new club in the city that we are going to check out."

Letticia was not dressed in a slinky, sequined dress like Sarah. Letticia didn't have Sarah's curves and probably wouldn't be comfortable in something like that. She wore black slacks and a satiny blouse that came up high on her neck. She wouldn't have looked out of place in church or a courtroom, but Reg wondered what kind of club Letticia would feel at home in. Maybe they had a seniors' night.

"Well, you girls have fun and don't stay out too late," Reg told them with a smile.

Sarah gave Starlight one final pet and nodded. "I hope your evening goes well. You really should come out with us one night and relax. Too much work will just burn you out. You need to regenerate too."

"Yeah. Maybe some night," Reg agreed, though she had no intention of going out partying with the older ladies.

"Marian is coming too," Letticia said. "It isn't all witches."

Marian was a psychic like Reg. Her competition. In the beginning, Reg hadn't gotten along with her. Marian had been adversarial toward Reg. Jealous of the work that she was picking up, maybe, or the reputation she was getting for being one of the better psychics in town. In Black Sands, there was no lack of psychics and other practitioners to compete with.

But they had reached a tentative truce. Marian had even sent a couple of referrals over to Reg recently and Reg was watching for the opportunity to send some business back Marian's way. It was better if they cooperated, or at least didn't openly compete with each other.

The two older witches were soon on their way, and Reg looked in the fridge for something that would be good for a quick bite to eat before Eugene showed up.

CHAPTER TWO

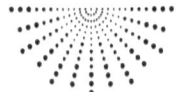

*E*ven after meeting the thin blonde, Reg kept thinking of her as Eugene, which didn't help the reading go particularly well. She tried not to be distracted by the woman's unusual name, but she kept worrying that she would slip out with "Eugene" during the reading.

Despite her distraction, Reg was able to give the woman a few tidbits that she thought were worth her money, so Eugenia went away satisfied with the session. At least, as far as Reg could tell. Maybe the woman thought she was just an idiot or a charlatan, but if she did, she didn't announce the fact or think it obviously enough for Reg to read. Hopefully, she would tell her friends that Reg was the real thing and get them to sign up. Reg had started to offer referral discounts so that if Eugenia got her friends to sign up for sessions, Eugenia could get a lower rate at her next reading. That encouraged repeat business and referrals, both of which were helpful to Reg in rebuilding her business.

Her next appointment was a seance for a group of friends, one of whom had received the session as a birthday gift. Oddly enough, seances were an increasingly popular birthday gift, at least around Black Sands. Reg was happy to take advantage of the trend. She enjoyed doing seances. The energy of the group was a boost, and in the odd event that there were not enough spirits around to provide commentary

—and Reg rarely lacked for extra voices in her head—it was easy to ad lib and keep the clients happy.

"This is Sharon," one of the women pointed to a dark-haired Latino girl. "She turns *thirty* today! At midnight! And this is Rachel, Sunny, Deb, and I'm April."

Reg blinked at the quick succession of names. "You might need to remind me if I get the names wrong," she apologized in advance. It might be a good idea for her to start supplying groups with stick-on name tags so that she didn't have to remember them all. It just wasn't a good idea to call people by the wrong name in the middle of a seance. It could be brushed off as the mistake of a confused spirit or perhaps the name from a past life, but it was always best to get them right in the first place.

"We'll let you know!" April laughed. "We're always confusing people. Should we sit down here?" She gestured to the dining room table, eager to get right to it.

"Sure," Reg agreed. "Make yourselves comfortable. Does anyone want tea? Drinks?"

"Drinks!" one of the women, perhaps Deb, echoed excitedly.

"You've already had enough margaritas," Sharon told her. "If you keep it up, you won't remember anything about tonight. How about tea?"

"No, drinks," the others protested as a group.

Sharon shook her head at Reg and rolled her eyes. "I guess it's drinks," she sighed.

"Shall I make you a tea? I can…"

"No, no point in going to the extra work. I'll have the same as everyone else."

Beverages were arranged and, in a few minutes, everyone was sitting at the table, drinks in hand, giggling nervously about the upcoming seance. With them so well-lubricated, Reg didn't foresee any problems. They would all be very suggestible. The only question would be whether they *would* remember it in the morning. If they didn't remember the seance, they couldn't exactly recommend her to others.

"Okay, if you are all ready, we'll get started. Is there someone in particular that you are trying to reach? Or a question that you would like answered?"

They all looked at each other, reluctant to speak up first.

"Birthday girl?" Reg suggested, looking at Sharon.

Sharon shrugged, blushing. "I don't know. I've never done anything like this before. It's just kind of a gag."

Reg nodded, smiling, so that Sharon would know that she wasn't offended. "A lot of people come just on a whim, to see what they get out of it. That's okay. Nothing then? Nothing special?"

Sharon shrugged and shook her head. "No... just, whatever. I guess. Will you do that thing where you say there is a spirit whose name starts with G and does anyone know someone who died whose name started with the letter G?"

"No. I don't do that. I can see who a spirit is attached to, if they are attached to someone. And sometimes, it's just one of the spirits that I'm familiar with, who might have a message or insight to be passed on. It just depends on who speaks to me."

"Does someone always speak to you?"

Reg shrugged. "That's what I'm here for."

"So you're a real medium? This is real?"

Reg pointed to the placard on the table. *For entertainment purposes only.* That little disclaimer that kept her from getting charged for fraud by people who decided they didn't like what she had to say or thought that she wasn't a real medium. She preferred to keep the police out of her life, if she could.

"Oh." Sharon nodded, looking disappointed.

"Let's join hands," Reg suggested. She sat down in her seat at the end of the table and held out a hand to each of the women sitting next to her. The girls quieted immediately, and everybody put down their drinks for the moment and grasped each other's hands.

Reg rolled her eyes upward and listened to the voices, waiting for one of them to come to the forefront.

"We reach out to the spirit world," she announced, "on behalf of this group of friends. Do any of the spirits have messages to be passed on?"

There were plenty of voices. A lot of them fought and bickered with each other like old married couples, they had been with her for so long.

"Perhaps someone here has recently lost a loved one?" Reg suggested. "Or maybe someone looking for love?"

There was a ripple of laughter around the circle, which seemed to be directed at April. Reg felt a surge in the energy level, and watched a rosy aura develop around April. A seeker. Reg could find one in most groups. The one person who was most likely to believe what they saw and heard. Not a dupe, exactly, but the one who really wanted to receive a message.

"April," Reg intoned. She listened to the voices whispering around her. She closed her eyes most of the way but could still see the faux candles flickering in their jars around the room. Little twinkle lights, because it was too dangerous for her to have real candles in the house without an experienced firecaster around to make sure that Reg didn't accidentally burn the whole house down around her. That would not impress Sarah. "April has come looking for love."

I see, a voice whispered in her ear, *let me tell you what I see.*

"Do you have a message for April?" Reg asked, wanting to make sure that she didn't give a message to the wrong person. It would be just like some impatient spirit to speak up and pass along a message intended for someone else. They needed a bit of managing.

Yes. A message for April, the spirit insisted.

"What message do you have?"

A stranger he is, but soon they will meet.

Reg spoke the words in her own voice and gave herself over to the spirit to give the rest of the message.

Handsome but dangerous. The man in black. He will come soon.

Handsome but dangerous. Reg gave a little shiver at the words, thinking of Corvin. She couldn't think of who fit the description better. The warlock was one of the most attractive men Reg had ever seen. Maybe the most handsome she had ever met in person. And his magical charms made him even more desirable. And for an unsuspecting woman who didn't know that he could steal magical gifts, he was very dangerous. He was very clever at getting his own way. Reg could not recall the morning she had woken up to silence in her head without a shudder and a sense of deep loneliness and loss. He had given her powers back to her, something that was never, ever done, but the circumstances had been unusual.

Reg never wanted to feel that emptiness again.

And she never wanted anyone else to experience it either.

"Be careful," she warned April, opening her eyes and being sure to meet the other woman's gaze. "Please beware."

April nodded. But her eyes were shining with excitement. She wouldn't be careful. She would be looking for this handsome stranger wherever she went now, eager to meet him and fulfill the prophecy.

Reg opened her mouth to inquire whether there were more messages for the group or whether there were other questions that the women hoped to have answered.

But something strange was happening in the living room. Reg blinked her eyes a few times and tried to focus on the dancing lights that had suddenly materialized. They swirled around like fireflies, or like moths around a light, but Reg couldn't tell where the light originated.

The women started to ask questions. Most just wanted to know what Reg had seen, why she was so distracted. Or wondering whether it was some kind of show she was putting on. But April gasped, her eyes focused on the swirling lights.

"What is that? How are you doing that?"

"It's not me," Reg told her.

They both watched the space, mesmerized.

CHAPTER THREE

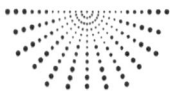

*A*s Reg and April stared, the lights multiplied, swarming around each other, with more and more of them appearing until they nearly formed a solid mass. And then they were solid. Or *he* was solid.

A man. Surely it wasn't April's handsome stranger already. The spirits' prophecies were rarely fulfilled quite so promptly.

The women were all silent, mouths hanging open. Reg gathered that even the less receptive ones could see him now. They were all wondering how she had made a man appear out of thin air.

And so was Reg.

He *was* handsome. Rugged, with long golden-brown hair, dark eyes that twinkled, and dark clothing that seemed to shift and change color as he looked around. He had a closely shaved beard that added just the right touch of masculinity to his gentle face.

But dangerous? Was this the handsome and dangerous stranger?

"Who are you?" Reg asked.

The man looked around at them all as if confused. He put on a pair of dark glasses, which couldn't have helped him to see, clothing the already dim room in complete darkness. He took them off again and looked at Reg, as if checking to see whether she were still there.

"I am Orri."

"Orri. Why are you here? Why have you appeared before us?"

"Well…" He looked around the table in consternation. "I didn't mean to appear to *all* of you."

Reg laughed. "They were prepared for a spiritual manifestation, so…"

He touched his chest. "But I am not a spiritual manifestation."

"Oh? What are you then?" Reg was not put off. Spirits frequently did not believe that they were dead until they were confronted with incontrovertible proof.

"I am physical." He blinked at her. "Aelf."

"What?"

"I am Aelf."

"I thought you said you were Orri."

"I am." He gave a nod of confirmation. "Orri. Of the Aelf folk."

"An elf?" Reg asked, trying not to let her voice rise in excitement at the possibility. It was rare for humans to see elves, and she had been visited by them once before. The odds of having a second visit from elves was astronomical.

"Yes," Orri nodded. "Elf."

Reg remembered the lights that had danced around and the sounds of bells that accompanied them on their last visit. She should have guessed that the dancing lights had something to do with elves.

"We are honored to have you here. Can I… get you anything?"

Fairies, she knew, liked milk. But elves? She had no idea what kind of a diet they ate, and whether they drank tea or alcohol or milk. Maybe they weren't even allowed to eat or drink in human houses. She knew next to nothing about their race.

"Perhaps… mead?" Orri suggested.

Reg was flummoxed. She looked at her human guests around the table, but none of them appeared to be capable of speech, let alone able to tell her what mead was. Reg knew it was sometimes served at the community parties, and that fairies were particularly partial to it, but she didn't know what it was. She was pretty sure there wasn't any in her cupboards and fridge, even with how well Sarah kept them stocked.

"Uh…"

Orri's eyes traveled over the women at the table and their cups. "Wine?"

Reg nodded with relief. "Yes. Wine. I can get you wine."

She stood up and went to the kitchen to pour him a generous glass of wine. She hoped that it wasn't too cheap. She didn't want to offend a person of another magical race by offering him an inferior beverage. Reg didn't buy the cheapest wine at the store, but it wasn't exactly premier stuff either. Nice enough to keep groups of women like April and her friends happy, but not anything a connoisseur like Corvin would compliment.

She walked over to the elf slowly, worried about scaring him off with any sudden movement. She was a bit anxious around creatures that could disappear in the blink of an eye. But Orri did not appear to be worried by her and did not disappear. He took the wine goblet from her with a polite nod. Reg bent her knees in a slight curtsy, not sure what else to do.

A curtsy? Reg had no clue what the proper protocol was. Why couldn't it have been a night where there were other practitioners present who could help her out and explain things to her? Reg never asked her clients whether they had any magical experience or not, but she could usually tell. And April and her friends gave no indication that they knew that real magic even existed.

"Is there... a reason you're here?" Reg asked tentatively, after the elf had a sip of the wine and didn't spit it back in her face. "Did you want to see one of these women?"

"You are Reg Rawlins?"

Reg nodded. She felt butterflies in her stomach over the elf knowing her name. She had a reputation among the elves? She hoped it was for something good, not something she had done wrong. He was there to see her. She assumed that if she had done something wrong, he wouldn't want to see her.

"Yes, I'm Reg."

"My message is for you."

"For me? Not for..." Reg motioned to the women seated around the table, "You're sure it isn't for one of them? They came to make contact with the spirits..."

"I am not a spirit," Orri pointed out. "I am corporeal." He patted his chest as if to demonstrate his solidity. Of course, he had already been drinking wine, which was a pretty good indicator that he had a physical body. If he didn't have a body, the wine would just dribble to the floor, wouldn't it?

"Yes, you are. I just thought that since they were looking for messages, maybe you had a message for them."

"No."

There was a little sigh of disappointment from April. She'd been hoping that the message was for her. Maybe more about the handsome stranger. Or maybe Orri *was* the handsome stranger. But he did not appear to be there for her. If she wanted to attract his attention, she would have to work pretty hard.

"Okay." Reg steeled herself. "What is your message?"

It probably wouldn't be good. In Reg's experience, unexpected messages from beyond were rarely good news. Why did omens always have to be of evil? Why couldn't they be good, at least half the time?

"This is my message," Orri announced. He held his hand up dramatically for silence. It wasn't as if there were a bunch of conversations going on around him. He took a deep breath and announced his message to Reg. "Beware fair folk bearing gifts."

CHAPTER FOUR

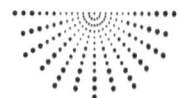

$\mathcal{R}$eg looked at him, waiting for more. That couldn't be the whole thing. She stared at Orri, waiting for him to finish. "That's... not it, is it?"

Orri nodded. He looked disappointed that this had not gotten a better reaction out of her. He had clearly thought that it would have an impact.

Reg smiled reassuringly. It was a good warning message; it just wasn't one that would be of any help to her.

Reg had already received a gift from the fairies. Orri was right, of course, she should have been more careful and maybe even not have accepted the gift in the first place. Fairy gifts, she had since found out, rarely brought the receiver any kind of joy or good luck. Fairies tended to take away at the same time as they gave, so that a person might end up with less than they started with. And might have a lot of bad luck or magic to contend with.

"It's good advice," Reg told Orri reassuringly. "It's just that... I already accepted a gift from the fairies. And I already figured out that it wasn't such a good idea. I appreciate you coming all this way just to let me know..." Who knew how long or far he had traveled? If he was supposed to give her the warning before she had received the gift, then he was months overdue.

"You already know?" Orri repeated.

Reg nodded.

Orri slapped himself on the forehead. "You already know! It's too late! This was the wrong time!"

"It's okay," Reg assured him. "I'm really grateful that you came to tell me. That was very thoughtful of you. It's just that I already know."

"The fair folk..."

Reg nodded. "The Papillon family of the fairies. I know. You're right. I should have been more careful. But it's all been straightened out now, so..."

Of course, claiming that it was all straightened out was more than a bit of a fib. Reg had managed to deal with some of the gems, but there would be many more trips and consultations needed before she could trace all of them... it was a big job, but hopefully Reg had the time she needed to do it.

Orri didn't need to know all the details. Just that Reg already knew everything she needed to and he didn't have to worry about it.

Orri took a large swig of the wine. Reg shrugged and grimaced. "I am sorry."

He looked at the table and the women interrupted mid-seance.

"You talk to spirits?"

Reg nodded. "That's what I do. These are clients, people who want to communicate with spirits or... otherworldly folk. Maybe you could give them a message too."

Orri looked doubtful, starting to shake his head.

"Come on," Reg prompted in a whisper. "You can just tell them something vague and mysterious sounding. They won't know what it means, but they'll think it's wonderful."

Orri hesitated.

"They were already told to watch for a handsome stranger." Reg fluttered her eyelashes at him. "And... here you are."

He actually blushed. Reg couldn't contain a laugh. She tried to keep a serious expression, but it was impossible.

"Maybe..." He looked at the women, trying to come up with something.

"Maybe you could give them my warning. It's a pretty general one.

No one should accept gifts from fairies without due caution, should they?"

He shook his head in agreement. He straightened, puffing out his chest slightly and looking at the women with a beatific expression. "Beware fair folk bearing gifts," he announced importantly.

There was a gasp from the women at the table. They started to whisper to each other. Reg glanced at them for a moment, and when she looked back at Orri, something was happening. The fireflies and moths were swirling around him again, bright spots of light swirling around and around, closing in on him until he was obscured from view, and then dissipating, the cloud of insects getting smaller and smaller until just a few stray lights floated around the room.

"Best birthday gift ever!" Sharon announced.

CHAPTER FIVE

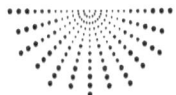

*R*eg slept restlessly after her guests were gone, wound up by all the excitement. She had pushed all thoughts of the fairy gems to the side while she'd been working on building up her business again. A person could only work on so many things at once. But the visit from Orri had reminded her that she needed to be dealing with the fairy gems, and not keep putting it off. It would take a long time to deal with all of them, so she should get started before they became a problem. Take one bite at a time. That was the way to eat an elephant. Or so she had been told.

Reg had never been very good at starting a big project. She got bogged down by the details and everything that she could see had to be done, and had problems breaking it down into smaller, manageable steps. One thing she had learned about herself was that she should just do *something*. Even if it were the wrong thing or started her off in the wrong direction, it was the easiest way to get some traction and to figure out whether she was going the right direction or not. Otherwise, she could be left fussing about a project for days, months, or years without any forward movement.

The first thing she could think of to do with the gems was to see whether she could liquidate a few of the ones that had already been cleansed. At least it would be possible to get rid of the cleansed gems, converting them into cash that she could deposit into her bank account. And the first people she thought of who might be interested in stones of power were the dwarfs. At least, the first people she could think of who would pay money for them. Plenty of others would try to steal them or to claim rightful ownership over them without giving anything in return.

She had the phone number for Gwythr, one of the dwarfs who she had talked to the last time she had visited the dwarf mountain with Corvin, Davyn, and the others. The phone rang a few times before it was picked up, and Reg wondered whether Gwythr might be out of range.

She had not expected the dwarfs to be able to get a good cell signal underground, but they had seemed to operate pretty well. She thought they might have some kind of signal booster underground. Or maybe they ran on a completely different service provider or kind of infrastructure.

Eventually, the call connected. "It is Reg Rawlins!" Gwythr announced enthusiastically.

"It is," Reg agreed, unable to suppress a smile at his excited tone. "How are you doing, Gwythr?"

"I am well! And thou?"

"I'm doing pretty good." And it was true. Reg had gone through some difficult times in the recent past, but she was in a good place with her business picking up and people talking to her again. Things would work out.

"You are calling to inquire after Nico, Warrior Cat?"

Reg hadn't been calling about Nico in particular, but she was interested in how he was faring with the dwarfs. And it was important to hear about him for other reasons.

Although Nico looked just like any other black cat, he was far from normal. Shortly after Reg's arrival in Black Sands, the Witch Doctor, an immortal going by the name Samyr Destine, had been raising a zombie-like race known as draugr to do his bidding. The draugr could shift into the form of a small black cat, a kattakyn, to enable them to get from one place to another unobtrusively. When Reg and the others had done battle with the Witch Doctor, he had sent what was left of his being out into the nine kattakyns to escape annihilation. Francesca, a charmer, had been able to bind the kattakyns in that form, so that they could not shift back into draugr again. Francesca and Reg had found new homes for the nine kittens around the world, each with a practitioner suited to their personality and abilities.

This would, Francesca promised, keep the witch doctor from being able to re-form for at least a thousand years.

But that had been on the assumption that no one would be able to undo the binding and that the kattakyns would be unable to find each other for a long time once the binding wore off.

But things had changed.

Reg took a deep breath. Nico was her favorite of the kattakyns. A mischievous, hyperactive, terror of a kitten who attacked her, broke lamps and vases, climbed the curtains, and defended her from the dwarfs when Reg had initially met them. The dwarfs, in turn, venerated the little black warrior cat and had made him custom armor. Nico had stayed to train with them when Reg and her friends had returned to Black Sands. It was the best home they could have found for him.

"Yes, of course," Reg agreed. "How is Nico?"

"He has learned much," Gwythr told her. "He is growing very strong and is getting bigger. We have had to refit his armor several times. You would hardly recognize him now."

Reg hoped with a pang that she would recognize him if she ever saw him again. And that he would recognize and remember her. He had never been her pet; she had known when she took him off Francesca's hands that it would only be for a short period of fostering before they found him a permanent home. But she still thought of him with fondness.

She understood Nico at a level that most others did not. His hyperactivity and distractibility. The way that he wouldn't or couldn't conform to the rules and type of relationship that seemed to come naturally to other cats. Reg knew what it was like to be different. She had never fit into the foster families she had lived with. She had always been an outsider, only there temporarily until her social worker could find her somewhere better. But the perfect home and family had never materialized, and when she had aged out of foster care, she was already on the street, trying to find a way to make it on her own.

But Nico had, hopefully, found his forever home.

"He's happy there?"

"Yes, very happy. He enjoys the training and the fighting. He is very skilled."

"That's good." She hoped that he had someone he could cuddle with at night too. That he was more than just a warrior cat that had to fight every day for his keep. He needed someone to take care of him too. "I'm really glad that he found such a good home with you."

"As are we," Gwythr agreed.

"I also was wondering…"

"What can the dwarfs do for the great Reg Rawlins?"

"Well, I thought that I might be able to do something for you."

"Indeed?"

"I have come across… well, I have some precious stones that I thought you might be interested in."

"Stones," Gwythr repeated.

In her mind's eye, Reg could see him nodding and stroking his long beard. When she had last seen Gwythr, he had been wearing a Cookie Monster t-shirt and jeans, with a sword on a belt. The mixture of modern and traditional dwarfwear was a little jarring.

"I could send you some pictures," she offered, "if you would like to look at them. And I have an evaluation from a jeweler, with the weight and cut and clarity and all that."

"Yes, that would be helpful," the dwarf agreed. "But why have you not sold them to this jeweler?"

"Well… that's a good question, I guess. You see… these gems have a bit of a history…"

"All gems have a history."

"Of course." Reg imagined that most of the gems that the dwarfs acquired were probably ones that they had mined themselves. Maybe they had been passed down from generation to generation over the years. Though maybe they had bought a few on Amazon or eBay. But the gems that she held had a more… storied past. "They were… uh… cursed for some time."

Gwythr cleared his throat.

"They aren't anymore. They have been cleansed. And I could sell them to a regular jeweler in the city. But some of them are more power-ful, and I would rather find them a good home with someone I know.

Somewhere I know they would be safe, and not be stolen again. Where their power would be used... in *positive* ways."

She did not want them to end up in the hands of a magical warlord like General Mbombo. She had seen the kind of harm that a man like he was could cause. The maimed villagers. The child soldiers. The poverty of the people who were pulling one of the world's most precious resources out of the mud.

"We appreciate that," Gwythr acknowledged. "Most humans do not understand how gems need to be properly cared for."

"Yeah. I didn't used to. But now that I know how they can be damaged by misuse and the trouble they can cause, I didn't want to sell them to just anyone. They could end up anywhere. I wouldn't have any control over it."

"You cannot control where they would go from here, either."

A heaviness settled in Reg's stomach. She had hoped that if she sold them to the dwarfs, they would be guaranteed to stay in the dwarf mountain. The dwarfs would keep them as heirlooms and not sell them anywhere else.

"No, I guess not. But I think that... someone like a dwarf who understood gems would be careful about who he sold such gems to, or how he used them."

There was a brief silence from Gwythr. She wondered whether he was thinking this over or had muted his mic and was talking to someone else in the background, going over strategies and negotiations. Eventually, there was a soft click and he spoke again.

"We will need to discuss this. Send me the pictures and specs. We might need to send someone to have a look at them firsthand."

"Okay. That sounds good. I'll send you the information." Reg let out her breath slowly, hoping the tension in her muscles would soften. "Give Nico an ear-scratch for me. He's really doing well?"

"He fares very well," Gwythr assured her.

"And... no one has come to see him?"

"Come to see him." Gwythr's voice hardened. "Who would come to see him? Has Reg Rawlins sent a delegation?"

"No. I haven't sent anyone. If anyone shows up to see him, it isn't because of me. I'm trying to make sure that no one bothers him."

"Why then? Who would bother him?"

"No one. I don't think." Reg thought of Harrison, and how to explain him to the dwarfs. Her immortal godfather? A powerful magical being with a penchant for cats and chocolate cake? Someone who didn't much care about human lives that could be lost while he and his kind amused themselves?

"Who?" Gwythr insisted.

"There is… a magical being. I don't know. I haven't told him where to find Nico, but I think he could search him out if he wanted to. He has… visited some of Nico's litter mates recently. I just want to make sure that he can't get near Nico."

"What does this being want with him?"

"I can't be sure. He likes cats. Maybe… he knew Nico in a previous incarnation. An old friend… I can't really understand it very well."

"When will he come?"

"I don't know whether he will. I hope not. But just… be aware."

"We shall," Gwythr agreed, his voice low and gravelly. "This person shall not bother our warrior cat."

CHAPTER SIX

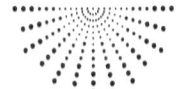

$\mathcal{R}$eg hung up the phone after talking to Gwythr. She focused on Starlight, who was sitting directly in front of her, staring at her intently. She hadn't even been aware of him during the phone call with Gwythr. But she was sure that he had heard every word and had probably understood the situation better than either of them.

"I'm sure it will be fine," Reg told him. "Right? I'm just worrying over nothing."

He blinked at her slowly, then opened his eyes again and stared at her, blue and green eyes drilling deep into her thoughts.

"The dwarfs will take the gems. I don't have any doubt about that. The only question is whether I can negotiate a price that both of us will be happy with."

The dwarfs were good at bartering. But they would want the gems once they had seen them. They would be ready to deal.

And Reg really didn't have anything to worry about as far as Harrison was concerned. She had already told him to stay away from the rest of the kattakyns. Harrison was her protector. He would not do anything that could cause her trouble. Not after she had warned him. The world was safe from the kattakyns and the danger of the Witch Doctor re-forming again in her lifetime. That wasn't going to happen.

The phone rang. Reg looked down at it, expecting to see a call back from Gwythr with further concerns or inquiries. But she hadn't even sent him anything about the gems yet. He wouldn't want to negotiate until he had seen what it was that he was buying.

And it wasn't Gwythr's name that she saw, but Corvin's name and incredibly handsome face. Something fluttered in Reg's stomach, and it wasn't worry and dread this time. She tried to keep her voice calm and relaxed and not give away that she was glad to hear from him. They hadn't spoken much since she had returned from her trip across the ocean to deal with the first batch of gems. He was kind of miffed by the fact that she hadn't waited for his help, hadn't even let him finish his research into how to cleanse the gems before her little excursion. Reg supposed that he had a point. She had asked him for help, and when things hadn't happened as quickly as she had hoped, she had found another way to deal with the problem. Corvin probably felt used. Unimportant.

"Corvin. Hi."

She shouldn't sound too friendly, since she was usually more reserved with him, trying to avoid being charmed by the warlock who could use his wiles to gain control over her if she weren't careful.

"Regina. We haven't… *talked* lately, and I was thinking of you…"

"Yeah, it's been a while. Everything going okay with you?"

"I am well, thank you. And you?" His voice took on a purring note. As if he really cared about her and wanted to know. That voice could get right under her skin and worm its way into her brain. Reg took a deep breath, trying to get air into her lungs. But she still sounded breathless when she answered him.

"Yeah. Things have been going a lot better for me, actually."

"Maybe divesting yourself of the cursed stones has had an effect."

"Maybe," Reg agreed. He didn't know how many gems she had started out with and how many she had been able to find new homes for. And how many gems were still sitting in a wooden box in her closet, waiting for her to take another trip. "What have you been up to lately? Working on any interesting projects?"

Not that she was really interested in any of his business. She didn't understand what he did as a warlock, when he wasn't stealing others' powers, and she found his collegiate studies to be extremely boring. But she felt she should at least inquire.

"I have applied to Davyn to reinstate me to the coven," Corvin told her.

It hit Reg like a punch in the gut. It shouldn't make any difference to her whether he were an active member of Davyn's coven or still being shunned by them. She had continued to be friends with him, despite the treacherous things he had done, so what did it matter whether he was being disciplined by his coven or not? If she, the victim in his case that had gone before the tribunal, was still on speaking terms with him, then why not the friends he'd had since before he even met her?

But that would mean that it was over. That the magical community felt that he had been fully punished for what he had done and was a full member of their order once more. He would be able to pick up more business, since he could now see and talk to the others in his coven without any restrictions.

Maybe he would stop calling her so often if there were other people he could call when he got bored with his solitary life.

It felt like a betrayal. Like the amount of damage that Reg had received from him had been measured and deemed to be compensated for. She should be over it now, since they had decided that he'd been shunned for long enough. No lasting harm.

Nothing they could see, maybe. That didn't mean that what he had done hadn't left scars that she would never get over.

"Are you still there, Regina?"

Reg considered just terminating the call. Why was she still on the phone with him anyway? Why had she even answered it to start with? Why would she even consider having anything to do with someone who had attacked her and taken something so precious from her in the past?

"Regina?"

"Yeah."

"Did you hear what I said?"

"Yes."

"You don't have anything to say?"

Reg licked her lips and swallowed. "What do you expect me to say?"

"I don't know. I expected you to go off, to be honest. Full-blown tirade about how I should never be released from my punishment after everything I have done. I expected… a lot of four-letter words, if nothing else."

"Well… however the coven wants to deal with you, that's their business." Reg cleared her throat. She felt very off balance but tried to act as if everything were normal. "I'm not the one who brought the charges against you in the first place."

"No, you didn't. I always thought that said something about you. And maybe about how you felt about me."

"Just that I didn't want anything more to do with you," Reg told him with a snap.

"Really, Reg. I think we're past that childishness, don't you? You and I have had some very enjoyable times together since then. We are far more alike than we are different."

Reg supposed he was referring to the fact that she was a siren and he was a warlock who had inherited certain abilities from his patriarchal line that allowed him—or to hear him tell it, forced him—to steal the powers and gifts from others to satisfy his unending hunger. Such things were not spoken of in the community, and that reluctance to talk about it had led to Reg being tricked by him into giving him her powers. She had never felt so empty and bereft as she had when she had woken up that morning.

In a bizarre twist of fate, Corvin had returned her powers to her, something that was previously unheard of. But he'd been trying to get them back ever since.

"We are not the same," she told Corvin coldly. "I am nothing like you are. What your coven does about you is their own business. It's got nothing to do with me."

"I'm sure Davyn will be calling you. You could, perhaps, happen to mention that you have no axe to grind. If you truly don't care whether I am readmitted to the coven or not, then tell him so."

It was a challenge for Reg to put her money where her mouth was.

"You could tell him that you are not afraid of me," Corvin prodded. "Inform him that you don't think I'm a danger to you any longer. That would go a long way to showing how much I have rehabilitated."

"You haven't rehabilitated. You haven't changed at all."

They had been psychically joined so many times that Reg couldn't ever fully separate from Corvin or keep him out of her own head. So even though he was only on the phone, she saw the smirk on his face and felt the chuckle that was too low to hear.

"Regina. I've changed so much. You know that. Look at how many times I have helped you. With the Witch Doctor and the draugar. With giving you the strength that you needed to help protect your younger self from Weston. Giving you strength to heal Calliopia and keeping you from blowing up the dwarf mountain. Can you really say that I haven't been the perfect gentleman, always willing to help you out whenever you called? Even if there was nothing in it for me?"

"No, I would not say that," Reg snapped.

"Well… I suppose everyone has a different perspective. But you can bet that I will be telling the tribunal of our many adventures together and how often you have called upon me to assist you. Whether you ended up taking my advice or not. I think if you look back at it, you will see that I have more than paid for one small mistake."

"Is that what you called me about? Just to gloat over how you are going to get reinstated into the coven? Because if that's all you're calling about, I have other things to do now."

"I'm sure you do. But I did want to give you a heads-up. It seems like the right thing to do. I wouldn't want you to get blindsided by this."

Reg breathed out slowly. Was she ever going to get to the point where she wouldn't react to Corvin's goading? Where she didn't care about what he was doing or thinking or had to say to her? It shouldn't matter to her what he did with his life. They were not a couple. They were not family. There was no tie between them, other than a psychic connection that both of them would prefer to break. Corvin was attracted to her, yes. Having once held her powers for that brief period, he didn't seem to be able to give up on the idea of talking her out of them again. But Reg knew too much now and she would never let him get the upper hand over her again. His powers had grown much stronger, but so had hers and, so far, she had been able to resist him.

And she would not give in to him again.

"You do what you have to," she said coolly. "It doesn't make any difference to me."

"I will, then," Corvin agreed smugly.

CHAPTER SEVEN

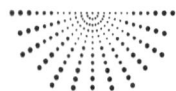

*R*eg was glad to get off the phone with Corvin. She didn't need the aggravation. He could go ahead and do whatever he wanted to. It was Davyn's problem to deal with, not Reg's. She didn't have to make any kind of decision about it. And she certainly wouldn't beg.

"What a pain in the neck," Reg told Starlight crossly.

Starlight, curled up on the couch with his nose touching his back feet, raised his head slightly to look at Reg. Who was a pain in the neck?

"Not you," Reg reassured him. "I'm talking about that warlock."

He blinked at her, then eventually closed his eyes and put his head down again, apparently satisfied that she wasn't criticizing him for something he had done.

"What would make me happy is if he just left me alone," Reg muttered to herself. She wasn't crazy. Not really. Talking to herself was just a way of sorting things out in her mind.

It wasn't as if she were talking to the voices in her head.

The voices had, unfortunately, been very loud recently. She thought it was her increased psychic activity. She was doing so many readings now that she was always open, always vulnerable to what the spirits had to say.

Or those who were not spirits but still, somehow, managed to worm their way into her head.

"That Corvin is lovely," one voice simpered, the accent and cadences as familiar to Reg as the sound of her own voice. "He is a wonderful specimen. You should get together with him. Go for a walk at the beach."

"Shut up, Norma Jean," Reg said evenly. "I can't even hear you."

"If you can't hear me, then how can you answer me?"

"You're not there," Reg pointed out. "You're all the way north in Maine or wherever you ended up. I'm just having a nervous breakdown."

"Of course you can hear the voices of your sisters."

Reg blinked, trying to process this. She petted Starlight, digging her fingers down into his thickest fur and trying to ground herself. "This is ridiculous," she told Starlight. "Even if I could hear Norma Jean, she is my mother, not my sister. Why would I think that?"

"We are all your sisters," Norma Jean's voice informed her.

"*All of you?*" Who else would Norma Jean be talking about? The other voices that Reg fought to ignore were not living beings like her mother, but those who had passed on. Reg had carried Norma Jean's voice in her head for a long time before Weston had changed the time-line, making it so that her mother had not died at the hands of Samyr Destine when Reg was four. Reg assumed that her familiarity with Norma Jean's voice after so long with her was the reason she could hear Norma Jean's voice even though it couldn't really be there. Reg had just gotten so used to it, that was the voice she had assigned to her internal voice.

At least, that was what she had been telling herself.

Everyone had an internal voice, right? She had heard writers talking about internal narrators. And that had to be what Norma Jean was now. No longer a ghost trying to communicate with her still-living daughter, but Reg's own brain, making observations about things around her. Helping her to make decisions.

But who else was Norma Jean talking about?

"No more. I'm tired. I need a break."

"You said he was yours. You claimed those waters, but you have not anointed them. You must seal your claim. Soon."

Reg shuddered. The last thing she needed to do was to take Corvin to the beach again. The last time she had nearly succeeded in pulling him into the water. Heart pounding loudly in her ears, she could almost smell the sweet scent of his blood that she had been able to sense that day. She had wanted so badly to just pull him into the water.

"Seal your claim," Norma Jean's voice insisted, losing the fake southern accent. "You must seal your claim with blood."

Norma Jean was joined by a chorus of creepy voices, most of them chanting words she could not understand, their voices starting low and hoarse and gradually rising until they were high-pitched and piercing. Reg poked her fingers into her ears, trying to drown them out.

Why couldn't she block them out? Why could she still hear Norma Jean's voice when she was miles away, and no longer a ghost, but attached to a physical body? None of it made any sense. Reg closed her eyes as tightly as she could, holding her breath, trying to force them to be silent.

CHAPTER EIGHT

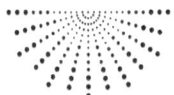

There was a whoosh of air, as if something very large had walked into the room or the door had been opened. Reg's eyes flew open and she looked at the door. There was no one there. It was still shut.

Reg looked around the room, spooked. It had felt like there was someone else there with her. She was sure she wasn't still alone.

"Norma Jean?"

"Do you want me to be Norma Jean?"

Reg turned all the way around to look into the corner of the living room, where Harrison was crouched down, looking at the TV and pressing buttons to try to make it do something.

"Harrison?"

"Regina?"

"What are you doing here? You startled me."

"Yes."

"What are you doing?"

Harrison pushed on the front of the TV. Not one of the buttons, just the TV screen itself as if it were a touch screen.

"I am experimenting."

"With the TV?"

"Yes."

"What are you trying to do?"

"Trying to play yesterday. There was a story I wanted to show you."

"You can't play yesterday. Unless you recorded it. And since you were not here yesterday, I am assuming you did not."

"Recorded it?" Harrison echoed.

"Yes. Onto the hard drive. If you didn't record it onto the drive, you can't play it back."

"I can be here yesterday."

Reg shut her eyes and pressed her temples with her index fingers. "Don't mess up my timeline any more."

"Mess it up? I would not do that."

"Whatever you call it. I don't want you changing my timeline at all. Got it?"

"How about me?" Weston suggested.

Reg whirled back around and saw the immortal bending down to look at Starlight and to scratch his chin.

"What are *you* doing here? When did you get here?"

"Yesterday?" Weston suggested, his tone tentative. He looked at Harrison questioningly, and Harrison nodded obligingly.

"You guys are not funny! Quit the comedy routine!"

The sad thing was, they didn't even know how ridiculous they were being. They could probably go back to yesterday, tape whatever show Harrison wanted to show to Reg, and then return to play it for her. If he had any understanding of technology. He would probably have more luck if he took her back in time and just showed her the movie himself. Or maybe it was a TV show or a documentary. Or even just a commercial. He might want to show her a commercial for underwear to ask her opinion of it.

As usual, Weston was the more conservatively dressed of the two; Harrison was the flamboyant dresser and could never quite get the styles that he wore *right*. Something was always missing, out of place, or worn the wrong way. He had on a Hawaiian shirt that she had seen him wear before, or one quite like it, and a sailor's cap like she had seen on an old TV show. And he wore long tan shorts. Going on a safari? Harrison put on a pair of dark sunglasses to complete the ensemble and looked at Reg for her response.

"It's... very nice," Reg told him. "You look great. And so does..."

She looked at Weston. She didn't even know what to call him. The immortal might be her father—and Reg was still not convinced of that fact—but he had never been a father figure to her. The immortals were extremely quirky. Self-centered, impulsive, and impossible to get any information from. If they were all-knowing, they hid it very well.

"So… why don't you tell me about the TV show?" she told Harrison.

"The TV show."

"You said you wanted to show it to me."

"But alas…"

"You can't. So why don't you just tell me about it? What was it about?"

Harrison made a gesture to wave it away. "Maybe we will go back there."

"No. Don't mess up my timeline. Listen, while you're here, I want to talk to you about—"

"Coffee?" Harrison suggested, walking into the kitchen toward the coffee machine. Reg turned toward it.

"I'll make the coffee. It's about Destine." She used the name that she had heard Harrison use for his old friend or enemy in the past. She still wasn't sure what the relationship between them was. If they had been rivals, then why was Harrison so interested in the kattakyns? Francesca was sure Harrison was going to try to free them to allow the Witch Doctor to re-form.

Harrison watched Reg put coffee grounds into the hopper. "The coffee?"

"The coffee what?"

"You said it is about Destine."

"No, I want to talk to you about Destine."

"Ah." He watched the coffee machine intently as Reg pressed the buttons and started the coffee brewing. "I thought it was about the woman."

"What woman?"

Harrison looked at Reg, and then over at Weston. Without his saying anything, Reg understood that "the woman" was Norma Jean. She put the discussion about the Witch Doctor on hold and thought about that. If Weston was in the mood to talk about Norma Jean, and could do it clearly, then it would go a long way to finding out why Norma Jean was in her head again. Maybe Weston had changed the past again, so that her mother was dead as she had been in the past Reg could remember. That would at least explain why she was talking to Reg again.

"You wanted to talk to me about Norma Jean?" she asked Weston.

"No."

"Why can I hear her again?" Reg asked, ignoring his answer. He obviously knew something. She couldn't give up the opportunity to find out what she could.

"You can hear sirens," Weston contributed. He looked around boredly.

"Sit down," Reg invited. She walked over to the living room to sit down, hoping to keep him there. She couldn't very well have a conversation if he disappeared into thin air again. Harrison stayed in the kitchen watching the coffee maker. "I know I can hear sirens. But why can I hear Norma Jean when she isn't even here?"

Weston followed her over to the living room, but didn't sit down. Reg wondered whether he had just followed Harrison there and wasn't really interested in visiting with Reg. Maybe the two of them were buddy-buddy now. They had been together when she'd seen them on her trip to the Everglades, but she hadn't seen Weston since then.

"Sirens can hear each other."

"So can humans. Why is that anything special?" Reg reconsidered her answer. Humans could hear each other when they spoke to each other aloud. They couldn't usually hear each other's thoughts, or she wouldn't be able to make any money as a psychic. But Norma Jean's voice was not actually audible. Maybe sirens, like gnomes, usually spoke to each other telepathically. "Do you mean that all sirens can speak with each other in their heads?"

Weston rolled his eyes to the ceiling. "Clearly."

"There's no need to be rude about it. I don't know anything about sirens and how they usually communicate."

Reg remembered Harrison saying more than once that "humans don't know anything." It was too true, in Reg's case in particular. Not having been raised in a community where paranormal powers and races other than humans mixed with them socially, Reg felt herself at a distinct disadvantage. Many things that might have been clear to the people who grew up in the community were completely unknown to Reg.

She looked at Harrison, who at least was more likely to talk to her and explain things than Weston. "Is that how sirens normally communicate? Telepathically?"

He shrugged. "Perhaps. I never paid any attention."

"How far can you communicate telepathically?"

"Me?" Harrison touched the side of the coffee pot, then jerked his finger back. "Distance is not a barrier."

"But you always come to see me in person. You don't just talk to me in my head."

He considered this for a moment. "When you were smaller, and there were many other voices, I had to visit you."

Reg nodded. There were still many competing voices and, as she had just demonstrated, she couldn't tell the difference between Norma Jean's spirit voice and her siren voice. If Harrison had just started speaking to her in her head, would she have known he was any different from the ghosts?

When she was little, she hadn't even been able to tell the difference between living playmates and ghostly ones. Or she hadn't known how to treat them any differently. Hadn't understood that playing with spirits would only make her a target to bullies and to grown-ups who thought she was too old for imaginary friends or thought she was psychotic.

"I like that you visit me," she told Harrison. "I like being able to see you physically."

"I like being able to see you too," he said generously.

"You are not as beautiful as the woman," Weston said bluntly. He clearly preferred his lover over his child. Reg had been surprised that an immortal could be charmed by a siren. Norma Jean was not a full-blooded siren, and her body and looks had been ruined by drug addiction and life on the street. But Weston had still been entranced with her, treating her like a beautiful princess.

If the immortals were all-seeing and all-knowing… but Corvin had corrected her more than once on this note. They did not have the attributes of the Christian God. They were very powerful and long-lived, but they didn't know everything and were quite naive in human matters.

"Have you seen Norma Jean lately?" Reg asked Weston, choosing to ignore the sting of his telling her she wasn't as beautiful as a drug addict living in squalor. Norma Jean didn't look like that anymore. In this timeline, she had recovered. Her skin was clear and her hair was thick and luxurious. Her rotting teeth had been replaced. She was a beautiful woman again, and her siren wiles meant that she was capable of ensor-celling pretty much any red-blooded male in her vicinity, including an immortal.

"I have seen her," Weston acknowledged.

"Recently?" Reg wanted to make sure that Norma Jean wasn't back in Florida. Just the thought of her mother being in the vicinity again set her heart beating faster and the anger and anxiety flooded through her whole body.

"All times are recently," Harrison reminded Reg.

To a being who lived forever, or at least for hundreds or thousands of years and who could travel back and forth in time as easily as walking into the next room, how could there be any long ago or recently? Reg knew from experience that trying to pin Harrison or Weston down to a human measurement of time would be impossible.

"Where is she right now?"

Harrison looked at Weston, passing the question back to him. Did that mean that Harrison didn't know? Or just that he wasn't interested?

Weston looked out the window, his hands loosely in his pockets, uninterested in Reg's question. Reg didn't know why he was there, why he had bothered to join Harrison. If he didn't want to talk to her, then why be there?

"Weston? Do you know where Norma Jean is right now?"

He looked at her, but his eyes were not focused properly on her face. Maybe he was remote viewing Norma Jean, checking in on her to answer Reg's question.

"She is… in her body. Where she always is."

"Yes, of course she's in her body. And where is her body?"

Weston made a vague gesture to the north.

Back in Maine, or a block away? Or outside the cottage?

Reg looked out the window Weston had just been looking out,

fearing she was going to see Norma Jean lurking outside. That would, at least, explain why her voice had been so strong in Reg's head.

"Is she in Florida?" Reg asked, turning back to Weston.

But he was gone. And so was Harrison. Reg was alone in the cottage once more. Just she and her cat. And a coffee maker that was dribbling onto the counter, the coffee pot mysteriously absent.

.

CHAPTER NINE

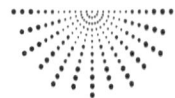

*R*eg tried to get the coffee maker to stop, but it was determined to keep dribbling fresh, hot coffee all over the counter and onto the floor. Reg shoved a coffee cup under the spout to catch the remaining liquid and tore a length of paper towels from the roll on the counter. She started mopping up, the hot coffee soaking its way through the paper towels and hurting her hands. Reg swore under her breath. Why would Harrison have disappeared with the coffee pot? He didn't even drink coffee. Chocolate, he liked, but he wasn't interested in coffee. He was just fascinated with the machine. He could have vanished the whole thing, so why hadn't he done that instead of just taking away the pot?

She muttered angrily to herself as she mopped up what she could, then ran cool water over her hands, which were turning a bright red.

Reg started to see bright spots in front of her eyes, and for a minute she thought that she was going to pass out. But they were not the bright sparklers that she saw when she was about to faint. They were sparking, glowing bugs—fireflies and moths and little things that Reg didn't have a word for. She turned away from the sink to look behind her, and saw a room filled with the brightly glowing insects, which gradually gathered and coalesced into a form that she had seen before.

Orri.

The day just couldn't get any better. A call from Corvin, Norma Jean's voice in her head, an appearance from Harrison and Weston that left her with a counter and floor covered with pools of coffee. And now the weird elf was back.

"Hi," Reg greeted.

Wasn't there any way to keep magical beings from appearing inside her house? With all the wards and charms Sarah had set, wasn't there anything that would keep the immortals and elves from coming and going as they pleased? It wasn't just malevolent humans and pixies that Reg wanted to keep out of the house.

Orri took off his sunglasses and looked around. "You are Reg Rawlins?"

"Yes… and you are Orri, the elf. I remember."

He cocked his head slightly, considering that. Did he really think that humans were so forgetful? That she could have a visit by an elf one day and have forgotten about it a day or two later?

His eyes moved from her face to the sink, where Reg was still holding her hand under a thin stream of cold water to relieve the minor scalding from trying to mop up hot coffee. The elf took a step toward her, looking concerned.

"It's fine," Reg said, pulling her hand away from the water and showing it to him. "Just a little bit of a burn. Nothing serious."

"I have a message for you."

"Don't take gifts from fairies?" Reg inquired.

He frowned.

"Sorry, go ahead." Reg told him. "Tell me your message." Even if he had already delivered his message once before, it was rather rude to upstage him. How many times had she gotten in trouble from foster parents for being a smart aleck? Even if she knew the answer, she knew better than to mouth off about it.

"I have a message for you," Orri repeated. He straightened, lifting his chin higher. "Waters be thy friend and foe."

"Oh." Reg nodded politely. She supposed that was why he had been concerned about her holding her hand in the water. Maybe he came prepared with a warning about water and seeing her standing there with her hand under the tap had confused him. "I see."

He waited, as if expecting some kind of reaction from her. Or maybe a tip. Did one tip elves who delivered warnings? Where did the warnings come from? Had someone paid him to deliver them? Or was it a compulsion?

"So… is this your job? Delivering messages to people?"

"No."

"Then… you're just doing it… for fun? As a hobby? What?"

"Waters be thy friend and foe."

"I know." Reg nodded. "Friend because it gives me strength, but foe because I can't control myself when I'm close to or in the water. I love the water; I always have. But with this whole siren instinct thing, I have to stay away from it to protect the people around me."

"Yes."

Reg nodded. "Well… thank you. Is that it, then, or was there something else?"

He frowned and looked around as if trying to figure out why he was there. "Have I been here before?"

"Yes. You showed up during a seance. Gave all my ladies quite a thrill. That time it was a warning about gifts from fairies."

He rubbed his forehead, frowning. "I'm not very good at this."

"You've done fine," Reg assured him. "Really. You found me, you gave me the message, what more could you do?"

He shook his head, clearly irritated with himself.

Did he have some kind of elf dementia? She hadn't even heard of an elf delivering warning messages before. If it wasn't his job, then why was he doing it? And it wasn't like the messages were wrong. They were apt, just… she'd already learned the lessons he was trying to warn her about. He was a bit late, that was all.

Orri strode up and down the room, scowling and looking around. He muttered something under his breath in elf-tongue. Finally, he shook his head at her, and the fireflies began flying around him again, and eventually, his shape dispersed.

CHAPTER TEN

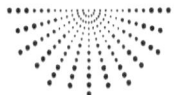

She thought that was the end of it. There were no more strange messages or messengers for the rest of the day, nor for the next day, nor the next. She started to relax again, not expecting to run into her mother or Harrison or the strange new elf at every turn. It was just a coincidence that she had heard from them all in a day. They didn't seem to have anything to do with each other and did not show up again to warn Reg of things that were to come.

Just a strange day. Nothing she needed to worry about more.

Reg sat in the garden behind the cottage with a cup of coffee. She had replaced her missing coffee pot within a day; there was no way she could get through life without coffee when she got up in the morning. It was a drowsy, warm, pleasant day, the garden buzzing with bees, birds cheeping away in the trees, and a mild wind blowing the branches and leaves.

"Hail, Reg Rawlins!"

Reg realized that she had shut her eyes to listen to the wind and the birds. She opened them and saw a little man in front of her, with a red cap and brown and green clothing. She thought in the first instant that it was Forst, the gardener, but in a split-second, she realized that it was his twin, Fir, who Reg had once done a favor for, delivering him from the clutches of human law-enforcement. Reg's experience with the police had come in handy and she'd been able to spring him from jail without much trouble.

Fir, how are you? Reg greeted, speaking to him in her head. The gnomes preferred to converse in their "inside words," and were awkward and terse when forced to resort to verbal communication with humans. That gave Reg an advantage over anyone who was not telepathic.

We are well, Fir advised, nodding pleasantly.

Reg took a more careful look around. He had said "we," so that must mean that Forst was there too. The gnomes were often difficult to spot in the garden despite their red caps. Reg had her own suspicions about how they managed to hide themselves so well.

She didn't find Forst, but Zinnia standing nearby, off to the side looking at Reg shyly. Reg smiled back at her. *And Zinnia. It's so good to see you. How is newlywed life?*

It was the first marriage for Fir and the second for Zinnia. They were an older couple, past the point where they would be bringing up children together. Forst, Fir's twin, had grandchildren. Six of them, because his daughter had twins and his daughter-in-law two sets of twins, very fertile for a gnome.

We are happy, Zinnia told Reg, her cheeks growing redder. *I am very glad your canna brought us such good luck.*

Reg doubted that they could credit the plant that she had grown from a seed planted during the spring equinox with their happiness. And even if the plant had been the cause, the magic that had made it grow and flower so quickly had not been Reg's own, but was, she thought, because of the equinox and the large magical population that had visited Black Sands during the Spring Games. There had been a lot of magic in the air.

Could I give you a gift? Reg asked, thinking about the gemstones that had been cleansed so far. She had enough that she could spare one for a newly married couple. They could keep it as a treasure, use its power, or sell it and decorate their house and garden together. *I have something for you.*

No, no, Fir interjected, shaking his head vigorously. *You came to our wedding. Brought the canna into the garden. That is what gnomen do. We do not give gifts like humans.*

You're sure? Not even something little? I would like to do something for you.

Reg Rawlins has already been most gracious, Zinnia asserted. *To do more would be an embarrassment.*

The gnomes were very retiring and did not seem to like to have attention brought to them. So Reg shrugged and smiled and turned her hands palms-up to indicate that she would give them nothing else. Zinnia smiled at this and nodded approvingly.

Do you know anything about the forest people and their wedding traditions? Reg asked them, thinking about the Bigfoot Etienne and his fiancée Ilka who had come all the way from Russia to meet him face to face and marry after being pen pals for some time. Empress Ilka was far above the station of humble Etienne, living by himself in the Everglades. Reg was sure there wasn't anything that Ilka would need that she couldn't buy for herself, but maybe there was something she would like for the house. Or some convenience that she would never ask for.

Zinnia and Fir looked at each other and shook their heads.

The forest people are very private, Fir said. *Do not share their nuptials with others.*

Not at all? No wedding? Even with their family members?

Very private. Maybe family. Mother, father, brother, sister. He shook his head. *No others.*

Wow. I guess I should probably be flattered that I met Ilka at all, then.

Fir nodded. He pulled a curvy pipe out of his pocket. It was just like the one that Forst used. Fir filled the bowl with tobacco. *Forest people are very large. Many humankind look for them and they be hard to hide.* He lit his pipe and smoked a few puffs. *They cannot gather.*

That's very sad... I'm sure they would like to have a lot of family members around them...

Zinnia nodded. She looked around the garden, maybe remembering their wedding and how many of their family members and friends had been able to come to watch and wish them well.

The breeze blew through the trees, and Reg watched the dappled sunlight shifting with the movement of the leaves and branches. A burst of white butterflies flew into the air all at once. There was something there, something coming out of the shadows.

Fir's eyes grew wide and round and he nearly dropped his pipe. *Elven folk!*

Reg groaned. *Not again!*

Zinnia gasped and covered her mouth, looking at Reg in shock.

I mean—elves are great. I love having them around the garden, but this one is starting to get on my nerves!

Zinnia giggled.

Elves helped to cure Starlight when he was sick and cursed, Reg went on. *They really helped him to start feeling better. Forst probably told you. But... Orri...*

The fluttering butterflies eventually resolved into the familiar shape. Reg shook her head.

"Orri."

He looked at her and took off his glasses. "Reg Rawlins."

"Another message? How many of these meetings are there going to be?"

He looked perplexed. "I do not know."

"Well... why do you keep coming to me?"

"To warn you."

"Why?"

"Reg Rawlins is a friend to the Aelfen folk."

"I'm a friend? Why?"

He raised his brows and looked at her. Reg squirmed under his gaze. She should be used to looks by now. The hungry looks that Corvin gave her. The looks that she had received as a child when she had done something particularly bizarre or since she had moved to Black Sands and people expected her to know about the magical world when she didn't have a clue. She should be used to people not understanding or believing her by now.

"You are a friend," Orri said.

There was another flurry of sunshine and butterflies, and another shape started to resolve near her. Regina figured it would be another elf, come to get Orri and maybe to take him back to whatever institution he had escaped from. But as she looked, she saw Orri forming again. She looked back at the one who was already there. There were minor differences in his dress, but otherwise he looked the same. A twin? A clone? Maybe, like gnomes, elves always had babies in pairs. They looked identical.

"Who are you?" Reg demanded.

Zinnia giggled again behind her hand. Reg supposed people didn't usually talk to elves that way. Elves were one of the races that were rarely seen, easily frightened away, so people probably didn't speak to them in a way that might be taken as harsh or rude. But Reg wasn't going to tiptoe around. This elf was taking over her life. He didn't just come and bring her a message once, so that she could learn from it and go on with her life. He kept showing up at inopportune times, warning her about things she already knew of. And he didn't seem to have a clue what he was doing or why.

The new elf said nothing. He looked at the first Orri, took off his glasses, put them back on, and looked around. Butterflies started to swirl around him, and Reg assumed that he was going to disappear as he had before. But rather than dissolving into the sparkling lights, something else was forming. Another elf. Another Orri. Triplets?

Reg bit her tongue and didn't announce "Another one?" She just looked at Zinnia, who giggled and shrugged as if she didn't understand what was going on either. At least that made Reg feel a little better. Elves must not typically come in identical triplets, or Zinnia would not have been surprised.

The elf started to speak as soon as he was solid. "Fall not to—"

The second Orri cleared his throat. The third turned to look at him, and startled. He looked at Reg.

"Reg Rawlins? I have a warning for you."

"Apparently it's going around."

He looked at her and then back at the second Orri, not under-standing Reg's comment. The first Orri raised his voice. "*I* have a message for Reg Rawlins," he said firmly.

The other two looked at him. Reg looked from one elf to the other.

"I assume you all have a message for me."

They nodded more or less in unison.

CHAPTER ELEVEN

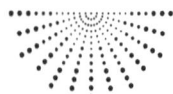

There was a buzz like a swarm of bees. Reg looked around, her skin crawling. She didn't like buzzing insects. Especially ones that stung. A fly buzzing against the window was irritating, but a bee or a wasp sent her anxiety into overdrive. Maybe she had listened to too many tragic stories of bee stings when she was younger. Not just about how much getting stung hurt, but about people being killed by an allergic reaction before anyone knew what was happening. Tragedies that came with a warning to stay away from bees and wasps and not to do anything to anger them.

Reg looked around and saw a swarm of bees drifting into the garden. She got to her feet. She'd heard of how entire colonies of bees would go out looking for a new home or queen. There were people who specialized in taking care of them. She wasn't one of them. In fact, she wasn't getting anywhere near a swarm of bees. She backed toward the house, trying to avoid attracting the attention of the swarm as she made her way back inside, where it was safe.

They started to coalesce into a dark shape. Another one? Maybe this elf had been sent for the Orri triplets. It was all just a misunderstanding. For some reason, three elves had been dispatched with her message instead of just one. There was a logical explanation for it. Bound to be.

But, as she feared, the fourth figure was Orri-shaped as well. Reg looked from one elf to the other, shaking her head in disbelief.

Do elves only come in one model? Reg asked Zinnia. She hadn't noticed when the elves had come into her house before. But she had been so worried about Starlight that she really hadn't paid much attention. She knew there had been men, women, and children, but she couldn't remember what any of them looked like and just how diverse they had been.

Zinnia shook her head. *No. Not like this,* she projected into Reg's thoughts. *Very strange.*

Well… I don't know what I'm supposed to do about this. Isn't there any way to make them stop? A way to chase them away? Pretty soon, this yard will be so full of elves that there won't be any room for the rest of us.

Fir and I go, Zinnia offered, *make more room for more elves.*

Reg chuckled. *No. No, I'll try to make them give their warnings, and then they will go. Right?*

Zinnia's eyes were wide and round. *I know not.*

"What are your messages?" Reg demanded of the four Orris. "Can you just give them to me and go back?"

They all looked at each other.

"Waters be thy friend and foe," the second offered.

Reg pointed at him. "Got that one already. You can go."

"This is not—"

"I got it. I know that. You can go back where you came from."

Lights began to swarm around him, and eventually the elf was gone. Reg looked at the others.

"Next!"

"Beware fair folk—"

"Bearing gifts," Reg finished. "That one too."

The first Orri looked offended. "I warn you…"

"I got it. Fairies with gifts. Don't accept them. Figured that out before you ever showed up. So you can go."

He turned into a swarm of lights that dissipated into the garden with a clash of discordant bells. Zinnia looked at Reg, eyebrows raised, worried about the trouble she was causing. Reg looked at the two remaining Orri's.

"That was mine too," the bee-swarm Orri said, putting his hand partway up like he was in a classroom. The bees started to swarm and his shape moved back out of the garden again. Reg was glad to see that one go. She hadn't wanted to deal with that annoying buzzing any longer than she had to. Her shoulders dipped a little as she relaxed. She looked at the final remaining Orri. The second who had appeared, she thought.

"Do you have a different message?"

He nodded. "I have a warning for Reg Rawlins."

"A different one."

Another nod.

"Okay. Go for it."

"Fall not to strange keys."

Keys. Reg had already learned the lesson of the keys as well. She had learned a lot more than she had realized since moving to Black Sands. Maybe the purpose of Orri's warnings was just to remind her of that fact. That she had learned a lot since she had gotten there, both about magic and about herself.

"Thank you," she told him politely.

Orri nodded in satisfaction. He dissolved into fluttering moths and dots of light and then was gone. Reg looked at Zinnia and Fir.

One does have to take care with strange keys, Fir advised.

I know. Keys can unlock things that you don't want unlocked. Like immortals that have been hidden away under the stairs for decades.

Well, Fir frowned, *I don't know about that.*

Trust me. They can. And you don't want to give someone else your own keys, because that gives them the ability to enter your house. Even if you have wards set against them.

Zinnia and Fir both nodded about this. It was probably basic stuff for them. But it had been an important lesson for Reg to learn. One that had almost come too late. It would have been nice to have been warned before the event. The same was true of the other warnings too. If they had come at the right point in her life, she would have appreciated them much more. Not hearing the warnings until after she had failed to protect herself or make the right decision was a real pain.

Learning from experience was only one way of learning life's lessons, but unfortunately it seemed to be the only one that worked for Reg. Try as she might to learn from other people's experiences, positive or negative, she just didn't seem to learn until she had been through something herself. A character trait that had made foster mothers despair.

We will… leave you to your thought and drink, Fir told Reg, motioning to her coffee cup, almost forgotten in all the drama. He tamped out his pipe and put it carefully back into his pocket. *Fare thee well. Pay heed to the warnings of elves.*

Reg nodded. *Okay. Will do,* she agreed.

Fir and Zinnia joined hands and pushed their way into the vegetation, and in a moment were gone from Reg's sight.

She had a sip of her coffee and rubbed the center of her forehead, which was pulsing with pain.

CHAPTER TWELVE

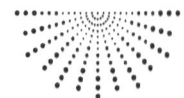

*R*eg was excited to be starting a new level of training with
Davyn, a warlock who was the head of Corvin's coven and a
firecaster. Being an experienced firecaster, he was helping Reg to develop
her own gift, which had been neglected and repressed for many years as
she had tried to keep out of trouble in foster care.

Lighting fires was not a way to endear oneself to foster families.
Even though Reg had thought that it was always the other children who
had lit fires in homes she had been in, she had realized that Davyn was
probably correct in his assessment that she had been the one to light
them without realizing it, knowing that such a thing was not allowed
but unable to completely suppress her gift.

So other foster children had been blamed for the accidents and
Reg's involvement in the fires had been overlooked.

And now, after several months of training with Davyn, Reg had
improved her control enough that Davyn had taken her out of Black
Sands to practice some new skills and techniques. Before, she'd had to
stay in the house, in an enclosed area where Davyn could quickly put
out any fires that got away from Reg.

"How are you doing today?" Davyn asked. "Feeling calm and
focused?"

Reg nodded eagerly. "Sure." She examined their surroundings. A farmhouse far from any prying eyes. The sweet-smelling citrus trees around them were green and well-watered, as most of Florida was. They didn't have to deal with the same risk of forest fires as California or other more arid locations.

"I want you to take the time to think about it," Davyn cautioned. "Really look inside and examine your feelings and motivations. You will need to be able to stay in control. This is not an amusement park."

Reg closed her eyes. More to feign concentration than to look inside herself. Of course she was ready. She'd been ready for weeks, but Davyn had been holding her back, insisting that she keep running through his preschool-level firecasting exercises until she could do them blindfolded and with her hands tied behind her back. So to speak.

She was ready to move on to more complicated exercises. Eager to build on the skills she had developed so far. She knew that her inner fire was very strong; she had proven that to herself and everyone else in the dwarf mountain.

"I'm ready," she told Davyn in a calm, even voice that he couldn't fail to recognize as being focused and teachable.

"Okay. Let's start with some of the exercises that you are familiar with, just to get warmed up and to make sure that you are able to keep your focus in this new environment."

Reg rubbed her palms together briskly, warming them up, and then drew them apart, slightly cupped, as if she were holding a basketball between them. She conjured a ball of fire, small and well-behaved, suspended between them. Davyn had her make it bigger and smaller, hotter and cooler, and Reg performed perfectly. There was no way he could find fault with any of her actions.

"Let's try a campfire," Davyn suggested. "You've done that before."

Reg nodded. She had done that plenty of times without his help, even before she had known that she was a firecaster. At camps in her childhood, she had always been the one who could build a fire and get it going the quickest, even if the fuel were wet. She had thought then that she was just really good at knowing how the fire would behave, what it needed and how to feed it the combination of fuel and oxygen that it needed. One match, and the whole thing would burn happily. Now she knew she didn't even need that one match. She'd lit a campfire when they went on their quest to the dwarf mountain and when she had been across the ocean to find the owners of the first bag of gems. Without any supervision by Davyn.

She made a space for a campfire in a flat, rocky area where there were not many green plants, just a few weeds that had pushed their way through the gravel and rocks. She surrounded it with a ring of larger rocks, although she knew that neither of them really needed any kind of firebreak. They would be able to keep the fire contained in the area they wanted to. Then she gathered firewood, bits of old lumber and building materials from outbuildings that had long since collapsed. Dry old wood that would light in an instant.

The hardest part was waiting until she had everything ready for the campfire. A couple of times, wood started smoldering in her hands before she even got it to the ring of stones, and she had to snuff it out.

Eventually, she had a small pile of tinder, kindling, and large pieces of wood ready to be lit. She looked at Davyn.

The way that he smiled at her, Reg knew that he was aware of the struggle she'd had in not lighting the fire prematurely. He nodded.

"Go ahead."

Reg didn't go through the exercise of holding a ball of fire between her hands to start with and then using it to light the campfire. She didn't point at the wood or bend down to touch it and ignite the pile. She just released the fire she had been holding inside and the wood was ablaze in an instant.

"Keep it contained," Davyn cautioned.

Reg monitored the size of the fire, the edges, and the embers that floated off into the air, tracking and mapping them all in her mind. The fire was an extension of herself, like a dream she controlled.

"Good," Davyn approved.

"I've done this before," Reg pointed out. "This isn't hard."

"I know that. We need to start with what you are comfortable with. Start with the skills that you already have."

Red rolled her eyes. But she stayed focused on the fire. She knew Davyn would test her, try to distract her or get her emotional, to see whether he could get her to lose her focus.

"So things have been good lately?" he asked. "You have been doing more business lately."

"Yes," Reg agreed. "More readings and seances. I had a dry spell for a while there, but I'm doing better now."

"People were worried about you being a siren."

Reg gritted her teeth. She didn't like the way that he put it. Reg wasn't a siren. Her mother was a siren. Or part-siren. Reg wasn't a siren, because she hadn't acted as a siren. She had kept her siren instincts suppressed and had not followed through on the impulses that the water brought out in her. So she *wasn't* a siren. She just happened to have a mother who was a siren.

"Yeah," she agreed. "That's what people were worried about. But they're starting to calm down now. And I've been able to find other clients. Non-practitioners who don't know anything about *that*."

"That's good. I'm glad you've found your place. Been out to the water lately?"

The campfire flared. The heat warmed Reg's face. She breathed in and out slowly and brought the size back down again.

"I'm mostly staying away from the water right now," she admitted.

Water be thy friend and foe.

She had been out on a boat with Corvin when she was trying to understand what to do about the gems. Corvin was one of the few people who had experienced the power of her siren instincts, but he wasn't afraid of her. He had his own power, and he had known when to back off and to put space between them so that Reg could not overcome his defenses. It had been a relief to go out on the water, to feel the waves rolling beneath her feet, but it had also been frustrating to be so close to fulfilling her siren desires and to have to back off, to leave the underwater world she could feel beneath her and go back to the land.

The thirst had been very strong. Stronger than she wanted to admit to anyone.

"Reg," Davyn prompted.

Reg focused back on her fire. She had expected to find it burning higher, out of her control because she'd let herself get emotional again, but instead she found that it was dying out. Just a few flames licking over the wood. Reg frowned.

"What...?"

She focused on building it up again. It took only a minute to get the campfire blazing merrily again. When it was the appropriate size and heat, Reg looked sideways at Davyn.

"Did you do that?"

"Me? No. Why would I do that?"

"To challenge me. You're always doing things to see how I respond."

"I did not quench your fire. Think about where your focus was. What were you thinking about? Where did your mind wander to?"

Reg sighed. "To the ocean. Water."

"You have a very strong affinity to two elements. An affinity for water is very rare in a firecaster. Just as I imagine it is very rare for a siren to have an affinity for fire. I believe that you can use both abilities to temper each other."

"I can control my fire by thinking about water."

Maybe that was how she had scalded herself on the coffee too. As a firecaster, it was pretty hard for her to burn herself. But maybe it was different with hot water.

Davyn shrugged. "That would appear to be the case. If so... it may be easier for you to quench your fire, even when you are angry, than it would be for the average firecaster."

It was funny to hear Davyn talking about the average firecaster, when she knew how rare firecasters were. Davyn was the only other one she had ever met, as far as she knew. Certainly the only one who had ever declared himself to her.

"Okay."

Davyn nodded. "I was talking to Julian the other day."

CHAPTER THIRTEEN

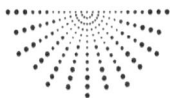

*R*eg's gut clenched and the fire leaped before she could suppress her reaction. Davyn had introduced the topic without any warning. If he had worked his way up to it, she might have been able to handle it better. Reg controlled the fire, keeping her focus on it.

"Yeah? What were you talking to Julian about?"

Davyn smiled. Maybe because he was pleased to see how Reg was able to keep her control now. Or maybe just because he was happy thinking about Julian and their conversation.

Reg didn't know what he saw in Julian. The magical investigator was still as much of a self-important bully as he had been when he had been Reg's foster brother many years before. He had physically abused her. Tormented her with his magic. And nearly gotten himself killed in the process. Coming back into her life to investigate what had happened in the Everglades, he had done everything he could to prod her into action, wanting to add another notch to his belt and prove to the Endangered Species Division what a good investigator he was. He had even drawn his wand on her, which really hadn't been a good idea.

But Davyn was attracted to Julian despite his dark side. Maybe because of it. Some people were just attracted to bad boys. He said that he saw something else in Julian. But Reg didn't know what. She knew that Julian was damaged. Whatever he had gone through in his early life before going into foster care had scarred him deeply, just as Reg's experiences had shaped her. Neither of them would ever be normal and whole on the inside. They would always be apart from everyone else.

"He mentioned you," Davyn said. "Asked how you were doing."

"That was nice of him."

"We might do something over the summer. A vacation of some kind. Get away from things."

"He's coming here?" Reg tried not to engage with the news, but to keep her emotions flat and the fire controlled.

"We haven't decided yet. Maybe we'll meet here and go to the Everglades. Maybe somewhere else."

"You should go somewhere else. He's already seen Black Sands and the Everglades. Go somewhere neither of you have been."

And keep Julian Sabat far away from her.

"We'll have to see," Davyn said pleasantly. "We haven't made a decision yet."

"Uh-huh."

Reg looked for some way to change the topic. She knew that Davyn was just trying to get an emotional reaction out of her, but she had herself under control now. He would not be able to push her into action.

"Have you heard from Corvin recently?" Davyn asked.

Reg swallowed. Davyn certainly was not making it easy for her. She focused on keeping the size of the fire down, but she let it grow hotter, hoping the intensity would relieve some of the stress.

"Yeah, I heard from him," Reg agreed. "He said he was going to give you a call. Or something. I don't know, maybe a formal letter. Did he send something by crow?"

"He talked to me directly."

"Great. So you're all over this application of his for reinstatement."

"It's on my task list," Davyn acknowledged. "I'm not about to rush it through, though."

Reg breathed steadily in and out, watching the flames, feeling the white-hot heat at the heart of it. "What's the process, then?"

"We will add the matter to the coven's agenda. Get feedback from what other members think. Talk to the parties involved." Davyn looked significantly at Reg. "And then the tribunal will be called to consider his application. As you know, this is not the first time he has applied to be reinstated."

The previous time had been mere weeks after Corvin had been kicked out of the coven. He figured that his fight with the Witch Doctor had proven his goodwill toward the community and he should be allowed back in immediately.

But they had turned down his application. Maybe they would again.

Reg wasn't counting on it. She remembered how she had been told before the hearing that removing Corvin from the coven had a negative effect on everyone in the magical community, not just him. He was a powerful warlock, and that meant that his powers would not be available for their use. They would have to do without him. And it had been long enough now that they probably really wanted him back. It wouldn't be as easy to turn him down a second time. There would be witches and warlocks who believed he had been disciplined enough for a minor failing.

"You think you'll approve it this time?"

"I've been keeping a close eye on him. I'm not sure that he has reformed as much as he would like us to believe."

"He hasn't reformed at all. He's no different than he was."

"And reformation is our goal. Of course... we can't change his nature. His condition is not his fault. We have to remember that what he is will never change."

Reg nodded. Corvin too had another set of instincts. She didn't know how much he could control and how much his predatory instincts took over his decision-making ability.

"How do you feel about it?" Davyn asked.

"I don't know. I haven't really thought that much about it."

"You and Corvin remain... friends."

"Not friends, exactly." Reg tried to explain it. "He's not someone I would pick out to be friends with... but we're connected. Like people in the same family. You don't get to choose whether you want to be family or not, and you're not responsible for what the other person does. But you're still... connected."

"He's like a brother to you?" Davyn asked, his tone dripping with sarcasm.

"No!" Reg's face grew hot, and it wasn't because the fire was getting out of her control. She would never have feelings like that for a brother. But she couldn't control the feelings he inspired in her. His magical charms and the pheromones he exuded had a physical effect on Reg that was difficult to overcome. That wasn't a moral weakness. It was just the power that his kind had over others.

Especially women.

And especially Reg.

"I'm just saying that we're connected. I can't help that. And since he's been shunned by the coven, there aren't many people that he can talk to."

"So you think that our punishment has had a negative effect on you? That it would have been better if he'd been able to remain in the coven, so that his attentions were not... directed elsewhere so much?"

"I don't know. I would have been really ticked if you hadn't punished him at all. And what else are you going to do? Give him a fine? A slap on the wrist? I know you were talking about binding him, but that would be harder, right?"

Davyn nodded. "It would take power away from the community. Binding a warlock of Corvin's power... I don't know if we could even have done it. Not for any length of time. And the negative implications on the rest of the community..." He shook his head. "You don't want to hear all this, I'm sure. You just wanted him to be punished. And maybe we didn't make the best choice for you."

"I don't know what would have been better," Reg conceded, shaking her head. "I guess you did the best you could. And now..." She pressed her lips together, trying not to show any emotion over the discussion. "Well, you do what you do, right? Whether you reinstate him or not doesn't really have any effect on me. He's still connected to me. He'll still keep coming back whether he's part of the coven or not."

CHAPTER FOURTEEN

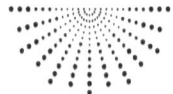

*D*avyn dropped Reg off in front of the big house that Sarah lived in.

"Make sure that you get plenty to drink," he advised. "You're going to be dehydrated after all the work you did."

"Yeah, I will."

"That's water, not alcohol. Alcohol will just make you more dehydrated."

Reg rolled her eyes. "I think I know that."

"I don't know what you know. Just stay away from the alcohol tonight. Or you'll be miserable in the morning."

Reg nodded. "Yes, *Dad.* I'm going in now."

Davyn snorted. He shifted the car into drive, gave a little wave, and pulled out into the street.

Reg walked along the pathway that went around the side of the house and into the backyard and the guest cottage. She was tired, but she was awake enough to keep an eye out for Corvin. He had ambushed her as she was going back to her house more than once, and it would not happen again. She might be superstitious, but she didn't want him showing up for a chat because she had been thinking about him.

All was quiet, and no one stepped out of the bushes or confronted her before she could get to the gate that marked the boundary of the wards and protective charms that Sarah had set. Reg stepped through the gate with a sigh of relief. She had left the evening clear, Davyn having warned her that she would probably be tired after their session. So instead of preparing for more client readings, seances, or other work, she could just relax with Starlight and not think about Corvin or Julian or anyone else she didn't want to think about.

Reg unlocked her door and went into the cottage. "Did you miss me?" she called out.

She heard Starlight jump down from wherever he was perched, and he came strolling out to see her, stretching first his front and then his back legs and giving a big yawn. He sat down and started to wash.

"Did you have a nice nap?" Reg asked him.

He stopped and stared at her for a moment before going on with his grooming routine.

"I figured we'll have an early supper, get into jammies, and then veg out the rest of the night. Just you and me. How does that sound?"

He gave another wide yawn that ended in a squeak.

"Great. Glad you approve. Now, what's in here?" Reg approached the fridge. She knew that she should eat something that was good for her body, before whatever Sarah had left in there went bad, but she wasn't a big fan of healthy eating. Truth be told, Sarah wasn't either, which was probably why so many of her dishes ended up in Reg's fridge. Reg browsed through the covered bowls and fast-food leftovers for anything that looked appealing, but wasn't inspired by anything she saw. It was time to clean out the fridge. She didn't even know how long half of the food had been sitting in there.

Reg pulled out a garbage bag and started tossing out all the fast-food cartons and bags. She even went so far as to pull out the larger bowls of Sarah's and to dump the contents into her garbage, then placed the bowls in the sink to rinse them out, hoping that way it wouldn't be so obvious that she had just dumped them instead of eating them. She looked back in the fridge.

Much better.

She could eat a few of the remaining items over the next few days. When she felt like making a sandwich or warming up some pasta. And that meant that she could order in something good.

* * *

With her belly nearly bursting with the excellent Chinese food from Tasty Lotus, Reg lounged in front of the TV, checking through the streaming media channels for something that she could watch for a few hours without getting bored. Starlight was curled up on her lap, purring away in his sleep, eyes closed tight.

There was little Reg found more comforting than a purring cat in her lap. She was sorry that she had missed out on it earlier in life, having never been able to have a pet before. But now she had Starlight, a cat that had chosen her more than she had chosen him, and all was well with the world.

* * *

Reg stirred.

A voice called to her.

She was so tired. Reg rubbed her eyes, trying to remember what she was supposed to be doing. Had she missed a client appointment? She didn't think she had meant to fall asleep where she was.

"Reg Rawlins."

Reg blinked, trying to bring the room into focus. She was pretty sure she hadn't had anything to drink. Davyn had told her not to, hadn't he? She wouldn't have gone ahead and had drinks anyway.

Not without a really good reason.

"Mmm." She tried to let the voice know that she wasn't dead, and give herself the time to wake up completely.

Had she gone out? Or was she still home?

Reg felt for Starlight and found him cuddled up against her. So he was there and she must be home because she wouldn't have taken him out anywhere.

Then who was in her cottage?

Reg forced her eyes open, alarmed. *Who was in her house?*

"Who's there? Who are you?"

She managed to pry her eyes open, and sitting up and squinting around, found a figure sitting in the chair across from her. Reg was stretched out on the uncomfortable wicker couch with Starlight, and he was sitting in one of the chairs.

An elf with twinkling eyes.

Aelf.

Orri.

"My name is Orri," he told her, leaning forward to talk to her in an intimate voice.

Reg shook her head, trying to get some perspective and to remember everything that had happened during the day. Had something happened since she saw Davyn? She was pretty sure that she had just been watching TV and vegging out.

Starlight stirred beside her, but he didn't seem alarmed. He stood up and arched his back and stretched luxuriously. She loved watching him stretch and always thought it looked so utterly satisfying. She would like to be a cat just once to know whether it felt as good as it looked. Starlight sat and started to wash.

At least if he weren't bothered by Orri, that probably meant that the elf was okay. He was not a danger to Reg, or Starlight wouldn't have been calm around him. He'd be hissing and spitting and nipping the elf's ankles.

"I know who you are," Reg said tiredly. "We have met."

"We have?"

"This morning, there were *four* of you. Are you identical quadruplets? Clones? Robots?"

"Four of me," Orri repeated thoughtfully.

"Yes. Four of you."

"I'm really not very good at this."

"Good at what? You seemed to have no problem appearing to me out of a swarm of bugs."

"This kind of travel can be very difficult."

"I would think so. I wouldn't want to travel in a swarm of bugs. How do you even steer them?"

She knew she was being mouthy, but she didn't really care. If Orri were going to keep appearing to her at random intervals with his useless warnings, then he would have to put up with a bit of sass.

"I am not in the bugs," Orri said with a frown. He looked as if he were going to try to explain his method of travel to Reg. She held up her hand to stop him.

"No. I really don't want to know. Just… give me your stupid warning and swarm out of here. And don't come back. I really don't want you to come back again."

"I can't help coming back. It's already happened."

Reg stared at him, blinking and trying to make sense of this statement.

"Just go home, okay? I don't need your warnings. Go warn someone else next time. Please. And don't wake me up. It's really rude to wake someone up out of a sound sleep."

He scratched his head and then fiddled with one of the rings on his fingers. "I have already come to you in the future. So, I can't… not."

"Oh, good grief." Reg ran her fingers through her braids as if it would help her to get her thoughts in order. She gathered up all the braids in one bunch and pulled them back behind her shoulders. Maybe it was time for a change. Maybe she should twist them into a knot or consider a different style. "How could you have already come to me in the future?"

He raised a finger and opened his mouth to explain.

Reg shook her head. "No! No, I'm not asking. I don't want you to explain it to me. I just want you to stop. So… whatever you are planning for the future, stop it now. Hasn't anyone ever told you that humans don't like people messing around with their temporal timelines?"

He rubbed his whiskered chin. "No."

"Well, we don't. So stop doing it. No more, you understand?"

"I have to do what has already been done."

"Argh!" Reg pulled on a handful of her hair, forcing herself to focus on the jolt of pain instead of trying to understand the convoluted story he was going to give her. She didn't want to hear anything about paradoxes or the unpredictable effects of time travel. She'd seen Star Trek, but had discovered for herself that things just didn't work out like they did on TV. TV had all the answers about time travel paradoxes, but they were all wrong. "Just stop!"

Orri looked down, nodding. "Yes, Reg Rawlins."

"I need some sleep. I need you to go, okay? So go home, and we're done. No more of this."

"I have a warning," Orri said apologetically.

"Of course you do. But you've already given them to me. Multiple times. I don't understand why you have to keep coming back and giving them to me."

"I want to help."

"If you want to help, then leave me alone. Driving me crazy won't help anyone."

Orri stood up and moved around restlessly.

"Well?" Reg prompted. She made a shooing motion with her hands. "Swarm away."

"I… can't."

"Why not?"

"I have a message for you."

"You can't leave because of the message?"

He nodded, looking chagrined.

Reg breathed out in exasperation. "Which one is it this time? Beware of fairies bearing gifts?"

"No…" Orri hesitated, looking at Reg's face, uncertain whether he should proceed with his message or make her keep guessing.

"Just tell me."

Orri straightened, preparing for his moment. Reg rubbed her eyes with the heels of her hands, trying to rub all the grit away.

"Be not ensorcelled by fair face," Orri announced.

It was a new message, at least. Reg was glad not to have to hear one of the old ones over again. She considered it as she waited for Orri to disappear. But Orri remained there, looking at her expectantly. What did he want? A tip? Gratitude? That moment where it all came together and she understood why he had kept coming to see her?

Well, she wasn't going to tip him. Help him to the door, maybe, but no tip.

"Okay, thanks."

He played with his rings again, not meeting her eyes.

"You've given me the warning, so you can go now, can't you?"

"Be not ensorcelled by fair face," Orri repeated.

"Yeah. I heard you. I'll be sure to take that into account when a handsome elf keeps transporting himself into my house." Reg gave a laugh.

Orri looked horrified. "No, not *me!*"

"I think I've learned my lesson about good-looking men. Since my experience with Corvin…"

Orri's face fell. "What? You and the warlock have already… met."

"Yeah, you're way late if you were trying to prevent that. That was when I first got here."

"But I thought I went back far enough."

Reg shook her head. "No. Sorry. But… don't try again. You can just stop now. You don't need to keep trying."

"But I *must* warn you. I *must* repay you…"

Reg didn't know what he thought he had to repay. She shook her head. "No, you and me are good. No need to keep warning me. I've had enough insights into the future. Okay? So you can go home now."

Orri stared at her, his face a picture of disappointment. Lights started to flash and dart around him, and eventually the swarm of fireflies swallowed him up and winked out, and Reg was alone with Starlight once more.

CHAPTER FIFTEEN

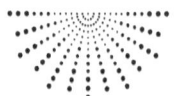

*R*eg looked out the window. It was late, the small hours of the morning. She was often still up at that time, so it was disconcerting to have been so soundly asleep before Orri's appearance. She still felt a little disoriented by his waking her up and then trying to give her his warning, as unnecessary as it was. Why did he feel the need to keep coming back to tell her to avoid things that she had already dealt with?

A light went on in the kitchen in the big house at the front of the lot. Sarah was up, back from whatever date or social event she had been out at, getting herself a cup of tea before retiring to bed. If she even slept. Reg wondered sometimes. Sarah certainly didn't seem to need as much sleep as Reg. How she found the time, Reg wasn't sure.

She pulled her housecoat on over the worn t-shirt and shorts that functioned as her pajamas and walked across the yard to the kitchen door.

"Come in, Reg," Sarah called out.

Reg opened the door and entered. Sarah smiled, her face pink as she bustled around the kitchen.

"How was your evening, Reg? Did you have a good rest?"

Sarah knew her schedule, of course.

"Yes. It was nice to have an evening to myself. I guess I need to remember to recharge now and then."

"Especially after a workout with your firecaster."

"Yeah. I like the firecasting lessons… so I don't really realize while I'm doing it just how tiring it is. How much it takes out of me."

"You need to make sure you stay hydrated." Sarah motioned to the tea kettle. "Can I get you something?"

"Sure." Reg looked at the packets of tea in the basket on the table and selected one of the commercial ones. Peppermint. While there were several bags of loose-leaf tea that Sarah had put together herself, Reg didn't have the palate for the herbs that Sarah used. They always tasted like cough medicine. Or worse. Reg had a sweet tooth, and that meant she used a lot of sugar or honey in her tea, which always made Sarah shake her head.

In a few minutes, Sarah was sitting across the table from Reg, watching as she spooned sugar into her tea. "I'm sure you need the extra energy for your firecasting," Sarah said pleasantly. "But as you get older, you may find that refined sugar is not the best thing for your body. Maybe some fruit? A banana?"

Reg glanced around Sarah's kitchen. Despite her words, Sarah indulged a little too much in restaurant food and delicacies imported from around the world. Reg did not see a bowl of fruit in evidence. Which was fine, since she wasn't big on fruit. She just shrugged.

"What can you tell me about elves?"

"Elves?" Sarah pursed her lips and stared off somewhere over Reg's shoulder. "Well, they are pretty shy. Humans don't see a lot of them. While we have some commerce and socialization with fairies, elves are different. Not haughty like the fairies… they just keep to themselves."

"So you don't see very much of them?"

"Goodness, no. Sometimes I see evidence they have been around. See lights or hear bells in the night as they are moving from one home to another, but no, the only time I have seen them face-to-face, in human form, is that day when they helped with Starlight."

"Hmm." Reg nodded.

"Why do you ask? Have you heard them again? Usually, they only move around winter solstice. Maybe summer if there were a reason for it, but it's still pretty early in the year."

"Well, no. I haven't seen more than one of them."

"More than one?" Sarah frowned.

"Yes…"

"So you have seen one."

Reg nodded.

"You are very lucky. It must be your psychic vision that has allowed you to catch glimpses of it. Him? Her?"

"Him."

"Was he very young? Maybe a child who hasn't learned how to avoid humans properly? Did he get separated from his folk?" Sarah looked concerned as she suggested this.

Reg shook her head quickly. "No. Nothing like that. Not a child. And not… trying to avoid me."

"He must be sick or injured, then. Something must be keeping him from being able to stay out of your sight."

Reg thought about that. She hadn't seen any sign that he was hurt. He didn't have any visible wounds or move like he was in pain. And he hadn't looked sick, but she couldn't discount the possibility. He had been quite nervous at times and had seemed unable to disappear when he wanted to.

"I don't know. I don't think he was hurt. Maybe he was sick. Some kind of… mental thing? Do elves get mental illness?"

Maybe he was suffering from some sort of elf dementia and that was why he kept appearing to her, talking his nonsense. Just because he said he was a time traveler, that didn't make it true. Though there were, of course, the other Orris. The ones who had appeared to her in the garden. Four identical Orris at once there to deliver their warnings to her.

If she went by what she had seen on TV, then the world should have imploded when the four of them had all appeared together in one time and place, but apparently things didn't work the same way in real life as they did on the sci-fi channels.

"I'm afraid I don't know very much about that," Sarah confessed. "I have never heard of any race other than humans having mental illness. But they might… call it something different or have remedies for it. Healing spells or herbs that don't work on humans."

Reg had seen signs of mental illness in other races. Calliopia the fairy, as one example. Ruan said she fought her demons. Reg didn't know how real the shadows Calliopia saw were. And how many of them were just in her mind, traumatized as it was by her kidnapping and the things that had happened to her as her pixie family had tried to prevent her from completing her transformation into a fairy.

"Hmm. I don't know. I don't think that mental illness is just a human weakness," Reg offered.

"Maybe not. Most of the races tend to keep to themselves and don't talk about their troubles to the meddling humans. While we are at peace with the creatures around here, it wouldn't do to reveal your weaknesses to a potential enemy. Susceptibility to any particular illness could be used against them." She took a sip of her tea. "Like the early inhabitants of this continent who were wiped out by the sicknesses the white explorers and traders brought with them."

Reg shuddered at the thought. She's always thought the settlement of the Americas was a pretty gruesome tale. The millions of innocent people who had been wiped out by men greedy for land, gold, and trade routes.

"But that's getting rather off-topic," Sarah observed. "Tell me about your elf. Where did you spot him?"

"Well… it wasn't as if I just happened to catch a glimpse of him in the garden. Though I did see him there, too."

"Too?"

"The first time was in the cottage, during a seance."

Sarah leaned forward. "Was it an elf spirit? Did he communicate with you?"

"He communicated with me… everybody there could see him; he wasn't just a spirit. He's solid enough." Reg tried to remember the word that Orri had used when referring to his physical body but couldn't recall it. "He drank wine, talked with us, he wasn't just an apparition."

"Oh, my!" Sarah's eyes were wide and round. "What I wouldn't have given to see that! As I say, the only time I have seen elves was at Yule at your house. And that was so brief, and we didn't get much of a chance to converse and to learn about them. To see and talk to one face to face like that…"

Reg nodded. "A little more than I would like, actually."

"What do you mean? You saw him in the garden, too? You're sure it was the same elf?"

"Oh yeah. Unless all elves are identical and go by the same name."

"Well, no. I haven't ever heard anything like that. And the ones that we saw in the cottage, they did not all look the same. They were all just as individual as humans."

"So, I saw them outside," Reg ticked off the appearances on her fingers, "inside during the seance. And tonight. And when Harrison stole the coffee pot and I was trying to clean up. And four in the garden."

Sarah blinked. "I've never heard of such a thing. Are you sure he isn't injured? Something that is preventing him from hiding?"

"I can't be sure. What part is it that makes them disappear? I don't have x-ray vision. I couldn't see any injuries, but that doesn't mean he didn't... hurt his chronometer or something."

"His chronometer?"

Reg's cheeks grew warm. "I know... I shouldn't steal ideas from sci-fi and think that they apply in real life. But a chronometer, that's something that measures or controls time, isn't it? So maybe the reason he keeps showing up is that whatever is inside of elves that helps them to stay in the right timeline is broken or damaged, so he keeps hopping all over..."

"What does time have to do with it?"

"He said he is coming back in time. He's trying to come back to a certain point in my life so that he can warn me. But he keeps getting it all wrong."

"He is traveling back in time?"

Reg nodded slowly. "Isn't that something elves do?"

Sarah frowned and rubbed at her temples. "I may have heard something about this before. I don't think it is something that they do regularly. Just some of them, under special circumstances."

"Like what?"

"I have no idea. I wish I could tell you."

"When they appeared in the garden—"

"They? Did you see more than one of them?"

"Well, I saw more than one of *him*..." Reg considered. Was it appropriate to say "they" when she was only talking about one person?

There had been more than one of Orri, so it seemed like the right thing to say.

"More than one… of the same elf?"

"Yeah. He kept appearing, until there were four of him. I guess they were all from the future, or from some other time. Trying to appear to me to give me a message…"

"Oh!" Sarah thumped her hand down on the table. "A harbinger!"

CHAPTER SIXTEEN

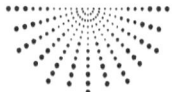

*R*eg shook her head. "What is a harbinger?"

Sarah took a long sip of her tea and put down her cup. "A harbinger is someone or something that brings you a warning of a danger that is down the road. A long time ago it literally meant someone who prepared the way ahead, booking you lodging and that kind of thing. But it changed to mean an omen or the bringer of a warning."

Reg nodded. "Okay. So that's what he is, I guess."

"I heard a story a long time ago about elves who were harbingers." Sarah closed her eyes, concentrating and trying to bring the details back to mind. "It has been so long. I believe that they are assigned or tasked with bringing an omen or warning. I don't know whether it is because of something they have done, or a gift they have, or a profession." She shook her head. "I don't know enough about elf culture to tell you."

"It sounded like it was some kind of assignment," Reg agreed. "He couldn't even go back until he had given me the warning, even though I told him I didn't want it."

Sarah's forehead creased. "Why would you not want the warning?"

"He keeps coming back. He gives me warnings about things that have already happened, or gives me the same one over again, and it's driving me crazy. I can't get away from him."

"What did he warn you about?"

Reg sighed, lounging back as much as the hard kitchen chair would allow. "About not accepting gifts from fairies. And... about water being a problem. Not using strange keys. And not being ensorcelled by Corvin."

Sarah raised her brows. "All good warnings."

"Yes, but a little too late, don't you think? I mean, I already learned not to do any of those things. I already had to deal with the consequences. So what's the point in him coming back again and again?"

"I suppose. But what about when he comes to you with a warning that isn't too late?"

"Do I have to keep putting up with him until he gets it right? What if he never does?"

"I don't know."

They sat in silence for a while.

"Maybe it's his first assignment," Sarah said. "He's just learning."

"Maybe. He said he's not very good at it. And he's right."

"We've all had missteps along the way. None of us can do our jobs the first time without making mistakes."

"Well then, maybe he should have a mentor or a supervisor. Someone to make sure that he learns how to do it the right way and doesn't keep screwing up."

"An apprenticeship would make sense. But maybe elves don't do that. Maybe it is all 'sink or swim.' Figure it out for yourself. Just because humans have supervisors and mentors, that doesn't mean that all cultures do."

"Next time he comes, I'm going to suggest it."

Sarah chuckled. "I don't see how it could hurt anything. You've already told him to go away."

"And not to come back, but he says he already has, so he can't not." Reg rolled her eyes. "I don't get how all this time travel stuff works."

"No one does, dear."

"Apparently, not even the ones who are doing the traveling."

"That would be awkward. They don't have any kind of map? No way to navigate through the tides of time?"

"I guess not. Or if he does, he doesn't know how to read it. Maybe he needs to stop and ask for directions."

* * *

Reg had eventually gone back to the cottage and managed to get back to sleep. She still felt groggy when she eventually got up around noon, but Starlight apparently decided that she'd been in bed quite long enough and would not leave her alone to sleep.

She groaned and pulled off her covers to climb out of bed, wobbling on legs that felt as if they belonged to someone else. She again felt hungover, when all she'd had was tea. She forced herself to have a glass of water before making her coffee, hoping that would do the trick, but it just sloshed around in her stomach making her feel seasick.

Starlight yowled.

"Yes, yes, I'm getting you something to eat," Reg assured him. "You just have to give me some time. I'm not a cat, you know, I don't always wake up all perky and ready to pounce on the day."

Starlight circled his dish. He had dry kibble, but Reg knew he wouldn't eat the dry food unless there were no chance of his getting anything else. And while Reg was there, there was still hope that she'd find him something better.

"Okay, let's see what's in here." Reg opened the fridge and browsed through the contents. Had Sarah been back to the cottage to fill it back up when Reg hadn't been around? Or while she had been sleeping? She thought she had cleared out most of what had been sitting in it, but it seemed like there was more than ever. Reg opened a few containers and found a tuna casserole.

Maybe the dairy and crunchy topping bits and spices were not the best for cats, but it was mostly tuna, so she knew Starlight would eat it.

"Here, have some of this." Reg took a large spoonful out and plopped it into Starlight's dish.

He complained once more, just to let her know she had taken too long, and then settled into eating it. Reg rubbed her temples and thought about the day ahead.

She didn't have any readings until the evening, by which time she would be feeling back to her usual self. But she should make the most of the afternoon before that. Maybe pick up some food from the grocery store. Put up some more advertisements on bulletin boards.

And she had told Gwythr that she would get him the information on the gems that she was interested in liquidating.

The gems were at least something she could sit down and do from home without showering and dressing. And maybe after doing that, her stomach and head would have settled down enough for her to eat something.

Reg went to the closet in her bedroom and pulled out the small wooden chest full of gems. The plastic bag that contained the gems that were not cursed was at the top. Reg picked it up and examined them through the plastic for a moment. She didn't expect them to be cursed again, but she had to check just to be sure. She touched them through the plastic, closing her eyes and feeling, using all her senses to be sure that everything was in order and the gems would let her sell them.

She took them out to the living room and put them down on the coffee table to take pictures and send the details to Gwythr.

CHAPTER SEVENTEEN

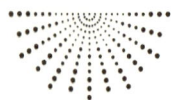

*I*t took Reg longer than she had expected to take pictures that turned out well and to compile the information she had from the various appraisers, matching each assessment up with the applicable gem, and then to send the information to Gwythr. What she had expected to be a five-minute job had ended up taking a couple of hours. Reg put the phone down and rubbed her eyes. Now time to have a bite to eat, shower, dress, and take a trip to the store. It would be evening before she knew it and she needed to be ready for her appointments.

The phone started to chime. Reg brushed moisture from the corners of her eyes and blinked to bring the screen into focus.

Gwythr.

That was quick. Reg hesitated, unsure whether to answer the call or not. Was he calling to say they would buy the stones? Or did he have more questions? She didn't really want to spend the whole afternoon in negotiations.

But he knew she had been at her phone or computer only moments ago, so it would be rude to ignore the call.

Reg sighed and picked up her phone. She swiped the call.

"Gwythr?"

"It be Brimir," another voice announced.

Reg frowned to herself. Brimir was the king's son and, as far as she could tell, he and Gwythr were not on friendly terms. So why was he calling from Gwythr's phone?

"Brimir. Uh… is everything okay? I thought this was Gwythr's number."

"Yes. He is attending to other matters."

"Oh. Okay. And did you need me, or did you just want to tell me that… he isn't available?"

"You sent him information on gems."

"Yes." Reg shifted uneasily. "Is that okay? I was asking him about whether the dwarfs would be interested in buying them. He said to send him the information. I don't think… that isn't going against some kind of protocol, is it? I didn't mean to disobey any rule."

"Whence came these stones?"

"They were held by the fairies. I can… give you more details if you want, the mines they came from initially. Gwythr didn't say he would need to know that."

Reg didn't want to get Gwythr in trouble if he'd been trying to do an end-run around the kingdom's laws, but she didn't want to end up under the bus either. If there were some other procedures she should have followed or person she should have talked to, then Gwythr should have told her that.

"They are good stones. The assessments are very promising."

"Yes. And I was hoping that they would find a good home in the dwarf mountain. I didn't want to sell them to someone who didn't know how to care for stones properly. Their history… they have been through enough without being mishandled further."

"This is true. Dwarfs would never abuse them."

"That's what I thought."

"You want to sell them to Gwythr, or you want to sell them to the king?"

"Uh… I don't really know. I don't want to disrespect either one of you. I am open to selling to both of you. I didn't mean to withhold something from you."

"We will talk. You will send me the same information you gave to Gwythr."

"Sure. What's your email address?"

Brimir gave it to her. Reg carefully tapped it into her phone for later use. "Okay, great. I look forward to doing business with you. If you're interested."

"Very good."

There was the sound of shouting in the background. Loud, angry voices. Reg held the phone more tightly.

"Is everything okay?"

"We are preparing for battle."

"Oh! I didn't know!" Reg was going to apologize for calling in the midst of their preparations, and then remembered that he was the one who had called her. "I'm sorry; you probably want to go deal with your duties."

"When do you expect the attack?"

Reg waited for the soldier that Brimir was addressing to answer the question and for Brimir to return to the phone call or to break the connection.

"Reg Rawlins," Brimir snapped.

"Yes?"

"The attack. When do you expect it?"

"The attack...? I don't know... what you are talking about."

"We are preparing for the attack on Nico. The warrior cat. When should we expect it?"

"Oh. Oh, boy. I don't... I don't think there will be an attack on him, just that someone *might* come to visit him. And if he does, that wouldn't be a good thing, but I don't think you want to start a war over it..."

"A powerful magical being coming to take our warrior cat. That is reason enough for war."

"I don't know that he's actually going to. I could be overreacting. I know he's gone to see some of the other—some of Nico's litter mates. That's all. He hasn't done any harm, but... I'm just a little worried..." Reg floundered, trying to express her concern without saying something that would push the dwarfs over the edge. If Harrison did go to see Nico, the results could be catastrophic.

Cat-astrophic.

Reg tried not to be distracted by the unintentional pun. She needed to carry on a serious conversation with the dwarf prince, not to start giggling at her own thoughts. It was a serious situation, but was preparing to do battle against an immortal the right response? Was there really anything that the dwarfs would be able to do if Harrison did show up and try to free Nico from the charms that held him bound?

"We are preparing," Brimir said sharply. "You do not know when he is coming?"

"No, I'm sorry. Maybe he won't even come, but… I don't trust that he won't. Francesca is very worried about it." She pressed her lips together, forcing herself to stop talking. She didn't want to voice Francesca's views or to explain to the dwarfs all about the Witch Doctor and the draugr and the kattakyns and the spell that held them bound.

She should probably have told the dwarfs about where Nico had come from when she realized that they wanted him to stay with them. They hadn't told any of the practitioners whom they had given the kattakyns to of their origins. They thought that it would be hundreds of years before the kattakyns could escape Francesca's spell, so what would be the point in telling their new owners what they really were?

The dwarfs, though, had recognized that Nico was something more than an ordinary cat. They didn't know what he was or where he had come from.

Or what danger there was in his breaking free from the spell that Francesca had woven around him.

"If you do not know, you do not know," Brimir growled. "At least you were able to give us a warning. You will tell us if you find out more?"

"About Har—about the being coming to see Nico? Yes, I'll let you know if I find something out. Right now, it is only a fear. I don't know for sure that he will. Maybe he'll get distracted and forget about him."

"Forget about a warrior cat? I do not think that will happen."

"Well, you don't know him… it is possible."

"You let us know when he is on the way. Or if you hear something else."

"Yes, Your Majesty. I will."

Reg didn't know if "Your Majesty" was the proper way to address a dwarf prince, but she thought it couldn't hurt. Even if it were an honorific that he didn't deserve, he would still be pleased that she had shown him that respect.

She hung up the phone and shut off the screen. Then she sat there looking at the blank screen, thinking it through. How did she manage to get in the middle of these things?

CHAPTER EIGHTEEN

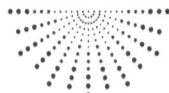

*T*he rest of the day and the evening passed uneventfully. But Reg still hadn't managed to get to the grocery store, and she knew that she had to at least get more kitty litter, even if she didn't get anything else to stock her cupboards and fridge. And she definitely needed food to stock her cupboard and fridge. It had been too long since she had bought anything herself and, while she had plenty of contributions by Sarah, Reg didn't have very much around that actually appealed to her.

She managed to get out of bed before noon and patted herself on the back as she watched the coffee drip into the new coffee pot at eleven o'clock. A *full hour* before noon. And she was barely even tired.

Hopefully, she would be able to keep that energized feeling for longer than an hour or two. She didn't want to conk out for a nap in the middle of the afternoon. Or worse yet, during a meeting with a client. Although, she could always say that it was a trance. A trance and sleeping could look a lot alike to the layman.

The coffee would help. Plenty of coffee.

She gave Starlight more of the tuna casserole, which didn't seem to have caused him any stomach problems the day before. Starlight happily chowed down and Reg checked her email, waiting for the coffee.

Nothing from the dwarfs regarding the gemstones. But she supposed she shouldn't expect anything if they were in the midst of preparing for battle.

How long would the preparations go on without an actual battle to fight? Would dwarfs get tired of playing dress-up after a few hours? A few days? Would they still be running scenarios and playing war games in a few weeks?

Or would Harrison show up before then?

Reg pushed the thought to the side. She didn't want to think of what might happen in that case. She remembered the Witch Doctor striking Damon down. Threatening to destroy them all. Bringing his power to bear against Corvin, who was well-matched due to the strength he had absorbed from the many magical artifacts that the Witch Doctor had been storing in the warehouse the showdown took place in. It had been terrifying.

The dwarf mountain was populated with not just dwarf warriors, but women and children as well. And Nico, the warrior cat. Reg didn't want any of them getting hurt. If Harrison showed up and the dwarfs attacked him, or if he tried to take Nico away or to unbind him…

Harrison might forget about the draugr kittens for a while. He was easily distracted. He might forget for a hundred years or more, and then the dwarfs would not be waiting for him and no one would know what harm he could do.

"Oh, Starlight. What am I going to do? You know him. Is there any way to stop him? What if I just ask him? He considers me his goddaughter. He would do whatever I asked, wouldn't he?"

Starlight looked up from his dish and studied her. Reg did not get reassuring feelings from him. She really wanted to feel him agree with her. She couldn't fight Harrison. None of them was strong enough to fight Harrison. He could only be matched by another immortal, and the only other immortal Reg knew, Weston, was his friend. Weston wouldn't oppose him in anything.

Immortals were unpredictable and dangerous. But Reg and Francesca could be completely wrong in their assessment of Harrison's behavior.

He might have no intention at all of doing anything to free the kattakyns and Samyr Destine.

* * *

It was afternoon when Reg got to the store, but she thought she was still making pretty good time. She pushed her cart up and down the aisles, looking for anything she might need. It was nice to have a little money in the bank account again so that she didn't have to worry about going without.

The lean years had left their mark on her. She often worried about not having enough food even when her cupboards and fridge were full. Things could change so quickly, and it really wasn't a big step from making enough money to provide for her needs to being out on the street with nothing.

That wasn't going to happen again. She had her business running again and, even if things went bottoms-up, she was sure Sarah would still let her stay at the cottage rent-free for a little while, until she figured out how to get back on her feet again.

Reg added a package of crackers and a box of cookies to her cart. Good, shelf-stable food that would keep for a long time. Just in case.

She turned down the next aisle. She needed more ice cream. And cat food and kitty litter in the pet aisle. Maybe she would get Starlight a toy, too. She didn't want him getting bored and fat because all he did was lie around all day cuddling with her or looking out the window. Indoor cats needed to stay active.

Reg picked up a bottle of olive oil.

It wasn't like she cooked. She just had the idea that if she had some things, like oil, that she needed for cooking, she might actually cook something. Maybe. Not that she knew what she would make with olive oil. French fries?

"Hail, Reg Rawlins!"

Reg jumped and looked up. Orri stood a few feet away from her. She hadn't seen lights or heard bells; he was just there. Maybe he had already been to the grocery store ahead of her or had materialized in another aisle before finding her.

There was a smash of breaking glass. Looking down, Reg saw a pool of oil spreading at her feet. Her hand was empty, the bottle shattered on the floor. Reg stepped carefully around it, looking around to see whether anyone had seen the accident.

She looked at Orri as she walked by him, trying to distance herself from the broken bottle of oil.

"Maybe you have a warning about dropping glass bottles this time?"

He raised his brows and looked at her.

"No, I suppose not," Reg sighed. She pushed her cart to the end and rounded the corner to enter the next aisle. Orri walked along beside her. "Well, what is it this time, then?"

"I have a warning for you."

"Yeah, I figured. What is it?"

He looked disappointed that she was not taking his appearance more seriously. Here he was, a time traveling elf, showing up to give her a special, personalized message, and she acted as though it were something that happened every day.

Which lately, it had.

Reg just waited, scanning the shelves for anything she might need. Who was she kidding? She wasn't going to cook anything. At best, she would warm something in the microwave. She even turned down food that required oven cooking. She didn't like the big, shiny oven and the blast of hot air that puffed up in her face when she opened the door. A person could burn herself trying to take out a pan of fries. She could forget that she'd left something in the oven and burn the house down.

Reg thought about that for a moment. How much of what was in her head were words that she'd absorbed from her foster homes? How would she burn herself? She was a firecaster! She wasn't going to be hurt by a little heat or fire. She should have a natural aptitude for cooking, given her powers.

Orri stopped Reg, holding his hand up to make her pay attention to his portentous announcement. A couple of other shoppers walking by gave him curious looks.

"Beware Janus and the cat with nine lives."

CHAPTER NINETEEN

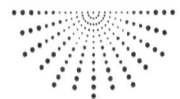

*R*eg looked at Orri. A new warning this time. One that she hadn't heard before. Janice?

Who was Janice? She didn't know anyone by that name.

And the cat with nine lives? Starlight, maybe? She knew that he had lived other lives before he had chosen Reg. He'd been powerful and important in the past. Maybe even one of the immortals. Harrison had told her that he was Bastet, an Egyptian god.

Reg found it hard to believe. He was her fuzzy, cuddly companion, who liked having his ears and chin scratched and got irritated if she didn't clean his kitty litter often enough. If he had been an Egyptian god, then what was he doing now, living with her, rubbing against the fridge door to beg for tuna casserole?

"Who is Janice?"

Orri gave a little bow, then fireflies began to blink in and out around him, swarming together, until she blinked her eyes and he was gone.

Reg looked around to see whether there were any more Orris hanging around. She saw only a couple of other shoppers, ordinary people, walking past the aisle.

* * *

Reg started putting the groceries away when she got home. Starlight jumped down from his spot in Reg's bedroom window and walked into the kitchen, arching his back to stretch, and then stretching each of his back feet out behind him in a way Reg always found charming. He'd obviously been sleeping the entire time she had been gone.

"I got you kitty food and litter," Reg told him. "Yeah. And do you really have nine lives, by the way? And is this your ninth, or do you still have a few left?"

Starlight ignored her, poking his head into the bags to see what else she had bought. Reg started putting items slowly into the cupboard and fridge. She threw out a few of the things that she thought Sarah had put there, foods that Reg wasn't ever going to eat, so she might as well reclaim her cupboard space for things that she would eat.

When there was a knock and the door opened, Reg startled guiltily and closed the garbage bin to hide the evidence. Sarah walked in, smiling and nodding at Reg pleasantly.

"Hello, Reg. Did you have a successful trip?"

Reg nodded. "Sure. Picked up a few things that I needed. I don't want you to think that you have to keep my cupboards stocked all the time. I can afford to feed myself."

"Oh, I know you can. I just end up with too much in my kitchen and figure maybe it is something that you would like." Sarah shrugged.

Or something Reg would throw out for her.

Reg put a few more cans in the cupboard. "I saw him again."

"You saw who, dear?" Sarah looked at her, then got it. "Oh, the elf? What did you say his name is?"

"Orri. Yeah. He showed up in the middle of the grocery store."

"Out in public? I've never heard of an elf appearing in public. Did anyone else see him?"

Reg wondered fleetingly whether Sarah believed her or thought that Reg was losing her marbles and hallucinating in the store.

Reg couldn't help wondering herself. Corvin had told her that the invisible friends she had when she was a child had probably been ghosts. He had told her how powerful she was. Others in Black Sands had agreed, and Reg had seemed to discover new powers and to have new adventures all the time. But what if it was all just in her mind? What if nothing was real and she was in an institution somewhere, experiencing everything in her head? Creating a new fantastical world in her own head.

What about that? What if none of it was real and she was just deluding herself?

"There were others around," she said vaguely, unable to remember specifically who might have seen Orri. Any of the clerks? The butcher at his counter in the back of the store? Friends or clients who had been there to get groceries at the same time? Black Sands was a small place. There were bound to have been people that she knew there.

"That's very surprising." Sarah picked a couple of items out of Reg's bags and put them in the fridge. "So what happened this time?"

"He scared the heck out of me. I didn't even see him materialize this time; he was just standing there."

"I imagine so. It would have scared me too. They really should be more careful. You can't just go around appearing to people and think that they won't have a heart attack or stroke."

"Or even just faint."

"Did you faint?"

"No. Thank goodness." Reg couldn't imagine what would have happened if she had fainted right in the middle of the grocery store. Would they slap her cheeks? Splash water on her? Call the police? Would she end up in an ambulance or the hospital wondering what had happened? "I didn't faint. Nothing happened."

If anyone had seen Reg drop the olive oil bottle, Sarah would probably hear about it sooner or later. The grapevine was alive and well in Black Sands.

"Did he have another warning? Or one of the same ones as before?"

"A different one this time. Janice and the cat with nine lives?"

"Janice?"

"Yeah. I don't even know a Janice. And the cat with nine lives? Is that Starlight? Francesca's Nicole? Some cat that is going to cross my path and I'm supposed to know about it ahead of time?"

"Maybe a black cat," Sarah suggested. "One that you don't want to cross in front of you, because of bad luck."

"Is it really bad luck for a black cat to cross your path?" Reg asked curiously.

"It is if you hit it. Especially for the cat."

Reg tried to stifle a laugh at the remark, snorting as she looked for a place for another box of cookies. Starlight yowled and looked at her reproachfully.

"I'm sorry," Reg told him. "But it is true. That's one of the reasons you are not allowed to go outside."

He meowed something again crossly and stalked out of the room instead of waiting to see whether she would feed him. Sarah watched Starlight's retreat.

"Well, if he's going to be so sensitive…"

Reg nodded. "He's fine. Don't worry about it."

"The cat with nine lives," Sarah mused.

"Don't all cats have nine lives? I mean, that's what they say, isn't it? It is really true?"

"Cats just have some close calls," Sarah said. "They get into mischief, and if they are lucky, they escape by the skin of their teeth. They don't *really* have nine lives."

"But they have more than one, right? Because I know Starlight has had others."

"Reincarnation, you mean? Yes, I suppose so. None of us knows how that might work, of course, or if it means that we all have an unlimited number of incarnations. There are many other traditions. Most religions believe in some kind of life to follow this one, whether it is as another person, or on another plane."

"Heaven?"

"That's one of them. There are many other names. And many other places our souls are said to go for their eternal reward."

Reg didn't want to think of those other places. She didn't believe in eternal punishment. She couldn't, not with the way she lived. She couldn't be a con and believe that people would be punished for every time they had lied and cheated.

"So do you think I already know the cat with nine lives?"

"You said that all the other warnings he has given you have already been fulfilled, so it would follow that this one has too. And the cat with nine lives might not even be a cat. It could be a person. A man who has been through several incarnations. Or who has been lucky to escape death in the past."

"Corvin? Do you think it's him?"

"Corvin." Sarah considered this. "No, I can't see that one. That doesn't mean he isn't, but I can't think of any reason that would point to him."

Corvin didn't even like cats. Reg thought about other people in her life. People that she had already known who had been threats to her. Because as Sarah had said, all the other warnings had been too late. Why would this on be any different?

"Oh!" It hit her with a flash of insight. "I know who it is!"

CHAPTER TWENTY

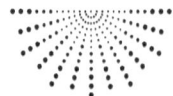

Sarah's eyes widened. "You know?"

"Of course. It's so simple. It's Jacky Lane. Maybe Janice was her real name, back in the beginning. It even starts with a J. Or maybe it's one of the aliases she took at some point."

"You think she was the cat with nine lives?"

"She had eight ghosts attached to her, right? That's eight lives. Plus her own. Nine. And she's a woman, so Janice could be her name."

"Well... yes. It's possible."

"And she was poisoning me. So of course Orri would warn me to stay away from her. It all makes perfect sense."

"You could be right," Sarah admitted. But she still sounded doubtful.

"I am. That's it."

"Then why would he say Janice *and* the cat with nine lives?"

"Because it is a riddle. That just makes it harder to solve. It doesn't mean anything."

Sarah pursed her lips. She shrugged. "Maybe. I don't know."

"Well, it's my warning, so I guess I'm the one who knows whether that's what it means or not."

Reg made herself sound confident because she didn't want Sarah to argue about it and to fill her mind with doubts. It was Orri giving her another warning about something that had already happened, just as he had done every time before. She hadn't told him this time that what he'd warned her about had already happened so, hopefully, he had gone home satisfied and would not be back. Without him reappearing in her life every single day, she could stop worrying and just go on with her life. She could work with her clients, relax with her cat and her friends, and afford to eat out or go to the grocery store when she needed to. That was a good life.

Sarah helped her to put the last few things away. She looked into the fridge for a moment. "It seems like you have an awful lot in here. We should probably clear some of it out."

Having cleared it out twice already, Reg didn't think there could be that much left. Certainly not enough for Sarah to complain about. She opened the fridge door and looked in. With the food that she had left behind, in addition to the things she had left in the fridge the last time, it was pretty full. Plus whatever else Sarah had added to it when Reg had been out. She supposed it was just a ploy to make sure that she looked through all the bowls and ate whatever Sarah had just added.

"Okay, I'll take a look later," she agreed.

Sarah nodded. "We wouldn't want anything to go bad."

Reg was tempted to wink at her and agree, but she didn't. She just nodded as if she didn't know what Sarah was up to.

"I'm glad you've worked out the warning by the elf." Sarah turned toward the door. Then she paused and looked back. "But if he warned you again about something that has already happened, then won't he come back again?"

"Not if I don't tell him."

"And you aren't worried that you still haven't been given the message that he was tasked with giving you?"

"He's given me all kinds of warnings. So, no. I'm not worried."

"You don't want to ignore a harbinger."

"I'm not. I've listened to everything he has to say."

"But you haven't received the *real* warning."

Reg rolled her eyes. "They were all real warnings. The timing was just off."

"To be a true harbinger, he has to tell you of something in the future."

Reg tried to ignore the knot in her stomach. "Then he's not a real harbinger. He just thinks he is."

Sarah tilted her head to the side and gave it a little shake. "You can think what you like, but I don't know. An omen is a sign of something to come. You don't eliminate the thing that is going to come or the omen by ignoring it."

Reg just pressed her lips together, waiting for Sarah to leave. There wasn't any point in arguing it anymore. Sarah knew her position. And Reg was sure that she was right.

Pretty sure.

* * *

Even though she had gone out for food, Reg wasn't in the mood to stay in and eat. She wanted to celebrate. Celebrate the fact that she had her business back and money in the bank. Celebrate the fact that she'd had her last visit from Orri. Life was good. Everything was good.

So she went over to The Crystal Bowl.

The last time she had tried to eat there, she had been turned away. Reg's siren parentage had only just been discovered, and the management had decided that they weren't going to serve "her kind" there.

But that was in the past now. People were forgetting about the revelation. Nothing had happened. Reg hadn't gone on a rampage. She hadn't dragged anyone to the icy depths of the ocean. She hadn't done anything exciting, but had stayed below the radar.

So she was confident that this time, they would allow her in. They had forgotten all about her history and would be happy for her patronage. She'd eaten there regularly ever since she had arrived in Black Sands, and she had missed it.

She went when she knew it would be busy. The more that was going on, the better the chances were that the staff would completely forget that they weren't supposed to be serving sirens.

Reg had to wait in the doorway for a few minutes while the hostess found tables for people. But it never filled up all the way so, in a few minutes, people were distributed to their various tables and the hostess turned to Reg. Her smile faltered slightly.

Reg gave her a determined, reassuring smile, and waited to be helped. She could go and find a table herself. She'd done it before enough times. Sometimes the staff were busy and the regulars didn't wait as the sign instructed. Reg looked around. She would just head to her regular table and the woman wouldn't stop her.

The tables in the corner she usually sat in were already occupied. It was the supper hour. Reg looked at the adjoining tables to see what was free. That was when she saw Corvin. He looked up and met her eyes across the restaurant. Reg wanted to turn away and leave but, if she did that, she might never have the confidence to go back there again. She couldn't run away.

Corvin stood. He nodded to the seat across the table from him. When the hostess turned around to see who Reg was looking at, Corvin gestured to the seat.

"Oh, there he is," Reg said hurriedly. "He's already been seated."

The hostess looked at Corvin, not sure what to do. She wanted to tell Reg that she wasn't welcome there, but Corvin tended to have an influence over the people around him. The same charms that made him so attractive to Reg also made it possible for him to get people to do things that they would not have done otherwise.

"I'll just go join him," Reg said casually, and slipped past the woman.

But the hostess followed, not willing to leave it at that. She stood beside the table as Corvin held Regina's chair out for her and then seated himself again.

"I'm sure Miss Rawlins would like a drink," Corvin told her, his voice oozing with charm.

The hostess drew out an order pad, though Reg knew that she didn't usually wait tables. "Of course," she agreed, in a faraway voice.

Reg placed her drink order. Just one glass. Alcohol and Corvin's charms together were a dangerously potent mix. The hostess brought Reg her drink and with reluctance drew away from the table again, leaving Corvin alone with Reg. Alone, but in a busy restaurant. He wouldn't be able to do too much with so many people around. As long as she could resist his taking her away from there, she should be fine.

"Well, I haven't seen you here for a while," Corvin observed.

"No. They haven't been that welcoming," Reg reminded him.

"Ah. I told you they would get over it. Once you've been here again a time or two, they'll forget all about that silliness."

"They should," Reg agreed. "They allow *you* in here, after all, and you're a lot more of a danger to the patrons here than I am."

He smiled. A silky-smooth smile that crept under her skin and made her break out in goosebumps. He knew what he was, despite his pretenses, and it did amuse him that he could charm the hostess and probably anyone else in the restaurant into giving him whatever he wanted. He was the one who could take all their powers away, but they were afraid of Reg.

She took a sip of her drink and let it burn all the way down. It felt good. She welcomed the alcohol taking the edge off her anxiety so that she could calm down and enjoy the evening. She didn't have to worry about omens and harbingers and whatever the time traveling elf had been trying to tell her. She could just enjoy a pleasant evening with a handsome man who always made her feel special.

CHAPTER TWENTY-ONE

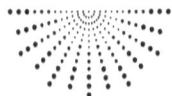

"**S**o how have you been faring?" Corvin asked after they had placed their orders with the waitress who approached the table and made moon eyes at him.

"I'm just fine," Reg said firmly. "No complaints."

"No? Well, that's good. You've had some interesting challenges lately. I'm glad to hear that they have been overcome."

"That's right," Reg agreed. "Smooth sailing now."

Corvin leaned forward slightly. "Maybe you would like to go sailing again sometime," he suggested.

"Yeah? You think I don't remember how you ran away last time? Seems to me that you were not so keen to get close to me then."

"Well…" Corvin shifted uncomfortably. Reg watched him try to come up with a manly explanation for why he'd had to separate himself from her. If he was so strong and had such an influence over her, then why had he found it necessary to retreat? "We *were* on the water," he admitted finally.

And they both knew what that meant. He knew that when her siren instincts kicked in and she touched him, he did not have the ability to resist her. So he had put distance between them while he still could.

Reg smiled. Score one for the "weaker" sex. "So maybe you don't want to go sailing with me?"

"Only under... carefully controlled conditions."

"Yeah. That's what I thought."

She enjoyed knowing that she could get the upper hand over him, even though she never intended to be ruled by her siren desires. It was just nice to know that she *could*.

"Have you talked with Davyn?" Corvin asked, turning his head away from her slightly and changing the subject.

"About you?" Reg shrugged. "Not much to say. He knows that I know about your application."

"And you told him that you don't care if I am readmitted to the coven?"

"Not in so many words."

Corvin's face tightened. Reg felt a definite cooling in his ardor.

"What did you tell him?"

"Nothing. They have a whole process. I'm not going to oppose anything, but I know that nothing has changed. You haven't changed."

"Everything has changed," Corvin countered. "You are not the same person you were when you first came here. You are not so... vulnerable. And me? I have acquired other powers, other abilities. I am not the same person I was either."

"You're more powerful. That doesn't exactly recommend you, does it?"

The waitress brought over their meals. She smiled and batted her eyelashes at Corvin, and coolly ignored Reg, doing nothing more than slapping the plate down in front of her.

If the waitress wanted Corvin, she could have him. Reg was not her rival.

They dug into their meals.

"What else is new?" Corvin asked after a while. "Your business is going well, you said?"

"Yeah. I'm really happy about that. Money in the bank is a *good* thing."

"Yes, it is," he agreed. "In days gone by, it was easier to live without cold hard cash. People could live off the land, barter for goods, trade, find a way to work things out. But now? Cash is king. No money means you're out of luck."

"Yeah, and believe me, you don't want to be there."

Corvin didn't ask her about what she knew of being down on her luck. But she had turned away his inquiries before, so he knew better than to ask.

"What do you know about elves?" Reg asked him. "Especially harbingers."

"Harbingers." He raised an eyebrow. "That's getting into some pretty esoteric stuff. Where did you hear about harbingers?"

"From Sarah. But she didn't know a lot about them. And with all your studies, I thought maybe you might have some information that you could share."

"Not much, unfortunately. The fables are very sparse on details about harbingers. The elves are a very secret people to begin with. They don't have much to do with humans or anyone else. To even have seen their lights or heard their bells in the garden... not many people have even experienced that. Having seen them face to face like you have is very rare."

"Well, I've experienced a little more than that."

"More?" Corvin popped a bite of steak into his mouth and chewed. "Do you mean that you've seen them again? Since Yule?"

Reg nodded.

He chewed slowly, intrigued. "And this wasn't just a fleeting glimpse or the lights and bells, was it? You mean a real... personal encounter."

"Yes."

"If you're asking about harbingers, then one of them must have given you a warning."

"Yes. Several of them."

"More than one elf gave you a warning?"

"No. One elf gave me several warnings."

"Several of them." Corvin poked his food around with his fork for a minute, then pushed his plate away an inch. "Did you... not listen the first time? I don't understand."

"Of course I listened," Reg protested. "I wouldn't just ignore him. But... he kept giving me warnings about things that had already happened."

Corvin snorted. "A fine harbinger he is to tell you the past."

Reg smiled and nodded. "Yeah. It's been kind of frustrating. What am I supposed to do? Just nod and say, 'oh yes, thank you for the warning'? Pretend that I haven't already dealt with it?"

"I don't know. What is he expecting?"

"He wants to give me a warning for something that hasn't happened yet. It seems like it is his mission. I think with the last warning, he was satisfied that he had told me something that hadn't happened yet. But thinking it over later... I think that it did happen. I just didn't know what he was talking when he gave it. Because he sort of talks in code, you know."

"Yes, omens are usually expected to be somewhat cryptic."

"I always thought that the reason fortune tellers talk that way is so that people can read whatever they want to into the reading. Like if I say you'll meet a handsome stranger, it's pretty much guaranteed that you will at some point. And then you'll know that I actually told your fortune. I thought that was just part of the con."

"And maybe it is in many cases. There are not a lot of prognosticators around who are on the up-and-up. Most of it probably is cold reading and guesswork. But a harbinger elf... well... I don't think there are a lot of elven cons around."

"There could be; you wouldn't really know, would you? They don't look that much different from humans. Maybe they like their greens and browns, but they could dress in modern style and colors and would you be able to tell them from humans?"

"Well, the fact that you rarely see an elf might be a tip-off."

"Maybe you do. Maybe they are just good at blending in with humans."

Corvin stared at Reg for a few minutes. Finally he shrugged. "Yes. I suppose if they were not afraid of people and were around them enough, they could learn to blend in. But sighting an elf is so rare, I highly doubt that would ever happen."

But if they were really good at blending in, he wouldn't know. They could be among the humans already.

"They are very shy and reluctant to communicate with humans," Corvin reiterated. "So I think that the odds that they would choose to do such a thing are pretty low."

"Maybe. But not impossible."

"Your harbinger, is he good at blending in?" Corvin asked, bringing the subject back around.

"Uh... no, not really. He keeps materializing out of nowhere, and he's got the whole 'twinkly' thing going on. I mean, he did appear in the grocery store and nobody screamed and fainted. He startled the heck out of me, but I don't think anyone else noticed." Reg took a few bites of her dinner. "The first time he appeared was in the middle of a seance."

"You're kidding. How did that go over?"

"Well, everybody figured they got their money's worth that night! I had him repeat his warning for them, so they had a real 'ghostly' warning from beyond the grave. When they tell their friends about it— you can't buy publicity like that."

Corvin chuckled and leaned closer to Reg. "You are a girl after my own heart, Reg Rawlins."

Reg felt warm and tingly all over. It was difficult to pull back from him and to put a psychic shield up around herself. She wanted to be there, close to him, warm and comfortable. The urge to touch his hand or arm to strengthen the connection between them was almost overwhelming.

"No," she said softly. "We can't go there."

She couldn't let him charm her. And she couldn't touch him and unintentionally bring him under her thrall. Why did things have to be so complicated? If he had been a man without any paranormal powers, and she had been just a regular woman, with no psychic stuff or siren stuff to worry about... it would have been different. But she wasn't sure whether there would even have been an attraction between them if not for their gifts. Corvin was handsome, granted, but did she see him as gorgeous because of his face or his charms?

CHAPTER TWENTY-TWO

*A*fter a moment, Corvin eased back from Reg as well, giving her space to breathe and allowing them both to get their equilibrium back. He toyed with his food for a moment, then started eating again.

"So what kind of warnings are you getting from your harbinger? Does he have a name, by the way?"

"Orri."

"Orri the oracle?" Corvin asked with a chuckle.

"What?"

"Seems like an apt name for someone who gives you warnings about the future, that's all."

"Is that someone well-known? Orri the oracle?"

"No, it was a joke. I'm sure he's not called Orri the oracle."

"Oh, okay." Reg shook her head. She was never quite sure when she had missed something that was from a fairy tale or was well-known in the magical community. It seemed like there were so many things she had missed by not only growing up in foster care, where her education was spotty and inconsistent, but also by not growing up in a community like Black Sands or at least a family with some knowledge of how the paranormal world worked.

"So what has he been warning you about?"

"Well… about you, for one thing."

Corvin looked up from his meal. He smiled. "Really."

"Be not ensorcelled by fair face. Sound like anyone you know?"

Corvin rubbed his whiskered chin. "Well… that could be anyone."

"Anyone good-looking, you mean."

"I wouldn't want to presume."

"You don't need to pretend that you don't know you're handsome. It's one of the ways that you charm women. There's no point in pretending to be modest about it. You're like a peacock."

"And a peacock knows that he's handsome?"

"Why would he spread his tail out like that if he didn't?"

Corvin chuckled. "I can't fault your logic."

"And it wasn't a warning about *anyone* handsome. It was a warning about someone who is handsome and can ensorcel me." She gave him a look. "And that would be you."

He had another drink of his scotch. "I don't know if I've ever been the subject of a warning by a harbinger before."

"I wouldn't be too surprised. Everybody who knows about you should be warning any unsuspecting women about what you do."

"Only those with powers."

That made Reg curious. "Do you only pursue women who have powers? Romantically, I mean."

It seemed like that would get tiring after a while. Like only eating sugary foods. Didn't he want to have a relationship with a woman who didn't have powers? To give him a break from just women whose powers he was interested in? To cleanse his palate and have a relationship with someone just because of who she was?

Corvin considered the question for a long moment. "I can… influence people whether they have powers or not and whether I am interested in them or not. Being able to persuade them to do what I want is part of my… condition. I've never had to live without that. So women without powers are interested in me."

"Yeah, but that's not really what I asked. I wondered whether you are interested in them."

He cocked his head slightly, blinking. "No…" he said eventually, "I don't think I am. Women without powers are just… uninteresting. Weak. They don't hold much attraction for me."

"Even if they're really gorgeous?"

"Despite what the media tells you, appearance is not the only thing that interests a man. There are a lot of things that enter into the equation. And for me, the woman's gifts are a very big part of that equation."

"So if a really gorgeous woman was coming on to you, but she didn't have any gifts, you wouldn't even be interested?"

Corvin's eyebrows went up. "No."

And did that apply to a woman whose gifts he had already taken? Reg thought about the way that he had behaved toward her after stealing her powers, back when she had first moved to Black Sands. He had been aloof. Gloating. Completely undisturbed by her distress over discovering that the voices in her head had been suddenly silenced and she was as hollow and empty as an eggshell.

Until Hawthorne-Rose had started to torture her. That had changed things. That was when Corvin had decided to return her powers to her, so that they could overcome him and escape to somewhere safe.

So maybe somewhere, deep down, he did have feelings for her that were separate from her powers. Only he'd never had the opportunity to explore his feelings, constantly hungering, always needing to find his next prey.

Corvin was watching Reg, his eyes calculating. Reg pushed the topic of discussion away. She didn't want to know how he felt about other women. She didn't need to know what it was about her that he found attractive, only that he would steal her gifts if given the opportunity.

"So Orri's latest warning, the one in the grocery store."

Corvin's eyes focused on her. "Yes? What was the latest warning?"

"Beware of Janice and the cat with nine lives."

Corvin's brows went up, and he shook his head. "And you think that refers to…?"

"It's pretty obvious, isn't it? Jacky Lane."

"No… I don't follow. How does that have anything to do with Jacky Lane?"

"Janice was probably her original name. She just changed it so that it wouldn't be easy to track her movements. An alias. She had a lot of different aliases. And she had eight ghosts attached to her. So… nine lives, get it? It makes perfect sense."

"Except she is not a cat."

"Yeah, but harbinger warnings are like that. Tricky. You have to be able to interpret them."

"Hmm." Corvin did not appear to be convinced. "He said Janice *and* the cat, didn't he? He didn't say 'Janice, the cat with nine lives.'"

"Well, no. But that's just… being tricky. Making it harder to figure it out."

"It is not the harbinger's intention to be unclear, though. If he's trying to warn you, he wants you to understand what the warning is about."

"Well… maybe. I don't understand his motivations. I think he just wants to give me the warning and disappear back to his own time. He can't go back until the job is finished."

"And his job is to warn you about something that has already happened?"

"As long as he thinks it hasn't already happened. How would he know? If he thinks he's done what he needed to, he can go home and be with his wife and kids and forget all about being a harbinger. Unless it's his job, and I really hope it isn't."

"And he thinks that he gave you a warning about something that hasn't yet happened."

"I didn't realize it was about Jacky at the time, so I thought that yeah, it was about something in the future. So as far as he's concerned, it was a warning about the future, not the past."

"If he can jump through time, then won't he know whether his warning had any effect or not? When he returns to his own time, won't he be able to tell whether you have acted based on his warning? If something has changed in his own time?"

"You don't know how time travel works," Reg said, waving her hand at him. "It isn't like in all those sci-fi movies and books."

"I *did* go with you on your little journey to the past. I know as much about actual time travel as you do."

He didn't say *and more* but Reg heard it in his voice.

"Well, all that stuff about paradoxes and not being able to see yourself if you go back in time and all that is just made up. It doesn't really work that way."

"But if he comes here and warns you, and you change something based on that warning, then won't he be able to tell that in the future?"

"Maybe. Maybe not. Maybe he'll just ask the me in the future, and I'll tell him that it did. Because I'll know that I want to stop the guy from going back in time and giving me another warning."

Corvin shrugged. He ate the last few bites of his meal and pushed it to the side.

"You really don't think it was about Jacky Lane?" Reg asked.

"No, I don't. It is a good fit, but not quite. Like forcing the wrong puzzle piece into a picture. It almost fits... but it doesn't."

CHAPTER TWENTY-THREE

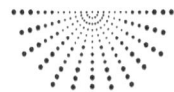

*R*eg opened the door to Francesca and let her in. Francesca had her black cat, Nicole with her. NEE-cole in Francesca's Creole accent. She released Nicole to go play with Starlight. Reg laughed as they watched the two cats greet each other enthusiastically, sniffing, licking, and play fighting. Until the two decided that they wanted some privacy and took off to the bedroom.

Nicole was not one of the kattakyns, though she was a pure black cat like they were. Reg couldn't tell Nicole and all the kattakyns apart physically, but when she thought about their personalities and felt their auras, they were quite easy to differentiate.

But the kattakyns had all been rehomed and now it was just Nicole. Nicole with Francesca and Starlight with Reg. Back to the cats they'd had initially, prior to the fight with the Witch Doctor.

"How has it been?" Francesca inquired politely. She was a white Haitian, blond with long spiraling curls. She attained a level of beauty that Reg would never achieve in a million years with thousands of dollars' worth of product.

Reg had made some tea, and she put the tray down on the coffee table where they both sat down, so they could pour their own drinks.

"Things are going well. Work has picked up. Lots of appointments for readings and seances."

"Very good. That must be a relief for you."

"It is. I feel much better. It's a lot easier to relax when you don't have to worry about where your next meal is coming from."

"It was not that bad, surely."

"It has been before. I didn't want to get back there. It doesn't take long, if you're not making enough money, for things to get really bad really fast."

"This is true," Francesca agreed. She sipped the tea she had prepared for herself. Reg spooned more sugar into hers.

"The real excitement that we've been having around here the last little while was an elf who kept appearing to me."

"An elf." Francesca looked impressed. Like the others, she knew that elves did not commonly appear to humans.

"Yeah. A harbinger, Sarah calls him. The kind that comes with a warning."

"Very rare. In Haiti—"

"Here too," Reg agreed, not really wanting to hear about elves in Haiti. Were there even elves in Haiti? "Did you ever see one?"

Francesca looked as though she would say something, then shook her head. "No. Not myself. But there are old stories. And my grandmother—"

"She saw a harbinger?"

"She told me stories."

"Did she know why they do it?"

"What do you mean?"

"I just mean... why do they appear to people to give them warnings? Why do they care what happens to humans at all? Do they give warnings to other magical races?"

"I do not know. Maybe it is penance for a wrong? Or a sense of justice that needs to be served?"

Reg nodded. She didn't get the feeling that was why Orri kept appearing to her. She felt like he was required to do it, but not as a punishment for anything he had done wrong. She would ask him if he appeared again. But hopefully he would not. It had been a couple of days since she had seen him last, and she hoped that meant that he had completed his task, or believed that he had, and he would not be back.

She couldn't help feeling a little guilty about that. Everyone else would be so excited to see an elf just one time, and she had seen him multiple times and didn't want him around.

But it wasn't like he was an entertaining guest. He didn't sit and watch TV with her or have a drink or share interesting stories. He didn't even gossip about his friends. All he did was appear, tell her that she was in danger from something or other that she really wasn't in danger from any longer, and then disappear again.

And to be honest, she didn't like the bugs either.

She was sure that elves were very clean. It wasn't like they were crawling with lice or shed cockroaches everywhere. But Reg didn't like the moths and other bugs flying around her face or in her house. They gave her the willies.

At least they weren't spiders. She really hated spiders.

"This harbinger of yours, what does he say?" Francesca asked.

"Lots of different warnings," Reg advised. She told some of the ones that she knew Francesca would find interesting. She didn't mention the one about Jacky Lane right away, because Francesca hadn't really known Jacky. She wouldn't understand the thing about the eight ghosts' lives plus her own life. Nine lives, just like Orri had said.

But Francesca showed interest in all the warnings and kept asking about more. Maybe she was more interested in Reg's experience than Reg had initially thought.

Reg told her the last couple of warnings. Francesca stared at her.

Reg squirmed in her seat and took a drink of her tea, pretending not to notice Francesca's intense stare.

"Did he say Janice or Janus?" Francesca asked, pronouncing the latter JAY-nus.

"Uh... I don't know. Janice, I think. Why does it matter?"

"Janus, he was a Roman god. An immortal."

"I've never heard of him before."

"The two-faced god. The beginning. The father."

"The father? I thought that was... Cronos. Or Jupiter."

Francesca shook her head. "Janus."

"Well, why should I beware of *him*?" Reg didn't like Francesca upending her theory that the omen referred to Jacky Lane. *Janice* might be Jacky, but *Janus* was not.

Francesca put her cup of tea down and squeezed her hands together.

"You know the immortals. They are unpredictable. They have great power. They cannot be trusted."

"That's just the Witch Doctor. He's the one who fought us. He's the one who had bad feelings against the human race."

"He is not the only one. The other immortals do not have regard for humans either. We are nothing to them. They don't consider us to be… individuals with feelings and souls. We are just… animals."

"No." Reg frowned and shook her head. "That's not true."

"It is."

"Weston was in love with my mother. He still is. He doesn't consider her an animal!"

"You romanticize them," Francesca said. "Just like the ancient peoples did. But they are not special because they are long-lived. Or because they have powers beyond what we can wield. They are *not* gods."

"You're the one who said he is."

"No, I was just explaining the name. Not saying that Janus really is… a god."

Reg rolled her eyes. "Okay. So beware the immortals. And I have already met the immortals. I've already learned that lesson too. It's just another warning that he is too late on."

"Janus and *what*? What did he say?"

"And the cat with nine lives. I thought that was Jacky, because…" Reg trailed off. If Janus was one of the immortals, then the cat with nine lives didn't mean Jacky. She hadn't had anything to do with the immortals.

Francesca didn't look happy about this. "The cat with nine lives. That could mean Samyr Destine. The nine kattakyns."

Reg remembered Weston picking up one of the kattakyns, laughing uproariously. *Destine, Destine, what have you done?*

He had been able to recognize the kattakyns as pieces of the Witch Doctor. Each of the kattakyns held a piece of him. And if all nine were put together and were no longer bound, then Samyr Destine could be whole once more. Like Weston when he was released, he could choose to go where and when he pleased, whether it was good for the human race or not.

338

"The Witch Doctor," Reg said finally, voicing what they were both thinking. "The cat with nine lives is the Witch Doctor."

"Samyr."

Reg's stomach knotted. "It could be." She kept her voice carefully even. "That would mean that Orri still has the wrong place in the time-line. Because he's talking about the Witch Doctor and the kattakyns being a danger. He was a danger to me back then, but he isn't anymore. Not now that he's bound by your spell. I'll be long dead by the time he can re-form."

Francesca did not look reassured.

Reg knew it was about the past. Everything that Orri had brought her had been about the past, not the future. It was all about lessons she'd already learned or battles she had already fought. Not anything new.

"Samyr Destine..." Francesca mused. "If he is the cat with nine lives, then he is not Janus."

Reg thought back to battling the immortal. He was the same being as had tortured and killed her mother when Reg was four years old. The Witch Doctor had recognized Reg when she approached, had gloated over the power that he had over her. If Reg were a harbinger, she would certainly have warned herself about that evil being and the fact that he was going to pop up in her life again. Seeing and recognizing him and the horrible feeling of dread that he brought with him had been terrifying.

"I don't know anything about Janus other than what you have told me. Are you sure the Witch Doctor isn't Janus? He can't be both Janus and the cat with nine lives?"

Francesca considered, rubbing the back of her neck. She was probably getting a headache. Reg was getting one herself. A great big one that wasn't going to go away very easily.

"He did not look like any of the images I have seen of Janus," Francesca said slowly.

Starlight didn't look anything like Bastet, either. The immortals could change their forms however they wanted to. If the form of the Witch Doctor was not one that would serve him, Destine could choose to appear as an animal, the doctor down the street, even Francesca herself. He could take whatever form he preferred, so saying that he did not look like Janus was useless.

"Janus is always shown with two faces," Francesca explained. "One looking forward, and one looking back."

"But that doesn't mean he actually has to have two faces."

"No. Of course not," Francesca agreed. "I am just thinking out loud. Trying to get it straight in my head."

"Right."

"Samyr Destine was very hungry for power. Very... angry. He did not want to wait. Violent. Raising draugar is not something that most people, even an immortal, would do. It violates the rules. Steals from death."

"So... he's probably not the god of death."

"No. Although... the god of death *could* raise an army of the dead."

"But Samyr Destine only raised one draugr at a time."

"True." Francesca nodded. "Death would, I think, have raised more of them and faster."

"So what is Janus like? Those Greek gods always had personalities. They weren't perfect like the gods in some other religions."

"No, the Greeks and Romans preferred gods that were imperfect, with vices like themselves," Francesca agreed. "Janus was not one of the ones who was always partying or chasing the women. He was the god of beginnings. He looked both forward and backward at the same time."

"The two faces."

"Right. Sacrifices were made in his temple. Not animal sacrifices, but offering up sweet cakes of spelt and honey and milk."

"Sweet cakes?" Reg repeated, her stomach beginning to do back flips.

"Yes. He was honored at the beginning of many ceremonies—"

"Like the Spring Games?"

"Well, there weren't any Spring Games yet. They came later..." Francesca leaned toward Reg, frowning. "What is it?"

"Harrison. You don't think that it's Harrison, do you?"

"Your Harrison." Francesca rubbed the frown lines between her eyes, the psychic third-eye position. "You said that he would not do anything to harm you. That he always protected you."

"Yes. He always has. I mean, he's a little flighty sometimes. Gets distracted by other things. I wouldn't trust him to keep a goldfish alive. But… yeah. He's always been my protector."

"And what if you were warned that you had to beware of him?"

Reg's headache was getting worse the more they talked about it. She wanted to go to her room and lie down in pitch-black silence. Maybe then her headache would recede again. It felt like she was going to have an aneurysm. Harrison? She didn't have to worry about Harrison.

If she were in danger from Harrison… she wouldn't believe it. Not if just anyone told her. It would take something big to make her believe it.

Something like a harbinger.

CHAPTER TWENTY-FOUR

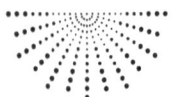

"You don't think that Orri was warning me about Harrison," Reg protested. "Harrison would never do anything to harm me."

"He does seem to like you... but that has not stopped the immortals from doing irreparable harm in the past. If something they do harms one human... or one million humans... what does that matter to them? How many of them killed their own lovers, parents, or children?"

"They have rules about not being allowed to harm their own kind."

"Perhaps. But they have not always obeyed those rules. And you are not their own kind."

"Harrison..."

He had always been so good to her. She couldn't believe that he would do anything to endanger her.

But when she had asked him to help her to fight the Witch Doctor he had refused.

He had told her that they could fight the Witch Doctor if they used all their assets, and that had proven to be true, so it wasn't as if he'd had to intervene. He hadn't had to break the rule against harming another immortal.

"And if Harrison is Janus...?" Francesca said delicately, and left the sentence hanging.

If Harrison is Janus?

The elf had told her to beware of Janus. So she would have to be careful. She would have to guard herself, even if she didn't think she was in any danger from him.

"The full warning," Francesca prompted.

"*Beware Janus and the cat with nine lives.*" Reg swallowed. "You said that Harrison had visited a couple of the kattakyns."

"And you thought it was nothing," Francesca said accusingly. "But it is not nothing. You cannot trust that he will not find and unbind each one of them. He has the power. Far greater than mine. My charms will not hold if he attempts to undo them."

"Then… what do we do?"

"What *can* we do?"

"How can we hide the kattakyns from him? There must be a way. You said that the immortals are not all-knowing. So we can keep things from him."

"You may be able to keep your thoughts from him. But to hide the kittens from him? I fear it is not possible."

Reg felt guilty, even though she had done nothing wrong. Could she keep her thoughts from Harrison? She had not done such a great job of that in the past. He appeared when she thought of him or called out to him in her mind. It was actually surprising that he had not shown up as they were discussing him.

CHAPTER TWENTY-FIVE

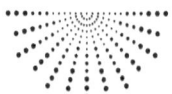

*T*here was a strange yowl from the bedroom. Reg had never heard Starlight make that kind of noise before. She was on her feet in an instant, tiptoeing toward the door to check on Starlight and Nicole. She didn't want to bother them if they were just playing together, or having a discussion, or if things were getting friendly.

Francesca was right behind Reg. They moved quickly to the bedroom, and Reg could see before she drew up even to the door that there was someone else there.

A tall, skinny shadow on the wall.

Reg looked at him. A tall, skinny man, not that much different from the shadow.

The mustached man turned his head to look at Reg, smiling pleasantly. He held a black cat in his arms.

Francesca gasped.

Reg looked at her, and then back at Harrison. There wasn't anything to be shocked about, as far as she could see. Other than his terrible fashion sense in combining a Scottish kilt that fell way above his knees with some kind of middle eastern robe. With a hood, because Harrison rarely went anywhere without some kind of hat.

Nothing horrible had happened. Harrison had a cat—one of the kattakyns, Reg assumed—but it appeared to be okay, just as when she had seen the kattakyns last.

"It's okay," Reg assured Francesca. "Everything is fine. Right, Uncle Harrison? There's nothing to worry about?"

"Why would I be worried?" he asked blandly.

Reg looked around the room. Everything was fine. Starlight and Nicole were on the bed, watching. They were both okay. Reg reached out her senses to the kattakyn. It was not Nico, but she had known that at a glance. Nico would not have been sitting comfortably in Harrison's arms. He'd be climbing up him, clawing to get away, or jumping from his arms to the curtains. She had reached out to the kattakyns before, helping to evaluate their strengths and gifts in order to match them with the most appropriate companions. They wanted the kattakyns to be happy, not to run away and look for the others. Not for their owners to decide that they had received the wrong familiar and to rehome them or send them back to Florida.

They had done everything they could to make sure that the kittens would all be happy in their new homes and not have any reason to leave. And Harrison had interfered. But all was not lost. The cat was in one piece, and they could take it back to its home or have Harrison do so. He just didn't understand why it was so dangerous. What the Witch Doctor could do if he were free again. He had nearly destroyed all of them; Reg didn't want to see what would happen if he were given a second chance.

The kattakyn was sleepy and relaxed, calm even though he had been plucked from his home by someone he didn't know. Maybe the Witch Doctor part of him knew Harrison, just as Harrison and Weston had been able to recognize the Witch Doctor in each of the kattakyns.

"Horace," Reg said to Francesca. The cat who had been sent to Egypt.

Francesca nodded her agreement. She was not psychic, but she had cared for the kattakyns in her home until they had found homes for each of them, so it was easier for her to recognize each of them by their physical attributes, even if at first glance they appeared to be nine identical black cats.

"Uncle Harrison, why did you take Horace from his home? He really should be back in Egypt where he belongs."

345

"I thought he should come here," Harrison countered, looking down at the cat in his arms. "This is much better."

"Why? It doesn't make any difference to you where he is, does it?"

"It makes a difference to him." A nod from Harrison indicated the cat.

Reg's stomach roiled. Did *Destine* have a preference? Was there enough of his consciousness in just one of the nine cats to tell Harrison what he wanted? Reg had thought that with Francesca's binding spell and the Witch Doctor's consciousness spread across nine different entities, Destine's self would be too diluted to be able to communicate with anyone. He was supposed to be bound for a thousand years, unable to communicate with anyone.

"To the cat? The cat likes to be with the people who feed him. With the people that he has grown to trust. He doesn't want to be here, in a home he's never known before."

"Maybe he wants to be with his mother." Harrison looked at Nicole.

"But she's not actually his mother, you know. She helped to take care of them, but she isn't really their mother. His mother."

Harrison looked at Reg. "You had other mothers."

"Yes, I did," Reg conceded.

"And a cat cannot have more than one mother?"

"He can. Of course. I'm just saying, he wouldn't really consider her his mother. He'd rather live in his home in Egypt. Where he's gotten used to the people and the way things run."

"He likes it here," Harrison said simply.

Reg looked at Francesca. She wasn't sure what to say.

"You cannot bring him here," Francesca said firmly. "And you cannot unbind them. They must remain bound for the humans to be safe."

Harrison turned his head to look at Francesca, as if he'd been unaware that she was there before. "You are the one who bound them?"

Francesca nodded. "Samyr wanted to kill Reg. You wouldn't have wanted him to kill Reg, would you?"

"He will not."

"Not if he remains bound. For at least as long as Reg lives. You can't unbind him."

"We cannot harm our own kind. It is against the rules."

"I'm not asking you to harm him. Just to leave things alone. To keep Reg safe. And the other humans."

"You should not have done this to him."

"It was the only way to make sure he could not do any harm."

"The immortals are not to be bound. They are powerful. They are to have free movement throughout the universe."

"Weston was bound, wasn't he?" Reg suggested. "And that was okay. Because it was to keep him safe. And me. You wanted to keep me safe, didn't you?"

"I did not bind him. He hid himself."

"But he couldn't get out until I released him with the key, right? So he was bound. He chose to be bound."

Harrison considered this.

"It was just for a little while," Reg continued. "He didn't mind being bound for a few years to make sure that he couldn't be punished for what he had done and I could grow up in safety."

"Weston hid himself," Harrison said slowly.

"Yes. Exactly. And we're hiding the Witch Doctor so that he can't do any harm. After a while, he'll be free again. Just like Weston. I'm sure he won't mind being bound for a few years."

"He did not choose this."

"He chose it by his actions," Francesca said, an edge to her voice that said she was not to be trifled with. "He is the one who created the draugar, a thing which is against nature. He is the one who sent his essence into the nine kattakyns, diluting his strength, when Corvin took so much of his power. He wanted to hide and escape. He wanted to be among all these cats so that he could rest."

"Where is the warlock?" Harrison asked, distracted by Francesca's words. He looked around. In a moment, there was a voice calling from the front of the cottage.

"Regina? Are you here?"

Corvin. Harrison had again transported Corvin, bringing him to Reg's cottage this time, a place Reg had done her best to keep him out of. But the immortal's powers were much stronger than hers and she couldn't prevent him from transporting himself or others right into the middle of her life.

"In here," Reg called.

Corvin appeared in the doorway of the bedroom. He looked around at the cats and people standing around. "I have dreamed about being in your room again," he told Reg in a husky voice, "but this isn't quite how I pictured it."

Reg snorted and shook her head. She looked at Harrison. "You can't just transport people into other people's houses without asking. I don't want Corvin here."

Harrison rubbed his chin. "Can I bring him?"

"You need to ask *before*, not after. Sooner or later, I would think you would get it! You understand the difference between before and after, don't you?"

He cocked his head slightly. "I don't think humans understand the sameness of before and after," he countered.

Reg didn't even want to think that one through. Her head hurt. "I don't want Corvin here. Put him back wherever he was before. *Before* you brought him here."

Corvin held up his hand to stop them. "Really, I can be on my way on my own. Don't bother."

Maybe he was right not to trust himself to the caprices of an immortal. He might end up in the middle of Siberia instead of back in his own home or wherever he had been when Harrison had snatched him up.

"This one tried to consume an immortal," Harrison said, glaring at Corvin.

"You knew about that already. In fact, you were the one who said that we needed to use all our assets if we were going to defeat the Witch Doctor. You knew what Corvin was and what he would do."

"Destine's power lies dormant. The warlock does not know how to use it."

Reg glanced over at Corvin. She didn't really want him figuring out how to access any more of the power he had stolen from the Witch Doctor. He was powerful enough without it. If he figured out how to access all that power, would he become an immortal? Had the immortals once been human, or could a human be transformed into an immortal? She knew that there were stories of half-humans becoming immortal in the Greek myths. Maybe some of the other pantheons too.

Or in reality, did a human always remain a human no matter what powers he managed to wield?

"Leave things as they are," she advised Harrison. "No good will come from stirring them up. They are... in a state of balance right now."

It was a stretch.

And saying that they were in balance was a risk, because what if Harrison didn't like things being in balance? Balance was boring. He like to stir things up. To change them. To see what would happen if he changed something in the past or interfered in some relationship. He always seemed to be playing around with something new, seeing just how far he could go in changing something.

"The warlock is no danger," Harrison decided, and Corvin was gone again.

Reg hoped that he had been returned to his house and not to Siberia. But Corvin was resourceful. Even if he found himself in the middle of Siberia, he would find a friend. He would ensorcel some woman and get whatever he needed from her to get home. A friendly smile and a shot of those pheromones, and pretty much any woman would give him what he wanted.

"Where did you send him?" Reg asked.

Harrison shrugged. Reg walked to the bedroom door and poked her head out to see whether he was just back in the living room, but it appeared he was not. Reg shook her head.

"I hope you sent him back home."

Harrison stroked Horace's head and whispered in his ear. Reg had often wondered if each of the kittens had gotten a different part of the Witch Doctor's personality. They were all very different from each other, and she thought that rather than being equal portions of the Witch Doctor, they were all different amounts of him and different aspects of his being.

Horace was probably the most innocuous of them. Quiet and content, which were not aspects of the Witch Doctor's personality that Reg had ever seen. A very small portion of the Witch Doctor with a very insignificant part of his personality. Maybe the safest of the kattakyns to awaken.

"He wants to go home," Reg tried, looking at the cat's face and speaking to Harrison. "He was probably right in the middle of a nap. You should put him back where he was. And just leave the kattakyns alone. It isn't really any of your business."

"You lie to me," Harrison accused. And for the first time, Reg saw anger in his expression. "I have always been a friend, and you lie to me."

CHAPTER TWENTY-SIX

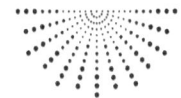

*R*eg's anxiety went through the roof.

Her heart was racing unbelievably fast, feeling like it would ram its way right out of her chest.

Harrison could squash her like a bug. She had thought that it was bad when they had gone up against the Witch Doctor? The Witch Doctor hadn't known her or understood her. He remembered her from when she was little, but back then his anger had been aimed against Weston, not Reg. Reg had only been a means of getting to him. Possibly.

He hadn't felt betrayed by her.

"I'm not lying to you," Reg said quickly. She looked for a way to convince him that he was overreacting and that everything was good between them, like it had always been. "What do you mean?"

"He does not want to be there. You sent him to the desert. To live with a warlock so old that he is turning into dust. Why would any part of an immortal want to stay with him?"

"We matched all the kattakyns up with their new owners very carefully. We matched their personalities, figured out who would work best with which cat. If Horace isn't happy there, we'll find a new home for him." Reg looked at Francesca. "Right? We can find him a new home. Our goal was to make all the kattakyns happy."

351

Francesca nodded. She took a hesitant step forward. "I am so glad that you brought him back here. If he was unhappy there, we will find him a new home. We want all the kittens to be happy with their new homes."

She reached out her hands as if to take the cat from him. Harrison pulled away.

"He is not yours."

"He's not yours either," Francesca pointed out logically. "One immortal cannot own part of another." She gave a tinkling laugh. "How could they?"

"You will not take him." Harrison turned away from Francesca slightly, and then she was gone too.

"Where did you send her?" Reg demanded, alarmed. It wasn't the same as it was with Corvin. Francesca was very strong-willed, but she did not have the power that Corvin did. And if Harrison were angry with her for having bound the pieces of Samyr Destine into the cats, then he might have done anything to her. He might have destroyed her. Or sent her back in time to choose differently this time and not bind the Witch Doctor as she had. He could have simply returned her to her house, where he had been once before, but considering his anger, Reg wasn't willing to bet on it. "What did you do to her? Is she okay?"

Harrison looked at Reg, his eyes icy instead of warm as they usually were. "You should not be friendly with her."

"I didn't mean to do anything wrong. We used the resources we had to beat and bind the Witch Doctor. We didn't do it to be disrespectful. He was raising draugrs. He was making zombies and making them do his bidding. People were being killed. I was almost killed by one of the draugrs. I would have been, if Starlight hadn't defended me."

"Humans are so obsessed with death." Harrison shook his head.

"Well... yes. Considering it is the end for us. Maybe it doesn't bother you because you expect to live forever, or close to it, but for us... our time here on earth is very short, and we want to get stuff done. We want to live our full lives and do all the things that we planned."

Harrison waved his hand as if brushing it all aside. "It is not the end."

"Well... maybe not." Reg had to admit that she had talked to spirits after death, which therefore meant that death was not the end of their existence. There was still something left behind, whether it was memory or an actual ghost or whether they went on to live whole new lives as reincarnated beings. "But it is a barrier that we can't see past. And we can't control what happens to us after that."

Harrison was looking at the two cats on the bed. Nicole was looking around as if confused by the various appearances and disappearances of the humans.

"Uncle Harrison," Reg wheedled. "You wouldn't want anything to happen to me, would you? You wouldn't want me to die?"

"The *little* Reg is already gone," Harrison pointed out.

"But she isn't dead, she has just grown up. Now she's me. I'm her. If you loved little Reg, then you still love me, right? You've always protected me. You've always tried to do the best thing for me."

"She wanted a kitty." Harrison looked at Starlight, and then at the animal in his arms. "And now she has one."

"Do you want... do you want to give me Horace too? Is that why you're here?" Reg smiled warmly at Harrison, trying to make him feel good toward her. "He's such a nice boy. I'm sure he would be very happy here."

She didn't want another cat. While she loved Starlight and loved having another creature around the house so that she wasn't all alone, and she loved Starlight's cuddles and the help that he gave her with her psychic readings, he also drove her crazy. Wanting to play when she wanted to sleep. Insisting that she feed him on his schedule whenever he asked her to. Getting underfoot. Even escaping or biting guests at various times in the past. He'd settled down since those early days, but he could still be annoying, and she didn't want another litter box to clean.

All of that was beside the fact that she didn't want a piece of the Witch Doctor in her house, no matter how small. She'd been happy to send the kattakyns away, all around the world. It had been tough to leave Nico with the dwarfs yet, at the same time, he had been a wild, rambunctious kitten who would sooner tear her cottage apart than to sit down and have a nap and a cuddle with Reg.

And Reg didn't want to be reminded about the destructive power of the Witch Doctor.

"You don't want him," Harrison countered, maybe sensing Reg's reluctance.

"I'd love to have him here." Reg put as much enthusiasm in her voice as she could. "Why don't you leave him here and we'll see how we get along together? I already have the food and everything else he'll need."

Harrison looked down at the languid black cat in his arms. Reg thought of him as being something like a young child who insisted that he wanted a pet, and then didn't want to take care of it. Harrison wanted the fun stuff, not any responsibility. Feeding someone and keeping them safe was not easy for someone who was so scattered and thinking of so many other things.

"He'll be fine," Reg coaxed. "You want him to have a nice time, don't you? If he doesn't want to stay in Egypt, then we need to find out what he does like. Maybe he wants to be with Starlight and Nicole. They can help us to figure out what's best for him."

Harrison looked at Nicole.

"You have the other one here as well? He can be with his mother?"

"She's not here all the time. She lives with Francesca, who you…" Reg made a motion to where Francesca had been standing until Harrison had decided to dispatch her somewhere else. Maybe Siberia. "Francesca takes care of Nicole. But she comes over here to visit with Starlight too. They like to see each other."

"They won't compete?" Harrison checked. "Eat each other?"

Reg tried to suppress a shudder. "No, they won't eat each other. And if they start to fight, we'll just separate them. But I don't think they will. They all know each other."

Harrison opened his arms and dropped Horace onto the bed, where he landed on his feet and looked up at Harrison for a moment as if he were offended that Harrison wasn't going to carry him around any more.

"He'll really like it here," Reg assured Harrison. "Horace, do you want to say 'hi' to Starlight and Nicole? This is nice, right?"

Horace eventually turned his attention to the other cats, and the three sniffed each other. Nicole tried to grab Horace by the scruff of the neck to move him somewhere else, but he was bigger than she was now. She couldn't move him around like she could when he had looked like a half-grown kitten. Reg was surprised by how big he was. Had Nico grown that much too? It was hard to think of him as being an adult cat instead of the wild kitten he had been.

Reg turned her head to make a comment to Harrison, but found that he had disappeared.

CHAPTER TWENTY-SEVEN

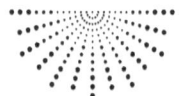

After checking again to make sure that Horace and the other cats were getting along and would take care of themselves for a while, Reg pulled out her phone and tried Francesca's number. Francesca picked it up right away.

"Reg?"

"Hi! Are you okay, Francesca? Where are you?"

"I'm back at home. He sent me back to the basement!" Francesca sounded outraged by this. Sending her back to her house was one thing, but back to the dark, damp, musty basement where Weston had been hidden was quite another. Reg wouldn't have wanted to be sent back there either.

"Good. I was afraid that he might send you somewhere else. Around the world. Or into nothingness. I had no idea what he might have done with you."

"Yes, I am fine," Francesca agreed grudgingly.

"Good," Reg repeated.

"Is Nicole still there with you? What about the immortal? Is he still there?"

"He's gone. Nicole is still here. And he left Horace too. Do you want to come get them?"

"I will come get Nicole," Francesca said slowly. "In a little while. I want to see whether I can figure out what we can do about your Harrison. We shall have to figure something out."

"Is there really anything we can do? I'm not so sure." She didn't add, "And he's not *my* Harrison." She'd told Francesca that enough times already.

And she hadn't failed to notice that Francesca had not offered to take Horace.

Francesca had been the one who had bound the kittens. She was the one who had fostered them until they had found a home for each of them, other than Nico. She was the one who was responsible for them, not Reg.

"So when are you coming? Do you know what you're going to do?"

"No. I need to figure out what to do. It is not so easy."

"No. I get that. I don't know how to handle this either. Now that we've got Horace back, we can make sure that Harrison didn't do anything to free the Witch Doctor? Find a way to prevent him from messing things up?"

"I do not know. I have to get into some books of mine and do some research. It is not as easy as you might think it is."

"I don't think it's easy. I couldn't do it on my own. I'm just hoping… that it's simple."

Something could be uncomplicated without being easy.

* * *

After ending the call with Francesca, Reg was still left with unanswered questions about Corvin. Reg could pretend that she didn't care. But she still wanted to know what had happened to him.

She tapped on his picture on the phone, but there was no answer.

Reg pondered this as she let the phone ring. Was he out of the service area? Usually if that was the case, Reg would have gotten a recorded message saying that he was out of the area.

"Come on, Corvin," Reg growled, concentrating on him and hoping that he would feel her query and make himself available for her. Psychically or on the phone, she didn't really care which one. What had Harrison done with him? *Had* he sent him to Siberia?

Reg hung up and tried again. Not only was the call not being answered, but it wasn't going to voicemail either. It just rang and rang. Maybe she had the wrong number or had reversed digits.

Again, it just rang and rang without going anywhere. Reg set the phone down, sighing. She didn't know what she would do. It wasn't as though she could do anything about it if he didn't answer the phone. She could try to see him in her mind—she usually could—but with the three cats there and everybody appearing and disappearing, Reg felt off-balance and wasn't sure she wanted to expend the psychic energy. Who knew if Harrison might change his mind and suddenly reappear, and she would have to try to talk him out of freeing Samyr Destine herself, without any help from Francesca or Corvin?

Reg watched the cats grooming each other and looking completely comfortable, as if they were a little family. But she caught Horace watching her, his head turning to examine her when the others were not paying any attention.

* * *

The phone rang. Reg looked at the face of the phone, but it wasn't a number she knew. It was a long number, international maybe, and Reg didn't want to end up talking to some salesperson from India or Pakistan about her phone plan.

As it rang, though, Reg realized that it could be someone else. Maybe someone whose phone didn't work outside his network. Reg swiped the call to answer. She could always hang up if it were someone she didn't want to talk to.

"Hello?"

"Regina." Corvin's voice came out in a huff, irritated, like she had taken too long to answer.

"Hi. Where are you? I tried to call you."

"My phone won't work."

"Did he send you to Siberia?"

"Not Siberia, no. A lot hotter here than it is there."

"Where?"

"Egypt."

"Oh. He sent you back to Horace's home?"

Corvin was silent for a moment. "I don't know. I don't speak the language fluently and I didn't stop to find out if someone with a black cat lived close by. I was just trying to call you or figure out a way to get back."

"Maybe you could talk to Horace's owner and find out… if something happened. Was Horace really unhappy there, or did Harrison just show up without any warning and take him away? Do they know… what Horace is and what Harrison is?"

"I'm trying to arrange passage back," Corvin growled.

And he wasn't interested in doing any investigating for her. Fair enough; Reg probably wouldn't have wanted to do anything for him either. But it wasn't her fault that he had ended up there.

"Okay. Fine. I'll see you when you get here."

"Regina."

"What?"

"I could… use some help."

"Oh, you called me for help, did you?" Reg couldn't help the sarcastic tone that entered her voice. "You have an interesting way of asking for it."

"I'm sorry. As you can imagine, it was a bit disorienting to suddenly find myself in another country, where I do not speak the language well or know the customs or how to find my way through the bureaucratic red tape to find my way home again."

"You speak Egyptian?"

"I know some Middle Kingdom. It… doesn't translate well to communicating with the people here. It would probably be better if I didn't know any at all."

"Just talk to them in English, then. Tell them you're American and someone kidnapped you."

Corvin considered this for a moment. "I'm not sure I want to get mixed up with the police here. It isn't exactly like at home. I don't want to end up behind bars in some hot, filthy cell while they try to decide whether I'm the victim or a criminal trying to pull some kind of con on them."

His voice went up just a little at the end of the sentence, as if he were asking Reg a question. She was the con man. Maybe she could give him some pointers on how to make people trust him.

"Why don't you just charm them?"

"That doesn't work so well on police and politicians. They are remarkably distrustful. Especially in a country like this."

Reg chuckled. "Aw, poor Corvin."

"Reg, do you think I would laugh at you if you were in this situation?"

"If I was in that situation... I wouldn't be talking to police and bureaucrats."

"Who would you talk to?"

"Some fly-by-night airplane pilot who could get me over a few borders into a friendlier country. And then... I don't know... I'd think of something."

"I'm here without a passport or any papers saying how I got into the country. It sort of throws a wrench into the works."

"There are always people willing to break laws for enough money," Reg offered.

"I didn't exactly bring cash."

"You must have credit cards. You can take money out."

"Regina." Corvin's voice was low, plaintive. Even across the ocean from her, it gave her goosebumps.

"There should be plenty of women over there you can charm into doing whatever you want. Call someone at your club. Don't they have connections?"

"Reg, I was hoping that you could help me. I know you can *call.*"

Reg had been able to use her psychic gifts to call Calliopia when she and Ruan had been far away, bringing her back through space to Black Sands to see her sister Karol Blackmoor. Corvin didn't know that Reg had done a call far more recently than that, when she had needed Ruan to help her with the cursed gemstones.

"You think I'm going to call you back into my house? There's no way I'm going to do that."

"It doesn't have to be into your house, although that would be the most discreet."

"It takes a lot of energy. If I do that, then how am I going to deal with clients? Or figure out what to do with these cats and Harrison?"

"Is he still there?"

"No. You know him. He appears, has a little chat, he disappears. But it isn't like we have solved the problem. He made you disappear and he made Francesca disappear. I got him to leave Horace here, but I've got no idea what to do next."

"He made Francesca disappear? Is she in Egypt too?" Corvin's voice rose hopefully.

"No. He sent her back to her house. I don't know why he sent her home and you to Egypt. Maybe because he's been to her house before."

"Well, nice for her. I guess I need to start inviting immortals over for dinner so when they disagree with me, they can at least send me to my room instead of halfway around the world."

"You haven't exactly been friendly with them before this. I wouldn't accept an invitation if I were one of them."

"Well, considering they can provide their own food, it isn't like they'd have to eat anything I had prepared." Corvin sounded a little more relaxed. Now that he'd asked for Reg's help, maybe he figured it was a forgone conclusion that she would help him.

"Where would I call you to?" Reg asked.

"Somewhere private. People tend to take a dim view of people just appearing out of nowhere. Despite the way Harrison and his friends seem to think that they can just appear and disappear anywhere and anytime they like."

"Well… they don't have to stay here and deal with people, so I guess it doesn't matter to them."

"Sarah's house?" Corvin suggested. "How about mine?"

Reg suspected that Sarah would take an equally dim view of Corvin appearing in her house. He had helped her in the past, and they were on reasonably good terms considering Corvin's "condition," but Reg suspected she would not want him in the house.

She had been to Corvin's house to drop him off once before, when he had been ensorcelled by Norma Jean and hadn't been able to drive himself, so Reg had an approximate idea where it was, though she would need the exact address to get her to the right place.

But meeting with Corvin alone at his house was probably not a good idea either. Especially if Reg were tired from calling him all the way across the ocean. Would she be able to resist his charms?

How could she call him somewhere that was both private enough to hide what they were doing and public enough that he would not be able to take advantage of her?

The last time Reg had been to the police station, she had seen a sign in the parking lot for a safe exchange area. When someone was buying an item from an online vendor and wanted to meet them somewhere safe to make the exchange, they could make use of the safe exchange area. It was not directly supervised, but was out in public and was on camera in case someone did get ripped off. Crooks didn't like to meet there because they knew they would get their pictures taken.

If she called Corvin there, it might cause some consternation for anyone reviewing the video feed because he would seem to appear out of nowhere. But it could easily be brushed off as an electronic glitch. Videos were often jumpy. Sometimes surveillance cameras didn't even take an actual video feed, but shot a frame every few seconds. Enough to catch anything that went down, but taking up far less storage space than a video shot at 30 frames per second.

If there were any issues, Corvin could ask Detective Marta Jessup to smooth them over. The two of them were friends, or Corvin was a consultant for Jessup, or some similarly murky arrangement. Enough that Jessup would probably do what Corvin asked of her.

"How about the police station?" Reg suggested.

"The police station?"

Reg explained about the safe exchange area.

"What if someone else is already there?" Corvin demanded. "Or you're wrong and it is under direct surveillance?"

"Then whoever is watching will have to explain to the authorities what exactly they saw and, if they don't want to be laughed off the police force, they can't exactly say that a man appeared out of thin air. They will have to leave off the fact that they didn't see you approach."

Corvin grunted.

"And if someone else is there, I'll just wait until they're gone. No one will stay around for long. You don't exactly stop for a long visit with the stranger you're buying a DVD player from."

CHAPTER TWENTY-EIGHT

*R*eg drove by the police station once. She told herself that she was just checking to make sure that no one was hanging around who shouldn't be and that the safe exchange area was as she had remembered it.

But she knew on another level that she was driving by because she was afraid. She didn't like to be at the police station. She had never called Corvin before and wasn't one hundred percent sure she would be able to. She didn't want to end up in any trouble or having to call on Jessup to smooth things over.

But she couldn't call Corvin to her house or his; it was just too big of a risk. And she couldn't think of another place that provided the same benefits as the safe exchange area.

She drove by a second time. Corvin would be getting very impatient for her to get there and call him. But she wanted to make sure that she was safe. There was no one else using the safe zone. There was a prominent surveillance camera, but no cops sitting around watching from cars or park benches or smoking a cigarette outside the building. It seemed like the perfect setup.

With a sigh, Reg eventually pulled into one of the parking spaces designated for users of the safe exchange area. She got out of her car and walked over to the open space. There were no eyes on her. She was sure she would be able to tell whether someone was lurking nearby watching. She was a little anxious of what a cop who was watching the video feed might think of her hanging around there on her own. Most people probably sat in their cars until the second party showed up.

But not everyone. Some of them must get up and smoke, or pace, or do something else to get some exercise or fend off the anxiety of waiting. Reg leaned against the wall of the police station. She took a few deep breaths and closed her eyes. She'd had Starlight there to help her with calls before. She hadn't thought about that. Could she do it without his help? She hadn't even thought to bring him with her. Cats tended not to take to car travel well, but she had taken him in the car a few times and he was pretty good about it.

She envisioned Corvin in her mind and reached out to him. They had a strong psychic connection, so she didn't anticipate having any difficulties with seeing him.

It took a few minutes of breathing and focusing before she started to see him. Dressed just as he had been when Harrison had made him appear in Reg's cottage. Standing on a quiet street looking around. It wasn't how she had pictured Egypt, all sand dunes and tents or a busy, colorful bazaar. It looked like the dusty streets of any other city she had been in. He could have been in Texas.

She could feel Corvin locking on to their psychic connection, strengthening it from his end. He was a powerful warlock, even if he couldn't access all the Witch Doctor's powers that he had absorbed. Maybe it wouldn't take so much energy out of Reg if he were helping from his end. As if he were pushing the heavy wagon that she was pulling.

Reg tried to keep her thoughts focused and relaxed. Corvin was impatient, angry, and irritated. He didn't like to wait, that one. He would not have done well on the street pulling a long con. Sometimes it took days to set something up. Hours of surveillance and setting up details.

"Just call," Corvin muttered aloud.

Reg took one more deep breath and let it out slowly. "Corvin, come."

She experienced a kaleidoscope of images, emotions, and the sensation of falling through empty space, and then Corvin was there, landing heavily beside her in a heap.

Reg steadied herself against the wall, trying to reorient herself in space after feeling like she had been flipped over. She sighed and bent down to offer Corvin her hand.

"Are you okay?"

Corvin didn't take her hand, but moved gingerly until he could sit up and look at her. Then he blinked and shook his head at her.

"Well… I've never done that before. It's a lot smoother when Harrison does it."

Reg had experienced travel with Harrison. It was definitely smoother, though it did leave her with a sense of disorientation and nausea.

"Sorry. I haven't had much experience. And I didn't bring Starlight to help."

Corvin pushed himself up to his feet. He too leaned against the wall for a moment to get his equilibrium back.

"That would have been one more thing for anyone looking at the video to explain. Why did this crazy lady bring her cat to the safe exchange area?"

"Yeah. I supposed we could pretend to swap him, but…"

"People do come to places like this to pick up kids who are visiting the other parent. I suppose… there's no reason you couldn't do the same with a cat that you share custody of."

"Yeah. But we don't."

Corvin looked mildly puzzled by this comment. "No, of course not. I'm not suggesting that we actually do it."

"Right." Reg was still feeling a little bit disoriented. "So you're good to get home from here? You can call an Uber or something."

"You could drop me somewhere."

"I think I've already done plenty."

"You're just going to leave me here? At the police station?"

"It isn't like I'm turning you in. You can go wherever you want. I just don't want to drive you."

"I thought the deal was that you would get me home."

"And I thought it was that you wanted to avoid all the red tape of trying to get out of Egypt and back to Florida without any papers."

Corvin made a growling noise in his throat, his lips pressed together in a straight, angry line. "After all this travel through space, you think I want to get an Uber? Your car is right there, Reg. I'm too tired to deal with strangers and having to wait for someone to show up."

He leaned against the wall as if he really were tired. Reg analyzed his face and body language and probed at his consciousness. He had pretended to be too tired to do anything to hurt her before. But Reg had been warned not to be fooled. He did seem to really be tired from his movements from one continent to another and trying to figure out travel arrangements while in Egypt, so maybe it would be safe...

She had taken him home once before, and he hadn't done anything.

Corvin waited, gazing into Reg's eyes, trying to will her into doing what he asked.

Reg sighed and looked around, looking straight at the video camera for a minute. "If you try anything, you've been caught on camera. I have proof that I came here to help you, and that you got into my car."

Corvin shrugged. "What do you think I'm going to do, Regina?" He leaned a little closer to her. "I'm grateful to you. Haven't you heard the saying about not biting the hand that feeds you?"

"Yeah, but I've never seen you follow it."

Corvin scowled. "Just drive me to my house. I'm not going to do anything to hurt you. I just want to get back home."

Reg rolled her eyes. She gestured toward her car and then walked over to the driver's side. "Fine. But you're on video. You try anything, and..."

"Why would I do anything to harm you when I'm trying to get reinstated by the coven?"

"I don't know. Because you're hungry?"

Corvin stopped at the passenger's side, looking across the roof of the car at her before either of them got in. His eyes glittered. Of course he was hungry. He was always hungry. Even when he had consumed the powers of the Witch Doctor and his artifacts, he had told Reg that he still had room for dessert. Her powers.

Reg slid into the car and put her key into the ignition. She pulled her door shut and didn't wait for Corvin to get settled and put on his seatbelt before pulling out. She remembered the general area of his house and pointed the nose of the car toward it. The sooner she could get there, the sooner she would be rid of Corvin and the danger that he would turn on her.

He made disapproving noises over her pulling out so quickly, and jabbed the tongue of his seatbelt against the buckle a few times before managing to get it inserted properly. Reg heard it click into place.

CHAPTER TWENTY-NINE

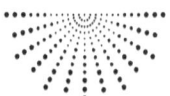

"Why do you think Harrison is doing this?" Reg asked Corvin abruptly, voicing the thought that had been running through her mind since Harrison had disappeared. "He knows that releasing the Witch Doctor would be dangerous and put a lot of people at risk, so why would he consider doing it?"

"I don't know what his motivations are. He has never struck me as being particularly close to the Witch Doctor."

"No, I don't think they are. They're both immortals, but I don't think they spend any time together or are friendly. In all the old myths, the gods are usually competing with each other and jealous and everything. I would think that he would be happy that Destine was bound to the kattakyns."

"Maybe he just enjoys causing chaos. Have you ever heard of the law of entropy?"

Reg glanced away from her driving to give him a look of disbelief. "What? What kind of law is that?"

"It's physics."

"And you think I know physics because…?"

"I just asked," Corvin said in irritation. "The law of entropy says that everything is becoming gradually more chaotic. Everything in nature tends to degrade over time. To break down instead of spontaneously becoming more organized."

"Okay."

"We can organize things. Plant a garden, build a house or a machine, impose our order on the things around us. But as soon as we step out of the picture, it starts to degrade again."

"Yeah."

"Maybe… Harrison just likes chaos. Maybe when things are going well and seem to be well-organized, he feels the need to upset the applecart. Impose some chaos."

It matched Reg's own theory that Harrison got bored easily and liked to stir things up. Imagine being able to do whatever she wanted to. How long would it take before it all got old? She nodded. "I think you're right."

Corvin raised an eyebrow, maybe surprised to hear her agree with him. Maybe he had thought that she would defend her Uncle Harrison and say that none of this was his fault.

"So do you think he's actually thinking about freeing all the kattakyns? Or is he being impulsive? Trying to get a reaction out of us?"

"You know him better than I do. What do you think?"

"I've known him longer… but I don't know whether I know him any better. I mean, I was only a kid before. I've seen him a few times now as an adult, but… I don't know if I understand him any better now than I did then."

"What was he like when you were a kid?"

"I don't know. Fun. We played games. A lot of hide and seek, which I guess was to teach me how to hide from the Witch Doctor. I would call him sometimes when I was scared." Reg shrugged. "He'd make me feel better."

"How?"

"Well… giving me food, stuff I wasn't allowed to have or that the family couldn't afford. Playing little games. Telling me stories."

"What kind of stories?"

"I don't know. Silly stuff." Reg thought about it. "Maybe some of it was stories from mythology. It's hard to tell, because I guess they've changed over the generations, but I remember him telling me about his friends and

369

the trouble they got into. It was nice to hear about adults getting in trouble. I always got in trouble, even if I was trying to be good. So it made me feel better to hear about these powerful grownups who still got into trouble."

Corvin nodded slowly. "You remember any of those old stories?"

"No... I don't really know. It was so long ago, and there were so many different people in different homes. It all blurs together. I don't remember any particular story. Just that somebody always got in trouble." Reg laughed. "And seeing Harrison now, through the eyes of an adult, I can understand that. He's just so..." Reg tried to think of a word or a phrase that would describe Harrison.

"Like an ADHD kid someone just gave a million bucks to?"

Reg laughed hard at that, trying to stop so that she could focus on her driving and not end up in an accident. "Yeah, just like that," she agreed breathlessly.

Corvin nodded his agreement.

When Reg pulled the car in front of Corvin's house, she turned to him, suddenly feeling serious.

"If he releases all of the kattakyns and the Witch Doctor reforms..."

"Yes?"

"That's really bad. If Destine keeps raising zombies and getting more power, like before... it could be the end of the world. He could destroy everything. He said he wanted to. That we were all like bugs he wanted to squash."

Corvin stared out the windshield, not looking at his house, but at something off in the distance. "There are many ancient texts that refer to an Armageddon. A last battle of humans against insurmountable odds. Sometimes against each other, but sometimes against a dragon or some other monster."

"So you think it could be the end of the world?"

"Not the end of the world..." Corvin hesitated. He put his hand on the door handle and considered for a few more seconds before popping the handle and pushing open the door. "But maybe the beginning of the end."

CHAPTER THIRTY

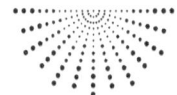

*S*leeping with three cats in the house was not nearly as easy as sleeping with just one cat in the house. Starlight was pretty quiet. He sometimes disturbed her sleep running and jumping onto the bed as if he were running away from something or chasing a mouse across her face. But usually, he just played by himself at night or watched out the window.

Having three cats in the house was a whole different story. Nico had been bad. When Reg had been taking care of Nico temporarily, with Starlight still there, things had been pretty tough. He seemed determined to break anything in the house that was fragile. Reg tried to put things away or out of reach, and he still managed to get at them. Starlight had been irritable with a kitten around demanding all Reg's attention and trying to engage Starlight in play or a fight.

Starlight and Nicole were fine when they had a play date. Reg enjoyed having Nicole over and she never caused any trouble. In fact, she would keep Starlight occupied and out from underfoot so that Reg could get things done without him always there watching her and silently passing judgment over what an inept human she was.

But she'd never had Nicole overnight. With Starlight, Nicole, and Horace all put together, looking for some fun to have while Reg was sleeping… There was not much sleep to be had.

"What's gotten into you?" Reg asked the big kitten as he sat on her nightstand looking down at her. "You were always so calm before!" That was one reason they had sent him to the old warlock in Egypt. They'd matched him with the kattakyn that was the quietest and most sedate, thinking that he would match the old warlock's needs the best.

Horace looked at Reg, a barely visible thread of green iris around his wide black pupils. She had owned a cat long enough to know what that meant. He would attack her at the first chance of weakness. All she had to do was to turn her back on him, drum her fingers on the counters, or flip her braids the wrong way, and he would be on top of her.

"You behave yourself. I'm not a bird. I'm bigger than you."

Horace just continued to watch her with those big black eyes. Across the bedroom, Starlight and Nicole started wrestling. Starlight ran away yowling loudly, and Nicole took off after him. She could hear both of them crashing around the cottage, knocking things over.

"You guys had better not break anything! And if either of you draws blood...!" Reg looked back at Horace again. "And that goes for you too. Especially if it's my blood. Why don't you go see what the others are doing? Supervise for me."

Horace didn't move. Reg reached over and shoved him off the nightstand. He meowed and headed for the door, turning to look at her to show her how disappointed he was in her behavior.

"Tell me about it," Reg muttered. "I'm not too happy with yours either."

* * *

When Francesca came back the next day, Reg was still in her bathrobe, sipping a cup of coffee which she hoped would wake her up enough that she would be able to do something constructive for the day. As it was, all she felt like doing was going back to bed. Where, of course, she wouldn't sleep anyway.

Although, the cats had finally settled down and gone to sleep after she had gotten up. Not all together, like when the kattakyns were new and had all slept in a heap, but all in their different spots around the cottage. So that Reg couldn't really find anywhere to sit down and relax without bothering at least one cat.

"Come in," Reg called out when Francesca knocked on the door. Reg had left it unlocked and she didn't have the energy to walk from the kitchen counter where she was leaning not-so-comfortably to answer the door.

Francesca tried the doorknob and peeked in to make sure she had heard properly before entering. "Regina...?"

"Yes, come in. Let yourself in."

Francesca obeyed. She looked at Reg for a moment, then looked around the cottage. She didn't make any comment about the various items scattered around the floor. Pillows, dishes, ornaments, candles, Reg's crystal ball, and various other knickknacks. On the couch, Horace was snoozing peacefully.

"Was everything all right?" Francesca asked.

"Not exactly. I don't think the three of them should stay together any longer than necessary."

"Well, I am here to pick up Nicole, so you won't have them all. I thought... did they not get along?"

Reg rolled her eyes. She took another long drink of her coffee. "Oh, they got along all right. But they were acting like the circus was in town and they were part of it. They were so loud. They were all over the place." She shook her head. "You wouldn't believe that three cats could be so loud. I was sure that Sarah would be over here any minute asking what all the ruckus was about."

"They were just playing?"

"I don't know whether I would say just playing. They were fighting, but they didn't draw blood, so I guess that counts as playing. And they were knocking things over. And Horace was looking for an opportunity to attack me."

"Horace?" Francesca looked at the snoozing cat with disbelief.

"Yes. Don't believe that innocent look. He was just as rambunctious as the others. I thought that he was the sleepy one. They don't change personalities when they get older, do they?"

Francesca scratched her head, looking at him. "Well... normal cats don't. They get quieter and more sedate as they get older, but they don't go through big personality changes. And they don't get wilder as they get older."

"Is it something to do with the Witch Doctor, then? Or did

Harrison put a spell on him to make sure that he caused me as much trouble as possible?"

"I will examine him." Francesca moved into the room, gliding across the floor as if she were on wheels. Reg didn't know how Francesca could always look so polished and glamorous. Reg felt like she'd been dragged behind a train. A speeding train.

She probably looked like it too.

Francesca sat down on the couch, taking care not to disturb the cat sleeping there. For a few minutes, she just sat looking at him. Reg didn't know what she could be looking at. Horace just continued to sleep. He was a pure black cat and looked just like any other pure black cat. What could Francesca tell just by looking at him? Reg expected her to pick him up and to examine him as a doctor would, listening to his heart and stomach, prodding and palpating.

After a few minutes of silence, Reg realized that Francesca was singing. A barely audible hum to start with. Reg thought that she was hearing things. But it got louder and louder until Reg could pick up the wandering melody. It wasn't any song that she knew. Nothing popular or on the radio.

It had to be a spell. She was a charmer and, when she had bound the kattakyns, she had done so by singing them a song and weaving her hands around them in a complicated way. And now she sang again, the notes rising and falling, questioning, exploring. Horace moved, curling into a tighter ball and turning so that he was belly-up.

As much as Reg would have wanted to rub his furry belly if she were closer to him, there was no way. She'd lived with Starlight long enough to know that even when a cat showed you its belly and looked as cute as a button, it was just waiting for the chance to rip your hand off.

Francesca continued the song for a long time. Then she stood up, silent, and walked around the room. She walked around the cottage without looking at Reg or saying anything to her. As if she were there completely alone. And Reg let her. It wasn't like there was anything Reg could do to help; she had no idea what Francesca was even doing.

Eventually, Francesca returned to the kitchen and stood close to Reg.

"You want some coffee?" Reg offered.

Francesca nodded. When Reg made no move to get it for her, Francesca moved to the coffee pot and poured one for herself.

"Thank you."

"So, did you find anything out?"

Francesca frowned, a tiny M appearing in the wrinkle between her eyebrows. "It is very strange."

"What is? That he was behaving so differently last night?"

"No. I do not think that was the strange part."

"What, then?"

"The part of the Witch Doctor that was bound to Horace… is no longer there."

Reg nodded. "Okay."

"I bound it there very tightly."

"But Harrison unbound it."

"Yes. Apparently." Francesca sipped her coffee.

"Then what is it that you find so strange?"

"If they are unbound… then where is that piece of Samyr Destine?"

"Uh… I don't know. Where do pieces of immortals go?" It was far too philosophical a question for Reg to answer.

"Even though it is no longer bound to Horace, I would still expect it to be with him. They are not bound anymore, but that is where the immortal sent the piece of himself, and I would expect it to stay there. Unless…"

"Unless what?"

"Unless… someone took it. Someone did something with it."

"Harrison, you mean."

"Yes… Harrison is the likeliest suspect. Who else would recognize it as a piece of the Witch Doctor? And what would they do with it. But Harrison…"

"What could he do with it? Does that mean that he is trying to get Destine to form again? Or is he taking the power for himself, like Corvin would…?"

Francesca looked at Reg sharply. "Oh!"

CHAPTER THIRTY-ONE

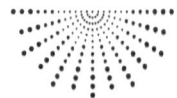

*R*eg nearly dropped her mug at the exclamation. She looked around to see what had startled Francesca, then looked back at her. "What?"

"Corvin was here. I had forgotten that."

"Yeah, he was here for a few minutes. But Harrison made him disappear, like you."

"Or he caused himself to disappear."

"That's not one of his gifts."

"Do you know what all of his gifts are? What he might have picked up recently in one of his liaisons? You don't know."

Reg had been ready to argue the point, but she reconsidered. It was true that she didn't know much about Corvin's gifts, other than his ability to steal others' powers. But the ability to steal others' powers meant that he could use the powers that he stole. His abilities were always shifting and morphing with each feeding. He had talked to Reg about her psychic powers and the voices when he had taken her powers. But he had never talked about what he had taken from anyone else. Or from the magical objects he was similarly able to absorb powers from.

"I know that Harrison sent him to Egypt."

"How do you know this?"

"Because I saw him there. I called him back."

"And you know that Harrison sent him there? He did not send himself?"

"Of course. If he could transport himself over there, why would he need me to transport him back?"

"Indeed."

"He was talking about how he couldn't get out of the country, couldn't get a plane ticket without a passport and other documentation. And he couldn't, could he? The laws don't make exceptions for people magically transported to other countries."

"You still do not know whether he sent himself there or whether Harrison did. Other people have the power to transport themselves somewhere, like you called Corvin. I did not know you could do a call."

Reg shifted uncomfortably. Not only could she do a call, but she could transport herself and others somewhere else. She had traveled with Ruan and Calliopia to return some of the gems to their source. Even Corvin didn't know that was what she had done to solve the problem of the cursed gems.

"If he sent himself over there, he could send himself back," Reg insisted.

"Not if he used up all his strength on the journey there."

"Well... I suppose."

"It takes a great deal of energy."

"I guess it would. But he could just take a nap until he felt better."

"Perhaps. Perhaps not."

"You think that Corvin went to Egypt on his own? Why?"

"He already absorbed much of Samyr Destine's life force. That is why Samyr sent himself into the kattakyns."

"Yeah."

"Corvin would be able to consume the portion of Samyr that was bound to Horace."

Reg's heart pounded. "How could he do that? Would he have to hold him? Or pet him?"

"I do not think so. I have not seen him in action as many times as you, but when we were at the warehouse, he was absorbing power from the artifacts without touching them directly. And he was able to begin to absorb power from Samyr before they were in physical contact with each other."

It was true. Reg breathed out hard. Was it true? Had Corvin disappeared not because Harrison had grown tired of him, but because he had taken the piece of the Witch Doctor which had been bound to Horace? Did he have to go somewhere else to assimilate it? Home or to Egypt?

"He wouldn't have to go to Egypt, would he? I mean, Horace was here, not there."

"Maybe he was hoping to find something in the old warlock's papers. Or maybe just misdirection. Maybe he never was in Egypt. Would you know?"

"Well… I don't know. He wasn't here; he was somewhere very different. Dry and dusty, not green and humid like Florida."

"But it could have been somewhere much closer. Did you see anything Egyptian?"

"No, just a street. It could have been any city, I guess."

Francesca nodded. She paced back and forth, thinking about everything. "You do not need to know where someone is to call them to you?"

"No. I never really know where they are. I think of them in my mind, picture them, and then I can see them and call them. I can see things around them, but I couldn't tell you what country they were in unless they were standing next to a road sign or a landmark I knew. Why would he want to mislead me?"

"So you would not guess that he had gone voluntarily? He had seen Harrison send me back. So he knew that if he disappeared, you would assume that it was Harrison too. You wouldn't guess that he had gone voluntarily and taken something with him."

"And if he didn't take that piece of the Witch Doctor, it would still be here. Attached to Horace."

"If someone didn't take it."

"But it might have been Harrison."

"Of course. It could be. But Harrison does not need more power. He is already an immortal. He has more power than he needs."

"You thought he was going to free all the kattakyns. So that the Witch Doctor could re-form."

"Yes."

"So maybe that is what he has done. Maybe he took that piece, and he's collecting all the other pieces, and then he will put them together."

Francesca nodded. "That is possible, yes."

"So it isn't necessarily Corvin. That's all I'm saying."

But then, she wasn't sure she liked the alternative either. She didn't want to think that her godfather was going to reassemble the Witch Doctor, someone who had wanted to destroy her.

"I will take Nicole home," Francesca said. "But I think we should start calling the owners of the other kattakyns. We should find out how many others Harrison has gone to see. And whether... any of them have changed."

"You think the change in Horace's behavior is because the piece of the Witch Doctor is gone?"

"When we first were trying to match them to the right owners, we thought that they had each inherited a different part of Samyr's personality. They weren't all the same; some had very different traits than others."

"Right."

"So the part of Samyr that went into them was what gave them that particular personality trait. And when it is gone..." Francesca looked around the room at all the things that the cats had knocked over that Reg hadn't yet bothered to pick up.

"Horace was quiet and sedate. You think that was part of the Witch Doctor's personality? He sure didn't strike me as calm."

"We do not always see what is inside. We only see the dominant personality traits. There could be many others that the person keeps hidden."

"I suppose so." Reg knew that there were parts of herself that she didn't share with others. And parts of her that could only come out when she was alone and didn't have the stresses and distractions of other people around her. She wasn't exactly the same person when she was by herself that she was when others were around. "So Horace had the quiet, calm part of the Witch Doctor. And now... he doesn't anymore. And that's why he has started behaving differently."

Francesca nodded. "That is my best guess. It isn't like there are a lot of cases of this happening that we can examine. I do not know of anyone who has put parts of his spirit into a kattakyn before. I know that the draugar can only be animated by the spell caster, but he does not send his spirit away from himself when he does."

Reg thought back to that day in the warehouse, when she had seen the Witch Doctor's body disappear in a bright starburst. She had felt his dark aura in the kattakyns before Francesca bound them.

"They have rules," Francesca said slowly, "but I do not understand them. And I do not know whether they are the natural rules of physics or imposed rules of their order that can be broken. They do seem to be bound by one physical manifestation... usually. But if they can step through time, then there could be many of them in one time and place, could there not? And if they were faced with destruction, could they not just go back to a different time? And as we saw, Samyr was able to leave his physical form to go into the kattakyns. Was that against their rules? Or natural laws?"

Reg's head hurt when she tried to understand it. Her brain told her that there had to be specific natural laws that the immortals were bound by. Just because a human had a difficult time understanding what the rules of that order were, that didn't mean that they didn't have the same natural laws of physics that humans did. They were just able to manipulate atoms or energy in a way that humans couldn't or didn't yet know how to.

They knew from what had happened that an immortal could be bound. Either in his body, as Weston had been when he had locked himself away, or dissolving his body and inhabiting another, or others, as the Witch Doctor had. They knew that the Witch Doctor would remain bound for as long as Francesca's spell lasted.

Francesca had said it would be at least a thousand years. She hadn't anticipated Harrison unraveling it before then.

CHAPTER THIRTY-TWO

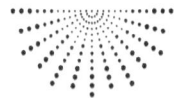

"What are you going to do about Horace?" Reg asked.

Francesca raised her brows. "What can I do about him?"

"I mean… where is he going to go? Are you going to keep him or return him to Egypt?"

"I am not going to do anything with him. We have eight other kattakyns to worry about. I need to focus my attentions on them."

"But you're going to take him with you. Him and Nicole."

Francesca shook her head. "You will need to look after him. I cannot at this time."

"But he was one of your kattakyns. You took care of them all before."

"When he was bound to Samyr, that was my responsibility. Now… it is not. And I have more important things to worry about."

"So you think you're just going to leave him here with me?"

"I'm sorry, Reg, but I have very important things to do. Can you not do this one small part?"

Reg opened her mouth, trying to marshal an argument. Of course she couldn't keep Horace. She already had another cat. All Francesca needed to do was to look around and see how much destruction the cats had wreaked in just one night. If she had to keep Horace for the longer term, who knew what problems he might cause? And Sarah, her landlord, would have something to say about it. She hadn't been too happy about Reg bringing Starlight home from the animal shelter and had made it clear that Reg was not to have any other animals.

"I... I can't."

"Then you need to find someone who can take care of him. Would you please do this thing? I cannot. If you cannot keep him here, then you must find somewhere else."

Reg looked for a way to make it Francesca's responsibility, but the fact that Francesca had looked after him before was all she could come up with. And she didn't have any way to research what they could do about Harrison releasing the kattakyns, and Francesca apparently could. Reg was in possession of the cat, which pretty much made it hers. Possession being nine-tenths of the law and all that.

On one hand, she wished that she hadn't gotten Harrison to leave Horace there but, on the other, Francesca wouldn't have been able to find anything out if Harrison hadn't left Horace behind. At least with Francesca taking Nicole, Reg would be down one cat.

Reg sighed and shook her head, but didn't argue. She couldn't change what had happened or convince Francesca to change her mind, so she would have to deal with it.

* * *

Horace continued to sleep, which was a relief. Except that it meant he would probably be up causing havoc all night again. Reg was determined to enjoy the peace while she had it so, when the phone rang, she was sitting on the couch with Horace beside her and Starlight snoozing in her lap, a cup of tea cooling on the coffee table, binge-watching a new sitcom series.

Reg looked down at the phone screen, hoping that it would be Francesca rather than Corvin, but it wasn't either one of them. It was not Gwythr's number, but it had the same area code and prefix, so Reg figured it was a call from one of the other dwarfs in the colony. She swiped the phone to answer the call.

"Hello?"

"Reg Rawlins, it is Brimir, son of Fraeg."

"Hi. Did you and Gwythr sort out whether you wanted to buy some of these stones?"

"I am the son of King Fraeg. I do not need to deal with the smithies."

"Okay. Does that mean that you're interested in them or not?"

Brimir grunted, probably displeased with the fact that she wasn't subservient to him. But Reg wasn't kowtowing to anyone, princeling or not. "We are willing to negotiate."

"Great. Do you have a starting offer?"

"I will send you an email."

Reg shrugged. He could have done that in the first place. He didn't need to call her just to say that he was sending an email.

"Great. I'll look at that. When we settle on a number, is there a courier service that you use? Or how do you want me to get them to you?"

"You would not bring them here?"

"I'm not going all that way on my own, no. Do you have someone you trust? I don't know anyone here that well."

"I will talk to the court. We will arrange for someone."

"Good. Okay. I'll get back to you."

"Do you have other stones? We are often looking."

Reg was cautious. "I have some others, but I am not ready to deal with them yet. I'm just starting with this lot."

"It would be good to know what else you might have. So that we know who to ask in the future. It could be quite profitable for you."

"Uh… yeah, let me think about that." Reg wasn't sure that telling anyone what else she had was a good idea. What if the courier who came to get the gems decided that he could get a little more for his time? Or if the dwarfs decided that they were entitled to all the gems, even though they hadn't made a deal for them? Pixies believed that all gemstones were theirs because they came from the earth. Dwarfs might have the same attitude. She didn't know.

"This could be a very beneficial relationship," Brimir encouraged.

"I'll definitely look into it."

"Hmmph. Reg Rawlins is very tight-lipped."

"I don't think you would tell me about all of the gems you have in your castle or in your colony either, would you?"

"Of course not. And what need would humans have to know such things?"

"What need do you have to know what gems I have that I'm not ready to sell yet?"

"You are not going to use them. It is best if they go to the kingdom. We know how to deal with such things."

"Doesn't matter. If I'm not ready to sell I don't need to tell you what I have."

"You are a heartless negotiator." Brimir's voice held a grudging note of respect.

"Thank you."

"I have further to ask of you."

"Okay, sure."

"It is about the devil that visited you."

"The... devil?"

"You warned that he might come here, to steal the warrior cat away."

"Oh. Him. I didn't say he was a devil."

"What else is a powerful practitioner who wishes to take our cat from us?" Brimir challenged.

"Well... okay. I don't know." Reg didn't want to tell them more about Harrison than she had to. If he hadn't shown up at the dwarf mountain, she didn't want to reveal that he was an immortal or that he had a relationship with her. "Has anyone come?"

"No. You still think that he will?"

Reg nodded, although he couldn't see her. "Yes. He was here yesterday... with another of Nico's litter mates. I don't know what his intentions are. And I don't know whether the dwarfs can do anything to stop him. I don't want any of your people getting hurt."

"We are ready to fight. The dwarf kingdom is strong!"

"I know. You are very tough opponents," Reg agreed, building his ego. She didn't want him to think that she was looking down on them, thinking they were helpless just because they were shorter than human beings. Reg knew very well that you could never judge a person's spirit or toughness by their body size and shape. People were too quick to make that assumption, and Reg knew better.

And she had seen the dwarfs' armor and weaponry, and some of the drills and training they did. They were very capable fighters.

But against Harrison?

Swords and shields would not be effective against him. Dwarf weapons were imbued with magic, of course, but she didn't know what or if they would have any effect against someone as powerful as Harrison.

"I just want you to be careful," Reg reiterated. "He is a formidable opponent and I don't want him to hurt anyone. And if he just wants to *visit* with Nico…"

Brimir laughed. "He does not just want to visit with the cat."

"Well… probably not, but you can't say you know that for sure."

"Has he merely visited the other cats?"

Reg thought about Horace. She didn't know the details of his visits with any of the other cats, but she knew that he had done something to Horace. Taken the piece of the Witch Doctor's soul, or unbound him, and removed him from the home that they decided was best for him. He hadn't just gone to Egypt to say hello.

"No."

"We will not allow him to take or harm our warrior cat."

"I'm just saying… be wise. Don't rush into anything impulsively. If you can negotiate with him… words are better than bloodshed. Maybe you can get somewhere with him, even if no one else could."

"We will not waste long on words."

Reg sighed. Hopefully, Harrison would know not go to the dwarf mountain until they had a better idea of how to stop him from freeing the Witch Doctor. Maybe Francesca could find something that would help them.

"We'll talk later, then. Email me your offer."

"Fare thee well," Brimir said brusquely, and hung up.

CHAPTER THIRTY-THREE

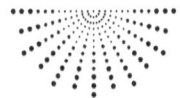

*R*eg checked her email and reviewed the detailed offer that Brimir had sent her, with a detailed itemization of each of the stones and their value for the dwarfs and how they would be used. It was on the low side, but she had expected that. The dwarfs were used to negotiating. You didn't go to a used car lot expecting to pay sticker price, and you didn't sell to dwarfs expecting to pay the first price that was bandied about.

She wanted to think about it for a while and see what she felt like after letting it simmer. She had only negotiated with the dwarfs once before and had to get a feel for it.

Reg did want to look at her other gems and see what else she had that they might be interested in. Future considerations were a big part of negotiations. It wasn't just a single deal they were working out. As Brimir had said, it was a relationship.

She pulled out each of the bags of gems, looking them over and remembering what she had sensed about each. She was not as good at reading the gems as a pixie or dwarf might be, but she could sense something about them. Their power, their affinity, where they had come from. The gems were grouped together by where they had come from, so that she would be able to return them to their rightful owners in their countries of origin. It seemed to be the only sure way that they could be cleansed from the curses on them. There were other ways that might work. She had been able to cleanse a few of them with fire or by other methods.

She was thinking of Egypt, of Horace being brought back from Egypt and Corvin being sent there by Harrison. Or saying that he had been sent there by Harrison. Her eyes kept returning to a bag containing a variety of precious and semiprecious stones, some of them lapis lazuli or turquoise. The blues were used in a lot of Egyptian statuary or decorations. The color of royalty for the Egyptians. Reg picked up the bag and examined the various stones through the plastic. She had forgotten that there were a few rings and other bits of jewelry among the unset stones. Two of them were in the bag of stones from Egypt. Something else she could sell to the dwarfs? They liked jewelry. They already had channels they could sell them through. Etsy. Amazon storefronts.

Reg opened the zip top and fished out the two rings. They were beautiful, the colors so pure. The lapis lazuli was the same shade of blue as one of Starlight's eyes.

They felt heavy in her hand. The weight was a good sign. They were not just thin slices of stone, but good, weighty pieces. She could feel the power that imbued them. It had taken her some practice, but she could sense both the power and the curses very easily now. She closed her eyes and communed with the stones.

Maybe she could go to Egypt to inquire after the warlock who had owned Horace. Maybe he could tell Reg something about what had happened. Why Harrison had gone there and why he had taken Horace away. Harrison said that Horace liked it better at Reg's cottage. If that was true, why hadn't he liked it in Egypt? Reg and Francesca had thought that they had matched the kattakyns and their owners quite well. Reg had studied the pictures on each of the profiles Francesca had written up, trying to read everything she could from their faces. They had discussed each of the assignments and had not rushed into it.

Horace had been one of the first kattakyns that they had placed. Had they failed to assign him to the right new owner? If so, had they made the same mistake for the others? Or had they only failed with Horace because he was the first and they didn't really know what they were doing?

The phone rang. Reg slipped the rings onto her fingers and picked up the phone. Corvin. Reg swiped to answer.

"Corvin."

"Regina." He sounded relaxed, more like his usual self. She didn't like it when he was irritated. She'd grown to expect him to be calm no matter what the circumstances, so it was disconcerting when he was not.

"Hi. Did you have a good night?"

"Slept like the dead. How about you?"

"No, not really. I'm not sure if I slept at all."

"Oh?" His voice was warm. "Something on your mind?"

"Yeah, three wild cats. It was chaos around here."

"Ah. Good reason not to have any cats! They always contribute to chaos."

Reg wasn't sure whether he was making a joke or referring to some other physics theory she wasn't aware of. She made a neutral sound in response. "So... were you really in Egypt?"

"Was I really in Egypt?" Corvin was silent for a moment. "Why would you ask me that?"

He didn't deny it, Reg noted. His question was thrown up in defense against her question, leaving it unanswered.

"I want to know whether Harrison really sent you there, or whether you just said that. Or whether you sent yourself somewhere else."

"Sent myself somewhere else? Where is this all coming from? You know where I was. You called me back from Egypt."

"But I can't tell where you were. I can find you in my mind, but it isn't as if you have a geolocator chip built into your head. I don't see you on a map with borders neatly marked out."

Corvin gave a short laugh. "Well, trust me, I was in Egypt. Did someone tell you I wasn't in Egypt? Harrison?"

"No." Reg did not feel a twinge of guilt at lying to him about Francesca's theory. "I just wanted to know. I can't see, so... I mean, you could have been anywhere. Anywhere hot and dusty, anyway. Could have been Texas, for all I know."

"Why would I be in Texas?"

"I don't know. You could have been."

"I... wasn't."

"What was it like in Egypt?"

"What it's always like in Egypt. Hot and dusty."

"Did you see anything interesting there?"

"Like... what?"

He was certainly being cautious about his answers. Reg would have expected him to have been more glib with his answers. Especially if he'd been up to something. When people knew they might get in trouble, they started rehearsing excuses. Explaining their behavior and coming up with cover stories. She'd seen it many times. She'd done it almost as many times. He seemed not to know what she was fishing for and was trying to avoid any potential traps. Throwing her questions back at her, avoiding committing himself to any particular story.

"I don't know. Did you see the Sphinx? The pyramids? King Tut's tomb?"

"No... I was not there sightseeing. I was just in the city for a few hours. It was noisy and smelly and hot. Crowded. Dealing with people who I did not want to deal with. Everyone trying to make a buck and rip me off if they could. Do you know what it would have cost me to get out of the country if you hadn't called me? How many people I would have had to bribe and pay off to get safely out without someone reporting me to the police? Prisons in Egypt are not nearly as nice as the ones in the United States."

"Did you talk to anyone?" She anticipated his next question. "Anyone interesting, I mean?"

"The people I talked to were very unhelpful. And... no one you would know. I don't know where these questions are going, Regina? Why don't you just ask me what you really want to know? Or explain what you're worried about. I'm a bit lost."

"Did you meet Horace's owner?"

"Who is Horace?"

"The cat. The one that Harrison brought back from Egypt."

"Oh. Him. How would I know? I wasn't looking for any cat owner. There wasn't anyone stapling up 'missing' signs or crying in the street."

"Well, if Harrison sent you back, then he would have sent you to where he had been, wouldn't he? To Horace's house?"

"I don't know. Maybe he went somewhere else after picking Horace up. Maybe he has a favorite restaurant in Egypt. You can't expect him to be logical."

"He sent you back to a restaurant?" That didn't sound right. Yes, Harrison enjoyed eating human food. But Reg was pretty sure that the warlock who owned Horace did not work in a restaurant.

Unless he had lied. Reg supposed that people inserted lies into all kinds of applications. Resumes for job opportunities, dating profiles, why not an application to become a pet parent? He said that he was the leader of a coven, but that didn't mean he really was. Had Francesca actually done any kind of background checks on the candidates? She supposed Davyn still had a day job, even though he was the leader of Corvin's coven.

"No, I didn't say he sent me back to a restaurant," Corvin said in exasperation. "I just said, you have no idea what Harrison had been doing before he appeared at your house and you have no idea what he might have been thinking of when he made me disappear. Who knows why he does any of the things that he does?"

"So where did he send you? He just dropped you in the middle of a street or on a sidewalk somewhere in the middle of Egypt."

"Pretty much, yes."

Pretty much. More waffling. Being imprecise so that he could take back the words later and say that he hadn't lied or misled her. She had just made wrong assumptions.

"You weren't in someone's house or place of business?"

"Well... initially, I suppose."

"And you didn't talk to the warlock who lived there?"

"What makes you think that a warlock did live there? Or that I would know him or approach him?"

"Why do you keep answering with questions? Why won't you just give me a straight answer?"

"You seem to think that I did something wrong. That I made myself disappear in order to get into some kind of mischief. Nothing could be farther from the truth."

"Then why don't you want to answer me truthfully?"

"I don't know what you're looking for."

"For the answers to my questions!"

But she wasn't going to get it from him. Whatever he had done while he was in Egypt seemed to fall into the category of "top secret."

"Maybe we can get together," Corvin suggested. "We could have a long and frank discussion about everything."

"You're not going to be any more honest to my face than over the phone."

She could see the slow curl of his mouth in her mind. Infuriating and attractive at the same time. Sometimes she hated how easily she was drawn to him.

CHAPTER THIRTY-FOUR

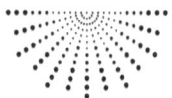

A plan was starting to form in Reg's mind. She could do several things at once. She could take the Egyptian stones with her to see whether she could pass them on to whoever was supposed to have them. Maybe it would even be Horace's owner. That would be very serendipitous. Sometimes things did come together like that. She would find out from Horace's owner exactly what had happened. Both when Horace had been unbound and when Corvin had been sent to Egypt. If he really had been. And if he'd been sent to the same place as Horace had come from. There was no guarantee, but Reg would feel better if she knew whether she could trust that Corvin was telling the truth about being to Egypt. She was sure he was, but Francesca had planted doubts in her mind and it was not helpful that Corvin wasn't answering her questions properly.

"Regina?" Corvin's voice reached Reg. Nudging her out of her thoughts.

"Oh. Sorry. I got distracted."

"I was asking about dinner."

"Oh. No, I think I'm going to be busy."

"You have clients tonight?"

"Um… I have to check; I'm not sure. I suppose I'll have to cancel them. Unless it doesn't take very long to talk to him and get things sorted out."

"Talk to who? Sort out what things? You're on a whole different plane than I am."

"I'm going to go to Egypt. Where you were."

There was a startled silence from Corvin. It seemed like a long time before he was able to find his voice.

"Why are you going to Egypt?"

"I have some things to do there."

"Just… a few errands to run? Have you ever even been out of the country before?"

"Yes." Reg smiled, thinking about her previous trip. Corvin knew nothing about it. He thought he was so superior because of his experience. But he didn't even know what she had experienced. "I have."

"Where?"

"That's none of your business."

"I think you're going to find that it's a lot harder getting to Egypt than you thought. There are a lot of arrangements to be made. You can't just go there on a whim like you might drive to Grandma's."

"It would be a lot harder to drive to Grandma's, since as far as I know, my grandmothers are both dead. Besides, it isn't like I'm *driving* to Egypt."

"Do you even have a passport? You'll need papers."

"Well, if I was going through the border, I suppose."

"And how do you expect to get there without going through a border?"

"The same way as I got you out."

"The same way…" Another silence as Corvin sorted this out. "You can't *call* yourself."

"No. But I know how to jump. I've done it before."

"When?"

"I don't need to explain myself to you."

"Well, no, of course not, but… how? Why haven't I heard of this before? How long have you had that ability?"

He was probably thinking of when he had held her powers. Wondering if he had been able to jump at that point and just didn't know it.

393

"I've only done it a couple of times," Reg admitted. "But I know how. So I thought… I would go to Egypt and talk to Horace's owner."

"By yourself?"

"Sure."

"You don't know anything about this warlock or his abilities."

Reg thought back to the profiles that Francesca had prepared on each of the candidates for kattakyn ownership. Reg hadn't done anything more than skim over it. She had studied the man's picture and Francesca had told her a few details in summary.

"I know some things about him. I know he's well-respected in his community and that he's the leader of his coven. Which is more than I can say for you."

That might be a bit of a low blow, but Reg didn't know where he got off acting so superior to her. Sure he had lived longer than she had and had grown up in a magical home, so he knew all the ins and outs of the community that Reg did not, but those were just practical matters that would be remedied with time. They didn't make him superior to her.

Maybe she shouldn't mention Horace's owner being the leader of his coven when Corvin couldn't even talk to anyone from his. But that was his problem, not hers, the punishment for his choice to break the rules of the community.

"I think you need to know a little bit more than that about him before you go over there. Don't be in such a hurry," Corvin warned.

"You were over there for a few hours and you were just fine. What do you think is going to happen to me?"

"A lot of things could happen. For one thing, it is not as safe for a woman to be there unaccompanied by a man."

"Really? You're going to play the gender card?"

"It's an important cultural factor to consider. And I at least know a little of the language. You haven't learned to speak in tongues without me knowing about it, have you?"

"Francesca talked to him on the phone and emailed with him in English."

"I still think that you would have better luck if I went with you. An old Egyptian warlock will have a lot of prejudices about women. He may refuse to talk to you at all."

"We are the ones who sent him Horace. So he'll talk to me."

"Reg. Let me go along with you. I really don't think it's safe for you to go alone."

Reg was actually reassured by the idea of his going with her. She was prepared to go on her own, but it would be easier if Corvin went with her. He could watch her back. Help her with any cultural or language issues.

But she wasn't going to tell him that. His ego was big enough without her pumping it up any more.

"Well… I suppose I could take you along if you really want to go. Are you sure you want to go back there so soon? I mean, you were just there and you didn't seem too keen on staying."

"And I'm not going to stay this time either. Just long enough for you to take care of your business. If I go with you, I know I won't be stuck without a way to get back." He paused. "Assuming you don't get yourself into some kind of trouble."

"If I get into trouble, I can still jump back."

"It depends on what kind of trouble you get into. What if you find that this warlock is more powerful than you think and he wants something from you?"

"Oh." Reg hadn't considered that. She had assumed that the warlock would be a kindly old man. "Well, yeah, I guess. But I don't think he will do anything to hurt me, do you? I mean… he's not like you, right? He doesn't have your 'condition'?"

"Very few do, but I don't know him. I assume that he does not, but I could be wrong. He might have been able to keep it a secret. Or he might have other powers that you don't know of. You don't know what kind of a person he is."

"Francesca did a background check on him. We wouldn't have given him Horace if there had been something wrong with him."

Corvin was silent.

Reg sighed. "How do you want to do this, then? You want to meet me somewhere?"

"Your safe exchange zone again? Why do we need to do something like that if you can jump? Just come here, or call me there, and we can go. You can save all kinds of money on transportation costs and commute time now that you have this ability," he teased.

"Yeah, except it takes energy. I can't just jump everywhere, or I'll be exhausted."

"Do you want to come here or should I come to you?"

"I guess… I'll come to you. I still don't want you in my house."

"There's no need to treat me like a pet who hasn't been housebroken," Corvin muttered.

"I wouldn't have to if you *were* housebroken."

He didn't have anything to say about that. "I'll see you soon, then?" he asked in a clipped tone.

"Yeah. I'll be there in a bit."

CHAPTER THIRTY-FIVE

*R*eg felt a little strange getting ready to go. She didn't have to pack her bags, since she would be back in an hour or two, not staying overnight. But she didn't feel like she should travel halfway around the world without some kind of preparation and packing. She carefully tucked away the bag of gems. No need for Corvin to see them before she was ready to reveal them. Maybe Horace's owner would be the right person to give them to and maybe he wouldn't. Hopefully, though, he would be able to give her some indication of where she should take them.

She decided to pack some granola bars and snacks, just in case she was there longer than expected and didn't have anything to eat. She didn't know what the hospitality rules were in Egypt, how much the food cost, or whether she would like it. And she didn't exactly have Egyptian drachmas or whatever they used for money.

Starlight followed her back and forth as she made her preparations. She thought at first that it was just because she kept going into the kitchen, and of course when she went into the kitchen Starlight thought that she was going to get him something to eat. Or that she would if he reminded her of his needs. But it occurred to her after a few minutes that he wasn't begging for food, and that the feeling she was getting from him wasn't concern for his own belly, but a worry about her and what she was doing.

"What is it?" Reg asked, stopping and crouching down to talk to him. "Everything is fine."

He stared at her with his one blue eye and one green, his gaze intense.

Reg raised her brows and shook her head, exaggerating her body language. "What?"

He bumped his head against her leg, rubbed his cheeks against her a couple of times, and then stood on his hind legs, putting his front paws on her leg.

"What? You can't come with me."

He bumped his head against her again and gave a low *mrrow*.

"You want to come with me? To Egypt?"

She got warm feelings of approval from him. Reg started to tell him again that he didn't want to go to Egypt, that he wouldn't like it there and he couldn't travel back and forth with her. But he had lived in Egypt before, had been a powerful being there, worshiped and venerated.

Maybe he just wanted to go back to visit his home country. To see how much had changed in the time since he had lived there, centuries ago.

"I doubt whether it's the same anymore."

He meowed again, more insistently. Reg looked down at him, thinking it through. She had taken him with her on a couple of other trips, and it had always turned out okay. There had been times when she hadn't taken him with her and had regretted it later, wishing that she had the extra psychic strength that he provided her with. He always helped to focus and strengthen her own abilities.

"I don't know. Are you sure?"

He meowed again.

"Corvin will be there," Reg warned.

He made a snorting, snuffling sound Reg took for contempt. But he kept looking at her, confirming that he wanted to go even if Corvin was going to be there.

"Well… okay. I guess. But you'll stay with me, right? You can't go running off anywhere. I won't know how to find you. And I'm not going to be staying for very long."

Starlight waited.

"Okay," Reg said again. "Do you want to go in your carrier? Or should I just take you…?"

He walked over to the door.

Even though he had agreed not to run off, Reg wasn't about to open the door and let him go where he pleased. He had run away once before and, even though that had been a long time ago and it had turned out that he was seeking out an herb that would help to heal her, she was still worried that he could run off and get lost.

She picked up her shoulder bag, then picked up Starlight and fumbled through her bag to find her keys. She locked the cottage door behind her, despite the fact that it was already protected by wards and anyone who could get by the wards could undoubtedly also get past a locked door. She had to do what she could to protect the gems, which she still had not put into a safe deposit box as Sarah had told her to do more than once.

Reg released Starlight in the car and he settled onto the passenger seat and started washing. He did not act startled or worried when she started to drive and, in a few minutes, stood up on his hind legs to be able to see out the front windshield and side window. He watched the scenery go by and did not yowl and complain.

"That's a good boy," Reg murmured in approval.

Starlight turned his head to look at her, then back to the window.

* * *

Reg had not expected to be at Corvin's house again so soon when she had dropped him off after his return from Egypt. She pulled up to the curb outside his house and wondered whether she was supposed to go in, or whether he would come out to the car. She supposed that he would not want to take the chance of their vanishing before the eyes of anyone who happened to be walking down the street, so she ought to go inside.

She was reluctant to cross his threshold. Who knew what kind of traps he could have set for her? She knew that letting him into her house granted him certain privileges and abilities. But she didn't know what risk she might be putting herself at by willingly walking into his lair.

Maybe it was a good thing she had Starlight with her. He could help to guard her against Corvin and warn her if she were walking into danger.

Reg slid the straps of her purse back over her shoulder, picked up Starlight from the other seat, and opened the door to slide out, awkwardly shuffling and climbing out of the car without the use of her arms, her shoulder bag bumping and catching on everything on the way out. Reg powered the locks and hip-checked the car door shut.

Corvin must have been watching for her or had sensed her approach. He was standing at the open door when she got up the sidewalk to his house. He looked at the cat in her arms with distaste.

"You didn't tell me you were taking that cat with you."

"I didn't tell you that I wasn't."

He shook his head. "And what about the other one? Did Francesca take him?"

"No... he's alone at my place still. He's sleeping, and hopefully won't get in any trouble while we're gone." She looked at Starlight. "Hopefully, we won't be gone too long, so he won't destroy anything while we're gone."

"I thought he was the quiet one."

Reg was surprised he had paid any attention to the fact. "Yes... he was."

She didn't tell him more than that and, while he looked like he wanted to know more, she pushed ahead.

"Are you going to invite me in so we can get on our way?"

Corvin stepped back and motioned for her to enter. "Please."

Reg stepped into the house. She paused for an instant, reaching out with all her senses. There was no one else in the house, of course. She didn't sense any traps or danger, but she hadn't always been the best judge of that. At least this time she was taking the time to check. That had to at least increase her odds of not being caught in whatever Corvin might have planned in the short time since she had hung up her call with him.

She looked around curiously. Although she had remotely viewed

Corvin in his home several times, she had never actually been there, and she had wondered how accurate her visions had been. It was an older home, but not ancient. The furnishings were a mixture of classic and more modern styles. Muted colors, as she would have expected. She didn't see any TV or computer, but thought that he must have one somewhere, maybe in his study or library. He would need some kind of computer for all the research he did. And he must communicate with other professors or scholars by email.

"Nothing too shocking, I hope," Corvin said, smiling at her.

"No. About what I had pictured."

"Maybe you'll feel more comfortable coming in now and then. There's no reason we can't see each other in a private setting."

There were several reasons that visiting with Corvin in a private setting was not a good idea. Reg shook her head and didn't answer him. She spun in a circle in the living room, looking around, Starlight still in her arms.

"Well… I guess we should go, huh?"

Corvin nodded. "I suppose you want to get your business over with quickly."

Reg drew in her breath a few times, trying to visualize the place they were jumping to. She had seen it when she had visualized Corvin in order to call him home. It shouldn't be too hard for her to reverse the process and jump both of them back. She looked at Corvin sideways.

"Do you mind if we hold hands to make it easier to stay together? I don't want to leave you behind."

"Of course. I love to hold your hand any time."

He touched her arm, ran his finger lightly down the back of it, then closed his hand around hers. Reg was braced for the electrical charge that flowed through the two of them whenever they made skin-to-skin contact, but she still jumped and had to steel herself not to pull away.

She tried to think of her destination instead of their contact with each other. She used her channel into Corvin's mind to strengthen the picture of Egypt and to drink in the other senses. The sounds, the smells, the feel of the air on her skin. Everything was different.

CHAPTER THIRTY-SIX

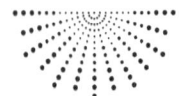

*W*ith barely a whisper, they were there. Reg had never called or jumped with such ease. One second, they were in Florida and she was imagining Egypt, and the next second they were there, the changed landscape flooding her senses. She opened her eyes and looked at Corvin. He looked back at her, eyes wide.

"That was... incredible. I've never traveled so smoothly."

Reg nodded. She let out her breath. "I'm getting better. But I think part of it was you."

"How?"

"Because you've been here before, so I could see and feel it through you."

"I always told you we make a great team."

Reg wasn't sure she'd ever heard him say that. The only time he talked about their doing something together, he was trying to get something from her. Trying to talk her into something that was against her better judgment. She pulled her hand out of his grasp.

"So..." Reg looked around. The streets were quiet. She could see, though, that it was not Texas. There were signs on buildings and litter on the street with letters written in a curly script that was completely unfamiliar to her. "When you came here, is this exactly where you landed?"

"No." Corvin shook his head. "This is where I was when you called me. But I had done quite a bit in the hours in between."

"Can you remember enough about where you landed to take me back there?"

"I think I can manage that."

Reg glanced at him. She wasn't sure whether that was sarcasm because she had asked him to do something that was simple, or whether it was more difficult for him and he was really sincere about thinking he could do it.

Either way, he was going to try. As long as he took her there, she didn't care.

"Why the place where I landed? I thought you had some specific tasks to do here? Why not go there, instead of relying on something that might be a wild goose chase?"

"It isn't a wild goose chase," Reg told him firmly, hoping she was right. Was he trying to distract her? Trying to keep her from finding something out?

Corvin looked at Starlight, still cuddled close in Reg's arms. "A wild cat chase, maybe?"

Starlight put his ears back and hissed at Corvin. He laughed.

"Starlight wanted to come along," Reg said. "I'm not exactly sure why. I think he wanted to protect me. Like you."

"From me, you mean."

"I don't know. But he didn't want me coming here without him. So..."

"The ancient Egyptians venerated cats and worshiped a cat god. Maybe he's hoping someone will worship him."

Reg didn't fill Corvin in on the details she knew of Starlight's past. As far as he knew, Starlight was just what he appeared to be. "Maybe," she agreed neutrally.

Corvin looked around, then began to lead her. "This way. Stay close. Egypt isn't well-known for the respect they pay to female tourists."

Reg didn't argue. Even though she had said that she was not afraid to go to Egypt alone, she was glad to have someone at her side. Especially someone with powerful magic and a knowledge of the culture and history of the place. Even if he didn't know the language well, at least he knew it better than she did. She knew exactly nothing about the Egyptian language, ancient or modern.

Corvin seemed confident in the direction he took. Hopefully it would not be difficult for him to find his landing place of the previous day. They would scout around, talk to Horace's owner, and Reg would find out what she could about what had happened with Harrison. And maybe find something out about where to take the gems. If she were lucky, maybe Horace's owner would even be able to do something with them himself. Some kind of ceremony or ritual he knew that would cleanse the gems so that they could be given back to the Egyptian people, with a portion going back to Reg in appreciation.

That was the way it had worked with the previous mission. Though she hoped that this time it wouldn't mean also going up against some powerful magical warlord.

They walked by a lot of businesses, with Corvin occasionally pointing one out to say that he had made inquiries there about money or a passport or other papers. Being dumped there so unexpectedly, without even any American cash in his wallet, it had been difficult or impossible for him to make any headway.

They covered quite a distance. Reg's arms were getting sore from carrying Starlight. Of course he could walk by himself, but she was afraid that he might take off if she put him down. Cats were not well-known for heeling. There were not many people out on the street, and those that they did see looked at Reg and Corvin with curious expressions. Clearly, Americans holding cats did not walk through their neighborhood very often.

Corvin pointed down a narrow lane. "Okay. We're close. Just down here."

Reg was nervous preceding him into the enclosed area. It felt too much like a trap. Only one way in and out, and it could be blocked by one man.

"You go first."

He looked at her, waving her ahead of him impatiently.

Reg shook her head.

"What do you think I'm going to do?" Corvin demanded. "This is where you wanted to go."

Why would Harrison put him into that close, dark alley? Reg

looked around, wondering whether Harrison was close by. Was he watching her? Waiting for her to show up there? Or was he completely oblivious, off doing something else. Maybe seeing Nico or one of the other kittens.

"Reg," Corvin encouraged, impatient.

"You go first."

He shook his head and stepped in ahead of her. Which of course meant that he blocked her from seeing anything as they moved forward. Maybe not such a good idea. But she still had a clear exit behind her, which she wouldn't have if she'd gone first.

The alley was dark and the piles of trash stank. Not exactly somewhere Reg would have chosen to go on her own. But she'd been in enough dark alleys and questionable circumstances previously in her life. She'd survived. And she would survive this time too.

They reached the terminus of the alley, the two buildings forming walls on three sides of them. Corvin turned and knocked on a wooden door set into the brick building. He rapped it hard with his knuckles. His blows boomed inside the house as if amplified.

Reg stood rigidly as the sound died away. It seemed ominous. She wondered if she should turn around and go the other way. Who said she had to come back to this place to find out why Harrison had sent Corvin there? It had just been the whim of a changeable, distractible god who didn't know what he wanted from one moment to the next. It meant nothing.

Corvin turned partway toward Reg, opening his mouth to speak. To make a joke about the situation or to ask her a question.

There was a sound on the other side of the door. Scratching. Bolts sliding. Chains jangling. An echoing click, and the door swung out of its frame slightly.

CHAPTER THIRTY-SEVEN

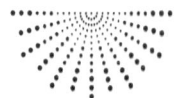

"*W*ho is it?" a hoarse voice inquired.

"It's me," Corvin replied "I was here yesterday."

The door opened a fraction farther. "You? I thought you left. You didn't go home?"

"I did, but I'm back, and I brought a friend." Corvin shifted to the side slightly so that the old warlock could see Reg as well. "She has some questions for you."

The man didn't open the door. Reg could not see him very well in the dimness of the evening, and there did not appear to be a light on inside the residence.

"Are you Horace's owner?" Reg asked. "I'm looking for the person who owned him."

"Horace? What do you know about Horace?"

"Are you?"

After another moment of consideration, he opened the door far enough to admit them. Corvin entered the house first, followed by Reg.

It wasn't a hovel, but it wasn't a modern place like Reg or Corvin lived in either. The building felt ancient. There was a woven mat inside the door with a couple of pairs of shoes beside it. The man pointed to them. It took Corvin and Reg a moment to get the idea and take off their shoes, and then they entered his home.

"Is that because this is a sacred place?" Reg asked in a hushed voice.

"It is to keep people from bringing the mud and sand from outside into the house."

"Oh."

Starlight twisted his head this way and that as Reg carried him through the house. She was glad that they were finally there, because she really wanted to put him down. Once she was seated in a dimly lit living room or sitting room, Reg rested Starlight in her lap and let go so he could decide whether to stay with her or to jump down and look around.

"Who is this?" the warlock inquired, looking at Starlight. He didn't get close or hold his hand out for Starlight to sniff. He didn't rush in and pet him as if he were a stuffed animal without any feelings of decorum or personal space.

"I'm sorry, I forget your name," Reg said. "This is Starlight, and I'm Reg."

While she waited for the warlock to answer, Reg studied him. She vaguely remembered seeing his picture in the profile Francesca had prepared. He was an older man. He looked older than Corvin, though she was learning that a person's appearance didn't necessarily reveal their true age. Some witches and warlocks seemed to know secrets that made them age far more slowly than others. Sarah had a special emerald that kept her young and healthy. Reg didn't know what Corvin did, but he claimed to be decades older than he looked, so she assumed he used some kind of potion or spell to keep him looking that way. The old man might be the age that he looked, in his sixties or seventies, or he might be ancient. His skin was dark, his face round. He had a sparse black beard, the rest of his hair gray and white. He was on the heavy side, but didn't look fat, just comfortable and settled. Someone who spent a lot of time sitting, but was still active. Maybe going for long walks in the evening as the day started to cool.

"I am Kareem," the warlock said finally, bending at the waist to give Reg a slight bow. He looked at Corvin.

"Corvin Hunter," Corvin said with a nod. He had apparently not introduced himself when he had seen the man the previous day.

"When you came yesterday, did you land inside or outside?" Reg asked curiously.

Had he surprised the warlock by making a sudden appearance inside his house? Or had Corvin knocked on his door to ask for help after being dumped outside by Harrison?

"And why are you here?" Kareem said, ignoring Reg's question and talking over her. He addressed Corvin. He was the man, after all. A warlock in the States would probably have assumed that Corvin was in charge too. Reg had found them to be remarkably sexist. "What brings you back to my home again?"

"Reg wanted to speak with you," Corvin said, nodding in her direction. "She asked me to accompany her."

Kareem looked in Reg's direction, but didn't seem to think much of her. He continued to address Corvin, eyes intent on him.

"You could not get back to the US and here again in a day."

"I did. But not on a plane."

"You said you had to catch a plane. That you needed help. You lied?"

"No," Corvin assured him. "I was looking for a plane in order to get out of the country, but that's not what I ended up doing. It turned out... there was no way I could get on a flight without papers or a significant amount of money, and I had not been prepared with either before I was sent here."

"Of course you cannot fly without papers or money. You should have known that."

"I didn't come here by choice. I was brought against my will."

"You are a warlock. I can feel that your powers are great. Why would you let someone do that?" His eyes flicked to Reg again. "It was her?"

"No. She brought me back today. With my permission, of course. Yesterday was... somebody with greater power than I."

The man scratched at his scrubby beard. "What are your questions?" he asked, finally looking at Reg and meeting her gaze.

"Are you Horace's owner?"

"Yes. I didn't call him that, but... yes. Do you know what happened to him?"

"I was hoping that you could explain it to me. I know where he is, but I don't know what happened before. What happened here before he was brought back to America?"

"You say he is in America?"

"Yes. He's at my house right now. He's safe, you don't need to worry about him."

"Of course I am very concerned. Everything that happened here was very confusing."

Reg nodded. She found pretty much everything Harrison did to be confusing. "Can you tell me what happened? Did Harrison just show up here and demand to see Horace?"

"He did not so much demand..." Kareem trailed off, thinking about it. "He was suddenly here. Without coming through the door or setting off my wards or any kind of warning. He was not here, and then he was. Like..." he looked at Starlight. "Like one of them."

Reg was going to say, "Like a cat?" But then she thought maybe he meant "like an immortal" and she didn't want to reveal anything about Starlight's previous life and history to him, so she kept her mouth shut. There were far more important things to focus on.

"What did he say?"

"He was here, petting Hassam. Horace."

"Yes?"

"He called the cat another name. Not Horace."

"Destine?"

"Yes. Yes, I think that was it. Destine. Why did he call him that? I thought that Hassam was owned by that other woman before me. That Haitian woman."

"Francesca."

"Yes. She was his owner before, was she not? She was the owner of the mother?"

"She owns Nicole. Yes." Reg looked at Corvin, asking him in her mind whether she should give Kareem the history, to explain to him about the Witch Doctor being joined to each of the kattakyns and their efforts to keep the kattakyns away from each other permanently. Or as permanently as magic and physics would allow.

Corvin gave a slight shake of his head. *Don't tell him.*

Reg shifted uncomfortably. She looked down at Starlight and petted him. He shook off her touch and jumped to the floor. Kareem said nothing. For a few minutes, they all just watched Starlight exploring the room.

"The man who came, he didn't say how he knew Horace?" Reg asked. "That is, Hassam?"

"He did not say he owned him," Kareem admitted. "I thought that must be why he was here and how he knew the cat. But... maybe I was mistaken. Or maybe he just knew Hassam casually, and the Francesca woman owned him."

Reg nodded. "Did he say why he was here? Did he do anything? Or did he just take Horace away?"

"He petted him, talked to him..." Kareem shook his head. He put his hands out, palms up, in a pleading gesture. "I do not know. I could not understand it."

Reg knew how Harrison behaved around Starlight and assumed he had been the same way with Horace. As if Starlight were an old friend, or an old enemy. An old acquaintance, anyway, one that he was apparently eager to talk to and engage with. Harrison always seemed too intimate with Starlight, too familiar with him. As if there were no social or species barrier between them.

"Yes. I know what you mean. Did he say anything in particular? Did he say that he wanted to take Horace away? Or to do something with him?"

"He just... petted him. Then took him. The two of them disappeared." Kareem shook his head. "That is all. He picked him up and talked to him, and then he took him away."

CHAPTER THIRTY-EIGHT

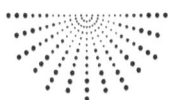

*R*eg sighed. She followed Starlight with her eyes while trying to figure out what else she could ask Kareem. He didn't seem to know anything at all. She had been hoping that he would be able to provide a little background and insight at least. But that didn't seem to be the case.

She looked over at Corvin, who didn't have any suggestions or questions of his own.

Reg was getting a prickly feeling from Starlight. He didn't like it there. Was it because something had happened to Horace there? Because Harrison had been there and taken Horace away? But Starlight liked Harrison. They were friends. He wouldn't have minded that.

But he didn't like Corvin, so maybe part of it was Corvin's presence there. And he didn't know the other warlock.

Reg looked at Starlight and waited until he turned and looked her in the eye. The sense of unease grew. Not just a wariness, but a sense that something was very wrong.

She supposed she had done what they had gone there for. To talk to Kareem and see if he knew anything. Unfortunately, he didn't. But Reg didn't want to turn around and go home again so quickly.

She still had the gems. Maybe Kareem could help her with those. Reg reached into the pocket of her skirt and touched the bag of gems.

She looked at Starlight's blue and green eyes, remembering the lapis lazuli and turquoise among the other precious stones.

"Can I ask you something else?" Reg asked. "Changing the subject. Do you know... about gemstones in Egypt? Where they come from? Who mines them?"

Kareem blinked at her, slow and thoughtful, like a cat. "Who mines the gemstones in Egypt? What does this have to do with Hassam?"

"Nothing. Like I said, it is a change of topic. Just something that I thought I would look into while I was here."

Corvin's eyes were sharp, his attention fully on her. He hadn't sensed her intention before that. Hadn't realized that she had gone to Egypt for something other than just asking Kareem about Horace and Harrison.

"There are mines here," Kareem said slowly. "I do not know much about them. They are mostly run by large corporations. Very few are privately-owned anymore. The mining for precious stones is done by big companies."

"And where do the workers live? Are they in the city? Or do they have a camp or a village somewhere else?"

He stroked the patchy whiskers on his chin. "I do not know... they do not circulate in my circles. Why do you ask this? What do you want with miners?"

"I have... something that belongs to them. Something that I wanted to return to the rightful owners."

Corvin's consciousness was pressing against hers. She tried to push him out of her head. He wanted to know what she was talking about, what she had, what she intended to do. None of it was any of his business, and she was regretting that she had brought him with her. She hadn't thought about how he was going to behave if he found out that she had precious gemstones with her. That she hadn't gotten rid of them all on her previous mission. Corvin was just as greedy as anyone else. Though more for the power of the stones than their monetary value. Maybe he would be interested in their history as well. He liked all that history stuff.

Reg turned her head to glare at Corvin. It had always been difficult to keep him out of her mind. And now he was even more insistent. He gave a slight shake of his head. Because, of course, he didn't want to be kicked out. He wanted more information. Much more than she intended to give him.

"I am not the right person to talk to," Kareem told her, shaking his head. "Perhaps... I can find those who can help you. But it will take time."

The stones were warm in Reg's hand in the pocket of her skirt. They were eager to be returned to their rightful owners. Reg had brought them all the way to Egypt and she hated to go back to the US without dealing with them. The stones would not be happy if she just turned around and took them back home.

"You're sure you don't know anyone who could help me today?"

"Tonight?" Kareem shook his head. "Everyone is closing up their businesses and going home. That hour is past. Even if I had someone for you to go to, I wouldn't be able to get you any help until the morning."

"Okay. Well. If you can't, you can't, of course. I guess... maybe I'll leave you my information, and then when you find something out, you can call or email me?"

He shrugged.

Reg dug into her purse, moving things around to look for her business cards. She'd had some nice ones printed when she had first come into possession of the gems. Not the cheap paper ones printed on a personal inkjet printer, but properly engraved cards on thick, glossy ivory stock. They looked and felt very sophisticated.

She found the card wallet and pulled one out. She passed it over to Kareem. It wasn't until she reached out to him with the card that she saw the rings on her fingers. She didn't even remember putting on the rings as she had looked through her stones and selected the ones to bring with her to Egypt. The rings should have been in the bag in her pocket, with the rest of the stones. She hadn't intended to put them on.

Kareem took the card from her, but he wasn't looking at it. He was staring down at the rings. Reg pulled back her hand and tried to fold her fingers into a position that looked natural and that hid the rings from sight. Of course, it was too late. Kareem had already seen them.

"Where did you get those?"

"They are not mine," Reg said quickly. "I'm just holding on to them."

"No, they aren't yours," Kareem agreed, his dark eyes getting darker and more suspicious. "Where did you get them?"

Reg didn't tell him. "I am trying to find the rightful owners."

"This is not something for someone like you to do. One would need to trace the histories of those rings. Where they came from. The genealogies of the true owners. Treasures like this, taken from tombs. Wars have been fought over them. They have traveled the world as men have fought over them."

Reg nodded. "I know all that. But I can find out. I can find out where they came from and who should get them." She glanced at Corvin and then away again. "I've done it before."

"Not stones as ancient and acclaimed as these."

Reg looked down at them self-consciously. "What is the difference? It is still the same thing. They were taken out of this country and traded between people who had no right over them. I want to make that right. Bringing it back to this country is what I need to do to cleanse them."

"Simply bringing them here does not wash the blood from them! And there are thousands who could claim to be the rightful heirs to these treasures. You will never find the one person who should hold them. It needs to be carefully researched and negotiated."

Reg had hoped that it would be easier. When she had jumped with Ruan, the stones had led her directly to the mines that they had come from. It had been easy to determine that the miners should be the ones who got the stones to try to care for their families, rather than the warlords, soldiers, and politicians who would have fought over them. But she had jumped to the location she had seen Corvin in, rather than letting the Egyptian stones guide her, so she had not arrived at the right place to find the rightful heirs of the gems and jewelry.

"I will have to look into it further," Reg said. "I'm not making a decision today. Maybe when you get back to me with the name of someone who knows about mines in Egypt…"

"You cannot be allowed to take those stones back out of the country. You must leave them here. I will safeguard them until you return with more information."

Like she would let him hold the stones.

Starlight's wariness and distrust of the warlock was starting to affect Reg. It was not a safe place to leave the gems. She wouldn't have been likely to anyway, not unless she'd had some reason to believe that Kareem knew about gems and was an appropriate guardian.

Even then.

Reg looked at Corvin, warning him mentally that they would be leaving soon, and it might be in a rush rather than a carefully prepared-for jump. She made kissy sounds to call Starlight back to her and put her hand close to the floor, rubbing her fingers together to encourage him.

Starlight looked at her hand, looked her in the eyes, and then walked directly over to her. He understood why she wanted to leave that place and he agreed. That made it easier. She wouldn't have wanted to be chasing around after Starlight trying to catch him while avoiding any attempts by Kareem to keep them there. Or to keep the rings there.

Reg had the rings turned around facing her palm so that they were out of sight. She folded her fingers over into a fist and crossed her thumb over. It didn't exactly do her any good, since Kareem had already seen them, but she hoped that if he weren't looking at them, his emotions would cool. He could remember what he had seen, but if he weren't looking right at them, hopefully those feelings would be transitory and he wouldn't be drawn to the power of the stones.

Corvin stood up. "We should probably be leaving, Regina."

"Yeah. It's getting late. We'll want to get home and have some supper. I have clients coming tonight." She was babbling, pretending that it had just been an ordinary visit and that they had other things to do. She could feel Kareem's anger and outrage building. She didn't want to still be there if he blew his top and decided to act.

"You must leave the rings here," Kareem insisted again, his tone sharp. "I will keep them safe until you are able to find the correct owners."

"No. I'm not leaving them here."

Maybe it would have been wiser to keep her mouth closed instead of broadcasting her defiance. Or pretended that she would give them to him, to allow her time to get ready for the jump and not botch everything up.

But Reg had always been a little bit oppositional. She hated people telling her what to do. Even if someone told her to do something that she wanted to do, a sure way to get her not to do it was to tell her she had to. Her instinct was to push back, to refuse to do anything just because someone told her to.

Reg picked up Starlight and stood beside Corvin. She was trying to quiet her mind, to picture home and to feel it with all her senses. It was not an ideal situation. She should be calm and relaxed in order to get to that meditative place where jumping across the ocean was just as easy as breathing in and out.

Corvin put his hand on her arm. Reg breathed raggedly in, unable to close her eyes because she had to keep looking at Kareem to make sure that he couldn't reach her before she managed to jump. She couldn't take her eyes from him and focus on something else, no matter how hard she was berating herself for it. Her body's instinct for self-preservation and her knowledge of what she had to do to escape were at odds with each other.

Corvin said her name from somewhere far away and encouraged her that it would be a good time to jump. Reg breathed in and out again as Kareem came toward her threateningly.

CHAPTER THIRTY-NINE

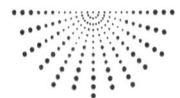

*K*areem was an old man, but he advanced on her quickly, pushing himself up from his chair and reaching toward her. Reg threw up a psychic shield around herself to prevent him from reaching her. It surrounded the three of them—Reg, Starlight, and Corvin. The warlock got closer, as close as he could to the shield. His face was an angry scowl, tight and hard and cold.

"You are a thief! You know that which you hold is not yours! You have no right to possess them or to use their power. I command you to turn them over to me. You cannot continue to hold them. You cannot take them out of the country. This is where they belong, and you know that. Give them to me!"

Reg shook her head. She kept the shield strong around her. She had fought people much more powerful than Kareem before. He was an old warlock, not someone who was used to fighting. He wasn't an immortal or another siren. He wasn't the most powerful wizard in the world. He couldn't do anything to her while she was within the shield.

But unfortunately, neither could Reg. She couldn't switch from holding the shield in place to jumping them back home. She could only do one or the other. Corvin would not be able to perform any magic outside the shield either, to hit Kareem with a spell that would disable him so that Reg could take them out of there. She hadn't thought; she had just reacted, and now Reg wasn't sure how to get out of the situation. She couldn't do anything without dropping the shield, and she couldn't drop the shield.

She swore under her breath, and then more loudly. There had to be a way out of it. Maybe Kareem would get tired and decide it wasn't worth attacking her over. Maybe he would have a heart attack and keel over. Or a stroke. Or an anvil would fall out of the sky, through the roof of the building, onto his head and knock him out. Anything would do, she didn't really care what it was.

"Reg, maybe you could—"

"I can't do anything," Reg snapped. "If I do something other than hold the shield, then the shield will go down."

"We could walk out. If you keep the shield around us."

"Where? He's just going to follow us."

"Let's at least get out of his house."

That resonated with Reg. Get out of Kareem's house. He had more power there. He might have ways of breaking through her magic. They were guests in his house, and there were a whole bunch of rules about magic surrounding guests and what they could and couldn't do. And Reg had no idea what all the rules were and how they would pertain to her.

"Yes," she agreed curtly. "Let's do that."

Corvin tugged her backward gently. Reg let herself be pulled along, letting him guide her, while she kept her eyes glued to Kareem to make sure that he couldn't do anything without her knowing about it. She didn't know what he could do while she had the shield in place. If he were very powerful, he might still be able to break through somehow and harm them.

She heard the door open behind her, and something banged into the backs of her heels. Reg stumbled over something placed behind her. How could Corvin be so inept in guiding her?

"Your shoes," Corvin said. "Put them on."

Reg glanced down. That was what she had tripped over. He'd been trying to guide her over to them to put them back on. She couldn't see whether he had put his back on, but assumed that he had. Reg slid her feet into her shoes, carefully watching Kareem the whole time. He continued to yell at her to stop, calling her a thief and worse.

When Corvin guided her over the threshold, Reg felt a sense of relief, and a lightening around her shoulders, as if a weight had been removed. There had been some kind of magic in the house that she had been fighting against.

"You will not leave!" Kareem howled, incensed. "You will not!"

"Can you leave now?" Corvin asked.

Reg shook her head. "Not while I'm keeping him back."

"Let me do that part. I'll hold him back, you jump us."

Reg nodded.

She intended to do exactly what he had said, but she could not drop her shield. Just as she had been unable to close her eyes and not watch for danger, she couldn't drop her shield and open herself up for attack. It was like not flinching when someone punched her in the face, not sneezing when the urge hit her. A physical impossibility.

"It's okay, Reg. I'm ready."

"I can't."

Tears of frustration broke free from Reg's eyes and started to trail down her face. Starlight made a meowing, growling sound in her arms. She knew that he wanted her to release him, that he was ready to take on the crazy old warlock himself, but Reg couldn't let him go and put himself at risk.

"We go together," she murmured to him.

The rings on her hand were getting warm, she was holding them so tightly in her fist. Was she willing to do all this for a couple of rings and a small baggie of gems? She could just give up and leave them with Kareem. He would be the one who would bear the curse on the gems. Maybe he would die some horrible death, like those who had opened the tombs of kings in the past.

There was a brilliant flash of light. Reg threw her arm up in front of her eyes to shield them, still holding Starlight in her other arm. The gems of the rings turned burning hot when they met with the white light that was too bright to look at.

"Now," a quiet voice said in her head.

CHAPTER FORTY

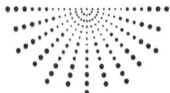

*T*hen there was silence. Reg still had her arm in front of her eyes and her lids squeezed tightly shut. Her whole body tense.

"Regina," Corvin's husky voice reached her ears. "It's okay. We're back."

Reg didn't believe it. She stood there in the darkness behind her lids for a time, listening to every tiny sound. She wanted to believe Corvin, but she didn't dare. She stood there, holding tightly to her shield, until Starlight squirmed to be put down.

She finally opened her eyes. She was in the space between her kitchen and living room, near the front door. It was her cottage. There were still objects scattered around the floor where the cats had knocked them down during the night. She hadn't yet bothered to pick them up.

"What happened?"

She turned to look at Corvin, who was still positioned behind her, as he had been as he led her backward out of the house. He jerked his chin toward the kitchen. Reg turned the other way to look into the kitchen and saw Harrison standing there. He absently stroked Horace's midnight black fur as the cat wandered around the top of the kitchen island sniffing at Reg's appointment book and being the king of the castle.

"Uncle Harrison? What are you doing here?"

Harrison raised his brows. He didn't seem as pleasant and amused as usual. "What were you doing in the land of the ancients?"

"Egypt?"

He just looked at her, waiting for the answer. Reg tried to come up with a logical explanation that wouldn't make it sound like she suspected him of doing anything wrong.

"I was just... I wanted to talk to Horace's owner," Reg nodded to the cat. "See if I could find out why he was unhappy there. If we need to find a new home for him, then I should make sure it is somewhere he'll like better, right?"

"I told you he did not like it there. He likes it here."

"Yes, you told me that. But he's not going to stay here. I already have a cat."

"People can have two cats."

"Yes, I know. But I have enough to do with just one. That's enough responsibility for me. We need to find someone else who will take him."

Harrison twirled the ends of his long, thin mustache.

"You should have stayed here with him."

"I was doing what I thought was best. You didn't say I had to stay here with him."

Harrison rolled his eyes. "Reg Rawlins does not stay when she is told to stay."

"Well... no, that's true." He was probably right. If he had told her to stay in the house to look after Horace and not to go anywhere else, especially back to Egypt, that was probably exactly where she would have gone.

Harrison nodded his agreement. "Now I must make sure you stay," he told her. "And do not go back there."

"I am not going to go back."

He stood there looking at her. Reg felt the rings, warm on her fingers, and looked down at them. She wouldn't go back to Egypt? She had to go back to take care of the gems and the rings. But she wouldn't go back to Kareem's house. She would go where the gems took her. To the mines or the people who should rightfully possess them. That was different.

"I'm not going back to see Kareem. I won't see him again."

"You do not know what you meddle with."

"I'm not meddling! Okay... maybe I *was* meddling, but I'm sorry. I didn't mean to cause any trouble, just to find out what was going on. What happened with Horace? You could explain it to me. Then I wouldn't have any reason to go back there."

Harrison shook his head. "He wants to live here."

"What happened to Destine? The piece of him that was bound to Horace?"

Harrison petted Horace. He held Horace's head to scratch his ears and kissed him on the top of the head. He didn't tell Reg what had happened to the part of the Witch Doctor that had been bound to the kattakyn.

"You will take care of him? Do not take him back to the warlock."

Reg didn't say anything. She wouldn't take Horace back to Kareem, but she would not promise to take care of him, either.

Harrison gave Horace one final ear scratch, then vanished. Reg looked around to make sure that he was really gone.

"Immortals," she said to Corvin in a light voice, as if it were something funny instead of something that frustrated the heck out of her. "Can't live with 'em..."

"He transported us from Egypt?"

Reg nodded. "It wasn't me. Like I said, I couldn't do that while I was trying to maintain the shield."

"You should have jumped before that. Before there was a danger."

"I didn't know."

"You shouldn't have gone there in the first place. I told you it wasn't a good idea."

"I needed to see if I could find something out from Kareem. Harrison clearly isn't putting all his cards on the table."

"No," Corvin agreed, looking over at Horace and the space Harrison had occupied. "But I think there would have been wiser approaches."

Reg shrugged. "I don't know where else I could have gone. Harrison and Kareem are the only ones who know what happened."

Corvin looked at the cat. "And Horace."

Reg considered that. "I guess so. But what is he going to tell me?"

"I don't know. You're the one who can communicate with these creatures."

"Well… not exactly. I mean, I can on a certain level, and I can see their auras or feel what they are feeling. But it isn't like with people… with words."

"Words are a very limited means of communication."

It was true. Reg could read far more from someone's face and actions and by their feelings and their unconscious psychic communication. But words were still preferable for some things. She knew when Starlight was hungry or tired or wanted to play games, but she wasn't so good at figuring out what he was thinking about or what his opinion was on different subjects.

"I don't know. Maybe there is something I can learn from him," she admitted. "But I'm feeling kind of out of sorts now. I don't think it's a good time for me to try to read him."

Corvin nodded. "It's been an interesting day."

Reg looked around. She was, once again, alone in the house with Corvin. She needed to get him on his way before he started getting ideas.

They had jumped from Corvin's house, so she needed to either drive him home, jump him home, or make him order an Uber or find another way to get home.

Corvin's eyes glittered, and she thought he sensed that she was trying to get rid of him. His gazed dropped to the rings on her fingers. "So are you going to tell me about those?"

Reg shrugged. "You already know about those. They're some of the gems that I'm trying to deal with."

Corvin gazed at her, considering the information. "You didn't tell me there were any set pieces. I thought it was all just loose gems. The gems that you showed me."

"There were a few more that I didn't show you."

"Any more jewelry?"

"I don't think I need to give you all the details."

"Of course they are your treasure, but it is curious… that you would show me some of them and leave these two pieces out. Two powerful rings like that. I would think they would be the first pieces that you would want to cleanse, to either use them for yourself or find a buyer."

"I figured it would be easier to liquidate the loose gems. Quieter. Not draw as much attention to myself."

"Well, that is true. You certainly attracted some attention today, wearing those when we went on our little trip." His eyes slitted halfway shut, like a cat sitting in the sun. "What was your reason for wearing them to Egypt? You wanted to see what the reaction to them was?"

"No. I forgot I had them. I was looking at them... and I just put them on my finger when I had to answer the phone. Then later when I put the rest away, I forgot they were there. Until I handed Kareem that business card, they completely slipped my mind."

Reg gazed down at the beautiful rings. Turned the right way around and no longer held in the middle of her fist, they were not as warm as they had been. But they did seem to have a glow and an aura that they hadn't before. They had seemed mild before. Pretty, certainly valuable, but not something that spoke to her. Now, they were completely different. The two rings demanded her attention, pulsed with a magic that made her want to examine them and find out their names and their purpose. These were not rings that someone had picked up at a Middle Eastern bazaar.

"I didn't know they were so powerful."

"Maybe they were dormant before. I didn't sense them before you showed them to Kareem. But now..." Corvin stared at the rings, apparently able to sense their power the same as Reg did. "Now it is unmistakable."

Reg rubbed her thumb over the face of each ring. "You think I activated them by taking them with me to Egypt? Ruan said before that some of the gems were at rest, but that they could become activated later, and I should deal with them before that happened. So that I wouldn't suffer the ill effects of the curses."

"I think that ship has sailed," Corvin confirmed.

Reg sighed. It wasn't easy trying to deal with the gems. She had thought that she would have all the time she needed. The gems had been dormant for a long time, maybe years or decades or even centuries. As long as they stayed asleep, she would be okay. Now her timeline was apparently sped up by quite a bit.

"Well… that's a problem for another day. I should get you home and get ready for my evening appointments."

"I thought that your comment to Kareem about having appointments this evening was a lie. You left clients scheduled for tonight when you didn't know what would happen in Egypt?"

Of course she hadn't. She didn't know whether she would have to stay overnight to deal with the gems, as she had before, so she had rescheduled her appointments for that day. But it was time to get Corvin home.

"Do you mind if I try jumping you there?" she asked, then held up her hand. "No jokes about that, please, I don't know how else to say it."

Corvin smirked. "If you are not too tired, then of course, feel free to take me home. I'd love to have company."

"I'm not staying." Reg didn't want to hold hands with Corvin, so she touched him on the shoulder and thought about his house. She focused on the sights and sounds and smells, the whole feel of the place. She opened her eyes, and they were still standing in her cottage.

CHAPTER FORTY-ONE

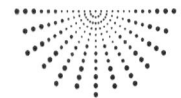

*C*orvin looked at Reg. "Anytime."

Reg frowned. "I thought... I was trying. Why didn't it work?"

He shook his head. "Maybe jumping twice in one day is all you can manage? You did expend a lot of power today."

"No..." Reg considered the way that her body and brain felt. She was a little tired, but not so much that she couldn't still perform.

Except that she couldn't.

"It must be something else," she murmured.

Corvin considered. "I could try boosting your power. You might be tireder than you think."

Without waiting for her to agree or object, he raised his hands and held them close to her without touching. Reg could feel the heat coming from him, filling her body with strength and vitality. She tried again, closing her eyes and picturing Corvin's house.

When she opened her eyes, she was still in her own house.

"Maybe it's because it is unfamiliar," Corvin suggested. "You've only been inside once. Maybe that isn't enough."

"I can jump places I've never been before," Reg pointed out. "I should be able to go back to your house without a problem."

She kept her eyes open, staring into Corvin's face and seeing and smelling and sensing everything about him. If she couldn't jump to his house by picturing the house, she should certainly be able to get there by filling her senses with Corvin. She'd been able to jump based on the almost indistinguishable smell of the stones when she had jumped with Ruan.

She still seemed stuck to the kitchen of the cottage.

"Try holding hands. Skin-to-skin contact," Corvin suggested.

Reg grimaced, but she took his hand anyway. It was strong and warm and her hand seemed to fit into it exactly, as if their hands had been made for each other. Reg resisted flinching at the electricity that buzzed between them and tried not to be taken in by his charms. The heady smell of roses rolled off of him, as he was clearly affected by her touch just as much as she was by him. Or else he was trying very hard to seduce her. Which, of course, wouldn't be surprising.

Skin-to-skin contact was proving to be more distracting than focusing. Reg pulled back from him.

"That's not working."

Corvin looked down at her hand as she let go. "The rings."

"The rings? But I was wearing them before and they didn't stop me."

"But now they have been activated. And removed from Egypt, which Kareem told you not to do. Maybe they are blocking you from taking them any farther."

Reg slowly took the rings off and pushed them down into the bottom of one of the pockets of her skirt, ensuring that they wouldn't fall out the minute she sat down. She put her hand on Corvin's arm once more and tried again.

Still, nothing.

How could it be nothing? There should at least be some sign. Some feeling. Even just a twinge. But there was nothing. Reg couldn't seem to move at all.

She shifted her feet experimentally, just to reassure herself that she wasn't pasted to the floor. She could still get from one place to another the old-fashioned way. Maybe Corvin would have to grab an Uber.

"I'm going to... put the rings away. Maybe if they're in the other room, in the jewelry box..."

Corvin nodded. She could feel his eyes on her all the way to the bedroom, hot on her neck, giving her goosebumps. She hurried into the bedroom and shut the door to keep his eyes off of her. She got out the chest of jewels and transferred the rings and the baggie of gems she had taken to Egypt back to the small wooden box. She took advantage of the time alone to slow her breathing.

The only problem was that she was distracted by what had happened in Egypt. Her powers were still all intact. It was just a matter of focus.

Starlight scratched at the door. He wasn't used to her shutting him out of the bedroom, except in the morning when she was still sleeping and he thought it was time to order breakfast. The rest of the time, all the doors in the cottage were always open.

Reg opened the door. Starlight sat looking up at her. He meowed loudly.

"Do you want to help me?" Reg asked.

Starlight was always a big help when she needed to concentrate on something or to extend her abilities. Corvin had given her more strength, but he was still a distraction himself. With Starlight to help her to focus, the jump to Corvin's house would be no problem at all.

"Thanks," Reg told Starlight. She picked him up and walked back over to Corvin. "Okay." She forced a cheerful smile. "I can do this now."

Corvin nodded.

Reg put her hand on his arm again and focused her being on Corvin's house. She remembered all the details she could of his furnishings, the smell of the place, Corvin's presence there. It was that easy.

Reg opened her eyes. She still hadn't moved.

* * *

She and Corvin looked at each other for a long time.

If it wasn't fatigue keeping Reg there, and it wasn't the rings of power or her distraction...

"Harrison said that he would have to keep you here," Corvin offered.

Reg swore. Yes, he had. She hadn't picked up on it, thinking that he was just telling her that she needed to stay put. That she needed to listen to him. She hadn't thought about his actually forcing her to stay there by preventing her from using her gifts to jump herself somewhere else. For all he knew, she could go straight back to Egypt again. And he'd decided he didn't want her investigating what he had done to Horace.

"Harrison!"

She looked around, but he didn't appear. Reg walked back to the bedroom to look for him, and checked the bathroom and the spare room, sure that he must be there somewhere. He came when she called. He had to be there somewhere.

But he wasn't. He didn't answer her call.

"This is crazy." Reg strode to the front door and opened it. She stood there, looking out at the pathway and the vegetation around her door.

"Not out there?" Corvin asked.

"I wasn't looking to see if he was out here. I was opening it to see whether I could..." Reg trailed off. It was a lovely day outside. Birds chirping, the sun low in the sky but the temperature still pleasant.

"What is it?" Corvin asked, his voice low, as he came up behind Reg.

Reg turned to look at him. "I can't leave."

"I know."

"No, I mean... even walking away. I can't leave the house."

"You can't physically step out of the house?"

"No."

He eyed her, expecting her to demonstrate. Reg didn't move.

"Is it like a force field?" Corvin asked.

"No, not like there's a barrier there. Just... I can't leave. I can't step out."

Corvin gave her a little push from behind. Reg stumbled forward, just an inch or two, not over the threshold. She turned to face him, blazing hot fury erupting.

"Don't *ever* do that!"

Corvin stepped back in surprise, putting his hands up defensively. "Regina, I was just seeing if—"

"You lay your hands on me or push me again and you're going to regret it!"

Corvin's cloak was suddenly engulfed in flames. Corvin yelped and struggled to quickly pull it off. He threw it on the floor and stomped out the fire.

Reg could have kept it burning. She could have made the fire larger and larger until it completely obliterated Corvin. She didn't have to put up with his bullying her or physically laying hands on her. But she let him stomp out the small fire and breathed slowly, trying her best not to reignite it.

Corvin glared at Reg, but she could see his surprise through the outrage. Reg hadn't lit him on fire since he had appeared before the tribunal. That had been before Davyn had taken her on and taught her how to manage her fire. She hadn't even believed back then that she was the one lighting the fires, though she had found the timing to be very propitious and his reactions quite satisfying.

"Don't ever do that again," Reg repeated, in a calmer voice.

"I hear you."

"You'd better."

They circled each other like dancers, watching each other and synchronizing their movements.

"So you can't leave," Corvin observed.

"No."

"He didn't say that *I* had to stay here."

Even so, Corvin made no movement for the door.

"Go then," Reg said.

"If I leave, I might not be able to return, and if you need my help..."

"I don't need your help." And she would make sure that he couldn't return. Harrison shouldn't have brought him into Reg's cottage to begin with. She had wards against intruders, and against Corvin in particular. There was a reason for that. Harrison should have respected those boundaries. If he felt he had to transport them from Egypt, he could have returned them both to Corvin's house. Or to the garden. Or somewhere else he had seen the two of them together. He shouldn't have brought Corvin into her sanctuary.

Corvin still looked uncertain about leaving.

"Go ahead," Reg encouraged.

Corvin stepped past her and over the threshold of the door. He looked back at her as if to see whether she would follow him or if he had gone far enough.

"Should I go for help?"

"Who would you get? Who is going to be able to break Harrison's spell?"

"We don't know if we don't try."

Reg shrugged. "I don't know. I assume he'll come back, and I can talk him into releasing me..."

"If he's not coming when you call him..."

"He'll get bored sooner or later, won't he? He doesn't usually stay gone for long if I need him."

"What if he is going after the other kattakyns?"

Reg's heart sank. That was what they had been trying to stop. She had half-forgotten why they had gone to Egypt in the first place due to the attack by Kareem. Or maybe Harrison had made her forget as well as sealing her into her house.

Reg thought about all the fairy tales where princesses were locked away in towers or dungeons. Those fun, romantic stories. When she had played as a child, she'd always been the knight coming to save the woman from her prison. She'd never wanted to be the princess.

"We need to stop him. But how are we going to do that if he won't even answer when I call him?"

"What does Francesca think?"

"She was going to call the other kattakyn owners. See if he had been around."

"Have you called her to see how that went?"

"No." Reg patted her pockets for her phone. "I guess I should do that."

Corvin tried to walk back into the cottage and was unable to step through the doorway. He looked at Reg. "Invite me in."

"I thought you were going to go home."

"Not yet. I'll stick around and help you to sort this out."

Reg found her phone and tapped to find Francesca's number. "I don't need you to stay here. You can go home and you can call if there is anything to tell me."

"Invite me in and we can at least see what Francesca has to say."

Reg tapped her phone, ignoring the request. Corvin was left standing on the doorstep while she placed the call.

"Reg, where have you been?" Francesca answered the phone immediately. "I have been calling you!"

"Sorry, I was away for a while."

"You need to keep your phone on! This is important work."

"I know. I just… had to go do some checking myself. And I guess I was out of cell range." Reg changed the topic before Francesca could continue on this line. "I wanted to know whether you were able to find anything out. From the other owners of the kattakyns."

"I did not reach the dwarfs, but otherwise… he has been to see *all* of them."

Reg tried to process this. "Harrison has been to see all the kattakyn owners?" she said aloud, relaying the information to Corvin. He looked grim.

"Yes," Francesca agreed.

"Has he… done anything? Taken them away or…"

"The only one he took away was Horace."

"And are they all still bound?" Reg worried at the problem even before Francesca answered. "That is the main thing, isn't it? If he just went to visit them, that's one thing, but if he loosed the parts of the Witch Doctor, if he is trying to restore Destine…"

"The other owners did not say there were any changes to the personalities of the other kattakyns or to their abilities. They are all witches and warlocks who should have noticed the difference, if there was a change."

"You don't sound sure."

Francesca sighed. "I am worried," she agreed. "It is very bad, the immortal going to see all of them. He knows where they all are. If he wants to restore Destine…"

"We need to stop him."

"You must talk to him. You said that you would."

"Well… I have talked to him, but… things didn't go very well."

"You must try again. Until you are able to convince him."

"You are the charmer, maybe you should try to talk to him."

Francesca considered this. "He does not know me like he knows you. He is your protector. It is not the same with someone like me, who he does not care about."

Reg sometimes wondered whether Harrison really did care about her, or whether he just liked to play that role on occasion. Until now, he had never done anything to harm her, but if he had changed his methods and was now going to lock her up to prevent her from doing anything to derail his plans, then she had to reconsider.

"But you could charm him. I don't have that ability."

"We would have to find a way for me to see him. And the last time... he just sent me home."

"I've called to him, but he hasn't come. I don't know where he is." Reg looked at Corvin. "Maybe with the dwarfs. Maybe I should call them to see... find out what's going on out there."

"I didn't know how to get them," Francesca said. "You are the contact with the dwarfs."

"Okay... I guess I'll call them. And maybe..." Reg shook her head. "I don't know *what* I'm going to do about Harrison."

CHAPTER FORTY-TWO

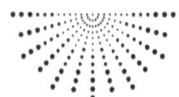

*R*eg hung up the call with Francesca, the knot in her stomach growing tighter and heavier.

"What am I going to do? He's really doing this, isn't he? He's going to resurrect the Witch Doctor!" She tried to keep the feeling of panic from overwhelming her. "How could he? I told him it was dangerous. I told him he couldn't do that."

"You can't expect an immortal to listen to you and believe that you know better than he does."

Reg breathed out heavily and shook her head. She raised her phone and opened the contacts.

Brimir or Gwythr?

Brimir might be higher in the kingdom's hierarchy, able to make decisions over anything his father gave him authority over. But it was Gwythr who had taken Nico in and was in charge of him. He seemed to be the one who was helping to prepare the dwarfs for war against Harrison. He probably had the on-the-ground knowledge of what was going on in the mountain.

Reg tried to relax the clenched muscles in her shoulders and stomach. She tapped Gwythr's name.

"Put it on speaker," Corvin suggested.

Reg hit the button before Gwythr answered.

"Reg Rawlins," Gwythr's voice boomed from the speaker. Reg turned the volume down.

"Gwythr. Hi. I wondered… how things are going there. I hadn't heard from you, so I assume that… no one came to see Nico."

"I should probably have contacted you earlier," Gwythr said, his voice grave.

Reg groaned. "Oh, no. What happened?"

"One of the ancient ones."

She gulped. "Harrison?"

"I do not know how he is known to humans. To the dwarfs, he is known as Far."

"Has he done anything? Did he try to take Nico?"

"He has seen Nico, but he has not taken him away. We would not allow this."

Reg wasn't sure how they would stop him if they tried. Not when Harrison could transport himself, Nico, or anyone in the dwarf mountain at any time. They could go to battle against him, and maybe their mages and sorcerers would be able to do something to shield Nico from him, but Reg wasn't confident about it. She and Corvin had fought an immortal. That was why they were so averse to Harrison allowing the Witch Doctor to re-form.

"What did he do? Did he… did anything change? Nico is very special."

"We know he is special," Gwythr agreed. "He is a warrior cat."

"And Harrison—Far—he didn't… change anything about Nico? Take that fire away from him?"

Gwythr's voice was very serious. "No, Reg Rawlins. He has not harmed the cat."

Reg blew her breath out. Horace was the only one, then. If she and Francesca were to believe what all the kattakyn owners told them, then Horace was the only one that Harrison had unbound. Why? And why had he brought him back to Reg?

"So everything is okay?" Reg asked. "Truly? You have not had to fight?"

"We are ready if he comes back. We will not let down our guard."

"He's not there right now?"

"No. Not now. Earlier today. But then he said he had to go see you."

Was that when he had rescued Reg from Kareem? "Okay. Thanks. I appreciate it."

"And Reg Rawlins is well? She has not had any trouble with Far?"

"Well…" Reg didn't feel like telling Gwythr that she had effectively been grounded. Harrison would be back. He would release her, and they would forget all about what had happened. "We have had some problems with him. One of Nico's litter mates… It appears that Far took something from him."

"His fire?" Gwythr demanded, returning to their earlier conversation.

"Well, it wasn't exactly fire in Horace's case, but yes. He took away part of him that… made him who he was. And we don't understand why."

"He is not there now?"

"Harrison? I mean, Far? No. He's not here now. But he could come back. I've been trying to get him to come back. I really need to talk to him."

And for him to release her from her house so that she could go other places if she needed to. Even though Reg didn't have anywhere to go at that moment, she couldn't help feeling trapped. Staying in her house when she wanted to was far different from staying in her house because she had to. Because some being had decided to keep her there against her will.

Reg made excuses to Gwythr and terminated the call.

"Can I come in, Reg?" Corvin asked.

Reg shook her head. "No. Um… you should go home, I guess. We need to figure things out, but I don't think there's any point in you staying here."

Besides the fact that she couldn't trust him if she let him back in, of course. Which Corvin knew full well was the reason she didn't invite him back in and let him past the wards.

"Reg, we can work together much better if you let me in."

"No."

Reg closed her eyes, frustrated. Sooner or later, he was going to have to figure out that she would not give in and he would leave in a snit. And that was fine with her.

When she opened her eyes, she was seeing sparklers. She put her hand on the door frame to steady herself, worried that she was going to pass out. The flashes of light did not clear, but multiplied. Until they started to gather, coalescing to become a recognizable figure.

"Orri."

CHAPTER FORTY-THREE

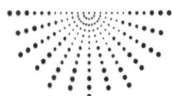

*C*orvin's eyes were wide, fixed on Orri as he materialized out of thin air. And fireflies.

"Your elf," he murmured.

"Yeah." Reg nodded. Although she was tired of Orri's appearances and bumbling around, she was a little proud that the elf had chosen her and that she had seen something so rare not just once, but multiple times. "My harbinger. *Orri.*"

Orri turned and saw Reg. "Reg Rawlins. I am here to give you—"

"A warning. I know."

He shook his head. "No. To give you assistance."

"Assistance." Reg blinked, surprised. "Assistance with what?"

"You are trapped? You are unable to get free from here?"

"Yes. How did you know?"

Orri nodded. He stroked his beard, and fireflies flew out from it. "I can help you."

"How?" Corvin demanded. "She cannot leave this house. She has already tried to leave, both by teleportation and by walking out."

Orri looked at Corvin. He gave a brief bow, and turned back to Reg. He indicated Corvin with his eyes and murmured so low that Reg could barely hear him.

"...fair of face..." Reg heard.

"I know." She told him. "I've already been warned."

Orri gave a nod. He reached a hand toward her. "Do you wish it?"

"Wish… what?"

"Do you go with me?"

"Yes, please, if you can get me out of here."

"Which direction do you wish to go?"

Reg was a little worried about his use of the word "wish." She had a certain aversion to the word, and he kept using it.

"What direction? Just… outside, I guess. I can get my car and go where I want, or I can jump. Whatever, as long as I'm not stuck inside."

"There are only two directions to go," Orri explained patiently. "Forward and back."

Forward and back? How could there only be two directions? Orri wasn't a train engine. Forward would take her through the doorway, so she supposed that was the direction she wanted to go. She nodded toward it.

"Forward."

Orri nodded. He put his hand on her arm. It didn't give her a buzz like when Corvin touched her, but it did feel very comforting. The elves had helped to heal Starlight when he had been sick, and maybe it was just her remembrance of that event that made her feel warm and comforted to have him touching her. Or maybe it was because of magic and healing in his touch. It soothed away the knotted muscles and nauseated stomach, so that she could feel calm and focused. Like a new person.

She saw the lights start to glow around Orri and around her. They seemed to be flying away from her, as if both she and Orri were dissolving into fireflies. Like a lit sparkler. She saw Corvin watching, eyes wide. And then he was gone.

For a long time, Reg felt as though she was suspended in space. In a nowhere place, where time did not pass, where she did not exist and neither did anything else. She couldn't sit and wait there, because there was nowhere to sit and nothing to wait for. Eventually, she started feeling her body. She could again see the fireflies and other brightly lit bugs swarming around her and Orri. They gathered in until they were all gone, and it was just her and Orri standing in the garden outside Reg's cabin.

Corvin coughed and cleared his throat. Reg looked around Orri and saw him.

"It worked!" she told him the obvious. "Why could you get me out of there when I couldn't jump myself out?" she asked Orri.

His raised his brows. "Because you were attempting to move through space."

"You moved us through space."

Orri shook his head. "I moved you through time and space." He looked back at the cottage, with the door standing open. "Janus did not prevent you from moving through time."

"Well, the joke's on him, I guess. Francesca says it's JAY-nus, by the way. Not Janice."

Orri shrugged. "Human pronunciation."

"Well, maybe I would have figured it out faster if you used human pronunciations. Or maybe if you didn't talk like a fortune cookie at all and just gave warnings straight out in normal human language. You could do that, couldn't you?"

"The rules are very exact."

"And you have to talk that way? You're not allowed to just give me a warning in plain language?"

"Your people and mine do not speak the same way," Orri told her slowly, obviously picking his words with great care. "Human language is very... blunt."

"Yeah. And that's the way we like it." Reg moved to the side so that she could see both Corvin and Orri. "So... I'm out. What should I do? Jump to the dwarf mountain?"

"Harrison isn't there. Your friend said that he had already left," Corvin pointed out.

"But he could go back. He didn't come back here. He didn't go to Francesca's. I don't think he would go back to Egypt; he already brought Horace back. It would help if he had actually told us what he was doing! Maybe we could help him, if it isn't something that wouldn't enable the Witch Doctor to re-form. I'd at least be able to predict where he might be."

"Do you know where he is?" Reg asked Orri. "Janus?"

"He has been here," Orri said. "And will be here soon. He will come back here."

Reg swore. She wanted to know what he was doing, but she didn't want him returning and finding her free again. What was the point in Orri releasing her if she was just going to be locked up again?

"We need to get out of here then."

There was a noise from the other side of the fence, the front yard of the big house. Reg thought at first that it was a caterwaul, it sounded so weird and otherworldly. Not like the noise that anything human would make. All three of them turned toward the noise, curious.

"What the heck is that?" Reg asked.

"Your other friend," Orri said, giving her a bow. "The other of the ancients."

"The other... who? Weston?"

"I do not know the human names."

Reg walked the path to the front gate. The back yard was protected from intruders by wards Sarah had set. There were beings who could get past it, obviously, Orri and Harrison, to name two. She wasn't sure why Weston could not get through it and Harrison could. Weston had been able to appear to her in the cabin before. But maybe he had approached the wrong way. Maybe he had to appear to her inside the cottage, not to approach it from outside. Or maybe he was prevented because of whatever Harrison had done to keep her there. Some kind of sealing power.

But the figure she saw outside the front gate was not Weston. Nor was it Harrison.

It was Kareem.

CHAPTER FORTY-FOUR

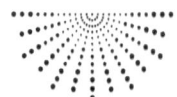

"*W*hat are you doing here?" Reg demanded. "How did you know…?"

"You invited me to contact you," Kareem reminded her. "If I knew anything about Hassam and your friend."

"Yes…"

"You gave me your card."

But Reg's address was not on her card. Her address was not published anywhere. She did give it out to clients when they made contact and wanted to set up a seance or reading, but she kept it off public records.

"How did you find me here?" Reg demanded again. "You didn't get my address from my card. And you didn't fly here on an airplane."

Orri had referred to him as another ancient. Was Kareem one of the immortals? If he was, then why hadn't Harrison explained that part to Reg?

"So… is that why Harrison took Horace away?" she asked aloud, following the series of thoughts. "Because he knew you were an immortal and you could take the part of the Witch Doctor from Horace?"

"You are a fool," Kareem sneered. "You still have no idea what it is going on. Even after activating the rings, you have no clue."

"I... haven't had much time," Reg explained. It was a lame excuse even in her ears. She was creative. She could come up with a lot better than that.

Corvin was thinking more quickly on his feet. He hadn't had to expend energy in maintaining a psychic shield and jumping halfway around the world and back. Of course he figured it out before Reg.

"Harrison went to see all the kattakyns, but the only one he took was yours. The only one that had been unbound."

Kareem rolled his eyes. He was an ugly man. An ugly man with an ugly attitude. Reg could tell him why it was he didn't have any friends. "You think I would not recognize the essence of an immortal when it was right in front of me? Rubbing against me every day?"

Reg pressed her fingertips to her temples. "*You* were the one who released the piece of the Witch Doctor from Horace? Why would you do that?"

"Why would I ignore that kind of power? I have lived many lifetimes longer than you, and this was my chance to increase my power. And now I know there are others. I only need to find them."

His eyes glittered and Reg followed his sight line to Starlight, who had apparently come out of the house when the door was left open. She tried to step between the two of them.

"Starlight does not have any of the pieces of the Witch Doctor. He's just a regular cat."

"A regular cat," Kareem scoffed. "There is no such thing as a regular cat. And *he* certainly is not one. Do you think I don't have vision?"

Sarah had shown Reg how to see the light around powerful objects, and Reg had been startled by the brightness around Starlight. She shouldn't have been, of course; more than one person had told her that he was powerful. But it was hard to understand sometimes that her cat was something other than a fuzzy little foot warmer who demanded fish.

She knew some of Starlight's history now. Maybe Kareem was hoping to take his power too.

"He is not one of the kattakyns," she told Kareem firmly. "The kattakyns are all pure black—"

Corvin nudged Reg. She scowled at him, turning to rebuke him for bothering her when she was trying to take control of the situation. He met her eyes, his consciousness burrowing into her brain, communicating with her as clearly as he could.

You are saying too much.

Reg opened her mouth to argue that she hadn't told Kareem anything he didn't already know. But maybe she was wrong. Maybe he was only guessing about the other kattakyns. Or maybe he knew that the Witch Doctor had gone out into several objects, but didn't know that they were all kattakyns. Maybe he didn't even know they were kattakyns, and had thought that they were just regular cats.

Except he said there was no such thing as a regular cat.

Instead of keeping her mouth shut, Reg had told him that there were others and had given him a basic description.

How do we get him out of here? Reg asked Corvin in her mind.

He shrugged with one shoulder.

Reg turned her attention back to Kareem. The wards that were set against intruders would not last forever. Especially if Kareem was stronger than Sarah. And if he were as old as he said he was and had acquired part of the Witch Doctor's power from Horace, then she needed to act while she was still able instead of waiting until he could break through the barriers and take them down one at a time.

"Why don't you go back to Egypt?" Reg told him. "There isn't anything for you here. I only have Starlight and Horace, and you already took Horace's power. So you might as well just go back to where you came from."

"You think yourself powerful. But you do not have the strength to fight me. Even in Egypt, still wearing the rings, you were barely able to hold me off. Now you have removed the rings..." He shook his head. "Why would you take them off instead of wielding their power?"

Reg looked sideways at Corvin. It was at his suggestion that she had taken them off. Now they were put away in the cottage. It didn't exactly make sense for her to run back into the house, dig under her bed for the chest, open it, and recover the rings from the plastic bag that held all the jewels from Egypt. It would take too much time and she would look foolish in front of Kareem. She needed to look as though she knew what she was doing, that she had a reason for everything she did, not that she was ignorant of the fact that she should have kept the rings on.

"I don't need the power of the rings," she told him confidently.

"Not in my own country. I will save them for the day that I require them. There is no point in wasting their power." She lifted her chin so that she was looking down her nose at Kareem. Not saying *no point in wasting their power on you,* even though that was what she intended to convey.

"You witch!" Kareem yelled. He kicked the fence and he held up his hands in front of the open gate, working on the wards that kept him from entering there. "You unschooled, incompetent witch! You don't have what it takes to fight someone like me! Not even with the rings!"

Reg could feel the power of his magic against the wards. She and Sarah had worked on them together, since the yard was their joint domain and Reg needed to be trained in the most basic of crafts. It felt as if someone were pushing her in the chest, forcing her back.

Reg hated being bullied. Hated the feeling of being overpowered. She had been in that position too many times as she grew up. Surrounded by people with greater physical strength, more authority, more experience, and more violence inside them. She'd been pushed around and abused enough times as a child and had sworn that it would never happen to her as an adult.

And here she was, taking it. Waiting for Kareem to break down her wards and invade her space. She wouldn't be able to stop him from hurting her, from trying to take Starlight's power. She would stand there, helpless, while he took everything that mattered to her.

"No," she said firmly. Her face was as tight and frozen as a mask. "You cannot enter here. You cannot do any harm here."

CHAPTER FORTY-FIVE

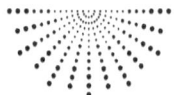

"*H*ow do you think you're going to stop me?" Kareem challenged. "What do you think you're going to do, *little girl?*"

Reg's anger flared. She was having trouble focusing her thoughts and keeping herself under control. That was how the Witch Doctor had addressed her. He remembered her from when she was small and she could do nothing to stop him from torturing and killing her mother.

And now he remembered her and the others challenging him in the warehouse, taking the immortal and his draugar minions on with their tiny force.

Little girl.

Reg hated to be called a little girl.

She wasn't that four-year-old child anymore. She had learned of her power and had been training and developing it. She had helped to defeat the Witch Doctor once already. She had also challenged Weston openly, and she and Corvin and her younger self had overcome him and forced him to leave Norma Jean and her child alone. She had overcome others who thought that she was a weak child or woman.

Being underestimated was one of her gifts. Like a mother bird pretending to be injured to lead a predator away, and then flying up in his face and leaving him far behind. She could use it to her advantage. *Appearing* to be weak wasn't the same as *being* weak.

Reg closed her eyes. They were swimming with tears, but not tears of distress or fear. Tears of anger. There was so much rage bubbling up inside her over the injustices she had suffered as a child and now faced again that she could not contain it. It had to get out somehow.

Kareem laughed.

"You are a child. Picking up rings of power as if they were baubles. Playing dress-up in vestments that are too powerful for you to even understand. You will fall here."

Reg opened her eyes. He had transformed. She was aware that it was only a trick of her mind, that he hadn't actually physically transformed, but she could see the Witch Doctor in front of her now, mocking and challenging, ignoring the fact that she had helped to overcome him once before. She could see the immortal's face superimposed over Kareem's features. Her mouth twisted into a grimace of pain and fury both at once.

"Stop! I am not weak. I'm stronger than you ever were, in all the centuries you have lived." She spat the words out, her inner convictions taking over. Her brain was still trying to sort and correlate all her scattered thoughts and impressions. "You cannot enter. You cannot find any more of the kattakyns. You have overestimated your own powers and have expended more than you should have."

She fought back against him, pushing back against the force on her chest. The fire inside her was raging to get out. Unable to contain it any longer, Reg released it. The Egyptian's cloak was in flames. He angrily shook his head and tried to pat out the fire.

"You think I'm afraid of a little party trick?" he demanded. "You don't have anything on me!"

"I do!" Reg argued, her voice strained as she tried to keep herself under control. "You are the one who doesn't know what he is dealing with."

"You think I can't fight a little girl?" Kareem's eyes went over the others. "And her little kitty cat? You think that this fallen warlock and bumbling harbinger can help you? They can't do anything. And neither can you."

"You've already lost. We've already beaten you once before. In fact," Reg looked at Orri, "we've already beaten you today, haven't we?"

Orri put on his dark glasses as if he would be able to see Kareem better with them on. He looked at his wrist, where he didn't wear a wristwatch, but a wide brass bracelet sparkled in the sun, nearly dazzling Reg.

"Yes," Orri agreed. "The child will prevail."

"No, she won't!" Kareem screamed. "You are *nothing* to me! My power is beyond anything you have ever encountered!"

"Isn't it the same thing I have encountered before?" Reg argued, "just one-ninth of the power?"

"No!" Kareem insisted "You cannot do anything to me! You have no idea of my power!"

Reg faced him, determined. He couldn't extinguish the flaming cloak, and eventually tore it away from himself and threw it down.

"Watch out," Corvin intoned. "She'll have your jacket next."

"Tricks," Kareem insisted. "You think that a few sparklers are going to scare me?"

"Sparklers?" Reg looked at the cloak on the ground, nearly consumed, and made it flare up, forcing the warlock to step back despite himself. Reg wanted to burn everything around him, but it was Sarah's yard, and she would not be very happy if Reg burned her trees, bushes, and fence to the ground just to prove a point.

She stepped toward the open gate. Corvin put his hand on her arm to stop her. "Regina…"

"You really think this guy can stop me? He can't even get past the wards."

Reg stepped through the barrier that prevented Kareem from entering the yard, feeling herself pass through it as if it were water or thickened air. She hadn't felt the full brunt of Kareem's attack until then. And Corvin was right, she should have exercised more caution. She wasn't prepared to face the full force of Kareem's power.

His magic seemed dark and sticky. Like something she didn't want to touch. The tacky floor in a public restroom. She would have to battle Kareem face on, but wanted to turn away from him in distaste.

Reg didn't put up a shield this time. She was tired of using shields, of passively trying to avoid or fend off attacks. People needed to know that she was dangerous in her own right. That she was strong and confident and would not be cowed by witches or warlocks who thought they were something special. Or even wizards or pieces of immortals.

She put up both hands and pushed Kareem back. He didn't like it. He resisted and stepped forward to gain the upper hand.

"No," Reg insisted. "You are not welcome here. You're not bugging me or my cat or any of my friends. You can go back to where you came from."

She wasn't sure whether she was telling Kareem to go back to Egypt, or the Witch Doctor to go back into hiding or to attach himself once more to Horace. But she didn't want him there.

"I don't take orders from little girls."

"You should!"

Reg held him, preventing him from moving. He couldn't attack her. He couldn't retreat or transport himself. All he could do was stand there, his eyes wide and angry, trying to overcome her by effort of will.

Gradually, he started to push forward, gaining ground on Reg a fraction of an inch at a time. He smiled. A tight, frozen smile filled with effort.

Reg could feel Corvin behind her. His hand was no longer on her arm, but she could feel his presence there and could feel his power. She turned her head slightly. Not far enough to look at him, just to acknowledge his presence. She felt for him in her mind.

Give me some power.

CHAPTER FORTY-SIX

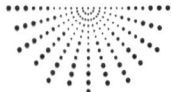

*S*he would not ask most people for such a favor, though she had skimmed from others' power before, but Corvin was different. He had helped her on several occasions, both by feeding her power when she was too weak and still needed to perform, and when she couldn't control the power she had and needed a relief valve before she ended up blowing everyone up.

He had chastised her before for not asking before accessing his power, so this time she did, though she fully intended to take it even if he did not agree. She knew that the two of them together could defeat Kareem, even with part of the Witch Doctor to help him. Corvin had drunk most of the Witch Doctor's power and it was only the dregs that had been able to go into the kattakyns.

She could feel warmth radiating from behind her and an immediate boost in her strength. She pushed back against Kareem, and like in a tug-of-war where one side suddenly overbalanced and was dragged through the mud, she forced him back several rapid steps without any apparent resistance.

"No!" Kareem howled. "You cannot!"

He drew back and to the side. Reg thought he was trying to figure out another avenue of attack, some attack that she was not expecting, but she was ready for him. He was not as strong as he thought he was.

She had thought that someone from Egypt would have been trained in many ancient arts that she had no idea about. He would have kinds of magic that she knew nothing of. He might put her into a trance or put a mummy's curse on her. Something she had never seen before.

But instead of attacking her, he went suddenly after someone behind her. Reg was too slow to turn around. Her first thought was that he had gone after Starlight. He had talked, after all, of her cat and how he was not strong enough to defend them. Reg had seen Starlight fight before, in several different forms, and she knew that he was a formidable foe. But still vulnerable to certain attacks. She didn't want him to end up sick or cursed again, as he had been at Yule.

At death's door.

She hadn't known from one day to another whether she would find him still alive when she next went to the vet's office. Reg's heart squeezed a little just thinking of it. So she turned as quickly as she could, prepared to protect Starlight against magical attack.

Orri stood there, his eyes wide, hands held up to protect himself. But it was too late, the warlock had clearly already struck. There was no blood or gore, nothing gruesome, but Orri's round, dark eyes showed his shock. His pale skin was paper white, as if all the blood had been sucked from him.

"Orri?"

He didn't respond to her, but slowly started to crumple on the spot. Reg hurried to him, trying to keep her eyes on Kareem at the same time. He would attack again given half a chance, Reg was sure.

"Leave the elf," Corvin advised. "You've got Kareem on the run. You have to finish him before he has a chance to retreat and gain in strength."

"Will you help him?" Reg obediently turned back toward Kareem, leaving Orri where he fell.

"I will aid *you*."

"No—Orri—" Reg wanted to turn back toward him, but she didn't have the time. Corvin was right, of course; she had to take care of Kareem before he had a chance to recover. There was nothing she could do for Orri until Kareem was out of the way. But she still felt like a traitor for turning her back on him when he had returned to her, over and over again, to try to warn her against danger.

"Give me back…" Reg didn't even know what to ask for. The piece of the Witch Doctor? Was it a soul? Powers? Essence? Was it something that could be trafficked between two people? Francesca had bound it to the kattakyn and Kareem had loosed it. Did that mean that it was now part of him? Could it be removed like a piece of clothing? Excised like a tumor? "It is not yours," she told him. "If you want to get out of here safely, you have to return that which is not yours."

"I give you nothing. I give no quarter. You cannot defeat me. You are weak and there are too many others I can hurt."

Reg's heart pounded hard. That was the one thing he could do. He could keep harming people that she cared about. Or even people she didn't care about. She would keep trying to fight him, but if he wouldn't face her and kept attacking others…

She closed in on him, her racing heart powering movements that were too quick for her body and had to be supernatural. She grabbed him and yanked him around, then clamped both hands over his arms to hold him still and prevent him from causing any more harm.

"No. You cannot," she insisted.

He squirmed not just in her hands but also inside her mind. He was not going to go easily.

"You are evil," Reg snapped, staring into his eyes. "You attack the weak and defenseless."

"Defenseless? You're not defenseless."

"I wasn't talking about myself."

Reg felt scattered, trying to keep her senses on everything at the same time. On Kareem and the Witch Doctor. On Corvin behind her, supplying her with strength, whispering prompts in her brain. She was aware of Orri, on the ground behind her somewhere, injured by whatever Kareem had done to him. Was he mortally wounded? Reg couldn't forgive herself if the elf died because of her, because he had kept coming back to warn her and she hadn't heeded him.

There was a movement in the trees beside her. Reg's mind snapped to Starlight. He was out there with her too. He also needed to be protected. And Horace? Where was he? If Starlight had left the cottage, then Horace could too. He might have followed Starlight or have gone off in his own direction. He might try to go to Kareem, his owner, not understanding that the man hadn't wanted anything to do with the cat, but had stolen something from him. Something that had given him power, and now he had none.

Reg glanced to the side to see if it was one of the cats. Instead of one of her four-legged friends, it was a child.

Where had a child come from in her yard? Reg tried to process the new information, while holding on to Kareem and trying to keep him pinned down both physically and psychically. Another glance to the side. The child was dressed in brown and green. He had slightly pointed ears and was creeping toward Orri. An elf child. Had Orri brought the child with him, or had one followed where he wasn't supposed to? Either way, there was yet another life in the balance. How could Reg protect all of them at once?

Finish him off, Corvin told her, directing her attention back to Kareem. *It is within our power.*

Reg didn't know what that meant. She felt there was enough on her conscience already with the death of the wizard in the graveyard. And then there was Vivian's disappearance when a sinkhole had opened up in the middle of the street. Reg knew that wouldn't have happened if she hadn't tried to help Vivian. And Jacky Lane.

She didn't feel bad about the Witch Doctor. Maybe if they had been able to do something other than bind him when they had bested him at the warehouse, none of the rest would have happened. But they hadn't been able to finish him off then, and that meant that he came back, and could keep coming back, in the shape of the kattakyns. And if they managed to band together? Or Harrison released each of them?

Reg renewed her attack, holding tightly to Kareem, squeezing his arms and drawing power from him. If she couldn't overpower him easily, then maybe she could de-power him, pulling strength from him until he couldn't fight her any longer. Until he had no strength to fight back or to hold on to the piece of the Witch Doctor.

Kareem tried to strike out at the elf child, laughing in Reg's face, knowing that she would protect him. That she cared more for the welfare of a child she had never seen before and who was of a completely different species than she did for herself.

"No!" Reg insisted. "You can't!"

He tried harder to break free of her and attack the child, and Reg fought harder to pull his strength from him.

Kareem's knees buckled. Corvin moved in. He raised his hands and tried to get in close to Kareem, pushing past Reg. Reg remembered his taking the essence of the dying wizard. And previously, of his sucking the massive power surge from the Witch Doctor, doing the best he could to destroy the entity completely. Reg put her arm out.

"No. He's weakened. Leave him alone."

"You can't stop there," Corvin insisted. "It's not safe. He needs to be neutralized."

Reg turned, looking for the elf child, who was still creeping towards his father's body, ignoring everything that was going on around him. Normally, the elves didn't travel in their bodily form, and Reg wasn't sure what had made him materialize when he was still so far away from his parent. Maybe it was inexperience. Or he might have been hiding there all along, left alone by Orri to blend in with his surroundings like a baby rabbit or deer.

"Corvin..."

Corvin looked in the direction that Reg was looking, but shook his head. "What?"

"The elf. We need to protect the little one."

Corvin blinked at her. "I only see one elf."

"But the little one..."

"No. I only see Orri. And when we have taken care of Kareem, we can make sure he's okay."

"But—"

Reg looked back at Orri and the young elf. Where was Harrison when she needed him? Why had he left her alone, grounded like a disobedient child, leaving her to handle everything all by herself? He should have been there to help fight the Egyptian warlock. Even if there were rules about the immortals not being able to hurt each other, she didn't need him to cause any harm to the Witch Doctor, only to help with Kareem.

"Reg."

Reg looked in the direction of the voice. Now he showed up? Now, right when they were in the middle of a heated battle?

CHAPTER FORTY-SEVEN

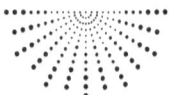

"*U*ncle Harrison!"

"What are you doing?" Harrison looked at Reg, then turned and looked at the guest cottage, where she was supposed to be locked in. He made a huffing sound and shook his head.

"I am trying to fight."

"This is not your battle."

"Well, Kareem made it my battle. What am I supposed to do, walk away?"

"Stay in the house." Harrison looked back at the house again. "Why are you no longer in the house?"

"I got out. So that I could do what I had to. We needed to overcome Kareem, the warlock who owned Horace. Because he—"

"He holds what was bound," Harrison acknowledged testily. "Why are you out here?"

Reg looked at Corvin, kneeling over Kareem, still sucking the life force out of him.

"You have to stop him. He's going to go too far!"

"When are you going to train this warlock?" Harrison said it as if Corvin were a puppy who should be trained but had just pooped in the house.

Reg snorted. "I'm not sure this one can be trained."

Harrison flicked his hand and Corvin went tumbling away from Kareem. "Hey!" he growled, baring his teeth at Harrison, more than just irritated at being stopped. He looked like a wild animal; a wolf-man stopped mid-feed. There was no blood, but that was the image that sprang to Reg's mind. An animal, fangs dripping with blood, snapping at the hand that got too close to his food.

Reg left Harrison to deal with Corvin and hurried over to Orri and the elf child. The child drew back immediately, frightened by the woman moving toward him. They were not used to being seen. They normally kept out of sight and, from what Corvin had said, even he hadn't been able to see the elf child as Reg did.

"It's okay," Reg murmured. "I'm not going to hurt you. I just want to see how Orri is." She hovered over Orri's long, slender body, holding her hands out over him, pushing the heat of her fire into him. She wasn't a great healer, but she knew the basics, and she hoped that all Orri needed was a little strength to get back on his feet again. Kareem hadn't had any chance to think of a strategy, so she had to assume that he had just struck out swiftly and reflexively, without really thinking about it. A quick blow and then retreating from Reg.

The smaller elf leaned forward, staring at Reg's hands and then looking up into her face, curious and questioning.

Reg couldn't feel anything wrong. The elf's heart and lungs were still operating, blood was still flowing through his veins, he was probably just stunned and low on energy. Reg fed more into him. She reached out to Corvin, supplementing her energy with his, so that she wouldn't collapse with the loss of her own strength. Corvin was an endless reservoir of strength, always getting more from somewhere.

After a few minutes, she could tell that Orri's face was getting pinker, regaining some of its ruddy coloring.

"See?" She smiled at the younger elf. "He will be okay."

The little one crept forward to his father's side and took his hand. He looked at Reg, waiting for her to pronounce his father healed. Reg rested her hand directly on Orri's chest for a moment, then went over to Corvin and Harrison who were having a heated discussion.

"Where is it?" Harrison demanded of Corvin.

"What?" Reg asked.

"The unbound essence. Where? It must be retrieved."

"No idea," Corvin said, raising his brows. "I'm sorry, things have been kind of crazy here."

"He had it."

Corvin folded his arms across his chest. "You left Reg alone and undefended. I helped her."

Harrison waved this away as if none of it mattered. "What happened to Destine?"

Corvin looked at Reg, shrugging. "Do you know? There was so much going on... I didn't feel any of the Witch Doctor passing through me. Maybe you? Or just into the universe..." Corvin made a gesture indicating the air around him, fingers graceful.

Reg looked back at Harrison with concern. "What does that mean? You didn't find him? That piece that was bound to Horace?"

Harrison nodded his agreement. "It is gone."

Reg looked over at Kareem, lying on the ground, still moving slightly. Not dead, as she had feared. Harrison had been able to stop Corvin before he had consumed all the man's life force. No more lives on Reg's conscience.

"Maybe he still has it?"

"No."

Reg shrugged widely. "Then it must be like Corvin said. It just... went out into the world."

Harrison looked at Reg, his mouth a straight, angry slash across his face. "Why did you not stay? How got you out?"

Reg ducked her head. "Well... the elf. He is a time traveler."

Harrison turned to look at Orri on the ground, beginning to waken. "A time traveler?"

"Yeah. So he kind of... moved me in time to where I wasn't in the house anymore."

"Where?" Harrison repeated

"When," Reg amended. "And then... for his troubles, Kareem attacked him too, to try to distract me."

"They should return to their time."

"They?" Corvin repeated.

"There is a young one too," Reg informed him. "His son, maybe."

"There are more of them," Harrison said.

Reg began to see other twinkles and movements around Orri and the child elf. The trees were alive with lights and the faint tinkling of bells. She hadn't noticed before. Reg looked around, but the others did not become visible to her. She returned to Orri's side.

"Wake up," she murmured, shaking Orri's shoulder gently. "Time to get up now."

Orri's eyelids fluttered and he opened his eyes, looking around him in confusion. He lifted his head, struggling to get up.

"It's okay," Reg said. "Just take a minute. Everyone is safe now."

"Jon? Where is Jon?"

Reg leaned back so that he could see the young elf beside him. "Is this your son?"

Orri relaxed, resting his head back down again. "Jon. You are safe."

"He's fine," Reg assured him. "You're the only one who took any damage."

"You protected him."

"Well... I did my best. I'm sorry that you got hurt, though."

"That does not matter." Orri closed his eyes for a moment and squeezed Jon's hand. "As long as my son is okay."

Reg smiled. They looked a lot alike; she could see Orri's features in Jon's face. "He's a very handsome boy."

Orri looked at him. "You should not have appeared," he chastised. "Elves must remain hidden to stay safe."

"You did not remain hidden," Jon pointed out.

"I had a debt."

"A debt?" Reg repeated. "To who?"

"To Reg Rawlins. Because you kept my son safe."

Reg tried to wrap her mind around this one. "You came to warn me, and to help me, because you knew I was going to help protect Jon?"

Orri nodded.

"But he wouldn't have been in danger if it wasn't for me. And for you appearing to me."

Orri smiled. He scratched his beard, fireflies twinkling in its strands. "Yes. It is hard for humans to understand," he admitted.

"Uh... yeah. It is. So does that mean this is the last time I'll see you? You won't be coming back anymore?"

"No more." Orri pushed himself up into a sitting position. He rubbed his temples, looking around. "It is a beautiful garden."

"Yes, it is," Reg agreed. "Forst has made it very beautiful and inviting."

"You must continue to protect it."

Reg hadn't thought about how the wards and protections they had placed might help other species who lived in the yard and garden as well. She and Sarah had only been thinking of themselves and their own safety.

"Yes. Of course. I'll make sure that we protect it."

CHAPTER FORTY-EIGHT

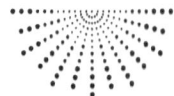

*H*arrison and Corvin approached, looking curiously at the elf. Reg could tell that there was still tension between Harrison and Corvin. But they had never really liked each other.

"So this is your elf," Corvin observed. "Your harbinger."

Reg nodded. It was sort of sad to think that Orri would never come back, that she was seeing him for the last time. But on the other hand, he had been driving her crazy with his appearances and she was glad she wouldn't have to listen to any more warnings.

"Fair face," Orri said, looking at Corvin. "And Janus."

"Why do you call him Janus?" Reg asked.

Orri raised his brows. "He is a human god. So you would understand."

Reg didn't tell him how difficult it had been for them to work the riddle out. "And you said that Kareem was an ancient. But he's just a warlock."

"He carried a piece of the Witch Doctor with him," Corvin reminded Reg, "So there was an immortal. Part of an immortal."

"I was mistaken." Orri shrugged. "The human world is… difficult."

Reg shook her head and ran her fingers through her braids as if straightening them could order her thoughts too. "You can see things in the future? You know what's going to happen?"

Orri didn't answer.

"So… now what is going to happen? Can you see where the piece of the Witch Doctor went and whether any more of the kattakyns will be loosed?"

She could feel Corvin in her mind again, cautioning her against saying more than she should to him, as she had done with Kareem. Reg looked over at the spot where Kareem lay to make sure that he was not conscious and listening to them. But he was gone. There was no sign of him.

If Orri could already see the future, then it didn't matter if she told him; he already knew what would happen. At least, if the world ended because Harrison or other witches or warlocks released the other kattakyns, Orri would know it. Because it would impact on his future.

"It is not our place to tell humans what will happen," Orri said apologetically.

"But that's exactly what you've been doing. What are you talking about, you can't tell us what is going to happen?"

"There are certain times when we are chosen to share what we know." Orri stroked his son's hair affectionately. "But normally… that is not something we may do."

"You could tell me what's going to happen with the Witch Doctor. You were already warning me about him, remember? About the cat with nine lives? Remind me again why I have to beware of the cat with nine lives."

"It is not done," Orri repeated. He put his sunglasses on. "Now, we must go."

As they watched, the lights started to sparkle around Orri and his son and, in a few seconds, they were gone. Corvin shook his head. "It's fascinating."

"It's confusing," Reg griped.

"Many things in the magical world are."

"I like things to be… simple and straightforward."

Corvin grinned. "You are in the wrong profession."

Reg looked over to where Kareem had lain after they had overcome him. "Where did he go?"

Harrison flicked his fingers toward the spot. "I sent him away."

"Where?"

He raised his brows at her. "He is no longer here. The question is," Harrison looked suspiciously at Corvin. "Where is the missing piece? Where is what Horace had?"

Corvin shook his head. "I told you. I don't know. Maybe he put it into some other creature before he attacked us. Maybe it was dispersed."

"You would know if Corvin had it, wouldn't you?" Reg prompted Harrison.

"Not if it was hidden well."

Reg couldn't help looking suspiciously at Corvin as well. But what reason would he have had to take a piece of the Witch Doctor away? This was the second time they had fought. He didn't have any reason to wish for the return of the Witch Doctor. None of them wanted that.

Well, maybe Harrison wanted it. And he could be deceptive if he wanted to be. He might just accuse Corvin when he himself knew the answer.

"Well," Reg sighed. "I'm beat. You're going home?" This was aimed at Corvin.

He looked disgruntled. "I suppose." His eyes slid over to Harrison. "And what about him?"

"He'll go home too," Reg said. "After we talk."

CHAPTER FORTY-NINE

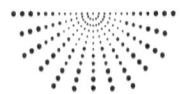

*C*orvin was past the gate and would not be able to return. Reg swept Starlight up in her arms, even though he yowled in protest at this handling. Reg and Harrison walked back into the guest cottage, each lost in thought.

Horace was waiting for them inside. He sat near the doorway, watching them with inscrutable eyes. Reg reached out to him with her mind, but was unable to read him. He didn't want to connect with her like Starlight usually did. He remained distant, not telling her what he was thinking and feeling.

"Know anyone who wants a cat?" Reg asked Harrison lightly.

"The cat does not want me."

"I'll have to find him something sooner or later. So... how did you know what had happened in Egypt? How did you know that Kareem had found out about the Witch Doctor's form being bound to the kattakyns?"

"The immortal can see many things. Things that humans cannot."

"I don't doubt it. Did you know because you went to visit him? Is that how you knew? Or did you go to visit him after you found out he had been loosed?"

"We can sense our own. If they are not hidden."

"And then you went to visit all of the others? To make sure that they had not been unbound too?"

Harrison tapped the tips of his fingers together. "If his power is unleashed, we must know."

"Because of his destructiveness? How evil he is?"

"His power needs to be balanced. Humans worry only about loss of human life. Immortals know... there is more at stake than human lives."

He was silent after that portentous revelation. Reg took a deep breath and tried to calm the pounding of her heart.

"So, what's for dinner?" Harrison asked brightly and opened the fridge door.

Reg was about to tell him that she had cleaned out the fridge—twice now—so there wasn't really anything in there he would be interested in. But she saw that it had been well stocked.

By Sarah? Harrison himself?

"I don't know. What's in there?"

They would have a feast. And they would worry about the Witch Doctor's power being unleashed on an unsuspecting world again some other time.

UNDISCOVERED TOMB

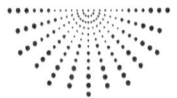

REG RAWLINS, PSYCHIC INVESTIGATOR
#15

For those who are seeking homes

CHAPTER ONE

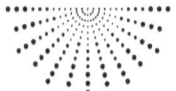

eg rubbed her eyes and yawned, not particularly ready to face her day and Sarah's disapproval. The gray-haired, older woman was usually pleasant and easy to get along with. Reg's landlord, she rented out the guest cottage in her backyard at a very reasonable rate, fully furnished in a rustic Florida style, and could frequently be found stocking Reg's fridge or writing new appointments into Reg's appointment book on the kitchen island, which Reg didn't pay her to do. She was helpful and grandmotherly and had helped Reg through some difficult situations.

But Sarah did not like cats, and that was a problem. She had an African gray parrot as her familiar and bird feeders in the beautiful gardens on the property, and cats were high on her list of pests to be eliminated.

Starlight, Reg's black and white tuxedo cat with a white marking on his forehead, had been lucky to escape Sarah's wrath. Reg had adopted him before she knew of Sarah's anathema, so Sarah had overlooked Reg's not consulting her first. Sarah even fed Starlight when she popped over—which was frequently. Too much, if the truth were told.

But the recent addition of Horace was another story. Reg had not gotten permission to take in another cat and had known that Sarah was strict in her rule that Reg was not to have any more pets.

Especially cats.

Of course, Reg knew that the pure black cat was not actually the usual, run-of-the-mill domestic short hair that he appeared to be.

And she hadn't adopted him. Not intentionally, anyway.

"I can't help it that Harrison left him here," Reg told Sarah for the hundredth time. She gathered her box braids into both hands to pull them all back behind her shoulders, and let the red strands fall. "I told him not to. But he did. And it's going to take me a little time to find a new home for Horace."

"You can't keep him."

"I know that. And I'm not planning to, I told you that from the start. He's not going to stay here. But... I need to find a new home for him. And I can't just dump him on someone."

Sarah's sour look indicated that she didn't see why not. "That's what you said last week."

"I'm trying. It isn't like I can return him to his previous owner. That warlock was in Egypt, and I don't even know if he exists anymore."

It seemed like a strange thing to say about a person, and maybe it was, but Reg didn't know how else to put it. Uncle Harrison had made the warlock disappear and, whether he had used his powers as an immortal to teleport him back to his house in Egypt or had annihilated him, Reg had no idea. And she didn't really want to know. Even if she asked Harrison, he would probably give her some nonsensical answer or ask her something about the nature of human existence and she would be no closer to the truth.

"Didn't he have heirs? Maybe the cat could go to his children."

"I hope he didn't have children." Reg gave a little shudder, thinking about the evil, power-hungry warlock. "And if he did, I wouldn't give Horace to them. He wasn't happy in Egypt."

"Egypt is a wonderful place for cats. They are worshiped there," Sarah pointed out.

"They *used to be* worshiped there. That was a long time ago. Now... who knows how they treat them. Probably let them wander the streets and get eaten by dogs."

"There is a natural order of things," Sarah said with a nod, as if this were a sad truth that nothing could be done about.

"Just like cats eating birds?"

Sarah's face got red.

Not the right thing to say. Not when Reg wanted Sarah to calm down and relax about Horace being around for a few more days.

"Sorry." Reg rubbed her eyes again. "I just got up. I need my coffee. Then I'll be in a better mood. I shouldn't have said that."

"You know that I said no more cats. Even having that other one over to visit..." Sarah rolled her eyes over the concept of kitty play dates. But Starlight really did like having Nicole over. Horace's adoptive mother, Nicole was also black all over, and she and Starlight were very close.

"I know. But I didn't take in another pet. You wouldn't want me to just open the door and shoo him out, would you? Have him stalking around your garden?"

"Certainly not!" Sarah's voice got noticeably shriller. "But we do have animal shelters. You could take him to one of those."

"You want him to be put down? How is that fair? He hasn't done anything to hurt anyone. His owner turned out to be an evil warlock who should never have had a pet. Who knows what kind of abuse Horace had to put up with while he was there. You think he should just be turned out and put down for something that wasn't his fault?"

Reg's own experiences with being abused and frequently moved from home to home in foster care meant that this hit much closer to home for Reg than it did for Sarah. It wasn't Horace's fault that he had been treated that way. Harrison had rescued him from a bad situation and dumped him on Reg, believing that she would be the best person to take care of him. And in other circumstances, maybe he would have been right but, as Reg couldn't take on another pet under the current circumstances...

Reg pulled the coffee pot out from the coffee maker, even though it was still dripping a little and the drips sizzled on the hot plate and filled the room with the smell of burning coffee. She sloshed a good amount of coffee into a mug and quickly put the pot back in place.

"I'll give Francesca a call later today," she promised. "She was going to be looking for some other homes too. Okay?"

"Yes, fine," Sarah agreed grumpily. "Why doesn't she take this cat in until she can find a new home for it? She had all of the kittens before. She can easily manage two."

"I've tried to get her to take him, but she says there is too much else going on and she needs to concentrate on the others… she's worried about… things."

Reg didn't want to get into it too deeply. She too thought that Francesca should be able to take one more cat. Even if it were just short term. But Francesca's worries about Horace and his eight litter mates were serious and not something that could just be brushed off. And Reg would prefer that Francesca were the one taking on that responsibility. Reg didn't want anything else to do with the Witch Doctor and the other kattakyns.

"Just see that you deal with it soon," Sarah reiterated, looking at the black cat who, for the moment, was curled up on the cushion of the wicker sofa, looking perfectly happy and at home.

"I will," Reg promised.

But she didn't know how she could find him a home any faster than she was already trying.

Sarah did a quick flip through the date book on the island, showing that she was moving on to other things and would not stop being involved in Reg's life.

"Let me know when you do."

CHAPTER TWO

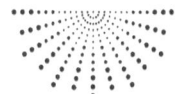

*R*eg decided to take a page out of Harrison's book and just show up at Francesca's with Horace. Maybe if Francesca actually had him in the house, and he showed how well he got along with Nicole (pronounced NEE-cole in Francesca's beautiful Haitian accent) she would let him stay there, at least until the two of them could find him another home. Then Reg didn't have to listen to Sarah's lectures three times a day and could focus on her psychic services business.

And they would find Horace another home. Eventually. Unless Francesca decided he could stay there permanently.

Francesca raised her brows when she saw Reg on her doorstep with Horace in the cat carrier. She swept long blond curls back over her ear, frowning.

"Why did you bring him here?" Francesca asked. She looked at her watch. "We did not have anything set up today."

"No, I know. But he wanted to see Nicole and has been moping around my place. So, I just took the chance that the timing would be okay. You don't need to do anything; he won't get in your way. He can just have a visit with Nicole…"

"You know I have other things to do."

"I know. You're a busy person," Reg agreed crisply. "Lots of responsibilities. I don't need to stop and visit. You can keep working on whatever…"

"I am not working on 'whatever.' I am working on preventing a disaster!"

Reg stepped toward the door and angled to get through it before Francesca decided to slam it in her face. As she expected, Francesca elected to be polite and stepped back, allowing Reg in. Reg put down the cat carrier and, as soon as Francesca closed the front door, Reg opened the carrier and let Horace out. He slunk out immediately and began smelling the floor around the carrier. He had lived there before and Reg was sure he would recognize the place and be happy to be there with his adopted mother again.

"Can you take a break from your work to have some tea?" Reg suggested.

Francesca sighed. She rubbed her forehead and nodded. "Come into the kitchen," she conceded.

Reg followed her in and sat at the kitchen table while Francesca turned the kettle on and got out cups. Bright sunlight was streaming in the kitchen windows, making the glass fronts of the cupboards sparkle.

"So, I take it things are not going as well as you would hope?" Reg hoped that sympathy would go a long way to greasing the wheels and convincing Francesca to take Horace for a few days.

"No. It is… difficult" Francesca puttered around waiting for the kettle to boil and thinking about what she wanted to say. When she sat down at the table, she was ready to talk. "This is the problem. First, we fought the Witch Doctor, who was raising draugar from the dead to do his will. Not just one or two of them, but an increasing army."

Reg nodded. "Nine zombie guys."

Francesca rolled her eyes and shook her head. But Reg's summary was correct, of course.

"We battle this immortal and together we are able to do what is not possible. With the help of Corvin and Damon, we are able to defeat him. Take most of his power away, until he flees, sending his essence into the nine draugar."

"Which have shifted form from huge zombie guys to cute little black cats."

"I use my charm to call them to me and bind them with a spell so that the being of the immortal cannot separate from the kattakyns and re-form as Samyr Destine."

"Which you figure should hold him bound for a thousand years."

"More or less," Francesca agreed. "But I did not count on any interference in the process. I thought that once we found homes for the kattakyns all around the world, we would be safe from them rediscovering each other and re-forming even when the binding spell wore off. So scattered, they would have a difficult time finding each other."

"But we sent Horace to Kareem."

Francesca sighed and nodded. She pulled a file out of a pile of papers beside her and opened it up. Reg saw the research profile she had done on Kareem before they sent Horace to him. Everything they needed to know about his background. Except for the fact that he had merely been waiting for opportunity to present itself so that he could make his grab for power. He was an older, well-respected warlock, the leader of his coven. He had recently lost his cat familiar and was looking for his replacement. They thought that he would do well with the sedate, often sleepy Horace.

But Francesca's profile had not suggested that the warlock might recognize the kattakyn for what he was and, even worse, recognize the portion of the Witch Doctor's power that had been bound to the kattakyn. And that he would have the knowledge and skill to unwind Francesca's charm and separate that piece of Samyr Destine from the creature for his own use.

"I cannot believe..." Francesca started. She stopped and shook her head sadly. "He seemed so *perfect* on paper. And I talked to him on the phone, corresponded with him in email. Everything seemed to be ideal."

"He's sneaky," Reg comforted. "He was being deliberately deceptive. How were you supposed to know that?"

"I should have sensed it. Things that he said, I should have known."

"You couldn't," Reg asserted. "Don't spend time beating yourself up. You have enough to do without that."

Francesca rubbed the bones around her eyes, looking tired. She nodded. "I know. You are right. So now... Kareem unbinds the kattakyn and takes that part of Samyr to himself. That is one thing. A powerful warlock with a portion of immortal powers—that is not good."

Reg nodded her agreement.

"But after losing that piece... *now* what are we to do?"

Reg didn't actually need a refresher on the problem. She knew that Francesca was just trying to lay it all out logically, to look at it again and find a solution they might have missed.

"It depends on where the piece went," Reg offered.

"If you are sure that Kareem no longer had it..."

"Well... yeah. Harrison wouldn't have *disappeared* him if he still had it."

"Why not?"

"Because... he and Samyr are both immortals. Harrison always follows the rule that immortals are not allowed to harm one another."

"Or so he says."

"So he says," Reg agreed. But she didn't think that Harrison would do anything to harm one of his fellows. That was one thing about him that had remained constant. Even when she had asked him for his help, he had refused to do anything that might harm another of his kind. Or even one-ninth of his kind.

"He wouldn't have done anything to Kareem if he still held a piece of the Witch Doctor."

"Not even to return him to Egypt?"

"Well... I don't know. But he said that Kareem no longer had that piece. And I believe him."

"Then explain where it went." Francesca took a sip of her tea and then folded her arms across her chest. She'd already heard the story from Reg enough times, there were no new details to give to her. They just kept going over the same facts.

"Harrison thinks that someone hid it."

"And he would not be able to sense it?" Francesca's tone was skeptical.

"He said that if it was hidden well enough, he would not be able to."

"He was able to find each of the kattakyns."

"But..." Reg struggled with magical concepts, not having been raised in a practicing home. "Were they *hidden*?"

Francesca considered. She chewed on her lip and had another sip of the tea. "I do not know how to hide something from an immortal. My skills are not in hiding."

"If Kareem could sense the piece attached to Horace, and he is just a human, just a warlock, then it couldn't have been hidden very well."

"No. Perhaps... just because I could not sense it after they were bound... that doesn't mean that *no one* could."

Reg nodded her agreement. They sat for a while, nursing their cups. Reg knew where the conversation was going next, but she really didn't want to go there. Talking about the past, about their battle with the Witch Doctor and finding the kattakyns homes; that was one thing.

Talking about what danger there might still be, a danger that was no longer a millennium away; that was something Reg didn't want to do.

"The options are very limited," Francesca said. She raised her index finger. "One, Harrison was lying, and he has the piece of Samyr."

"If he does, I'm sure it's just for safekeeping," Reg said immediately. "I explained to him how dangerous it would be for him to put the pieces of the Witch Doctor back together again. How it was dangerous to me and the whole human race."

Francesca didn't look impressed by this. Harrison was not well-known for an overwhelming concern for the human race. Reg had caught his fancy, or at least, the child that Reg had been years before when he had tried to protect her from the Witch Doctor. Reg was no longer that little girl, and she feared he might be withdrawing from her, recognizing that she was no longer an innocent little child but had powers and gifts of her own. She wasn't helpless any longer.

But against the Witch Doctor if he were re-formed and came after her? Reg shuddered at the thought of what he might do to her.

"Possibility two," Francesca raised the next finger, "Someone is hiding the piece of Samyr. Namely Corvin Hunter."

Reg nodded.

This was entirely possible. Corvin had been sucking the powers from Kareem, intent on his destruction. He might have taken the piece of the Witch Doctor during that process. And as a creature hungry for power and who already had absorbed much of the Witch Doctor's powers, he would be loath to give it up. He would hide it from

Harrison and anyone else who was able to sense it. He did not have control of all the powers that he had absorbed from the artifacts and the Witch Doctor the day of their battle, but he might control enough of them to access memories and powers that would allow him to hide what he had stolen.

"Or," Reg held up three fingers, "it just dispersed out into the universe, like Corvin suggested."

Francesca shook her head. "That seems very unlikely. The more I research… the more certain I am that these final pieces of Samyr cannot be destroyed or dispersed. They must remain intact somewhere."

Reg thought of mythology stories she had heard in school. Very powerful beings were difficult to kill. Even if you cut them into little pieces, those pieces had to be scattered or burned to prevent them from resurrecting, re-forming, or reincarnating.

"It isn't like the pieces are his physical body," she countered. "His spirit or powers or whatever is left of him… it isn't like a body that has to stay the same size and shape."

"No," Francesca agreed thoughtfully. "They could be present in many different forms."

"I don't think that Corvin took that piece and hid it. I would know if he did that."

"How?"

"Because… he can't hide from me. We are connected."

"He cannot hide *anything* from you?"

"Well…" Reg wavered.

Of course he could.

Francesca read Reg's expression and nodded. "You do not even know all the powers he has absorbed. From Samyr and his artifacts and… anyone else he has drunk." She grimaced as she said it. The thought made Reg a little queasy as well. She had been one of Corvin Hunter's victims. He had charmed her and tricked her into agreeing to his proposition, which did not realize meant taking her powers from her.

She had awakened empty and hollow, the silence as loud as a klaxon in her head. But he had returned her powers to save her from torture, and she had guarded them carefully—or *tried* to guard them carefully—ever since.

"It's either Harrison or Corvin," Francesca told her. Her lips pressed together in a line as Reg shook her head, not wanting to attribute the theft to either one of them. "If it isn't them, then the only other person who could have taken it was… you."

CHAPTER THREE

Reg's jaw dropped. She stared at Francesca in disbelief, trying to come up with the words to protest this accusation. The ridiculousness of it! The very suggestion that she would take a piece of the Witch Doctor and hide it from Harrison and everyone else…

Why would she even want to? She had a hard enough time controlling her own powers and learning what her abilities were, what things were dangerous, how she could defend herself without blowing anything up or burning anything down. How to avoid her siren instincts being triggered so that she wouldn't try to drown the nearest human male.

"I wouldn't—I would never!" she sputtered.

"I don't think you would. I don't think it is something that you seek. But… you have surprised me before. You have abilities and a heritage that is… suspect. You were there. You were the one who attacked Kareem."

"I defended myself; I did not attack."

Francesca shrugged. "I was not there. You and Kareem fought, did you not?"

"Yes. Because he forced the issue. He was attacking me, threatening me and my friends. Orri, the elf. I had to fight him. It wasn't my choice."

"But you did. And in that fight, you might have taken what he held."

"No."

Francesca nodded and sipped her tea. "I think not. But... if not you, then who?"

* * *

When Reg prepared to leave, Francesca didn't forget that she needed to take her furry companion with her.

"You need to take him, Reg. You cannot leave him here."

"I can't keep him at the cottage. Sarah will kick me out. She lets me stay even though I have Starlight, but if I keep another cat there, she won't let me stay."

"She can't evict you without notice. You have thirty days to find a home for him."

Reg opened her mouth to protest again. Francesca shook her head and held up her hand. "If you leave Horace here, I will take him to the animal shelter."

"What?"

"You heard me. I cannot take him."

"You had him before. You had all nine of them before, plus Nicole."

"And I cannot take him back. I simply cannot, Reg. I am sorry."

"You would take this poor, defenseless animal to the shelter."

"Yes."

"And what would happen then? You would let them put him down? He isn't even really a cat, Francesca. What would happen when they tried?"

Francesca tilted her head to the side slightly. "I do not know. Do you want to find out?"

"No." Reg stomped off to find Horace. She found him in the laundry room where Nicole's litter box and dishes were, pawing at her empty dish. Reg bent down to pick him up. "Did you eat all Nicole's food, you little pig?"

He made several noises of protest and squirmed, trying to get away from her. Reg kept away from his powerful back legs, marched back to the kitchen, and pushed him into the cat carrier.

Horace hissed and turned around to face the gate as she closed it, growling and spitting at her.

"I'm sorry. It's time to go." She felt a little bit bad for just grabbing him and shoving him into the carrier. She wouldn't have liked to be treated that way. She should have given him a warning that it was close to time to leave. And then called him and given him time to say goodbye to Nicole. Then maybe given him a treat in his carrier so that he would walk into it willingly.

She sighed. "I'm sorry, boy. I really am. I'll do better next time."

Francesca raised an eyebrow, as if she thought it was silly that Reg would apologize for her treatment of him.

"Let me know if you figure anything out," Reg told her. "About... how to keep Harrison or anyone else from unbinding the kattakyns. And maybe... about how to find the missing piece." She scratched the back of her head. "I really don't like the idea of it being out there somewhere, whether someone else has it or it's free-floating. The Witch Doctor... he's dangerous."

"And you let me know if you discover something about Corvin or Harrison. Because I can't think of anywhere else it would be."

Reg nodded. She thought they should set up another play date between Starlight and Nicole, but the timing felt wrong.

Reg stepped out the door and Francesca closed it behind her. As Reg walked down the sidewalk toward her car, she felt a heavy sense of sadness. She wasn't sure why until she put the cat carrier in the passenger seat beside her and saw Horace looking out at her from behind the bars. It was his sadness she was feeling.

"Did you think you were going to be able to stay there?" Reg asked. "With your mama cat? I'm sorry, Horace."

She poked her finger between the bars to pat his head or scratch his ears, and he snarled and swiped at her with bared claws.

Reg jerked her finger back. "Hey. I know you're upset, but you don't have to attack me. We'll see Nicole again, okay?"

But after she said it, she regretted that she had. When was he going to see Nicole again? She had to find him a new home soon, and Nicole would not be there. Francesca wouldn't take Horace in. Horace's new owner, whoever he or she was, would probably not agree to set up play dates between Nicole and Horace on a regular basis. Or ever.

She shifted the car into drive and headed back home.

* * *

Does the cat wish to visit the garden?

Reg was a little startled by the voice in her head as she prepared to unlock her front door. She hadn't seen Forst, the garden gnome, in the yard. But then, she rarely saw him if she weren't looking for him. And even when she was, he was easy to miss despite his red cap.

Reg turned her head and saw him watching her from the corner of the house, by one of the bushes that had flourished under his care, growing thick and wild and producing beautiful pink blossoms.

Forst. Reg answered him telepathically as well. The gnomes usually spoke with each other in their "inside words" and had a difficult time with spoken communication. She looked down at Horace, looking miserable inside the cat carrier. *Maybe he would. Couldn't hurt to give it a try. I'll keep him in the carrier so he doesn't try to run away, but maybe if he can just get some fresh air and watch the birds and the bugs flying around...*

Forst nodded his agreement. *Wild things need wild places.*

Horace had been pretty wild lately. His personality had changed so much since his rescue from Kareem. He'd been so quiet before. Francesca attributed it to the fact that he had been separated from the piece of the Witch Doctor.

Reg wasn't so sure about that. She hadn't seen anything quiet or sedate about the Witch Doctor. Francesca said that everybody had sides of themselves that they hid, and it was just a side of the Witch Doctor that they hadn't seen. Reg wondered if there was more to it than that.

Reg followed Forst around the guest cottage to the back garden, where there was a fountain and a bench to sit on. She looked for just the right spot to set the cat carrier down, positioning it so that Horace could see the pool and the trees and long grasses and plants, and would get some of the light breeze that was blowing across the yard. She looked in at him to assess how he felt about it.

Horace's ears were no longer back and he wasn't hunched over in a tense, angry position. His whiskers were forward and his nose worked as he smelled everything around him, stepping forward to put his face against the grill of the carrier, as close to being free as he could be.

"How's that?" she asked softly. "You like that? Do you smell the birds?"

Sarah would probably be horrified if she realized that there was a cat in her garden. But he was safely in the carrier. He would not catch any of the colorful birds that stopped at the bird feeder.

The sadness and heaviness that she had felt from Horace as they left Francesca's house had dispersed somewhat. He was enjoying his exposure to the outdoors, even if it was through the bars. He had probably never had a chance to spend any time outside since he had been trapped in his kattakyn form. Did he remember being outside in his previous life, before he had been raised as a draugr? Had he been an outdoorsman before he had died? Had he lived other lives before then?

Reg had never thought much about reincarnation before learning that Starlight had lived other lives before he had been a cat. She didn't know whether he was reincarnated or had changed his form voluntarily or if something else had happened to him. She didn't know how prevalent reincarnation was. Had everyone lived other lives, or was it just something that happened occasionally? Everything she learned only prompted more questions.

She sat there, feeling Horace's emotions settle, enjoying the scent of the sea and the flowers on the wind. She closed her eyes and just rested for a while.

CHAPTER FOUR

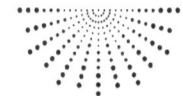

*R*eg could hear Forst as he dug around the bushes and flowers in the garden beds. It was just as soothing as the cool breeze and the smell of the growing things. The "living," as the gnomes described it.

You see more elven folk? Forst asked.

Reg opened her eyes and looked at him. She smiled. *No. Not since Orri appeared the last time. I don't think he will be coming back.*

They are still here, Forst observed, looking at the bushes around him.

How do you know that? Do you see signs of them?

A gnome can feel them. Sometimes hear their bells.

Reg nodded. She had seen lights in the garden and heard tinkling bells, before she had known what it meant. *It must be quite a compliment to have them living in the garden that you tend.*

Forst nodded, his rosy cheeks growing even pinker. *A great thing to have elves in your garden.* He plucked dead blossoms off a couple of plants with practiced fingers.

Are there other creatures in the garden too? Reg asked, looking around. *Orri said that we need to keep the garden protected with the wards and charms, to protect all the creatures.*

Forst spread his hands apart, indicating all the plants around them.

Plants do not live alone. They need sun and soil and water, but they also need companions. Elves and gnomen and human. And many others. Birds, bees, bugs...

Reg nodded. *But birds and bugs don't need magical protection. Maybe there are other creatures who do.*

He smiled and nodded, but did not elaborate. Reg resolved to take it up with him again in the future.

* * *

Reg found herself getting drowsy in the warmth and peacefulness of the garden. She decided she'd better go inside before she fell asleep and fell off the bench. She picked up the cat carrier and said her goodbyes to Forst, and went back inside.

She hadn't been sleeping very well lately. Of course, when did she? It seemed like there was always something on her mind or disturbing her dreams. She had thought all of that would stop when she had a safe place to live and a regular income. But her worries had just changed from where the next meal would come from to zombies and spiders and entities like the Witch Doctor. Each time, she told herself that once the current situation was resolved, she would sleep better and wake up feeling well-rested each morning. But it didn't seem like the current situation ever resolved into a better situation, just a different one.

The voices of her foster mothers of the past were all stored in her brain, and sometimes it was hard to remember that they didn't live there like the other voices. Foster mothers had always told her that if she went to bed in good time and just lay still in her bed, that she would have a good sleep and be able to wake up well-rested in the morning and ready for school like the good kids. But it had never worked that way for Reg. She was always too restless and hypervigilant at night and couldn't settle down to sleep until the small hours of the morning which, of course, meant that she wasn't ready to get out of bed at six-thirty or seven like the *good* boys and girls. She would not be ready for school on time, would fall asleep during morning classes, and would be grumpy with her teachers.

She no longer tried to go to sleep at a decent hour. Night was a good time for psychic readings and seances. People were much more receptive and the spirits' voices were that much stronger. Reg could work at night, sleep until the late morning, and then manage to roll out of bed and start her day again.

Lately, though, she had been waking up a lot. She couldn't blame it all on Starlight and Horace, although they did make too much noise after she went to bed. Sometimes it was something else that woke her up. A dream. A noise in the night. Waking up with a feeling of dread. She would lie there awake, listening to the house around her, trying to discern whether someone or something were there. She was safe in her house; she knew that. There were plenty of charms and wards to keep away those who had evil intentions. But still…

Reg let Horace out of the cat carrier. He didn't bolt out of it and hide under the bed as she expected him to, but exited slowly, rubbed against the carrier and her leg, and wandered over to Starlight's dishes with an inquiring meow. Maybe the time in the garden had helped him to calm down and mellow out. Maybe she needed to take him out there more often. Starlight might enjoy a few excursions too. She could even get a harness and leash and take them out for walks around the garden. That would be even better than going out in the carrier.

As long as Sarah didn't freak out about it. She wouldn't like the idea of a cat in her yard, even if he were on leash.

Starlight jumped down from the bedroom window and galloped out to the kitchen to stand by his dish, shouldering Horace away. He was polite enough not to hiss and growl at Horace for getting close to his dishes, but he didn't just stand by and let him claim that space, either. He yowled loudly at Reg to hurry up and find them something good in the fridge, before both of them died of hunger.

Reg opened the fridge and looked over the numerous dishes and takeout cartons. She had tried to clean out the fridge, but it seemed like every time she turned around, there was more food in there. Some of it was from Sarah, she knew. Sarah always made too much food when she cooked, and she wanted to mother Reg and make sure that she was eating properly. Which she wasn't. Even with healthy food around, Reg always went for the junk.

"What's in here? I don't even have a clue where most of this came from."

Reg started opening containers at random, looking for something that the cats would enjoy, her own supper a secondary consideration. One smelled like tuna casserole, so Reg plopped some into a bowl from the cupboard, which she put down on the floor for Horace, and some into Starlight's dish. Both cats immediately started to chow down.

The casserole smelled good, but wasn't really what Reg was looking for. She looked through some of the takeout containers. Uncle Mike's Ribs? When had she gotten ribs? Had Sarah ordered them and not been able to finish? Reg pulled the cardboard container out, put it into the microwave, and started it warming.

Ribs were good. It had been a long time since she had gone to the little rib shack with Corvin.

CHAPTER FIVE

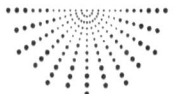

"We like ribs," Harrison commented.

Reg jumped about two feet in the air. She suppressed a shriek of surprise at his sudden appearance.

"Ah! Warn me before you do that?"

"Do what?" Harrison asked, raising an eyebrow in query.

He was a tall, thin man with a dramatic long mustache usually curled at the ends, but now drooping down. He wore a pink silk shirt and striped black and green shorts. And a perky little cap like the one from a police uniform.

"You scared me," Reg scolded. "You can't just appear out of nowhere and start talking to me. I wasn't expecting it."

"It wasn't out of nowhere."

"Well, I don't know where you were, but suddenly appearing here is startling." Reg blew her breath out, trying to calm her racing heart. The microwave beeped and she pulled the ribs container out. She got two small plates out of the cupboard and set one on the island in front of herself and one closer to Harrison. They each helped themselves to some ribs.

"We like ribs," Harrison repeated.

"Yes," Reg licked her fingers. "We do. Is that where they came from? You left them in the fridge?"

Harrison nodded. He put one of the ribs in his mouth and gnawed the meat off. "You do not need to go with the soul sucker to get them."

Reg nearly choked on her mouthful. She swallowed strenuously and filled a glass of water from the tap to wash it down.

"No," she agreed. "I could go there myself."

"Or eat with me."

Reg nodded. She watched him as she ate, looking for any sign of a change in him. He seemed eager to please her lately, looking for ways to show her that he had her welfare and happiness in mind.

"You don't like Corvin Hunter, do you?" Reg asked.

Harrison shook his head. "A spirit drinker cannot be trusted."

"He has helped me out a lot of times. I mean… I know he does it because he wants to get close to me, because he wants my powers, but… he has been helpful."

"He cannot be trusted."

"And I don't trust him. I'm always careful."

"Always?" Harrison repeated. He shook his head.

"Well, I always try…"

Harrison picked up another of the ribs and pulled the meat from it. He looked at Reg. "We do not need forks?"

"No. You can eat ribs with your fingers. It's not rude."

He continued to eat, apparently filing this information away for the future. Another of the strange quirks of human society, how some food had to be eaten with a fork and some did not.

As Reg watched him, she tried to determine if there were anything different about him. If the piece of the Witch Doctor had made Horace sleepy and sedate, would it affect an immortal in the same way? Or would he be unaffected by it because it was only a small piece of Samyr Destine and they were of the same kind? Harrison had a strong personality himself, and his own seemingly endless reservoir of powers and abilities. Too much for the Witch Doctor's spirit to affect him? Or did he just hide its influence well?

She had only Harrison's word for it that the piece of the Witch Doctor that had been bound to Horace had disappeared. Reg didn't think that he had the guile to lie to her and hide something like that from her, but he often surprised her and she couldn't be sure.

"How have you been lately?" she asked him. "Everything… going well in your world?"

She had no idea where he was or what he did when he was away from her. Was he somewhere? Or nowhere? Or everywhere? Was he somewhere with other immortals, like Weston, or was he alone? Or were there others in the mortal world that he visited, supplying them with tasty food, protection, and extra power when they needed it?

"Everything always goes as it should."

Another of Harrison's impossible answers. Did that mean that he controlled the outcomes? Or that it was all up to fate? That everything was predesigned? Did the fact that he could travel to other times mean that he could see the future and already knew what would happen before it happened, or could he only travel to the past and not see the future? Was he subject to fate or did he control it?

"Are there a lot of immortals?" Reg asked. "I haven't met very many of you."

Harrison licked sauce from his fingers, looking remarkably like a cat as he did so. "More than you think."

"How many?"

"They are not numbered."

"Does that mean that there are more than you can count? Or what?"

Harrison shrugged. "I cannot tell you that."

"You're not allowed? Or it isn't possible?"

"Yes."

"Why do you come here if you are never going to answer my questions?"

He looked surprised. "I did answer your questions."

"But not in a way that I can understand?"

"I am not responsible for your human brain."

"Well… no. But I think you could explain better."

"Perhaps."

But he didn't make any attempt.

* * *

Reg made a stop at the Sandy Claws Thrift Shop to pick up some new items for her wardrobe. One thing about living out of a suitcase and not really having a permanent address—she hadn't had to worry before about any variety in her wardrobe. Now that she had a place of her own, and the same people were seeing her week after week, Reg felt the need to expand and diversify her clothing choices. She didn't want people to think that the options were quite as limited as they were. There were only so many different combinations and ways to accessorize her outfits. A scarf could be worn a dozen different ways, but it was still the same scarf.

She felt better after picking up a few additional items at the thrift shop. As she left, she saw Marian's store front. She also ran a psychic service business but, instead of having it out of her home like Reg, had her own little storefront where people could come for consultations. Reg could see the benefits of not running her business out of her home. Unexpected callers would be reduced. She wouldn't have to worry about having her home address on business cards. There was opportunity for walk-in traffic. And at the end of the day, Marian could just go home and relax, with a clear separation between business and non-business life.

But a storefront had to have a lot more overhead too. Reg wasn't about to lease a storefront or office space. And while Marian operated during daylight hours, Reg's late-night work would mean that she was traveling between work and home in the dark, when it was lonely and predators were more likely to be out. She would stick to her home-run business for the time being.

She decided to pay Marian a visit. While the two had started out as rivals, Reg had broken the ice a little when she had asked Marian for a consultation on the dreams and visions she had been having during one particularly difficult case. Since then, the two were nodding acquaintances. Reg didn't feel like Marian wanted to run her out of town every time they saw each other. They could at least be civil to each other.

A bell jingled as Reg pushed the door open into Marian's business. There was no one in the consultation area but, in a moment, Marian came out of the back room, a welcoming smile on her face. It wavered only slightly when she saw who it was. She was a tall woman, with a scarf turban and a sagging, pouchy, jowly face. She wore a bright skirt that made her skin look drab and colorless.

"Reg. How nice to see you."

"I was just in the area and thought I would stop by and say hi."

"Wonderful… would you like some tea? It's a few minutes before my next appointment."

"Oh, you don't need to put yourself out for me."

"I'm going to make some tea anyway."

Reg shrugged. "All right. Sure."

Marian nodded. She walked to a little nook and turned on the kettle and busied herself with the tea things. "So, how are you? Having problems?"

"No. I really didn't come here because I wanted anything. Really."

Marian pursed her lips and kept fiddling with the teabags while she waited for the kettle to boil. Reg tried to read her expression and her aura. She was very careful not to infringe on Marian's consciousness. The psychic would be sure to realize if Reg ventured where she wasn't wanted.

"Are *you* okay?"

Marian lifted her brows and nodded. "Yes. Why do you ask?"

"It's just… you seem a little sad. It isn't any of my business, of course. I just wondered whether you want to talk about it."

The kettle whistled. Marian poured the boiling water into mugs and brought them to the table with a basket containing tea bags, sugar, and powdered creamer. Reg helped herself to a generous amount of sugar, making her selection of tea almost as an afterthought.

"I don't know what you might have heard…" Marian started.

"Nothing. I just… well, I'm a little bit psychic, if you want to know," Reg offered with a laugh.

Marian chuckled, the tension easing a little. "Well… it's nothing, really. Just one of those trials that everyone goes through. A loss…"

Reg reached across the table to touch Marian's hand, trying to convey her sympathy and to push a little warmth into Marian, hoping to boost her spirits.

Marian made an expression that was part smile, part grimace. "Thank you, Reg. You're very kind. You came at a very fortuitous time."

"I want to help. Is there anything I can do?" Reg cast around for some idea. "You could come over for a movie. Or ice cream. Just hang out for a while."

"Oh, no, no. You don't need to do that. We're not used to seeing each other socially, it would be awkward."

"A drink?"

Marian gestured to their mugs. "Tea is fine. Really, this is probably better for me than anything else you could have done. Just having someone here who recognizes that I'm going through a tough time and can sympathize."

Reg quit trying to dissolve all the sugar into her tea and took a long sip. "Well, good. I'm happy to help however I can. You really helped me that day. With the visions."

Marian nodded. "I told you then… we can do things for each other. We are a community. Not everyone can understand what it is that we deal with every day, so intimately involved with others' thoughts, feelings, hopes, and dreams. It can be a burden."

"It can," Reg admitted, a little surprised. "I'm always tired after a few sessions, and I thought it was just the amount of energy that it takes to see or hear what others can't."

"It's more than that. That part probably isn't even hard for you, you're so very gifted. But taking on others' burdens, feeling their feelings, even for just a short time, does sap a lot of energy. You can't let yourself be gloomy all day just because you did a reading for someone that didn't turn out to be very positive. But when you feel what they feel…"

Reg nodded slowly. It gave her more insight into what happened inside her during those sessions with clients, helping them to make decisions, or to see a vision for their life, or to contact a loved one who had already passed death's door. Maybe it should have been clear to her without Marian's insight, but Reg had always talked to ghosts and exercised her powers without even knowing what she was doing. She hadn't had anyone to teach her about the world she was a part of. Only parents and teachers and social workers and therapists telling her that she needed to pay attention, be obedient, and at least *try* to fit in.

"Do you want—" Reg started impulsively, and then stopped herself.

Marian took another drink of her tea and shook her head. "Do I want what?"

"No, nothing. I was just thinking…"

"If you don't tell me what you were thinking, I have no idea. How do you know whether the answer is yes or no?"

"Well… okay. But you can say no."

Marian gave her a dry smile, which lifted the wrinkles on her pouchy face a little. "I am more than capable of saying no," she agreed.

"Okay…" Reg had to bite her tongue to keep from adding any other reassurances or excuses. "I wondered if… you wanted a cat."

CHAPTER SIX

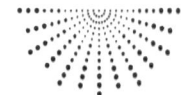

$\mathcal{M}$arian stared at her.

Reg sipped her tea and looked away. She cleared her throat. "It's just that I have an extra cat right now... I know, it's weird to just ask you if you want one. But he's looking for a home. I can't keep him. And I thought... maybe you could use some company around the house."

"I recently lost my cat." Marian sniffed and wiped her nose. "How could you know that?"

"I didn't, exactly." Reg's spirits lifted. She could help Marian and find a new home for Horace at the same time. "He's a lovely little cat. All black, short hair. He's not a kitten anymore, and you know it's so hard to find people to adopt older cats."

"Where did he come from? How did you end up with him?"

That was a longer story that Reg wasn't willing to reveal to Marian. She didn't need to know about the zombies and the kattakyns and trying to keep the parts of the Witch Doctor away from each other.

"Do you know Francesca St. Martin? Blond hair, from Haiti?"

Marian nodded. "Not well, but I know who she is."

"She has a cat, Nicole. She had nine kittens, all pure black. We found homes for them, but Horace's new owner didn't work out. And I ended up with him. But I can't keep another cat. I'm lucky Sarah lets me keep Starlight. She really doesn't like cats. And Francesca says that she can't take Horace on right now. Which kind of leaves me in the lurch…"

"Maybe… I could come meet him. See what I think of him."

Reg hoped that Horace would be in a quiet mood when Marian came over, not one of his crazy, knock-everything-off-the-shelves moods. "Of course. Anytime. Do you want to come over now?"

Marian looked toward the door. Reg supposed she still had clients coming in. "Well… I suppose so. I don't have anyone coming in until later. And I haven't really been feeling very well. Kind of off my game the last few days."

Reg nodded understandingly. It was hard to connect with someone and be empathetic when she was going through a crisis of her own.

"Why don't you come? I'm sure you'll like him."

Marian nodded tentatively.

"I'll give you the address." Reg dug into her shoulder bag to dig up a pen and some paper.

"I know where Sarah lives. You're just in the back, right?"

"Yes."

"Okay. I'll be a few minutes closing up here, and then I'll be over."

* * *

Reg had enough time to worry about whether things were going to work out or not. She wanted to believe that everything was falling into place for a reason and Horace was meant to be with Marian.

But there were so many things that could go wrong. She didn't want to get her hopes up and she didn't want to jinx it by believing it wouldn't work out. Why did everything have to be so complicated?

She tried to brush Horace before Marian got there so that he would look his best, but Horace objected and swiped at her hand, drawing blood when his claws snagged her wrist. Reg sucked on the wound, trying to explain to Horace how important it was.

"You want a new owner, don't you? A home where you can stay and be happy? Marian is looking for a new cat. She just lost hers. If you're a good kitty and show her your best behavior, she could be your forever home."

A wave of vertigo went through Reg, flashing back to Mrs. White, one of many social workers, trying to talk her into behaving at her new foster home. "Just be quiet and be on your best behavior. Didn't you brush your hair this morning? You have to try, Regina. This could be your forever home."

But there had never been a forever home. After a few years, Reg had stopped believing the promises. Stopped hoping for things to get better and just trying to survive until she aged out of the system and didn't have to live with anyone else and pretend to be something she was not.

She bit her lip, trying to keep herself present with the pain. She petted Horace. Long, soothing strokes to calm him down. It was okay if Marian said no. They would find him another home. She would try harder and find him the place where he belonged.

Horace purred and rolled over, offering his belly to her. Reg knew better than to be taken in and scratch it. Any cat worth his salt would just be waiting for her to fall into the cuteness trap and would attack at the first opportunity.

"Oh, no. You're not getting me with that one," Reg told him, choosing to scratch his ear instead. Horace made a low trill, enjoying the attention. Reg didn't just sit and pet him very often. She usually left him alone if he was settled down and behaving himself, and chased and scolded him when he was not. Not much of a relationship. But then, she had never intended to take him in. She didn't want to get attached and then to give him up.

The doorbell rang. Horace flipped back over and put his ears back. He looked toward the door to see who it was.

"It's going to be okay," Reg told him. "Just see whether you like her."

She opened the door and ushered Marian in, pointing her toward the couch where Horace was sitting, bunched up uncomfortably, no longer sprawled out relaxed and happy.

"Marian, this is Horace."

"Horace." Marian approached slowly, her feet quiet. She sat at the opposite end of the couch from the cat. "Hi, Horace. I'm Marian."

He watched her suspiciously. Like any cat being introduced to a stranger. They were always reserved, unless the person was allergic and didn't want a cat in her lap. Then that's where the cat would be.

They sat apart for a while. Horace's nose was twitching as he inspected the new woman sitting beside him.

"Reg told me you were looking for a new home. And I'm looking for a new cat to share mine with. Do you think you might like to come and live with me?"

Marian clearly knew cats. She talked with Horace and gave him time to get used to her. He eventually let her scratch his ears and chin and purred away while she crooned to him. She petted him and gave him a few kitty treats she had brought in her pocket, which made him crawl into her lap excitedly and snuggle and nuzzle her for more. Yes, Marian knew cats.

Reg was happy to see Horace letting go of his suspicions and becoming more natural with her, the red aura around him dissipating until she could no longer see it. She could feel warm, hopeful thoughts from him, like when they had gone over to Francesca's house.

Marian nodded to Reg. "Yes, I think this will work out. I'll take him."

"I can lend you my carrier and you can take him with you now. If you have everything you need?"

"My carrier is in the car. I didn't bring it in because..." She shrugged.

Because she didn't want to jinx it. She didn't want all of them thinking that it would work out, and then to change her mind and walk off with the empty cat carrier.

"Do you want me to go get it out?" Reg offered. "I don't want Horace to think that you're leaving without him..."

Marian chuckled. "Here we all are, all worried about how the cat will feel if he isn't chosen."

But Reg knew what it felt like not to be chosen. And she had a feeling that Marian did too. She might feel silly assigning human feelings to an animal, but with the way she had connected with Horace, Reg was sure she could feel his feelings and knew how hopeful he had become that he could go with her.

"Do you want to give me your keys?" Reg pressed.

Marian got them out of her purse, a much smaller and neater receptacle than Reg's cavernous shoulder bag. She handed them over to Reg, keeping Horace on her lap, warm and comfortable, blissful under her gentle strokes and attention.

"Thank you." Marian smiled.

Reg could feel that Marian's mood had lifted too. She had been feeling very bad when Reg had popped in to see her, but now she was happy and a bit excited, buoyed up by the new little fur person who had come into her life.

Reg hurried out to Marian's car. She unlocked it with the fob and grabbed the cat carrier from the seat. There were supplies in bags in the back seat too. Marian had obviously stopped in at the store before her arrival. She had really wanted to take Horace home with her. Reg felt light and happy. They would make such a good pair. They were already bonding.

She shut and locked the door and returned to her house with the cat carrier. Marian and Horace were right where she had left them. Reg opened the carrier and placed it on the floor near Marian.

"He's pretty good about traveling. Doesn't make a big fuss."

"That's good. It's always so distressing when they are upset and don't understand what is going on."

Reg nodded. She bent over to give Horace a final pet. He swiped at her arm and sank his teeth into her wrist.

CHAPTER SEVEN

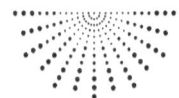

*R*eg sat bolt upright in bed, gasping from the intensity of her dream. She looked around her, disoriented at first, thinking that she was somewhere other than her own bed in her own room. But where else would she be?

Still, there were pictures in her head. Strange pictures on the wall. A long, narrow bed that was hard and cold. A woman who was angry with her.

The woman was probably some iteration of one of the foster moms. She still had nightmares about not being able to perform to their expectations. About trying to hide some disaster that she had created or the fact that she had not been able to find her classes at school. Trying to avoid punishment, whether it was a lecture or a beating. She could never tell for sure which it would be. Even the ones who seemed patient and loving when talking to the social workers could break, letting go of all the good intentions and lashing out.

Reg gulped a few times and tried to relax her body. It was just a dream. She had a lot of dreams; this was no different from any other.

Starlight jumped up onto the bed and rubbed against her, his tail tickling her nose. Reg laughed.

"What are you doing? That tickles!" She sneezed and rubbed her nose. "How are you, boy? Are you doing okay? Are you lonely now that Horace has found a new home?"

But she didn't think Starlight was lonely. He had put up with the new cat as well as he could, but they weren't best friends. They played and got into mischief together, but when it was time to sleep, they went off to opposite corners, and Reg had never seen them groom each other. A couple of guys hanging out together, but then wanting their own space to chill in after.

Starlight continued to rub against Reg and make inquiring trills.

"I'm okay," Reg assured him. "Everything is fine. Just a dream."

She rubbed her eyes and looked around the room once more to make sure that everything was where it should be and that she was alone. Although she liked Harrison, it freaked her out that he could just appear in her house, bypassing all the wards that she and Sarah had set. Sure, it was fine if all he was doing was making chocolate cake or Uncle Mike's ribs appear, but if he were angry with her or used his powers to trap her, as he had when he'd wanted her to just stay home and look after Horace, there was nothing she could do about it. Francesca was right that being as powerful as he was made him dangerous, even if he did like her and was trying to protect her. Immortals were fickle and his feelings could change in an instant. Or he could do something to her, not realizing that it could harm her. He was remarkably ignorant of many things concerning humans.

But she didn't see Harrison or any sign that he had been there. Not in her bedroom, anyway. She couldn't speak for the kitchen or living room, and she wasn't going to get up and check. She would work on the assumption that if he'd materialized in her house, it was because he wanted to talk to her, and he would have come to the bedroom to find her.

"Everything is fine," Reg repeated, rubbing her forehead.

Reg had left the closet doors open, as she usually did, and the moonlight shining into it made it look as though something was glowing. It gave Reg a weird, uncomfortable feeling. She was too tired to get up and close the doors, but she would make sure that they were closed the next time.

* * *

She tossed and turned for a while, trying to find her way back to sleep. Other people made it look so easy. She remembered other foster kids she had shared a room with. When it was bedtime, they lay down in the bed and in a few minutes were asleep. No special rituals. No lying awake for an hour or two before being able to convince their bodies to go to sleep. And that was how it was on TV too. People turned off the light, lay down in bed, and fell asleep. No fuss or drama. Sleep just stole into the room and carried them off to dreamland. And no one ever had nightmares unless it moved the plot forward.

When an hour had passed and she still had not been able to get back to sleep, Reg picked up her phone from the side table and unplugged it. She intended to just check her email and social networks until her eyelids started to get heavy again, but her fingers moved as if of their own accord, tapping and swiping to find Corvin's contact card in her list and to initiate a call.

He wasn't even on her favorites list. She had hoped that by not setting up a shortcut for him, she wouldn't be tempted to call him impulsively. Apparently, that didn't work. Her hands and brain still knew how to access his record on her phone.

"Hello?" Corvin's words were thick and drowsy. "Regina."

"Yeah. Sorry, I guess you were asleep."

He didn't point out that sleeping was what he generally did at five in the morning, or whatever time it was. Reg looked at the time on the face of her phone, then promptly ignored it.

"Yes. But I'm awake now."

"Do you ever have trouble sleeping?"

"On occasion. I could recommend a sleeping potion, if you like. There are some very good ones."

"No. I used to have to take pills to make me sleep when I was a kid. I don't like the way they make me feel."

"It wouldn't be the same. Potions don't have the same side effects as medications."

"But they still have side effects, right? I don't want to be having weird magical symptoms either."

"No. Well, sometimes a potion can have unintended consequences, but…"

"I'm bound to be one of those people who would have them. Seems like that's just the way my life works."

Corvin grunted. "Well... I suppose it's not outside of the realm of possibilities."

"And how do they affect... other species? Because with my heritage..."

"You are still more human than anything else."

She knew it was meant to reassure her, but she wasn't sure it was true, and it irritated her that he would say so.

"So, what were you doing today?" Reg asked, changing the subject. If she got him talking about himself or one of his academic projects, then it would be sure to put her to sleep...

"I don't think you're interested in any of my pet projects," Corvin dismissed.

"I am. What are you working on?"

"Nothing. Just some ancient tales and mythologies."

"Roman?" Reg asked.

"No."

"Which country?"

"I really don't see how that would be of interest to you."

"Mythology is interesting. Unless it's one of those weird ones, I kind of get lost on the Norse stuff."

"There are a lot more countries with stories to tell than just Greece and Rome."

Thinking about it, Reg realized she knew next to nothing about any of the mythologies of the Asian countries or even the Americas. How bad was it that she didn't even know the stories from the country she had grown up in? But she didn't remember their teaching that in school. Just the ones that Corvin had mentioned, Roman and Greek mythology. Maybe she could look up some of the other stuff on YouTube. There were some informative videos there. Maybe she could learn more about Bastet and the other Egyptian gods.

"Do you know much about Egyptian mythology?"

Corvin made a choking noise.

"Does that mean you don't?" Reg asked. She mentally reached out, trying to sense his mood.

"Stop doing that," Corvin ordered.

"What?"

"Reading me."

"I wasn't... I didn't do it intentionally. You said not Greek or Roman, and I was thinking about Egypt because, you know, we were just there..."

"You thought about it because that's what I was thinking about."

"Well... not on purpose. And... there are other reasons." Reg stroked Starlight, looking into his blue and green eyes.

"Your gems, you mean?"

"Oh." Reg hadn't been thinking of them. She glanced toward the closet. "Yes. That too. Sooner or later, I'm going to have to take them back to Egypt. Sooner, since the rings have been... activated."

"You know it isn't safe."

"I wouldn't be going back to see Kareem. Tourists still go to Egypt..."

"There are other dangers. I would not recommend that you go by yourself."

"If these rings are so powerful, then it shouldn't matter. I can use them to protect myself, right?"

Corvin was silent.

Reg thought about the two rings. They had just been curiosities to begin with. Most of the gems that she had been given by the fairies had been loose, cut gems. There were only a few that were set into jewelry like the rings. Reg had worn them on her last trip to Egypt, more by accident than anything else, and that had apparently not been such a good idea.

She didn't actually know what powers the gems had, or how to use a stone like that. She was still woefully uninformed about the magical world around her. For someone like Corvin, growing up in a magical home, it was second nature but, for Reg, everything was new, and people expected her to know things that she didn't.

"Have you used the rings?" Corvin asked.

Reg didn't know whether he was expecting a yes or a no answer, or what implications either would have. Would not using the rings mean that she was ignorant and uninformed? Was using them taboo?

"What difference does that make?" she hedged.

"You are playing with powers you know nothing about."

"Well, that's par for the course," Reg pointed out. "Since I hardly know anything about anything."

"You shouldn't use them without knowing their history and the proper way to use their powers. You already know that they are cursed."

Reg did know that they were cursed, but she didn't think that they were evil or would do anything to harm her. She saw the cursed gems more as being sad or broken. Like a child who had been traumatized or moved through too many different homes. Lashing out because they were hurt, not bad.

"I know. That's why I want to get them back to Egypt."

Home, where they belonged. Where they could rest. Back to the people who were supposed to own them. That was what they wanted.

CHAPTER EIGHT

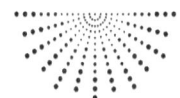

"*A*re you still there, Reg?"

Reg took a deep breath in. Her eyes were closed and she didn't open them. "Yes. I'm here."

"Thought you might have dropped off to sleep."

It sounded like a good idea. But part of Reg was too awake. Too watchful. "I don't know whether I'm going to go back to sleep tonight."

"What did you dream about?" Corvin's voice was rich and resonant. Like he was in the same room with her, leaning in to talk to her as she'd seen him do so many times. Getting just a little closer. A little too close.

She opened her eyes just a sliver to make sure that he wasn't there with her, although she knew that he couldn't be. The wards were enough to keep Corvin away. He couldn't come into the house or even into the yard without her invitation.

Or some sly trick. But Reg thought she knew all his tricks now.

Hopefully.

"What?" she said, forgetting what it was that he had just asked her.

"What were you dreaming?"

"I don't know; a lot of it has disappeared already." Reg let her eyes close all the way again and thought about it. "Um... a room. A dark, empty room. Strange pictures on the walls. An uncomfortable bed." Maybe she had been dreaming about foster care. Moving into a new room was always a little scary, everything unfamiliar when she woke up. Everything different from the last place and from what she would have liked it to be.

Or one of the institutions. They didn't usually have pictures on the walls, but some had art installations. A mural on the wall rather than pictures hung there.

Maybe that was it.

"Hm." Corvin sounded uninspired by Reg's dream. "Nothing... portentous, then."

"I'm not even sure what that means. Nothing *important*."

"Portentous is like... ominous. An omen. A vision of something to come."

"Oh. No. I don't think so. Just... a dark dream. And when I woke up, I couldn't get back to sleep."

"So you called me."

"You said I can call you anytime," Reg reminded him. "You always look forward to my calls."

Corvin chuckled. "That sounds like something I might have said," he admitted. "But I'm afraid I'm going to have to cut it short tonight. I have a lot of work to be done tomorrow if I'm going to... get anywhere on this project. I can't let myself get sidetracked by a siren's call."

He thought he was so clever. Reg rolled her eyes.

"More work on Egyptian mythology?"

"Stay out of my head," Corvin warned. "A man's thoughts are his own. Private."

"Yeah. Well, goodnight, then. Talk to you some other *more convenient* time."

"Good," Corvin agreed. "Talk later, then."

He hung up. Reg shook her head. Corvin was in a strange mood. Usually, he was happy to hear from her, teasing and seductive. But during the call, he had been irritable and impatient. Maybe it was just because he was tired and she had woken him up after a long day of studying.

* * *

She never did get back to sleep. Every time she started to get close, a noise would startle her awake, or she would think she saw something moving in the shadows. Or she had one of those sleep starts where she thought she was falling and her whole body clenched in panic.

Eventually, Reg got up and wandered around the house, unsure of what to do with herself. She made coffee and stood in front of the TV, flicking through channels, but there wasn't anything on that she wanted to watch, and she didn't even feel like going to YouTube to watch her favorite channels or to look up more information on Egyptian mythology.

Horace wandered over and meowed at her, looking for attention or wondering why she was standing in front of the TV instead of sitting on the couch where she could be comfortable. Reg bent over to pick him up, and then realized before she wrapped her hands around him.

"Horace? What are you doing here?"

Reg looked around the room, disoriented. Had she only dreamed that she had given the cat to Marian? Or was she dreaming that he had come back? She hated having dreams where she didn't think she was dreaming. They were the most disorienting of all.

"Horace, you can't be here. Where did you come from?"

He meowed and stood on his back legs to rub against her hand, coaxing her to pick him up. Reg did, and stood up with him in her arms, trying to figure out whether she was dreaming or awake. Nothing changed. She didn't start dreaming of something else. Horace didn't morph into Starlight or someone else in her life. She didn't dream of any unbelievable creatures. She just stood there in the living room with Horace purring in her arms.

Reg raised her phone to check the time. She didn't know what time Marian usually got up, but it was probably too early to call her to find out what was going on.

Was she losing her mind? Maybe the whole day had been a dream. Maybe she never had found a home for Horace. But now that she had thought of Marian in her dream, maybe she could contact Marian in real life and see whether she wanted a cat. And then she would probably find out that Marian didn't even like cats and certainly didn't want one in her house.

Despite Horace's contented purrs, she put him down on the floor.

She went to the window and looked up at the brightening sky. Of course, there was no way to tell just by looking at the sky what day it was. She looked at her phone again and checked the date and the day of the week. But then she wasn't sure what day it was supposed to be. She often lost track of the day, so she had nothing to anchor herself to. She went over to the appointment book on the kitchen island and opened it up. Checking through the sessions, she could see which ones she had completed—or thought she had—and that it should be Thursday. She looked at her phone again to confirm that it was Thursday.

Then she hadn't dreamed an extra day. Had she dreamed that it had happened differently than it really had? Had she skipped to a parallel time, where things had unfolded differently and she hadn't given Horace away to Marian? Reg rubbed her forehead, where pain throbbed in the third eye position.

She fed the cats, moving automatically while she tried to figure everything out. They didn't usually get fed that early in the morning, but they certainly were not objecting.

"What is going on here?" Reg murmured to no one in particular. She didn't expect an answer from the cats. Though maybe Horace could tell her what was going on if he wanted to.

"It's just one of those things. It will all make sense later. It's just because I haven't slept. Because I woke up from a nightmare. Once I've been up for a while..." She trailed off, looking around. What would change? When she had been awake for a while, how was it going to make any sense?

CHAPTER NINE

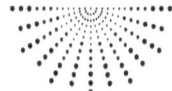

Once Reg deemed it late enough that Marian should either be getting ready for her day or already be at her storefront, she phoned for a chat. She didn't have to mention anything that had happened in the dream or the alternate reality. She would just let Marian bring it up. If she didn't, then Reg would know that it hadn't really happened.

"Reg!" Marian answered the phone almost immediately, sounding upset. "Reg, I don't know what to do. I don't know what happened!"

"What is it?"

"Horace is gone! I don't know how he could have gotten out; there wasn't a window or door left open. But I can't find him. If he's hiding in the house somewhere… I just don't know how he could be. Could he have somehow gotten into the ceiling or wall? Into a vent? He's not crying. I tried to sense him, but I can't…"

"It's okay," Reg assured her. "He's back here."

Marian was silent, too shocked to speak. Reg gave her a few minutes. Eventually, Marian spoke again.

"He's there? How did he get there? Did you come and get him? You should have told me. I've been worried sick."

"I didn't come and get him. I have no idea how he got back here. Or into the house. No more than you know how he got out of yours."

"A cat can't just teleport himself somewhere else."

Reg thought about that. When Nicole had been taking care of the nine kattakyns, they had all disappeared more than once, reappearing in another part of the house that they couldn't logically have gotten to. There had been a wormhole between Sarah's garden and Francesca's house, some kind of passageway, and it had, Reg and Francesca had assumed, also enabled the cats to get from one part of the house to another when they shouldn't physically have been able to. Was there a similar passage between Reg's cottage and Marian's house that Horace had made use of? Or did Horace himself have the ability to make wormholes, and the passage that they had assumed had been made by Weston had actually been made by Horace?

"I don't know," she said slowly to Marian. "Maybe he has powers that we don't know of."

"You don't seriously think that he just decided to go back to your house and teleported himself there? I've heard of cats having strong gifts, but not like that. That can't be possible."

But Starlight's powers were as strong or stronger than Reg's. He had once been one of the immortals. And Horace was a kattakyn, not an actual cat. He had been bound to a piece of the Witch Doctor and maybe it had conferred some residual power on him. But Reg couldn't tell Marian that. They were being careful not to tell the kattakyn owners about the kattakyns' true origin. Which might be a bad idea, considering that Kareem had figured some of it out himself anyway and had taken advantage of the situation. Francesca had assumed that the owners would be better off not knowing the nature of the cats. Maybe she had been wrong.

"I don't know what happened," Reg told Marian. "I can only tell you that I didn't come over to your house—I don't even know where you live. And I didn't leave any doors or windows open either. But... here he is."

"You're sure it's him?"

"Who else would it be? What other black cat would suddenly appear in my house and act like he lived here? Of course I know it's Horace. I can *feel* him."

"That doesn't make any sense."

"It makes more sense that a random cat off the street showed up inside my house without any way to get in? And that Horace disappeared from your house?"

"He must be hiding here somewhere. Or else someone came here and got him."

"It wasn't me," Reg told her evenly.

But it could have been someone else. What about Harrison? He was the one who had originally brought Horace to Reg's house, telling her that she had to keep him and that was where Horace wanted to stay. And Reg *might* have promised to keep him when she had never intended to, just to get Harrison out of her house.

"Some kind of magic is at work here," Reg pointed out the obvious. "I can't explain it, but that's kind of the point of magic, isn't it? That it is things that cannot be explained?"

"I can't perform any magic. All I have is some psychic ability. Unlike *you*."

"I'm just a psychic too," Reg insisted. She'd never been able to consider herself anything else, despite what others had said. All of her gifts were just an extension of her psychic gifts.

Except that her mother was part siren. And her father, if Weston really was her father, was an immortal. And psychics didn't have fire-casting abilities. That was a witch craft.

Still…

"You're not fooling anyone but yourself," Marian snapped. "You're playing cards from all the decks."

Reg shrugged uncomfortably, a gesture that Marian couldn't see. "The question is… what do we do now? Do you want to try again?"

"Would you let me?" Marian asked, surprised. "I thought that…"

"I didn't come and get him back. I can't keep him here; I told you that. I need to find him a new home. If we have to take him to your house a few times before he gets used to the idea… then let's do that. Sooner or later, he'll figure out that he's supposed to stay there, right?"

"It's worth a try," Marian conceded. "But… I'm a little bit worried about taking on a cat who apparently has such strong gifts. I can't control them."

"Um… I don't know anything about that. Maybe you could talk to Sarah about it. Maybe she would have some ideas. I know she doesn't like cats, but it must be something that witches deal with. You can't be the first person to end up with a cat with stronger powers than she has."

"I suppose. Maybe I can find something on the internet."

How exactly did someone search for that? *My cat has magical powers; what should I do?*

"Okay. So, do you want me to bring him over? Are you going to be home for a while, or do you have to go open your shop?"

"I don't normally open for a couple of hours yet. People don't like to see psychics first thing in the morning for some reason."

"Great. I'll put him in Starlight's carrier and bring him over. What's your address?"

Marian gave it to her, sounding slightly surprised and suspicious, as if she still believed that Reg was gaslighting her and had come to her house in the middle of the night to get Horace after all.

* * *

Reg waited for the cats to finish eating and then, as the two of them were completing their after-breakfast baths, got out the cat carrier. Starlight eyed it and then looked at Reg.

"Not for you this time," Reg explained. "I'm just going to take Horace back to his new owner."

Horace stopped licking and stared at Reg, one hind foot still raised in the air.

"Yes, that's right. You need to stay at Marian's. You can't keep coming back here. I can't keep you."

He stared at her for a minute longer, then resumed his ablutions.

When he was finished, Reg showed him a treat and put it inside the carrier. Horace was not fooled. He knew exactly why she wanted him to go into the carrier. He'd done it enough times to recognize what was going on.

"Come on," Reg coaxed. "I'll take you to the garden for a few minutes first. Then just a short ride over to Marian's. It's not very far, you know. I can come over and visit you sometimes, if that would help you to make the transition."

She didn't think he was really attached to her, though. He'd wanted to stay with Nicole, not with Reg and Starlight. Which made Reg all the more suspicious that Harrison was behind Horace's return to Reg's house. Horace hadn't done it himself.

Eventually, she coaxed Horace into the cat carrier and shut the gate. She said goodbye to Starlight and, as she had promised, took Horace into the garden for a few minutes. He definitely found the garden calming. His body language started to relax as he sniffed the air and sat in the green grass and leaves, even if he had to be inside a cat carrier to do it. It was like a little cave in the wilderness. Other than the bars on the door.

CHAPTER TEN

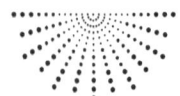

*A*fter returning Horace to Marian and staying with them for a few minutes to make sure that Horace was settled and would not immediately vanish, Reg stopped in at Witches' Brew, a coffee shop she and Corvin had previously visited. She really needed a large mug of very hot, very good, very caffeinated coffee. The stuff from the machine at home would just not cut it after the day and night she'd had.

A cat that could jump from one location to another that was a great distance away was definitely a problem. They had thought to be able to keep all the kattakyns apart, and thus prevent the Witch Doctor from re-forming again for hundreds of years. But if the kattakyns could jump from one side of the country to the other, or one side of the world to the other, then it would be impossible to keep them from visiting each other and gathering in one location.

Reg had no idea what to do about it.

Was there a way to stop a creature from teleporting from one location to another? Was there a way to stop Harrison from gathering up all the kattakyns if he decided to do so? He said that he had been trying to keep Horace safe and to get him away from the warlock in Egypt, not that he had been trying to gather the pieces of the Witch Doctor to re-form him. But Reg wasn't sure she believed that.

Not sure at all.

"Reg? I don't think I've seen you here before!"

Reg turned her head to look at Detective Marta Jessup.

Dang.

She had not intended to run into anyone at the coffee shop. Least of all Detective Jessup.

They had been friends. Or building a friendship. They had done a few things together like friends. But after Jessup's suspicions had fallen more than once upon Reg for a crime, and she hadn't believed Reg or protected her from a police investigation, Reg had started to avoid her. A friendship between a con and a police officer was not really a good idea, no matter how many fun TV movies they made about it. And while Reg was currently running a legitimate "entertainment" business and was not trying to con anyone out of their money, Reg wasn't prepared to say that she never would. If she were desperate, or the right opportunity presented itself, she might take the chance.

A person didn't simply move to Florida and go legit, giving up a life of crime forever.

"Hi," Reg greeted. She sipped her coffee, holding the large mug in front of her face so that she didn't have to meet Jessup's eyes, hoping that the woman would just get the hint and move on. Get her coffee and be on her way.

But Jessup did not take the hint. She smiled, her pretty Asian features softening a little. Her *friendly* face. The one she used when talking to her friend Reg, rather than the suspect, Miss Rawlins. But Reg would not take the bait. Jessup had proven that she wasn't willing to overlook indiscretions on Reg's part, that she was quick to suspect her when things looked bad, and Reg could not let herself be taken in by a friendly word and smile.

After Jessup placed her coffee order, she sat down next to Reg without an invitation.

"It seems like forever since we saw each other. I really miss our talks."

Reg had never treated her as a confidante, so Reg wasn't sure where Jessup was getting this script.

"Things have been busy," she said tersely.

"Yeah. For me too. It seems like things just never stop happening, do they? You think that you'll be able to get together after this particular case is resolved or crisis is past, and then something else pops up in its place." Jessup laughed. "But that never happens."

Reg said nothing. She kept her mug in front of her face and didn't look Jessup in the eye.

"So… how did that thing with the gems end up?"

Reg had been trying to get rid of the cursed gems. But that hadn't worked out too well when she had been caught on several surveillance cameras dumping them. As people had turned the gems in to the police, they had identified Reg as the rightful owner, and Jessup had dumped them all back on Reg's doorstep when she had refused to go to the police station to claim her property.

"Nothing to tell."

Jessup fished for more information. "I never could figure out why you did that… it was crazy. And why everyone turned the gems in. If you'd asked me what percentage of people would turn gemstones in to the police instead of keeping them and cashing in… the number would have been very low. But so many people brought them in… it must have been pretty close to a hundred percent."

It had, in fact, been more than a hundred percent. Somehow, Reg had ended up with more cursed gems than she had "lost" in the first place.

"Yup. People are more honest than you think," Reg said, getting in a little dig. Friends should believe each other. Especially when friends were telling the truth and hadn't had anything to do with a murder. No matter how bad it looked.

Jessup shifted and sipped from her large travel cup. "We should get together again sometime. Make some time."

Reg didn't respond. A friendship with a cop had been a bad idea from the start. She had thought that maybe in her new life it was something that could work out, but that had been a fantasy. She shouldn't have even considered it. It was too much of a risk.

Jessup tried a couple more times to convince Reg that nothing had changed and the two of them were buddies. Reg concentrated on remembering how confrontational Jessup had been the first time they had met, and how she had threatened to bust Reg for fraud for running a psychic consulting service. All Reg's literature and the sign on her table said, "for entertainment purposes only," so it wasn't like Jessup could have followed through on that. And then there had been the trouble with Sarah's stolen emerald necklace. And the dead man in the cemetery. She needed to stay focused on Jessup's track record, not on the possibility of having a friend to hang out with.

* * *

She should have been in a good place mentally and emotionally when she got home. She had taken care of the problem with Horace. She'd had a really good cup of coffee, and caffeine usually settled her nerves. She had been firm in not letting herself be pulled back into a relationship with someone who could be a danger to her. Unlike with Corvin, she wasn't psychically connected with Jessup and Jessup didn't exercise any magical influence over her, so it was just a matter of setting boundaries.

All of that meant that she should have been calm and focused when she got home. Not unsettled.

Starlight met her at the door, meowing and rubbing against her legs. Reg put the cat carrier down, and he sniffed it.

"Horace has gone back to Marian's," Reg told him. "Hopefully… permanently this time. You don't know how he got back here, do you?" She focused on the white spot on Starlight's forehead and reached out to him. "You didn't have anything to do with him being able to come back here?"

As far as she knew, Starlight could not teleport himself back and forth through space. But he had helped her to call or to jump on more than one occasion, so she couldn't discount the possibility that he had the power to do so on his own.

She got only warm feelings of concern from Starlight, not an explanation of how Horace had come back. No vision or sudden insight.

"Well, I don't know either. Probably Harrison. Was Harrison here last night?"

Again, no emotional response from Starlight. Starlight liked Harrison, so she figured she would get something from him if Harrison had been there. But did Harrison need to actually physically appear in Reg's house to transport Horace from Marian's house? Reg suspected not. He could make food from Uncle Mike's Ribs appear in her kitchen in an instant. He didn't seem to go there and bring them back in his hands. Julian had said that what Harrison did to make food or other objects appear out of thin air was impossible, against the laws of physics, and yet he did it. As far as Reg could tell, their human understanding of natural laws didn't apply to magic or immortals.

Reg heard a fluttering noise and looked around the room. What was that? A fly that had gotten in when she had opened the door? Some other bug or creature? She didn't see anything when she looked around, which made her a little nervous. Her cottage was supposed to be her safe place, protected by the wards. She hoped it wasn't the beginning of another series of visions. She'd had visions of spiders and of snakes previously, and they freaked her out. Especially when actual live spiders or snakes put in an appearance.

She walked through the house, looking and listening. The noise seemed to be coming from the bedroom but, when she entered and looked around, she couldn't see or hear anything out of place. No bugs or flying critters.

Reg went to the closet to move the clothes around and make sure that nothing had landed on them and was just hiding from her. Nothing flew out. Reg looked down at the small wooden box that held the gems. Sarah had told her repeatedly that she needed to put them into a safety deposit box at the bank, but Reg hadn't. She couldn't countenance being separated from them like that. She needed them close by so she had them when she needed them. A person never knew when she would have to move at a moment's notice. She didn't want to be tied down to bank hours to make her escape if something happened.

She knelt down and picked up the box. She also had to make sure that they were safe. Storing the precious stones in the cottage, she could check on them at any time to be sure that they were all there and… settled. She couldn't think of another word for the feeling she got knowing that they were safely stored in the box, "tucked in" like a child going to sleep.

But when she opened the box, she didn't get that calm feeling of reassurance. Instead, she felt anxiety and uncertainty. She ran her fingers restlessly over the bags of gems, grouped together by the country or area from which they had originated. The Egyptian gems and rings, which Corvin had told her had been activated when she took them with her to

Egypt in the hopes of finding their rightful owner, gave her an unsettled, hollow feeling.

"Hey. It's okay," Reg murmured, handling the bag and studying them through the plastic. "I'm going to go back. We'll find out where you belong. Soon."

How soon?

She acted as if she didn't care when Corvin told her that it wasn't safe for her to go to Egypt alone, but she was a little worried about it. She had been on the streets enough to know how dangerous it could be for an unaccompanied woman in the good old USA; she really had no idea what other dangers she might be up against in Egypt. She had been nervous when she had gone with Corvin. And of course, dealing with Kareem hadn't turned out at all as she had planned. He had been dangerous. And she'd been told he was well-respected. How would a rogue warlock or a street thug act?

She had powers to protect herself, but Egypt was an ancient land, rife with magic. Maybe stuff she'd never seen or heard of before. Which wasn't hard, considering her lack of experience.

Maybe she should ask someone to go with her. Davyn? She and Damon weren't really seeing each other, so she couldn't ask him. And Corvin… he would be eager to go, which was part of the reason she wouldn't want to go with him.

Soon.

CHAPTER ELEVEN

*R*eg's phone rang. She kept her fingers resting on top of the gems. Of course she knew who it was.

Even people who didn't consider themselves psychic still had experiences when they thought about someone, and then that person called or got into contact with them. If they were not practitioners, they just laughed and brushed it off as a coincidence.

But Reg and Corvin were closely connected and it wasn't hard to figure out that if the phone rang as she was thinking of him, it would be Corvin on the other end.

She let it ring for a minute or two and go to voicemail. Maybe he would think that she was with a client and would just leave her alone.

But her phone buzzed with a voicemail or text message. Reluctantly, Reg picked it up. A text message.

Where are you?

Reg breathed slowly, thinking about it. He wouldn't give up. He might wait half an hour in case she had an appointment, but then he would call again. Text again. Maybe show up at the gate, demanding to be let in. He really could be annoyingly persistent.

Obsessive, even.

She chewed on her lip for a minute, then swiped the missed call to dial him back.

"Regina." Normally, he breathed her name, laying on the charm. This time, he sounded anxious and distracted, as if she had pulled him away from something, when he was the one who had called her.

"I missed your call."

"Where are you?"

"At home."

"I'll come over there. We need to talk."

"You're not coming here," Regina told him firmly.

"Don't start that nonsense with me again. We both know very well that you're perfectly capable of protecting yourself."

"No. Not here."

"This is getting tiresome."

"You called me. I'm not playing games with you. You're the one who wants to get together. It has to be on my terms."

"You can't tell me you're not playing games."

"I can hang up. What's gotten into you today?"

"I didn't exactly sleep well."

"Well, neither did I. Sorry, next time I won't bother to call you."

There was a pause as Corvin considered that; then his voice was a little softer the next time he spoke.

"No… I don't mean that. I enjoy our late-night talks. *So what* if you woke me up one night? I just got up on the wrong side of the bed. It's not your fault."

"Because if you don't want me to…"

"I do want you to."

Reg was silent. She let him consider his next move. Eventually, he continued.

"I suppose we could go out for dinner. That would suit you better than meeting at your house?"

"Yes."

"A private room this time."

"Still no."

He grumbled under his breath, not loud enough for her to hear his complaint. Better if he kept it to himself.

"Where do you want to go?" he asked.

"The Crystal Bowl?"

"It's not exactly quiet there."

Reg shrugged. She liked the Crystal Bowl. It was a pub and restaurant and was more her kind of place. Corvin liked his fancy club, but it always made her uncomfortable. She didn't like the way that the hostesses fawned over Corvin and that everybody watched them. At the Crystal Bowl, where it was busy and noisy, she didn't feel as though everyone was watching them and listening in on their conversation. And the waitresses were too busy to do anything more than smile stupidly at Corvin.

"I like it. It's my kind of place."

Corvin grunted, but didn't come back with an insulting retort, so he was obviously trying to keep himself under control.

"Six?" Corvin suggested.

"Sure. That should give me time to get back to my clients."

"Can't you clear your calendar for one night so that we could… spend more time together?"

"No."

"You are impossible."

"Then why don't you give up? There are plenty of fish in the sea. You could ensorcel a dozen women in the time you've taken to pursue me."

"I don't want them." His mouth was close to the microphone on his phone, maybe touching it. "I want you."

"You want my powers. It's not exactly the same thing."

"Your powers are part of you. The most—one of the most important parts of you. The way that you grew up, that your personality was formed, the person you turned out to be. They were all influenced by your gifts."

"They are because of my history," Reg disagreed. "My mother being killed when I was four. Growing up in foster care. Sure, some of what I became was because of the way they tried to keep me from talking to ghosts. Trying to convince me that I couldn't see what I could or that there was something wrong with me. But there were a lot of other things going on in my life."

She reminded herself that her mother, Norma Jean, had not died in the current timeline. Even though that was what she remembered, everything had changed when Weston returned. Single events, even ones that she thought were life-defining moments, apparently didn't have as much effect on a person's destiny as she would have believed.

"Suffice to say, I am still interested in more than just your powers," Corvin assured her.

But she doubted it was true.

He might believe it, but she didn't.

"I'll see you at six at the Crystal Bowl?" Corvin asked, filling the awkward space.

"Yeah. Six o'clock. And I do have clients later in the evening, so don't even bother asking about having a nightcap or coming back here after. Not that it would do you any good anyway."

CHAPTER TWELVE

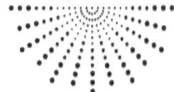

*I*n person, Corvin was just as he had sounded over the phone. Moving around restlessly, his eyes darting back and forth while he and Reg talked rather than staying focused on her as they normally did. He was irritable, quick to snap or to disagree with her. She wanted to ask him what was going on, why he was being so difficult, but she held her tongue. He'd already said that he'd gotten up on the wrong side of the bed. Best to leave it at that. She hated it when she was having problems and people tried to dig down into her psyche, insisting that they had to know what was going on with her. People's thoughts were private and, even if she and Corvin did have a strong psychic connection, that didn't give Reg the right to know everything that was going on in his head.

Corvin flicked through the menu. Which he probably didn't need to do. He'd lived there longer than Reg, and she already knew everything good on the menu at the Crystal Bowl. It wasn't exactly a wide range of cuisines. Corvin would probably have preferred a thick, rare steak at his club, but he would have to settle on a burger, roast beef sandwich, or fish fillet. She'd seen what the Crystal Bowl served as steak, and he might as well chew on his shoes.

"Where are the kattakyns?" Corvin asked, leaning forward as he grumpily tossed the menu to the side.

"They all have new homes." Reg was a little surprised at the question. He already knew that.

"I know that. But where?"

"All over the world."

Corvin rolled his eyes and shook his head. "Are you being deliberately thick? Where? Where is each one?"

"I don't know," Reg evaded. "I don't have all that information at my fingertips. Francesca was in charge of that. I just helped out a little when she wanted advice as to which cats to place with which people."

"And look how well that turned out," he said with a sarcastic snarl.

"Francesca was the one who picked people out and screened them. I didn't have anything to do with that. All I did was try to match the personalities of the cats with the personalities of the witches and warlocks and their needs."

"You must remember where they are. Most of them, at least."

Reg shook her head. "It isn't like I knew addresses. Maybe countries. But I don't know that I could even give you those. You should talk to Francesca. She could tell you all the details."

Corvin shook his head. The waitress approached and took their orders. Corvin tapped his glass impatiently. "And a refill. I've been waiting."

She nodded politely and removed the empty glass from the table. Corvin was usually very gracious and friendly with the staff. He wasn't the kind who raised a ruckus if there were a problem with his meal or he had waited for too long.

Corvin turned his attention back to Reg. His eyes were weird. Bright and fixed on her, but easily distracted. Like he was high on something.

"I don't know where they all are," Reg said with a shrug. "Sorry."

"Horace was in Egypt," Corvin said. "Nico is with the dwarfs."

"Yes."

"Where else did they go?"

"There was one to China." Reg shook her head, unable to remember which kattakyn it was or what city she had been sent to. But there were too many holes in her memory still. Things had been disrupted and misfiled during some of her recent experiences. She knew she should be able to remember more, but she couldn't bring the memories up.

Trauma could do that, cause all kinds of memory issues. She had been very scattered and unpredictable as a child. Her grades had been awful and teachers were always complaining that she couldn't attend to the work or to remember what she had been told just five minutes before. And recently she hadn't just been traumatized; she'd actually had to live with someone else in her head, and that wasn't nearly as much fun as it sounded like.

Meaning not at all.

"Yes…?"

"And I think, one to South America."

"Only one? Which country?"

"I don't know. Honestly, Corvin. You need to talk to Francesca, not to me. I don't remember much about it, and I didn't know a lot at the time. I was just a sounding board. Giving her my thoughts on some of the different applicants."

Corvin's mouth was a thin, downturned line. He was still incredibly handsome, but the sour look did something to him. It made him feel like a different person to her. Someone dangerous. He'd never seemed dangerous before, even though she had known that he was.

The waitress returned with a glass, which she set in front of Corvin without a word. Then she turned and walked away without so much as an acknowledgment by him.

Reg looked at Corvin with sudden understanding. "You've already talked to Francesca."

Corvin just stared back at her, his dark eyes glittering.

"And she wouldn't tell you anything," Reg guessed.

Francesca didn't trust Corvin. Of course, she was right not to, but Reg was still surprised. Corvin had a very strong effect on most women.

"*You* can tell me," Corvin said firmly.

She could feel his charms working on her. Waves of warmth flowing over her, the scent of roses making her giddy. Corvin moved his hand over hers and the buzz of electricity sent her heart racing.

"Back off," Reg told him weakly. "We haven't even eaten yet."

Corvin smiled, looking like his old self for a moment. He withdrew his hand.

"Just tell me everything you know about where the kattakyns are. It's important, Reg."

"Why?"

"Why? You know why. Because if anyone can get to all the kattakyns, they might be able to unravel Francesca's charm and bring the Witch Doctor back."

He leaned forward.

"You know how bad that would be. All the work we did before… destroyed. The Witch Doctor back among us, raising havoc. Raising draugar, smuggling, slaving, killing. He will stop at *nothing*."

He withdrew slightly, watching her face.

"And he knows you. He knows you from when you were a child. Do you think that he won't come back looking for you? He knows that you are one of the humans who overcame him. He may not know who the rest of us are, but he knows *you*."

Reg felt a chill.

She had known this. But she had avoided thinking about it. It was just a hypothetical. No one had unbound the other parts of the Witch Doctor, so he couldn't return. It was something that could happen, but not necessarily something that would happen. And if it did, it might be long after she had died.

She had not wanted to think about what impact it would have on her personally. Maybe he would go somewhere else. He wouldn't necessarily come back to where he had died. In fact, since it would bring back bad memories, he would probably avoid it, wouldn't he?

But Corvin was right. He knew that Reg had been involved in his downfall. The first thing he would probably do would be to come after her.

Reg felt suddenly exposed. She had hidden from the Witch Doctor in the Crystal Bowl once before, under Corvin's protection spell. But when that spell had broken, the Witch Doctor had seen her.

He knew that she had been there. He could come back. If anyone released him, he would come after her, and he knew where to go.

She drew back from Corvin and looked around. "Maybe we should go somewhere else."

"You're the one who suggested the place," Corvin reminded her. "Now you'll have to at least wait until we've been served. I'm not leaving without my dinner."

"But what if he comes back here?"

"It's not going to happen before dessert."

It was a process. It would take time for anyone to find and release all the kattakyns. So far, the only one that had been compromised was Horace. And no one but Francesca knew where the kattakyns all were.

"You think it's good that only one person knows?" Corvin asked. "What if something happened to her? How could you be sure that the kattakyns were all safe? You wouldn't even know where to start."

"But if I don't know, no one can come after me for the information. I can't give them anything. I can't give *you* anything, no matter how hard you try to charm me. Because I don't know."

"I think you do know."

CHAPTER THIRTEEN

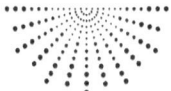

"*I* told you I don't," Reg told him firmly.

"You can't remember. That's not the same as not knowing."

Reg shook her head. "I don't see how. If I don't remember it, I don't know it."

"No. If you don't remember it—and I'm not sure you're not just withholding it—that just means that you can't currently access it. It doesn't mean that the information isn't there. In your mind."

Reg immediately saw where this conversation was going and tried to slam shut the doors to her mind. But her experiences with Corvin had bound them together so closely that she could not keep him out entirely. No matter how hard she tried, he could still worm his way in.

"I can help you, Reg. I can access the information."

"No, you can't. If I can't access it, then neither can you. It's just not available."

"You're just muddled. That doesn't mean that I can't find it with some diligent searching. Maybe it's misfiled. Maybe it is blocked. Either way, I *can* bring it to light. It just takes a little patience and someone who is truly motivated."

"No. You can't."

"Don't make this harder on yourself, Regina. We both have the same goals in mind. You don't want the Witch Doctor returning any more than I do. You're the one who stands to lose the most."

But Reg saw for a moment, just the briefest of flashes, that she wasn't the one who had the most to lose. Yes, she could lose her life to the Witch Doctor. She was a fragile human being without the ability to fight an immortal by herself. But Corvin, he was the one who had stored up all the Witch Doctor's powers. He was the one who had a massive treasure trove of magical gifts that he hadn't even begun to delve into. If the Witch Doctor stole *that*, Corvin would be empty.

And as someone who had been empty before, he did not want to be put into that position again.

Reg just stared at him. Corvin looked away, avoiding her searching gaze, his eyes flitting around the room. He was looking for danger, perpetually vigilant in a way that she had never seen him before. Corvin was always cool and relaxed. They had fought together; she had seen passion and intensity from him before, but he wasn't a worrier. The new vigilance was concerning.

The waitress arrived with their meals.

Reg was no longer hungry. It was time for her to eat. If she didn't, she would end up famished later. She couldn't let a good meal go to waste. But she was worried about Corvin's words and behavior.

She picked up her sandwich and held it in front of her face, breathing in the hearty, spicy smell and hoping that would do the trick and change the heaviness in her belly into hunger.

Corvin took a few bites of his burger and looked at her. "I just want to do what's best for everyone."

As usual, what Corvin wanted was what was best for himself. But he was right in one thing; their interests were aligned. She didn't want the Witch Doctor to rise up again in power any more than he did.

Reg toyed with her food. The more she thought about it, the less appetite she had. She wanted to go home, where she was safe. Corvin couldn't do anything to her there.

But he had been able to sense her thoughts when he had called her when she was thinking about him. That might have been unconscious, but it still showed that he had access to her mind while they were apart, and she was in a place that was supposed to be protected.

She could use a psychic shield to keep him out. But that required energy and she could not keep it up all day long or while she slept. Sooner or later, she would have to let it go, and when she did... he would have access to her thoughts, her dreams, her memories. He could search for the answers he wanted. And if he were patient enough, he could find them.

She thought about the rings she had left at home with the gems from Egypt. A lot of good they did her sealed up in a plastic bag in a wooden box in the closet. Or under the bed, which was where she generally moved it when she started to think that the closet wasn't a safe enough hiding place for them.

With a powerful ring, she could protect herself from Corvin. She had not been trained in using the rings, but she had worn them for a short time, and she knew that they would help her to keep Corvin out of her head. They could provide a shield around her that she didn't need to consciously maintain and that didn't draw power from her all the time.

Why had she left them at home and not brought them with her? It was ridiculous. She should be using the tools available to her, not hiding them in the closet.

"I have to go."

Corvin's eyes met hers. He frowned, looking at her meal, barely touched.

"Uh, to the restroom," Reg said. She stood up. Maybe if she stood up, got some air, had a chance to think on her feet for a few minutes...

Corvin stood as well, a gentleman as always, standing when she stood, helping her with her chair, taking her by the arm.

Reg jerked away from him. It wasn't as though she needed to be escorted to the bathroom. He wanted to hold on to her, to make sure that he didn't lose her, but she would not put up with his attempts to control the situation. She was strong too. She could be the one in control. As long as she thought things through and didn't act impulsively.

"Thank you," she said sweetly. "I'll be right back."

She headed to the restaurant's ladies' room. She looked back over her shoulder at Corvin once, feeling his gaze on her. His eyes were glued to her. He would not glance away so that she could slip out one of the other doors instead of into the bathroom.

Reg went into the bathroom. At least farther away from him she could think more clearly. She didn't need his pheromones muddling up her thoughts and his own psychic powers trying to break down the barriers of her mind to access the information that he needed.

She paced up and down the aisle in front of the stalls a couple of times, too agitated to sit down. She needed to keep moving to get her brain working.

Reg hadn't thought to put the rings on or even just to bring them in her purse. That had been a mistake. Knowing that the rings had power, she should have put some thought into how to handle them and what they could do for her.

But what if she could call them? She had been able to see and call Calliopia and Ruan from across the country. That had to be far more difficult than a ring or two. They were such small objects and she knew exactly where they were. She could envision them even without any psychic knowledge. They were hers, so she should be able to call them to her at any time.

Reg closed her eyes and stood still. She thought about the rings in the box. They weren't far away. She remembered how they had felt on her fingers. The smoothness of the insides of the bands. The shine of the gems. They had fit her fingers perfectly. Was that because of her magic? She imagined that rings of power would have been made for a man, not a woman, and would have been far too large for her fingers.

She ran her thumb over the bands, feeling how they fit her so perfectly. As if they had been made just for her.

Reg opened her eyes and looked down at them. There was no feeling of having exerted power, and she had not seen or felt them flying through space to her. When she called a person, she experienced the sensations that they did. With the ring, there was no outward sensation. Just *not there*, and then *there*.

She studied them for a long time, gazing into the crystalline depths of the gemstones. One ring was carved into the shape of a beetle, with the gemstone the main part of the beetle's body.

"Are you okay?"

Reg was still standing in front of the stalls, staring down at her hand. A woman stood in the doorway looking at her uncertainly.

"Oh." Reg forced herself to move. She looked around the room and decided she should get out of the way. "Yeah. Sorry."

"It's okay, I just wondered whether there was something wrong."

They passed each other. Despite her words, the woman gave Reg a look that suggested she wondered what substance Reg had retreated to the bathroom to get high on.

Reg's face got hot, but she didn't say anything to defend herself. A person could go to the bathroom to have the peace and quiet she needed for a few minutes to get over an upsetting conversation or event. People did it all the time.

She put her hands over her cheeks, waiting for the flush to subside before going back to talk to Corvin. He would tease her and want to know what was wrong.

Finally, Reg took a few steadying breaths and went back to their table. Her dinner was still there, largely untouched. Corvin was nearly finished his, though he laid down the remainder of the burger when she approached, and he rose to pull out her chair for her.

"You don't need to do that," Reg told him irritably.

"I know I don't need to. But I want to do things for you." He leaned close while she sat down, so close that she could feel his breath on her neck.

"Well, don't. It's annoying and it attracts attention." Reg looked around at the other patrons. They weren't exactly staring, but they were watching Corvin and Reg with interest. It was better if they didn't do anything to attract attention to themselves.

"Are you unwell?" Corvin asked, returning to his own seat. He nodded to her plate. "You've hardly eaten anything. And you spent quite a bit of time in there."

"I just needed to think for a few minutes. Where... you weren't."

"Fair enough." Corvin picked up his burger. "And what did you decide?"

"Nothing. Like I said, I don't know anything about the kattakyns. And you know that you're supposed to stay out of other people's heads. If you're going to go where you're not wanted, I'll tell Davyn. What do you think that will do to your reinstatement application?"

Corvin's face flushed red. The waves of heat that poured off him were not enticements this time, but a warning to stay back or she would get hurt.

"You don't have any right to interfere with my relations with the coven."

"Oh, no? Davyn asked me for my input. Considering that it was because of your previous assaults on me that you were shunned by the coven, I think it would be of great interest to him that you were trespassing on my mind." Reg forced a smile. She didn't want to betray how anxious his rage made her.

Show no fear.

"I haven't done anything against the rules. And Davyn knows that we are... intertwined. That the nature of our relationship means that the psychic connection between us can't be broken by will."

"If you do what you said, trying to go through my memories and find the ones that will help you find the kattakyns, I will report you."

His anger was so great that he couldn't even speak to her immediately. Reg could see a black, shadowy aura around him. She was dealing with a dangerous warlock. She both knew and didn't know how great his powers were. She knew that he didn't respect boundaries and had no compunctions about flouting the laws that were imposed on him when it suited his purposes. Would that extend to forceful intrusion on her mind?

There was a knot in Reg's stomach. She was already dealing with the aftereffects of having had someone else possessing her mind. The fractured and misfiled memories were just one of the consequences. She didn't need to be dealing with even more damage from an attack by Corvin.

CHAPTER FOURTEEN

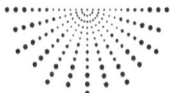

The beetle ring was warm on Reg's finger, growing hotter and demanding her attention. As a firecaster, heat was unlikely to hurt her, but she did notice it. She touched the band with her thumb, feeling the smoothness of it, stroking it. Her thoughts became clearer. The anxiety eased. She was not as worried about Corvin's anger. Yes, he was powerful, but so was she. She had immortal blood in her veins. She already knew that her touch as a siren could enchant Corvin. He couldn't do anything she didn't want him to.

Corvin's gaze dropped to Reg's hand. He looked at the two rings, his brows drawing down.

"Where did those come from?"

Reg raised her eyebrows. "Egypt."

Corvin grunted in irritation. "Clearly. I mean how did you come to be wearing them now? I thought you had decided not to use the rings."

Reg shrugged. She didn't owe him any explanation. She could do what she wanted to. Change her mind. Wear the rings. Use the rings against him if he decided to make good on his threat to invade her psyche.

"You weren't wearing them when you arrived here."

"How could you be sure? You just didn't notice them."

"Didn't notice them? How could I help but notice them? They are like beacons."

Reg looked down at them. If she thought about it and used all of her senses, she could see the glow that emanated from the gemstones. Corvin was right, they were pretty bright, hard to ignore. Was Corvin able to see power all the time, like a cat was able to see in the dark? It would make sense that a power drinker, would be able to quickly identify any sources of power that came into his presence.

"Maybe they were in my bag."

"I would still have been able to feel them." Corvin shook his head. "Did someone bring them to you? They were already here? I don't understand how you came to hold them."

Reg didn't enlighten him any further. If he thought about it, he would probably realize that she had been able to call them to her.

Reg looked down at them. They were old and plain, not like some of the modern jewelry she had seen. The carving was fairly primitive. But she was drawn to them like a moth to a flame.

"Do you like them?" she asked. "The little beetle is cute."

"A scarab," Corvin corrected. "It is a powerful symbol of power in Egypt, not just 'cute.'"

"But it's cute too."

Corvin rolled his eyes. His rage seemed to be settling as they talked about other things. It had gotten away from him momentarily, but he was doing better now, back under control.

"Do you know anything about Egypt?" Corvin demanded. "You can't just go back there without knowing anything about the place. It's an ancient land, full of magic and power."

"I know it's hot and sandy," Reg offered flippantly, which she figured would probably set him off in another rocket-blast of rage.

Corvin suppressed his reaction, grimacing, but keeping his eyes steadily on hers. "Yes, it's hot and sandy," he agreed. "And it's full of unknown and unknowable dangers. You don't have a clue what you're going to find there."

"Well... I have a clue. Several clues. But I don't see what any of this has to do with you."

"You can't go there alone."

"I think I can. But I'm not going to today. So you can relax."

"Does that mean… that you have set a time? You are making your plans?"

"No. I just have other things going on tonight." Reg waited several beats. "Do you know much about Egypt?"

"Do I—? Of course I do! I have always been interested in the ancient lands and legends. And since we came back from there, I have been studying, trying to work everything out in my mind…"

"About what?"

Corvin pointed to the rings on Reg's fingers. "These rings, for one thing. Do you have any idea how old they are?"

Reg used her thumb to spin the smaller one around her finger. "No. What difference does that make? Because it will be so hard to find out who the rightful owner is?"

"I have been looking through all the literature, everything I can find about early Egyptian jewelry discoveries. These would appear to be contemporary with rings that have been dated to 2500 BC." He stared at Reg, his eyes drilling into hers. "That makes them more than four thousand years old."

Reg gazed down at the rings, raising her eyebrows. "Wow. I don't know whether I've ever even *seen* anything that old."

Corvin nodded. "A find like this is almost unheard of. I don't know where the fairies got it from or how long they had it. But actually getting something like this into your hands… they are priceless, Reg. And not just because of how ancient they are."

Reg glanced around her at the other restaurant patrons. Their eyes were no longer on Reg and Corvin, but she wanted to be sure that no one would overhear the conversation. She knew what could happen when the right—or wrong—person overhead information like that. She would be in constant danger of having the rings stolen. And of possibly being killed herself in the process. It would be a thief's dream, getting his hands on something so rare, priceless, and untraceable.

"What do you know about them? Other than the fact that they are old?"

"Not much without examining them, maybe taking them to some experts. May I…?" Corvin made a gesture toward the rings, opening his hand for Reg to give them to him.

"No." Reg shook her head. "You can look, but that's all." She put her hand a little closer to Corvin, with her knuckles up so that he could see the faces of the rings. She watched Corvin carefully. He could grab her hand and pull them off. Leave town or just deny to the police that he'd ever seen them or knew what Reg was talking about. As long as he had a place to hide them for a few months, any investigation into the theft would peter out. The police had better things to do than to search for lost jewelry. Especially when Reg couldn't prove she'd had them—or that they were rightfully hers—in the first place.

But Corvin put his hand down and didn't grab Reg or try to take the rings by force. She could feel his disappointment that she didn't trust him enough to hand them over, but he probably recognized that in her position, he would never have let them out of his hand either.

He leaned closer to look at the rings. He also glanced around to make sure that no one was paying too much attention to them. But no one appeared to have noticed his intense interest in Reg's jewelry.

"When you brought me the gems before, you had a magnifying glass."

Reg pulled her bag closer to dig around in it, looking for the tool. She really did need to clean out her purse of everything but the essentials. The trouble was that to her, everything was essential. She needed to have things with her, within reach, in case something happened. If she had to run or wasn't able to get home for some reason, she would be starting over with nothing but what she had on her. Just like when she had gone to a new foster home as a child.

After a few minutes, she found the jeweler's loupe and handed it across to Corvin. He held it above the rings, studying them closely. Then Reg saw his eyes close to slits and knew that he was feeling the power the rings emanated. He could pull power from artifacts, so she watched him carefully and kept herself attuned to the rings in case he tried to pull from them.

"I see Egypt," Corvin said in a murmur. "Egypt as it was, long before cars and phones and men with white skin. They have been through many hands. Men who wielded their power, even when they had not earned it."

Reg nodded. His words resonated with her. The rings responded to his acknowledgment. *Yes. Yes, there had been many unworthy hands.*

"I want to take them back," she said. "I know they need to go back there. They won't rest until they are back there."

Corvin shook his head. "You don't feel the curse."

"I know they're cursed," Reg said. "Or what you call cursed. But I don't think it feels the same for me as it does for you and the others who have examined the stones. They don't feel… malevolent."

Reg gazed down at the rings, feeling the stones and connecting with them. They wanted her attention. They wanted her to hold them and to put them on her fingers and to use them. And they wanted her to take them back to Egypt. Reg touched each stone with her thumb, gently.

"You treat them more like a dwarf would," Corvin told her. "You will hear them talking about gems like they are their children. As if they have personalities and feelings and preferences. And you don't want to admit how powerful and dangerous they are."

"They're not dangerous to me."

"Until they are."

"They don't feel that way toward me," Reg insisted. She closed her eyes, focused on the stones. "I understand them."

"You don't know anything about them. How can you understand them?"

"I don't need to know everything about them."

"You should know *something*. It's very irresponsible to meddle with things that you don't know anything about."

"Who is meddling? How is it meddling to take them back to where they belong?"

"Why did you bring them here? And *how* did you bring them here? I don't think you are taking this seriously. You didn't have any idea how old they are. You don't know anything about who owned them or the history behind them. What they were used for, what the symbols signify. There is so much to learn about them, and you don't seem at all interested."

"And… why do you care? Why does it matter to you where they came from or who owned them before? They aren't yours. What I do or don't do doesn't have anything to do with you."

"I'm coming with you to Egypt. So of course it makes a difference whether I know about them or not."

"Oh. You're coming to Egypt." Reg shook her head. "We've never discussed that."

"We don't need to. It's the only sensible thing to do."

"What if I don't want you along?"

"You need someone to go with you. You can't go alone."

Reg rolled her eyes. She picked up her sandwich. She was starting to relax and feel better. Corvin couldn't do anything to her while she wore the rings. She should have realized that when she had been in Egypt, under attack by Kareem. He couldn't really have done anything to her while she wore the rings.

Reg's appetite returned as she relaxed. She took a big bite of the sandwich and chewed, thinking about Egypt.

It was more than hot and sandy. With the rings on her fingers, she could see and feel a much richer tapestry woven by the history, the people, and the buildings. There was a deep spiritual undercurrent to everything. Ancient, running through the blood over everyone who had come through that stock, permeating everything.

The sandwich was really not that good. Not when she was dreaming of the richness of Egypt. Soft white bread, limp lettuce, bland tasting fillings. Not like the food that had been grown there anciently or was now sold on street corners all over the country. Spicy and hearty and rich.

Reg ate it anyway. She wasn't into Egyptian food.

CHAPTER FIFTEEN

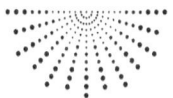

"I don't know what I'm going to do with this cat!" Marian complained. "I've had cats before and they were always pretty quiet and kept to themselves. Horace is… different."

"He just needs some time to settle in," Reg assured her. "He's only been there for a day. It might be a while before he gets used to it. We don't have any idea what it was like for him in—at his last owner's. It was probably very different from the way that you live."

"He's always underfoot. I've almost fallen flat on my face a few times when he has tripped me up. Except for when I'm looking for him. If I want him for something, then he's gone. Hides and won't come out when I call or even when I shake his treats. He just tucks himself away somewhere and won't come out. I keep thinking that he's gone back to your place again, without me realizing it."

Reg looked around her, verifying that there was no pure black cat hanging out there again. "Nope. I haven't seen him again."

"No, he's still here, I just keep thinking that he must have somehow escaped."

Reg wondered if Marian were exaggerating. She'd had cats before; she must know how they could behave when they got in the mood. Underfoot or racing around the house like they were on crack. Cute and cuddly one moment, and then trying to take your hand off the next.

"So... other than that, has he been okay?"

It had only been a day, and Marian had probably been working for half of it. How could she make any judgment based on a few hours? Horace hadn't had any time to get acclimated. It wasn't really fair to judge him based on a few hours.

"He's pushed things off my shelves. Must have gotten behind my books to push them all off onto the floor. He dumped his water bowl across the kitchen floor. Why would he do that? Did he object to the water or just do it out of general principle?"

"It probably wasn't on purpose."

"Did he drink out of a water bowl at your house?"

"Well... yes."

"And he must have drunk out of one wherever he was before that. Then why tip it over at my house?"

"I don't know... maybe it was a different kind of bowl? Or something scared him? Maybe he was just racing around and bumped into it. Cats can be clumsy sometimes."

Starlight, who had been kneading the couch cushion in front of him with his eyes closed while he settled in for a nap, opened his eyes and looked at Reg. She mouthed "sorry" to him. She wasn't saying that he was clumsy. Just that cats were not always the graceful creatures they were portrayed to be on TV and in poetry. Sometimes they ran into things, fell off of things, or fell over in the middle of having a bath.

"Maybe," Marian conceded. "It's just that with everything else..."

"What else? Just with him disappearing last night?"

"No, not just that. He practically ripped my easy chair to shreds. I don't know how he could be so destructive in just one day."

Maybe Reg should have found somewhere the owner would be home for most of the day. A retired person or someone who worked from home like she did. She hadn't thought about Marian being at her shop and leaving Horace home alone all day. He might have felt bored or abandoned, suddenly all alone for hours on end.

"Well... I hope you'll give him a little longer to see if he can settle in. Once he adjusts to your schedule and his surroundings..."

Marian sighed. "Yes, I'm not going to just bring him back to you after one day. But I'm not very happy with him so far. I may not be able to keep him if things keep going like they are."

Reg thought of all the families who hadn't wanted her. All the supposedly experienced foster parents who had declared her too much of a handful, or not a good match, or disruptive to the rest of their family. She had known after a few homes that no matter what the social worker said, she was not going to find her forever home someday.

"Let's give him some time. I'll come over tomorrow and see how he's doing... see if I can make him understand that he's safe there and that he can calm down."

Marian was silent for a few moments. "Of course he's safe."

"He might not feel as if he is, though. Moving around might be making him anxious. And he wasn't... it was a little traumatic for him, the last home he was in. The warlock that couldn't take care of him anymore... Horace probably doesn't understand what happened and why he had to leave."

"You're being very cryptic."

"You don't think he's scared?" Reg asked. "What is he feeling?"

"Well, I don't know. How am I supposed to be able to tell that? It isn't like he can tell me."

"But you're a psychic."

"I'm not a *cat* psychic."

Reg blinked. She looked at the phone, then over at Starlight. He had stopped kneading and was just watching her.

Couldn't all psychics read cats just as well as humans? It wasn't exactly the same, of course. There weren't words to describe what was going on in a cat's head. But there were auras and feelings.

"You can't tell what he's feeling at all?"

"No, Reg. I've never had a gift with animals."

"Oh. Okay. Well. I'll come over and see him. Maybe I'll be able to help him understand what's going on. Or find out why he's acting the way he is. Maybe he's not feeling well. If he can't communicate with you, he might do things that don't make sense."

"We'll set up a time, then. In the evening tomorrow?" Marian sighed. "If my whole house hasn't been ruined by that time. Giving that animal free rein for another full day..."

"Give him some attention tonight. Maybe if he can spend some time with you, things will work themselves out. He'll be able to relax."

* * *

Reg had clients to deal with until the early morning, so she didn't give much more thought to Horace and the problems he was causing for Marian. After the last client was gone, she opened the fridge to look for something good to eat.

Although she had lectured herself several times about needing to start a diet and quit eating all the junk food and sugary treats she could get her hands on, the first thing her eyes landed on was a cake. A big, luscious-looking black forest cake. Reg pulled it carefully out of the fridge. There was one slice taken out of it. Had Sarah had a craving for chocolate cake but had only been able to buy a whole cake when all she wanted was one slice? Or had she planned to hold coven at her house and no one had been able to come? A failed book club meeting?

Reg cut a larger slice than she really needed and put it onto a plate. She put the rest back into the fridge. Sarah really was not helping her to keep her diet goals. Reg couldn't eat an entire cake by herself without putting on a few extra pounds. And her impulse control was not good enough to ignore the fact that there was a big cake topped with creamy white icing and cherries in her fridge. Willpower was not her strong suit.

Starlight complained that he didn't get anything to eat, forcing Reg to go back to the fridge to look for something that was good for him. Not chocolate cake. He might like the thick piles of buttery icing, but it wouldn't be good for him. Not that it was good for her either.

She managed to find some leftover roast beef that must also have come from Sarah, and chopped some up for Starlight. "There you go. Now let me eat my snack in peace. Neither of us should really be eating right before bed."

But Starlight was already noisily digging into the dish and ignored her advice.

* * *

In the morning, Reg woke up with a cat snuggled on either side of her. She looked in dismay at Horace, who looked peaceful and angelic curled up in a ball against her.

"What are you doing here again?"

Horace snoozed heavily. Reg poked him to try to wake him up. He started purring, but didn't open his eyes. Reg petted him and scratched his chin and ears. He purred away, a picture of happy contentment. Reg turned to Starlight on her other side.

"How did he get back here? Can you tell me that?"

Starlight opened his blue eye and looked at her.

"Was it you?" Reg asked. "Do you know how to call him here? Or how to make a wormhole for him to go through?"

The membrane of Starlight's inner eye slid back over his eye before he closed it all the way.

"Hey!" Reg scratched his ear, unable to help herself even if she were trying to get answers from the two of them. He was just so cute and cuddly. "I'm talking to you. Was it Harrison, then? Did he bring Horace back here again?"

Starlight began to purr. Reg was trapped there, between the two purring cats, not wanting to wake either of them up. If she did, then they would just be demanding breakfast in loud voices and wrapping themselves around her legs until she complied.

Reg grabbed the phone from her side table and pulled off the charge cable. She dialed Marian's number.

"Reg. Well, I did like you said and gave him some treats and cuddled with him last night, hoping he'd feel more at home and not act out today. But this morning, he was hiding again. I couldn't find him before I left for work. I left him food and water, of course, but he's sleeping behind the furniture or in some closet somewhere. I couldn't look everywhere before I left the house. I had appointments."

"He's back here again."

"He's back there? How did he get back there?" Marian sounded just as astonished as she had been the first day. Hadn't she at least suspected that Horace might have found his way back to Reg's house again, since it had already happened once?

"I have no idea how he's doing it. Or I have some ideas, but I don't have any proof yet as to how he's doing it or who is transporting him."

"I don't know how long I can put up with this. It might be best just to leave him at your house. I'm sorry, I was willing to help, but…"

"Can we give it one more try?" Reg coaxed. "I'll bring him back once you're home from work, and I'll explain it to him. If I keep bringing him back there, then he'll get the idea sooner or later, won't he?"

"Hmmph. You tell me. It seems to me that he knows exactly where it is he wants to be."

"But he can't stay here," Reg said firmly. She understood Marian's frustration; she was feeling it too. "Sarah will not let me stay here with another cat. If I can't find a new home for Horace where he'll stay, then I'm going to have to move out. And if it turns out that he's attached to the cottage instead of me, I'm still going to have some explaining to do!"

"Bring him back tonight. But I can't keep going on this way."

"Okay," Reg agreed with a sigh. "Maybe just one more time will do it."

But she was worried that it wouldn't.

CHAPTER SIXTEEN

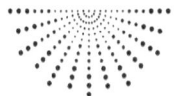

*R*eg eventually managed to tear herself away from the purring cats in order to go to the bathroom and afterward find some coffee. It was earlier than she usually was up, and she thought she might want to just go straight back to bed, but her need for the coffee was strong, so she would try breakfast first.

With the cats meowing around her feet, Reg was just getting the coffee on when Sarah's key turned in the lock of the front door and she let herself in.

"Well, you're up early. I wasn't expecting to see you yet."

Reg nodded. She looked down at Horace guiltily. Sarah's eyes followed her gaze.

"Reg! I thought you had found a home for that cat."

"I did… Marian took him. But… there's just one small problem."

"What? If Marian took him, then what is he doing back here?"

"He… keeps showing up again. I'm going to take him back tonight when she is off work. But…"

"Why is she letting him out? Tell her to keep him inside the house. At least until he gets used to it there."

"She isn't letting him out. He's… letting himself out."

Sarah rolled her eyes. "A cat can't get out of the house all by himself. They don't have fingers, Reg."

Reg's face got hot. She shook her head and punched the start button on the coffee maker much harder than she needed to. "I know that. And don't ask me how he's getting out and getting back here, because neither of us knows that right now. I talked to Marian before I went to bed last night, and he was fine. She gave him some extra kitty treats and tried to make him at home. But this morning, Horace was back on the bed next to me."

"He can't just materialize there."

"Well… it seems like that's what he's doing. I can't explain it. I guess he has some powers that we don't know about. How do you *know* that cats can't have… the power to teleport themselves somewhere else?"

"I think that we would know if they did. Cats and humans have been living together side by side for thousands of years. If they could teleport, we might have noticed that by now."

Except that Horace was not a normal cat. He was a kattakyn. And that might be completely different.

"I've already talked to Marian and told him that he can't stay here," Reg said, hoping to head off any further lecture. "She knows that, and I'll take him back there after she is finished at work. He's not staying here."

Sarah considered this, her mouth turned down, displeased. But there wasn't much point in continuing to tell Reg what she had already acknowledged, so she gave a stiff nod. "I hope this will be worked out soon."

"Me too!" Reg sighed. "I like the little guy, but having two of them around here, especially when he gets wild, is too much for me to handle."

After Sarah had gone, Reg fed the cats.

"You really can't stay here," she told Horace sternly. "This isn't your home. Marian wants you to stay at her house now. You have the whole place to yourself; she'll make sure that you get enough to eat and have your own place to sleep and a clean litter box. I'm sure she has some sunny windows, and she'll play with you. What more could a cat want?"

Horace continued to eat his breakfast, ignoring her. Reg knew that he could hear what she was saying. But he didn't like it.

"What is it that keeps you coming back here? Is it because you like to play with Starlight? I can bring him over for a play date now and then. And Francesca can bring Nicole, too. Just because you're the only cat living there, that doesn't mean you have to be lonely."

Starlight looked up from his bowl briefly. Reg sipped her coffee, even though it was still too hot.

Reg fingered the rings she wore. Could they really be as ancient as Corvin had suggested? Or was he just trying to make her believe that they were more precious than they were or that he knew more about jewelry and ancient Egypt than she did? He might have just been showing off, hoping that it would ensure his place at her side when she went back to Egypt to return the gems.

The scarab ring was hot. Horace looked up from his bowl and stared at her, his pupils getting big and black like they did when he wanted to chase something.

"No," Reg warned. "You aren't going to attack me."

He stayed where he was, staring at her, his eyes big and round. Starlight looked from his bowl to Horace's and, seeing that his was all gone and Horace still had some left, moved toward it to help himself. Horace hissed and swiped at Starlight.

"Horace!" Reg warned. "And Starlight, you have your own dish, leave Horace's alone."

Starlight looked at Horace and growled. The two had gotten along before, so Reg was a little thrown by the sudden animosity between the two. But Horace was just protecting his food dish. Reg bent down to move Starlight's dish farther away from Horace's. She could add a few kibble to keep Starlight happy and away from Horace's food.

But as soon as she reached down to move the dish, Horace's paw flashed out like lightning, and he ripped several bloody red lines across Reg's skin.

"Oh! Ow!" Reg brought her hand up to her mouth and sucked on the deepest cut. "No, Horace! Bad boy! Ow!"

He crouched down closer to his dish, eyeing her.

"I was just going to move Starlight's dish farther away," Reg told him. She nudged Starlight's bowl with her toe, separating it from Horace's. "Ouch. That was nasty. Bad cat!"

She looked down at her hand, the stripes welling up with beads of blood. He'd gotten her really good, and she'd let him, not expecting any trouble.

"No scratching. Sheesh. Ouch."

Starlight followed his bowl as Reg pushed it farther away. She used her good hand to scoop a little kibble from the bag of dry food and scattered it into his bowl. Starlight bent over the dish to eat. Horace looked up from his dish to Starlight's, his green eyes alert. He looked at Reg and meowed.

"You still have food in your dish."

He looked down at his, and then over at Starlight's.

"No," Reg told him sternly. "You're not being very nice. You finish what you've got. I'm not going to give you more."

He went back to eating, emanating resentment that she would give Starlight a treat and not him. Reg didn't try to point out again that there was food in his dish already and that she wasn't showing favoritism. But that was a bit abstract for a cat to be expected to understand, even if he was a kattakyn. He no longer had the Witch Doctor's consciousness to help him to evaluate a situation. He was all on his own.

Reg ran cold water over the back of her hand to wash away the blood and ease the stinging of the scratches. It was a good thing that Horace was just a small domestic cat rather than a panther or something bigger and more dangerous. He could have done some real damage. As it was, those scratches would take days to heal. They were pretty deep. As she thought of a panther, she pictured Horace as one, remembering the one she had run across in the Everglades. He had, luckily, been on her side and had helped her rather than stalking her.

Horace as a panther... she was glad that he wasn't any bigger than he was. That was when she had a flashback to the draugrs when they had been in their other form. When they had been giants. Huge, hulking black man shapes in the shadows and darkness, full of malevolence, stinking of rot. She shuddered at the memory. It was a good thing that Francesca had bound them in their much cuter kattakyn form.

CHAPTER SEVENTEEN

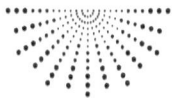

*W*orrying over finding Horace an appropriate home if Marian didn't work out, Reg's mind was drawn to Nico. It had been a while since she had seen him. She missed him, even though he had raised havoc when he had been around. Horace was nothing compared to Nico. Nico had been the type to climb the curtains, to hide under the furniture in order to jump out at Reg and attack her, had knocked down and broken things way more than Horace, and had clawed, scratched, and bitten her at the least provocation, or even without a reason, as far as Reg could tell.

He had seemed unplaceable, and yet, the dwarfs had been delighted with him. They had not coddled him and tried to explain to him, as Reg had, that he was safe and didn't need to attack her. She had told him he needed to settle down so that they could find an appropriate home for him. Instead, the dwarfs had been pleased with his nature. Gwythr had declared him a rare warrior cat. They had made cat-sized armor for him and had trained with him, teaching him how to fight in battle.

Reg wasn't quite sure how useful a cat would be in battle. It seemed like it would be too much of a distraction and not really be able to cause any damage. The dwarfs would have to watch him and protect him, because a cat would be vulnerable to swords, spears, arrows, and other weaponry. Even with his armor on, they would still have to protect him rather than his being an asset.

But that was their business. Just because Reg didn't understand how a cat would participate in battle, that didn't mean they were wrong about Nico or shouldn't take him. However warlike the dwarfs were, she didn't think they were actually going to go to battle with anyone. They had rallied their troops to fight Harrison in case he should come and try to take Nico away from them, but Reg didn't think they stood a chance against an immortal. And she didn't know of anyone else who would go against the dwarfs to battle.

But it might be a good idea to check in anyway.

Reg found Gwythr's name in her contact list and tapped it to call him. The call started to ring through, and Reg waited for him to pick up.

"Reg Rawlins!" Gwythr greeted heartily. "Great sorceress! You honor us with your call."

"Uh... hi, Gwythr. I'm just wondering how things are going. With Nico. Whether there have been any issues."

"Nico is well. Grown very large, into a formidable opponent. You would be very proud."

Reg thought again of the panther. Just how large did kattakyns grow? She had always assumed that he would stay the size of a domestic house cat, but maybe that wasn't true. She couldn't be sure.

"I am proud," she assured Gwythr. "And... I might come see him one of these days."

Having learned how to use her gifts to transport herself from one place to another, Reg didn't have to worry about what a long drive it was to the Blue Ridge Mountains. She could jump herself to just outside the dwarf kingdom's doors, make sure everything was good with Nico, and then jump back home again, all within the space of minutes instead of having to cover the distance by car as they had the last time.

"Reg Rawlins will come here?" Gwythr asked, his voice cautious.

"Maybe. If that would be okay. I don't want to put you out."

"Of course not." But his voice was reserved, not inviting her to immediately come and have a feast with them.

"I wouldn't take him away from you," Reg assured them. "I would never do that. I just want to see for myself how things are going. Make sure there aren't any problems."

"Gwythr would tell thee if there were problems."

"Probably," Reg agreed lightly. "But I would be more reassured if I could see for myself."

"*Far* has not been to see him the last few days. The ancient one has not been here."

Far was the name that Gwythr told her the dwarfs had for Harrison.

"And Nico... nothing has changed? I mean... his personality? His behavior?"

"No, the warrior cat is fine, Reg Rawlins."

"Good. I'm glad. I would like to see him one of these days. He must really have grown since I saw him last."

"Very much," Gwythr agreed. "And perhaps you would like to continue our discussion of the stones of power you wish to sell. It has been some time since I last heard from you."

"Oh." Reg chewed on her lip. "I communicated last with Brimir. I sent a counter to his offer."

"Brimir," Gwythr repeated, sounding surprised. "Why would you have talked to Brimir?"

The son of King Fraeg had taken over the negotiations on the stones the last Reg heard. Reg shifted uneasily. "He told me to deal with him. That he spoke on behalf of the king..."

"He has no right to negotiate for the gems you offered me," Gwythr growled. "Why would you go to him?"

"I didn't. He... answered your phone. He said that he was the one I was supposed to deal with, that you were busy looking after the war preparations against Harrison—Far, I mean. He said... I'm sorry, I didn't realize he was trying to scoop you."

Though Reg had wondered at the time. She didn't understand all the politics that went on in the dwarf kingdom, but it had not been hard to discern the tension between the chief of the smithies and the prince. Gwythr had withdrawn when Brimir had taken over the negotiations on Calliopia's fairy blade, and so Reg had assumed that he'd had the authority to take over on the negotiations for the gems as well. But she'd had a feeling...

"I'm sorry," she repeated.

Gwythr grunted. "You knew not. I understand. Are your negotiations with Brimir binding?"

"Uh... no, I don't think so. I haven't... signed anything. We haven't come to a landing on price, so I could pull out at any time, right? I don't really know about your legal system, so I don't want to say something that isn't true. I don't think I've said or done anything that was binding."

"Good. When he contacts you next, tell him you have changed your mind. He does not need to know why. You can continue to talk to me. What was his offer?"

Reg hesitated for only a moment before quoting him Brimir's first offer.

"It is low." Gwythr said immediately. "I will send you better."

"Okay. Thanks. And I am sorry, I thought that he was the one I was supposed to talk to."

"He is devious. I do not think he will live long enough to take the throne."

Reg worried that Gwythr's words might be treasonous. Was he making a threat on the life of the prince? Or just observing where his underhanded ways might take him? She didn't want Gwythr to get in trouble or for Brimir to get killed over something she had done. If she had misjudged the situation and somebody got killed for it... Reg did not want to bear the responsibility for something like that.

"I look forward to receiving your offer," Reg said neutrally. "Thank you. And... let me know if anything happens with Nico. If you have any worries about him... let me know. If Far shows up again. Or if there is something wrong. When we talked before..."

"I recall," Gwythr agreed. "We will protect him with our lives. It will not be easy for even one such as Far to take any part from him."

"Thanks. Hopefully... it won't come to that."

CHAPTER EIGHTEEN

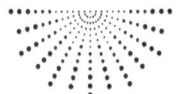

*R*eg checked her date book and noted that she had a firecaster training session with Davyn in the afternoon. Davyn was the only other firecaster that Reg knew, and he was the head of Corvin's coven. One of the people who would be dealing with Corvin's reinstatement decision. Something that Reg did not want to talk to him about.

But she was eager for another training session. She was getting better about handling fire, and Davyn was allowing her to attempt more difficult tasks in spaces that were not enclosed and controlled like her cottage. It was more dangerous, of course because, if Reg let her fire get away from her, she could do real damage. She was strong, and if things got out of control, it would be more difficult for Davyn to deal with.

But Reg knew that she could handle it. She was up to the task. Davyn had really put her through the paces the last time and, while she probably couldn't say that she had passed with flying colors, she had done reasonably well. She would do even better as she continued to improve her control.

Davyn had said that he would meet Reg at the cottage, and then they could go somewhere else for the training session. Reg was watching for him and opened the door before he reached it, eager to be on her way.

Davyn smiled. "Good to see you, Reg. How are you feeling today?"

"Good. Ready to get started."

"Well rested?"

Reg hesitated. "Well… sleep is not exactly something I have mastered."

Davyn chuckled. "You're going to need good control today. Strong focus. Do you think you can manage that?"

"Yes."

"No distractions?"

"There are always distractions. You don't exactly try to eliminate them."

They both laughed. On the contrary, Davyn did the opposite, trying to provoke Reg by bringing up things that might upset her to see whether he could break her focus. Things he knew would make her angry or upset or that would tempt her to let her fire burn hotter. That was how he built up her resistance.

Horace jumped down from the couch, where he had been sleeping in the sun earlier. The patch of sunshine had since moved on. He yawned and stretched his front legs and then his back legs and arched his back, quivering all over. He started off in Reg's direction but, before she could call his name or reach out to pet him, his head snapped around to look at Davyn. He stopped, frozen, for a moment, looking at the stranger.

"It's okay," Reg told him, amused. "Davyn's just here to help me. We'll be gone in a minute."

"I don't know this one," Davyn commented. He reached out a hand toward Horace. "Kitty, kitty?"

"This is Horace."

"Funny name for a cat."

He continued to reach his hand out to the motionless cat.

Then in an instant, Horace broke free of his inertia. He dashed toward Davyn, then leapt into the air and fastened claws and teeth into the outstretched hand. Davyn was too slow to avoid the attack. He gave a howl as Horace chomped down on his hand.

Reg dashed in to save him. She grabbed Horace around the middle and tried to pull him away.

"No, no! Bad kitty! Let him go, Horace!"

Horace writhed, his hard muscles snakelike under his fur and skin.

Reg could barely hold on to him. He was heavy in her grip and felt more like a crocodile or fighting fish than a pussycat. Reg separated the two with difficulty. Once Horace was free of Davyn, she let him go. But instead of running away, retreating to hide under the bed like Reg expected him to, he went for Davyn again, attacking his legs this time. Reg dove in and again grabbed him and pulled him back. "No! No, Horace!"

She couldn't hold him for long, but dashed toward the bedroom to put him down somewhere she could lock him up. He escaped her grasp before she managed to get him there. Reg kept between him and Davyn, with her arms out, trying to herd him backward into the bedroom. Eventually, Horace gave a huff and a growl and slunk into the bedroom. Reg shut the door.

"I'm so sorry! He's never done anything like that!"

Reg looked with dismay at Davyn's arms, where Horace had raked him with powerful back legs. They were ripped and bloody.

"I don't know what happened. He's never attacked anyone."

Davyn was pale, looking down at the bloody shreds.

"Sit down," Reg told him, pulling a chair away from the kitchen table and shoving it behind Davyn, so that he was forced to fall into the seat. "Can I try healing? Is that okay?"

Davyn had taught her the basics of pushing heat into someone to speed the healing process. She'd been allowed to use the technique even when he was away from her, as long as she only used her heat and didn't directly kindle fire.

Davyn nodded his mute agreement.

"I'm so sorry," Reg repeated. She rubbed her hands together briskly, feeling the warmth of the friction to start with, and then the growing heat of her internal fire. She held her hands a foot apart, like she was holding a basketball between them. A small ball of fire started to form, and she extinguished it. Just the heat. Not the fire itself. Though perhaps with Davyn, the fire would be okay. She couldn't light him on fire, being a firecaster himself.

Reg traced a path above Davyn's arms, hovering just an inch or a fraction of an inch away from his skin, pouring healing heat into him. She didn't need to worry about it being too hot for him to take, so she pushed more than she normally would have been able to. She watched as the cuts stopped bleeding, sealed, scabbed over, then started to fade. She wasn't able to completely eliminate the lines where Horace had scratched him, but the scars that were left were faint and would probably disappear over time. They didn't look painful anymore. Reg pulled another chair away from the table and sank down into it, looking at Davyn's hands and arms.

"I can't believe he did that. I don't know why he would do such a thing."

If it had been Starlight, she would have been suspicious. Starlight tended to be quite intuitive about people, not trusting people who intended harm to her, scratching or biting in order to protect her. Not like that, though. Just a quick nip and then running away to evaluate the response.

"Where did you get him?" Davyn asked, sounding breathless. "Do I need to get a rabies shot?"

"No. No, he doesn't have rabies." At least that would be an explanation. "He's—" She had been about to say that he wasn't a real cat, but didn't want to explain that. "He's up to date on all his shots."

"Thank goodness for that." Davyn ran his fingertips over the healed scratches. "He's very... strong."

"Yeah. I've never had him react that way before. When I've picked him up, he's always been pretty chill, even when I put him in the carrier. Today..." She recalled the feeling of Horace's muscles and his sudden weight. That hadn't been the cat she knew. Even when he had been racing around the house knocking things down, he hadn't been like that with her. She shuddered. It was like trying to hold a demon or Tasmanian devil.

She remembered how it had felt to try to hold on to a pixie, when she had first met Ruan. The inhuman strength in his deceptively thin limbs. Was Horace something other than a cat? Even as she asked herself, she shook her head at the ridiculous question. Of course he was something other than a cat. She had known that from the start.

But why had he attacked Davyn without any provocation? He had never behaved that way before.

"Maybe he doesn't like men," Davyn suggested. "Has he been around other men?"

Reg considered the question. "Well... no, not a lot. Mostly me and

Francesca and Marian. His last owner was a man, but…"

Maybe that was it. Maybe Horace had remembered something that Kareem had done to him while he was living there, or as he had removed the piece of the Witch Doctor bound to him. Having something that was bound to him torn away must have been traumatic, even if Kareem had been an ideal owner otherwise. And he had been bounced around from one home to another; to Francesca's, then Kareem's, then Reg's, then back to Francesca's for a visit, then Marian's. Too many homes in too short a time. It was disruptive.

"We had to remove him from his last home," she explained to Davyn, trying to give him a coherent explanation for what had happened. "It was with a man… he might have been abusive. I never thought…"

"Well, cats don't normally behave that way when they don't like someone," Davyn conceded. "Normally, they run away and hide. You had no way of knowing. But… you'd better be careful after this. Maybe shut him away if you are expecting company. You can't let him savage your guests. Even if you can heal someone afterward," Davyn looked down at the pink marks on his arms again, "You don't need anyone suing you or passing it around town that you own a dangerous animal."

"He's not even supposed to be here. He's not really mine."

Davyn shook his head. "And I suppose I should be more careful about trying to make friends with unfamiliar felines. I must have done something that made him feel threatened."

Reg was relieved that he wasn't ranting about how she needed to keep her cat under control or threatening to call animal control and have Horace put down.

"Thanks for understanding. I'll be really careful. It won't happen again."

Davyn nodded. He took a deep breath in and out. "Okay. Are you still up to training, or did that take all your energy?"

"I still want to go. If you're okay with that. If you want to go home and rest, I'll understand…"

"I don't need to rest. I'm fine. You didn't use any of my energy for the healing. You're sure you still have enough?"

"Yeah. I'm fine. It was just…" Reg shrugged. "Just the skin, mostly. It wasn't really deep. Not like when Calliopia was injured."

CHAPTER NINETEEN

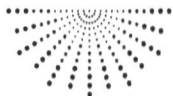

*D*avyn drove Reg out to a remote location for their training. Not the same dilapidated property that he had previously taken her to. There were skeletons of some old buildings on the land, but mostly it was just open fields filled with weeds and trees. Or what Reg assumed were weeds, since they grew there by themselves without any cultivation.

"Let's do a couple of practice exercises first, just to make sure you're in the right frame of mind and not having any trouble focusing," Davyn suggested.

Reg stifled a groan. She hated the basic exercises that they had been working on over the preceding weeks. She felt so constrained. So held back. She wanted to burn things. To really "play with fire," as Davyn put it.

But she didn't argue with him. She needed to be on her best behavior after the attack by Horace. She didn't want Davyn to be reluctant to return, thinking there was no point if she wouldn't do what she was told and he had to worry about being attacked by an insane cat. She went through the basic exercises with him, one step at a time, showing that she was ready and would do what she was told.

"Okay," Davyn agreed, nodding. "We worked on a campfire last time. That was pretty easy stuff. Something a little more challenging today. I want to see a grass fire, but kept confined within the boundaries that I set."

Reg knew how easily grass fires could get out of control. She bit her lip. Was he really going to trust her to do that? What if she lit half of Florida on fire?

"I can help contain it, but I will set my boundaries outside of yours," Davyn explained. "A safety fence, if you like. But I still need you to be focused. This kind of burn can very easily get out of control."

Reg nodded.

Davyn gave her step-by-step instructions and pointed to each of the boundaries that he wanted Reg to keep the fire within. Reg started the fire. Though the area was green, there was a lot of drier grass under the fresh growth, and it went up quickly. Reg focused, trying to keep it from getting too high, which might allow it to skip over the boundaries she was keeping.

"Has your new cat ever met Corvin?" Davyn asked.

Reg knew it was an intentional distraction. One that she was expecting. Davyn often asked her about Corvin.

"Um, not for very long. A couple of quick meetings. But there were other things going on and... Horace certainly never attacked him."

"That honor belongs to me."

"Yeah. He's never done it to anyone else." Reg was happy to see that she was able to keep her fire low and under control, still within the set boundaries.

"I don't suppose Corvin called him or tried to get close to him, though."

"No," Reg agreed with a laugh. Corvin didn't like cats. He still referred to Starlight as "the cat" without calling him by name. If Horace had attacked him... Reg wasn't sure what would have happened. Corvin had quite a bit of power. He probably would have used a magical attack on Horace without even thinking about it. "He and Sarah are both like that. They like birds but not cats. Is everyone like that? They like one particular kind of animal over another?"

"I think it is pretty common to like one kind over another... but some people like all animals... or don't like any."

"And it's the same in the magical world? I thought that witches were supposed to like cats and use them as familiars. I never heard of them having any other kind of animal instead."

Though Erin's friend Adele, who had warned Reg against playing with powers that she knew nothing about, had had a bird. A big black bird that was always close by. They hadn't told Reg that Adele was a witch, but she thought it was pretty obvious. Who else but a witch would have warned her about using her powers without understanding them?

"That's just popular media," Davyn said. "You know you can't believe everything you see or hear on TV."

"Yeah, I know. They don't get it right."

"You know that we're considering Corvin's application for reinstatement."

He would not throw her off with any mention of Corvin this time. Not even about his being reinstated into his coven. They'd already talked about it before. What difference did it make to Reg whether his discipline was terminated? She wasn't the one who had charged him in the first place for what he had done. Maybe if he had someone other than her to talk to, he wouldn't be calling her at all hours.

Though Reg knew that the last call had been from her, not him.

"Is he... stressed out about the application?" Reg ventured.

"Stressed out? I don't think so. Corvin usually keeps a pretty cool head about things. Outwardly, at least. Why do you ask?"

"It's just that he seems a little different lately. More irritable." She remembered his threatening to read her mind, going through all of her memories to find the information he wanted, without her permission. "And... I don't know. Acting differently than usual. Not so... charming. More serious and... what's the word when someone gets angry easily?"

Davyn considered, his expression serious. "Volatile?"

Reg nodded. It was a good word. One that could refer to fire as well as to people. Reg couldn't help liking a word that meant something that caught fire easily. Davyn grinned, clearly thinking the same thing.

"Volatile. Yeah. I mean, I've seen him angry before, but it seems like he's really on edge, and doing things... he normally would not."

Davyn's smile was gone again. "About anything in particular? I know that he sometimes gets that way when he's... hungry."

Reg's fire flared. Corvin's hunger was something she had experience with. Both because he had taken from her, and because he had put his hunger into her mind to demonstrate what it was like for him. That painful, hollow feeling was not something she wanted to feel again. She tamped down her emotions and managed to keep the fire controlled.

"I don't know. Maybe. How could I tell?"

"Aside from asking him, I don't know. The two of you are connected, so maybe you could notice some sign if you were thinking about it. Of course, he may show increased… hunting behavior."

Reg nodded slowly. Corvin had not been trying harder than usual to charm her at the restaurant. On the contrary, he had seemed more interested in other things. In the kattakyns and in her rings. She hadn't had to fight him quite as much as usual, and he hadn't been showing the waitresses the attention he usually did.

"It didn't seem like that. More like he was off his game. Anxious. Maybe he's not sleeping very well."

"It's possible. Maybe he *is* worried about his application. It is something that has a fairly large impact on his life. Who he can associate with, his business, his mental state."

"Yeah. Well, I hope it doesn't take too long. I never thought I'd say this, but I prefer his old charming self to this new version."

"I'm sure everything will go back to normal fairly quickly once we've heard his case."

CHAPTER TWENTY

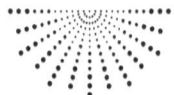

*R*eg knew she'd made a mistake as soon as she stepped in the door. She could hear Horace yowling in the bedroom, where she had shut him in after detaching him from Davyn.

"Dang. I'm sorry, Horace!" Reg hurried to open the door and let him out.

Starlight was in the bedroom as well, but he sat on the windowsill and acted as if he didn't even know that the door had been closed. Horace streaked out of the room immediately and bounded around the cottage, meowing at her several times to express his displeasure.

Reg set her jaw. "I'm sorry you didn't like being shut in, but if you're going to attack guests like that, you're going to have to be shut away where you can't hurt anyone."

He stopped running and licked his back several times, as if she had petted him and gotten his fur fluffed up. He glared at her.

"You can't attack people. You really hurt Davyn. He was bleeding. I had to heal him."

Horace licked his back a couple more times. The feelings she was getting from him when he resumed glaring at her were a mishmash of negatives. Angry, anxious, upset that she'd locked him up and then left the house.

Obviously, he couldn't teleport himself from one place to another, or he would have transported himself out of the room while she was gone. Maybe even out of the house. Someone else must be involved in his reappearances.

Harrison.

Reg decided that the best course of action was to just give Horace some space. He'd settle down once he'd had a chance to move around a bit and seen that everything was back to normal. She wasn't going to shut him back in the bedroom or leave.

"I'm going to clean out the fridge," Reg decided aloud. Every time she had opened it lately, it seemed to be stuffed to the gills. She blamed Sarah, who was always bringing her food, but Sarah had been irritated with her for not leaving any space for healthy dinners. Would she be irritated if she were the one who had filled it in the first place?

Maybe she would. Maybe it was irritation over Reg not eating everything she had brought over, but leaving it in the fridge to go bad. Or maybe she was getting forgetful and didn't remember that she was the one who had put all that food there to begin with.

Whatever the reason, the fridge was full, and Reg figured she'd better thin it out before things went bad and she had to deal with moldy, stinky, rotting food. She thought she and Harrison had finished the ribs the other day, but there was a pretty hefty takeout box from Uncle Mike's Ribs still in the fridge. And that chocolate cake that she had started on. It had been pretty good too.

Surprisingly, most of the things in the fridge were Reg's favorite foods. Usually, the offerings from Sarah took up most of the space and were things that she either threw out or gave to the cats. She could have ribs for supper and the cake for dessert. Though what would go really nicely with the cake would be some ice cream…

Reg opened the freezer door to see whether she had anything left. There were several boxes and tubs of ice cream in varying flavors. Reg looked through them and pulled one out. The freezer was too full too. She would need to clean it out. Finish off one or two boxes of the ice cream.

"We like ice cream," Harrison announced from behind her.

Reg jumped and nearly dropped the box of Cookies & Cream ice cream she had chosen.

"Crap! You scared me!"

Harrison looked at her steadily, unapologetic. "You like that kind?" He nodded to the box in her hands.

"Yes, I like that kind. This kind."

Harrison nodded. He looked at the other containers that she had pulled out of the fridge. But she wasn't eating those, she had gone straight for the ice cream. Reg's face warmed. But what did Harrison care? He wasn't worried about following human conventions and probably had no idea that she should eat dinner before dessert.

"Do you want some?" she offered.

Harrison nodded. "Yes." As an afterthought, he tacked on, "Please."

Maybe he was starting to better understand human interactions. Though by the looks of his clothing… Reg turned away from him before rolling her eyes at the horizontal black and white stripes on his shirt and breezy paisley pantaloons.

She got out a couple of bowls. They would eat like civilized people instead of straight out of the carton standing in front of the fridge. Harrison watched her prepare the two bowls of ice cream. She put a spoon in each and passed a bowl to Harrison.

"Do you remember ice cream?" Harrison asked as he took the bowl from her. He took a large bite of ice cream that would have given Reg an instant headache, and looked at her, waiting for a response.

"Do I remember ice cream? What do you mean? Of course I remember ice cream." He had mentioned her memory more than once lately. Reg knew it had been bad since the possession, but it hadn't been that bad. Of course she knew what ice cream was.

"Little Reg," Harrison explained. "Do you remember little Reg liked ice cream?"

Reg took a small bite of her ice cream and swirled it around her tongue. She tried to remember when she was younger and Harrison had come to visit her when she was living with Norma Jean or one of her early foster families. Ice cream? She could remember hiding under the table or in the cupboard, licking ice cream from her spoon. Making it last as long as she could. She remembered Harrison sitting with her, apparently not visible to the others, laughing and stirring his melting ice cream with a spoon, making a soupy mess.

"Yes. You brought me ice cream when I was hungry."

Harrison gave a delighted smile. "I did!" he agreed. "We like ice cream. And cake." He looked at the fridge, anxious for Reg to open it and serve him a piece of cake as well. Reg did so. Why not? She shouldn't eat the whole thing herself. She had put on enough weight without eating whole chocolate cakes.

Harrison mixed ice cream and cake together and put a big spoonful into his mouth, closing his eyes and savoring it.

"Are you the one who has been filling my fridge?" Reg asked.

"I do not want you to go hungry."

"I don't think there's any danger of that. It isn't like when I was little and Norma Jean spent all her money on drugs and didn't have anything to feed me. Between what I buy and what Sarah puts in here, I'm pretty well-fed."

He frowned a little, nodding.

"Now that I'm grown up, you don't have to worry about me as much. When I was little and you had to protect me from the Witch Doctor and my mother and other foster kids and parents. Now…"

"There are still dangers," Harrison pointed out. "The soul drinker. Sirens. Witches and warlocks. Other creatures."

Reg had to admit that she had faced a lot of challenges since moving to Black Sands. Things that she had never anticipated dealing with. She no longer had to scrounge from one day to the next, wondering where her next meal might be coming from, so it didn't feel like as much of a struggle. But she'd never faced so many things that wanted to kill her. Or at least, she didn't think so. She didn't remember all of what had happened when she was with Norma Jean.

"Well, you don't need to give me quite so much food. It will go bad before I can eat it all. And I should be eating stuff that's good for me, not all ice cream and cake and Uncle Mike's ribs."

"They *are* good."

"They taste good, and I really like them. But I need to eat things that my body needs too. Vegetables and stuff that isn't full of sugar."

Though Reg's brain rebelled against this idea. She *liked* foods that were full of sugar. She did not like vegetables. She shook her head at the unruly child that still lived in her head, despite her best efforts to act like a grown up.

"He is not polite," Harrison said.

Reg blinked at him, trying to figure out what he was talking about.

Corvin? The Witch Doctor? She followed Harrison's gaze to Horace, who was creeping around the corner, watching them.

"Horace isn't polite? How is he not polite?"

Of course he *wasn't*. It certainly wasn't polite to go around mangling Reg's guests. She wouldn't be able to have him out when her clients showed up for their appointments. And he wouldn't like being locked up again. But maybe that would encourage him to stay at Marian's instead of returning to Reg's house.

"Did you bring him back here?" she asked. "Something keeps returning him here when I take him to his new home. If it's you, you need to stop so he can get used to Marian's house."

"He likes it here."

"I know he does. But he can't stay here. My landlord won't allow it."

"Because he did *that*?"

"What are you talking about?" Reg frowned, looking at Horace and trying to figure out what Harrison was trying to tell her. "He did what?"

Horace was sitting in the middle of the floor having a bath. Which was something cats did. They weren't embarrassed about licking their toes or backsides around other people.

Harrison gestured, not at Horace, but farther away. Reg looked past Horace into the living room, at something dark on the floor. She put her ice cream down and went a few steps closer for a better look. The odor hit her. Reg wrinkled her nose and looked at the black cat.

"Horace! Tell me you didn't!"

Horace continued to lick, unconcerned with what she thought about his behavior. Or maybe secretly happy to have put her in her place. Reg got closer and gagged.

"You know how to use the litter box! Oh, yuck!"

Reg tried not to breathe through her nose as she gathered the supplies she would need to clean up after Horace. When she looked around, Harrison was gone.

CHAPTER TWENTY-ONE

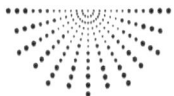

$\mathcal{A}$fter she had finished cleaning up, Reg put Horace into the cat carrier and called Marian to see what time she would be home.

"I'll be closing up soon," Marian assured her. "I'll let you know what time I'm at home so you can bring Horace back over. I hope he's settled down…"

"Well, he's been kind of a pain while he's been here." Reg didn't want to tell Marian about any of the worst behavior, in case Marian decided not to take Horace back. Maybe he would behave better at Marian's. "I think maybe he's ready to go back to your house."

Marian laughed. "I wouldn't count on it. He hasn't been there long enough to miss it. He just keeps going back to you. If you didn't have to worry about being kicked out…"

Earlier in the day, Reg might have had a difficult time saying no to Horace if Marian wouldn't take him and Sarah wasn't an issue. Even though she hadn't gone looking for a second cat, it might be nice to have two of them around the house to keep each other company. And two cats weren't that much harder to take care of than one. Until they started behaving the way Horace did.

"Maybe he's sick," Reg suggested. "Sometimes kids act out when they're not feeling well."

"It's possible, I suppose," Marian said. "But I haven't seen anything to indicate that he isn't feeling well."

Reg had done a couple of searches on her phone that suggested one reason that cats sometimes stopped using their litter boxes was because they were sick.

"Keep an eye on him, just in case. Maybe I'm wrong. But if he is sick, then we should get him looked at sooner rather than later."

"Yes," Marian agreed, her voice a little wistful.

Reg had forgotten that Marian had just lost another cat. She didn't want to make her sad by suggesting that they could lose Horace too.

"I'm sure it's nothing. I'm wrong. It isn't like he's just been lying around not doing anything. He has… lots of energy."

"That's one way to put it," Marian laughed. "In fact, I could do with a little less energy, if you could somehow manage that."

"I don't think so. He hasn't exactly been quiet here."

* * *

Reg wasn't sure how long it would be until Marian was actually home. She said she was closing up the shop, but Reg had worked a few retail jobs and knew that closing procedures could take a long time. And Marian might need to run some errands or pick up supper before she went home, too. "Soon" might be a few hours away. She already had Horace in the cat carrier and had nowhere to take him.

"We could go visit the dwarfs."

Horace lifted his head and looked at her. Reg was pretty sure that he hadn't understood what she had said and was just responding to her voice or her mood.

"Would you like that? Would you like to go to the mountains and see the dwarfs for a few minutes? I could check on Nico. Do you remember Nico?"

Horace bumped his face against the barred gate of the cat carrier. He emitted a low yowl. Not surprising that he didn't like to be penned up in the cage. Reg wouldn't like it either. But she couldn't risk what he might choose to do next. She had clients coming later and her house needed to be in good enough shape to receive company. And that meant that all the furniture and decor were intact and there weren't little kitty surprises left in strategic places for someone to step in.

"Yeah, let's go," Reg agreed. She called Starlight with a kissy sound. "Starlight? Do you want to go visit Nico?"

There was no answering thump as Starlight jumped to the floor. Reg waited for a minute to see whether he would come out, then went to the bedroom to look for him. He was curled up on the bed and lifted his head just enough to look at her through one eye as she approached.

"We're going to the dwarf mountain," Reg told him. "Where Nico is. Do you want to go with us?"

He put his head down and closed his eye.

"You sure? You liked it there. The dwarfs were pretty good to you."

Starlight didn't get up or acknowledge her. Reg shook her head and sighed. "Fine, then. Your loss. Just don't get mad at me for not bringing you along."

He didn't look like he was going to. It wasn't like Reg would be there for long or would be doing anything exciting. Just seeing a few dwarfs. And Nico. And to touch base with Gwythr on the gems. There was no reason, given her skills, that she couldn't pop in and visit them for a few minutes, just as if they were staying next door.

Reg went back out to the living room where the cat carrier was. She picked it up and closed her eyes.

She thought about the dwarf mountain and all she had seen there. All of the dwarfs; men, women, and children. Dressed in cartoon and superhero t-shirts and children's pants, their long beards incongruous with the popular media images they wore. She thought of the smell of the food in the cafeteria they referred to as their feast hall, and the heat of the forge where she had fired Calliopia's necklace. In a few breaths, she opened her eyes and looked around her, recognizing a change in the atmosphere around her.

She had, unsurprisingly, materialized in the crafting room that the forge was in. That was the place she had the strongest sensory memories of. She had not thought to ever go back there again, but there she was. The air was heavy and warm, and she was surrounded by the crafting tables of the dwarfs who were crafting jewelry and mementos for sale on Etsy. There was a kanban board on the wall showing various projects and what stages they were in.

The room was unnaturally quiet. The dwarfs, who should have been busy working away and chattering with each other, were all looking at her, silent and still. Of course they were. Reg had jumped directly into the middle of the kingdom with no warning or permission. That wasn't something that people normally did. She stood there with her cat carrier in her hand, trying to think of what to say to them to break the ice. *Hello? I was just in the neighborhood?*

"Intruder!" someone across the room shrilled, and he must have pulled an alarm, because a klaxon immediately began to blare, so loud that it hurt Reg's ears. She looked down at Horace, feeling sorry for him and his extra-sensitive cat hearing. And Nico, wherever he was.

"No," Reg said, holding up her hand, trying to reassure them. "I don't mean any harm. I just stopped in for a visit…"

Dwarf crafters streamed to the doors, casting frightened looks over their shoulders at Reg. Others turned toward her, baring their sword-hilts or pulling weapons free of their scabbards.

"I'm not here to hurt anyone!"

"No one may appear in the dwarf kingdom without leave," said a dwarf woman with a clipboard, staring sternly at Reg like the meanest librarian she'd ever crossed.

"No. I'm sorry. I should have called ahead…"

"Put down the cage," one of the older men ordered.

Reg bent down and set the carrier carefully on the floor. She raised her hands to her shoulders, hoping that they would not attack without provocation.

"It's a cat," one of the other dwarfs reported, bending down to examine Horace in the cat carrier. "Kitty, kitty, kitty?"

"Careful—" Reg warned as he stuck his finger into the carrier to scratch Horace's ears.

With a snarl, Horace attacked the offending digit, making the dwarf holler and jerk his hand back, finger bleeding. He put it into his mouth, his eyes wide.

"A formidable foe!" he exclaimed around the finger.

"Yes, please be careful, I don't want anyone to get hurt. I can heal that for you…"

The dwarf shook his head, taking his finger out of his mouth to study it. "It is a battle scar!"

"Um… okay. If you want."

Reg could hear the pounding of approaching feet over the sound of the alarm. A lot of approaching feet.

"Oh, man. I didn't mean to cause any trouble. Please tell the others —I'm not here to do any harm!"

A contingent of dwarfs streamed into the cavernous room, spreading out in formation, surrounding Reg on all sides. Swords flashed in the light of the forge. Reg was anxious, and she had forgotten how the forge pulled her, calling to her inner fire. She was sweating, not because of the heat, but because of the effort to stand there, unmoving, and not release her fire.

"Halt!" One of the dwarfs who had just arrived, a helmet of iron obscuring his features, called out and held up his hand. "It is Reg Rawlins, great sorceress!"

They all stopped and looked at each other. Reg waited, wondering what the protocol was. Was she off the hook because they had recognized her? Or would she be taken before the king or even thrown into prison?

She should have known better than to appear there. She had badly miscalculated.

The dwarf removed his helmet, revealing long hair and a familiar face.

"Gwythr!"

"Hail, Reg Rawlins." He spoke stiffly. "How came you here without permission?"

"I'm sorry. I didn't even think about it. I just wanted to come and see Nico, and to see you. I didn't mean to cause a whole…" Reg gestured at the army around her and the blaring klaxon, and the dwarf woman with the official schedule clipboard.

"A friend of the kingdom may approach the outside door and request entry," Gwythr advised. "And it is best if you arrange something ahead and get onto our Google calendar. Appearing inside is…" He shook his head somberly. "It is a great breach of etiquette."

CHAPTER TWENTY-TWO

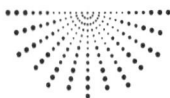

*R*eg bowed her head, trying to look suitably humbled. "I'm so sorry. It was stupid. I should have known that."

"Reg Rawlins is a great sorceress, and oftentimes a sorceress does not think she needs to follow the rules like everyone else."

"It wasn't that. I'm just... inexperienced. I was so overwhelmed with your hospitality the last time that it didn't even occur to me that you would need some notice that I was coming, and security checks and all that."

"You said you would visit," Gwythr said, acknowledging that Reg had mentioned it in their last call. "I should have told you the proper procedure then. I did not think that you would just... appear. We would normally... have several discussions first to make the arrangements."

Reg nodded. "I'm sorry."

Gwythr made an expansive gesture. "It was an oversight." He gave several sharp commands to the rest of the dwarfs in his contingent. They stood down, lowering their weapons, taking off their helmets or raising their visors, and relaxing.

Reg breathed a deep sigh of relief.

Gwythr came closer and peered into the cat carrier. "You have brought us another warrior cat?" he asked eagerly.

"No, not this time. I just thought he might like to see Nico. They are litter mates."

"Ah. Is this the one who…" Gwythr trailed off and didn't finish the question. He raised his brows questioningly. Reg had talked to him about what had happened to Horace in broad terms, though she hadn't expected at that point to take him there to see the dwarfs.

"Yes. This is the one," she said in a quiet tone that she hoped would not carry.

"Poor creature." Gwythr patted the top of the cage and was not silly enough to stick his finger between the bars.

Reg picked up the carrier. "I shouldn't be in here," she said, looking toward the forge, which was still trying to draw her in. "Can we go somewhere that is more private to visit? And to see Nico, if he's not too busy?"

She had no idea whether they had him on a training regimen or whether he was allowed to nap on his own schedule. She hoped that he would not have forgotten her already, but he had probably been very busy and had a lot of interesting experiences since he had joined the dwarfs.

"Come," Gwythr agreed. He led the way toward the door. The dwarf warriors parted in front of him and Reg was able to walk through without jostling any of them. They watched her with curious eyes, some of them whispering to each other. Maybe explaining who she was to anyone who hadn't seen her the last time she had been there.

She felt awkward walking with all of their eyes on her. She didn't want to trip in front of them and make a fool of herself. She really didn't like to be the center of attention.

She followed Gwythr through a few tunnels before she recognized the route to the feast hall. They cut through it to get to a cluster of meeting rooms on the other side where she had previously met with her company while they waited for the dwarfs to formulate a plan to unmake Calliopia's blade.

"Have a seat," Gwythr invited, motioning to the chairs around the table. "Would you like a beverage? Water? Ale?"

"Just water is great, thanks." Reg could tell that she had expended energy just trying not to be drawn into releasing her fire. She was learning that she needed to monitor her hydration level. Too much firecasting would leave her dehydrated and unable to function. Drinking too much water would quench her firecasting ability. She supposed it was the same with athletes. They needed to drink enough to operate at peak levels, but not so much that it weighed them down.

Gwythr went to the mini fridge and pulled out a bottle of water for her and a tall silver can for himself. She glanced at the label as he placed it on the table. *Dwarf Ale straight from the mountain*, it proclaimed in big, old-style lettering.

"Good product," Gwythr told her, following her eyes. "We have a campaign running right now to target D&D players. They love this kind of thing."

He sat down on one of the chairs and pumped a lever on the side to raise himself closer to Reg's level.

"I didn't offer anything to the cat. Should we let him out?"

"Uh… not a good idea to let him have free rein in the kingdom. We can shut the door, maybe, and just let him walk around in here. Maybe if Nico comes…?"

Gwythr hadn't made any effort to arrange for Nico to be brought. He leaned forward, ignoring her comment, eyeing the rings on her fingers.

"Whence came these?" He asked, eyes glittering. "You did not tell me you had anything like this."

"I can't sell these ones. They are cursed. They need to be cleansed before they can be sold. They don't rightfully belong to me."

"No," he agreed. "Egyptian. Very ancient."

"That's what Corvin said. He said maybe five thousand years old."

Gwythr nodded his agreement. "And how came they into your hands?"

"I can't really talk about that. I'm not here to trade them. I just wanted… to keep them close. I can't leave them unattended. Someone might try to steal them."

"Indeed."

"I did bring these, though," Reg offered. She reached into her pocket and pulled out the gems that she had previously offered to him via email.

"Ah!" Gwythr's eyes lit up and he picked up the plastic bag that held them. He fingered them through the plastic and held them up to the light. "They are beautiful, are they not? See how they sparkle."

Reg smiled at his obvious delight. It would be hard for him to be parted from them now that he'd held them in his hands. Negotiations should go much more quickly. He wouldn't want to stretch them out and have her go home with the gems still in her possession.

Gwythr caught her look. "Oh, you are a canny negotiator. Very smart, Reg Rawlins."

She smiled innocently.

Gwythr attempted to hand the gems back to her, but she didn't take them, waiting for him to take the next step.

"You were modest in your description. The assessments were..." Gwythr searched for an appropriate word. "They were technically correct."

Was he going to play hardball now? Pretend that she was asking too much or that they were dealing with a hardship that would prevent them from paying as much as she would like?

"There is a word we have," Gwythr said. "I do not know if there is an English word for it." He said the word in dwarfish, a sort of a guttural clicking. "Human assessors do not account for it when they are examining gems. It is a combination of the gem's history and power... its *personality*. The closest that I can think of in English would be... flavor?" His dark eyes bored into Reg's, trying to see if she understood his meaning. "These gems have a very rich, deep flavor. Is that right?"

Reg knew a bit about valuing gemstones, but only in the technical aspects that Gwythr had mentioned. Size, cut, clarity. She had never heard of this other aspect, but it made sense to her. There was something about the gems when she held them or was near them. Not just warmth or power, but a feeling of wholeness and rightness.

When she held the cursed gems, the feeling was different. She could still sense their power, but there was something unsettled and fractured about them. A need to be filled. While some of the gems could be cleansed using other methods, some of them could only be cleansed by returning them to the source they had come from. To the people who were the rightful owners. Only the rightful owners could give or trade the gems without a curse accompanying them. Then they were transformed, and she could feel that fullness again. She thought that Gwythr was right, but in her mind, she identified two separate qualifications, not just one. The flavor of the gems, the power and history and personality, but also the wholeness of them, the fullness.

"Yes… I guess flavor makes sense," she agreed.

"As such, these gems are worth more than… some of the flavorless pap that you find in human markets. Especially the grown gems."

At Reg's questioning look, he clarified. "The ones created in labs?"

"Oh." Reg nodded. She didn't have much experience in that regard, though she had heard of such a thing.

"They can be technically perfect, but worthless."

"Because they were made artificially."

"They do not have any soul."

Reg nodded again. All this was leading up to something, but she wasn't sure what.

"I must revise my offer for these gems," Gwythr concluded finally. Reg had been expecting this. "It is not high enough."

CHAPTER TWENTY-THREE

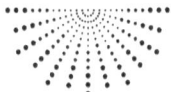

*S*he looked at him, his words clicking through to her brain, but unable to decide what he meant. She was expecting him to bargain harder, to tell her that she had overpriced them and that they could not be expected to pay so much. She had not been expecting to be told that they were worth more than he had previously offered for them.

"You're… *increasing* your offer?"

He nodded. "Dwarfs can be cunning too. And we always like a bargain. But if I were to give you too low a price, it would be robbery, and it would hurt my reputation. I must pay a fair price."

"Oh. Okay. Well then… do you have a price in mind, or do you have to think about it?"

"I will need to look over my accounts, talk to some others, and get back to you." Gwythr laid the baggie of gems down on the table reluctantly, eyes shining as he looked at them. "I will be as quick as possible."

Reg could tell that he didn't want to leave them behind. Hopefully, that meant that they could come to a landing before she had to go home.

"And can you… see if you can find Nico? I'd like to see him."

Gwythr looked around. "He comes."

Reg looked out the door and saw a dark shape approaching.

"Nico?" she asked uncertainly.

The proportions of the rooms in the dwarf mountain distorted Reg's sense of size. Tall ceilinged rooms with smaller furniture than she was used to as a human threw off her ability to judge scale. The shape approaching the room looked disproportionately large, and she was sure it would resolve when he got closer.

But the cat shape that came through the door was not small like the kattakyn she had left with the dwarfs. It was not the size of Horace, who had grown and put on weight while he had been with Kareem. It was the size of a panther or a small bear. Armor plates protected his body and long spikes protruded along the spine, making him look even larger.

Nico gave a trill of recognition and galloped toward Reg. She gasped as he leaped toward her, putting out her hands to stop him and protect herself. But he stopped with his front paws on the table in front of her, powerful hind legs planted firmly on the floor.

"Nico!" Reg was relieved and flabbergasted. What had the dwarfs done to make Nico grow to such proportions? Horace was the shape of a normal cat, and Francesca had not said that any of the other kattakyn owners thought that they were too large or had strange qualities. They all thought that they owned normal house cats, which would not be the case if they were as big as Nico. "Look at you! My goodness!"

Gwythr smiled as he slid down from his chair. "He is a warrior," he informed Reg, slapping Nico's armored side. "You are impressed?"

"Wow. Am I ever. What are you feeding this guy? It must be the big spiders down here."

He laughed heartily. "We know how to take care of a warrior cat."

"I guess so. Are you in charge of him, or does someone else take care of him and do his training?"

"I am responsible for him, but there are many who are involved in his care and training. As Chief of the Smithies, I do not have the ability to put all my time into his care. And there are others better suited to train him in combat."

"Yeah, I guess your calendar must be pretty full." She remembered the way he had entered the forge when the alarm bell rang. "You command part of the dwarf army too?"

Gwythr gave a little bow. "Only the protectors of the forge. As Chief of the Smithies, that duty falls to me."

"Wow. You really must be busy. I had no idea how much being the Chief of the Smithies entailed."

"Time blocking," Gwythr said. "That is the way to ensure you get things done when you have so many responsibilities." He assessed Reg's blank look. "On your calendar. Blocking off specific times for different tasks."

And he probably hadn't expected the interruption of whatever he was currently supposed to be doing, dealing with a breach of security and Reg showing up with her gemstones.

"And here I am interrupting you. I'm sorry about that. I wasn't thinking."

"It is an honor to be able to visit Reg Rawlins. But I do have other things to do… and I will need to revise my bid for you quickly, before you have to leave. Will you be here for a little longer?" He looked at Nico and gave him another ringing pat. "You will want to visit with Nico and give him a chance to see his litter mate."

"Yeah. I guess. I'll be here for a while longer."

"Good. I will do my best to work within your time frame."

* * *

Gwythr left, pulling the door shut behind him so that Reg would be able to let Horace out of his carrier.

But Reg wasn't so sure that was a good idea now. Horace was much smaller than Nico. What if Nico decided that he was a rat or some other kind of prey? She couldn't imagine how he had gotten so large. Was it something they were feeding him? A spell? Gwythr didn't seem to think that it was anything unusual.

From the beginning, they had seemed to recognize him as something different, but familiar. Had they once had kattakyns in the dwarf kingdom? It seemed unlikely. But by now she should be used to dealing with things that were unlikely.

Reg reached her hand out to Nico tentatively. She remembered how he had often slashed at her or fought back against her before she had brought him to the dwarfs. If he were to slash her now with those bear-like claws, the results would be far worse. A scratch from a kitten was something she could handle. Considering the injury, she would get from Nico now was sobering.

"Hi, Nico. Do you remember me? Remember how I used to feed you treats and how I brought you to the mountain?" Hopefully, these happy memories would make him well-disposed to her and he wouldn't be thinking of the way that she had yelled at him when he had intentionally knocked things down or broken something of hers.

Nico sniffed her hand and rubbed his jaw against it, his rough fur brushing it gently. Reg scratched tentatively, and he started a loud, rumbling purr, rubbing his face, cheeks, and ears against her like a kitten.

"Yeah? You remember me?"

He gave her hand a brief lick with his long, rasping tongue.

"Yeah, you're a good boy. Gwythr says that you are a very good warrior cat. He is very pleased with you. And look at how big you have gotten."

Nico continued to rub against her and purr. He even flopped onto his side and lifted his front leg for her to rub his belly, but Reg knew that trick. He might enjoy having his belly rubbed for a minute, but then he would attack, and she did not want those big, powerful back legs raking down her arm. Ouch.

"You're just a big kitten, aren't you? Do you want to see Horace? Do you remember your brother?"

Reg tapped the cat carrier, and Nico turned his attention to it. He sniffed the carrier and shuffled closer to it, looking in through the grill on the front. Reg couldn't see Horace, but could hear him snuffling inside the carrier as well. Was he afraid of Nico? Or was he just interested? Did he recognize his fellow kattakyn? Since he no longer bore a piece of the Witch Doctor, was there a relationship between them? Or was Horace just like any cat Nico might meet in an alley?

"Nico and Horace," Reg said softly. "Two kattakyns from the same litter. Do you remember?"

She wondered if it was right to call them littermates, since they weren't actually kittens born to the same mother. She had called them that to Gwythr to avoid having to explain where they had come from.

Keep the story simple. But was that the word she should use when she talked to the kattakyns?

They were draugrs raised from the dead by the Witch Doctor to serve him. Comrades in arms? That might be closer.

Nico nosed against the grill of the carrier and turned to look at her, waiting for her to open it. Reg read him the best she could. He didn't seem angry or as though he wanted to hunt. He seemed friendly enough toward Horace. Gwythr hadn't seemed to be worried that he might attack Horace. It seemed natural to him that they would want to visit and that Reg would let Horace out of his cage once Nico arrived.

"You want me to open it?"

He moved over, rubbing against her hand again, nudging her toward the carrier.

"And you're going to be nice? You're not going to do anything to hurt Horace, right?"

He purred loudly, still encouraging her. Finally, Reg nodded. She released the catch on the front of the carrier and carefully swung the door open. She could see Horace's black, furry face, but he didn't dart out once he had the opportunity. He sat hunched over where he was, watching Reg and looking past her to Nico.

"Do you want to come out and see Nico? Do you remember you used to play together? When you lived with Francesca?"

Horace's eyes went from Reg to Nico and back again, looking remarkably like a worried child.

"It's okay," Reg assured him. "He's not going to hurt you."

And she really hoped that she was right. They would get along just fine together. They were happy to see each other and would play together and renew their acquaintance, just like when Starlight and Nicole got to have a play date.

Horace's nose wiggled and his nostrils flared as he sniffed and sniffed, gathering all the information he could from the air in the room. Reg had often wondered what it would be like to be an animal, able to sense danger by the smell, able to seek out even the smallest scent trails to track down what they were looking for. Smelling the grass where other animals had been and knowing all about them just from their smell.

But Reg had also lived with Erin, the super-smeller, and had quickly learned that being able to smell things that no one else could was not a superpower. Erin was always the first one to get sick around a putrid smell. She would be running to the bathroom to throw up before anyone else was even aware of something nasty. And that did not impress Reg as a talent she wanted. Better to have a gift like hers, being able to cold read people and make quick judgments about them. That was far more beneficial than being able to follow a scent trail.

CHAPTER TWENTY-FOUR

*H*orace poked his face out from the carrier. He and Nico touched noses. Reg felt suddenly dizzy and had to hold on to the chair to keep from tipping over. She sat very straight, trying to keep herself focused on the two kattakyns. But both of them seemed to be vibrating, blurring in front of her eyes.

Reg shook her head. She closed her eyes for a few seconds and then opened them, hoping her vision would clear. What was wrong? Had she expended too much energy without realizing it? Let herself get dehydrated? She had eaten before she had jumped to the dwarf mountain, so she should have been just fine. Maybe she was coming down with something.

She rubbed her eyes and looked at the kattakyns again, wanting to keep an eye on them and make sure that everything was okay. If Nico showed any signs of bullying or stalking Horace, or if Horace looked afraid, she needed to be able to react, not to be swooning in her seat.

Horace's fur was puffed out. Reg reached down to touch him. "Are you okay, Horace?"

He turned his head to look at her, but did not lay his ears back or look upset. He just looked puffier than usual. But when Reg touched him, his fur did not seem to be standing up, but was lying flat as usual.

"You're okay, then?"

He made a soft noise in his throat that Reg thought was meant to reassure her. She withdrew her hand and left him alone so that he and Nico could get reacquainted. There was a lot of sniffing, and some meowing and licking. The two of them seemed to be getting along together just fine. Reg relaxed. It was okay. Nico hadn't become a monster during his time with the dwarfs. He had grown bigger, but he didn't appear to have become vicious. Maybe he was even calmer than he had been when he'd been living with her. He'd had some quiet moments with Starlight in the days that he had spent at Reg's house, but most of the time he'd been climbing the walls. Or the curtains. Or the bookshelf. Or Reg's leg.

He was a little large to be climbing up her leg now!

Maybe the training regimen with the dwarfs had calmed him down, had allowed him to work out his energy and aggression in an acceptable way so that he could be calm the rest of the time.

"You're just a big pussycat now, aren't you?" Reg asked him.

Nico shot her a look. Big pussycat was clearly not the way that he preferred to be addressed.

Reg giggled.

Horace was sniffing the floor and starting to explore the room, apparently having completed the prolonged greeting ritual with Nico. Just two tomcats out having a good time. He stepped on her foot as he went by her, and Reg pushed him away and pulled her foot back.

"Ouch! You're heavier than you look. Watch where you're going."

Horace didn't even look at her. Reg looked at him and looked at the carrier. She had been holding the carrier not an hour earlier. She knew how heavy he was. He was a large cat, but he wasn't that big. Not like Nico. But his weight when he had stepped on her seemed disproportionate to how much he had weighed when she was holding the cat carrier. And looking at him, she wasn't even sure whether he would fit back into the carrier again when it was time to go.

"Did you *grow?*" Reg demanded, having difficulty believing what she was seeing. Horace wasn't a kitten anymore. He was a full-grown cat. He shouldn't still be growing. And he certainly shouldn't be growing fast enough for Reg to notice a difference from one moment to the next.

But surely he was bigger than he had been just a few minutes earlier.

Was it something about the dwarf mountain? Starlight hadn't gotten any bigger when he had visited. Horace hadn't eaten or drunk anything, so it wasn't something he had consumed. He had just made friends with Nico, a very large warrior cat. Had they put a spell on him that was affecting Horace? Maybe he was radioactive. Reg couldn't think of any other explanation for what she was seeing.

Hopefully, Gwythr would be back before Horace got so large that he would not fit back in the carrier again.

* * *

Reg's phone rang. She looked at the caller ID. Marian. Reg swallowed, thinking about what she would say. She answered the call and sounded as casual as possible.

"Hi, Marian."

"I'm home now, Reg. You can bring Horace over any time."

"Great. He and Starlight are just playing right now, so I'll wait until they're done. Better if he gets plenty of exercise before coming over to your house. Then maybe he'll be quiet tonight. And I don't want to take him away in the middle of their game. I think Horace is already having enough trouble with the back-and-forth without making it worse by interrupting him in the middle of something."

"That's fine," Marian agreed. "Anytime is fine, as long as I can still get to sleep in good time to get up in the morning."

Reg was sure that Marian didn't sleep as long as she did. Not when she opened her store in the morning, even if it were late morning. "Yeah. What time is bedtime for you?" She did a quick check-in with herself. Were the dwarf mountain and Black Sands both in the same time zone? She was pretty sure that they were.

"Say... eleven o'clock?" Marian suggested. "You won't have any trouble getting here before then, will you? I thought when we talked the last time that you were in a hurry."

"I guess I was. But things have settled down since then and the cats are having a good time, so I'm more relaxed. I can have him there by eleven o'clock. No problem. I have clients coming before then anyway."

"Okay. See you in a while."

* * *

Gwythr had said that he would get back to her as quickly as he could, so Reg wasn't too worried that he would keep her for hours. He wanted the gems in his hand again by the time that she left. If the way that Reg felt about water and fire were at all similar to the way that dwarfs felt about gemstones, the gems would be calling to him now. He would be intent on making sure that she did not leave before he could negotiate a fair payment between them.

She watched the kattakyns. They didn't do anything else of concern. She swiped on her phone and scrolled through videos, looking for something to entertain herself until Gwythr's return.

Eventually, the door opened and Gwythr entered. He looked at the cats and nodded. He took his seat at the table again, and slid a stapled stack of papers over to Reg.

She looked down at it and flipped past the cover page and table of contents, looking for the bottom line. On the third page was a bold number in a box, with details around it. Reg blinked at the number and read the words above it. It was, in fact, Gwythr's offer for the gems.

"Is this right?" she asked, pointing to it.

Gwythr nodded. "As you can see, the flavor of the gems did increase the offer significantly. I can't afford to go too high. I can't jeopardize my family's wealth for one purchase. But I hoped that this would be enough to... keep you interested."

Reg nodded. She feigned a frown, pushing her brows down as she studied the paperwork. She flipped through the pages slowly but wasn't actually reading anything else. This part was all for show. She would take the amount that he had offered in an instant. It was significantly higher than the jeweler she had gone to had appraised the gems at.

Gwythr made comments as she looked through the details of the offer, pointing out similar transactions that he had reviewed, as much as he could discern about the origins of the gems, their powers and personalities.

"How long will it take you to get this much together?" Reg asked eventually. He would need to at least make a deposit before she would leave the gems with him. Even a deposit would be a nice little injection into her bank account.

"My sons are getting it together now." Gwythr pulled out his phone and looked at the face. "I think… another twenty minutes or so. You will excuse them if it takes a little longer… I do not wish to keep you here longer than you intended…"

"Twenty minutes is fine."

He was going to give her the entire amount right away? Reg's face flushed. She'd never had a windfall like that before. It was one thing to receive the gems from the fairies. It had been pretty exciting once she had realized that they were real gems and not just glass. But she had discovered that having the gems wasn't nearly as beneficial as actually being able to do something with them. Merely owning them and keeping them hidden in her closet or under her bed didn't bestow any advantages. They didn't pay the bills.

CHAPTER TWENTY-FIVE

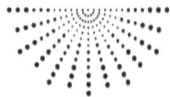

*a*fter Reg signed the formal document accepting his offer, Gwythr's gaze wandered to the cats. He watched them interacting with each other. Like Reg, he looked at the cat carrier and then back at Horace. He frowned.

"Your new cat…"

"Horace."

"Horace. He has… has he grown?"

Reg nodded. "Yeah. I was wondering about that. I thought that maybe it was something to do with Nico, with whatever it was that made him grow so big."

Gwythr considered this thoughtfully. "I am not sure… it does not usually work this way. It takes time and training for a warrior cat to grow."

"But you must have done something to make Nico grow so large, and that somehow… rubbed off on Horace?"

"It is very strange."

Gwythr watched Horace for a while. He looked at Reg, and she caught him staring at her rings again.

"Do you want to see them?" Reg asked. He was obviously curious about them. But maybe handing such a thing to a dwarf would not be a good idea. Gwythr had been fair with her about the gems, giving her more than they had been appraised at, but that was no guarantee that he wouldn't try to take the rings from her on some pretext. If she handed them over and he took off with them, there wasn't much she would be able to do about it. With so many armored dwarfs at Gwythr's command, and who knew how many others in the mountain, she didn't stand much of a chance, even if she used her powers.

Gwythr made a motion for her to keep them to herself. "They would be difficult to resist," he informed her. "Difficult for any dwarf."

"I'm not trying to tempt you. But I couldn't really leave them at home."

"No. You could not leave something so valuable so vulnerable to thieves." His eyes were fixed on the rings. "Though, I am not sure that they are safe on thy fingers, either."

Reg squirmed at this observation. What could she do if someone did try to steal them? She had powers. She could not be overcome by just anyone. But if she were taken unaware? If someone attacked her before she knew what was happening, they might be able to kill her or make off with the rings. And if there were more than one attacker, that was another possibility. She couldn't be sure of being able to fight off a physical or magical attack if there were enough attackers banded together, like the dwarf army or a few magical beings allied together, as when she and Corvin, Damon, and Francesca had fought the Witch Doctor. Several kinds of powers originating from several different directions... There was definitely a danger in being overwhelmed.

"I'm going to Egypt soon," she explained. "To return them to their rightful owners. Until then... I think this is where they are safest, even if it isn't ideal."

"You know to whom they belonged?"

"Well... no. I hope to find out once I get there."

Gwythr opened his mouth and closed it again. Reg had a pretty good idea what he was thinking. "I know... I should plan better. Be less impulsive. Get someone to do the research before I go over there..."

"Perhaps," he agreed with a nod. "But it is thy choice. They are powerful. They will call to someone." He stroked his long beard. "Hopefully... not a *lot* of people. It could be very difficult if there are many people who would claim them. And with symbols so ancient and powerful... there may be many who feel their pull."

Reg hadn't thought very much about what would happen when she got back to Egypt. She hoped that by using the rings and the gems to jump her there, that she would land in the right location. The proper owners of the treasure would be close at hand and it would be quick to complete their transaction. In and out in just a few hours, like Reg's trip to the dwarf mountain to see Nico and talk to Gwythr about the stones.

"Take care," Gwythr warned. "One must take great care in a case such as this."

"I will," Reg agreed. But was she? Or was she expecting the universe to come to her aid again? Harrison appearing and taking over if she were attacked. Friends helping her and advising her, knowing what she needed to know at just the right moment. Inspiration in the face of danger.

She wasn't exactly well-known for carefully planning things out ahead of time.

* * *

Before they could get too deeply into the conversation about avoiding dangers in Egypt, there was a soft knock on the door.

"Enter, my sons," Gwythr called.

Two men entered. They were noticeably younger than Gwythr, but Reg wasn't sure of his age or theirs. Gwythr's beard was long and gray, and his two sons had shorter, black beards. They were trimmed and groomed, and it would be some time before they could grow beards as long as their father. They stepped into the room and bowed formally to Reg.

"The great Reg Rawlins," one of them intoned in a serious voice.

Reg rolled her eyes but didn't correct them. While she didn't like to be addressed in such honorifics, she was getting used to it. And she supposed that knowing her gave Gwythr and his sons a good rep with the other dwarfs, so she was careful not to disparage the title. She gave them each a nod, hoping that was enough.

"I'm... honored to meet you," she told them, stumbling a little. "Your father is a very great dwarf."

Their eyes shone at this and smiles twitched under their beards. They stepped forward in unison, each bearing a business envelope on outstretched hand. Reg glanced at Gwythr, and took both envelopes, keeping an eye on each dwarf to make sure she did not misstep.

One envelope was thinner, and she opened that one first. It was a certified check in her name. The numbers on it didn't quite match the offer she had signed, but there was the second envelope.

"Banks sometimes hold funds such as this for ten business days to make sure that it clears," Gwythr explained. "Even though the funds have been certified."

Reg nodded. She'd never had a check for so much money before, but she had heard of things like that. Anti-fraud measures. She opened the second envelope, which was filled with hundred-dollar bills.

"The cash portion, as per our agreement." Gwythr nodded toward the offer that Reg had signed, apparently agreeing to the payment being split between cash and certified check. "It is our practice to always make sure that part of the payment is liquid and can be used immediately."

Reg folded the cash and the check and put them into opposite pockets in her skirt. "That's very thoughtful. Thank you."

"There are often expenses that must be paid. We do not agree with banks holding money that has been certified, but that is the world we live in. So we try to reduce the inconvenience."

"Very wise," Reg agreed. "It has been a pleasure working with you."

"I hope that Reg Rawlins will come to us again, if she needs to liquidate more gems such as these."

The two sons nodded their agreement. Reg smiled and let out a slight chuckle. "I might have others. But this will keep me afloat for quite a while."

She let her mind wander to the number on the check. She hadn't thought about what she would do with a windfall like that. Buy a house of her own? A new car? Invest in something that would bring in even more money later? She'd never been in a position before to consider long-term savings and investments. When she got the gems, she had started to dream of world travel. Not just going back to see Erin if everything seemed to be quiet in Tennessee, but maybe going on a cruise or a flight around the world taking her to far-flung destinations she had only heard of before. Or maybe a few that she had never heard of, seeing sights that she had never imagined. With the addition of magical species, the world was even bigger and more interesting than she had thought. She had gotten a very small taste of that in Black Sands and at the Spring Games.

"You will keep us in mind," Gwythr said with another bow.

Reg nodded. She stood. "Now... I'd better get this cat back in the box."

CHAPTER TWENTY-SIX

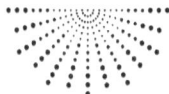

They all looked at Horace. Reg hoped that he only looked so large because of his fluffiness. She didn't want to have to actually squeeze him into the carrier.

"Another warrior cat?" one of the sons asked.

"I think he was just influenced a bit by Nico," Reg explained.

"And the power of your ring," he commented, nodding to Reg's hand.

"Shh." The quick warning came from Gwythr like the air escaping from a bike tire when Reg pulled the pump from the valve. A sharp hissing sound, quickly cut off.

The dwarf who had spoken turned red. Reg looked at him and then at Gwythr.

"*What* about my ring?"

"It is very poor manners," Gwythr said, shooting a glance at the offender.

"I want to hear anyway. You think it is my ring that made Horace grow?"

Gwythr looked uncomfortable. "These rings are powerful. They might magnify the magic of another spell."

"What spell? Whatever made Nico grow so big?"

"It would not be usual…" Gwythr shook his head, looking at the two cats. "A spell does not expand or rub off on another creature. But... perhaps. Your cats are... unusual, and the rings are very powerful. Ancient magic... the curse upon the rings... They can behave unpredictably. Perhaps in ways that we are not familiar with."

So he had noticed that the cats were *unusual.*

Not just two identical black cats from the same litter, but something unexpected and different. He hadn't asked her what that was. Perhaps that would have been poor manners. But it was clear from his words and his glances toward the cats that he knew there was something going on that she hadn't told him about.

"Can you tell me anything about the rings?" Reg asked, holding her hand toward Gwythr so that he could examine them again if he needed to refresh his memory. "Other than the fact that they are ancient and from Egypt?"

He took her hand gently in his strong, roughened fingers, but didn't touch the rings. His lips twitched as he studied them carefully. He raised his eyes to her face and didn't let go of her hand.

"They are powerful. The coronation rings of a ruler. A symbol of his office. When whole, they will do the bidding of their owner. But cursed as they are, I would not try to wield them."

"Does that mean I shouldn't wear them? Or just that I shouldn't... try to make them do anything? I don't even know how you command a ring."

He chuckled softly. "You know much more than you think you do, Reg Rawlins. Or else you toy with me."

"But I can wear them? That isn't a danger?"

"As you said, it would be more of a danger to leave them somewhere unprotected. But you need to be cautious. They will enhance your powers, which are already great. And you may find them doing things... that you do not wish." He looked down at Horace again.

Reg sighed. She knew she needed to get to Egypt as soon as she could. Before the rings disrupted anything else. Who knew what else they could do? If they could take the magic that had been used on Nico to make Horace grow, what might they do with Corvin's power? Or Harrison's, the next time he came to visit her? Filling her fridge with cake and ice cream was one thing. But Harrison's powers extended far beyond that. She didn't want to inadvertently use his power to go back in time, put a curse on someone or make them disappear, or any of the other powers she had seen Harrison exercise. He might play the fool sometimes, but he was cunning and knew and understood far more than he pretended to.

"Thank you. You've been really helpful."

"I look forward to doing business again in the future," Gwythr agreed with a bow.

Reg stood up. She bent down to pet Horace. "Did you have a nice visit? It was nice to see Nico again, wasn't it?" She extended her fingers to Nico and, when he sniffed them and then rubbed against them, she scratched his ears. "I'm glad to see how well you're doing here," Reg told him. "You are so big and strong, and you look great in that armor. The dwarfs must be very proud of you."

Nico purred loudly.

"Now, let's go home," Reg told Horace. She pressed his side, directing him back toward the cat carrier. He resisted, which didn't surprise her. Of course he didn't want to go back inside the little cage when he had grown so much. It would be very tight quarters. "It's just for a short trip," Reg encouraged. "Just to make sure that you can't get lost along the way. I would not want anything to happen to you."

He yowled at her, not pleased. Reg pressed him again, alert and ready for him to try to bite or claw her. He might not be as big as Nico, but he still had larger than usual teeth and claws, and she wasn't in any mood to find out if they were proportionally sharper and more powerful.

"Come on, Horace. Just hop back inside for a few minutes."

One of the rings on Reg's finger grew warm and Horace's coat crackled with static electricity. Horace gave a sharp yap that sounded more like a dog than a cat, and he allowed himself to be herded into the carrier. Reg shut and latched the door.

He was too large to turn around inside the carrier to face the door, as he had done earlier. She hoped that he didn't feel too claustrophobic. But she didn't want to try transporting him without the carrier. If he got it into his head to cause mischief, he could do a lot of damage in a very short period of time.

"Good boy," she told him. "Thank you. That's very good."

Horace sneezed.

Reg patted Nico on the side, thumping his armor. "Bye, Nico. Be good and listen to the dwarfs."

She bent over to pick up the cat carrier, which was much heavier than it had been since the last time she had held it. She hoped that everything was well-constructed so that the bottom would not separate from the top. She braced the muscles in her arm. She closed her eyes, and pictured being home.

CHAPTER TWENTY-SEVEN

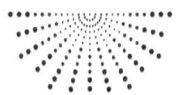

*R*eg opened her eyes and looked around her cottage with satisfaction. Traveling by magic was so much easier than having to drive for hours on end. It took a little of her energy, but not enough that she felt weak or wanted to sleep. Just a bit of fatigue, as if she'd been lifting weights and then stopped.

Speaking of lifting weights…

Reg put the cat carrier down and stretched her arms and shoulders. Horace definitely was not all fluff. While she could have jumped directly over to Marian's house, Reg didn't think it would be advisable. Just as she didn't know all the proper etiquette for dealing with dwarfs, she didn't know what the unwritten rules were about appearing in someone else's house, even if Marian had told Reg to come over any time. She had meant to come over in the car, not magically. Reg didn't particularly like the fact that the immortals could appear in her house without warning, despite the protective wards. She assumed that Marian would feel the same about Reg using her powers to get into her house.

After resting her arms for a few minutes, Reg picked up Horace's carrier with the opposite hand. It felt even heavier on that side. Taking quick, short steps, Reg went to the door and let herself out. She put the carrier down to lock the door, then picked it up again and headed to her car.

She didn't make it.

The carrier was very heavy, and Reg had to stop to put it down and take another break. She was doing the best that she could, but it was a much more difficult job than it had been the last time she had taken Horace to Marian's.

"Where are you going?"

Reg startled at the voice that came from the gathering shadows. She instantly thought of the Witch Doctor, Wilson, Weston, and finally settled on Corvin. Of course Corvin. Lurking around her yard, hoping to be able to sneak past the wards or catch a glimpse of her.

"Don't you know how to use the phone?" Reg snapped. "You're not supposed to be around here."

"I wanted to see you."

"I have things to do. As you can see."

They both looked down at the cat carrier.

"Where are you taking him?" Corvin asked, stepping out of the shadows. He picked up the carrier and started to walk toward Reg's car. "Did you find him a new home?"

"To Marian's. She's agreed to take him... but he keeps coming back."

"Like a bad penny," Corvin said. He switched the carrier from one hand to the other and marched more deliberately toward Reg's car. "Good grief, what are you feeding this guy, Regina?"

Reg didn't try to explain. She didn't understand well enough herself what was going on with Horace. If the dwarfs, who could grow humongous cats, did not understand what was going on, then how was she supposed to know?

They reached the car and Corvin put the carrier down on the sidewalk beside it.

"Are you going to Egypt?" he asked suspiciously.

"Yes. Oh, you mean now? Not now. Just to Marian's right now."

He eyed her as though he didn't believe it for a moment. He knew that she must be trying to pull something over on him. Reg looked directly back into his eyes, challengingly.

"I told you where I'm going. If you don't like it or don't believe me, that's your problem. Not mine."

"Do you have any other luggage?" Corvin looked around.

Reg offered her empty hands. She had only the big purse over her shoulder. "Do you see any?"

"You might have already sent it on ahead. Or you might think that you won't be in Egypt long enough to need anything but your shoulder bag. Which looks suspiciously hefty…"

Reg straightened a turn in the strap of the purse so that it lay flat on her shoulder. She didn't like the look in his eye, the suggestion that he would dig into her purse and find out the truth. Just as he had said he would search through her memories to find what he wanted.

"You're not welcome here," she told him sternly. "Go back to your own house or I'll call the police."

"You wouldn't call the police."

"I could."

Corvin shrugged. "I could do a lot of things. I could be on the next flight to the moon. But you know what? I'm not. Just like you won't call the police on me."

He looked very sure of himself. Reg was tempted to call the police just to prove him wrong and to show that she didn't have to do anything he said. But she held herself back.

"Thank you for helping me with the cat."

She picked up the carrier and put it onto the front passenger seat. It would be too awkward to wrap the seatbelt around it. She would have to just be a careful driver and make sure she didn't make any sudden starts or stops that might make it slide on the seat.

"You should put it in the back," Corvin advised. "On the floor behind one of the seats. That would be safer."

"It's fine there," Reg told him. "There isn't space behind the seats."

"It could slide off the seat."

She glared at him. What business was it of his? He just wanted to tell her what to do.

"Okay, okay," he held his hands up. "No need to freak out about it. Just trying to help."

"I didn't ask for your help, okay? I'm just fine how I am. You're not supposed to be hanging out in my yard waiting to ambush me. You're supposed to be at your house, doing whatever it is that you do."

"I wanted to talk to you about Egypt."

"I'm not talking to you about it. You just get all controlling."

"I do not," Corvin protested haughtily.

"You're always telling me what to do. I'm not taking you. It doesn't have anything to do with you."

"But your safety is important to me. The only reason I want to come is—"

"I'm not sure why you think you should come along with me, but I know it's not because you want to keep me safe."

"Regina." He used that hurt-puppy look and injured voice that she hated. She knew that she hadn't hurt him. His ego didn't depend on her strokes. She knew that he was lying about just wanting to keep her safe, and so did he. She shouldn't have to act as if she believed his lies.

Reg stepped back from the car and slammed the door. "I'm leaving. Goodbye. Take yourself home. You'd better not still be here when I get back."

"Maybe I could help you. Escort you to Marian's."

"You are *not* escorting me," Reg snapped. He just wanted an excuse to keep an eye on her, and she'd had enough. He didn't need to know what she was doing every minute of the day. And he didn't need to go to Egypt with her.

Reg went around to the driver's side, slid into her seat, and slammed that door too, eliminating the possibility of any further discussion. She started the engine, then made sure that the cat carrier was all the way back on the seat before putting the car into drive. As irritated as she was by Corvin's appearance, she drove slowly and carefully. She didn't want to make it any more stressful on Horace than it had to be. She certainly didn't want to get into an accident where he could be injured.

They made it safely to Marian's house. Reg sat there for a few minutes, just breathing and trying to slow her rapidly beating heart and calm herself down.

Horace gave a low meow. He wanted out. Hadn't he spent enough time in the cramped carrier already? Reg had said it would only be for a few minutes and it had been longer than that.

"Yes. I'm ready. Let's go inside."

Motion-activated lights went on as they walked up the sidewalk to Marian's front door, and she opened the door shortly after Reg rang the doorbell. Though Reg still had to wait a minute and put the carrier down to ease the muscle fatigue she was getting from carrying it. Marian obviously wasn't standing at the door watching for her.

"Come in." Marian watched Reg pick up the carrier again and bring it inside. "How has this little beggar been behaving?"

"He's fine," Reg assured her. "Everything is just fine."

She opened the cage and, since Horace did not have the space to turn around, he backed out.

"Well, he'd better stay here now. This is where he is supposed to be. If he keeps disappearing... I won't be responsible for him."

"I'm sure he'll be okay now."

"Reg... what happened to this cat?"

Reg looked at Horace, trying to think of something to say. Something funny like that he had shrunk in the wash. But of course, he had gotten bigger, and she couldn't think of an appropriate joke to say for that.

"He's... uh... put on a little weight."

"In a *day?*"

"Yes."

"This is not Horace," Marian insisted. "It couldn't be."

"Check for yourself," Reg suggested.

"How am I supposed to tell him apart from any other black cat? I know because he doesn't look the same. He's huge."

"You can feel that he's the same cat, can't you?" Reg suggested. "Use your psychic senses and you'll recognize him."

"I can't do that. My gift does not extend to cats."

Not that Horace was a cat. But she wasn't about to tell Marian that.

"Then you'll have to trust me. He is the same cat."

Marian shook her head, looking at Horace.

"He's the same cat," Reg insisted.

"Then how did he get so big?"

Reg floundered for an explanation. "Have you ever heard of a warrior cat?"

"A warrior cat? No. Are you trying to tell me that he is one?"

Reg hesitated before shaking her head. It would make sense. It would be a good explanation. But Reg didn't really want Marian asking questions about dwarfs and cats and finding out that Reg wasn't exactly telling the truth.

"No, but he was visiting one today. And they think that... some of the magic that they use when training Nico might have accidentally rubbed off on him while they were visiting."

"Who is *they*? And Nico? I thought you were at your house; you said he was playing with Starlight."

"He was... but earlier, we went to visit Nico. I thought they might have some answers about Horace's behavior," Reg lied. It might not have been a bad idea to ask, but then she would have had to explain about the kattakyns and what if they said that they wouldn't keep Nico? She couldn't exactly take him back. Especially now that he was so large.

"They?" Marian prompted again.

"Oh. The dwarfs."

"The dwarfs," Marian repeated in a tone of disbelief. "There are no dwarfs around here."

Reg shrugged and didn't try to give an explanation. If she said that they had gone to the Blue Ridge Mountains and back, then Marian would think she was crazy or lying. Or else she would have to explain about her ability to magically transport from one location to the another. And she really didn't want to explain all of that. Marian was already somewhat jealous of Reg's gifts. She didn't need to know how much more there was to it that she hadn't been told about.

"Are you hungry?" Marian asked Horace.

Horace's ears perked up and he looked at Marian eagerly.

"Let's go get some dinner," she told him.

Horace trotted ahead of Marian toward the kitchen where his food bowl was located. Marian shot a glance toward Reg. That was, at least, one sign that Horace was who Reg said he was. Of course, any cat might find his way to the kitchen by smell, but Horace plopped his wide behind down next to his food bowl and waited expectantly. Reg smiled.

"You see? It is Horace."

"That being the case," Marian looked at him. "I'm not sure he needs anything else to eat."

Horace let out a mournful howl. Reg laughed. "He didn't get big from eating too much. It isn't his fault."

Horace meowed, looking at Marian and licking his lips.

Marian gave in and put some food in Horace's bowl. He chowed down immediately.

"I have a feeling he is going to be expensive to feed," Marian commented, hands on her hips, looking down at him.

"He'll probably be extra hungry for a few days and then settle down," Reg suggested. "You know, like a kid going through a growth spurt."

She spoke this as if she were an expert in giant cats and raising children, when she didn't have experience with either one. Marian eyed her, but didn't point out this fact. But Reg couldn't help feeling Marian's doubt and her reluctance to take Horace back. It was, Reg suspected, the last time she would be able to take Horace back. If he came back to her one more time, Marian would say no. She'd had enough.

"Thank you for taking him," Reg told her. "I really appreciate it. I know it hasn't been easy."

"No, it hasn't. He'd better be on his best behavior tonight."

Thinking about the mess outside of the litter box earlier, Reg couldn't help but be anxious about how it would work out. Where was she going to take Horace if Marian wouldn't keep him? And what was she going to do if he kept reappearing in her cottage? How exactly was she going to explain that to Sarah? And how could she stop him from returning?

How was it she could fight immortals and other beings with great powers, but she couldn't persuade one black cat to stay at his new home and stop reappearing in hers?

CHAPTER TWENTY-EIGHT

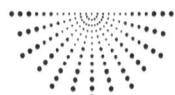

*I*t had been a long day. After everything else, she'd had several readings and a seance to lead, so it wasn't until early in the morning she could relax and make her way to bed. It took a while for her to unwind, and she knew it would be getting light out just as she was falling asleep.

But that was fine. She wouldn't have any more meetings until the next evening. She could sleep however long she wanted. She didn't have to get up for Starlight or Sarah or anyone else who thought there was something wrong with her sleep schedule. It was what worked for her and that was all there was to it.

She tossed and turned restlessly for some time, halfway between dreams and waking. She sank deeper into the dreams, trying to make sense of them. She recognized the funny looking script on the signs. That and the piles of garbage in the street and the dress of the people around her told her that she was back in Egypt. That was good. She had known that she needed to go back to Egypt to find the rightful owner of the gems. Now she was there. A tall Black man with a turban wrapped around his head walked beside her, just slightly in front of her, leading the way through the crowds. Reg didn't like having so many people around her. She had never had a problem with crowds or claustrophobia, but she couldn't shake the feeling that they were watching her. They were all watching her.

Why? They too could sense the gems. They knew she was carrying something valuable. Even with the rings turned in toward her palm so that no one could see the gems in the settings, she knew they still shone like a beacon, calling out to any magical practitioners in the immediate area.

They were all just watching for the opportunity to take the gems and the rings from her. Waiting for her to get distracted. Lying in wait. They were all around her, knowing who she was and what she carried, knowing that when she found the rightful owner of the gems, she would give them away. *Give them away. Something as precious as that. Who would do such a thing?*

"They aren't mine," Reg explained to the people hemming her in. "I am just holding them temporarily. They were stolen, taken away from their rightful owners. They can't be used by anyone else. They are cursed!"

It felt like the rings were writhing on her fingers, trying to work themselves loose. Reg closed her hands into fists, trying to hold on to them.

There were so many people, they were kicking up the dust and breathing all the oxygen. Reg couldn't seem to catch her breath.

"Come on. Give me some space," she puffed. "I can't breathe."

Still the crowds pressed in on her. Reg put her hand on her chest, straining. There was a dull ache spreading across her chest. Was she having a heart attack?

"Can't... help?"

There was a caterwaul in response, startling Reg out of her sleep. She took a huge breath in, but still couldn't seem to get any air. The pressure on her chest grew.

More cat voices. It sounded like a fight. Two cats arguing over territory.

Then the pressure was suddenly gone. Reg sat up. She panted, getting as much air in as quickly as she could. There were a few more yowls, not as angry, and then they tapered off. Starlight jumped up on the bed and nosed at her.

"Hey, Star," Reg puffed. "How are you, bud?"

She was dizzy and lightheaded, black spots dancing before her eyes. But she would be okay in a few minutes. It was just a bad reaction to a nightmare.

Starlight rubbed against her and pushed his way into her lap so that she would hold him and pet him.

Sunlight was streaming in through the window. It would make sense for Reg to get blackout blinds, considering that most of the time she spent in bed it was light outside. But she didn't like to block out the sun. And Starlight wouldn't like it if she blocked the sunbeams he liked to sleep in.

Reg startled when one of the shadows in the closet moved.

"What? What's that?"

Starlight put his ears back, looking at the shape, and gave a low growl in his throat, reminding Reg of the caterwauling she had heard as she woke up from the dream.

"Was that you growling? Is there something in here?"

The shape moved again, and Reg laughed in relief. It was Horace. Horace had come back yet again, and was sniffing around the closet, probably looking for somewhere dark to hide and get some sleep. With Reg talking or shouting out in her dreams, she was probably keeping him awake.

"Horace! What are you doing here? I told you that you were supposed to stay at Marian's. That is your home now, not here."

He meowed in response. A soft, almost kitten-like mew. Reg tried to analyze it, reaching for his feelings.

They were unexpected. Shame, fear, a restlessness and sadness that nearly broke her heart. *Didn't anyone want him? Why couldn't he stay where he wanted to?*

But he couldn't. That was Sarah's decision, not Reg's.

"Come here, Horace. Come get some pets and cuddles. I'm sorry you can't stay here. You need to stop coming back in the night. It isn't because I don't like you, just that I'm not allowed to keep you here. Harrison shouldn't have brought you here to begin with."

After a bit more coaxing, Horace jumped up onto the bed. Reg laughed at the way that it shook when he jumped up. Starlight watched the other cat with suspicion. He knew, of course, that Horace was not an ordinary cat. Horace tried to crawl into Reg's lap like Starlight, but he was too big. He was no lightweight, either. He was good, solid muscle.

She remembered the dream she'd had when they were trying to figure out what the Witch Doctor was doing. Corvin had told Reg about the draugrs, but she didn't really understand what he was talking about. And he hadn't told her everything he knew, just hit a few of the high points.

He had explained to her that the dead that the Witch Doctor raised to become zombies could grow into giants or could shrink down into cats. They could look like a man, or be indistinguishable from any of the other stray cats out there.

Reg didn't know whether the draugr cats—the kattakyns—came in colors other than black. All the ones that the Witch Doctor had created had been pure black, but that didn't mean that other practitioners of the dark arts couldn't give them other markings, like Starlight's tuxedo, socks, and star. Or like a tabby cat. Or maybe they could be ginger cats or calicos instead of black.

She'd had a dream about one of the kattakyns. In the dream, it had lain on her chest. That was fine when it was the size of a small house cat. But as it had lain there, it had grown heavier and heavier, and Reg had experienced that same shortness of breath as in the Egypt dream. Until Starlight had attacked and chased the kattakyn in her dream away.

Others had not been so lucky. There had been several reports of people who had died in their sleep behind locked doors from asphyxia and crush injuries. Reg had been the one to suggest that the draugr cats might have done it, as one had tried to do to her. Corvin had confirmed the legends that the draugrs could kill that way, and that was all the proof that Reg needed. Her own experience, backed up by Corvin's studies.

Reg scratched Horace's ears, looking at him with fresh eyes. Had he been lying on her while she slept and dreamed of Egypt? She petted him in long, even strokes, thinking about it. While he was calming as she petted him, his foremost emotion was still the same.

Shame.

Why shame?

Because he had lain on her and cut off her breath? Because he had put her life in danger until Starlight had chased him off?

"Is that what happened?" Reg asked softly.

How could a creature who seemed so harmless do anything to hurt her? She understood that he was scared and wanted to stay with her, but why hurt her? He might have killed her if Starlight hadn't intervened. Just like those other people had been killed.

Horace buried his nose in Reg's palm and continued to rub against her, purring and drinking up the attention. Reg's eyes burned. What was she going to do with him? How could she manage such a creature?

Draugrs could enter a house through someone's dreams. That must have been how Horace had returned to her night after night when there was no physical way into the house.

She had completely forgotten all of that. Francesca had bound them into their cat form so that they could not shift into the giant draugrs. But none of them had considered that the kattakyns themselves might be dangerous. They were not just cats. Even though they might look like and act like cats, there was another side to them.

And Horace had been unbound. They had all focused on how that meant that a piece of the Witch Doctor was out there, maybe held in the hands of someone who meant to gather all the pieces back together and re-form the Witch Doctor. They had talked about the changes in Horace's behavior.

But they hadn't talked about the fact that he might no longer be bound to his kattakyn form. What if as well as being able to smother her, he could now shift into giant form? Was his growth—and Nico's, for that matter—an indication that he still had some power to shift his form? Or was it just dwarf magic and the power of her rings?

"This is not good," Reg murmured. She continued to pet and cuddle with Horace, trying to give him all the love and assurance she could. It wasn't his fault. He hadn't chosen his nature any more than she had chosen her parentage or Corvin had chosen his condition.

But what were they going to do if Horace were a dangerous draugr? And what about the rest of them?

CHAPTER TWENTY-NINE

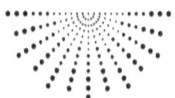

*O*nce both cats were reassured, fed, and snoozing on the bed, Reg started making her plans.

She put aside her worries about the kattakyn, focusing instead on Egypt. She had been promising herself and the gems that she would take them back to Egypt at the earliest possible opportunity, but she kept putting it off. Now she was going to get down to business.

It wasn't because she was avoiding the question of what to do about Horace. She'd been planning to go back to Egypt again for a while. It wasn't anything to do with avoiding more immediate, unpleasant responsibilities.

She wasn't sure how long her trip to Egypt would be. The travel itself was instantaneous, but she didn't know how long she would need to be there to find the rightful owners of the gems. It could be a few days, so she needed to be prepared for that instead of assuming, as she had before, that she would be back in time for supper. She needed to consider food, clothing, and how she would get lodging. She didn't know exactly where she was going, so she couldn't make a hotel reservation ahead of time. But maybe she should at least go to the bank and get some Egyptian money. She wouldn't be able to liquidate any gems on her arrival. She would need cash for food and lodgings. It would be too dangerous to just sleep on the street or find a shelter.

As she packed items into a bag, her phone vibrated in her pocket. Reg considered ignoring it, then decided it might be important and slid it out of her pocket.

Corvin. Of course.

"Hi."

"Regina."

"What do you want, Corvin? I'm kind of busy."

"I did sense that."

"If you know I'm busy, then why are you calling me? I have things to do."

"You're leaving?"

"I didn't say that."

"You don't need to."

She wasn't sure how strong the psychic connection was for him, whether he could see her face or what she was doing. Or could he just sense her restlessness or her intent to leave? It took all of her focus to make her preparations. It shouldn't surprise her that he could sense that.

"You're going to Egypt?" Corvin demanded.

"If I am, it's none of your business."

"I should be there with you. You'll need someone who knows the country. Some of the language."

Though Corvin's language skills had proven not to be quite adequate the last time they had gone to Egypt. He knew some ancient Egyptian. He wasn't so good at the modern stuff.

"I'll be fine."

"Reg, it's too dangerous for a woman to go there unaccompanied."

"For a normal woman, maybe," Reg agreed. "But that's not taking my gifts into account. I can manage myself."

"Like you did when we went to see Kareem?"

Kareem had wielded part of the Witch Doctor's powers. And that, combined with his own natural gifts, had been too much for Reg. She had put a protective shield around herself and Corvin, but then had realized that she couldn't perform any magic from within that bubble of protection. She couldn't jump them back to Florida. She couldn't counterattack. It was a difficult lesson to learn—that a shield was not always the best solution and should not be her first line of defense. She needed to keep herself open to act, preserve her options.

"That's different. And I learned something from that."

"Yes. We both did," Corvin agreed.

"I'm not taking you," Reg reiterated. "Is that everything?"

"You're not thinking clearly. If you were, you would realize that this is a bad idea. You can't just go hopping all over the globe and expect to be able to handle whatever situation you put yourself in."

"Okay, gotta go now." Reg hit the red button to cut off the call. She watched the phone and waited for a moment, knowing that he would call right back. When he did, she rejected the call, sending it directly to voicemail. He tried one more call, and then a series of texts. Reg put down the phone and continued packing.

* * *

Reg made all the arrangements that she could think of. Francesca could come by and feed the cats. Reg took her date book over to Sarah and explained that she'd be gone for a day or two, but everything was taken care of and she didn't need to worry about taking care of Starlight or anything else at the cottage. Hopefully, that would keep Sarah from popping by the house while Reg was gone and discovering that Horace —a bigger and more dangerous Horace—was back once more. It was only for a day or two. Then Reg could get everything straightened out.

Even while she prepared herself for the leap to Egypt, Reg couldn't totally banish the problems that Horace presented from her thoughts. How was she supposed to keep him from entering her dreams—or anyone else's—in the future? Starlight had protected her from death by kattakyns twice now, but could she really expect him to always be keeping an eye on her? How could she keep Horace from returning to her house, no matter what kind of home she found for him?

She knew that she was avoiding the real question. Corvin had talked to her, back in the beginning when they first became aware that the Witch Doctor was raising draugrs, about the difficulty of fighting them. There were only a couple of ways to completely kill a draugr. Since they were dead already, most methods didn't have any effect on them. The Vikings had tried to bury bodies deep down underground, with a big tombstone over the grave, to make sure that bodies could not rise again. But that hadn't stopped them.

There was such a disconnect in Reg's mind between the kattakyns and the hideous draugr giants. As if they were two separate beings instead of two different physical forms of the same creature. She couldn't imagine using one of those methods on the cats that she had grown to love. Horace could kill her. It was part of his makeup. But she couldn't even think of hurting him.

She picked up her bag and closed her eyes, trying to calm the rapid beating of her heart and to focus her thoughts on Egypt instead of worrying about Horace. Horace would have to wait until she got back. Maybe if she let the problem simmer in the back of her mind for a couple of days, her unconscious mind would come up with an effortless solution all on its own.

Reg held the gems in the plastic bag in her hand, deep in the pocket of her skirt. With the other hand, she touched the rings, stroking across them with her thumb. She inhaled deeply, remembering the feeling and the smell of the drier air in Egypt. She remembered the heat of the sun on her skin. The pungent smells. The cadences of the language she couldn't understand.

And then she was there.

CHAPTER THIRTY

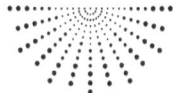

*T*he heat and the dry air. The sounds of the voices around her. All as she had remembered and imagined them. And not all of it was from her previous visit to Egypt. Some of it had come to her in her dreams. She had been dreaming about Egypt since the time she had left and hadn't even realized it. Those dreams seemed almost more real than the memories.

Reg looked around, hoping for some sign of where she was supposed to go. There must be a reason the gems had brought her there. Some person she was supposed to talk to or sight she was supposed to see. There had to be something to lead her back to the origin of the gems or the rightful owners.

No one appeared to have noticed her materializing out of thin air. Had everyone blinked at the same time? Been distracted by something in a shop or stand? Or had they seen her, but denied the possibility of a human being appearing out of nowhere and had explained it away?

Whatever the reason, everyone around her went about their own business as if they hadn't noticed her, other than a tall Black man with a turban whose eyes remained on her for a few seconds. Reg walked around for a bit, looking at the store windows and street vendors, waiting for something to occur to her. She was beginning to get worried, thinking that she would not be able to find her purpose for being there. She fingered the rings, trying to decide on a course of action.

"A tour of the pyramids for madam?" a man asked, leaning in close and flashing a folded brochure in front of her eyes.

Reg startled and withdrew slightly, putting a little more space between her body and the man, feeling crowded. She looked him over. He gave her a big smile that showed several gaps between his teeth. Older than she was, brown-skinned, slender. He gave a little bow. "You would like to see the pyramids, would you not?"

"How did you know I speak English?" Reg asked.

He beamed at her. "You look American. Are you not?"

"Yeah. But I didn't know I looked any different from anyone else." Reg looked down at herself. She had changed out of her usual fortune teller garb, exchanging bright skirts and scarves for khakis and a loose white t-shirt with long sleeves. She knew it would be hot in Egypt, but the videos she had watched on sightseeing in Egypt had advised that all women should wear long pants and sleeves so as not to attract unwanted attention from men who would see her bare skin as an invitation.

She didn't think that she looked all that different from the other women around her. She wasn't wearing any kind of headscarf or veil, but she certainly wasn't the only one. Something about her, though, had given her nationality away.

"Well, yes," she admitted. "I am."

"You like to see the pyramids?"

Reg hesitated, not sure that was where she was supposed to go. But maybe this was the invitation she had been looking for. The sign pointing which way to go next.

"Tombs of the great pharaohs? Where they were buried with great splendor in preparation for the afterlife?" the man suggested.

Great splendor. Definitely a sign pointing toward the possible origins of the gems. If the rings were so ancient, then it made sense, didn't it, that they had come from a tomb? So many of the tombs of the kings had been raided over the years, stripped of gold and jewels and other finery. She'd even heard that it had once been in vogue to have mummy unwrapping parties.

Reg shuddered at the idea of a group of women nattering away and squealing as they pulled away the burial shrouds from a brown, desiccated body. How could such a thing ever have been considered proper?

"Yes," she told the man, who was still hovering, waiting for her answer. "That sounds very interesting."

He bowed, pleased. "My name is Ahmed, madam. I am very pleased to make your acquaintance."

"I'm Reg. Reg Rawlins. Good to meet you too. So where do we go? Do you have a car?"

"I will make arrangements for us to take a tour tomorrow. It is too late in the day to begin now. That would be acceptable?"

Reg looked at the sky. It was later in the day than she had thought. She had forgotten about the time zone differences.

"Yes. Of course. Do you have a card?"

He pressed the brochure into her hand. "All on here. Do you have a phone?"

"I do, but..." Reg pulled her phone out to look at it. As she had expected, there was no service provider named in the top corner. No service bars.

Ahmed stretched his neck to look at her screen. He nodded. "You need a SIM card." He pressed her shoulder to turn her around and pointed at what might be a grocer or convenience store. "You can get one there. Would you like me to help you?"

"Uh, yeah." Reg gave him a grateful smile. Despite planning ahead, she had not understood all the ins and outs of phone service when jumping across the ocean. She had hoped that her phone would recognize a service partner in Egypt and she wouldn't have to do anything. She could go into the store by herself, point at her phone, and hope that the owner charged her a fair price for whatever equipment was needed to make it work. But it would be better if someone local could help her out.

"Of course, madam." Ahmed bowed again. "It would be my pleasure."

Already, Reg was experiencing greater hospitality than she had when she had arrived there with Corvin. No one had approached her and offered to help then. The difference was probably Corvin. When people saw him with Reg, they assumed that she was taken care of. On her own, she would get more offers of help.

Probably more people trying to scam her too, but she was a psychic. She would be able to weed out the con artists. She had plenty of experience in that regard.

Ahmed walked with her over to the store and negotiated with the man at the counter. They argued back and forth about the price and, eventually, Ahmed told Reg the price. She took out the Egyptian currency she had purchased at the bank before leaving Black Sands and showed him, unsure of the denominations. Ahmed took what he needed from the bundle, handed it to the cashier, and returned the change to Reg.

The cashier displayed the SIM card that Reg had purchased and asked a question. Reg looked at Ahmed.

"He can install it for you," Ahmed said. "If you give him your phone."

Reg handed over her phone and watched the man pop out the SIM card drawer and replace her old SIM card with the new one. He carefully put the old one into the folder the new one had come in, patted it, and said something to Reg.

"To keep it safe," Ahmed said. "You will need it when you go back home."

"Thank you!" Reg received her phone and the folder back and put them into her purse. "You have both been very helpful."

Both men nodded and bowed. Ahmed indicated the brochure and pointed to the phone number on it. "This is my number. We will meet early tomorrow so that we have plenty of time to tour the tombs. You would like to see the pyramids *and* the Valley of the Kings?"

"Sure. Will we have time for both?"

"With an airplane ticket, yes."

"Oh. That sounds expensive." Maybe she could do just the pyramids and then jump to the Valley of the Kings later if she needed to. She could find another guide there.

"No, not expensive," Ahmed assured her. He showed her packages listed in the brochure. "You see? Very reasonable."

Reg tried to breathe through her anxiety over spending so much. She had the money from the dwarfs. She didn't need to worry about the cost. It really wasn't bad for a full-day tour, including airplane tickets. And she could get everything done in a day and, hopefully by the end of it, have rehomed the gems, or at least she would know where she was supposed to take them. And then she could go back home to Black Sands.

And deal with Horace?

She pushed thoughts of Horace away. She could only deal with one problem at a time. Horace was safe in her house. As long as he stayed there, she didn't have anything to worry about. Maybe he would knock things down or break things while she was away. Maybe he would refuse to use the litter box. But he would be safe and so would everyone else.

Ahmed was looking at her face anxiously. "It is okay?" he asked. "Or you do not wish to go to the Valley of the Kings? You could catch a bus or rent a car, but it takes eight hours and would not be much cheaper than by plane."

"It's okay," Reg said. "It's perfect. What do you take? I don't think I have that much cash with me."

"You can e-transfer," he assured her. "Just text it to my phone number. You can use this currency converter." He took the brochure back from her, pulled a pen from his pocket, and wrote down a URL. "Just send US dollars. That is perfectly fine."

"Very efficient." Reg nodded. It was a good thing that she had deposited Gwythr's cash portion into her bank account before leaving, because she didn't know whether the bank would freeze the certified check for ten days as Gwythr had suggested. With the deposit, she knew she could make the e-transfer to Ahmed. "How early do we need to start?"

"Seven o'clock?" Ahmed suggested. At the look on her face, he quickly revised. "Eight o'clock? Nine?"

"Uh," Reg sucked air in through her teeth. It was still really early for her. But her body was on Florida time, so maybe it would be okay. And if she didn't sleep well before going, she could sleep on the plane halfway through the day. Have a little siesta. "Eight-thirty?"

"Eight-thirty." Ahmed agreed. "What hotel are you at?"

"I don't know yet."

He gave her the tolerant sort of look that she might get from Corvin when she didn't know something that he thought was basic magical knowledge, or from a foster mom who thought she was missing some vital life skill despite all the families that she had been through.

"How much you want to pay?"

Reg tried to come up with a reasonable price range. She didn't usually stay at hotels. Sometimes at a shelter or a hostel, a room to rent in someone's apartment. Whatever she could afford to get herself off the street. She made a tentative suggestion to Ahmed, and he nodded quickly. Apparently, she had not given a price that was so rock bottom low he thought she was crazy.

"You should stay at the Cleo," he told her. "Very clean, nice rooms, Wi-Fi, breakfast. I can meet you there and take you to the pyramids without having to go through traffic." He rolled his eyes. "You would not believe traffic in Giza."

Reg made agreeable noises.

"You want to go there now? I will get you a taxi?"

"Sure. Is there somewhere to eat?"

"Good restaurant. Some bars and clubs on the street." He spread his hands wide. "I would not recommend them for an unaccompanied lady. Best to stay in the restaurant. Good food. You will like."

"Egyptian food or American food?" Reg asked uneasily.

"They have some American. Plenty to tourists' tastes."

"Okay. Yeah. That sounds good."

He nodded and stepped out into the street, whistling shrilly and waving down a taxi. The car pulled over and the driver looked at them both.

Ahmed gave the driver rapid instructions Reg couldn't understand, but she did hear the word "Cleo" among the rest. Ahmed made a gesture in Reg's direction, rubbing his fingers together and looking expectant. Reg frowned. "What?"

"Your money? I pay him now, you don't have to negotiate when you get there. I get you fair price."

"Oh, okay. Thank you." Reg pulled out her money again, Ahmed stepping between her and the taxi to shield her money from the driver's view. He took a couple of bills and waited until Reg put the rest back away before turning to the driver. He dickered over the price for a few minutes and then handed the money over and shook hands with the driver. He turned back to Reg.

"It is all arranged. He will take you to the hotel. Get yourself a nice room. It is very reasonable. If you have any troubles, you call me." He indicated the brochure. "You have my number. I will deal with anybody who gives you trouble."

Reg smiled. "You've been so helpful, Ahmed. I will see you tomorrow."

CHAPTER THIRTY-ONE

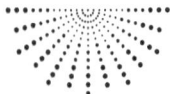

*R*eg was relieved when the taxi pulled up in front of a hotel with Cleopatra splashed all over the signs and let her out. He did not demand any further payment. Two more marks in Ahmed's favor. He had been a godsend, eager to help her with whatever she needed.

She thanked the driver and nodded at him a couple of times as she climbed out of the car with her purse and her luggage and leaned down to close the door again. He seemed pleasant and satisfied with the transaction.

That just went to show Corvin. She could take care of herself without him, even in Egypt.

Reg walked through the lobby and approached the front desk. The desk clerk nodded at her, smiling, and waited expectantly.

"Do you speak English?" Reg asked, suddenly nervous.

"Of course, madam," he spoke with perfect British diction, "How may I help you today?"

"I need a room for the night. My... guide said that this was the best hotel." She smiled, hoping this would help her get a good rate.

"We are honored. What were you thinking, and how many nights?"

"I'm hoping just one night." Ahmed had said to get a good room, so Reg tried to envision what that might be. "Uh... queen bed?"

"We are happy to oblige." He tapped a query into the computer on the desk and scanned the screen. "We have the princess suite available. Always very popular with the Americans."

"That sounds expensive. I really just need a room…"

"You will be very happy with the princess suite. A queen bed separated from a sitting room and kitchenette. Jetted tub, very nice at the end of a long day of walking. Very good Wi-Fi signal in that part of the hotel."

It sounded very nice, but Reg was still worried about the price. He quoted her a number, and she tried to figure out what that translated to in US dollars. Sensing this, the man gave her the US price.

"Really? Well… yeah, that sounds really good. Is that all-in? All the room taxes or whatever?"

"Of course." He smiled. "Perhaps at that price you will be willing to spend more than one night with us?"

Reg smiled. "Maybe. I really don't know how long I will be yet; it depends on how things work out. Is that room available for a few days, if I end up needing it for longer?"

"It is. Shall I ring that up, then?"

Reg nodded. "Yes, thank you."

He did so, fingers working busily over the computer keyboard. He made pleasant small talk, asking her about where she was from and which sights she planned to see.

"It is your first time in Egypt?"

"No… I mean, it's my first time as a tourist. I was here before, but just for a few hours. I didn't get a chance to see anything."

He nodded understandingly. He printed off forms and prepared a folder for her with the room card key slotted into a special holder. As he handed it to her, his eyes strayed to her hand, looking at the rings. Reg touched them and tried to think of what to tell him. He hadn't actually asked anything, but clearly wanted to know how this American woman came to be wearing ancient Egyptian rings. Reg wanted to tell him that they were not hers and she would be trying to find the rightful owner, but it didn't seem like the right time. She closed her mouth and said nothing.

"It has been a pleasure, madam. Please give me a call if there is anything you need."

"Thanks." Reg looked around, checking out where the various amenities, including the restaurant, were.

"The elevator is over there. Your room is on the third floor."

Reg nodded and headed in the direction he had pointed, not seeing the elevator alcove until she was practically on top of it. She pressed the up arrow and waited.

A man approached. Tall, very black skin, with a turban. His face was aged, but she couldn't be sure whether he was fifty or seventy. He looked as though he'd spent a lot of time in the sun. Reg glanced around, wondering why he was walking directly toward her. Maybe it was just for the elevator. Like Reg, he was going up to his room. But then she saw her duffel bag on his arm.

"Oh!" She looked at her shoulder and saw that she had her large purse, but had put down her luggage. "Thank you!"

He handed it to her and gave a bow. Reg studied him. He seemed very familiar. But how could anyone in Egypt be familiar to her? Other than Kareem or Ahmed. But it wasn't either of them.

"Thank you very much. I guess I wouldn't have gotten very far without this."

He didn't say anything, only nodded again, bowing very slightly. The elevator opened. Reg got on and nodded to him, feeling awkward. She had already thanked him and didn't know what else to say. Have a nice day? Thank you again? She didn't even know whether he could speak English. She felt like she should say something, but couldn't decide what it was before the elevator doors closed again, Reg inside and her helper outside.

Reg smiled and shook her head, and hit the button for the third floor. So far, her trip was going well. She had met some very nice people who had been more helpful than she could have asked for. She walked down the hall looking at the room numbers and found the princess suite a few doors down the hall from the elevator. Close enough to be handy, but hopefully not so close that she would be hearing it and all the conversations of people who got on and off the elevator all night long. The desk clerk had said that it was a popular room for Americans. Americans tended to be high-maintenance guests, and she expected that if the room were too noisy, they would have complained about it.

She used the card key to let herself in. It was a beautiful suite. As

Ahmed had promised, it was very clean, as if the maid had just given it the full treatment, not a stain or speck of dust to be seen anywhere. The sitting room was lovely, furnished in sand and pastel colors that echoed notes of the desert. The furniture looked soft and comfortable, and there were a couple of paintings and pieces of decor that were there just for the pleasing effect. There was a large armoire which she assumed held the TV behind its closed doors, and the remote was not screwed into the side table that held a lamp handy for someone who wanted to read. The lamp was not screwed down either.

"Very nice," Reg murmured.

She opened the door to the bedroom, which continued the soft color scheme and tasteful decor. The bed and bedding looked comfortable. The coverlet and linens did not look like they had come from a bulk warehouse somewhere but, instead, as though they had been hand-crafted just for that room. Reg was sure she would be very comfortable there. She put her bag down on the bed.

Her stomach was rumbling. She hadn't had much to eat that day, and was kind of getting tired of cake and ice cream. The restaurant had a grill and looked like it would have a good range of savory selections. The Cleo had been a good recommendation by Ahmed.

* * *

When Reg went down to the restaurant, she walked past the Black man who had retrieved her bag when she had forgotten it. He was just standing around the hotel lobby and, while he didn't have a name tag or anything else to identify him, she supposed he was probably security or maybe a concierge or other employee of the hotel. That would make more sense than his just being a guest or other passerby. She nodded to him as she went past, but he made no response.

In the restaurant, she ordered herself a drink and perused the menu, which had a combination of both local dishes and good old American and English classics. Hamburgers, fish and chips, pasta, grilled vegetables. Something for everyone. A waiter and waitress both waited on Reg, even though the restaurant was pretty full and they could probably have been used elsewhere. At least one of them. She certainly didn't need two people waiting on her.

She ordered a steak sandwich and, while she waited for it to be prepared, people-watched the other patrons of the restaurant. They were mostly tourists, as she had expected. Maybe a few who were there on business, but the overwhelming majority were tourists, mostly American and European. She tried to guess the stories of each of them, but it wasn't really fair, since she could not only see their auras and read their faces, but could also hear the inner thoughts of many of them. A place like that would have made a great location to pick up new clients. She would dress as an Egyptian mystic, offering to tell people about their ancestors who hailed from Egypt, and would tell them some great stories to make them feel good about themselves. She'd make a killing. Until the management caught on and kicked her out.

But she wasn't there as a psychic or a con. She wasn't there to read their stories or to make anything up.

Which made the ghosts who crowded in around Reg groan with disappointment, as they wanted her to tell their stories.

CHAPTER THIRTY-TWO

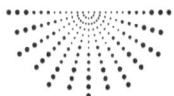

*R*eg eventually made her way back up to her room, where she watched a little TV until she thought she could fall asleep, and then lay in bed thinking about sleeping and restlessly tossing and turning. She watched some more videos on her phone, telling herself that it didn't matter what time she fell asleep. She would be able to have a nap on the plane anyway. It was just one time she was expected to get up early in the morning, and with the time difference between Florida and Egypt, it wasn't really even early.

But she kept thinking about the rings, warm on her fingers, and what she would be able to find out the next day. Would Ahmed lead her directly where she needed to go? Would she find a place in the pyramids that she was supposed to leave the gems? Or was she supposed to ask Ahmed or give them to him? He was the one who had shown up when she had needed to know where to go, and maybe all she had to do was to give the gems to him to be cleansed. He hadn't given her any signals that he was a practitioner of magic, but he might know a holy man who was able to cleanse the gems for him, or they might be cleansed simply by giving them to Ahmed, if he were the rightful owner.

But she didn't get the feeling he was the one to give them to. They had provided her with a guide, but she didn't think he was the final destination.

Reg punched her pillow into shape and tried again to just let it go and float away into sleep. But she was so distracted by the unfamiliar place, the bed and sheets that didn't feel like hers, the lack of cats, and the noise of people walking up and down the hallway talking to each other. Even when they didn't speak loudly enough to disturb her, she could still hear random thoughts and found it very distracting when she was trying to empty her mind for sleep.

She had pretty much given up on sleep when she started to fall into dreams. Wild, restless dreams that made her feel unsettled and like she hadn't really gotten any sleep at all. She was finally in Egypt, but her dreams were still filled with images of walking the Egyptian streets or exploring the sites that she had only ever seen on TV or in books. How many times as a child had she wondered whether she would ever get to see anything like the pyramids up close? She had known that it was very unlikely, as a child with no family and no means. No education because she would never be able to pay for it. What kind of job was she going to get that would provide her with the money she needed to travel the world? There was always the possibility of marrying someone with money, but the thought had never appealed to Reg. She valued her independence too much and couldn't imaging fawning over a man and marrying him just because he had the means to provide her with the material things that she wanted in life.

She kept falling asleep, dreaming she was in the pyramids or some other tomb, and then waking up and finding out that she hadn't even begun her journey. It was frustrating to be so close and yet not to have started. She wished it was morning so that she could just get ready and meet Ahmed. She wanted to get started.

There was a heaviness on Reg's chest that she recognized and, even in the light state of sleep that she was in, it took her a few minutes before she could wake herself up to deal with it. She couldn't let him smother her in her sleep, getting heavier and heavier until the breath was crushed out of her.

Reg awoke and tried to turn onto her side to tip Horace off of her. She couldn't move. She ran her fingers through his fur and murmured to him, trying to coax him into getting off. If Starlight were there, he would have chased Horace off, but she had left Starlight back in Florida, thinking she would not need him in Egypt.

There was a loud knock on the door. Horace startled, leapt from her, and darted around the room looking for somewhere to hide. Eventually, he pushed his way under one of Reg's rumpled blankets and was still, his hindquarters and tail exposed. Reg chuckled at his hiding place. She got up to answer the door, wondering who it could be so early in the morning. She hadn't left a wake-up call, though maybe she should. It wasn't light enough yet outside the window for it to be time to get up. What, then?

She padded across the sitting room area to the hallway door and peered out through the peephole. There was no one there. Reg hesitated. Was someone waiting in the hallway for her to look out, in order to take her off guard? She stretched out her senses, searching for anyone close by, but could only sense the people sleeping in the next room on either side. No one in the hallway. No one lurking around with evil, predatory thoughts. She left the chain on the door and opened it a crack, and then as far as it would go with the chain on. She still couldn't see or sense anyone. There was no notice under or in front of her door. It was as if whoever had knocked on the door had simply walked away afterward, leaving no sign as to why he had disturbed her sleep.

It was lucky he had, though.

Reg put a "Do Not Disturb" sign on the door handle, closed the door, and bolted it. Then she returned to the bedroom. She gently uncovered the big black cat on the bed.

"Horace… what are you doing here, huh? You weren't supposed to come here to Egypt."

He started to purr, rubbing against her hand.

"Horace. You wanted to be at my house, so I left you at my house. I'll find you somewhere new. But you can't… follow me halfway around the world. You need to stay in the house, where it's safe." Reg looked around the bedroom. It wasn't exactly like there was anything dangerous there, but she couldn't help feeling like he had put himself in jeopardy coming back to Egypt. That was where he had lived with Kareem. That was where he had been taken advantage of, the powers of the Witch Doctor that were bound to him unwound and taken away. He had been robbed of something that was a big part of him. She didn't have any doubt that he might have been abused or neglected in other ways. Kareem obviously hadn't cared about him. He'd had cats before, but he hadn't shown any special affection or affinity to Horace. There was no sign that he put the cat before him in anything.

"I want you to be safe, and this isn't the right place for you. Do you understand? You shouldn't be here. And I can't leave you here in the hotel when I go out with Ahmed. You can't stay here."

Horace just purred and cuddled against her as closely as he could. As if by doing that, he could make up for the fact that he kept trying to kill her. She stroked and scratched and tried to let him know that she didn't hold it against him. He couldn't help what he was. But she didn't know what to do about him. There was no way that she could trust him. But she could never hurt him either. How could she protect him and protect herself and others from the dangerous draugr?

CHAPTER THIRTY-THREE

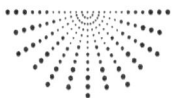

*B*y morning—real morning when it was actually light outside —Reg had made the decision to take Horace back to Black Sands. He would be safer there than in Egypt. She couldn't stop him from coming to her again if she fell asleep and dreamed, but she didn't think that would happen again before she returned home. She had every chance of being able to return the gems and rings to their source during the day, and then her quest would be complete. She could return home, knowing that she had done the right thing and no longer dealing with the disruption that the rings were causing. The money from the sale of gems to Gwythr would clear her account so that she would be able to buy whatever she needed. She would continue to work as a psychic, not necessarily because she would need the money, but because she enjoyed it. She liked working with people and helping to answer their questions and to make contact with the other side. It was important work and people appreciated working with someone with real talent, not just someone trying to take them for a ride.

She could jump Horace back to Black Sands, jump herself back to Egypt again without him, and then continue with her quest. No one would be any the wiser that Horace had returned briefly to Egypt.

It was too bad that cats were no longer worshiped in Egypt. Then maybe she could have just taken him to a temple there and made a new life for him with people waiting on him hand and… paw. Maybe he would have liked that and would have been convinced to stay there instead of following Reg. And they would love him because he was so big and friendly and had some powers, even if they were sort of dark.

But, no more cat temples in Egypt, as far as Reg knew. Maybe she could have Harrison take Horace back in time to sometime that was better for him. A time where he would actually like to stay. Maybe they could move all the kattakyns around in time and across multiple realities. That would be more likely to keep them from being reunited as the Witch Doctor than just trying to separate them in space, wouldn't it?

With Horace heavy in her arms, Reg closed her eyes and imagined herself back in her bedroom in Black Sands. She saw the picture in her head and focused on the smell of her room, the feel of the sheets against her skin in the heat of the Florida morning, the humid air tinged with the smell of the ocean.

She opened her eyes and released Horace into her bedroom. "You need to stay here now where it is safe. Understand? I don't want you back in Egypt again. It's too dangerous for you. You don't want to run into Kareem again, do you?"

She didn't even know whether Kareem still existed, or if Harrison had made him vanish from the face of the earth.

But she didn't want to take that chance, and she assumed that Horace wouldn't want to either. "You're safe here. And I'll be back. Probably tonight. Okay? You have to stay here until I come back."

Horace yowled unhappily. Reg went out to the kitchen to put a little food in both of the bowls. Francesca would still be coming by to feed them, but Horace could use a little treat. Because of the amount he needed for his larger body, if nothing else. She didn't want to starve him.

She put a little tuna in each of the bowls. She looked around. Where was Starlight?

"Star! Starlight! Come and eat."

She hadn't seen him in the bedroom. He hadn't been in his usual sunny morning spot. She had expected to see him in the living room window or hanging out with his bowl in the kitchen. But he wasn't in either place. The house felt cold and empty, not like it usually did.

"Starlight?"

She made a quick tour of the cottage looking for him, but there wasn't that much more to see. He wasn't in his litter box or hiding under the bed or the couch. The door to Reg's spare room was still shut like usual, but she opened it anyway just to make sure that he hadn't managed to get locked in there.

Where else could he have gone? Had he slipped out the door when Sarah or Francesca had been there? She couldn't imagine that either of them would have been careless enough to let him escape. There was no note telling her what had happened. He just wasn't there.

Reg made sure that she didn't let Horace out as she left the cottage to take a quick look outside.

"Starlight? Where are you, Star?"

There was no answering meow or sign of the cat. Reg looked through the underbrush, hoping to spot him hiding underneath, playing that he was a wild jungle cat. But there was no sign of him. Reg wandered into the garden. Sunning himself in a bright beam of sunlight in the garden? Seeing if he could fish anything out of the fountain or pond? There was no sign of him.

She reached out with her mind, calling to Forst.

Are you here?

Reg Rawlins! Forst pushed his way through some tall plants to reach her. *It is wonderful to see you. I thought... you were away.*

I was. I came back for just a minute because of the cats. But I can't find Starlight. You haven't seen him outside, have you?

No, Forst shook his head with certainty. *He is never outside.*

Yeah. That's what I thought. But I can't find him inside and there's no note to say that Francesca took him to her house or that he escaped. I don't know what to think.

You could perhaps call her on your device. Forst held his hand up to his ear in explanation.

Reg pulled out her phone to do just that. But there were no service bars. Reg stared at it for a moment before it made sense. The US SIM card was still back in Egypt in her luggage. She couldn't make any calls until she put it back in.

Oh, right. It isn't working right now.

Forst nodded. *Perhaps she will come here. I can watch for her.*

Would you? She must just have taken him to her house for a play date with Nicole, I think. Of course she wouldn't leave me a note, because she wasn't expecting me to be back in the time that he was gone.

Yes. I will watch for her. She will bring the cat back. If she returns and does not have him, I will ask her.

Reg knew how difficult it was for Forst to use his "outside words" and speak out loud to communicate with humans, so she knew he did not promise lightly.

You're a lifesaver. Thank you so much. I really appreciate it.

Forst smiled more broadly and nodded at her. *Of course. The cat is part of your family.*

Yes, he is, Reg agreed. *I wouldn't have left if I had thought that anything might happen to him while I was gone. I thought he would be safe at home with Francesca looking in on him.*

He is surely safe. He is a very wise creature.

That helped to reassure Reg too. The last time that Starlight had escaped, he had returned with an herbal remedy that she had needed. He had not been harmed. She was sure that if he had gone off, he must have had a reason, and he would intend to return to her safely.

But probably he was just hanging out with Nicole.

You're right. He wouldn't just take off and run away, she agreed with Forst. *He can take care of himself.*

He had powers, Reg knew. She didn't know what those powers were and why he normally didn't choose to use them, living with her just as a regular house cat. But if there were a need for him to use his powers, then he would, wouldn't he? He would protect himself and he would come back to her.

Reg's phone vibrated and she pulled it back out of her pocket to look at it. She knew it wouldn't be a call, because she was too far away from the Egyptian service providers. It was a calendar appointment she had added to make sure that she wouldn't sleep through the eight-thirty appointment with Ahmed.

You must go, Forst observed.

Yes. You're right. I have to get back there… to finish what I started.

Starlight will be fine. You go and be safe.

Thank you. I'll try not to be too long. Hopefully I'll be back some-time tonight.

Reg returned to the cottage. She had a feeling it probably wasn't considered polite to disappear in front of people. Though she hadn't told Forst anything about what her quest was or where she was going, she had a feeling that he understood exactly where she was going. Perhaps he had a better idea of it than she did.

CHAPTER THIRTY-FOUR

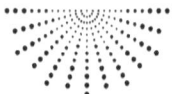

*I*n a few moments, Reg was back in her hotel room at the Cleo. She looked around carefully, making sure that Horace hadn't managed to return with her somehow and that Starlight wasn't there. Was it possible for him to dream travel as well? Or to hitch a ride with Horace? But she didn't see any sign of Starlight in the hotel room. He had not been there.

It was just her.

Reg tried to focus on the job at hand. She stroked the rings on her fingers, thinking about what she was there for. She would find the rightful owner of the rings and the other gems, and she would hand them over, and then return to Florida. Very simple. She was already well on her way to finding out what she needed to know.

Her phone vibrated again. Reg picked up her purse and headed down to the lobby to look for Ahmed. There was a continental breakfast spread in the lobby. Reg grabbed a muffin and a coffee to go. She wasn't a breakfast person, but she figured she'd better have something to sustain her. She took a bite of the muffin as she stepped out of the hotel to check the cars and taxis that were waiting outside. She thought of Harrison. Once again, she was having cake for breakfast. She smiled and shook her head.

"Madam Reg Rawlins?"

Reg looked around and found Ahmed. He gave her a brief bow.

"I trust you slept well?"

Reg rolled her eyes and shook her head. It felt like she'd gotten no sleep at all. "No, not well at all. It wasn't the hotel," she assured him quickly, seeing his head turn toward the Cleo as if he were going to give the manager a piece of his mind. "It was a beautiful room and, as you said, very clean and comfortable. It wasn't anything like that. I just had so much on my mind, and the time zone differences… my body didn't think it was time to sleep yet. And I normally sleep quite late. Or what normal people think is late."

"Perhaps… did you want to postpone, do something else today? And do the tour tomorrow?"

"No. I don't think so. I want to get it done as soon as possible."

Ahmed raised his brows but didn't ask her for her reasons. She supposed that most tourists probably didn't want to get everything done in one day. They probably spread the various sites out over a week or two and did what they felt like each day, doing less if they were tired and more if not. But she wasn't actually a tourist like he thought she was. She wasn't there for her own enjoyment. She had a job to do.

"As you say," Ahmed agreed. "We will begin, then." He looked at her muffin and coffee. "Did you want to finish eating first?"

"No. My stomach isn't really ready for breakfast yet, so I thought I would take it slow. Is it okay? Or you don't like food in your car?" She'd been at several foster homes where food was not allowed in the car. She could understand how parents didn't want to be cleaning up food ground into the upholstery. It didn't take much to make a big mess.

"No, it is fine. You may bring it." He nodded quickly. "Come along, I will show you the car."

Reg followed him to a small white compact car. She wasn't big on cars and couldn't tell whether it was an American or European brand. Or even something from China. When Ahmed opened the door for her, she saw that the interior was spotless, as if it had just come from the dealer. She slid into the passenger seat, regretting the fact that she had only picked up a napkin to catch the crumbs from her muffin and not a proper plate. She didn't want to get crumbs all over Ahmed's car. Even the floor mats were spic and span, and she didn't want to mess anything up.

"Wow, this is beautiful. Is this your car?"

It could be a rental. But Reg didn't get that feeling. "I own it with some other guides," Ahmed explained. "We share it, depending on who needs it on a particular day. Today I have you to take to the pyramids, so I get the car for the morning. When we go to the airport to go to the Valley of the Kings, one of my co-owners will pick it up and he will use it this afternoon for driving around an American couple here for their thirtieth wedding anniversary."

"That sounds like a good arrangement. It's so clean, I wouldn't have guessed that it was a shared vehicle."

Ahmed smiled. "Yes. We keep it very clean. Top working condition, too. No mechanical problems."

Reg thought about her own vehicle and nodded. Every time she had to go very far from the house with it, she always worried that it was going to break down at the worst possible moment. It was an old clunker and she'd put some money into it to try to keep it in good working condition. But it was a failing battle and she knew she would have to replace it soon.

"That's great. You probably put a lot of miles on it too."

"Yes, many kilometers," Ahmed agreed, correcting her subtly. "Now we should go. The pyramids will already be busy by the time we get there."

"Sorry." Reg shrugged. "I know you wanted to get there earlier, but I really don't sleep very well... I needed the extra time."

"Of course. I am not to judge. Different people follow different schedules. Maybe even some want to look at the pyramids at night. Who am I to judge?"

"Can you see them at night?" Reg asked, surprised. "I thought they closed at night. That's why we had to wait until today."

"They are closed," Ahmed agreed. "You can see them in the night, rising up out of the desert... but you cannot go inside." He paused, thinking it over. "It would be very expensive to get someone to open them up late at night."

But maybe if a person had enough wealth, they could arrange for things like that. Reg had never thought of using her money that way. It was strange to think of all the things a person could do with money, if they knew its power.

Reg put on her seatbelt. Ahmed opened the sunroof and pulled out.

It was a pleasant morning. Reg didn't know what the weather usually looked like in Egypt at that time of year, but it was a nice day, cooperating with her needs.

Ahmed chattered to her while he drove, pointing out landmarks and historical sites, filling her in on celebrity gossip, the political situation, and details of how he had gotten into the position of giving people tours. He was independent, clearly, and he obviously knew what he was doing.

Reg could see the pyramids in the distance almost immediately. They were stunning, rising up from the desert, as if they had grown there rather than being built by human hands. How had humans built something so massive without any machinery or blueprints? It was an impossible feat.

The rings on her hand were growing warmer. Reg rubbed them with her thumb, trying to keep them calm. It wasn't as if they were going to burn her. But they kept getting warmer.

"Can we go any faster?" Reg asked, trying to put the feeling from the rings into words.

Ahmed looked at her sideways. He thought she was just being impatient. He had no way of knowing how important it was to identify the proper place for the rings. They were ancient. They needed to be dealt with properly. They had waited a long time to be returned to their native country.

"Of course," Ahmed agreed, giving a nod. He pressed his foot down on the pedal and increased their speed. Reg watched the scenery race by outside her window, a blur of brown.

Traffic slowed as they got closer to the pyramids and Ahmed could not keep up his speed. He shrugged at Reg. "Now we wait."

Reg looked around at the gridlock. She should have gone early, as Ahmed had initially told her. "Maybe there's a back way?"

Ahmed eyed her. Like he would have kept going the way he was going if he knew of a better way?

"There could be," Reg said. "Sometimes there's a different way in. One that most of the tourists don't know about. An access road that the delivery trucks use."

"The pyramids are not Disneyland. We do not have concession stands."

"Staff parking? There must be security, a director or guide or something. They don't just leave the pyramids open for everyone to wander through without any supervision."

"No," Ahmed admitted. "But even if there is another route in, we will not be able to use it. They'll just tell us to turn back around and come back to the public entrance."

"I might be able to talk them into it." Reg kept her thumb rubbing across the rings. They gave her more confidence. And it was working with Ahmed, he was listening to her, considering what she had to say instead of treating her like some crazy American tourist. He wasn't just placating her; she knew the difference.

Eventually, Ahmed conceded. He pulled out of the long lane of traffic he was in and started scanning for roads that led to non-public locations. He knew where all the parking lots and ticket booths were; now he had to think differently. Think about the other roads he had seen and where they might lead to. If one of them would get them closer to the pyramids before the crowds, where Reg would then do her magic and talk someone into letting her in.

For no particular reason.

Just because she was going to talk them into it.

It was a pretty tall order. Reg was thinking through her approach, trying to figure out what she would say to them when they got there. *Please let me in because I have these powerful rings from five thousand years ago and I wanted to bring them home?*

CHAPTER THIRTY-FIVE

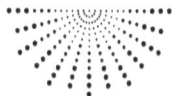

*A*hmed looked in his rear-view mirror a couple of times. Looking back, Reg could see that another car had pulled out of the queue and was following them.

"Maybe security," Ahmed said. "Maybe coming to tell us to get back in the line."

Reg nodded. She watched through the window, but the glare of the sun on the windshield would not allow her to see the driver. If it were a security vehicle, the driver gave them no sign. He didn't flash lights or turn on a siren or honk his horn. Just followed them a car length or two back. Obviously following. Maybe it was just some other tourist who thought that if it worked for them, he could get in too. Someone willing to leave his place in line and take a risk.

Reg turned her attention back to the road. Many of the road signs she had seen had English on them as well as Egyptian, but the ones on the side road that Ahmed had taken did not. They were only in Egyptian, so she couldn't read them and give Ahmed advice as to which one to take.

"What do you think?" she asked. "Is there somewhere back here where we can get in?"

Ahmed shook his head. "Maintenance. Security. Why would any of them let us in?"

"Maintenance, try that. At least they're more likely than security to let us in."

"Really?" Ahmed shook his head. "They do not have the authority to let anyone in. Security at least has the ability to make their own decision on what is safe and who might just be breaking in to write graffiti or break into an off-limits area."

"You think so?"

He nodded.

Reg pressed her lips together, thinking about it. "Okay," she agreed. "Try that, then."

"What are you going to tell them? That you need to get in because...?"

"I don't know yet. I'm working on that."

Ahmed didn't express his disapproval out loud. He just drove until they pulled up to a gated lot. He looked at her.

"Just drive around the bar," Reg advised. "Get us right up to the door inside."

There were a number of smaller buildings at the base of the pyramid, out of the sight of the public. This one was clearly a security center.

"I can't do that."

Reg looked. "There's plenty of room to get by. And there aren't any of those spiky things on the road to pop your tires."

"We are not supposed to go in there."

"Fine. Stop here and I'll walk."

Ahmed looked torn. Eventually, he conceded and drove around the security gate, leaving the guard in the booth yelling after them in Egyptian. The following car performed the same maneuver and the two of them drove up to the doors of the building. Reg smiled weakly at Ahmed and opened her car door. "Wish me luck!"

"Good luck, Reg Rawlins." Accompanied by a head shake of disbelief. The gall of the American to think that she could just walk up to the pyramids and gain entrance based on her charming smile. Reg laughed at him.

The man in the car behind them got out as well. No passengers, only the driver. Reg studied him. It was the same Black man as had helped her with her luggage the night before when she had accidentally left it at the check-in desk in the lobby. The same man as had been watching her when she went to and from the restaurant later. And apparently, he had followed her all the way to the pyramids.

Reg looked at him. His eyes were intense and she was sure she had seen him before. Not just the day before at the hotel, but some other time. "Who are you?"

He gave a little bow and just stared into her eyes without blinking. He didn't say a word.

"You've been watching me. Following me. Who are you?"

He still said nothing. But Reg was not afraid of him. She knew she should be concerned about this tall, dark-skinned man who was following her everywhere. She didn't want to end up another statistic. Women who went to Egypt unaccompanied and thought that they could just act like they were back in the USA. It was a different country. A different culture.

She rubbed the rings, worried, anxious about what was going to happen next. But not at all worried that the man was going to hurt or abduct her. She knew that he was only there to watch over her. He wasn't there to cause her any harm. Just like Ahmed had appeared when Reg had touched the rings and wished that someone would notice her and help her out. There was a reason they were there. She had a mission to perform, and they were both there to help her.

She turned away from the tall Black man and to the door that they had stopped in front of. She pushed the door open and walked into the small, blue-carpeted lobby of the security building. A uniformed guard at the desk scowled at her.

"Who are you and what are you doing here? You can't just ignore all the signs and the gate."

Reg smiled as if he had complimented her. "Thank you. I'm glad I found this place. You will be able to help me out."

He looked uncertain about her reaction. "The public is not allowed to be back here."

"No. Not normally," Reg agreed pleasantly.

He looked at her, clearly wondering what this strange American was up to. Reg continued to smile, trying to think of what to say to him. She touched the rings, closing her eyes briefly.

"But I think you will let me through," she said confidently.

The guard stared at her. "I will let you through?" he repeated in a doubtful voice.

"Thank you."

He blinked at her. "What?"

"You said you will let me through. Thank you."

He walked around the desk to where Reg was, looking at her, then turned and motioned to a door on the other side of the lobby. "I will need to show you through. It isn't an area normally accessed by tourists."

"That would be great. Thanks. And can my guide come too—?"

The guard looked behind Reg and nodded. "Of course."

Reg turned and saw the tall Black man standing behind her. He had followed her into the lobby, quiet as cat's paws. Ahmed was still sitting in the car, waiting for her to come back out, or maybe to be thrown out by a couple of armed guards.

"No, I meant—"

It was too late; the guard was already escorting her to the back door. The other man followed close behind them.

"It's just that—"

The guard hustled her through the door into the dingy hallway behind. Reg had to walk briskly to keep up with him and was glad that she had worn comfortable shoes. They worked their way through a series of corridors without comment. Eventually, they emerged into a dark passageway built out of sandstone blocks. The guard closed the door behind them and escorted Reg around a rope security barrier to the other side, where members of the public were lined up to purchase tickets. He took her to the cashier.

"A special pass for Miss…" He looked at Reg inquiringly.

"Rawlins. Reg Rawlins."

He nodded. The cashier looked puzzled by the turn of events, but began tapping commands into her computer, and printed off a couple of security name tags to be attached to her lapel and that of her mysterious companion. Reg looked surreptitiously at the other tag to see what it said. While hers had her name on it along with the "special guest" designation that of the man merely said, "Escort."

"Don't you have a name?" she asked him jokingly.

He looked at her and didn't answer.

Reg didn't know what to make of the apparently mute man. She didn't feel threatened by him, but he had an obvious interest in her, having been helping and watching her since the previous evening. He had followed her there and presented himself as her guide when Ahmed had not believed that she would be able to get in.

When she tried to explore his consciousness to find out more about him, She found a closed door. While he let his feelings of interest and protectiveness toward her be felt, everything else was hidden. She couldn't identify him or what his intent was.

But he wasn't trying to deceive her or hurt her, as far as she could tell, so she would just have to accept that he had a reason to be there that would be revealed later. It was certainly something to do with the rings and the other gems. Maybe he was the one who was there to lead her to the rightful owner of the gems. She had believed that someone would show her the way, and he had attached himself to her.

With their visitor tags fastened to their shirts, they were ready to begin their tour of the pyramids. The guard nodded to them. "Okay... if you have any problems or questions, there are docents and security staff throughout the monument."

Reg nodded. "Thanks. You have been very helpful."

He blinked at her, looked at the cashier who had printed off their tags, and then retreated in the direction they had arrived. The cashier nodded.

"You can go ahead."

Reg hesitated. She thought she should probably wait for a tour guide to take a group of them through the pyramid. It didn't seem right to just walk in by themselves and start exploring. But the tall man touched her arm and guided her to a passage beyond the cashier, nodding toward it.

"We're supposed to go in there? You know... why I'm here?" Reg asked awkwardly.

He nodded again toward the hall. Reg walked with him.

"I've never been anywhere like this before," Reg said as they walked down the stone passage. "I never thought I'd be able to come somewhere like this. Just... rich people."

Her silent guide led her through a couple of public passages, then indicated an area that was blocked off with security ropes.

"I don't know whether we should go there."

He waved her on and, when she slowed, uncertain, he again took her arm and guided her past the security ropes and into a smaller passageway. The floor was sloped down. Reg gripped the man's arm, feeling a bit of vertigo in moving from the flat surface to the downhill.

"Are you sure we're allowed to go this way?"

He made no response. Reg didn't know why she was expecting him to, why she kept asking him questions when it was clear that he would not or could not answer. She wanted a response from him, whether it was telepathic, like she would converse with Forst, out loud, or some kind of gesture. But the only gestures that he made were to indicate that she should go on.

CHAPTER THIRTY-SIX

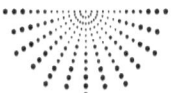

*I*t was quiet away from the public. No one discussing the pyramid as they walked through it or complaining about how long they'd had to wait in line to get a ticket and then had to wait for a tour guide as well. No crying children or raised voices.

Nothing at all.

But as they walked along, descending through the dimly lit passageway in silence, Reg could hear other voices.

Not from the tourists or their guides, or the staff or security personnel.

Other voices. Ghostly. Rising up through the back of her head and making the hair on her arms stand on end. Reg looked around.

Of course there were spirits there. A pyramid housed a burial chamber. Not just for the king, but also members of his household, favorite servants, soldiers. Whoever the king wanted to be with him in the afterlife. Someone would need to feed and serve him and protect him from harm. Things were no different in the afterlife the Egyptians envisioned than in one's first life. Except that the afterlife lasted much longer, and if a person was not properly prepared and equipped, it would be a long, torturous afterlife instead of the pleasant one that it could be with a little planning.

"Are there mummies here?" Reg asked anxiously. Her mind flashed through popular media, everything from Scooby-Doo mummies to those of graphic horror movies.

She had dealt with real life zombies; she wasn't so sure she wanted to contend with mummies as well. She was already holding the cursed gems. If they belonged to whatever king was interred in the pyramid, would he come and get them? Or could she just leave them as an offering in some small side chamber that no one would ever go into, hoping that they would remain safe there forever?

They couldn't be safe forever if she just hid them somewhere in the pyramid. Only if she gave them to the rightful owner personally.

She just hoped it wasn't a mummy.

In Africa, the rightful owners had been the villagers, the descendants of those who had originally mined or owned the gems hundreds of years before.

She really hoped that she didn't have to return them to the original owner whose tomb had been plundered. She wasn't sure how she would manage walking up to a mummy to hand them over.

The draugrs had stunk, rotten and vile. Would the mummies smell worse because they were older, or would the smell be gone by then, turned to dust centuries earlier?

Her companion was waiting for her to return her attention to him. Reg struggled to rein in her thoughts and pay attention to his answer.

It came, not in words, but in vibrant pictures that filled her mind. The queen and young prince following the soldiers carrying a large and colorfully decorated sarcophagus. It gleamed with touches of gold paint. Actual gold, Reg was sure, not just the craft paint like she got at Michael's. She couldn't see the man within the casket and hoped that she wouldn't. Hopefully, he was at rest in the bottom of the pyramid and would not be waking up to ask her for the gemstones and rings.

She wondered, briefly, if the rings had been stolen off of the fingers of the corpse. The idea gave her a little shudder of horror. But she didn't see the rings anywhere in the vision her guide had given her. She looked at the fingers of the queen and young prince and saw that they both had signet rings. But not the ones that Reg had on her fingers. She was glad she wouldn't have to put them back onto the shriveled black fingers of some desiccated corpse hundreds of years old.

"Do I have to see him? Talk to him?" Reg demanded.

One of the spirits was close by, doing all he could to impose himself on Reg's mind. "I am here. Why would you come here except to talk to me?"

"Umm…" Reg looked around, hoping for a quick way to get out of it. While she enjoyed the seances she did for her customers, she rarely actually channeled a spirit for her clients. When she did, it was always a bit of an unsettling experience, even though she brushed it off as perfectly normal when speaking with her clients.

"Don't delay," another told her. It was a younger, gentle voice, and she glanced around, looking for the owner.

She could see a younger man just at the edge of her vision, dressed very much like she had seen ancient Egyptians portrayed on TV shows. She knew that it was the boy who had followed the sarcophagus into the tomb in the vision from her guide, but he was older, a young man rather than a child.

"I just don't want to talk to the mummy," Reg clarified. I'll talk to *him*. She looked around, but could not see the ghost of the dead king. He was there, though; she could still feel him in her mind. "Just talk."

"It has been a very long time," the young man said.

"Well, yes, I would guess so. The rings and gems are very old. But I don't know… did they come from here?"

She closed her eyes and tried to expand the vision. Not just to see what the people were wearing on their fingers, but expanding to other chambers in the pyramid where the jewels might have been stored. They believed they could take their wealth to the afterlife, so it would be there somewhere. He would have wanted it all close at hand.

The young man shook his head slowly. "They were not my father's."

"Do you know where they came from? Were they from one of the other pyramids? Or from the other place that Ahmed is going to take me? The Valley of the Kings?"

"You will need to find out."

"You don't know? Do you recognize them?" Reg held up her hand, displaying the rings.

There was hissing around Reg, making her jump. She tried to see who the sound came from, but it seemed to come from various sources around her, not just one direction. She thought about the young man's father. The dead king. He wanted something from her. He wanted to get into her head. Because he wanted to use her voice and her body as other ghosts had? To be able to feel and speak again? Or because he wanted something else?

"You cannot command me," the old pharaoh's voice hissed.

"I wasn't... I didn't mean to command you," Reg explained. "I'm just trying to get these gems back to the place they came from and, if that's not here or one of the other pyramids, then maybe I'd better go on, not waste so much time here."

"You must come see me."

Reg rubbed her arms and neck, trying to get rid of the gooseflesh and the creepy, sticky feeling that someone was watching her every move.

"Why?"

"You come to my land and do not want to see me? I was the greatest of my time. You do not come here and command and not pay your respects."

"I didn't mean to be disrespectful. But I don't have a lot of time in this land. I am sure you were very powerful when you were in power here. It must have taken a lot of time and money to build these things." Reg looked at her guide, his black skin taking on a blue sheen in the dim artificial lighting. Why didn't they have stronger lights? Was it the cost? Would light damage the artifacts there? Other than the paintings on the walls, Reg hadn't seen anything left over from the time of the king. Was that because everything had been looted, or because it had all been locked up in a museum, safe from people who would use it the wrong way?

"You should come," the young man urged. He put his hand on Reg's arm. He was insubstantial, so she could not feel his touch, but she felt a sudden chill. Like the cold of a grave.

"I don't know. Do *you* think I should?" Reg looked at her guide. She assumed that he could see the ghosts and their whispered conversation.

He made a gesture to her, a sort of "Go on, then" urging her to continue down the sloping passage.

"I don't really like this. I don't want to stay here very long."

But she went. She and the guide walked close together. Reg was careful of every step she took. Didn't they set booby traps? She was pretty sure she had heard that somewhere. And what if she walked right into one because she wasn't being careful enough? She tried to sense ahead of her, both in space and in time, hoping that she could foresee any hazards that lay ahead.

Even though she was sure the lights were all the same all the way, she felt like the passageways were getting darker and more oppressive. "Is it much farther?"

If they could show her where it was, maybe Reg could jump herself there instead of having to go through all the hallways, taking so much extra time and energy.

The ghost and the guide just continued to take her down and down and down through winding passageways.

CHAPTER THIRTY-SEVEN

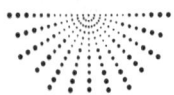

There were locked doors, but her guide stopped at each, resting his hand on the doors, until Reg could hear the lock click open, and he would open it for her. The pyramid security clearly hadn't thought that they would have to deal with magical beings getting past the doors. Or maybe they had known that those who had the powers would still get through and didn't worry about it. If they could do nothing to keep people out, why go to a lot of trouble to try?

"We are here," the young man told her, stopping and looking around. Reg tried to reconcile the vision she'd had of the Pharaoh's burial with what she saw before her.

The room was bare, but for the hieroglyphics on the walls. Even those were faded and hard to read after so many years. Reg wandered around, looking for some sign of all the wealth and artifacts that had originally been housed in that small vault. It was so bare now. She hoped that the pieces were in museums or in display cases that people could tour in the public area of the pyramid.

"This is it? This is where the mummy was?" Reg asked.

A man stepped into the room, through the same entrance that Reg and her guide had just used. He had apparently been following her.

At first, Reg took him for the ghost of the dead king. An old man. He looked ancient, like he'd lived a thousand years. But ghosts usually looked either like they had when they had died or were in their prime. They didn't keep getting older after they died.

She waited for him to hiss something at her, to confirm that he was the pharaoh who had been buried there, but he advanced, eyes fixed on her, looking as though he would prefer to take her head off. This wasn't a ghost who wanted to talk through her. He seemed to be very real, very much a physical being.

"Who are you?" Reg asked. She took a step back away from him and avoided him the best she could. He was spry for an old guy, but she managed to stay out of his reach, studying him, trying to evaluate him and to decide whether he was a danger to her or not.

"You don't know me?" he growled. "You can't even recognize me after a few short days?"

A few short days? Reg tried to picture him in her life. How had she known him? Was he someone who lived on her street? A client? Someone she'd sat next to in some public place who had decided that they were acquainted with each other?

"I'm sorry..." She looked at her guide and caught the flash of the young man's ghost in the corner of her eye. But she still didn't see the old ghost and couldn't figure out who the man was. "I know I should remember, but..."

"You stole my powers."

Reg stared at him. She hadn't stolen anyone's powers. She couldn't. Well, she could to an extent, but she didn't. She wasn't like Corvin, hunting down the weak and helpless and consuming their powers.

"*I* stole your powers?" she repeated, her voice challenging.

"You and your servants. All of you, ganging up on a helpless old man..."

Reg sucked in her breath. She studied the old man. She was getting an inkling, but it didn't seem possible. The old man who stood in front of her didn't look anything like the black-haired man they had originally met in Egypt when they had gone there to find out what had happened to Horace before Harrison brought him to the house.

Horace's old owner.

Kareem.

"It's not possible," Reg murmured. She couldn't see any of that man in this old man's face. He was utterly changed. He had seemed old when Reg and Corvin had gone to meet him. Not ancient, just like an old warlock, someone who had likely lived for far more years than he appeared to have. Witches and warlocks aged slowly. Sarah claimed to be hundreds of years old.

"Look what you did to me," Kareem complained. "Taking my power away from me. What did you think would happen when you had drained me?"

"I didn't… all I did was to defend myself. You were the one trying to kill the elf's child. How could you do something like that?"

"Why should the child of some other species be of any concern to me? I didn't care what happened to it. I was trying to gain leverage over you. It's your fault."

"My fault? I didn't attack you. You're the one who attacked me!"

Kareem spat. "You came to my home to show off your rings and to command me to tell you all I knew. You're the one who wanted the spark."

Reg bit her lip. She *had* wanted the piece of the Witch Doctor that Kareem had held. Not for herself, but to safeguard and make sure that no one could gather the pieces he had sent out to the kattakyns and re-form the Witch Doctor once more. She had been promised a thousand years. A thousand years before the binding spell would wear off. Longer still before the kattakyns could move around the world to gather together in one place. Multiple levels of complexity to make sure that the Witch Doctor would never be back in her lifetime.

But one of the pieces, the spark that Kareem spoke of, was lost. They didn't know where to find it. Harrison had said that Kareem no longer had it, but he didn't know where it had gone. Kareem's words seemed to verify this. He was playing the victim because someone had stolen from him what he had taken from Horace.

And it was Corvin who had drained Kareem's power, not Reg. And Kareem knew that. But he needed someone to blame and Reg had returned to Egypt, giving him a target.

"How did you even know I was here?" Reg asked. She continued to stay as far away from Kareem as was possible. He didn't appear to be able to move quickly and, if his powers had also been drained enough by Corvin that Kareem was aging that rapidly, then Reg assumed he would not have the strength to wield any power over her. But she couldn't be sure. She still needed to be careful.

"Do you think I cannot feel your rings of power?" Kareem looked greedily at the rings on her finger. "Do you think I cannot recognize your aura when you come into my part of the world? You can't hide those things from me, even if I have been crippled by what you have done to me. I can still *feel* you."

Reg shifted uneasily. Her instinct was to throw up a shield around herself and her guide, to protect them against any imminent spell from the warlock. She had a feeling that, like a bird faking a broken wing, he was pretending to be far more pitiable than he really was. He wanted to take her off guard. When she wasn't looking, then he would attack.

But she had learned that maintaining a psychic shield around herself also prevented her from using her powers outside of that shield. She could not attack while she was defending, it was one or the other. She remembered the attack and defend exercise she had seen at the Spring Games. The defender had used a very small shield, which he could then move around to counter any move by the attacker. Could she do that? Defend with one hand and use offensive moves with the other? She didn't think that she was well enough coordinated to pull it off. Not without practice, which she didn't have. She was limited to one or the other.

"What do you want from me?" she asked Kareem.

"I want what you took from me."

"I didn't take anything from you. That was Corvin. The other warlock."

"He was in your service. He would not have been there or attacked me without you. You might not do your own dirty work, but that doesn't mean you're not responsible."

Reg wanted to argue it but, on at least one level, he was right. Corvin would not have been there if not for her. And he would not have had any reason to attack Kareem. He wouldn't have gone back to Egypt to question Kareem without Reg leading the way. He hadn't been too keen on going back.

Of course, that had changed recently. He had been angling to go along with Reg ever since he had fought Kareem. Did he know that Harrison had sent Kareem back to Egypt and he wanted to take the rest of Kareem's power? Or did he think that Harrison had done away with Kareem and that he wouldn't have to face the other warlock upon his return?

"How about you leave me alone, and I'll leave you alone?" Reg suggested. If she could negotiate a treaty with him, maybe he would be satisfied. "I'm not here to see you. I'm not doing anything to harm you. There's no need to start a fight."

Kareem shook his head, baring his teeth, which were few in number and looked like they were rotting out of his head. Maybe he was just grumpy because he had a toothache. "I am here to get what is mine," he said, looking again at the rings.

CHAPTER THIRTY-EIGHT

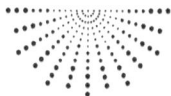

"*H*ow are these yours? I didn't take them from you. I didn't even get them from Egypt. I just brought them back here."

"They are not yours."

"No, I never said they were. But they are not yours either."

"You know nothing about my heritage. I am descended from the kings. I have more right to them than anyone else."

Reg hesitated. She looked out the corner of her eye at the ghostly young man, looking for some sign of agreement or disagreement. He looked at Kareem with disdain, shaking his head. "This warlock is not of our family."

Could he know that for sure? Or did he just figure that Kareem was disgusting and he didn't want the valuables being given to him?

But then, the ghost had not lain claim to the jewelry either. He had not said that they had belonged to him or his father, and Reg had not seen them in the vision. Someone might have stripped the tomb bare of everything else of value, but if the rings and jewels had not come from there, then Reg was wasting her time standing around having discussions with ghosts and warlocks who had nothing to do with her quest.

"Bring back my treasure," the old king's ghost whispered inside Reg's head. "You make things whole? Bring back what belongs to me."

"I don't have anything that belongs to you. I can't give you what I don't have."

"You must go find them. They have taken it all away. You must find it and bring it back."

"I can't," Reg insisted. "I have stones that must be returned to their rightful owners, but I do not have anything of yours."

"You see what they have done to me. You know it is wrong."

"Yes... it's wrong," Reg agreed. She pictured his sarcophagus on display upstairs in the public area, tourists gawking and taking pictures. Archaeologists taking pictures and doing special scans of the mummy inside. She wouldn't want her corpse to be treated that way. "But I don't have any authority over them."

"You have the rings. You can command."

Reg looked down at the rings. She ran her thumb over their surfaces. "You know where they come from? What they can do?"

Images flashed through her head too fast for Reg to be able to process them. She closed her eyes, bringing her hands up to her head as if she could physically block them from entering her mind. "No, no! You can't do that. Stay out of my brain!"

Another sharp hiss from the old ghost and the pictures stopped. Reg tried to recover. She couldn't process even part of what she had seen, it had been a flood of images and memories too complex to sort out.

"What was that?"

"You command an answer and then you command I stop. You don't know your own mind."

Reg rubbed her thumb between her eyebrows in the third eye position, a pounding headache making it difficult to think straight. "I'm sorry. I'm not commanding, I'm just... asking questions. I want to understand. But it's like drinking from a fire hose; it is too much."

"You want answers."

"Yes. No."

Reg's guide put his hand on her arm. She was distracted from talking to the old king's ghost. Had it all been in her head or out loud? Could the guide understand what had been happening, or was he lost at sea, trying to figure out if she had lost her mind. Kareem crept closer, his hand in his pocket, his manner furtive.

"You, stay back," Reg ordered. She focused her attention on the rings to make sure that this time it was a command, hoping that Kareem would be bound by it. "Don't come any closer."

She looked at the guide, deep into his eyes, wondering where she had seen him before. Because she was sure she had seen him before. She was sure he was someone she should know. There was a fleeting, familiar feeling that she was almost able to put her finger on, and then it was gone again. Reg groaned. "Who are you? Can you speak? What if I command you to speak?"

He shook his head. Did that mean that he couldn't or that she shouldn't command him? It was too hard for Reg to sort out. She should only ask one question at a time. That way maybe she could sort out the answers.

"Do you know where the gems came from?"

Steady eyes, an affirmative feeling, nothing else.

"Did they come from here?"

A slight turning away from her. Like a cat turning away from attention he didn't want. No, negative. Reg let out her breath in an angry puff.

Then what was she doing there? Why was she wasting her time climbing all the way down to the depths of the pyramid? She would not find a place to leave the gems, because they didn't belong there. Reg supposed that the Egyptians had, like all countries, gone through several different ruling families. Maybe related, maybe not, but whatever number of families there were, Reg was not in the right place.

Had he known that before they talked to the ghosts and had just followed her to keep an eye on her, or had he just figured it out like she had?

"Where should I go, then?"

As if an open-ended question was one that he would be able to answer. But Reg reached out with her mind, hoping that he would show her another vision or help her to understand another way. She closed her eyes to focus better. After a moment, a vision started to form, but it was dark and indistinct. Another tomb, another room somewhere. But where? There were not limestone blocks as there were in the pyramid Reg was in, but the room seemed to have been carved out of the rock.

Not one of the other pyramids, then, Reg decided. But then, where? The other site that Ahmed had told her he would take her on a tour of?

"Is this that Valley? The Valley of the Kings?"

An indecisive response. Maybe, but maybe not. No, but close. Yes, but not where she was thinking. Reg tried to sort through the feelings to pin one down, but that was as far as she could get. Yes, but no. No, but yes. She shook her head.

"Okay… so I'll go to the Valley of the Kings… at least it is closer."

The room around her was silent. Reg looked around at the occupants. Her silent guide. The ghost of the young man she could see out of the corner of her eye. She couldn't feel the old king's ghost, but she could still feel him there. He was unhappy with her decision to leave, and not to leave the rings and other gems there for him. All his treasure had been taken from him, and Reg felt sorry for him to be left with nothing, after all that planning and work to make sure that he would be well-supplied in the afterlife. But in the end, he was a ghost, not someone who could actually make use of all the amenities he had provided for himself. Or was he only a ghost because he had not moved away from that place, progressing along the appointed timeline for his afterlife?

And then there was Kareem. He seemed to have stopped when Reg told him to, but she didn't know how long the command would hold. Until they were separated again? Until she left the room? The pyramid? Forever?

He still had his hand in his pocket, close to whatever weapon he carried with him.

"What if I command you to stay here?" she suggested to him.

Kareem's watery eyes widened. "Taking my powers is not enough for you?" His voice was loud and querulous. "You would leave me here to die of starvation?"

Would he? It wasn't as though he had told her the truth from the beginning. It wasn't like he'd ever told her the truth at all. He'd even twisted what she knew to be the truth, what she herself had witnessed.

"Someone would come down here sooner or later," she suggested. "We could call in later and tell them to have a look."

"You can't do that!"

It did seem like a cruel thing to do, even if Reg was concerned about her safety. Putting someone else's life or mental health in jeopardy for her own convenience didn't seem right.

"Then…" She pressed her thumb against one of the rings. "I command you to stay here for one hour."

She looked at the tall, Black guide, seeking his approval. He gave no indication one way or the other. Reg hesitated, wondering if she had done the wrong thing. Too little or too much? Corvin had told her the last time that they needed to dispose of Kareem permanently. But he was too quick to disregard the lives of others. He took everything that was precious to a person and left behind the shell. What did it matter to him whether the shell survived or not?

She would see Kareem again if she did not do something to stop him permanently. But he was an old man now, ancient, with no more power that she could sense, other than the ability to feel her and follow her. And if it was actually the rings that he was following, he would stop when she divested herself of them.

Kareem swore and cursed in his own language. Reg didn't need a translator to understand his venom.

"Maybe you can keep the ghosts company," Reg suggested. "Maybe they could tell you where another treasure is located."

Kareem looked around the room, but was apparently unable to see either the old, dead king or his son. No powers.

Reg looked at her guide, and together they retreated from the tomb room. The unsettled vibe Reg had felt since arriving there gradually lifted.

Reg hadn't been thinking, as they had taken their downward path, that she would have to climb up the way she had come. Her leg muscles were burning before long, her breathing ragged and uneven.

"It didn't seem this steep when we were going down," she told the guide between wheezes.

He gripped her arm and helped her along, but he wasn't really providing any support, just urging her forward. After what seemed like hours, Reg stopped for a rest, leaning against one of the walls and breathing hard, wondering if the burning muscles would ever be the same again. She really did need to take up some kind of exercise routine and get herself into shape.

"What I wouldn't give to be back in Ahmed's car," Reg gasped out.

The man looked at her, eyes steady. As if reminding her of something she should know. Reg considered her statement and what he might mean by his mild reproof.

"Oh, brother." Reg couldn't believe that she was being so dense. There she was, trying to climb all the way up the passages of the pyramid, out of sheer habit. Because that was what she had done her whole life. Gotten herself from one location to another using her feet. She had covered many miles on foot, not always able to afford or "borrow" a car.

But she hadn't gotten to Egypt by walking.

CHAPTER THIRTY-NINE

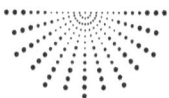

"*D*o you want me to jump you out as well?" she asked the man watching her with serious dark eyes.

He reached out and touched her hand. Reg thought about Ahmed's car, and where he had parked outside the security door. She didn't know whether he would still be there or whether he would have moved to a less obvious location to wait for her. Or whether he had just given up on the crazy American and decided to find another prospect. She switched her focus to the inside of his car, wherever it was. The spic and span surfaces, the smell of the carpet shampoo and the air freshener. Ahmed's reassuring presence, always eager to help her out.

Then she was there with him. Ahmed yelped and dropped the book he was reading, turning to stare at her wide-eyed.

"Sorry," Reg apologized. She wondered if she should try to explain the whole magic thing to him, then decided it would be too much. People tended to create their own version of reality when what they saw did not reconcile with their experience. If Ahmed did not have any experience with magical practitioners, he would just decide that he had been immersed in his story and hadn't seen her approaching the car, or opening the door and getting in. "Thanks for waiting around."

He blinked several times and shook his head. "You are back early if you went through a tour."

"We did our own behind-the-scenes thing. There's a lot to see in there, and we didn't have time for everything. What time is my flight to the Valley of the Kings?"

He produced a folder with the tickets in it. "It is an airbus; you can take the next one with available seats when you get there."

"Great! So we can go now."

"Yesss…" Ahmed drew the word out, doubt in his voice. Still trying to figure her out. She clearly wasn't behaving like the average tourist.

Reg looked around the car. Her other guide was standing outside the car. She didn't know where his car was or how far away from it Ahmed had parked. She opened the door.

"Do you want to go get your car, or come with us?"

He opened the back door and climbed in. Ahmed made a noise like he would object, then closed his mouth. Whatever the crazy lady wanted was fine with him. Better if there were someone else to deal with her nonsense. But he stopped and took a long, assessing look at the tall Black man before starting the car's engine.

"Who is he?"

"A friend."

Ahmed waited for more information, but Reg didn't have anything else to tell him. He looked at the other man, then back at Reg. "Does he have a ticket for the plane?"

"Uh… I don't know. I guess probably not. Can he get one there?"

Ahmed nodded. "It is more expensive."

Reg looked at the man. He didn't object to this. Did he have money, then? Or was Reg supposed to pay for his ticket? She shrugged, supposing that she had enough to cover it.

* * *

Ahmed guided Reg through the various queues and procedures to get them on the airbus to the Valley of the Kings, and Reg picked up a brochure about what they would see when they got there. She was absorbed looking through the pictures when she felt a familiar warmth. She straightened and looked around.

"Regina."

Reg stared at Corvin, taking in his self-satisfied expression. "Corvin? What are you doing here?"

"Looking for you. And now I found you."

"What do you mean? How did you get here?" Reg looked at her two guides, but neither of them seemed to have any idea where Corvin had come from.

Corvin raised his brows. "I flew."

"You flew here?" Reg repeated stupidly.

"How else would you expect me to get here when you didn't bother to take me along?"

"Well… I didn't expect you to get here at all. That was sort of the point."

Corvin looked smug. "And yet, here I am."

Reg couldn't believe that he had flown from Florida to Egypt to find her. Who did that? It was crazy.

"I don't know why you would do that. I'm just fine." Reg looked pointedly at her two guides. "I have people to help me out. We're making progress. I'm sure that by the end of the day…"

Corvin studied the two men. His eyes lingered on the tall Black man. He frowned. Reg felt immediately defensive of her guardian. He hadn't done anything but help her. He certainly did more than Corvin to make sure that she was kept safe. Corvin looked out for one person, and that was himself.

"You're going to the Valley of the Kings?"

Reg shrugged. "Seemed like a good idea."

"I don't see what you're going to find there. Everything has already been picked over. There are no more artifacts there."

"I'm not looking for artifacts." Reg looked at Ahmed and shook her head to disabuse him of any idea he might get from Corvin that she was there hoping to raid a tomb. She wasn't there looking for national treasures. She wanted to return the gems and rings she had.

Corvin and the guides measured each other. Reg got the idea that Corvin and the Egyptians didn't like each other, but Ahmed seemed to be willing to put up with the silent guide. Reg wasn't too pleased about Corvin being there. She had done her best to leave him back in Florida.

"Well... I can't stop you from going where you like," Reg said finally, "but you're not part of our party. I didn't invite you along."

"We're old friends. Why wouldn't you want me along?"

"Old friends or old enemies? You're not a part of this. I don't know why you think you should be."

"I'm just looking out for you..."

"You wouldn't come all the way here on your own dime just to look out for me. You're looking out for yourself. Like you always do. And you can look out for yourself somewhere else. Not with us."

Corvin could apparently see that he would not be able to get anywhere with her, so he shrugged. He would obviously not just turn around and go home. He could do the tourist thing all around Egypt if he liked; it didn't have anything to do with Reg. He could stay there permanently, for all she cared. Maybe that would be good for him. He could continue his studies of ancient Egyptian artifacts and whatever else he was researching and would be far away from Reg when she returned to Florida. So she didn't constantly have to be on her guard with him.

There were not assigned seats on the airbus so, of course, Corvin charmed the flight attendants and managed to get a seat just across the aisle from Reg. He smiled smugly at her, pleased with himself. Reg just closed her eyes and put her head back to go to sleep. She hadn't gotten very much the night before, and she had promised herself that she would have a nap on the flight.

She drifted off quickly once they were in the air, fatigue from her short night and long morning and the climb through the pyramid quickly taking over. She didn't awaken until a flight attendant shook her by the arm to tell her that they were landing, and she needed to put her seatbelt back on. Reg blinked sleepily and buckled up, then watched out the window closest to her, waiting for the plane to land. It took longer than she expected to complete its descent.

"You were talking in your sleep," Corvin told her. "And drooling."

Reg wiped her chin. She couldn't help herself. It was dry, no sign of drool. She shouldn't have reacted to him. "Talked about what?" she asked, keeping her voice casual and steady to signal to him that he hadn't thrown her off and she didn't really care what he had to say. She was just being polite, since she had to sit with him.

"You said something about Kareem. I couldn't make it out. Something like 'stay in bed' maybe?"

Reg's cheeks heated. She ignored her reaction, hoping that if she did, she wouldn't draw Corvin's attention to it.

"Oh. We saw him earlier. He asked about you." Reg decided to get in a little dig of her own. See whether she could get him off of *his* game.

Corvin's eyes widened, and he looked around. "He what? You what? Where?"

"At the pyramids."

"You saw Kareem at the pyramids."

"Yeah." Reg looked away from Corvin, watching the blue sky and clouds out the window.

"What did he look like? What did he say? After what happened, I thought that Harrison… I thought that we would never see him again."

"I guess Uncle Harrison just sent him back home. And… yeah, he didn't look too good. He was blaming me about you taking his powers. He aged… maybe because of that? Is that the way it works?"

"How much older did he look?"

"As old as anyone I've ever known. I don't know. A hundred. He didn't look good, but he got around okay. Followed me all the way down to the bottom to the tomb."

"He followed you."

"Yeah. Said that I should have known that he would be able to feel me there. And…" Reg tapped one of the rings but didn't do anything else to draw attention to it. She didn't want to get mugged when she got off the airplane.

"But he didn't do anything? Try to… harm you?"

"How could he? You took all his powers."

"Not all," Corvin hedged.

"How much did you leave him with? Not enough for him to do anything."

"If he followed you and the scent of those stones to the pyramid, then he still had some powers. What did you do? How did you get away?"

"I just commanded him. Apparently, people here have to obey when I tell them what to do, if I'm wearing the rings. I wonder if it works on everyone." Reg eyed Corvin. What should she tell him to do? Go away and leave her alone? Never try to trick her into giving up her powers again? What would be of the most benefit to her, if he had to obey?

"Don't try it," Corvin warned.

"Why not? You don't want to listen to me?"

"What would you tell me to do?" Corvin raised his brows suggestively. "I could give you some ideas…"

"I would be in charge," Reg said, "I wouldn't need any suggestions from you." She caught a glance from Ahmed and wondered if he picked up on Corvin's charms aimed in her direction. Her face warmed again. "Maybe I would just tell you to go home," Reg said, by way of example. Clearly, she and Corvin were not a thing. Ahmed could see that. They were not together and they were not discussing anything tawdry.

"And to wait for you, where…?" Corvin asked, still trying to embarrass her.

"No, to go to your home and to stay out of my life. I don't know why you think that you have any part in my life."

"I think that both of your companions have already figured out that isn't true."

"It is!" Reg insisted, flashing looks at the guides. "I do not have a relationship with Corvin."

Ahmed nodded and studied the air vents above him. The other man just looked at Corvin, unblinking. If only that were all it took to put him in his place.

The wheels of the plane touched down and, with one bounce, the plane settled on the runway and coasted, decelerating and then turning around to drop them in the right place. Reg's stomach lurched a couple of times with the plane's movement. After it stopped, she was happy to sit for a couple more minutes while the flight attendants organized their egress.

"So…" Reg rubbed her eyes and pulled out the brochure she had been looking at about the Valley of the Kings. "This whole valley in the middle of the desert, it's full of tombs of kings. A whole bunch of the pharaohs were all buried there."

Ahmed nodded. "They were not all kings. We do not know who all of them were. Some of them were lower in the government, or perhaps wealthy merchants. But to pay for a tomb like this and furnish it in the

Egyptian manner, it did take a lot of money. Slaves and gold and all the trappings."

"And they were all buried here."

"Many were buried in this valley. But not all of them. As you saw, there were the pyramids, and there were many other tombs, most of which are probably gone now. But there have been 63 tombs discovered in Wādī al-Mulūk. And they are still looking for more."

"How could there be more that they haven't found yet? Aren't they… pretty easy to find with modern equipment?"

"No, not necessarily. Radar and other technologies do make it easier, but you have to tunnel through rock to find them. And much of this space is protected now; you can't just go out to the desert and start digging holes wherever you please. And any tomb that is discovered… they have to be properly documented and reported to the government, and you cannot just take whatever you find. Any valuable archaeological artifacts belong to Egypt and must be properly preserved in Egypt."

"That's fine, that's fine," Reg said, wanting to reassure him again that she wasn't out to rob a grave. "I'm not going to be digging around and trying to find one."

Ahmed looked slightly relieved at her reassurance. After the display that the crazy tourist had put on at the pyramids, insisting that she be allowed in through the back door, she might do almost anything. And he didn't want to be responsible.

"We will go on a tour of the tombs that are open to the public," he told Reg. "I have been here many times before, and I can tell you all about them. We can stay the rest of the day, and then go back to your hotel. If you want to see more tomorrow…"

"No, hopefully I'll be done today and I'll be able to head back to Florida tonight."

He gazed at her. Reg knew he was puzzled about what her purpose there actually was and what it was she had to do before returning home. She obviously didn't behave like the other tourists. She had something more going on.

And then there was this new American.

Ahmed flashed a look to Corvin.

"Ignore him," Reg said firmly. "I can't stop him from going wherever he wants to go, but he isn't with us."

"Yes, madam."

"You might as well call me Reg."

He nodded politely. The flight attendant reached their row. Reg and the others stood up to disembark together.

Outside the sun was bright. Reg put on a pair of sunglasses, but she wished that she were wearing one of her colorful scarves so that she could wind it around her head to keep the sun off and shade her eyes from the glare of the sand a little. Who knew that the sand could be so bright?

Ahmed led the way, and Reg and her guardian followed. Corvin stayed close, but he didn't try to get closer to Reg to charm her or make demands about what she was doing there or what she should do. She wasn't sure she understood why he was even there. The jewels had nothing to do with him.

CHAPTER FORTY

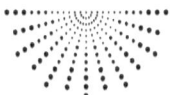

The first couple of tombs that they visited were fascinating. Reg got to see some of the kinds of artifacts she had missed in her backroom tour of the pyramid. Beds and Coptic jars and decorated sarcophagi like she had seen on TV and in movies. More hieroglyphics on the walls. Ahmed told her what some of the depictions meant, and Corvin corrected him in a couple of cases, giving detailed explanations in his professorial voice about what they really said or meant, leaving Ahmed red-faced and sputtering over being shown up by an American. But Corvin was apparently not wrong; he just liked the longer, more detailed explanations, when Reg was fine with an overview even if it did gloss over a few points.

But as they went on, Reg's fatigue returned. The nap on the plane had not made up for the amount she had lost the night before, and after a while all the tombs and the displays started to look the same to her. Not only that, but in each one she had a fresh bunch of ghosts to deal with.

She didn't know why she hadn't foreseen this difficulty. She should have realized that all of these mummies who'd had their rest disturbed and their tombs raided would not be happy and would be looking for someone to complain to. Some of them just crowded in, wanting to tell Reg their troubles, and others wanted to dive right into her mind and take control of her. And she wasn't there to be channeling a bunch of disrupted pharaohs. She didn't have that kind of time.

Corvin could not only see her distraction, but could feel it when in close quarters with her. He probably felt as if he were climbing out of his skin too, absorbing some of her feelings.

"Can't you tell them to just leave you alone?" he asked impatiently. "Just block them out."

Reg rolled her eyes. "Is that what you did when you held my powers? Just turned it off?"

"Well... no," Corvin admitted, thinking back to it. "I seem to remember that some of them were fairly persistent."

Reg nodded. "And those weren't fresh new ghosts, either. Those were mostly old friends. They're quieter."

"But you must be able to suppress them somewhat."

Reg shook her head. "You know, I spent almost all my teenage years trying. And social workers and foster parents trying to get me to shut up about the voices and visions. And doctors trying to drug them to death. And you know what? They didn't go away."

As if to emphasize the point, one of the old kings seized her by the arm, putting so much energy into the motion that she could actually feel his fingertips restraining her, and he got in her face and tried to channel through her. Reg pulled back.

"I need... somewhere quieter," she told Ahmed. "I just can't do it here with so many of them around me."

There was a deep frown line between his brows. The tomb was filled with tourists, but the numbers were carefully controlled and people were not allowed to talk too loudly. And exactly what was it that Reg was trying to do? What made her so different from the rest of the tourists?

"I can't be in here," Reg insisted. "Let's go back out."

Ahmed nodded his agreement and led her out of the cave, back out into the bright desert sun, with heat waves reflecting off of the sand and stone. Reg covered her eyes, tears welling up and dripping down her cheeks.

"What is the oldest tomb?" she asked.

Ahmed motioned to the tomb that they had just come out of. But Reg already knew that wasn't the one that she wanted.

"No, not that one."

Corvin also shook his head. While he couldn't point out which tomb was the right one, he had placed the ring at 2500 BC or earlier, and none of the tombs they had seen were that old.

"That is the best I can do," Ahmed protested. "I am sorry if it is not what you would like, but I cannot take you to the undiscovered tomb."

Reg pulled her hands away from her face and looked at him.

"The undiscovered tomb?"

Ahmed shrugged. "There are other tombs out there. Maybe in this valley, maybe somewhere else in the desert that no one has seen in a thousand years because the sand buried it. Something from the ancient days may have been preserved by the gods and nature, but I cannot show it to you. If man has not found it, how could I take you there?"

Reg stood there for a moment, thinking about it. She scanned what she could see of the desert. Of course Ahmed couldn't show her anything but what was already known. And the rings and the gems in her possession had not come from any of the known tombs. She didn't think so, anyway.

Then how was she going to get there?

* * *

"Regina. Are you okay?"

Reg looked at Corvin, barely seeing him. "Yeah. I'm fine. Why?"

"Because you've been sitting here for… longer than I have ever seen you be still before. Do you have heat stroke? I could get you some water…"

"No. It's not heat stroke. I'm just trying to think."

"Don't try too hard," he joked. "You wouldn't want to burn anything out."

"Oh, ha ha," Reg snapped. "What I need is… somewhere I can be alone. Or just our group, anyway. I can't think with all these people coming and going. Their thoughts are like hamsters in a wheel. Add in all the other voices, and I just can't get everything sorted out." She ran her fingers through her thin red braids. "When we were in the pyramid, the old king there gave me a vision, but it was too much information too fast, and now I'm trying to remember it and sort through it all, but there's just too much going on."

"Let's see if we can find you somewhere quieter, then." Corvin strode away from her to go talk to some of the staff who supervised the tours through the tombs.

Reg put her face in her hands and rubbed her temples, trying to think through everything that was relevant to her quest.

In a few minutes, Corvin brought back with him a dark-complexioned, professionally dressed man with a look of concern on his face.

"You are not feeling well, madam?" he asked.

Reg opened her mouth to object, irritated that Corvin had told someone that she was having heatstroke instead of attending to what it was that she really needed. He projected a thought toward her to just follow his lead and not argue. Reg closed her mouth and considered.

"I think that if she just had somewhere quiet to lie down for a few minutes, she would probably be okay," Corvin suggested.

"Yes, yes; of course," the doctor agreed. "It can all be very overwhelming for someone who is not used to our climate. The heat, the brightness of the sun, the dryness of the air. Many tourists have problems going in and out of the tombs, alternating between the bright and the dark."

Reg put her hand over her eyes. "Yes," she agreed. "It gives me a headache, going back and forth."

Corvin nodded. "Maybe a bottle of water and somewhere she can lie down with a cold compress over her eyes?" he suggested firmly.

"Yes. Are you feeling well enough to walk a short distance?" the doctor asked Reg solicitously.

"Yeah, sure." Reg got up quickly, and then feigned a head rush, wobbling a little before straightening up again.

Corvin reached out to take her arm and Reg shook her head. Her guide took up the position instead. His touch was warm and soothing, unlike Corvin's, which always electrified her. They walked with the doctor, Corvin following behind, seething that the guide was the one at Reg's side. Ahmed followed behind him, uncertain about what he was supposed to do and staying out of the way of Corvin as much as possible.

There were several prefab buildings in a cluster, like the ones used at a school for overflow rooms or on a construction site. Not a trailer, exactly, but something similar. Reg was led to an infirmary, away from the hustle and bustle and much quieter than anywhere she had been all afternoon. She sat down on the bed initially; then, at the doctor's urging, she lay down with her feet off the end so that they wouldn't dirty the white sheets. The doctor retrieved a water bottle from a mini fridge and cracked the top. He handed it to Reg.

"Make sure you drink that. It's important to stay hydrated. You might not even feel thirsty, but you still need the water."

"Okay."

Reg knew if she drank too much water it would hamper her ability to kindle fire, but she didn't foresee the need to set fire to anything at the moment, so she wasn't too concerned. It was all for show anyway, since she wasn't really sick. She just needed some quiet and space to sort out her next step.

"Thank you." Reg touched the rings. "You can go now."

The doctor raised his brows and looked at her, confused by the dismissal. He didn't make any move to obey. Maybe because the infirmary was his domain, she didn't have any right to command him there. But Reg didn't like this apparent change to the circumstances, when everyone else had obeyed the requests and orders she had made while wearing the rings. She smoothed the faces and bands of the rings with her thumb, focusing her concentration on them. They grew warmer on her finger. She looked at Corvin. "How about you go back outside and give me some space."

He didn't move either. Reg didn't bother giving Ahmed a command; he would obey her whether the rings were still giving her additional powers or not. She looked at the other guide. He gazed back at her with clear eyes, unconcerned.

"Isn't it working anymore?" Reg asked him.

The doctor frowned at Reg's odd question and looked at the guide for his response.

The guide turned his face away slightly. *No.*

Reg sat up, worried. "Wait... why isn't it working anymore? What has changed?"

He couldn't answer those questions, of course. The doctor pressed Reg back, encouraging her to lie down again. "Don't exert yourself.

Wait until you are feeling better, and even then, I want you to move slowly and be careful. Sometimes people don't realize how sick they are. You don't want to faint."

"Don't touch me." Reg squirmed away from him. "I'll be fine. I'll stay still; just leave me alone. I need to think. There are still too many people in the room."

"Someone needs to stay with you to keep an eye on you."

Reg pointed to the tall, Black guide. "You. Please."

Ahmed and the doctor prepared to leave. Corvin didn't look like he was going to.

"I need to think," Reg insisted. "When you're here, you interfere."

"How do I interfere? I'm not doing anything. I can be quiet."

"You still interfere with my brain," Reg pointed out. "Your charms and our psychic connection are too strong, too disruptive."

"You've never said this was a problem before."

"I haven't ever been in Egypt, surrounded by ancient ghosts, trying to figure out how to get to a tomb that has never been discovered before."

"Well…" Corvin cocked his head to the side slightly as he considered this. "Fair enough, I suppose."

"You're the most distracting. You need to wait outside, at least. And don't hang around my window." Reg glanced toward the small window nearby. The shade was pulled down to keep the room from getting too hot or bright, but they could still see the outline of the sun shining through the blind.

"How long?"

"I don't know."

"How will we know when you are ready for us to come back in? Your… friend… doesn't seem to be too talkative."

"He can still come out and get you. Or I can come out. Once I've figured out what to do, I don't have to stay in here any longer. I'm not actually sick."

"I suppose not," Corvin admitted reluctantly.

Reg waited. Corvin let out an irritated sigh and left the room. Reg looked at the guide. He shut the flimsy door to the infirmary.

They were alone.

CHAPTER FORTY-ONE

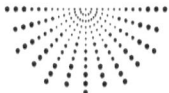

"*D*o you know what I am looking for?" Reg asked him.

He looked back at her, giving no indication one way or the other.

"I need to give these back," Reg said, indicating the rings. "And the rest of the gems I have from Egypt."

He expressed no surprise over this.

"I think that… I need to find an older tomb. These rings and stones are very ancient, and the tombs we have seen so far are too new. If I tried to leave them in one of the tombs we have been in, they would just be stolen. If we tried to give them back to the rightful owner… well, I don't think I've found the rightful owner yet, unless it is you."

He turned his head slightly.

"So I don't have anyone to give them to. If I give them to the wrong person, they might still come back to me, or they might cause a curse on the lives of the person I give them to, and that wouldn't be right. The stones have come to me, so it's my job to return them to their rightful place. Right?"

Yes. She could see that. She could feel that was right.

"I need to find an older tomb. Maybe… *the* oldest tomb. Do you know where it is?"

She got the feeling that the answer was much more complex than a yes or no.

"Can you take me there?"

Head turned. *No.*

Reg felt the frustration welling up inside her. She spun the rings on her finger, staring at them, focused, waiting for them to get hot.

"Take me to the undiscovered tomb," Reg commanded.

There was no flash of light. No sudden change to Reg's surroundings. The rings started immediately to cool.

"No! Take me to the tomb," Reg tried again. "Please. If that's where I need to go, then why won't you take me?"

But maybe the rings only allowed her to command others, not the rings themselves. And for some reason, even that ability seemed to have worn off.

If her guides could not take her, and the rings could not take her, then what was Reg left with? She couldn't take herself.

Or could she?

Reg closed her eyes partway, thinking about it. She could jump herself to places that she had never been before; that was how she had found the rightful owners of the previous bunch of gems. Ruan had taught her how to use her senses to see and feel and smell the gems and jump herself to where they had come from.

But when she had done the same thing with the Egyptian gems, she had jumped to the middle of the city and, when she asked for help, she had found Ahmed, or Ahmed had found her. The other guide had also found her, though she wasn't sure where or how she had picked him up. He had remained in the background at the hotel other than when he was needed.

Why hadn't she jumped to the tomb, so she could return the gems and jump straight home again? Why had she needed to find the guides instead? Was facing Kareem part of the quest she needed to fulfill before she was allowed to hand over the gems? Or meeting Corvin? Was he required for that part of the plan? She couldn't be sure what parts of all that had happened had been designed to bring her closer to the resting place or rightful owner of the gems and which were just things that had happened to occur along the way.

But now, all of that was past. She had met her guides. She had gone to the pyramid and to some of the tombs open to the public in the Valley of the Kings. And now she knew—or thought she knew—that she needed to go to an undiscovered tomb, one that was older than all the rest. One that was as old as the rings.

"Can I find the undiscovered tomb?" she asked the man who stood there silently waiting for her next question.

Cautious affirmation in his eyes. Why cautious?

Because she had said *find*? Maybe find wasn't the right word.

"Can I jump there? I don't need to dig it out or to find my way in through the front door, do I?"

A steady gaze, with a tiny fan of amused wrinkles in the outside corners of each eye.

"I can jump there. If I try to use the rings or the gems this time, I can jump there, instead of wandering around looking at all these modern artifacts. What about the others? Do I need to take everyone with me?"

He stood watching her.

"You. I need to take you with me."

A tiny nod, the strongest confirmation he had given her so far.

"And Ahmed? Do I need to take him?"

Less certain this time, but no head shake. Ahmed too.

"And Corvin?"

The guide lifted his head slightly and stepped back, as if he had just smelled something foul. He didn't like Corvin. But he didn't turn his head away. He kept looking at Reg, waiting for her to finish her questions and to take action.

"And Corvin," Reg sighed. Maybe that was why she had not jumped directly to the tomb the first time. Corvin had needed a day to follow her to Egypt, taking a plane instead of the instant jump that she had, because she had refused to take him along. "Well… I guess we should get ready, then."

He waited for her to make the first move. Reg went to the door and opened it. She motioned for him to lead the way, but he hesitated in the doorway, looking out and then back at her. Reg supposed he was being chivalrous, letting her go out before him. Egypt seemed so far out of step with the society she had grown up in as far as women's roles were viewed. Dark ages. She rolled her eyes and went through the door ahead of him.

* * *

Reg looked around when they stepped out of the building. It was still just as hot and dry and bright as it had been earlier. She'd had a bit of a break from the sun and some of the water, so she was feeling pretty good. She didn't see the doctor or any others standing around outside. He might have been in another room inside or might be on call somewhere else in the historic site. It didn't really matter, as long as he wasn't there to witness her dematerialization.

As far as Reg could see, no one was watching or trying to listen in on what she was doing. Why would they? Everyone had their own jobs to do, or else they were tourists who wanted to see Egyptian artifacts, not some pasty-white American tourist who had succumbed to the heat.

"Well?" Corvin's voice was immediately inside her head. His facial expression was just as demanding. She wouldn't have had any trouble cold reading him even if she hadn't been able to hear his voice in her head.

"Okay. I have a plan," Reg advised.

Corvin looked expectant. Ahmed, somewhat nervous. He'd already seen her break all the rules at the pyramid site. She could only imagine the things he was worried she might do in the Valley.

"I don't know… if we all need to touch. But it might be the best, to make sure that no one is left behind."

This only ramped up Ahmed's anxiety. The other guide and Corvin seemed to take it in stride, unsurprised by the suggestion.

Corvin took one side, touching her on the shoulder so that there was still a layer of clothing between them, rather than jolting her by touching her bare skin. The guide could have touched Corvin, but chose instead to take Reg's other arm, his hand resting lightly behind her elbow. Ahmed looked at them.

"You should come too," Reg told him.

He looked at the other two men. One on each arm. What was he supposed to do?

"You can touch one of them or get in closer." Reg stretched her hand for him to take.

Ahmed eyed the others, then gently took Reg's fingertips between his. Reg realized that the gems were in her pocket. Luckily not on the same side as Corvin and Ahmed; she still had the ability to move her other arm, as long as the silent guardian matched her movements and stayed in contact. He kept his fingertips on her as she touched the bag of gemstones in her pocket.

Without taking them out of her pocket, Reg found the edges of the mouth of the bag and gently opened the plastic zip seal. She reached in and touched the gems, trying to sense them as deeply as she could. She didn't want to display them to Corvin or Ahmed, so she couldn't see them, but she could feel them with her fingertips and her extra senses. And while she was not sensitive enough to be able to smell them as Ruan did, she thought that there might still be enough microscopic particles escaping the bag that her brain could process them, even though she couldn't consciously detect anything special.

She couldn't visualize the place she was to jump to, yet she could. She had seen the other tombs. She had a rough idea of what it would look like. A cave deep in the rock, rough-hewn walls, hieroglyphics and scenes on the walls. She didn't know whether there would be riches there already. She had to assume if it was an undiscovered tomb that it still contained whatever riches the mummy had been buried with. She pictured the beds and jars and other items she had seen on display.

CHAPTER FORTY-TWO

$\mathcal{I}$t was suddenly difficult to breathe. Reg hadn't realized that she had closed her eyes. She opened them, expecting the bright Egyptian sun, and saw nothing. She could still feel the men around her.

Ahmed gasped. "What happened? Am I dead?"

"You're not dead," Reg assured him. She tried to see through the darkness. There had to be some flicker of light in the place that would allow her to see where they were. But it was as if her eyes were still closed.

"Where are we?" Corvin asked, his voice calm and even.

"In a tomb, I think," Reg explained. "The undiscovered tomb."

"That would explain the darkness."

Reg snickered. She looked around, still expecting to be able to see something. On TV when people discovered caves and treasures, there were always torches burning in holders on the walls, which lit by magic as they approached or had somehow remained burning for decades or centuries. She supposed that was just Hollywood taking a shortcut.

But if there were torches around...

Reg moved to free herself from the touches of the three men and held her hands close together, quickly kindling a small fire between them. After the total darkness, it was shockingly bright. Reg held it between her hands and looked around, shining it this way and that to get a better view of the cave they were in.

It was a little more roughly hewn than some of the tombs they had seen, but the walls were still covered with carvings, pictures, and statues. Reg wondered where they were geographically. Was the tomb within a pyramid? Buried under the sand for years? Or had it been carved out of the stone in the Valley of the Kings? In some other valley that had never been discovered? She could be anywhere in the world, but she assumed it was in Egypt. Or what had been Egypt millennia ago. Who knew what the geographical area of Egypt had been that many years ago? Reg didn't know whether they'd ever had an empire that had stretched across the known world, like the Roman Empire.

Corvin looked around at the hieroglyphics and scenes on the walls. When he stepped closer, his own shadow obscured what he was trying to look at.

"Can you get closer, Reg? Shine it over here."

Reg got closer to the wall and held the light so he could see the symbols clearly. She glanced around, looking for those torches in wall brackets that they had in all the movies. But there obviously weren't any. The dead king hadn't had enough foresight to ensure that he and his retinue would be able to see anything in the afterlife.

"This is... very ancient," Corvin observed, his eyes moving over the symbols and pictures, his hand just an inch from the wall as if to guide his eyes in a certain direction. "Archaic Egyptian."

"Well, that's good, isn't it? You said you studied ancient Egyptian. It was the modern stuff you had trouble with."

"Yes." Corvin looked uncomfortably at Reg. "But this is... even older than what I have educated myself in. My studies were of Middle Kingdom. Maybe one of your guides would be better able to take a crack at it..."

The silent guide remained so. Ahmed shook his head, looking at the wall. "I never made any study of the ancient tongues. This is... beyond me. Very obscure."

"It isn't gibberish," Reg objected. "It's just something that's hard to read. The pictures are pretty clear, though."

The men widened their viewpoints to look at the larger pictures that also told a story.

"They are not necessarily literal," Corvin warned. He studied the pictures. "In the Valley of the Kings, the earliest pictures were what was called the Book of Gates. But this is... not."

"This must be the king," Reg indicated one of the figures, sitting on a throne.

"Yes..." Corvin drew the word out as if he doubted Reg's conclusion.

"Well, he is, isn't he? He's on the throne. He has a scepter." Reg leaned closer in to the hand that was outstretched, pointing off in the distance as he gave an order. "And the rings. Look."

Nods from both Corvin and Ahmed. Reg looked at the other guide, but he seemed more reserved, not jumping right in to agree with her interpretation.

"This has to be the right tomb," Reg affirmed. "The rings are right there. This is the right place."

"But the right place for what?" Corvin asked. "What do you plan to do?"

"Well... I guess the first thing would to be to find the tomb. This isn't it." Reg looked around. There were several passages leading off from the room they had materialized in. There was no sarcophagus or any of the other trappings, so she must have to follow one of the passages to find it. They had landed in this anteroom so that she could see the rings on the wall painting and know that she was in the right place.

"*Then* what are you going to do?"

Reg scowled at Corvin. He was suddenly planning ahead? Now? It wasn't even his quest.

She went to each of the passages leading out of the room to look at the passageways and see whether there was any indication of which one she should take. A hieroglyphic that said, "this way" or a feeling pulling her in one direction. Maybe the rings would heat up.

They all looked very similar. But the floor sloped in one. Reg looked at it and tried to sense what was beyond. Did it lead to the tomb?

"The downslope suggests that this is the way to the tomb," Corvin said.

"We go down?" Ahmed questioned.

Reg looked at the passageway and turned her head to look at her guide. "Do you know where it is? You should lead the way."

"How would he know?" Corvin's voice was a growl. Was he jealous of the guide? Embarrassed because with all his studies about ancient Egypt, he still wasn't sure of himself?

Reg scowled at Corvin. "Don't be rude. So you can't read the old kind of writing. Nobody cares. You wanted to come along."

"I can read more than you think. *He* can't."

The guide didn't make any sign whether he agreed with this or not. At any rate, he wasn't going to read the writing aloud to Reg, and she didn't want to go through a whole long series of yes/no questions to try to figure out the interpretation.

"Do we go this way?" Reg asked.

The guide turned his face away from the passage.

"He doesn't know what he's talking about," Corvin insisted. "This is the only passage that slopes down; there has to be a reason for that. The tombs in the Valley were all at the lowest point. We should go look."

Reg shook her head. "We'll go where he says."

"That's not a wise choice."

"You don't know anything about him or whether it is a wise choice or not."

Corvin was insistent, hot anger pulsing behind his almost expressionless face. If she hadn't been connected with him and able to read him, she would never have guessed how angry he was. It seemed out of scale.

But the guy was probably jet-lagged. And humiliated that he couldn't do what he said he could do in the first place.

The guide moved away from them. Reg followed. Corvin and Ahmed didn't have much choice but to follow along, since Reg's fire was the only light. They went slowly down the passage, Corvin trying to read the signs and writing on the walls, trying to figure out the story that it told. Reg watched for the larger pictures, which gave her a better idea of whose tomb it was.

Corvin stopped when they reached one fork, putting his hand out to stop Reg from following the guide to the right-hand passageway.

"Look at that," he said sharply, pointing to an inscription on the wall. "I can read this one. It is a warning not to enter."

Reg looked at it. Of course, the symbols meant nothing to her. She looked at the guide. "Do we need to be worried about this? I'm

P. D. WORKMAN

not keen on getting trapped forever in someone else's tomb, you know."

The guide made a motion, inviting Reg to go forward, continuing in the direction he had chosen.

"Maybe it's just a warning to people with bad intentions," Reg told Corvin. "Like how the wards around my cottage will keep out someone who intends me harm. But not a friend."

"You're not exactly a friend with whoever is laid to rest here."

"But I am. I'm bringing back his rings and jewels. Why wouldn't he welcome me for that?"

"Reg…"

"He says it is safe."

"He doesn't know."

"He seems like he knows."

"You are too trusting. You can't believe that someone is safe and knows what they are talking about just because you think they look trustworthy. What do you know about this guy? Really know about him? Just that you met him here. You don't know anything about his family, where he came from, even his name. How can you trust someone like that? He has no past. He has no way to tell you anything. Why would you put someone like that in charge of your future?"

"I know him. He's not going to lead me into danger."

Corvin shook his head, huffing angrily. But he followed Reg as she continued down the right-hand passageway.

CHAPTER FORTY-THREE

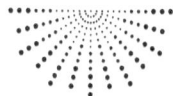

*R*eg had to admit that she was a *little* anxious following the tall Black man in the dark passage of the tomb. She didn't believe that he was leading her into danger, but she felt a little uneasy at Corvin's warning, and tried to reach ahead with all of her senses to determine if they were going to walk into a trap.

It wasn't like she and Corvin hadn't ever run into a trap together before. They did tend to run headlong into things.

"Do you sense anything?" she asked him quietly.

Corvin shot her a look. He looked ahead to their guide, then back at Reg. "No. Why? What do you feel?"

"Nothing, I just wanted to make sure. We should still be careful."

"You may be a little late on that."

"What do you mean?"

"We are stuck in the middle of a warren of caves, with warnings on the walls, and little air or light. It is sort of the definition of recklessness."

Reg was quiet, thinking about that for a while. She didn't like to be reckless, but it was something that had plagued her from childhood. Impulsive behavior. Doing things that parents had warned her against just to see what would happen. Thinking that she knew better and could control the outcome, only to find out that they had been right in the first place.

Some people learned from the mistakes of others. Some, like Reg, had to try everything themselves. She sighed and followed the guide, flitting like a shadow just at the edge of the light her fire cast.

He stopped before another doorway and waited for her. Reg and the others caught up.

"Is this it?" Reg peered into the room, brightening her fire for a moment to visualize more of the room.

It looked promising. There were more murals, a lot more hieroglyphics and, as they entered, she saw that there were dishes, furniture, and other practical items that the dead would need in the afterlife.

But as Reg entered and looked around, everything felt wrong and out of scale. She looked at Corvin and then looked around the room.

It was smaller than she had guessed. All of them inside would make it quite crowded. And the rectangular stone box sarcophagus was tiny. A prince who had died while still an infant? Reg stood still, feeling for any ghosts, for something to explain what they were seeing. She looked around at the pictures on the walls.

Corvin too was making a careful study of the symbols and pictures. Reg, looking only at the pictures, drew her conclusion before Corvin.

"A cat?"

She looked down at the small sarcophagus and saw that it also had a picture of a cat on the side and the wrapped bundle was about the right size. Reg got closer to the carvings on the side with her fire to look at the details of the cat picture. A cat which looked remarkably like Starlight, even down to the tuxedo vest markings on his chest. Reg gazed at it, a feeling gradually growing in her chest, warm and then hot.

"These hieroglyphs are about Bastet," Corvin advised. He pointed at a couple of pictures and inscriptions. "Defender of the king and goddess of the sun." He indicated several of the pictures on the wall. "Pictured as a lioness, as a god with a cat head, and as a domesticated cat." He shook his head slowly. "I did not know that cats were domesticated so early."

Reg looked back down at the sarcophagus. She raised her eyes to look at the other figures on the walls. Were they all representations of

Bastet? Or were some of them another cat? Maybe this was the tomb for the king's cat, a beloved pet that he had promoted to a god.

"Was Bastet always a female god?" she asked Corvin.

"That's a strange question. She was generally portrayed as a lion or a woman, yes."

"Who are the other figures? Are they all Bastet?"

Corvin looked around at them. "Perhaps some are the king. Others are probably servants or members of the family."

Reg looked at her guide to ask him his opinion. He seemed to know more about the ancient Egyptian than Corvin did, despite Corvin's bragging. Living in Egypt, he had probably been taught in school and been exposed to other myths and histories that Corvin hadn't studied. She opened her mouth and then closed it, looking into the guide's face.

Something had changed. The guide's appearance had visibly shifted since the last time she had looked him in the eye. Reg knew that it had to be just a trick of the light. He hadn't actually changed; she was just having one of those moments when something familiar suddenly seemed different and alien. It had happened more than once before, and she had been told that it was perfectly normal. Just one of those little brain hiccups, like deja vu.

Corvin noticed Reg's distraction and looked back at the guide. He too stopped and studied the guide, frowning.

"A trick of the light." Corvin didn't say it out loud, but inside Reg's head.

Reg raised her fireball higher, so that the light struck the guide directly in the face instead of underlighting it.

But Corvin was wrong. It wasn't a trick of the light. The guide's face had morphed into something much more feminine. Reg recalled Harrison's amusement over her difficulty with the idea that Starlight had been Bastet in a previous incarnation. Reg couldn't understand how a female goddess could have become a male cat. And one occasion, when Starlight had leaped to Harrison's defense, he had taken the form of a warrior, a full-sized man, instead of a cat. Harrison was amused that Reg had a hard time recognizing Starlight in another form or not understanding how fluid his physical identity was from one life to the next.

And then there was the time that Harrison had appeared to them as the proto-goddess Eostre. Sarah had been perfectly willing to identify him as a female goddess instead of a male immortal, since that was the form he had taken, but Reg could hardly wrap her mind around it. People were individuals. They didn't shift between species and genders and names.

Only, apparently, they did. She should have known that from her early days in Black Sands, when she had discovered that the fairies changed children of other species—both human and pixie, as examples —into fairies. Not just that they adopted them and treated them as if they were members of the family no different from anyone else, but actually used magic to transform them into something completely different. Calliopia had completed her transformation to a fairy, and would never again be pixie, even though she had taken a pixie mate.

All those different things should have prepared Reg for the fact that her guide was now clearly a woman rather than a man. Still tall and Black, with much the same lean body shape as he—she—had had before. But an identifiably feminine face. Reg looked around the room, taking it all in, trying to put all the pieces together.

"Is this… this is the tomb of Bastet," Reg suggested.

Corvin looked at her, rolling his eyes. "I highly doubt that. If there was an actual Bastet, and she wasn't just an invention of the people, then she was an immortal, and wouldn't have had a tomb."

But Reg looked back at her guide, a handsome woman watching her with clear, perceptive eyes. No longer two brown eyes, but one blue and one green. Suggesting that changing form from man to woman was not the only shift she was capable of. "You. Are you Bastet? Is this your tomb?"

The woman's gaze was approving, but she still gave no audible answer.

"Can I call you Bastet?"

There was no indication that she should not or that it would be considered sacrilegious. Corvin was still doubtful about the whole thing. But he didn't know Reg's previous relationship with Bastet. Reg was just starting to make the connections. Why Starlight had not been home when she went back to Florida to return Horace. Why her guide did not speak. How she had known where the tomb was and that Reg would be able to jump there.

Reg looked down at the small mummy again. If Bastet had been an immortal who sometimes took the form of a cat, then how had she died? Reg didn't even want to think further along this path, like how Bastet had then been reincarnated, and if so, how many times, and whether she still had power in each of those forms that would allow her to change her form. Was her death really a death, or just leaving behind one previous form?

Reg shook her head. She would not think about all those questions, or she would remain in that tomb for the rest of her life trying to sort it all out in a way that made sense.

"Do I give the rings and gems to you, then? You could have told me that before."

Bastet turned her head to the side slightly. *No.*

"Then the picture we saw to start out with in the first room, that was not you?"

No.

"The person in that picture was a man," Ahmed pointed out. "It was not Bastet."

Reg liked the way that he said *Bastet.* Even though he was speaking English, it had a slightly different intonation and pronunciation from when Reg had heard it used before. More intimately familiar.

"But…" Reg indicated Bastet. Ahmed had surely not missed her transformation from a man to a woman.

"And I am not so sure," Corvin said slowly.

They all looked at him.

"Sure of what?" Reg asked.

"The king with the rings on his finger… I was not sure, when we looked at it, that he was a man."

"He looked like a man," Reg objected.

"But there were subtle variations from the traditional Egyptian depiction of a king."

"He had a beard."

"But when women took the throne in Egypt, even as regents, they often wore a fake beard as a symbol of their authority. A beard on the picture does not necessarily mean that it was a man. Also, he was painted with yellow ocher."

Reg looked at the pictures of Bastet on the wall. The skin tone was yellowish. "So…?"

"Typically, men were painted with red ocher, and women with yellow ocher."

Reg considered this. "Well… okay. Maybe the king was actually a queen. But it wasn't Bastet, because Star—Bastet says that we are not to give them to her."

"Do we have to go to another tomb?" Ahmed suggested.

"No, I don't think so," Reg disagreed. "The picture of the queen at the beginning had the rings. There must be someone else interred here in a different room…"

She looked at Bastet, who watched and waited with crystal-clear, steady eyes.

"Is there another room?" Reg inquired. "Or a ghost or somewhere else to leave an offering?"

There was no disagreement. *Yes*, then.

"We keep looking," Reg told the others.

"What about the downward passage? Now that we have seen this room, maybe we can take that one. We know that a tomb is most likely to be at the bottom of that passage."

Reg looked at Bastet. "Will you lead the way? Is that the one we are supposed to take?"

Bastet stepped toward the doorway.

CHAPTER FORTY-FOUR

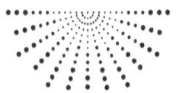

*R*eg walked with Bastet, since she was the one with the light. Bastet could, presumably, see in the dark, but it seemed to be polite for Reg to walk with her to share her light. Both of the men seemed to be feeling a little put out by the events of the day. Finding that their other guide was a woman as well as or instead of a man. And that she was Bastet, which neither of them fully believed. Ahmed was somewhat superstitious and was therefore more likely to believe that one of the ancient gods might have appeared to them. While Corvin had seen other immortals like Harrison, Weston, and the Witch Doctor, he didn't have much faith in the idea that their guide was Bastet. Why not? Because she was in the form of a woman? Because he thought that she was less in some way than the immortals that he had previously seen? He was the one who was studying ancient Egypt, so it seemed like he should be the one most excited to see her. He hadn't given any good reason for rejecting the idea that she might be Bastet.

They reached the intersection that met up with the down-sloping passage and stopped at the head of it. Reg looked at Bastet, not sure why they had stopped. Bastet looked at the walls. Reg held her light up and looked at Corvin, wondering whether he would be able to interpret this inscription.

He cast his eyes over it, mouth pressed into a thin line.

"Can you read it?" Reg prompted.

"It is not as clear as Middle Kingdom would be to me. The syntax has changed, and some of the glyphs are different... but the meaning is fairly clear."

Reg looked at him, waiting.

"The tomb is cursed." Corvin said it as if Reg should have figured that out already. And maybe she should have.

"But so was the one for Bastet, and we were safe to go in there."

"Maybe. But," Corvin looked grudgingly at their guide, "that could be because we went in with Bastet, if that's really who it is. But going farther than this... unless *he* is also going to turn into someone else, we may be inviting a curse upon ourselves. And your whole purpose in coming here was to rid yourself of the cursed stones."

They both looked at Ahmed, as if he might morph into the pharaoh who was entombed there. Ahmed just blinked at them and shook his head.

"I am who I said I am," he objected. "I am not one of the ancients." He sounded somewhat peeved that they would even think it.

Reg shrugged. "If Bastet believes we are safe to go down there, then we can go."

Bastet was at the head of the group, waiting for them to follow. Corvin still hesitated. Ahmed did not look too keen on going down to a cursed tomb either.

"I do not believe in curses," he said. "Yet... why would one take the chance?"

"You two can stay up here, then," Reg said. "In the dark. Bastet and I will go down and deal with this, and then we'll be back."

"Or you won't," Corvin pointed out.

"I will be."

"Do you know what you are going to find down there?"

Reg looked at the pictures on the walls. She looked at the floor that sloped down into darkness. She closed her eyes and reached out her senses, trying to identify anything that was ahead of them. She should look for traps. She should think ahead and consider the matter before going on.

There would be ghosts. She could feel more than one entity ahead. She'd always had trouble differentiating between the dead and the living, but she thought it was pretty obvious that anyone else there in the tomb was going to be dead. No one else had entered the tomb in millennia.

She searched for other magic, wards or triggers that might have been placed to await their arrival. Bits of magic that she couldn't understand or account for.

But the place was laced with magic. She could see it woven through the hieroglyphics written on the walls. At the doorway of every passage and room. Imbuing the objects that had been left there to accompany the dead in their afterlife. And of course, in the mummies themselves. Everything was awash in magic, and she wasn't accomplished enough to understand it.

"There is a tomb," she said finally. "A very old one. And I'm going to go down for a visit." She looked at Bastet. "And hopefully, with an old friend along, the Pharaoh won't mind."

Corvin and Ahmed looked at each other, neither one willing to say that they refused to go, but at the same time, reluctant to join. Maybe Corvin had learned something from their past adventures. The Corvin she had met when she first arrived at Black Sands would already be halfway down to the tomb, ready to see what magical artifacts he could get his hands on. Of course, it was that propensity that had landed them both in trouble in the past.

"Let's go," Reg said to Bastet.

Bastet stepped forward. She had a smooth and silent gait, seeming to skim over the stone floor like a ghost. Reg might have thought that she was a ghost, if she hadn't been so substantial. At least now she knew why the guide had seemed so familiar to her. She had seen Starlight transformed into a man once before, but she couldn't remember enough details of his appearance as a soldier before to know whether he had put on the same face as her guide, or if it was just his manner and his aura that had been familiar.

Reg didn't say anything else to Corvin and Ahmed, but she could hear them following her. So they had decided that they didn't want to stay in the pitch black after all. She wondered which of them had been the first to step forward to follow her. Or whether they had counted to three and stepped forward together. She shook her head.

There was not a square foot of the wall that was not covered with carvings and symbols. They were not as bright as the walls in the tombs she had visited in the Valley of the Kings, but they weren't as brightly lit, and maybe the ones in the Valley were cleaned regularly too, to keep the colors bright. Or maybe they even touched them up. Or maybe the pigments that they'd had available when this ancient tomb had been painted just hadn't been as bright or well-wearing as the ones several thousands of years later in the Valley of the Kings.

Corvin was murmuring something behind her, or maybe whispering inside her head. She wasn't sure which and she didn't want to turn to look at him. A spell? A lecture? Reading aloud the symbols that he could interpret?

"Is it far?" Reg asked Bastet, even though she knew that she wouldn't answer. She just wanted to hear her own voice for a minute. It was small in the dimly lit, cavernous space. There was the whisper of an echo, trailing off into the distance. Reg could no longer see the ceiling above her, unless she made her fire brighter, and she didn't want to do anything that would startle or upset any entity that remained there after so many thousand years.

The pictures on the walls were not particularly cheery. They detailed the wars that the Pharaoh had apparently fought, orders given, slaves managed, goods traded. It had been a powerful and wealthy empire, if the pictures were to be believed.

CHAPTER FORTY-FIVE

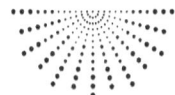

The slope of the floor suddenly changed, and Reg stumbled for a moment before she got reoriented. It had, she thought, evened out, so that she was now walking on the level instead of a downslope. She waited for the men to catch up and, once more, they surveyed their surroundings.

"You're sure you should go on?" Corvin asked once more.

"What else am I going to do? Give the gems to you?" Reg challenged. "This is what I came here for. I don't even understand why you are here. You didn't have to come to Egypt or to come with me to the tomb."

Corvin grumbled, but it was not loud enough for Reg to make out the words, and she was sure that if she heard them, she would be even more angry with him. What right did he have to show up and tag along with them and then to complain about what they were doing? He could have stayed in the Valley of the Kings and looked at the other artifacts. Maybe he would find something that still retained a small amount of magical powers that he could suck up.

She looked back at Corvin suddenly. Was that it, then? All the artifacts that had been on public display for the last century had been long-since drained of any special powers they might have had. But the artifacts in a tomb like this, that had lain undiscovered for thousands of years? It could be filled to the brim with powerful objects that Corvin would want to drink.

"You aren't to touch anything," she told him firmly. "If you have any concerns about the curse being real, then you won't take the chance of touching anything and having the mummy come after you, or catching some ancient disease and dying next week."

"I'm not touching anything," Corvin said mildly, his mouth curling up slightly in the corner.

Reg wished that he didn't look so cute when he was being oppositional. She kept her gaze as hard and unyielding as she could, channeling all of those foster moms that she had been exposed to who could freeze a hardened juvie hood in his tracks with one look.

"That means taking anything from here. Even powers that you can suck out from three feet away. You are not to take anything from here."

He cocked his head slightly, looking not the least bit cowed by her attempt at sternness. "What about the air that I breathe? I suppose you want that back too."

Reg shook her head. "If you get cursed because you're stupid and can't keep your hands off anything with magical powers, that's on you. Not on me. Everybody here is a witness that I told you not to take anything. You're the one who forced your way on this trip. So you'd better be on your best behavior."

He was still smiling. "I'm always on my best behavior with you, Regina."

Sheesh, even in the middle of a thousands-of-years-old tomb, he still poured on the charm, figuring he could cloud her mind and sway her into doing whatever he wanted to.

Reg turned away from him and continued down the passageway, faster than they had been walking before. Bastet looked back and picked up her speed as well, looking a bit spooked that everyone was suddenly moving so fast behind her. Reg let herself slow back down gradually. She didn't want to be scaring anything in the tomb.

* * *

There was a boom far off down the tunnel, as if something big had just been dropped or a big door closed tight. Reg's step faltered. She looked at Bastet for her reaction.

"What was that?"

Bastet took another step along the passage, indicating that she would continue. Reg hesitated. Whatever was down there, it sounded pretty big. Most ghosts were not able to manifest that strongly. It took a lot of energy to be able to move objects in the physical world, and most ghosts did not have enough energy stored up over time to do much more than appear or make a few noises. Even coming to a seance to speak through a medium like Reg took an enormous amount of energy and they probably had to be saving it up for a while before they could make another appearance.

"What is it?" Reg asked, hoping that Bastet would give her some sign or reassurance. Reg studied the walls around her, raising her fireball to study some of the ominous-looking pictures.

But Bastet did not answer or make any sign. She just waited, taking another step and looking over her shoulder for Reg to follow her. Just like Starlight often did when trying to lead Reg step by step to his empty food dish. *Come on. Come on. This way. Another step...*

Reg wanted to be sure that she wasn't going to *become* someone's dinner this time.

She kept walking, her heart pounding hard, scenes from every mummy and horror movie she had ever seen flashing through her brain. All of the *don't go in there* moments. She had mocked heroes and heroines who seemed to lose all brainpower and walk into the most dangerous situations possible without regard for their own health and safety.

And there she was, acting like she was one of them. Walking toward something big and powerful in hopes of appeasing it with a bit of jewelry.

"I sure hope I'm not going to regret this."

"So do I," Corvin intoned dryly.

"Okay. So I am getting a little nervous now. But what are we going to do? Turn around and go back now? Then we'll be cursed for sure. I brought the gems here to offer them to the rightful owner, I'm not going to back out now."

Shhhh!

Reg wasn't sure whether it was a command to be quiet or just a puff of wind that raced down the corridor making a rushing sound. But it sounded like the shushing of Mrs. Perth, a high school librarian who had been out to get Reg. She had always been within hearing whenever Reg had said a word in the library, acting like she was the noisiest, most disruptive student in the school. Mrs. Perth peered through her old granny glasses down her long, bony nose while she hushed Reg and gave her a fierce, quelling look.

Reg wondered whether Mrs. Perth would have had any effect on Corvin, or if he would just have turned on the charm and she would have melted into an old-lady puddle at his feet. She stifled a giggle.

Regina! The rebuke from Corvin was inside her head. He hadn't dared to voice it aloud.

Giggling after being quieted by an ancient mummy was probably not the brightest thing she could do. If she wanted to stay on the good side of this pharaoh, then maybe she should guard herself a little bit better.

Sorry.

Bastet looked back again. That same beckoning, overly-patient look. The humans were being too slow again. The humans were likely to let a cat starve if they didn't get a little bit of encouragement. Maybe a nip on the ankles.

Coming. Reg directed this reassurance at Bastet, following at a slightly quickened pace to make up for lagging and giggling. It was just because she was nervous. Plenty of people giggled and got silly when they were nervous about something. She remembered one girl going into hysterical laughter and tears before the big final exam in... one of the classes that she'd managed to fail before aging out of foster care and leaving it all behind.

Her feet were too loud in her own ears. She could barely hear Corvin and Ahmed, and could hear nothing at all from the cat-footed Bastet, but her own feet sounded like a giant stomping down the hall. Ruan would have called her a buffalo. Or maybe an elephant. Humans were so clumsy and noisy, and Reg Rawlins worst of all.

She was almost laughing by the time they reached the end of the hall. But keeping in mind that girl who had eventually had to be taken off to the nurse's office to recover from her hysterics, Reg kept it under control and was careful not even to smile.

CHAPTER FORTY-SIX

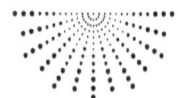

*T*he doorway before them was open. Reg had half-expected it to be shut, after the big boom. Slamming the door before she could get to it. Sorry, Miss Rawlins. Try again in another century.

But maybe it had been the door slamming open. Maybe that *shhhh* had been the rush of fresh air as a ventilation shaft was thrown open so that they wouldn't run out of oxygen before they finished their quest. Who could tell? That boom might very well have been a good thing.

There was a chanting coming from the dark room beyond the doorway. Reg stopped and listened to it.

She didn't know any Egyptian, modern or ancient. Maybe this was where Corvin's knowledge of conversational Middle Kingdom would come in handy. Hopefully there were enough words that were still the same between Archaic and Middle Kingdom that he would be able to get their mission across to the angry mummy waiting for them.

"Reg?" Corvin prompted.

"Yes?"

"Are you going in?"

Reg glanced back at him. "I was hoping you could translate that."

Corvin looked around at the walls. "The inscription?"

"The chant."

Corvin looked at her blankly. Ahmed didn't give any sign that he could hear the chant either.

"There's…" Reg motioned to the room. "A…"

"A chant," Corvin repeated.

"You can't hear it?"

"No. Not me. Must be something you are picking up psychically."

"Dang." Reg tried to discern the individual words or sounds so that she could repeat it back to Corvin with some accuracy.

He put his hand lightly on her shoulder, giving her a jolt. Then he closed his eyes. Reg realized there was no need to repeat the chant back to him. She just needed to channel it to him. Their shared bond was close enough that it didn't take any extra energy for her to do so. It seemed like the natural thing to do.

Corvin's head went up as he listened and tried to make it out. He shook his head. "I don't… hear any words. It might just be a meditation chant, empty sounds to try to clear the mind. Or it could be something that I'm not familiar with. Sumerian, maybe, or some offshoot of archaic Egyptian that I've never heard before. I assume there were probably different accents and dialects in different parts of the land. They didn't have the same communication abilities that we have now. Populations that were isolated developed language along different paths and became more distinct—"

"Yeah, I don't want to hear it, professor," Reg said, stopping him.

Maybe when Corvin got nervous, he switched into intellectual mode to cover his anxiety. He looked at her for a moment, face red with anger or the light from the fire. Then he nodded. It was not, of course, the time for a lecture on the way that languages developed.

"Do we go in?" Reg asked Bastet. That's who she should have spoken to in the first place. At least Bastet could understand the language of the time. "Is it… a prayer? Something that we shouldn't interrupt?"

Bastet stepped into the doorway and looked back. She looked into the room, and then back behind her again. The same behavior as cats around the world when presented with an open door? *Do I go in? Do I stay out?*

Reg waited, trying to curb her impatience. She had asked the question; she should wait for the answer. It was only fair. Whether it took Bastet a million years to make the decision or not.

Eventually, of course, Bastet stepped into the room, and took short steps into the darkness, then looked back at Reg, waiting for her to enter as well. She hadn't set off any booby traps and hadn't been immediately struck down by whatever entity was down there. So far, so good. Reg stepped into the room. She too remained herself, not turned into a beetle or a toadstool. Always a good sign. This seemed to encourage Corvin and Ahmed as well, and they stepped in behind her.

Reg paused. In a horror movie, that would be the point at which the big stone door closed behind them, once they were all in the trap. But no door closed.

Reg enlarged her fire slightly so that they would be able to see around the room without having to go any farther. Get the lay of the land and decide on their next step.

The walls were adorned with many carvings and pictures, as they had been in the rest of the tomb. Studying the pictures, Reg thought that these ones were more discernibly female. Despite the fact that most of the pictures showed the Pharaoh with a beard, the face was more feminine than Reg had initially perceived. And the skin tone was yellow ocher.

"Do we know… the name of the Pharaoh?" Reg asked in a low voice. It would be best if they could address her with the right name and titles. Ghosts liked that. To know that they were remembered after their deaths and that their lives had not been so insubstantial that they were immediately forgotten.

Corvin was studying the walls. He swallowed and looked at Ahmed, as if expecting him to speak up. But Ahmed had said that he didn't know ancient Egyptian.

"Bastet?" Reg prompted, hoping that now that they were in the final chamber, it would all be revealed. Just because Bastet was drawn as a lioness, that didn't mean she really couldn't talk. Why would something as powerful as a god be unable to speak aloud? And if she chose not to speak aloud, then why didn't she at least put the answers into Reg's head?

"Mer…" Corvin started, and for a moment, Reg thought that he was trying to say *meow* or *purr* to communicate something to Bastet.

Maybe in legend she could only communicate in cat speak. "Merneith," Corvin finished finally.

He stopped. He looked at Ahmed,

"Merneith?" Ahmed's eyes widened. "This is not Merneith."

"That is what the cartouche says," Corvin insisted.

"Who or what is Merneith?" Reg demanded.

I am Merneith.

CHAPTER FORTY-SEVEN

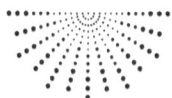

*R*eg whirled around, looking for the source of the voice that resonated down to her breastbone. She felt suddenly light-headed, as if her blood were no longer reaching her brain. She reached out to steady herself on the nearest shelf.

She hadn't really taken stock of her surroundings, and pulled back immediately after steadying herself. There was a raised box beside her, similar to the one that she had seen in Bastet's tomb, but bigger. A huge stone box that presumably held the mummy of the Pharaoh. Not something that you stuck your hand into. She hadn't touched anything disintegrating inside the box, but all the same, it probably was not good etiquette to stick her hand into someone else's casket without permission.

"Merneith?" Reg looked around. Looking for a figure, for the shape of the spirit somewhere nearby.

She was glad to see that Corvin and Ahmed looked just as shaken as she felt. That at least meant that the voice was outside her head. The manifestation was not limited to only her.

"Do you want to show yourself?"

"Who disturbs my rest here?"

"This can't be the tomb of Merneith," Ahmed insisted.

Reg glared at him. She didn't ask him "Why not?" but it was certainly implied.

"Scientists have already found *two* tombs of Merneith. This would be a *third* tomb."

"How could she be buried in three different places?"

"She couldn't," Corvin said. "I mean, she could—part of the body in one place and part in the other, but the Egyptians were pretty keen on keeping the corpse intact, for obvious reasons."

"So, what…? One was the main house and one was the summer-house? So she could go on a little vacation?"

"No," Corvin smiled at that, despite how tense they both were. "More like one was a red herring, a big, obvious tomb, and the other was where she would really be entombed, where no one would find her."

"A secret tomb."

"Yes." Corvin nodded quickly. "Long entrance passageways that could be collapsed or filled with stone once she was interred, and all the slaves who had been used to build the secret tomb would be… disposed of so that they couldn't tell its location."

"But why a third?"

Corvin shook his head. "I never heard that Merneith had three tombs. It's news to me, too."

"But you said that the… name tag said Merneith."

"It does."

"Then… were there more than one? Maybe it was a common name back then."

"Who disturbs my tomb?" the resonant voice demanded again.

"Well, whatever Merneith she is, she's certainly cranky," Reg observed. She looked around, hoping again for a physical manifestation to address her remarks to. "Merneith. I apologize for disturbing your rest."

"Who are you?"

A wind hissed through the tomb, cold and biting, snatching Reg's breath away so that she couldn't answer at first.

"I am Reg Rawlins. I have come looking for the rightful owner of these rings and stones."

There was no response. Maybe the ghost was thinking this over. Reg looked at the others, eyebrows raised for any suggestions.

"I am here with Bastet," she said. "Bastet said that it would be okay for us to come down here. You two are friends, right?"

"Bastet?" the voice repeated. "After so many years?"

There was another wind, and this time the ghost did manifest, appearing near Bastet. A tall, dark-skinned woman with rough-hewn features. She was not wearing the fake beard, and had markings on her face emphasizing her eyes.

Reg bowed her head slightly and tried to look small and insignificant. Which wasn't too hard. She was feeling very small and insignificant.

"Merneith. It is an honor to meet you."

Merneith did not have eyes for Reg. She saw Reg but immediately discounted her. Her eyes skipped past Corvin and Ahmed as if they weren't even there and fastened on Bastet.

"Bastet!" She reached out and touched Bastet's cheek, then laid her face alongside Bastet's for a moment in greeting. Not quite a kiss, but not the barely-touching bussing of cheeks that Reg had seen in the society set either.

"The rest shall go!" Merneith ordered. Wind pushed through the room, driving them the way they had come.

"No, no!" Reg protested. "We came here on a mission!"

"Your mortal affairs are none of my concern," Merneith waved this aside. "I care not."

"Don't you care about these?" Reg held her hand out, displaying the rings.

Merneith stepped closer, looking at the rings, the shadows on her face dancing in the flickering of Reg's fire. Her nose cast a long, dark shadow. Reg tried not to stare at it.

"I was hoping these are yours," she explained. "I have been trying to take them home. There was a mural in the first room we arrived in. I think it was you, with these rings on your finger. They're yours, aren't they?"

Merneith held out her hand. In her hurry to remove the rings, Reg scraped her finger. They were just a bit too tight around the knuckle.

She was surprised that Merneith, such a tall woman, would have such narrow fingers.

Reg handed them over to the ghost, and neither of them anticipated that the ghost was not solid enough to take them. They fell to the floor.

"Stupid mortal!" Merneith shrieked. "You disrespect me by throwing them on the floor! I would have killed anyone who did such a thing to me in life!"

"I'm sorry! I was just trying to hand them to you. I didn't mean to." Reg's stomach tightened. She felt like she had as a little girl when Norma Jean would scream at her for something she had done, something that was rarely within Reg's control and, more often than not, actually Norma Jean's fault. Merneith shouldn't have put her hand out to receive them if she wasn't material enough to hold them. Reg had just obeyed her command. "Do you want me to pick them up?"

"Imbecile! Of course! You would just leave them lying on the floor in the dirt?"

Reg bent swiftly over to retrieve them. She looked around the room. "Where would you like me to put them? Do you have a chest or a bowl or something you would like them to be in?"

"Look at this place," Merneith growled. "I spent years building the tombs, decorating them, furnishing them, getting everything just right. I made sure that only my closest family members would know where my body was really laid to rest."

Reg looked at the mummy in the sarcophagus, her skin crawling. "Yes, that seems like a very smart thing to do."

"Do you think so? Do you really think so?" Merneith's voice rose in a shriek.

Reg winced and looked around at the others. Couldn't one of the men who knew more about Egypt and its history and traditions step in to help her? But Corvin and Ahmed both seemed frozen.

Bastet stayed close to Merneith, gazing at her with clear eyes, exuding calm and reassurance. Reg wasn't sure that the feeling was helping at all. Merneith seemed pretty worked up about something.

"I'm sorry. I don't know what happened."

"Does this look like the place you would like to spend eternity?"

Reg looked around at the room. It was very old. And despite the richness of the carvings and paintings around them, there was little of value in the room. Some Coptic jars set into a niche in the wall. A few broken dishes and a goblet. No piles of food or treasures. And Reg hadn't seen the bodies of dead slaves on the way in, slaves who might have been intended to protect the tomb or to serve Merneith in her afterlife. No family members. No other sign of another soul, other than the mummy of Bastet.

"What happened?" Reg asked. Maybe there had been an earthquake and the tomb had been buried. Maybe there had been war or an outbreak of plague and Merneith had died at a time when it was inconvenient for everyone to complete the arrangements that Merneith had made, having to compromise by just laying her mummy there alone, with no ceremony, wealth, or company.

"You want to know what happened?" Fury sped across Merneith's features, making her flicker in and out several times as she tried to stay in control.

The broken plates spun and flew around the room like they were in the middle of a whirlwind. Reg and the others put their hands up in front of their faces to try to prevent sharp bits of debris from cutting their skin. Reg tried to think of a way to dampen Merneith's anger. Like Bastet, she did the best she could to exude feelings of calm and comfort that Merneith would be able to feel and absorb. Positive energy to replace the negative energy. Merneith had been there for a long time, stewing over what had happened to her. She'd had hundreds of years to work herself up into a lather.

"I do want to know," Reg confirmed. "Do you want to tell me? I'm sorry it's so painful…"

"I am not hurt. I am not a weeping woman. I am a king!" Merneith shouted. "I am the greatest king this country has ever known! Not a queen," she said, her voice lower, threatening, "not a regent to someone else. I myself was the king. The first of my sex that this world has ever known. And the best, the most powerful, the most effective king in the history of humankind!"

Reg widened her eyes at Corvin and Ahmed, who knew more about the history, encouraging them to step in.

"Even now, thousands of years later, your name is still known," Corvin assured her. "Five thousand years, and the world has not forgotten."

Merneith looked at him for the first time, nodding proudly.

"You were the first," Ahmed agreed, his voice a little squeaky and breathless. "The first reigning quee—female ruler in recorded history. Even today, women cannot hold the type of powerful position that you did. Which you administered so well."

Reg bowed her head, hoping that would suffice to demonstrate her respect for Merneith. She was astounded that in all she had heard about Egypt, she had never heard of this woman. A king in her own right? Ruling a powerful country five thousand years ago? Why was her name not spoken in every girl's ear? Instead, they heard of Hatshepsut. Cleopatra. And in modern time, the Queen of England. Where were the other female rulers?

Had they removed Merneith's name from history? Ahmed seemed to know who she was; he was the one who had said she had two tombs. So her name couldn't have been wiped out, like she'd heard other rulers' names had been.

"They stole from me," Merneith addressed Reg again, her anger seething. "My own closest family members stripped this tomb. Took my gold and my rings of office and my gems of power." She shook her head, quaking with anger. "Can you imagine such treachery?"

No wonder she was so angry. They stripped everything that she had managed to keep for the afterlife, and then had forgotten all about her, burying the tomb so that it would never be found, and their treachery never revealed to anyone but the dead Merneith.

Reg looked around and found a bowl that was nearly whole. She put it on the edge of the stone box that held Merneith's body. She reverently put the two rings into it. She reached into her pocket and pulled out the baggie of gems.

Corvin's and Ahmed's eyes got very wide. Neither had known the extent of what she had when she'd said that she needed to return the stones to their rightful owner.

Reg held the plastic bag in the direction of Merneith for a moment. Then she slowly poured the gems into the bowl. Everybody watched the stream of jewels flowing into the bowl, covering up the rings.

"These were wrongfully taken from you," Reg said. "I return them to you, to do with as you please, to comfort you in your afterlife."

Merneith's eyes glowed more brightly than Reg's fire, which she was juggling around as she tried to restore everything to its rightful order.

"You have done well," Merneith admitted. "You have come far to restore this treasure."

"Yes. All the way from Florida."

The name obviously meant nothing to Merneith. But then, Reg hadn't expected it to.

"You must do more," Merneith announced.

CHAPTER FORTY-EIGHT

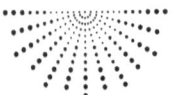

*U*h-oh.

Reg did not get a good feeling in her stomach when Merneith said that.

She had pretty much expended all of her mental energy getting the gems back to Merneith. She didn't want to do anything else.

"Why do I need to do more?" she asked. "Haven't I done more for you than anyone else in the last five thousand years?"

"You have returned what is mine. But you also made use of them."

Reg grimaced. She looked at Corvin, who raised an eyebrow. She had, in fact, used the rings. She had done it unintentionally to begin with. She had slipped them on in a moment of distraction and had activated them by returning to Egypt to talk to Kareem. On returning to Florida, she found that the rings and the gems had changed. Still, other than the different feeling she had around them and the dreams of returning to Egypt, they had not made much difference in her life.

Each request and demand she had made since going back to Egypt had been fulfilled. And that wasn't Reg. A few people might be kind to a tourist from the States, but not everyone. They wouldn't all go out of their way to do what she asked them to, no matter how strange.

That wasn't Reg's power. That was the rings. Merneith's power, even after thousands of years.

"Okay," she admitted cautiously. "I used them a little. But not that much. Just a few times, to help me to find you."

So what Merneith asked of her could not be too big. It had to be reasonable, in proportion to what Reg had done with the rings. Which had really been for Merneith's benefit anyway. Maybe the rings wouldn't even have worked if it hadn't been for Merneith's benefit.

"You must bring me a body."

"What?" Reg recoiled, her mind filling with pictures of zombies, blood sacrifices, children or animals on an altar. She wasn't doing anything like that. No matter what Merneith asked of her. She wouldn't commit violence to some innocent.

Merneith's eyes went over each of them in turned, examining each member of the party as she evaluated their strengths and weaknesses. Reg's stomach clenched. Did Merneith expect her to sacrifice one of the members of her party? The scenario was getting worse and worse.

"No," Reg told her, before she could make any suggestions as to how the bargain would be struck. "You can't have anyone from my party. I'm not doing anything to harm anyone."

"Harm?" Merneith repeated. "I ask you to harm no one."

"But you said… I don't know what it is you want." Reg didn't want to put words into the ghost's mouth. With her luck, suggesting that she'd thought Merneith meant a blood sacrifice would make her think that it was a good idea. And it wasn't. It definitely wasn't.

"I have been a wanderer all these years," Merneith told Reg. "I need a home."

"Isn't… this your home?" Reg looked around. "Maybe we could bring you a few things to make it more comfortable."

"This no home for my *sah*. I need a receptacle. A *khet*. To be able to hold my being. Like this one." She motioned to Corvin.

Reg turned wide eyes toward Corvin. "I'm sure you would enjoy possessing Corvin, but… isn't there another way? I can't really leave him behind here."

She remembered asking Bastet whether she should take Corvin along, and her affirmative answer. Had Bastet known that Merneith would ask for his body for her to inhabit? Bastet still said nothing, just watched and listened to her old friend.

Reg was still having a hard time wrapping her mind around the idea that her cat Starlight had been an Egyptian god and had known this first queen of five thousand years before.

"Before Bastet died, we had a bargain," Merneith told Reg. "She promised me that I would be able to use her cat form."

"Use it... how?"

Merneith let out an exasperated sigh that the living humans were being so stupid. "She would allow me to join with her, when my body died. We had a plan."

"But that deal was with your Bastet," Reg said sternly, getting an inkling of what Merneith was talking about. "You cannot use my cat."

That was all she needed, some ancient queen stomping around the house in Starlight's body. Reg thought the cat demanding now; how much more demanding would he be with this woman's ghost inhabiting him?

"No," Merneith agreed. She gave a little bow of her head instead of arguing as Reg had expected her to. "I understand my bargain was not with Bastet's current incarnation."

Reg sighed with relief. One disaster averted. What was it that Merneith wanted her to do? To provide her with someone else who would make room for her? Perhaps Reg herself? Reg already had enough voices in her head. She couldn't make room for another person, especially one with as strong a personality as Merneith.

"So, you want me to..."

"You must bring me a cat," Merneith said simply.

Reg looked around as if there might be kittens playing around her feet like in the statues of Bastet. Obviously, there were no cats in the tomb, or Merneith would not be asking for one. Cats were still much beloved in Egypt; surely it wouldn't take Reg long to find one and take it back to her. Although she felt a little queasy at the idea of leaving a kitten shut up in the tomb with the ghost. Who would take care of it?

"It cannot be just any cat," Merneith warned.

"I don't know about this," Reg said. "I'm not really good at matching up cats and their owners."

She'd tried to help with that once, and look at how it had turned out. Horace had ended up with someone who had unbound the piece of the Witch Doctor attached to him and had traumatized him. Kareem had been exactly the wrong person to match a kattakyn to. Who knew if the damage done to Horace had been permanent, or if it were something he would eventually get over? Reg had no idea how she would find Horace a home if he was just going to keep coming back to her in her dreams.

"It must be a cat who was willing to be joined with me," Merneith went on, ignoring Reg's protest. "Like Bastet agreed to."

"How... would you do that?"

"I don't know whether any of us have access to that kind of magic," Corvin warned.

Ahmed just blinked at them, maybe considering the word magic, and what he had seen and experienced that day. The people who had stepped into his world were very different. He would probably decide never to have anything to do with anyone who might potentially be magic again. He'd been through a lot.

"I can do this," Merneith told Corvin with a shake of her head. "I do not need *your* magic."

The first woman to rule a country, and Corvin still thought that she needed his help. Reg rolled her eyes. At least the next time he insisted he had to do something for Reg, she would know it wasn't personal. He just thought that all women were helpless.

"How will you know...? How will you talk with this cat to make sure that it doesn't mind?" Reg asked haltingly. "I can communicate some with cats, but that's a pretty difficult concept. I'm not sure how I would communicate that with it, or how it would tell me that it was okay with the idea." She paused. "Not all cats are Bastet."

"Bastet will help. Perhaps she already knows a candidate. She surely knew she would be coming back here and has been looking for a suitable host."

Reg turned her gaze to Bastet. Maybe she could talk to the queen in a way that Reg could not. Maybe their previous relationship and a shared language and culture years ago would allow them to communicate much more freely than Reg.

Bastet looked Reg in the eye and cocked her head to a slight angle.

Reg licked her lips, thinking. She had that awful feeling of having forgotten to answer everything on a test. No matter how she had done

717

on the portion that she had completed, she would fail it anyway. What was the question? Or what was the answer that she already knew but didn't know she knew?

CHAPTER FORTY-NINE

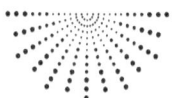

*R*eg tried to keep her gaze steadily on Bastet's eyes, to communicate all of her feelings and to pick up the slightest changes in Bastet's.

As Reg stared, Bastet suddenly seemed to be melting, shrinking down to a fraction of her size and folding over into a shape that Reg recognized. Her Starlight.

Reg bent over to pet him as he rubbed against her leg. Corvin made a choking noise. "Your cat?" He took in Reg's demeanor. "How are you not surprised by this?"

"I already knew," Reg pointed out the obvious.

"You knew? How could you know? When did you know?"

"I found out… through a client. And Uncle Harrison. A little while back."

"You knew that your cat was Bastet."

"Or had been… yes."

He shook his head in amazement. "This is… unbelievable. So, you will leave him here, so that he can be joined with this spirit."

"No. Didn't you hear? She already agreed that she didn't have any contract with Bastet in this form."

"But…"

"No, Corvin. Starlight is not staying here. He's coming home with me."

Corvin considered this. "Your other cat, then?"

"I don't have another—you mean Horace?"

He waved a hand. "I don't bother to learn their names. What point is there in that? Cats don't answer to their own names."

He looked at Starlight and didn't say, "Stupid creatures," but Reg heard it in her head. She glared at him. The worst part was that she knew that he knew the cats' names. As many times as he'd heard Reg and others refer to Starlight, he had never mentioned him by name to her. It was always "the cat." And he certainly knew Horace's name after all of the back and forth to Egypt.

"She wouldn't want Horace," Reg said slowly. "He's been... quite a problem lately. Because of... what he is. You know."

Corvin thought through the issues. Eventually, he shrugged. "Maybe he's just the thing for her. He could grow or shift on her command. And he's used to being joined with another entity. Maybe part of the reason he's having so much trouble is because he doesn't know how to govern himself by himself. He needs that... other prompting."

It would solve two problems at once, if Horace were amenable to joining with Merneith. Reg could be more sure of getting out of the tomb, with Merneith's anger sated and demands met. And she would have found another home for Horace. He wouldn't keep traveling back in her dreams if he were somewhere he was happy. He couldn't very well lie on Merneith's chest until she smothered, since she was already dead. It was a win-win solution.

If it worked.

"Maybe," Reg murmured. "Should we try? Should we tell her... *you know?*"

"I think she'll probably know what he is once we bring him. I don't think we'll need to tell her anything."

Reg kind of liked the idea of not having to tell Merneith anything. Just to give her the cat, say, "Nice meeting you," and go back home. Well, probably jump Ahmed back home, then pick up her stuff from the hotel, and then go home. Corvin could catch the plane back to

Florida. And Starlight would, of course, jump with Reg. All neatly fixed and tied up with a bow.

"I have a cat who might agree to your plan," Reg told Merneith. "I don't know for sure. I will have to talk to him first. And if he doesn't want to…"

"Then you will need to find me another," Merneith said archly.

Reg couldn't help raising her brows in disbelief at Merneith's cheek. It was one thing to ask for help, but it was another to try to order people around when she didn't really have any authority anymore. She had been dead and gone too many years to just pick up where she'd left off.

She wanted to mouth off to Merneith, to declare that she had never agreed to do anything for her, that Merneith already owed Reg for bringing the rings and gems back to her, not the other way around. There was no reason for Reg to serve her.

Except, of course, that she was stuck in a small room with a ghost that had been gaining in power for five thousand years and appeared to have built up some pretty good reserves. All she had to do was to take the last of the air from the room, and Reg would be dead. The atmosphere was already pretty thin. And there were four of them breathing it. Well, three and a half, now. Starlight would not need as much oxygen as Bastet.

"Go get this creature, then," Merneith said impatiently.

Reg could just imagine if she had to retrace all of her steps that day, and even to fly back to Florida to fetch Horace and bring him back. As far as Merneith knew, Reg might have to do all of that to bring Horace back. It wasn't exactly a simple process.

But Reg didn't have to do all that.

There was no proper furniture in the room, and Reg's legs and feet were killing her. Walking for so long, in and out of tombs, her flat feet slapping against all of the stone floors of the passageways, Reg's feet felt as though they'd been beaten to a pulp.

She sat down on the floor, with Merneith's stone box behind her. She needed to get comfortable. Or as comfortable as she could be. The stone wasn't particularly forgiving to her sitting bones or back, either.

Reg arranged herself the best she could and closed her eyes. She didn't have her crystal ball this time, which she always found helpful when doing a call. She wondered whether she would need Corvin's help to extend her range. She'd been able to jump back and forth between Florida and Egypt, and it shouldn't be that much more difficult to call Horace that far, should it?

Starlight rubbed against Reg and settled into her lap, rubbing against her encouragingly. Reg pressed him down gently until he snuggled into her lap. She slid her fingers through his fur and felt his warmth and encouragement, the little bit of an extra boost that she got whenever they joined their psychic powers together.

She wondered whether he had been holding back on his powers to avoid overwhelming her. It seemed like he had quite a bit more power than he had previously shared with her.

But she put all of that out of her mind. Those were considerations for another time. Another day. She needed to focus on only one thing. Horace. The pure-black cat back at the cottage. She pictured her home. The inside furnishings. The place where Starlight would have been snoozing and looking out the window if Reg had been home instead of jumping all the way to Northern Africa. The various places that Horace sometimes settled down to go to sleep, or things that he regularly got into or knocked over when he was out of control.

Then she saw him. Sitting right in the middle of the kitchen island. Where, of course, cats were not supposed to be sitting. Except that it was true that she sometimes let Starlight get away with it if he really wanted to look at something or talk to her, or if she were busy and couldn't be bothered to go over and move him off.

"Horace," Reg whispered. *"Come."*

He was, perhaps, more startled than Ruan or Corvin would have been. They could at least have understood what she was going to do and prepared themselves. But a cat had no way of understanding what was going to happen. Reg saw the world in a kaleidoscope through Horace's eyes, everything upside down and wonky, racing through space, and then eventually falling into the darkness at Reg's feet.

Reg reached out to pet and reassure him immediately. "It's okay, Horace. I know that was scary, but it's done now."

Horace pressed his furry cheek against Reg's hand, and then looked around, trying to figure out what had happened. He tensed, fur standing on end, as he looked at his surroundings and the people around him. Reg felt his terror at being back in Egypt. Back to where Kareem was. With Corvin, the soul-drinker and others that Horace didn't know. He was glad to see Starlight, but even he didn't look and feel like he was supposed to. Something had changed in him.

"It's okay," Reg assured him, reaching out both hands to try to corral Horace before he bolted. If he escaped, they might never be able to find him again. "It's okay, you're safe here. No one is going to hurt you. And if you don't want to stay after I tell you everything, then you don't have to. I'll take you right home before anything else. Just like I did last time. Remember how I took you back the last time?"

He hissed and spat, not liking her hands so close to him. He wanted to know that he had an escape route, but it was blocked off, not just with her hands but with fire. She was really serious about keeping him in that dreadful place.

Reg hadn't even thought about how the fire would scare him. It hadn't bothered Starlight, but then, he'd seen her playing with fire plenty of times with Davyn. She couldn't put it out, or they would all be plunged into darkness. Reg pushed the fire away from her, finding a slight depression in the floor where it nestled naturally. Horace relaxed a bit with the fire farther away.

"It's okay." Reg stroked him, trying to calm his fear and the anger that would naturally result from it. A being who had been abused would expect more abuse and would try to use the defenses he had learned in the past before he could be hurt again. Reg scratched his jaw and ear. "You're safe. You don't have to worry. I'm just going to tell you why you're here, okay? And if you don't like it, I'll take you straight back home."

Horace didn't move. He wasn't calming down as much as she had hoped, but he was definitely not on such high alert as he had been previously. Cautious and guarded, but not terrified.

She supposed that was progress.

"There is a ghost here," Reg explained. "A very old ghost. You see the symbols on the wall and the pictures? That is her. Merneith."

Horace wasn't particularly interested in the pictures. He could smell the ghost. And he'd probably smelled other ghosts around Reg at other times. It wasn't as if she managed to stay away from them all the time.

"Merneith is Starlight's friend."

Starlight got up from Reg's lap and he moved around Horace, going slowly and being careful not to do anything that would startle him. Horace bumped faces with Starlight, and the two of them sniffed and snuffled and groomed each other. Reg waited, wondering how much Starlight could convey to Horace through these actions. She knew it wasn't the same as direct language, but there was much that could be conveyed about their feelings with these social behaviors.

"Merneith has a problem. And you have a little problem. And I wonder if the two of you might be able to solve each other's problems."

Horace was calmer. He looked at Reg, waiting for more. She was glad Starlight was helping.

"Merneith has been a ghost for a long time and wants to rest in a body. She needs to be anchored. And you... have been in this body, but you are maybe missing that part of you that Kareem took away?"

Horace's alarm returned, his fur puffing out as if electrified.

"No, it's okay. Kareem is not here. And he won't come here. If he showed up here uninvited, Merneith would send him away. She's a very powerful ghost. She wouldn't let him hurt you anymore."

Horace calmed a little, but was still on edge. He didn't like even the mention of Kareem's name. Reg determined to proceed without mentioning it again.

"You have been feeling bad ever since he did that, and Harrison brought you to my house, hoping you would feel better there."

And he kept returning to her house, even though it was not the right place for him.

"I am hoping that you would feel better, more whole, if you were joined with this ghost."

Horace began licking his fur back down again. Reg sat there and listened to him and tried to feel his feelings as he groomed himself, thinking of all that Reg had said and Starlight had explained. The two men watching were impatient, shifting and sighing and acting like if they were restless enough, it would hurry along Horace's decision. But a washing cat could not be hurried.

Eventually, Horace stopped and was still. He sat like a statue, looking at Merneith's ghost.

"I think he is ready to try," Reg said. "But if he doesn't like it, then you have to leave him. I'll look for another host for you."

"He is a fine specimen," Merneith observed, noticing how large Horace was, Reg was sure. As Corvin had said, if Horace could grow and shift for her, that would probably make her very happy. She didn't actually have to protect herself from anyone in the outside world, because no one but Reg had discovered her tomb since it had been sealed, but it would probably make her feel better to know that she could grow Horace to monster size to protect her if she so wished.

CHAPTER FIFTY

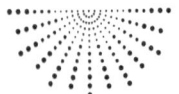

*M*erneith faded from sight. Reg continued to follow her progress by feel, as she moved slowly across the room toward Horace, taking care not to startle him by simply jumping in and taking over. Gradually, the two auras began to merge. Reg was waiting for the finish line, the point at which she could tell that Merneith had snapped into place and the two of them were one. But it was so gradual that she couldn't detect the line. Horace-Merneith looked around, surveying the room with his physical eyes.

Reg and the others waited. Horace-Merneith didn't start racing around the room like a devil-cat, or attack anyone, or puff out again and try to shake the ghost loose. He seemed to be contemplating the new feeling of being joined to the ghost, and the ghost of being joined with a physical body after so many millennia of waiting, neither in a big hurry to judge whether it would work or not.

"How is that?" Reg asked, prodding for some reaction.

Horace-Merneith looked at her, but didn't answer audibly. Reg waited some more. Horace began to walk around, picking his way delicately like the floor was wet. He walked over to Starlight, and the two cats rubbed against each other, bumping heads, rubbing cheeks, sniffing, and eventually grooming each other.

Reg couldn't feel any anger or alarm coming from Horace-Merneith. The cat's fear and anxiety seemed to have subsided, and the ghost's anger at the world with it. The combined entity seemed to be calm and satisfied with the state of things.

Horace-Merneith left the mutual grooming and jumped up to the edge of the stone box, where Reg had left the bowl of gems and the rings. Reg's breath quickened in anticipation. Now that the stones had been returned to their rightful place, they should no longer be cursed. If Horace-Merneith decided to give her any of them, Reg would be set for the next time that she wanted to negotiate with the dwarfs for more cash. Or she could choose to have them set in jewelry and wear them. Maybe she would make a ring of her own.

Horace-Merneith nosed at the gems, shifting them around. Eventually, he turned away from the bowl and Reg heard a slight *tick* as something hit the stone floor. She brightened her fire and brought it in closer. There was a large, sparkly diamond beside the sarcophagus. Reg picked it up, displaying it to Horace-Merneith.

"You dropped this. Did you want me to take it?"

Horace-Merneith sat on his haunches and looked at Reg. She reached out to touch his thoughts, now a strange mixture of catly feelings and Queen Merneith's words. She felt the calm *yes* answer, which reassured her that the diamond was meant for her.

Horace-Merneith bent down over the bowl once more. Twice more, he delicately picked out a gem with his lips and dropped it, though he deposited it directly into Reg's palm instead of on the floor. Then he sat up again and looked away from Reg.

That is all.

Reg nodded. She took in a deep breath, still feeling like she wasn't getting quite enough air, and let it out slowly.

"We will go, then, and leave you on your own." Reg looked around. "You will be okay here? Are there... mice? How will you eat?"

Horace-Merneith shook his head quickly, making the ear-flapping sound that always made Reg giggle. She wasn't sure whether that meant that the entity wouldn't need to eat, or that there was food present or he would find it somewhere else, but it didn't seem to be of concern, and wasn't any of her business.

"Okay... well, I'll be going home, then. I hope that everything works out the way you are hoping."

With the return of some of Merneith's riches and the emblems of her office, and a body to anchor her once more, hopefully she would be happy. Reg had done her part and received her payment.

Reg picked Starlight up. He snuggled comfortably in her arms. She looked at Corvin and Ahmed. "Ready to go back home?"

"Where will you take me?" Ahmed asked anxiously.

"Where do you want to go? Back to the airport where you left your car?"

Ahmed nodded. "That would be most gracious."

"Okay. Sounds good."

"Are you forgetting something?" Corvin prompted.

Reg frowned at him. "What?"

"You received three gems. There are three of us. Doesn't it seem logical to..."

Reg couldn't believe his gall. "Are you serious? You expect me to give you one of the gemstones?" She shook her head. "You were not even invited to come along. You weren't supposed to be here. You just took it upon yourself to fly to Egypt and track me down. That's your own business. And Ahmed..." Reg looked at the guide, hoping that she was not offending him. "I paid him for the tour already. I e-transferred his fees last night."

"I'm sure he wasn't expecting to be dragged to some remote tomb where he faced danger and—"

"I didn't drag him. He didn't have to come with me. And he wasn't in any danger." Reg chose to suppress the memories of Merneith throwing her dishes around the room in a whirlwind. Or the warnings and threats in the hieroglyphics on the way to the room. His life hadn't ever been in any *real* danger. "I'm sure he is glad that he got this education. What other guide has ever actually visited Merneith's third tomb? The one where her body really rests?"

Reg looked over at Ahmed, and he didn't object. He, at least, didn't seem to be angling for what was rightfully Reg's.

Reg glared at Corvin, daring him to try again. He shook his head, face red with suffused blood. "I came all the way here to protect you—"

"From what? Heat stroke? You could hardly even read most of the inscriptions. You didn't protect me from anything. Bastet-Starlight is the one who led and directed me, not you. And he doesn't care about jewels. I'll take him home and give him a tin of tuna. That will make him happy."

CHAPTER FIFTY-ONE

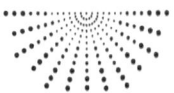

*R*eg jumped with everyone back to the airport so that Ahmed could pick up his car and carry on with his day. Probably to go home and have a good stiff drink.

Reg turned her attention back to Corvin. He was still angry, his mouth set in a scowl and the red flush still visible on his throat. She considered whether she should just leave him there and let him find his own way back to Florida. Sixteen hours in an airplane should give him plenty of time to cool off.

"You're not leaving me here," Corvin warned, catching the edge of her thoughts or reading her expression.

"I could, you know. You came here on your own. You can go home the same way."

"You're not that cold-hearted."

Reg would like to think that she was. She looked after herself first and, if Corvin was a threat to her, then why wouldn't she just leave him behind?

But she knew that she had stepped in and saved him before when others would not have. Standing up for him in spite of what he had done to wrong her. Taking him home after he'd been ensorcelled by Norma Jean, at her own peril. Other times when her friends had said that she had too much to do with Corvin and should stay away from him.

She was too warm-hearted for her own good. She'd been able to justify looking after herself first in other situations, but for some reason she couldn't leave Corvin alone.

"Fine. Where do you want me to take you?"

"Back to your place would be nice." Despite his anger at her not sharing her wealth with him, he couldn't help but fall back into the familiar pattern of engineering opportunities to charm her whenever he could. His voice was once again a low, intimate purr.

"No. Starlight and I will go home after we drop you off."

She felt as if she were taking a school child home after a particularly long field trip. The whole adventure in Egypt seemed a little distant and surreal.

"What about dinner?" Corvin suggested. "You could drop the cat off and then you and I go out to eat."

He knew he could often tempt her to go out to eat. Reg might have to start eating at home to try to break the pattern. She resisted the offer. "Not today, I need to spend some time at home…"

She didn't know why she always felt like she had to give him a reason. He never accepted her excuses anyway. Unlike Damon, Corvin wasn't a diviner, but he had a direct connection with her brain, and he could often tell when she was lying.

"Now that you've dealt with the gems and the other cat, why do you need to be anywhere? You've had a long day and should just be giving yourself time to relax."

"I am. At home, with Starlight."

"I want to hear all about what happened before I got to Egypt. You running off like that, I missed all of the first day…"

"Later. Tonight, I'm at home. Now, you want me to take you somewhere, or leave you here?"

Corvin grumbled. "Fine. Back to my house, I suppose. I really couldn't tempt you with something to eat? Some nice fresh fish? A walk on the beach?"

Reg just shook her head. He knew how dangerous the beach was. "Back to your house, then."

She touched his arm, remembered all of the sights and sensations of his house all too quickly and, in a moment, they were back there. Corvin leaned in toward Reg, so close that she could feel the warmth of his breath on her cheek, the smell of roses already strong. He was really laying on the charm, trying to ensorcel her the moment they arrived, while he was in his own territory.

Reg's mind immediately started to cloud. She pictured her house, pressing her face down into Starlight's fur to block out Corvin's pheromones. It took a few seconds for Starlight to focus her enough that she could make the jump, and then she was finally back at home.

Just Reg and Starlight. No other psychics, witches, or warlocks. No other cats. Just the two of them.

CHAPTER FIFTY-TWO

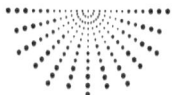

*R*eg awoke to the sounds of Sarah banging around in the kitchen late the next morning. At least, she assumed that it was Sarah. It could, of course, be Harrison. He didn't usually bother with the cupboards, since he could just materialize whatever he wanted. But he had been known to rummage through the fridge from time to time.

Reg rolled herself out of bed and was rubbing her eyes with her fists as she walked out of her bedroom and into the kitchen.

"Morning," she greeted croakily.

Sarah turned around to face Reg, smiling pleasantly. "You're back. I wasn't sure."

"Oh, sorry, I guess I should have called you yesterday. I didn't really think about it."

"No need. It isn't like it is a long trip to get here!"

Reg chuckled. Just across the back yard. Not too far at all. She caught Sarah looking around at the floor suspiciously.

"Just Starlight," she told Sarah. "Only one cat. As promised."

"Well, good. I'm very pleased to hear that. You got Marian to hold on to the other one, then?"

"Well, no, he wouldn't stay there. I'll have to give her a call and update her on the whole thing. But I found someone… elsewhere to take him. That should be the end of it."

Reg was pleased with the way things had turned out. Despite all odds, she'd been able to find a permanent home for the large, misbehaving cat.

With just one cat again, and more cleansed gems in her possession that could be sold, everything was perfect.

No more worries.

CHAPTER FIFTY-THREE

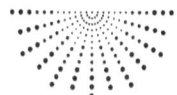

*R*eg was studying her client's hand, focused not only on the fine lines that mapped its surface, but also on Susan Petrovich's aura and emotional state, and what Reg could gather from her clothing, face, and the way she talked. There were no helpful spirits attached to her to tell Reg part of her story, so it was mostly what Reg could read and speculate from what she could see.

The woman's hands were thin and strong. Not calloused, but they felt like she had done a lot of physical labor in her lifetime.

"You are a hard worker," Reg speculated. "Goal oriented." This, based on her strong, determined aura. Reg had met people like that before. People who rose up from the mire and made a way for themselves. They found an escape and pulled themselves up out of poverty and other adverse circumstances they were in.

"Yes," Susan agreed crisply in her strong, Russian-accented voice.

"You will—"

Reg was seized suddenly with emotion. A jubilant, exultant feeling that thrilled all the way through her body from her heart outward. She gasped at the shock of it and was disoriented.

She was sure that it hadn't come from Susan. Reaching out to Starlight, Reg knew that it hadn't come from him, either. He hadn't captured some disgustingly wonderful prey that he was thrilled about.

He was still on her bed, snoozing peacefully. Reg expanded her search, trying to identify what direction the triumphant euphoria came from.

"Miss Rawlins?" Susan inquired, sounding like she was very far away. "Is everything okay? What's going on?"

"Something…" Reg gave Susan's hand a squeeze and pushed it away from her. "We'll have to reschedule. Something… unexpected has happened. I'm so sorry. I'll call you later."

There were more questions and expressions of concern, but they just flowed right past Reg. She was too focused on the rapture and where it was coming from. Susan made her way out and was gone. Stumbling over her own feet, Reg got up and retrieved her crystal ball from the shelf. She didn't even get back to the coffee table with it, just stared into it, searching for the answer to her query.

She had been staring into its depths for some time when her phone started vibrating in her skirt pocket. Reg set the crystal ball back down gently into its place on the shelf. She searched through the folds of her voluminous skirt to find her phone and pulled it out. With numb fingers, she tried to swipe to answer the call before it went to voicemail.

"Hello?"

"Reg, it's Davyn." There was hesitation in Davyn's voice. Reluctance to tell her what he had called to say. "I just wanted to give you a heads-up that the tribunal reconvened to rule on Corvin Hunter. And it was decided—"

"I know," Reg interrupted, not needing to hear the rest. "He has been reinstated to the coven."

Did you enjoy this book? Reviews and recommendations are vital to making a book successful.

Please leave a review at your favorite book store or review site and share it with your friends.

Don't miss the following bonus material:
Sign up for mailing list to get a free ebook
Read a sneak preview chapter
Other books by P.D. Workman
Learn more about the author

Sign up for my mailing list at pdworkman.com and get
Gluten-Free Murder for free!

PREVIEW OF GLUTEN-FREE MURDER

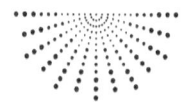

AUNTIE CLEM'S BAKERY #1

More Reg Rawlins, Psychic Investigator books are in the works! In the meantime, have you read the Auntie Clem's Bakery culinary cozy series? Check out what has been going on with Reg's foster sister, Erin Price, in Bald Eagles Falls.

CHAPTER 1

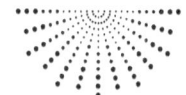

*E*rin Price pulled up in front of the shop and shut off her loudly-knocking engine. She took a few deep breaths and stared at the street-side view. She hadn't seen it since her childhood, but it looked just the same as she remembered it. Maybe a little smaller and shabbier, like most of the things from her childhood that she re-encountered, but still the same shop.

Main Street of Bald Eagle Falls was lined with red brick buildings, pasted shoulder-to-shoulder to each other, in varying, incongruous styles. Each one had a roofed-in front sidewalk to protect shoppers and diners from the blazing Tennessee sun they would face in the coming summer. All different colors. Some of them lined with gingerbread edges or whimsical paint jobs. Or both. Some of the stores appeared to have residences on the second floor, white lacy curtains drawn in windows that looked down at the vehicles, mostly trucks, nose-in in the parking spaces. There was no residence above Clementine's shop. She had lived in a small house a few blocks away that Erin had no memory of. She had spent most of her time at the shop and did not remember sleeping over at her aunt's when her parents had brought her for a visit.

A US flag hung proudly on a flagpole in front of the stores, just fluttering slightly in the breeze. It was starting to get dark and she knew she'd have to find the house in the dark if she were going to stop and take the time to explore the shop.

With another calming breath, Erin unbuckled her seatbelt, unlocked the door, and levered herself out of the seat. She felt like she'd been pasted into the bucket seat of the Challenger for three days straight. She had been pasted into the bucket seat for three days straight, other than pit-stops and layovers. She wasn't tall, so she wasn't crammed into the small car, but she'd been in there long enough to want to get out and straighten her body and stretch her legs. And to go to bed, but bed was still a long way off.

Erin walked up to the shop and put her key into the lock. It ground a little, like it hadn't been used for a long time. Maybe it needed a little bit of lubrication to loosen it up.

The air inside the shop was too still and too warm. She remembered when the little shop had been filled with the smells of exotic teas and fresh-baked goods, but Clementine had retired and closed it years ago. It had been a long time since anything had been baked there. It just smelled like dust and stale air. Erin left the front door open to let some fresh air circulate while she took a look around. There wasn't much space to explore in front of the counter. She would need a couple little tables, with a limited number of chairs, for the few people who wanted to eat in. Most of her business would just be stopping in to pick up their orders. She walked behind the counter. Everything seemed to be in good shape. A good wipe-down and some fresh baked goods in the display case and she'd be ready to go. Maybe a fresh coat of paint on the wall and a chalk board listing the daily specials and prices.

She walked into the back. A kitchen with little storage and a microscopic office that might once have been a closet. The back stairs led to a larger storage area downstairs, she remembered. And what Clementine had always called the commode. There was a second set of stairs from the store front down to the commode for customers. Not exactly convenient, but it was a small, old building. The arrangement had worked okay for Clementine. As a girl, Erin had always been a little afraid of the basement. She would creep down the stairs to use the bathroom and then race back up again, always drawing a warning from Clementine to slow down or she would trip and catch her death on those stairs.

All the old appliances were still there in the kitchen. Even a decades-old industrial fridge stood unplugged and propped open. There was no microwave and Erin was going to need a fancier coffee machine, but everything else looked usable.

* * *

"What are you doing here?"

Erin turned around and saw a looming figure in the kitchen doorway at the same time as the clipped male voice interrupted her thoughts. She just about jumped out of her skin.

She put her hand on her thumping chest and breathed out a sigh of relief when she saw that it was a uniformed police officer. But he wasn't looking terribly welcoming, jaw tight and one hand on his sidearm. There was a German Shepherd at his side.

"Oh, you scared me. I'm Erin Price," she introduced herself, reaching out her hand and stepping toward him, "and I'm—"

"I asked you what you're doing here."

Erin stopped. He made no move to close the distance between them and shake her hand, but remained standing there in a closed, authoritative stance. His tone brooked no nonsense. Erin couldn't imagine that she looked anything like a burglar. A little rumpled from the car, maybe, but she hadn't been sleeping in it. Was a slim, white, young woman really the profile of a burglar in Bald Eagle Falls?

"I own this shop."

He raised an eyebrow in disbelief, but he did let his hand slide away from the weapon and adopted a more casual stance. Erin allowed herself just one instant to admire his fit physique and his face. He was roguish, with what was either heavy five o'clock shadow or three days' growth, but his face was also round, giving him an aura of boyishness and charm.

"You own the shop. And you are...?"

"Erin Price. Clementine's niece."

"If you're Clementine's niece, why haven't we ever seen you around here?"

"It's been years since I've seen her. My parents died and I lost all my family connections years ago, living in foster care. A private detective tracked me down."

He considered this and took a walk around the kitchen, looking things over. His eyes were dark and intense. "You'll be selling the place, then? Why didn't you just hire a real estate agent?"

"No, I'm not selling," Erin said firmly. "I'm reopening."

The eyebrows went up again. "This place has been sitting empty for ten years or more. You're reopening Clementine's Tea Room?"

"No, I'll be opening a specialty bakery, once I get everything whipped into shape." She folded her arms across her chest, looking at him challengingly. "I assume you don't have a problem with that?"

"No, ma'am."

But he didn't give any indication of leaving. Erin swept back a few tendrils of dark hair that had slipped from her braid, aware that she was probably looking travel-worn after several days in the car. She had put on mascara and dusty rose lipstick before getting on her way that morning, but she felt gritty and sweaty from travel and would have preferred a shower before having met anyone in her new hometown.

Erin strode toward the front of the store and the policeman moved out of the doorway and then back around the counter toward the front door.

"You shouldn't leave the door wide open."

"I wanted some air in here. I've only been here five minutes. Do the police always show up that fast in Bald Eagle Falls?"

"I just happened by. Thought it was strange to see Clementine's door hanging open. Didn't recognize the car."

"Well, thank you for looking into it." Erin waited until he stepped out onto the sidewalk and then followed, pulling the door shut behind her. He watched as she locked it again. "You see? I have the keys."

"Where did this detective find you?"

"Maine."

"Is that where you're from?"

"I'm from a lot of places. Now I'm looking at settling back down here."

Erin looked at the German Shepherd, doing the doggie equivalent of standing at attention.

"I've never heard of a small town like this having a K9 unit."

"Well," he looked down at the dog, chewing on his words, "this is the extent of our K9 contingent."

"He looks… very well-trained. What's his name?"

"K9."

Erin cracked a smile. "Seriously?"

He kept a serious face, nodding once.

"Okay. Well, again, thank you for checking in on my store, Officer…?"

"Terry Piper."

"Erin Price." Erin offered her hand and this time Piper took it, giving her hand a brief squeeze as if he were afraid of crushing it.

"Pleased to meet you, Miss Price. Or is it missus?"

"It's Miss."

"Keep safe. Give us a call if you need anything." He produced a business card with a blue and yellow crest on it. "We don't exactly have 9-1-1 service but there's always someone on call."

Erin nodded her thanks. "I'll keep it handy. A lot of crime in Bald Eagle Falls?"

"No. It's a sleepy little town. Not too much excitement. Rowdy teenagers. Some of the drug trade trickling down from the city. The occasional domestic."

"Not a lot of break-and-enters?" she teased.

He didn't look amused. "You can't be too careful. Where are you headed now? There's a motel down the way…"

"No. I got the house too. I'll be staying there."

"You can't sleep there tonight. Won't be any water or power."

"They've been turned on. Thanks for your concern."

He looked for something else to say, then apparently couldn't find anything, so he nodded and walked down the sidewalk with his faithful companion.

* * *

Erin kept one eye on the GPS and the other on her rearview mirror to see if Officer Piper had any ideas about hopping into his car and following her home to make sure that she was properly situated. But apparently, he couldn't think of any laws she had broken and he never appeared behind her. Clementine's house was only a few blocks away. Erin parked on the street in front of it and took it in. It was a pretty little house with white siding and green shutters, roof peaks, and accents. The living room had big windows to let in the light and a window up at the top peak hinted at an attic bedroom or study. Beside and behind the house, beyond the fence line, were shimmering green, dense woods.

Erin got out of the car and grabbed her suitcase before walking up to the heavy paneled door and inserting her key in the lock. This one didn't stick, but turned smoothly like it was welcoming her home. Erin lugged her suitcase into the front entryway and closed and locked the door behind her. No point in inviting more visitors. She really didn't want to have to deal with anyone else until morning.

The AC was on, so the house wasn't stifling like the shop had been. Erin hadn't been sure what to expect. Burgener, the lawyer, had informed her that the house was furnished, but she hadn't known what kind of state it would be in. But it was neat and tidy. Furnished, but not cluttered. There were a couple of magazines on the coffee table in the living room that were months old, but other than that, Clementine might have just left it a few days before. Or still be in the other room just awaiting Erin's arrival.

She wasn't a believer in ghosts or restless spirits, but Clementine's smell and flavor still clung to the place.

Erin left her suitcase at the door and explored the house slowly. Living room, small dining room, kitchen, Clementine's bedroom, a guest room, and what Erin thought she might call a sewing room. There was fabric, rolls of wrapping paper, partially finished crafts, and post-bound books of genealogy, painstakingly written in longhand.

There were pull-down steps to the attic. If there had only been a ladder, Erin probably wouldn't have explored any further, but the stairs were well-made and modern and raised her hopes that the attic had been properly developed and wasn't just a storage space full of boxes, bags, cobwebs, and dust.

She mounted the stairs. At the top, there was enough light from below to find a light switch. Erin switched it on and had a look around.

It was a beautiful, bright room. Erin knew she was going to be spending a lot of her free time up there. White paneling and built-in cabinetry, soft, natural-looking lighting; it consisted of a reading nook, a writing desk, a comfy-looking couch, and various other touches that would make it a paradisiacal oasis at the end of a tiring day of baking.

Or driving.

After exploring the attic, Erin shut off the light, descended, and pushed the stairs up until the counterbalance took over and raised them to snick softly into place in the ceiling.

Erin returned to the kitchen for a glass of water, not looking forward to the fact that she was going to have to go out and pick up groceries if she wanted anything to eat. She found a sticky note on the fridge on notepaper preprinted with the lawyer's logo and phone number.

Welcome home. You'll find some basic supplies in the fridge. JRB

Erin opened the fridge door and sighed. Milk, juice, eggs, bagels, jam, and some precut fruit and vegetable packs. That and the coffee maker on the counter would do just fine. If James Burgener had been there, she would have hugged him.

A quick snack and then she would be off to the guest room for some shut-eye. Ghosts or not, she wasn't going to be sleeping in the master bedroom until she had made it her own.

* * *

Never one to let moss grow, Erin set to work immediately the next morning. She found a sort of a general store which carried both the small appliances she needed and painting supplies. With the back seats folded down, she filled the cargo area of the Challenger with as much as it would hold. She went back to the shop, opened the windows, and prepped the walls to start painting. Best to get a fresh coat of paint on before installing anything new.

"Knock, knock?"

Erin was startled out of her thoughts. She yanked the earbuds out of her ears and turned to face the woman who was trying to get her attention.

"I'm sorry," the woman said, giving her a tentative smile. She had a pleasant face; a middle-aged woman with ash blond hair. Either she had the perfect figure, or her clothes were hand-tailored. "I didn't want to startle you, but you were pretty engrossed…"

Erin wiped her forehead with the back of her hand. "Yeah. A little caught up in my music and my work."

"My name is Mary Lou Cox. I heard a rumor that you were here. So, I just had to come over and extend a good old Bald Eagle Falls welcome."

"Erin Price. I, uh… Clementine was my aunt."

"Well, if you're kin to Clementine, you're kin to half the mountain. Welcome home."

Erin nodded awkwardly. "Thank you. That's very kind of you."

"So…" Mary Lou took a look around the kitchen. "A fresh coat of paint and then I hear you're opening up Clementine's Tea Room again? I'll tell you, this town has surely missed the tea room."

"Uh. No. I'm not reopening the tea room." Erin enjoyed a cup of tea at the end of the day as much as anyone, but she was much more interested in baking. The groove she got into while painting was nothing compared with the nirvana she would achieve while baking. "I'm opening a specialty bakery."

Mary Lou patted her hair. "We already have a bakery in Bald Eagle Falls."

Erin ran the roller down the wall, watching carefully for seams or drips.

"I'm sure the town can support more than one bakery."

"But we already have The Bake Shoppe. We don't need another bakery."

Erin gave her a determined smile. "I'm opening a bakery."

"Angela Plaint owns The Bake Shoppe and does a really nice business, I'm not sure any of us would go to another bakery. It wouldn't be a very loyal thing to do."

"You could go to The Bake Shoppe for… whatever Angela Plaint is best at and then come to my bakery for gluten-free muffins."

"Gluten-free?" Mary Lou echoed.

"I assume you don't already have a gluten-free bakery."

"No, we do not. If you want that kind of baking, you have to drive into the city."

"Well, now you'll be able to get them in town."

"There aren't that many people that want that gluten-free stuff in Bald Eagle Falls. I don't see how you could make a living off it."

"We'll just have to see. I do other specialty baking as well. Dairy-free, allergy-free, vegan."

"We don't have a lot of *those* kind of people here. We like our meat. Whoever put meat in muffins anyway?"

Erin studied Mary Lou for a moment, trying to divine whether she was teasing or being sarcastic. "You might not put meat in a muffin, but you would probably put eggs and dairy."

"And you could make it without all those things? Who would eat such a thing? It would be like eating cardboard."

"Not when I make it."

"I guess we'll just have to see," Mary Lou said. "I sure don't cotton to the idea of you trying to take Angela's business."

"I guess we'll just have to see," Erin echoed.

* * *

Mary Lou was the first citizen of Bald Eagle Falls to express her opinion and welcome Erin to town, but she wasn't the last. Next came Melissa Lee, a woman with curly dark hair and a wide, even smile. And then Gema Reed, with her long, steel gray locks and a girlish complexion.

Erin did her best to explain to them that she wasn't there to horn in on Angela's business and take money out of her pocket, but to offer a new service that hadn't previously been available. But it was like talking to the wall. Or yelling at an avalanche. It didn't stop them from dumping advice all over her, while smiling and telling her she was welcome in town.

She didn't feel welcome.

At least Terry Piper did not show up with his K9 to give his input on the matter.

It was a long day and Erin never did meet Angela, her competition. The end of the day, the walls were freshly painted. Everything looked fresh and new. Exhausted though she was, Erin spent a few more minutes in the tiny office, going through the papers and plans in the folders she had brought with her from Maine.

Then she locked everything up tight and headed back home.

CHAPTER 2

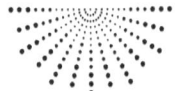

$\mathcal{T}$he day dawned bright and clear. Erin woke up earlier than she expected after her hard work of the day before. She was looking forward to each new day, rather than dreading another day of work.

Starting the day in her attic study, Erin wrote up lists of things she would need to get in the city. Not only did Bald Eagle Falls not have a specialty bakery, the general store did not carry any of the specialized flours or other ingredients that she would need. Erin had no intention of taking months getting outfitted. The store and the appliances were on hand and ready for use, so why wait?

It was late when Erin returned to the shop at the end of the day. Darkness was settling over Main Street and the streetlights were few and far between. As she juggled her first armload of goods while trying to unlock the front door, chiding herself for using the front door instead of the back—even though she would have had the same problem at the back—a voice spoke in her ear.

"Can I help you with those?"

The bag of flour she was pressing against the door with her body in an effort to hang on to it while unlocking the bolt was removed from its position. Erin laughed a little and unlocked the door, turning to get the bag of flour back from him.

She froze, looking into the dirty, sweaty face of a man she had never met before. He was white, though the word white did nothing to convey the color of his skin, dirt ground into it as if he had been working in a coal mine or living on the street for weeks. He had a fringe of a mustache and a few bristles on his chin, looking more like he was careless with his shaving than that he had intentionally trimmed his facial hair in a particular style. He had a filthy, army-green cap pulled down low so she could just make out his dark eyes.

"I can take this in for you," he offered. His voice was gravelly and low, but polite. He didn't have the drawl that would indicate he was native to the area.

"Oh, no, let me take it back," Erin said, encircling the bag with her arm and taking its weight.

He looked at her with a sullen expression that told Erin he understood that she didn't want him in her store. She turned her back on him to take the supplies into the kitchen, mentally sorting out possible weapons and escape routes. She was sure he was going to follow her in. Would a scream bring Officer Terry Piper or whoever else might be on shift?

When she went back out to her car for the next load, the man was still hanging around, as she had expected. He took bags out of her car and handed them to her.

"Really," Erin told him politely, "I'm okay. I don't need any help."

He didn't react with anger or violence, but his dark eyes glittered under the bill of his cap. "Just trying to be neighborly."

"I appreciate it. You're very kind. But you're making me nervous."

She surprised herself by telling him that. Was she acting like a victim? Encouraging him to menace her further? She knew from self-defense classes that predators looked for shyness and low self-esteem. Did she sound weak saying he was making her nervous?

But the man immediately backed off, shaking his head. "Not trying to make anyone nervous, miss."

"Then please leave me alone."

He stood there looking at her for a minute, then turned without a word and walked away. Erin blew out her breath, relieved. Here she had thought that moving to a small town in the South, she would be safe from crime and unwanted attention, but obviously nowhere was completely safe. She needed to be realistic instead of idealizing small-town living as being something it wasn't. Next time, she would not be unloading her car after dark. She would plan ahead and be better prepared.

Erin took the rest of the supplies into the kitchen and put them away. She stopped in the office to pick up one of her folders, frowning. She had a strange feeling of vertigo, like everything was slightly out of place. She couldn't identify any one thing that would make her feel that way, but couldn't help feeling like her things had been touched and moved around. She found the folder she was looking for on signage and took it home with her, locking up carefully.

* * *

Traffic was even quieter than usual in the sleepy town when Erin got to the shop to finish organizing her ingredients and to make plans for what she would make to kick off her opening and really wow her customers.

She was sitting at her desk in the tiny office, scribbling away and flipping back and forth between recipes when she heard the bells over the front door jingle. She didn't want anyone sneaking up on her today.

Erin reluctantly stood up from her work and went out to the front of the shop. It was Gema Reed, the beautiful gray-haired woman.

"I thought I saw your car outside," Gema declared. She couldn't very well have missed it. It wasn't exactly camouflaged. And it was one of the only vehicles parked on sleepy Main Street. "So, I thought I would drop in and make sure everything was okay?"

Erin tilted her head slightly, trying to figure out where Gema was going with the inquiry.

"Umm, yes. Everything is fine. Why wouldn't it be?"

"Well, being as it's the *Sabbath* and you're at work. I was worried maybe you had a water main break or vandals. Maybe even a fire. You never know what's going to happen."

"No, there's nothing wrong. I just wanted to get some work done. There's lots to do before I open."

They stood there looking at each other awkwardly for a few

moments. Erin knew she was moving into the Bible belt, but she hadn't expected things to be that different from the way they had been in the North. Some people were religious and some people were not and everybody observed their beliefs as they wished. But apparently, things were not quite so straightforward in the South.

"Well, maybe no one invited you to Sunday morning services. You probably don't even know the schedule!" Gema proclaimed. "Now there are lots of churches to choose from, of course, but if you want to join us at First Baptist, just down at the end of Main Street and Garity, why, we'd *love* to have you!"

"I'm going to have to pass..." Erin said slowly, feeling her way through. "I'm not really the churchgoing type."

"Not the type? Why, bless your heart, dear, you don't have to be a type to join your fellow Christians at worship on Sunday! You... *are* a Christian, aren't you? Not one of these... other sects? I don't mean to put down Jews or Muslims or anyone else, but here in Bald Eagle Falls, we're Christian. Baptists, Catholics, Protestants, it doesn't matter, as long as you're Christian!"

Erin cleared her throat. She wished she had brought a cloth with her out to the front, so she could occupy herself with polishing the glass and chrome display case and counter. Just to have something to do with her hands and somewhere to look other than Gema Reed's benevolent Christian face. "Actually, Mrs. Reed. I'm not."

"You're not... what? You don't look like a Jew or one of those... pagan people. Not everyone goes to church every Sunday, but..."

"I'm... not Christian. I'm atheist."

"Atheist!" Gema was aghast. She held her hand dramatically at her throat, halfway to covering her mouth in horror. She stared at Erin pleadingly, as if she thought it might just be a clumsy joke and Erin would change her tune. "You're not! Really?"

"Yes. I am. I'm sorry if that upsets you..."

"Well, Jesus loves every humble seeker of the truth. You are a seeker, aren't you? Not everyone can be converted, but as long as you're looking for the truth, you will find it in the end..."

Erin took a deep breath and let it back out again. As much as she wanted to smooth Gema's ruffled feathers, to just reassure her and send her on her way, she wanted to get it out in the open. Her real beliefs, not just rumors or half-baked explanations.

"Mrs. Reed—"

"Gema, sugar…"

"Gema. I am an atheist. Not an agnostic. Not an investigator or a seeker. An atheist. I'm not looking for something to believe in. I already have a belief system. And it doesn't include God."

Gema gasped audibly and this time she did cover up her mouth. "Oh, my dear…"

Erin forced a smile. "I'm not a witch or a devil-worshiper. And I won't try to talk you out of your beliefs. But I, myself, do not believe in God. Not a god of any sort. Not the universe, or Mother Nature, or a higher power, or Jesus. I'm sorry."

"Well." Gema looked for a moment as if she would flee without another word. Instead, she smoothed her waves of silver, took a calming breath and gave a polite nod. "Everybody is entitled to their own opinion, no matter how wrong. I'd better get on my way, or I'll be walking into service late. I just hope… that you won't be encouraging others to break the Sabbath by your blatant disregard for it. You won't have your bakery open on Sunday, will you?"

Erin gave a little shrug. "Didn't my Aunt Clementine have it open after services on Sunday?" she asked tentatively. Her memories of Clementine's Tea Room were startlingly clear in some respects and shrouded by fog in others. She was sure she remembered helping to serve the church ladies after Sunday services. They had all thought her such a cute, pretty young thing. She remembered her resentment over being treated like a puppy or a baby instead of a person with a mind of her own. She loved helping Clementine in the tea room, but she didn't like that part of it.

Gema made a noise of indecision, not wanting to admit that Erin was right and yet compelled by her Christian morals not to tell a lie. "Mmmmm… yes, it is true that she opened up for an hour or two after services on Sunday, so the ladies would have somewhere to go to discuss Christian services required in the upcoming week…"

"So, it would be okay, as long as I waited until after your worship services?"

"As an atheist, I'm not sure it would be the same…"

"I would be shunned for opening my restaurant, but a Christian would not? When it's against a Christian's beliefs, but not mine? Wouldn't it be worse for a Christian to do it?"

"I just don't know," Gema snapped, shaking her head in confusion. "I must get on now, but I'll... I'll think it over."

"Okay..." Erin gave her a little wave. "You be sure to let me know what you ladies decide. Someone mentioned that Clementine's Tea Room had been sorely missed and I thought that if I could provide a similar service..."

Gema Reed gulped. She shook her head and retreated. The bells tinkled behind her and Erin stood there, watching her get into her big red truck and pull out into the street. Then she was gone.

Erin went back to her office to continue working on her opening and marketing strategy. She added 'Sunday social tea' to her list with a wry smile and continued to look through her recipes.

* * *

After Erin finished her plans, she carefully filed her folders in the cabinet beside the desk. There was no reason to leave her lists scattered all over her desk and take the chance of losing something when she had a perfectly functional file drawer to put everything neatly away. She emptied the dregs of her cold coffee from her mug and washed it out, leaving it upside down on a towel to dry.

When she stepped out of the shop onto the sidewalk, she nearly collided with a woman coming the other direction. Sunday had been so quiet, she hadn't expected any foot traffic and hadn't even looked before stepping out the door.

"Oh, I'm sorry!" she apologized.

The other woman was ruddy, a redhead, on the plumpish side. Her hair fell in waves around her head, partially obscuring her face. She stepped back from Erin, folding her arms across her chest and staring at Erin as if she had just committed a mortal sin. Which, given Gema's reaction to Erin working on a Sunday, was probably the case.

"I didn't see you coming," Erin apologized. "That was my fault. I'm sorry."

The woman ignored the apology. "You're Clementine's niece."

"Yes, I am."

"You don't favor her, do you?"

"I don't remember her too clearly," Erin admitted. "And I don't really know what she looked like in later years."

"If you don't remember her, then what are you doing here? Why come to Bald Eagle Falls?"

Erin's mouth was dry. She tried to put together words that made sense, flummoxed by the woman's attack.

"I inherited the store and the house. I wanted to reopen the shop."

"Only you're not," the redhead hissed. "You're not reopening the tea room, you're opening a bakery."

"Well, yes. That's what I do, I bake. I'm still planning on serving tea after Sunday services each week, so the women can get together…"

"We don't need another bakery."

Erin sighed and shook her head. "It's a specialty bakery. It means people won't have to go into the city to get gluten-free or allergy-friendly baking. It doesn't directly compete with the other bakery."

"You are competing, little Miss Out-of-Towner. And you're not going to last a week!"

With that, the redhead marched on, shouldering past Erin with a force that staggered her and made her catch herself on the side of the building.

Looking across Main Street, she saw Officer Terry Piper watching her, K9 at his side. She considered calling him over to vent about the rude woman, but decided that would just be sour grapes. She didn't really want to charge the woman. There was no point in reporting the encounter to the police.

* * *

Erin yawned as she pushed open her door, sending the little bells tinkling in welcome. She was going to have to get used to getting up early if she were going to be running a bakery. She was going to have to get up while it was still dark and everyone else was sleeping in order to have freshly baked goods in the display cases when people started walking in for a little something to go with their coffees or office meetings.

Her day would start way before anyone else's and, if she were going to stay open past afternoon, she was going to need to find an assistant to split shifts with. It wouldn't have to be another baker, just someone who could answer questions about ingredients and work the cash register.

Taking into account the not-so-warm reaction she was getting from the women of the town, she might have to go to the city to find someone willing to work the bakery.

Erin juggled her keys and her bag of groceries to turn on the kitchen light and put her bag on the counter.

Her coffee mug lay on the floor, shattered. Erin frowned and looked around. A shiver ran down her spine. Had someone been there? Had her shop been broken into?

For a few moments, she just stood there, frozen, listening for any movement.

There was only silence. She considered the situation. Had she put the mug too close to the edge of the counter and it had fallen off by itself? Were there earthquakes in Tennessee?

The imprint of the mug was still in the towel she had left it sitting on. Close to the edge of the counter, but not over it.

She heard the bells on the front door ring and hurried out to see whether someone was leaving the shop. Had she actually walked right past an intruder? Maybe hiding behind the counter, below her eye level while she yawned and juggled her groceries in the morning dimness?

She stopped stock-still. Nobody had left the shop; wild-haired Melissa Lee had come in. She was all smiles and sweetness, launching into a long-winded description of some fundraiser that she and some of the other women were running. She cut herself off abruptly.

"My dear, you look like you've just seen a ghost. Are you okay?"

"I... I think someone has been in here."

"What do you mean, in here?" she asked doubtfully.

"I think someone broke in..."

"You have been burgled?" Melissa's voice rose, a mixture of disbelief and alarm. Such things were probably unheard of in sleepy little Bald Eagle Falls. "Honey, you stay right there while I get the police."

Melissa hurried back out the front door and, without a clue what else to do, Erin obeyed, standing there like a statue. It was only a few minutes before Melissa returned, Officer Terry Piper in tow with his K9. Melissa was babbling on about crime rates and burglaries. Piper ignored her and focused on Erin.

"The place was broken into?" he demanded.

"I don't know. I think someone has been here."

Feeling embarrassed that she might be overreacting, Erin took him into the kitchen and showed him the broken mug and where it had been sitting on the counter. Piper nodded and looked around, his brows drawn down.

"Anyone else have a key?" he asked.

K9 sniffed at the broken mug with interest, but didn't lead his master along a scent trail. He just sat back on his haunches and panted.

"No. I haven't given anyone else a key."

Piper looked into the small office. "Anything been touched in here? Anything missing?"

Erin hadn't yet had a chance to look. She gave a little laugh and slipped by him to see. The room looked untouched. Erin checked her file drawers.

"There was one other time… when I thought things had been moved in here. I put everything away in my drawers, this time…"

"Do you have petty cash in here? A safe?"

"No. Nothing like that. And no cash in the register yet, either. I haven't opened for business yet." She knew she didn't really need to add that part. Terry Piper was undoubtedly aware that she hadn't yet opened to the public. If there had been any doubt, the fact that there were no baked goods in the display case or in the oven would pretty much be a giveaway.

"When are you opening?" he asked. "Assuming you still are?"

"Yes, of course. I'm just putting together my plans for a small opening celebration right now. A few days…"

He raised an eyebrow. "That quickly? I thought it would take longer to get things up and running."

"Everything is already in place. I've bought supplies. I am still waiting on signage and a few little things like that, but for the time being, I'll just put a handmade sign in the window."

He pursed his lips and nodded. He and K9 went to the back door and examined it to confirm it was still locked and had not been tampered with. He looked at the steep stairs to the basement.

"What have you got downstairs?"

"Storage and the commode. I haven't been down there yet this morning…"

K9's ears pointed down the stairs curiously.

"Does he hear something?" Erin asked.

"No… not yet. Come on, K9. Let's go investigate."

The dog eagerly led the way down the stairs. Erin realized she was holding herself tense and she tried to relax. There wasn't anything downstairs. She already knew it. There had been no sign of forced entry at either door. No open windows somebody might have crawled in through. She was going to have to accept that there had been a tremor or something else that had made the counter shake and caused her coffee mug to go crashing to the floor. The shops were all connected; perhaps someone had dropped a pallet of books with enough force in the bookstore next door that it had shaken the shared wall and sent her mug on its kamikaze journey.

There were no sounds of conflict downstairs. No sign that the officer had found anyone lurking below them. He was back up the stairs in a minute.

"All clear."

They went back out to the front, where Melissa was anxiously waiting. Piper examined the front door and frame.

"There aren't any signs of forced entry," he said with a shrug. "Is it possible you left it unlocked last night?"

"No, I'm sure I…" Erin remembered colliding with the woman on the sidewalk as she left. Had she locked the door afterward? Erin knew she had unlocked the door in the morning. And it could only be locked from the outside. If she'd had to unlock it in the morning, then she had locked it the night before. "Yes. I'm sure I locked it. It was locked when I came in this morning."

"Maybe you knocked the mug down without realizing it, last night or this morning. Or maybe a crosswind or the building shaking for some reason?" Piper shrugged.

"It's a mystery!" Melissa said in dramatic tones.

Piper gave her a tolerant smile. "Yes, Mrs. Lee. It surely is."

"Maybe it's a ghost! The tea shop is haunted."

"Bakery," Erin corrected, aware she was nitpicking, but irritated about the community's opposition to a second bakery opening.

"We haven't had a ghost here before," Melissa enthused. "I wonder who it could be. There are a lot of civil war ghosts in the area. We have a rich civil war history, you know. Why, the library is practically famous in these parts. There are so many legends of lost and buried treasure in the hills around here, a person can hardly go for a hike without tripping over one!" She laughed.

"If there hasn't been a ghost here before," Piper said gravely, "then the ghost must be of a more recent vintage, wouldn't you say?"

Melissa stopped and considered. "Well, yes, I suppose. Unless you've somehow awoken a restless spirit. You haven't been digging down there in your basement? Or in the back?"

"No," Erin assured her. "The basement floor is concrete and so is the parking lot in back."

"Then we need to think of who might have died recently that would have a reason to haunt the store." Melissa pondered the problem.

Erin exchanged looks with Piper. He appeared to be suppressing a smile.

"Maybe... the owner?" he suggested.

"Erin?" Melissa said blankly.

"The... previous owner...?" Piper prompted.

"Oh, Clementine! Why, of course it would be Clementine! Silly old me!" She put her hand on Erin's arm. Her dark curls quivered with her movement. "You are being haunted by your Aunt Clementine. Did you have any unfinished business with her? Something that she would be expecting from you?"

"Just opening the bakery. And why, if there was such a thing as ghosts, would my aunt's restless spirit want to break my coffee mug?"

"She's trying to reach you, dear. Ghosts are very limited in what they can do. Move things, appear to you, maybe make noises. It's not like on TV, where they can just walk up and talk to you and explain themselves in words. All she can do to reach you is to move things around."

Erin nodded. "I see. Well, I don't believe in ghosts, so I'm going to look for more earthly explanations. You can… believe what you like."

"Oh, I do," Melissa agreed. "I am going to talk to the others and we'll see if we can sort this out. After all, we all knew Clementine. I knew her my whole life. We'll figure out what it is that she wants to reach you for. Mary Lou's sister-in-law, she's very good with spirits. We'll see if she can come here and make contact with your poor dead auntie."

Erin glanced over at Piper, widening her eyes, sure she was being played. But Piper gave no sign that Melissa was joking. And Melissa continued to look earnest and excited about the whole ghost business.

"Isn't contacting ghosts considered sorcery in Christian circles?" Erin suggested.

"No, no! Mary Lou's sister-in-law won't be using a Ouija board or any other devil's tool. She just uses prayer. There's nothing wrong with that."

"Ah." Erin nodded. She looked at her watch as obviously as possible. Time was trickling by and she had work to do. "Did you want to leave me a flyer about your fundraiser, Melissa?" At Melissa's blank look, she indicated the woman's clipboard. "That was why you came in here, wasn't it?"

"Oh, yes!" Melissa pulled a fuchsia-colored page from her clipboard and handed it to Erin. "Of course, no one is required to donate or put time into it, but every little bit is appreciated! I'd better get on my way! If I stop to yap at every store, it's going to take me all day! I'm already busier than a one-armed paper hanger."

Erin nodded and gave a little wave, and Melissa went on her way. Erin sighed and looked at Officer Piper. He had a gorgeous smile, when he let it show.

"Miss Price, I'm sorry I couldn't be of more assistance. You feel free to call on me if you have any more troubles. Hopefully, your ghost won't cause any more trouble."

"Thanks," Erin said dryly. "Just tell me… everyone in town doesn't believe that, do they? In the existence of ghosts, I mean? And that they can just… be contacted?"

"Not everyone is quite as literal as Mrs. Lee, but… I do imagine most of them will agree that your shop might be haunted. They might not be willing to say that it is, but they won't say that it isn't…"

Erin shook her head. "I suppose it's harmless, as long as they aren't demanding to hold séances in here."

* * *

Gluten-Free Murder, Book #1 of the *Auntie Clem's Bakery* series by P.D. Workman can be purchased at pdworkman.com

ABOUT THE AUTHOR

Award-winning and USA Today bestselling author P.D. (Pamela) Workman writes riveting mystery/suspense and young adult books dealing with mental illness, addiction, abuse, and other real-life issues. For as long as she can remember, the blank page has held an incredible allure and from a very young age she was trying to write her own books.

Workman wrote her first complete novel at the age of twelve and continued to write as a hobby for many years. She started publishing in 2013. She has won several literary awards from Library Services for Youth in Custody for her young adult fiction. She currently has over 80 published titles and can be found at pdworkman.com.

Born and raised in Alberta, Workman has been married for over 25 years and has one son.

* * *

Please visit P.D. Workman at pdworkman.com to see what else she is working on, to join her mailing list, and to link to her social networks.

* * *

If you enjoyed this book, please take the time to recommend it to other purchasers with a review or star rating and share it with your friends!

facebook.com/pdworkmanauthor

twitter.com/pdworkmanauthor

instagram.com/pdworkmanauthor

amazon.com/author/pdworkman

bookbub.com/authors/p-d-workman

goodreads.com/pdworkman

linkedin.com/in/pdworkman

pinterest.com/pdworkmanauthor

youtube.com/pdworkman